THE CRADLE IN THE GRAVE

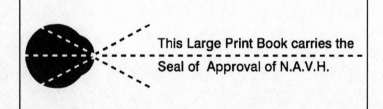

This Large Print Book carries the
Seal of Approval of N.A.V.H.

THE CRADLE IN THE GRAVE

SOPHIE HANNAH

THORNDIKE PRESS
A part of Gale, Cengage Learning

Detroit • New York • San Francisco • New Haven, Conn • Waterville, Maine • London

GALE
CENGAGE Learning®

Copyright © Sophie Hannah, 2010.
"Anchorage" by Fiona Sampson from *Common Prayer* (© 2007) is reproduced by permission of Carcanet Press Ltd.
Thorndike Press, a part of Gale, Cengage Learning.

Thorndike Press® Large Print Basic.
The text of this Large Print edition is unabridged.
Other aspects of the book may vary from the original edition.
Set in 16 pt. Plantin.

LIBRARY OF CONGRESS CATALOGING-IN-PUBLICATION DATA

Hannah, Sophie, 1971–
  [Room swept white]
  The cradle in the grave / by Sophie Hannah.
    p. cm. — (Thorndike Press large print basic)
  ISBN-13: 978-1-4104-4418-9 (hardcover)
  ISBN-10: 1-4104-4418-X (hardcover)
  1. Women television producers and directors—Fiction. 2. Sudden infant death syndrome—Fiction. 3. Mothers—Crimes against—Fiction. 4. Large type books. I. Title.
  PR6058.A5928R66 2012
  823'.914—dc22   2011036223

Published in 2012 by arrangement with Penguin Books, a member of Penguin Group (USA) Inc.

Printed in the United States of America
1 2 3 4 5 6 7 16 15 14 13 12

For Anne Grey, who introduced me to, among many other invaluable pieces of wisdom, the motto 'Take nothing personally, even if it's got your name on it'. This dedication is the exception to that generally sound rule.

Ray Hines

Transcript of Interview 1, 12 February 2009
(First part of interview — five or so minutes — not taped. RH only allowed me to start recording once I stopped asking about the specifics of her case. I turned the conversation to HY thinking she would talk more freely.)

RH: I met Helen Yardley once, that's all. What do you want me to say about her? I thought you wanted to talk about me.

LN: I do, very much. You don't seem to, though.

(*Pause*)

LN: I don't want you to say anything in particular about Helen. I'm not trying to —

RH: I met her once. A few days before her appeal. Everyone wanted her to get out. Not only the women. All the staff too. None of them believed she was guilty.

That was down to you.

LN: I was only a small part of the effort. There were —

RH: You were the public face and the loudest voice. I was told you'd get me out. By my lawyers, by nearly everyone I met inside. And you did. Thanks to you, and because of the timing, I had it relatively easy, in Durham and in Geddham Hall, give or take a few minor run-ins with idiots.

LN: The timing?

RH: Public opinion was turning by the time I was convicted. Your hard work was having an effect. If my case had come to court a year later than it did, I'd have been acquitted.

LN: Like Sarah, you mean?

(*Pause*)

RH: I wasn't thinking of Sarah Jaggard, no.

LN: She stood trial in 2005. A year after you. She was acquitted.

RH: I wasn't thinking of her. I was thinking of myself, in the hypothetical situation of my trial taking place a year later.

(*Pause*)

LN: What? Why are you smiling?

RH: The group identity is important to you. As it is to Helen Yardley.

LN: Go on.

RH: Us. The women you campaigned for. You say 'Helen' and 'Sarah' as if they're my friends. I know nothing about either of them. And what little I do know tells me we have nothing in common, apart from the obvious. Helen Yardley's husband stood by her throughout, never once doubted her innocence. That's one thing we don't have in common.

LN: Have you had any contact with Angus since getting out?

(*Long pause*)

LN: It must be difficult for you to talk about. Shall we go back to Helen and Sarah? They don't know you any better than you know them, and yet, from speaking to both of them, I can tell you that they feel a strong affinity with you. Because of what you call 'the obvious'.

(*Pause*)

LN: Ray, you're unique. Your tragedy is something that only happened to you. I know that. I'm not trying to chip away at your right to be an individual. I hope you understand that. I'm simply saying that —

RH: Sarah Jaggard was acquitted. She was accused of killing one child, not her own. There's even less common ground between me and her than there is between

9

me and Helen Yardley.

(*Pause*)

LN: Ray, you know, I'd understand completely if you said you'd had moments when you hated both Helen and Sarah. *They* would understand it.

RH: Why would I hate two women I don't know?

LN: Sarah was acquitted. All right, she had to endure a trial, but she got a 'not guilty' verdict. That's the verdict you should have got. Meanwhile you were stuck inside, wondering if you'd ever get out. If you resented her — even if you wished in your darkest moments that her verdict had gone the other way — it'd be only natural. And Helen — you said it yourself, everyone knew she wasn't guilty. Her appeal was coming up just as you landed at Geddham Hall. When you heard she was going home, and you knew you weren't, you might well have hated her, wanted her appeal to fail. No one would blame you.

RH: I'm glad you're recording this. I'd like to say very clearly, for the official record, that I felt none of these feelings you're attributing to me.

LN: I'm not —

RH: I didn't resent Sarah Jaggard's acquittal. I didn't want Helen Yardley's appeal to fail. Not for a fraction of a second did I want either of those things. Let's be absolutely clear on that. I would never wish for anybody to be convicted of a crime they hadn't committed. I would never want anyone to lose their appeal if they hadn't done what they'd been convicted of doing.

(*Pause*)

RH: I knew the appeal had gone her way when I heard cheers coming from everywhere at once. All the girls had been glued to the TVs, waiting. The screws too.

LN: Not you?

RH: I didn't need to watch it. I knew Helen Yardley would be going home. Was it her that put the idea in your head that I was jealous of her?

LN: No. Helen's only ever spoken of you in the most positive —

RH: I didn't meet her by accident, the one time I met her. She came to find me. She wanted to speak to me before her appeal, in case she didn't come back to Geddham. She said what you've just said, that it would be natural for me to envy and resent her if she walked free, and she wouldn't blame me for doing so, but she wanted me to know that my time would

11

come: I'd appeal too, and I'd win. I'd get out. She mentioned your name. Said you'd helped her and you were equally determined to help me. I didn't doubt her on that. No one could doubt your commitment, no one who's heard of you — and who hasn't, by now?
(*Pause*)

LN: So perhaps Helen is your friend, after all.

RH: If a friend is someone who wishes you well, then I suppose she is. She's part of JIPAC, she campaigned for my release. I don't understand it, really. She was out, free. Why didn't she just get on with the rest of her life?

LN: Is that what you would have done?

RH: It's what I'm trying to do. There's nothing left of my old life, but I'd like to try and start a new one.

LN: Of course Helen wants to get on with her life. But, having been the victim of a terrible injustice, and knowing you were in the same boat, you and many others . . . Dorne Llewellyn is still in prison.

RH: Look, I don't want to talk about anyone else, all right? I don't want to be part of your gang of miscarriage-of-justice victims. I'm alone, which isn't that bad once you get used to it, and if I ever choose not to be alone, I want it to be my choice. I don't want to think about other women. It's better for me if I don't. You've got your cause — don't try to make it mine.

(*Pause*)

RH: I don't want to rain on your parade, but justice and injustice? They don't exist.

(*Pause*)

RH: Well, they don't, do they? They patently don't.

LN: I believe very strongly that both do exist. I try to prevent one and bring about the other. I've made it my life's work.

RH: Justice is a nice idea and nothing more. We invented it — human beings — because we'd like it to exist, but the fact is that it doesn't. Look . . . For the benefit of the Dictaphone, I'm holding a coaster in mid-air. What will happen if I let go of it?

LN: It'll fall to the floor.

(*Sound of coaster dropping on rug*)

RH: Because of gravity. We believe gravity exists; we're right about that. I could pick up that coaster, and that one, and that one, and let go of them, and they'd all fall to the ground. But what if only one fell and the rest floated at eye-level, or scooted up to the ceiling? What if you saw that happen now? Would you still believe in gravity, if it only *sometimes* made things fall down?

LN: I see what you're trying to say, but —

RH: Occasionally, good things happen to good people. And bad things happen to bad people. But it's chance — pure random coincidence. As it is when it happens the other way round — bad things to good people.

LN: But that's what I call injustice — when the system treats good people as if they were bad.

RH: Justice doesn't exist any more than Santa Claus does.

LN: Ray, we have a whole legal system devoted to . . .

RH: . . . seeing that justice is done. I know. And when I was a child, I sat on the knee of a man in a red and white suit with a long white beard, and he gave me a present. But it was a fantasy. A fantasy that makes people feel better. Except it doesn't — it makes them feel worse when the illusion is shattered. That's why I try to think of myself as someone who's had appallingly bad luck, not as the victim of a miscarriage of justice. Why should I torment myself by believing there's this amazing force for good at work in the world, but that it failed me, or ignored me? No thanks. And people? They don't commit unjust acts in the service of an opposing evil force. They blunder along to the best of their abilities, doing their best — which, mostly, is not good enough — or in some cases not even doing their best, and their behaviour has repercussions for other people, and . . . The point I'm trying to make is, life is chaotic and indiscriminate. Things just happen, and not for any reason. (*Pause*)

RH: You'd be better off ditching justice and concentrating on truth instead.

LN: You believe in truth?

RH: Absolutely. The truth always exists, even while people are believing the lie. The truth is that I didn't murder my babies. I loved them, more than you can possibly imagine, and never harmed either of them in any way.

LN: I know that, Ray. And now everyone else does too.

RH: The truth is that Helen and Paul Yardley are people who will pour all their time and energy into helping strangers, and maybe Sarah Jaggard and her husband — I can't remember his name . . .

LN: Glen.

RH: Maybe they're that sort too. But I'm

not. And it doesn't matter, because you've got them to help you make your programme. You don't need me around to mess it up by saying what I inconveniently think.

LN: You won't mess anything up. The opposite. Your story's —

RH: My story will muddy your waters. I'm a drug addict who either lied in court or lied before I got to court — take your pick. Your average middle-England viewer's going to feel all buoyed up with self-righteous indignation after hearing about Helen Yardley — the respectable, happily married childminder, adored by her charges and their parents, by everyone who knew her — and then you'll move on to me and lose your advantage. A lot of people still think I did it.

LN: Which is why it's all the more important for you to be part of the programme and tell the truth: that you didn't lie, in court or out of it. That you were traumatised and your memory let you down, as people's memories tend to when they're under a massive emotional strain. Tell the truth in this context, Ray — in the context of my film — and people will believe you. I promise you, they will.

RH: I can't do this. I can't get sucked in.

16

Turn that thing off.

LN: But Ray . . .

RH: Turn it off.

www.telegraph.co.uk, Wednesday 7 October 2009, 0922 GMT report by Rahila Yunis

WRONGLY CONVICTED MOTHER FOUND DEAD AT HOME

Helen Yardley, the Culver Valley child-minder wrongly convicted of murdering her two baby sons, was found dead on Monday at her home in Spilling. Mrs Yardley, 38, was found by her husband Paul, a roofer aged 40, when he returned from work early in the evening. The death is being treated as 'suspicious'. Superintendent Roger Barrow of Culver Valley Police said: 'Our inquiries are ongoing, and the investigation is still at an early stage, but Mrs Yardley's family and the public can be assured that we are putting every possible resource into this. Helen and Paul Yardley have already endured intolerable anguish. It is vital that we handle this tragedy discreetly and efficiently.'

Mrs Yardley was convicted in November

1996 of the murders of her sons Morgan, in 1992, and Rowan, in 1995. The boys died aged 14 weeks and 16 weeks. Mrs Yardley was found guilty by a majority verdict of 11 to one and given two life sentences. In June 1996, while at home on bail awaiting trial, Mrs Yardley gave birth to a daughter, Paige, who was placed with a foster family and subsequently adopted. Interviewed in October 1997 on the day that he heard the family court's decision, Paul Yardley said: 'To say that Helen and I are devastated is an understatement. Having lost two babies to crib death, we have now lost our precious daughter to a system that persecutes grieving families by stealing their children. Who are these monsters that decide to tear up the lives of innocent, law-abiding people? They don't care about us, or about the truth.'

In 2004, the Criminal Cases Review Commission, which reviews possible miscarriages of justice, referred Mrs Yardley's case to the appeal court after campaigners raised doubts about the integrity of Dr Judith Duffy, one of the expert witnesses at the trial. In February 2005, Mrs Yardley was released after three judges in the court of appeal quashed her convictions. She had always maintained her innocence. Her husband had stood by her throughout her ordeal, working '20 hours a day, every day', according to a source close to the family, to clear his wife's name. He was helped by relatives, friends, and many parents whose children Mrs Yardley had looked after.

Journalist and writer Gaynor Mundy, 43, who collaborated with Mrs Yardley on her 2007 memoir *Nothing But Love,* said: 'Everyone who knew Helen knew she was innocent. She was a kind, gentle, sweet person who could never harm anyone.'

TV producer and journalist Laurie Nattrass played a major role in the campaign to free Mrs Yardley. Last night he said: 'I can't put into words the sadness and anger I feel. Helen might have died yesterday, but her life was taken from her 13 years ago, when she was found guilty of crimes she didn't commit, the murders of her two beloved sons. Dissatisfied with the torture it had already inflicted, the state then robbed Helen of her future by kidnapping — and there's no other word for it — her only surviving child.'

Nattrass, 45, Creative Director of Binary Star, a Soho-based media company, has won many awards for his documentaries about miscarriages of justice. He said, 'For the past seven years, 90 per cent of my time has been spent campaigning for women like Helen, trying to find out what went so dreadfully wrong in so many cases.'

Mr Nattrass first met Mrs Yardley when he visited her in Geddham Hall women's prison in Cambridgeshire in 2002. Together they set up the pressure group JIPAC (Justice for Innocent Parents and Carers), formerly JIM. Mr Nattrass said: 'Originally we called it "Justice for Innocent Mothers", but it soon became clear that fathers and babysitters were being wrongly charged and convicted too. Helen and I wanted to help anyone whose life had been ruined in this way. Something needed to be done. It was unacceptable that innocent people were being blamed whenever there was an unexplained child death. Helen was as passionate about this as I am. She worked relentlessly to help other victims of injustice, both from prison and once she got out. Sarah Jaggard and Ray Hines, among others, have Helen to thank for their freedom. Her good work will live on.'

In July 2005, Wolverhampton hairdresser Sarah Jaggard, 30, was found not guilty of the manslaughter of Beatrice Furniss, the daughter of a friend, who died aged six months while in Mrs Jaggard's care. Mr Nattrass said: 'Sarah's acquittal was the indicator I'd been waiting for that the public were starting to see reason. No longer were they willing to let vindictive police and lawyers and corrupt doctors lead them on a witch-hunt.'

Yesterday, Mrs Jaggard said: 'I can't believe Helen's dead. I will never forget what she did for me, how she fought for me and stuck by me. Even in prison, not knowing if and when she'd get out, she took the time to write letters supporting me to anyone who would listen. My heart aches for Paul and the family.'

Rachel Hines, a 42-year-old physiotherapist from Notting Hill, London, had her convictions overturned in the court of appeal after serving four years for the murders of her baby son and daughter. Julian Lance, Mrs Hines' solicitor, said: 'If it wasn't for Helen Yardley and JIPAC, we wouldn't have been granted leave to appeal. We were lacking key information. JIPAC found it for us. Helen's death is a devastating blow to everyone who knew her, and a huge loss.' Mrs Hines was unavailable for comment.

Dr Judith Duffy, 54, a paediatric forensic pathologist from Ealing, London, gave evidence for the prosecution at the trials of Mrs Yardley, Mrs Jaggard and Mrs Hines. She is currently under investigation by the

GMC, pending a hearing next month for misconduct. Laurie Nattrass said: 'Judith Duffy has caused unimaginable suffering to dozens if not hundreds of families, and she must be stopped. I hope she'll be removed from the list of home office pathologists and struck off the medical register.' Mr Nattrass is currently making a documentary about the miscarriages of justice for which he believes Dr Duffy to be responsible.

PART I

1
WEDNESDAY 7 OCTOBER 2009

I am looking at numbers when Laurie phones, numbers that mean nothing to me. My first thought, when I pulled the card out of the envelope and saw four rows of single figures, was of Sudoku, a game I've never played and am not likely to, since I hate all things mathematical. Why would someone send me a Sudoku puzzle? Easy: they wouldn't. Then what is this?

'Fliss?' Laurie says, his mouth too close to the phone. When I don't answer immediately, he hisses my name again. He sounds like a deranged heavy-breather — that's how I know it's urgent. When it isn't, he holds the phone too far away and sounds like a robot at the far end of a tunnel.

'Hi, Laurie.' Using the strange card to push my hair back from my face, I turn and look out of the window to my left. Through the condensation that no amount of towel-wiping seems to cure, across the tiny courtyard and through the window on the other side, I can see him clearly, hunched over his desk, eyes hidden behind a curtain of messy blond hair.

His glasses have slipped down his nose, and his tie, which he's taken off, is laid out in front of him like a newspaper. I stick out my tongue at him and make an even ruder gesture with my fingers, knowing I'm completely safe. In the two years I've worked with Laurie, I've never seen him glance out of his window, not even when I stood in his office, pointed across the courtyard and said, 'That's my desk there, with the hand cream on it, and the photo frames, and the plant.' Human beings like to have such accessories, I restrained myself from adding.

Laurie never has anything on his desk apart from his computer, his BlackBerry and his work — scattered papers and files, tiny Dictaphone tapes — and the discarded ties that drape themselves over every surface in his room like flat, multi-coloured snakes. He has a thick neck that's seriously tie-intolerant. I don't know why he bothers putting them on at all; they're always off within seconds of his arriving at the office. By the side of his desk there's a large globe with a metal dome base. He spins it when he's thinking hard about something, or when he's angry, or excited. On his office walls, up among the evidence of how successful and clever and humane he is — certificates, photographs of him receiving awards, looking as if he's just graduated from a finishing school for heavy-featured hulks, his grade-A gracious smile fixed to his face — there are posters of planets, individual and group portraits: Jupiter on its own, Jupiter from a different angle with Saturn next to it. There's also a three-dimensional model of the solar system on one of his shelves, and four or five large books with tatty covers about outer space. I asked Tamsin once if she had any idea why he was so interested in astronomy. She chuckled and said, 'Maybe he feels lonely in our galaxy.'

I know every detail of Laurie's office by heart; he is for ever summoning me, asking me questions to which I couldn't possibly know the answers. Sometimes, by the time I arrive, he's forgotten what he wanted me for. He has been into my office twice, once by accident when he was looking for Tamsin.

'I need you in here now,' he says. 'What are you doing? Are you busy?'

Move your head ninety degrees to the right and you'll see what I'm doing, you weirdo. I'm sitting here staring at you, in all your weirdness.

I have an inspired idea. The numbers on the card I'm holding make no sense to me. Laurie makes no sense to me. 'Did you send me these numbers?' I ask him.

'What numbers?'

'Sixteen numbers on a card. Four rows of four.'

'What numbers?' he asks more abruptly than last time.

Does he want me to recite them? 'Two, one, four, nine . . .'

'I didn't send you any numbers.'

As so often when I'm talking to Laurie, I'm stumped. He has a habit of saying one thing while leaving you with exactly the opposite impression. This is why, even though he's said he didn't send me any numbers, I have the sense that if I'd said, 'Three, six, eight, seven' instead of 'Two, one, four, nine', he might have said, 'Oh, yeah, that was me.'

'Bin it, whatever it is, and get in here, soon as you can.' He cuts me off before I have a chance to reply.

I swing my chair from side to side and watch him. At this point, surely, anyone halfway normal would glance across the courtyard to see if I was obeying orders, stealth, allowing her to believe she's in charge.

'What's that?' She nods at the card in my hand.

I look at it again, read it digit by digit for about the twentieth time.

2	1	4	9
7	8	0	3
4	0	9	8
0	6	2	0

A grid, Tamsin said. There's no grid here, so it can't be a Sudoku puzzle, though the layout is grid-like. It's as if the lines have been removed once the numbers were filled in.

'Your guess is as good as mine,' I tell Maya. I don't bother to show her the card. She's always gushingly friendly, particularly to lower-ranking Binary Star employees like me, but she has no interest in anyone but herself. She asks all the right questions — loudly, so that everyone hears how much she cares — but if you take the trouble to reply, she blinks at you blank-eyed, as if

which I'm not: I'm not binning the card, I'm not leaping to my feet. All of which Laurie would see if he turned his head in my direction, but he doesn't. Instead, he pulls at the open collar of his shirt as if he can't breathe, and stares at his closed office door, waiting for me to walk through it. That's what he wants to happen, and so he expects it to happen.

I can't take my eyes off him, though on the physical evidence alone, I really should be able to. As Tamsin once said, it's all too easy to imagine him with a bolt through his neck. Laurie's attractiveness has little to do with his looks and everything to do with his being a legend in human form. Imagine touching a legend. Imagine . . .

I sigh, stand up, and bump into Tamsin on my way out of my office. She's wearing a black polo-neck, a tiny white corduroy skirt, black tights and knee-high white boots. If something isn't either white or black, Tamsin won't wear it. She once wore a blue patterned dress to work, and felt insecure all day. The experiment was never repeated. 'Laurie wants you,' she tells me, looking nervous. 'Now, he says. And Raffi wants me. I don't like the atmosphere today. There's something not right.'

I hadn't noticed. There are a lot of things

I don't notice when I'm in the office these days, and only one thing that I do.

'I reckon it's something to do with Helen Yardley's death,' says Tamsin. 'I think she was murdered. No one's told me anything, but two detectives came to see Laurie this morning. CID, not your regular bobbies.'

'Murdered?' Automatically, I feel guilty, then angry with myself. I didn't kill her. She's nothing to do with me; her death's nothing to do with me.

I met her once, a few months ago. I spoke to her briefly, made her a coffee. She'd come in to see Laurie and he'd done his usual trick of vanishing without trace, having confused Monday with Wednesday, or May with June — I can't remember why he wasn't there when he ought to have been. It's an uncomfortable thought, that a woman I met and spoke to might have been murdered. At the time I thought it was strange to meet somebody who'd been in prison for murder, especially someone who looked and seemed so friendly and normal. 'She's just a woman called Helen,' I thought, and for some reason it made me feel so awful that I had to leave the office immediately. I cried all the way home.

Please let her death have nothing to do with why Laurie's summoned me.

'Do you know anything about Sudoku?' call after Tamsin.

She turns. 'As much as I want to. Why?

'Does it involve numbers laid out in square?'

'Yeah, it's like a crossword puzzle g except with numbers instead of letter think, anyway. Or maybe it's an empty and you fill in the numbers. Ask some who's got swirly patterned carpets an house that smells of airfreshener.' She w and heads for Raffi's office, shouting her shoulder, 'And a doll with a ski cover up the spare loo roll.'

Maya leans out of her office, holdin door frame with both hands as if hopi block the strong smell of smoke wit body. 'You know those knitted-doll bo holders are highly collectable?' she say the first time since I've known he doesn't smile, try to hug or pat me me 'honey'. I wonder if I've done som to offend her. Maya is Binary Star's though she prefers 'head honcho' — her nickname for herself, always de with a giggle. In fact, she's only third pecking order. Laurie, as Creative D is the supreme power in the organ closely followed by Raffi, the Fi Director. The two of them control N

you've bored her into an upright coma. And I can tell from her frequent glances over her shoulder that she's eager to get back to her burning cigarette, probably the tenth of the thirty she'll get through today.

Sometimes when Laurie walks past her office, he shouts, 'Lung cancer!' The rest of us pretend to believe Maya's story about having given up years ago. Legend has it that she once burst into tears and tried to pretend it wasn't smoke billowing from her office but steam from a particularly hot cup of tea. None of us has ever actually seen her with a cigarette in her hand.

'I've worked out how she does it,' Tamsin said the other day. 'She keeps the cig and the ashtray in the bottom drawer of her desk. When she wants a drag, she sticks her *whole head* in the drawer . . .' Seeing that I wasn't taking her theory seriously, she said, 'What? The lowest drawer's twice the size of the other two — you could easily fit a human head in there. I dare you to sneak into her office and —'

'Yeah, right,' I cut her off. 'I'm really going to commit career suicide by ransacking the MD's desk.'

'You'd totally get away with it,' said Tamsin. 'You're her baby, remember? Maya's got an underling fetish. She's going to love

35

you whatever you do.'

Once, without irony and in my presence, Maya referred to me as 'the baby of the Binary Star family'. That was when I started to worry that she didn't take me seriously as a producer. Now I know she doesn't. 'Who *cares?*' Tamsin groans whenever I mention it. 'Being taken seriously is seriously overrated.'

Maya quickly loses interest in me and withdraws into her smoky lair without so much as a 'Bye, sugar!' Suits me fine; I never asked to be the object of her frustrated maternal urges. I hurry down the corridor to Laurie's office. I knock and walk in simultaneously, and catch him whizzing his model globe round on its axis with his right foot. He stops and blinks at me, as if he's struggling to remember who I am. In his head, he's probably already had whatever conversation he wanted to have with me, I've agreed to whatever he wanted me to agree to, and done it, and maybe I've even retired or died — maybe Laurie's mind has transported him so far into the future that he no longer knows me. His brain works faster than most people's.

'Tamsin says Helen Yardley was murdered.' *Nice one, Fliss. Bring up the thing you least want to talk about, why don't you?*

'Someone shot her,' Laurie says expressionlessly. He starts to manipulate the globe with his foot again, kicking it so that it goes faster.

'I'm really sorry,' I say. 'It must make it even harder . . . Than if she'd died naturally, I mean. To cope with.' As I'm speaking, I realise I have no idea how to pitch my condolences, towards what sort of loss. Laurie spoke to Helen Yardley every day, often more than once a day. I know how much JIPAC means to him but I've no idea whether he cared about Helen personally, whether he's mourning her as a fellow campaigner or as something more than that.

'She didn't die naturally. She was thirty-eight.' The anger in his eyes still hasn't reached his voice. He sounds as if he's reciting lines he's memorised. 'Whoever murdered her — he's only partly responsible. A whole string of people killed her, Judith Duffy for one.'

I don't know what to say, so I put the card down on his desk. 'Someone sent me this. It came this morning in a matching envelope. No explanatory letter or note, no indication of who it's from.'

'The envelope also had numbers on it?' Miraculously, Laurie seems interested.

'No . . .'

37

'You said "matching".'

'It looked expensive — cream-coloured and sort of ribbed, like the card. It was addressed to "Fliss Benson", so it must be from someone who knows me.'

'Why must it?' Laurie demands.

'They'd have written "Felicity" otherwise.'

He squints at me. 'Is your name Felicity?'

It's the name that goes on the credit sequence of every programme I produce, the name Laurie will have seen on my CV and covering letter when I applied to Binary Star for a job. Seen and then forgotten. On a good day, Laurie makes me feel invisible; on a bad day, nonexistent.

I do what I always do when I'm in his office and there's a possibility that I might get upset: I stare at the miniature solar system on his shelf and list the planets. *Mercury, Earth, Venus, Mars . . .*

Laurie picks up the card and mutters something inaudible as he aims it across his office at the bin in the far corner. It whizzes past my ear, narrowly missing me. 'It's junk,' he says. 'Some kind of marketing teaser, waste of a tree.'

'But it's handwritten,' I say.

'Forget it,' Laurie barks. 'I need to talk to you about something important.' Then, as if noticing me for the first time, he grins and says, 'You're going to love me in a minute.'

I nearly drop to my knees in shock. Never before has he used the word 'love' in my presence. I can say that with absolute certainty. Tamsin and I have speculated about whether he's heard of it, felt it — whether he recognises its existence.

You're going to love me in a minute. I assume he's not using the word 'love' in the physical sense. I imagine us having sex on his desk, Laurie utterly oblivious to the large window through which everyone whose office is on the other side of the courtyard can see us, me anxious about the lack of privacy but too scared of upsetting him to protest . . . *No. Stop this nonsense.* I shut down the thought before it takes hold, afraid I might laugh or scream, and be called upon to explain myself.

'How do you fancy being rich?' Laurie asks me.

Part of the reason I find talking to Laurie so exhausting is that I never know the right answer. There's always a right one and a wrong one — he's very black and white — but he gives you no clues and he's disturbingly unpredictable about everything apart from what he calls 'the crib death mothers witch-hunt'. On that, his views are fixed, but on nothing else. It must be something to do with his brilliant, original mind, and it makes life hellishly hard for anyone who's secretly trying to please him by second-guessing what he'd like them to say while at the same time wanting to look as if they're just being themselves, acting with a hundred per cent integrity and to hell with what anyone else might think. Actually, that's unlikely to be a significant constituency of people, come to think of it. It's probably just me.

'I'd like to be well-off,' I say eventually. 'I don't know about rich. There's only so much money I'd need — a lot more than I've got now, but less than . . . you know . . .' I'm talking rubbish because I'm unprepared. I've never given it a second's thought. I live in a dark, low-ceilinged one-bedroom basement flat in Kilburn, underneath people who have sound-amplifying wooden floors in every room because to lay a carpet anywhere would threaten their upper-middle-class identity, and who seem to spend most evenings jumping around their living room on pogo-sticks, if the noise they make is anything to go by. I have no outside space whatsoever, though I have an excellent view of the pogo-jumpers' immaculate lawn and assortment of rose-bushes, and I can't afford the damp-proofing my flat has urgently needed since I bought it four years ago. Funnily enough, wealth isn't something I dwell on.

'I suppose I'd like to be rich-*ish,*' I say. 'As long as I wasn't getting my money from anything dodgy, like people-smuggling.' I play back my answer in my head, hoping it made me sound ambitious but principled.

'What if you could do my job and earn what I earn?' Laurie asks.

'I couldn't do what you —'

'You can. You will. I'm leaving the company. From Monday, you're me: Creative Director and Executive Producer. I'm on a hundred and forty a year here. From Monday, that's what you'll be on.'

'*What?* Laurie, I —'

'Maybe not officially from Monday, so you might have to wait for the pay-rise, but effectively from Monday . . .'

'Laurie, slow down!' I've never shouted an order at him before. 'Sorry,' I mumble. In my shock, I forgot for a second who he is and who I am. Laurie Nattrass doesn't get yelled at by the likes of me. *From Monday, you're me.* It must be a joke. Or he's confused. Someone as confusing as he is could easily be confused. 'This makes no sense,' I say. Me, Creative Director of Binary Star?

I'm the lowest paid producer in the company. Tamsin, as Laurie's research assistant, earns significantly more than I do. I make programmes that no one but me has any respect for, about warring neighbours and malfunctioning gastric bands — subjects that interest not only me but also millions of viewers, which is why I don't care that I'm regarded by my colleagues as the light relief amid all the purveyors of earnest political documentaries. Raffi refers to my work as 'fluff stuff'.

This has got to be a joke. A trap. Am I supposed to say, 'Ooh, yes, please,' then look like an idiot when Laurie falls about laughing? 'What's going on?' I snap.

He sighs heavily. 'I'm going to Hammerhead. They've made me an offer I can't refuse, a bit like the offer I'm making you. Not that it's about the money. It's time I moved on.'

'But . . . you can't leave,' I say, feeling hollow at the thought. 'What about the film?' He wouldn't go without finishing it; there's no way on earth. Even someone as hard to fathom as Laurie leaves the odd clue here and there as to what makes him tick. Unless the clues I've picked up have been planted by someone determined to mislead me — and it's hard to see how that could happen, since most of them came from Laurie's own mouth — then what makes him tick at a rate of a hundred and twenty seconds to the minute rather than the usual sixty is the film he's making about three crib death murder cases: Helen Yardley, Sarah Jaggard and Rachel Hines.

Everyone at Binary Star calls it 'the film', as if it's the only one the company need concern itself with, the only one we're making or are ever likely to make. Laurie's been working on it since the dawn of time. He insists that it has to be perfect, and keeps changing his mind about the best way to structure it. It's going to be two hours long, and the BBC has told Laurie he can take his pick of the slots, which is unheard of. Or rather, it's unheard of for everyone but Laurie Nattrass, who is a deity in the world of television. If he wanted to make a five-hour film that knocked out both the *News at Six* and the *News at Ten,* the BBC higher-ups would probably lick his boots and say, 'Yes, Master.'

'You're going to make the film,' he tells me with the confidence of someone who has visited the future and knows what happens in it. 'I've emailed everyone involved to say you're taking over from me.'

No. He can't do this.

'I've given them your contact details, work and home . . .'

I want nothing to do with it. I *can't* have anything to do with it. I open my mouth to protest, then remember that Laurie doesn't know my . . . well, it's something no one here knows. I refuse to think of it as a secret and I won't allow myself to feel guilty. I've done nothing wrong. This cannot be a punishment.

'You'll have Maya and Raffi's full support.' Laurie stands up, walks over to the tower of box files by the wall. 'All the information you need's in these. Don't bother moving them to your office. From Monday, this'll be your office.'

'Laurie . . .'

'You'll work on the film and nothing else. Don't let anything get in your way, least of all the filth. I'll be at Hammerhead, but I'll make myself available to you whenever . . .'

'Laurie, stop! The filth? You mean the police? Tamsin said you spoke to them this morning . . .'

'They wanted to know when I'd last seen Helen. If she had any enemies. "How about the entire fucking judicial system, not to mention you lot," I said.' Before I have a chance to remind him that Helen's murder convictions were overturned in the court of appeal by that same judicial system, he says, 'They asked about the film. I told them you'd be exec-ing it as of Monday.'

'You told them before you asked me?' My voice comes out as a high-pitched squeak. My stomach twists, sending prickles of nausea up to my throat. For a few seconds, I daren't open my mouth. 'You emailed everyone and told them I'm . . . When? When did you do that? Who's everyone?' I dig my fingernails into the palms of my hands, feeling horribly out of control. This wasn't supposed to happen; it's all wrong.

Laurie taps the top box file. 'All the names and contacts you need are in here. I haven't got time to go through it all with you, but most of it's self-explanatory. Any more detectives come sniffing around, you're making a documentary about a doctor determined to pervert the course of justice, and three women whose lives she did her best to destroy. Nothing to do with the investigation into Helen's death. They can't stop you.'

'The police don't want the film to be made?' Everything Laurie says makes me feel worse. Even more than usual.

'They haven't said that yet, but they will. They'll trot out some guff about you com-promising their —'

'But I haven't . . . Laurie, I don't want your job! I don't want to make your film.' To clarify, I add, 'I'm saying no.' There, that's better. Perfectly in control.

'No?' He stands back and examines me: a rebellious specimen. Previously compliant, though, he'll be thinking, so what can have gone wrong? He laughs. 'You're turning down a salary that's more than three times what you're on now, and a career-launching promotion? Are you stupid?'

He can't force me — it's impossible. There are some things one can physically force a person to do. Making a documentary is not one of them. Focusing on this helps me to stay calm. 'I've never exec-ed anything before,' I say. 'I'd be completely out of my depth. Don't you want to cooperate with the police, help them find out what happened to Helen?'

'Culver Valley CID couldn't find tennis balls at fucking Wimbledon.'

'I don't understand,' I say. 'If you're going to Hammerhead, why isn't the film going with you?'

'The BBC commissioned Binary Star, not me personally.' Laurie shrugs. 'That's the price I pay for leaving. I lose it.' He leans forward. 'The only way I don't lose it is if I give it to you, and work with you when I

46

can behind the scenes. I need your help here, Fliss. You'd get all the credit, you'd get the salary . . .'

'Why me? Tamsin's the one who's been working on it with you. The woman's a walking miscarriage-of-justice encylopaedia — there's not a detail she doesn't know. Why aren't you trying to force this promotion on her?'

It occurs to me that Laurie's been patronising me. *How do you fancy being rich?* He's always moaning that he can barely afford the mortgage on his four-storey townhouse in Kensington. Laurie comes from a seriously wealthy family. I'd bet everything I've got — which is considerably less than he's got — that he regards his salary at Binary Star as acceptable, nothing more. The offer Hammerhead made him, the one he couldn't refuse, obviously knocked a hundred and forty grand a year into a cocked hat. But of course a hundred and forty a year would be wealth beyond the wildest dreams of a peasant like me . . . I stop in my tracks and realise that, if that is what Laurie's thinking, he's entirely correct, so perhaps it's unfair of me to quibble.

'Tamsin's a research assistant, not a producer,' he says. 'Look, you didn't hear this from me, okay?'

At first I think he's referring to what he's already told me, about the promotion I don't want. Then I realise he's waiting for me to agree before telling me something else. I nod.

'Tamsin's being made redundant. Raffi's talking to her now.'

'*What?* You're joking. Tell me you're joking.'

Laurie shakes his head.

'They can't get rid of her! They can't just . . .'

'It's industry-wide. Everyone's tightening their belts, making cuts where they can.'

'Who made the decision? Was there a vote?' I can't believe Binary Star would keep me and lose Tamsin. She's got loads more experience than I have, and unlike me, she isn't constantly pestering Raffi for a dehumidifier for her office.

'Sit down,' says Laurie impatiently. 'You're making me nervous. Tamsin's the obvious choice for redundancy. She's earning too much to be value for money in the current economic climate. Raffi says we can get a new graduate researcher for half the price, and he's right.'

'This is so out of order,' I blurt out.

'How about you stop worrying about Tamsin and show me some gratitude?'

'What?' Was that the great crusader for justice who said that to me?

'You think Maya wants to pay you what she's paying me?' Laurie chuckles. 'I talked her through her options. I said, "If there's a line in the budget for me, then there's a line in the budget for Fliss." She knows there's no film without my cooperation, not for Binary Star. Ray Hines, Sarah and Glen Jaggard, Paul Yardley, all the solicitors and barristers, the MPs and doctors I've got eating out of the palm of my hand — one word from me and they walk. Whole project falls apart. All I need to do is bide my time, then sign a new contract with the BBC as MD of Hammerhead.'

'You *blackmailed* Maya into agreeing to promote me?' So that's why she was less gushy than usual when I passed her in the corridor. 'Well, I'm sorry, but there's no way I'm —'

'I want this documentary made!' Laurie raises his voice to a level some might describe as shouting. 'I'm trying to do the right thing here, for everyone! Binary Star gets to keep the film, you get a package that's appealing enough to make you get off your arse and do the work . . .'

'And what do you get?' I feel unsteady on my feet. I'd like to sit down, but I won't, not after Laurie ordered me to. *Not when he's just made a snide remark about my arse.*

'I get your full cooperation,' he says, so quietly that I wonder if I imagined his outburst a few seconds earlier. 'Unofficially I'll still run the show, but my involvement will be strictly between you and me.'

'I see,' I say in a tight voice. 'You're not only blackmailing Maya, you're blackmailing me, too.'

Laurie falls into his chair with a groan. 'I'm bribing you. At least be accurate.' He laughs. 'Fuck, did I read you wrong! I thought you were rational.'

I bite my lip, struggling to take in this latest revelation: that Laurie has an idea of what sort of person I am. It means he's spent time thinking about me, even if only a few seconds. It has to mean that.

'You deserve a chance,' he says in a bored voice, as if it's tiresome having to convince me. 'I decided to give you that chance.'

'You want control of the film even after you leave. You chose me because you thought I'd be easier than anyone else to manipulate.' I hope he's impressed by how calm I am. On the surface, at least. Not in a million years did I ever imagine that I would stand in Laurie Nattrass's office and accuse him of bad things. What the hell am I doing? How many innocent citizens has he sprung from their jail cells while I've been whiling away my spare time leafing through *heat* magazine on the sofa, or shouting abuse at *Strictly Come Dancing?* What if I've completely misread the situation and I'm the one in the wrong?

Laurie leans back in his chair. Slowly, he shakes his head. 'Fine. You don't want to exec the documentary that's going to win every prize going? You don't want to be Creative Director? Then why don't you make Maya's day: tell her you want out of the deal, and watch her lose any respect for you that she ever had.'

'The *deal?*' I am bloody well not in the wrong here. 'You mean the deal I wasn't party to, the one that involves my life and career?'

'You'll never be offered anything again,' Laurie sneers. 'Not at Binary Star, not anywhere. How long do you think it'll be before you're standing behind Tamsin in the dole queue?'

Mercury, Earth, Venus, Mars, Jupiter, Saturn, Neptune, Uranus, Pluto.

'I don't feel comfortable getting a pay-rise of a hundred grand a year when my friend's losing her job,' I say as unemotionally as possible. 'Of course I'd like more money,

51

but I also like being able to sleep at night.'

'You, lose sleep? Don't make me laugh!'

I take a deep breath and say, 'I don't know what you imagine you know about me, but you're wrong.' Then I feel like a scumbag for implying that I might have an active social conscience, when in fact all the sleep I've lost has either been love-related, or . . .

Or nothing. I can't let myself think about that now, or I'll start crying and blurt out the whole story to Laurie. How hideously embarrassing would that be?

How much would he hate me if he knew?

'Jesus,' he mutters. 'Look, I apologise, okay? I thought I was doing you a favour.'

What happens if I say yes? I could say yes. No, I couldn't. What the hell's wrong with me? I'm panicking, and upset about Tamsin, and it's affected my brain. The state I'm in, it's probably sensible to say as little as possible.

Laurie swings his chair round so that I can't see him. 'I told the board you were worth what I think you're worth,' he says flatly. 'They nearly shat themselves, but I made a good case and I talked them round. Do you know what that means?'

A good case? *Do what I say or I'll put the kibosh on the film* — that's his idea of a good case? He can't even be bothered to put a convincing gloss on it; that's how little he values me.

Without waiting for my response, he says, 'It means a hundred and forty a year is now officially what you're worth. Think of yourself as a share on the stock market. Your value's just gone up. If you tell Maya you don't want it, if you say, "Yes, please, I'd like a pay-rise but not *that* much, because I'm not *that* good, so can we please negotiate downwards?" — do that and you plummet to rock-bottom.' He spins round to face me. 'You're worthless,' he says emphatically, as if I might have missed the point.

That's it: my limit. I turn and walk out. Laurie doesn't call after me or follow me. What does he think I'm going to do? Take the promotion and the money? Resign? Lock myself in a toilet cubicle for a good cry? Does he feel at all guilty about what he's just done to me?

Why the hell do I care how he feels?

I march back to my office, slam the door, grab the damp towel from the top of the radiator and wipe away condensation until my arm aches. A few minutes later, the window is still sopping wet and now so is my jumper. All I've succeeded in doing is flicking the water all over myself. Why doesn't someone think to put an end to world drought by collecting condensation? My window alone could irrigate most of Africa. Why doesn't Bob Geldof sort it out? It must be Bob Geldof I'm angry with, since it can't be Laurie. I've got a typed document buried somewhere in my desk, instructing me, among other things, never to allow myself to get angry with Laurie.

I used to look at it all the time when Tamsin first gave it to me. I thought it was hilarious, more hilarious still when she told me she gave a copy to every woman who came to work at Binary Star. About a year ago, it started to lose its appeal for me, and I stuffed it in my desk, underneath the flower-patterned lining paper that someone who worked here before me put in all the drawers.

No point trying to kid myself that I can't remember which drawer it's in; I know exactly where it is, even if I've spent much of the last twelve months pretending it isn't there. I pull out the files and the drawer-liner, and there it is, face down. Steeling myself, I pick it up and turn it over.

It's headed, in capitals, 'TAMSIN'S SEVEN COMMANDMENTS', with a subheading in italics, *'To be borne in mind at all times in relation to Laurie Nattrass'*.

The list reads as follows:

1) It's not you. It's him.
2) Have no expectations, or, alternatively, expect absolutely anything.
3) Accept what you can't change. Don't waste time getting angry or upset.
4) Bear in mind that it's only because he's a man that he's got a reputation for being 'brilliant but difficult'. If he were an equally talented woman who behaved in exactly the same way, he'd be ridiculed as a mental old bat instead of headhunted for all the best jobs.
5) Beware of imagining that he has hidden depths. Assume his true self is the bit that you can see.
6) Don't be attracted by his power. Some people are powerful in a good way, enhancing the confidence of others and making them believe anything is possible. Not him. Get close to him and you'll find that, as his power seems to grow, yours rapidly diminishes. Look out for a feeling of helplessness and the growing conviction that you must be fairly rubbish.
7) Whatever you do, DO NOT FALL IN

LOVE WITH HIM.

According to at least one of Tamsin's criteria, I have failed spectacularly.

2
7/10/09

'Unusual, yes,' said DS Sam Kombothekra. 'Suspicious, no. How could it be?' If trying to be fair to everyone ever felt like too much effort, Sam hid it well.

He and DC Simon Waterhouse were on their way to today's second briefing. It had probably started by now. Sam was walking a little too fast, trying to look as if being a few minutes late didn't make him nervous.

Simon knew it did. Lateness belonged to that vast super-set of things that displeased Detective Inspector Giles Proust, known unofficially as the Snowman because his regular avalanches of disapproval descended as tangibly as boulders of ice, and were as hard to shake off. After long years of trying, Simon had finally succeeded in insulating himself against Proust's condemnation: the inspector's opinions no longer mattered to him. Sam was a newer addition to Culver Valley CID and still had a long way to go.

The incident room was packed by the time they got there, with nowhere left to sit and hardly any space to stand. Simon and Sam had to make do with the doorway. Between the bodies and over the heads of dozens of detectives, most of whom had been drafted in from Silsden and Rawndesley, Simon could see Proust's trim, immobile form at the front. He wasn't looking in their direction, but Simon could see the Snowman noticing his and Sam's lateness. A tilt of an eyebrow, a twitch of the jaw — that was all it took. Wasn't it supposed to be women who were passive aggressive? Proust was both: passive aggressive and aggressive aggressive. He boasted a full repertoire of noxious behaviours.

It was clear from the noise in the room that they'd missed nothing; the meeting hadn't got going yet. 'Why now?' Simon addressed his question to Sam's ear, raising his voice to be heard over the mix of murmured conversations and the irregular drumming of feet against table legs. He was still suspicious. More so, if anything, for being told there was no cause. 'Two briefings a day? It's not like this is the first murder we've ever worked. Even with the multiples we've had in the past, he's barely stuck his nose out of his box apart from to carp at you or Charlie, whoever's been skipper. Now he's leading every —'

'Helen Yardley's the first . . . celebrity's the wrong word, but you know what I mean,' said Sam.

Simon laughed. 'You think the Snowman's keen to get his carrot nose and coal eyes in the papers? He hates —'

'No choice,' Sam interrupted him again. 'A case like this, he's going to get publicity one way or another, so he might as well get it for taking a strong lead. As SIO, case this visible nationally, he's got to step up.'

Simon decided to let it lie. He'd noticed that Sam, who normally was courtesy itself, cut him off mid-sentence whenever he talked about Proust. Charlie, Simon's fiancée and former sergeant, put it down to Sam's concern for proper professional conduct: you didn't badmouth the boss. Simon suspected it had more to do with the preservation of self-respect. Even someone as patient and hierarchy-conscious as Sam could barely put up with what he had to put up with from the Snowman. Denial was his coping mechanism, one that must have been made all but impossible by Simon's constant dissection of Proust's despotism.

Ultimately, it came down to personal preference. Sam preferred to pretend he and

his team weren't abused daily by a narcis-
sistic megalomaniac and helpless to do
anything about it, whereas Simon had long
ago decided the only way to stay sane was
to focus, all the time, on exactly what was
going on and how bad it was, so that there
was no danger it would ever start to seem
normal. He'd become the unofficial archi-
vist of Proust's abhorrent personality. These
days he almost looked forward to the inspector's offensive outbursts; each one was
further proof that Simon was right to have
cut off the goodwill supply and all benefits
of the doubt.

'You'd think Proust had an evil ulterior
motive whatever he did, even if he dragged
sacks of grain across the desert to famine
victims,' Charlie had teased him last night.
'You're so used to hating everything about
him, it's become a Pavlovian response — he
must be doing something wrong, even if you
don't yet know what it is.'

She's probably right, thought Simon. Sam
was probably right: there was no way out of
the limelight for Proust on this one. He had
to be seen to care, so he was doing it with
gusto, while secretly counting the days until
he could revert to his usual mode of doing
as little as possible.

'He's bound to feel responsible, like we all

do,' Sam said. 'Professional considerations aside, you'd have to have a heart of stone not to want to pull out all the stops in a case like this. I know it's early days and there's no proof this murder's connected to the reason we all know Helen Yardley's name, but . . . you have to ask yourself, would she be dead now if it weren't for us?'

Us. By the time Simon had worked out what Sam meant, Proust was banging his 'World's Greatest Grandad' mug on the wall to get the room's attention. *Sound to silence in less than three seconds.* The Silsford and Rawndesley lot were quick learners. Simon had done his best to warn everyone yesterday. It turned out none of them needed the tip-off; spine-chilling tales of the Snowman's mercilessness had done the rounds at both nicks, apparently.

'Detectives, officers, we have a murder weapon,' Proust said. 'Or, rather, we don't have it yet, but we know what it is, which means we're closer to finding it.'

That was debatable, Simon thought. He allowed no statement the inspector made to pass without rigorous scrutiny; everything had to be challenged, albeit in silence much of the time. Was this or that fact a genuine fact, or merely a dogmatically expressed opinion masquerading as the one and only truth? Simon saw the irony; he had the Snowman's perennially closed mind to thank for his determination to keep his own open.

'Helen Yardley was shot with an M9 Beretta 9 millimetre,' Proust went on. 'Not a converted Baikal IZH, as Firearms told us on Monday, nor a 9 millimetre Makarov police gun, as they told us on Tuesday. Since it's now Wednesday, we have no alternative but to believe them a third time.'

An angry-looking Rick Leckenby stood up. 'Sir, you forced me to speculate before I'd —'

'Sergeant Leckenby, while you're on your feet, do you want to tell us a bit about today's gun of choice?'

Leckenby turned to face the room. 'The M9 Beretta 9 mil is US army standard issue, and it's been in circulation since the 1980s, which means it could have come back from Iraq, from the first Gulf War or more recently, or from any other war zone, any time in the last twenty, twenty-five years. Obviously, depending on how long it's been in the UK, that potentially reduces traceability.'

'So we're looking for anyone with links to the American armed forces?'

'Or the British,' said DC Chris Gibbs. 'A

Brit could have got it off a Yank and brought it back.'

'No, sir, that's the point I'm trying to make,' Leckenby answered Proust. 'I'd say there's no grounds for assuming the killer's got links with the military. If the gun entered the UK in, say, 1990, there's a good chance it's been through several owners since then. What I would say is —'

'Don't tell us what you *would* say, Sergeant — just say it.'

'The gun on the streets at the moment, used in more than half of urban shootings, is the Baikal IZH gas pistol. You buy them in Eastern Europe, convert them, and you've got an effective short-distance murder weapon. My first thought, at the scene, was that since Mrs Yardley was killed at close range, and since Baikals account for the majority of guns we're seeing lately, and based on the amount of residue on the wall as well as on the body and the carpet around it, the likelihood was that a Baikal killed her. It was only after the bullet was retrieved from her brain and we had a chance to examine it that we were able to link it to the M9 Beretta 9 mil.'

'Which means what?' Proust asked.

'It could mean nothing,' said Leckenby. 'Either gun, Baikal or Beretta, could theoretically be in the possession of anybody. But my gut feeling is, street shooters don't have M9 Beretta 9 mils. They just don't. So . . . this killer's as likely to be anybody as he is to be gang-connected or a known offender.'

'He or she,' a female DC from Rawndesley called out.

'If the murder weapon is standard US military issue, Sergeant, then we're going to look for anyone with links to the American army, and, as DC Gibbs sensibly suggests, to our own,' said Proust. When he spoke with this sort of slow deliberation, you were intended to understand that he was taking care not to allow the dam of his disgust to burst. 'You've no way of knowing how many hands it's passed through. Guns are like cars, presumably — some sold on every three years, others loyally tended by one careful owner over a lifetime. Yes?'

'I suppose so, sir,' said Leckenby.

'Good. Make sure you have a full resumé of the M9 Beretta, complete with colour pictures, by tomorrow morning, to distribute to everybody,' the Snowman ordered. 'Assuming you haven't changed your mind by then and decided the murder weapon was a turbo-charged pea-shooter from the shores of Lake Windermere. Interview teams — you'll need to start from scratch. Everyone you've already spoken to, Helen Yardley's friends, family, neighbours, etc — you'll need to speak to them again and find the military connection if it's there to be found. CCTV teams — you're looking for any cars with number plates that are either American or armed forces or both. Or — and I hope this goes without saying — anyone known personally to the Yardleys. CCTV could have been a sizeable headache for us, given that the two cameras nearest to Bengeo Street are on the busiest stretch of the Rawndesley Road, but thankfully we've done well with witnesses — more of which in a moment — so for the time being we're prioritising Monday morning between 7.45 and 8.15 a.m. and Monday afternoon between 5 and 6.10 p.m. for the camera outside the Picture House. For the one by the entrance to Market Place, the times we're looking at are slightly different: 7.30 to 8 a.m. and 5.15 to 6.25 p.m. Of particular interest is any car going in the direction of Bengeo Street during one of the earlier time slots and away from it in the later ones.'

The DS with overall charge of the CCTV team, David Prescott from Rawndesley, raised his hand and said, 'A lot of people driving down the Rawndesley Road at rush

65

hour are going to be people Helen Yardley knew. She was a childminder. How many children did she mind whose parents lived in Spilling or Silsford and worked in Rawndesley?'

'I'm not asking your team to red-flag anybody on the basis of CCTV footage alone, Sergeant. I'm simply suggesting that it's an avenue of enquiry.'

'Yes, sir.'

'We don't even know if the killer drove to Bengeo Street or walked, not for certain,' said Proust. 'If he walked, he might have come from Turton Street or Hopelea Street.'

'He could have cycled,' said DC Colin Sellers.

'Or perhaps he fell out of the sky and landed in the Yardleys' front garden,' the Snowman snapped. 'DS Prescott, instruct your officers not to bother with the CCTV footage until we've contacted all the hot-air-balloon suppliers in the Culver Valley.'

The silence in the room was as thick as glue.

Another one for the archive, thought Simon. The killer might have driven or walked, but the idea that he could have cycled to the murder scene was laughable and far-fetched, because cycling wasn't something Giles Proust ever did. Therefore

it was contemptible and not worth mentioning.

'Moving on to witnesses, then,' said the
inspector glacially. 'Mrs Stella White of 16
Bengeo Street — that's the house directly
opposite number 9, the Yardley house —
saw a man walking up the Yardleys' path to
the front door at 8.20 on Monday morning.
She didn't see if he got out of a car — her
first sighting of him was on the Yardleys'
property. Mrs White was strapping her son
Dillon into the car to drive him to school,
not paying much attention to what was happening on the other side of the road, but
she was able to give us a general description: a man between the ages of thirty-five
and fifty with dark hair, wearing darkish
clothes including a coat, smartly dressed,
though not in a suit. He wasn't carrying
anything, she said, though an M9 Beretta 9
millimetre gun would easily fit in a large
coat pocket.'

A description like that was about as useful
as no description at all, thought Simon. By
tomorrow Mrs White, if she was anything
like most witnesses, would be saying that
maybe the dark hair wasn't so dark, and
maybe the coat was a dressing-gown.

'By the time Mrs White drove out on to
the road, there was no sign of the man. She

67

says there wasn't long enough for him to have gone anywhere but inside number 9. We know there was no break-in, so did Helen Yardley let him in? If so, did she know him, or did he say something plausible enough to get himself inside when she opened the door? Was he a lover, a relative, a double-glazing salesman? We need to find out.'

'Did Mrs White see or hear Helen Yardley open her front door?' someone asked.

'She thinks she might have, but she's not sure,' said Proust. 'Now, at number 11 Bengeo Street we've got eighty-three-year-old Beryl Murie, who, in spite of her partial deafness, heard a loud noise at 5 p.m. that might well have been a gunshot. She said it sounded like a firework, which is an easy mistake to make if you're unfamiliar with the sound of an M9 Beretta 9 millimetre being discharged, as I think we can safely assume most retired piano teachers are. Miss Murie was able to be precise about the time because she was listening to the radio and the five o'clock news had just started when she heard the loud noise. She said it startled her. She also said it sounded as if it had come from Helen Yardley's house. So, assuming we've got a man entering the house at 8.20 a.m. and the fatal shot fired at 5 p.m., what's happening in between? We can't assume the man Mrs White saw is the killer, but until we track him down and find out for certain, we have to consider the possibility that he might be. Sergeant Kombothekra?'

'Still no joy, sir,' Sam called out from the back of the room.

Proust nodded grimly. 'If another day passes and we haven't found and eliminated Mr Morning Visitor, I'll put my money on him being our man. If he is, and he was in Helen Yardley's house with her for more than eight hours before he shot her, what was happening during those hours? Why not shoot her straight away? She wasn't raped or tortured. Apart from being shot in the back of the head, she wasn't injured. So, did he go there to talk to her, thinking he might or might not shoot her, depending on the outcome of the conversation?'

Simon raised his hand. After a few seconds of pretending not to see it, Proust nodded at him.

'Don't we also have to consider the possibility that the gun belonged to the Yardleys? We can't assume the man brought it with him. It might already have been in the house. Given the Yardleys' history —'

'The Yardleys have no history of illegally

69

possessing firearms,' the Snowman cut him off. 'There's a thin line between exploring all reasonable avenues of possibility and squandering our resources on tosh that, in our desire to be egalitarian, we've elevated to the status of hypothesis. Everyone in this room needs to bear that in mind. We're forty-eight hours into this investigation and we're without a suspect — you all know what that means. We've already alibied and eliminated Helen Yardley's friends, family and close acquaintances. This is shaping up to be a stranger murder, which, for us, is about as bad as it gets, and all the more reason to channel our efforts in the right direction.'

'You were right to raise it,' Sam muttered to Simon. 'Better for us to focus on it and dismiss it than not to think of it at all.'

'Paul Yardley returned from work at 6.10 p.m., found his wife's body and phoned the police,' said Proust. 'He found no one else in the house and neither did the first officers to the scene. Some time between 5 and 6.10 p.m., the killer left 9 Bengeo Street. Someone must have seen him. You know what that means: house-to-house is top priority, and let's extend it. Someone come up with a new mile-radius.'

The Snowman walked over to the board

where the enlarged crime scene photographs were displayed. 'Here's the input wound,' he said, pointing at a picture of the back of Helen Yardley's head. 'Look at the scorch marks. The gun was so close it might even have been touching her. From the position of the body, it's a strong possibility that she was in the corner of the room facing the wall when she was shot. A 9-mm bullet in the brain at close range doesn't spin a person round. But there's nothing on the wall next to where she fell, so what was she doing standing there? What was she looking at? Had he marched her over there to kill her because it's the only part of the room that can't be seen from the window? Or was she standing there for some other reason, and he came up behind her, knowing she wouldn't see the gun?'

Simon had missed some of that. He was still thinking about what Sam had said to him. 'Better to focus on it and *dismiss* it?' he said behind his clenched fist so that Proust wouldn't notice. 'Why are the Yardleys less likely to have a shooter than this dark-haired man we can't find?'

Sam didn't sigh, but he looked as if he wanted to. He shook his head to indicate that he wasn't going to risk answering. It occurred to Simon that Sam might find it a damn sight easier to work with the Snowman than he did at present if he didn't also have to work with Simon.

Stand in the corner. Face the wall. Simon considered drawing attention to the symbolism — a teacher punishing a child — then decided against it. Today was one of those days when everyone would disagree with him whatever he said. And he would disagree with the world, as he so often did. A stranger murder? No. Proust was wrong. Collective police responsibility for Helen Yardley's death because eleven out of twelve civilian jurors voted to send her to prison for murder? *Fuck off.*

'Where are we with fingerprints and swabbing?' Proust asked.

DS Klair Williamson stood up. 'Fingerprints — no matches with any on our database. Lots belonging to friends and family, quite a few sets unidentified, but that's only to be expected. We've swabbed everybody for forensic evidence of weapon discharge and got nothing so far.'

'Predictable,' said Proust. 'Gunpowder residue perishes easily. If our killer knows that, he'll have had a thorough wash. All the same, I'm sure I don't need to tell any of you that it would be a grave mistake to drop this angle prematurely. Do your utmost to preserve every possible forensic opportunity. Keep up the swabbing until I say otherwise, and make a note of the names of anyone who gives you an argument about it.'

'Yes, sir,' said Williamson.

'We also want the names of any unsavouries who have raised their heads above the parapet, so keep going through emails, letters, anything you can find — to JIPAC or to Helen Yardley personally. Our killer could have been unknown to her but obsessed with her.'

Simon heard grunts of agreement; people seemed to like this idea. He didn't. Why was no one pointing out the obvious? It wasn't the simple either-or of someone close to the victim versus total stranger, not in this case. There was a third possibility. Surely he wasn't the only one it had occurred to.

'Moving on, then, to the most inexplicable aspect of this killing,' said the Snowman. 'The card protruding from Helen Yardley's skirt pocket.' He jerked his head in the direction of the picture on the board. 'Her fingerprints are on it, as well as another set we can't identify. It's likely the killer put it in the pocket after he shot her and left the top half visible to draw our attention. Also likely is that the sixteen numbers on the card, arranged as they are in four rows of four, have some meaning for the killer. Any new ideas on this — from anyone?'

All over the room, heads were shaking.

'Right, well, we'll wait to hear back from Bramshill and GCHQ.'

There was a general groan and mutters of 'waste of time'.

'What about seeing if there's anybody in the Maths department of a university who knows anything about codes?' Proust suggested. 'And I mean a proper university, not a former polytechnic or an accredited branch of Pizza Hut.'

The reaction to his suggestion was disproportionately enthusiastic. Simon wondered how many tyrants questioned the rapture with which their every utterance was received. The sixteen numbers had been going round in his head all day: 2, 1, 4, 9 . . . Or maybe it was 21, 49, or perhaps you were supposed to start at the bottom and read backwards: 0, 2, 6 . . .

'As a last resort, there's always the press,' said Proust. 'We let them print the sixteen numbers and see what happens.'

'We'd have every loony in the Culver Valley ringing in, saying they'd got the numbers off an extra-terrestrial's lottery ticket,' said Colin Sellers.

Proust smiled. A few people risked laughing. Simon pushed down a rising swell of anger. Any sign that the inspector might be enjoying even the briefest moment of happiness made him want to do damage to somebody. Luckily, such signs were rare.

'What about a profiler?' someone called out. *Someone else who doesn't think the Snowman deserves a lighthearted moment and knows how to put a stop to it.*

Simon waited for Proust to breathe frost, but, surprisingly, he said, 'If we make no progress on the card in the next twenty-four hours, I'll be asking for a profiler to be brought in. In the meantime, while we wait for the code teams at Bramshill and GCHQ to get back to us, we do the dull legwork: which retailers supply this kind of card? What sort of pen does the ink come from? *Well?*' he roared suddenly. A collective shudder rippled through the room.

'Sir, we're still pursuing that,' said the unfortunate DC from Silsford who'd been tasked to find out. 'I'll chase it up.'

'You do that, detective. I want two hundred and fifty per cent effort from all of you. And don't forget your ABC. Let's hear it, DC Gibbs.'

'Assume nothing, believe nobody, check everything,' Chris Gibbs muttered, his face colouring. Simon was the one the Snowman usually nominated to make a tit of himself in front of a crowd. Why had he been spared this time?

'Our mystery caller at 9 Bengeo Street might turn out to be a false lead, so let's make sure he's not our only lead,' said Proust. 'As someone's already pointed out, we could be looking for a female. I want brains switched on and fully serviced round the clock. I don't need to tell you all why this case matters more than any you've worked before.'

'Don't you?' Simon murmured. Beside him, Sam was nodding. And yet the thing that marked out Helen Yardley as different from other murder victims had barely been mentioned, not this morning and not now.

'It's been forty-eight hours,' said the Snowman. 'If we don't get a result soon, they'll cut this squad in half, and that'll just be for starters. You'll all be going back to your own nicks — something I'm sure at least those of you from Rawndesley are keen to avoid. All right, that's it for today. DS Kombothekra, DC Waterhouse — my office.'

Simon was in no mood to wait and see what Proust wanted. 'How come you're happy to ditch the "assume nothing" part when it comes to the gun?' he asked, as soon as he'd slammed the door behind him. This time Sam did sigh. 'Why's Helen or Paul Yardley less likely to own an M9 Beretta than this dark-haired man we can't find?'

'Sergeant Kombothekra, explain to DC Waterhouse why a killer is more likely than his victim to bring a gun to the party.'

'The Yardleys fought to keep their only surviving child, and they lost. Think about what that must have meant to them. You've got a daughter . . .'

'Mention her name, Waterhouse, and I'll yank your tongue out by the root. My daughter has nothing to do with this.'

You ought to hear what Colin Sellers has said about her over the years, what he'd like to do to which bits of her. Simon tried again. 'Paige Yardley lives less than two miles from Bengeo Street, with new parents who've changed her name and won't let her birth family anywhere near her. If I was Helen or Paul Yardley in that situation — someone stole my kid and, to add insult to injury, the law was on their side — I might get myself a shooter. If I'd had to stand in court and watch helplessly as my wife got two life sentences for crimes I was sure she hadn't committed —'

'You've made your point,' said Proust.

'I've made part of my point, and I'll make the rest of it now: Helen Yardley spent nine years behind bars. If she wasn't guilty, revenge might have been on her mind once she got out. And even if —'

'Enough!'

Simon ducked as something flew past his head. Proust's 'World's Greatest Grandad' mug hit the corner of the filing cabinet and smashed. Sam bent to pick up the pieces. 'Leave that!' the Snowman bellowed. 'Open the top drawer of the cabinet. There are two copies of Helen Yardley's book in there. Take one for yourself and give one to Waterhouse.'

The only way Simon could keep his mouth shut was by vowing to do what he should have done years ago and put in an official complaint. He'd do it first thing tomorrow morning. Proust would come back at him with counter-accusations of disrespect, sarcasm, disobedience. *True, true, true.* No one would speak up for Simon apart from Charlie, and she'd only do it because of her personal feelings for him, not because she would disagree with Proust's portrayal of him as every line manager's nightmare.

Sam handed him a copy of *Nothing But Love* by Helen Yardley and Gaynor Mundy. Simon had interviewed Mundy earlier today. She'd told him Helen had written most of the book herself and been a dream to work with. The cover was white, with a picture of a pair of knitted baby bootees at its centre. Curls of yellow paper protruded from the sides of several pages: Post-it strips. Simon glanced at Sam's copy and saw that it was the same.

'Let's start again,' said the Snowman, loading each word with a hefty dollop of patience in the face of provocation. *Not asking for another chance; bestowing one with self-conscious generosity.* 'I called the two of you in here because you're my best detectives — personality disorders notwithstanding, Waterhouse. I need to know that I can count on you.'

'You can, sir,' said Sam.

'Count on us to do what?' Simon asked. He could only occasionally manage a 'sir'. Less and less often these days.

'I want you both to read that book,' said Proust. 'I've read it, and I don't think there's anything in it that adds to what we know already, but you might spot something I missed. The sections I've marked are the parts where I'm mentioned by name. I arrested Helen Yardley three days after the death of her second child, and charged her with the murders of both her children. I gave evidence at her trial. I was a DS at the time. Superintendent Barrow was my DI.'

Not looking at Sam, not reacting at all, took all Simon's willpower.

'As far as I'm concerned, nobody working this murder needs to read the book apart from the two of you. At the briefing tomorrow morning, I intend to tell everyone about my . . . involvement. However irrelevant it is to the business at hand, I'd like it to be out in the open.'

Irrelevant? Was he joking? Testing them?

'I won't be mentioning the role played by Superintendent Barrow, whose name does not feature in the book.'

Had Barrow told Proust to leave his name out of it? Had the two of them been arguing behind the scenes about what to reveal and what to withhold? The Snowman had never bothered to conceal his hatred for Barrow, but it had blended so seamlessly, over the years, with his antipathy for everyone else he knew that Simon had never questioned it or wondered about its origins.

'Ordinarily, as I'm sure you're aware, any officer who charged someone with murder as a DS would not then lead the investigation into the murder of that same person as a DI. The Chief Constable, the Assistant Chief Constable and Superintendent Barrow didn't want me as SIO on Helen Yardley's murder. And yet here I am — SIO on Helen Yardley's murder. Go ahead, Waterhouse. You look as if you have a question.'

'Am I getting the wrong end of the stick, or are you implying that Barrow, the Chief and the Assistant Chief don't want it known that they were instrumental in sending Helen Yardley to prison?' Simon stopped short of asking Proust if he'd threatened to go public about their role in an extremely visible miscarriage of justice if they assigned the investigation into Helen Yardley's murder to any DI but him.

'The Chief and the Assistant Chief weren't involved,' said Proust. 'Though as Superintendent Barrow's superior officers, they have his best interests at heart, as well as the best interests of Culver Valley Police Service.'

Sam Kombothekra cleared his throat, but said nothing.

'So . . .' Simon began.

'In so far as your hypothesis applied to Superintendent Barrow, Waterhouse, I *would say*, to borrow a phrase from Sergeant Leckenby, that your purchase on the stick needs no lateral adjustment.'

'What . . . ? Oh.' Simon got it, just in time to avoid making an idiot of himself.

'Will you both read the book?' Proust

asked. 'It's not an order. I'm asking you as a favour to me personally.'

'Yes, sir,' said Sam.

Simon had ordered *Nothing But Love* from Amazon this morning, after talking to Gaynor Mundy. He would read his own copy when it arrived, because he wanted to — nothing to do with being asked. *A favour.* He'd have preferred it to be an order. Friends asked favours; the Snowman was no friend.

'Tomorrow morning I want the two of you standing on either side of me for the briefing and tasking, so get in early,' said Proust, more relaxed now that the meeting seemed to be going his way. 'I want everybody to see that I have your full support when I announce that from now on, anyone who makes a remark along the lines of "No smoke without fire" or "Just because they let her out doesn't mean she was innocent" will be formally disciplined, no matter where and in what circumstances that remark is made — as somebody's idea of a joke, under the influence of alcohol. Any bobby who so much as whispers the words in his bedroom in the middle of the night, with his head buried in his duvet — he'll rue the day. From now on, you two are my eyes and ears. You hear any comments like that, you report them to me, whether the commentator is your closest friend or someone you hardly know. You pick up on any bad attitudes, I want to hear about them.'

Simon couldn't believe Sam was nodding.

'I know I can count on your support, and I'm grateful for it,' said Proust curtly. 'Waterhouse, any other points you want to raise, now I've said my piece?'

There was plenty more Simon could have said — had been planning to say — about where he thought the investigation was going wrong, but until he'd had a chance to think about what he'd just heard, he didn't want to say another word in the Snowman's presence. *Count on nothing, shithead.*

'Let's call it a night, then,' said Proust, who would have called it whatever he wanted to call it, whether it was morning, night or the middle of the afternoon.

3
WEDNESDAY 7 OCTOBER 2009

'It's exactly the kick up the arse I need —
that's the way I'm looking at it,' says Tamsin, taking a gulp from her sixth gin and
tonic of the evening. 'Control freak like me,
any sort of disruption to my routine has to
be good for me.' She's started to slur her
words. Her top lip keeps slipping on her
bottom one, like a smooth-soled shoe over
snow.

I could sneak off to the loo, phone Joe and
tell him to come and pick her up, but if I
leave her unattended she's bound to accost
a stranger, and there are at least two men at
the bar who look likely to have chloroform-
soaked hankies in their pockets. The Grand
Old Duke of York is the only pub within
walking distance of work that can be guaranteed to have nobody from Binary Star in
it, which is why we've braved the bad beer
and creepy loners. Tonight, anything's better than bumping into Maya, Raffi or Laurie

at the French House.

'My life's been too safe for too long,' says Tamsin decisively. 'I should take more risks.' That's it: no way am I letting her get the tube home. I'll have to wait until she passes out to phone Joe. Another fifteen minutes, half an hour maximum. 'There are no surprises — you know what I mean? Up at seven, in the shower, two Weetabix and a fruit smoothie for breakfast, walk to the tube station, in work by half past eight, running round all day after Laurie, wearing myself out trying to . . . *decipher* him, home by eight, eat dinner with Joe, snuggled up on the sofa by half nine to watch an episode of whatever DVD box set we're on, bed at eleven. Where's the spark? Where's the dyna . . . dianne. . . . ?'

'Dynamism?' I suggest.

'Whereas now I've got a real challenge: no job!' She tries to sound upbeat about it. 'No income! I'll have to find a way of keeping a roof over our heads.'

'Can Joe cover the mortgage?' I ask, feeling terrible for her. 'Temporarily, until you find something else?'

'No, but we could rent out Joe's study to someone chilled-out who wouldn't mind having to walk through our bedroom every time he needed a wee in the middle of the night,' says Tamsin brightly. 'He might become our friend. When was the last time I made a new friend?'

'When you met me.' I try to prise the gin and tonic from her grasp. 'Give me that. I'll go and get you an orange juice.'

Her hands tighten around her glass. 'You're a control freak too,' she says accusingly. 'We both are. We need to learn to go with the flow.'

'I'm worried the flow might be of vomit. Why don't I ring Joe and he can —'

'*Nooo.*' Tamsin pats my hand. 'I'm *fine.* I whole-heartedly embrace this opportunity for change. Maybe I'll start wearing blue or red instead of black and white all the time. Hey — know what I'm gonna do tomorrow?'

'Die of alcohol poisoning?'

'Go to an exhibition. There must be something good on at the National Portrait Gallery, or the Hayward. And while I'm doing that, you know what you're gonna do?' She burps loudly. 'You're going to be in Maya's office saying, "Yes, please, I'll take that extremely well-paid job." If you feel guilty about earning too much money, you can give some to me. Just a little bit. Or maybe half.'

'Hey — did you just suggest something

that makes sense?'

'I believe I did.' Tamsin giggles. 'Socialism in miniature. There'd only be two of us involved, but the principle's the same: everything you have is mine, and everything I have is yours, except I haven't got anything.'

'You need an income. I've just been offered more than three times what I'm on now . . . No, that'd be mad. Wouldn't it?' I haven't drunk as much as she has, but I've had a fair bit.

'What's the prollem?' she slurs, wide-eyed. 'No one needs to find out apart from you and me. Laurie's right: if you blow this chance, everyone'll think you're a dick. And if you hoard your wealth like a Scroogey miser . . .'

'So this is the great challenge that was missing from your life? Forcing me to take a job I don't want so that you can nick half my salary?' I'm not even sure she means what she's saying. I wait for her to tell me she's only kidding.

'You wouldn't have to fund me for ever,' she says instead. 'Just until I sort myself out with a new career. I'd quite like to work for the UN, as an interpreter.'

I sigh. 'Do you speak anything, apart from English and Pissed?'

'I could learn. Russian and French is a good combination, apparently. I did some Googling before I left the office. For the last time *ever,*' she adds pointedly, reminding me of her hard-done-by status. 'If you've got those two languages . . .'

'Which you haven't.'

'. . . then all you need's a translation qualification, which you can get at Westminster Uni, and the UN'll snap you up.'

'When? In four years' time?'

'More like six.'

'How about I support you while you look for a job *in your field?*' I stress the last three words. 'With your track record, you could get one tomorrow.'

'No, thanks,' says Tamsin. 'No more TV for me. TV's the rut I was stuck in until today. I'm serious, Fliss. Ever since I left university, I've been a wage-slave. I don't want to rush out and find new shackles, now that I'm free. I want to do some living — walk in the park, go ice-skating . . .'

'What happened to learning French and Russian?' I ask.

She waves away my concern. 'There's plenty of time for that. Maybe I'll see if there's a local evening class or something, but mainly I want to . . . take stock, walk around, soak up the atmosphere . . .'

'You live in Wood Green.'

'Could you stretch to a flat in Knights-bridge if I'm willing to settle for one bedroom?'

'Stop,' I tell her, deciding the joke has gone on long enough. 'This is exactly why I don't want to be rich. I don't want to turn into the sort of person who thinks it's my God-given right to have more cash than I know what to do with and keep it all for myself. Here I am listening to you witter on, thinking, "Why should I give half my hard-earned fortune to an idle waster?" I'm already turning into that Scroogey miser you mentioned earlier and I haven't even said I'll take the job!'

Tamsin blinks at me, her powers of com-prehension impaired by alcohol. Eventually she says, 'You'd resent me.'

'Probably, yes. The ice-skating might just tip me over the edge.'

She nods. 'That's okay. I wouldn't hold it against you. You can call me a feckless scrounger to my face, if you like, as long as I get my share of the money. I'd rather be insulted by you than have to tout myself round prospective employers feeling the way I do now — unwanted and worthless. What am I talking about?' She slaps herself on the wrist, then hits my leg, hard. 'Look what

89

you've done — your negativity's totally dragged me down!'

'I'm turning down the job, Tam.'

She groans.

'Which means I'll probably get my marching orders too by the end of the week. We can go to the National Portrait Gallery together.' *Tell her the truth. Tell her why you can't make Laurie's film. You have nothing to be ashamed of.*

'Bollocks to that!' Tamsin bangs her fist on the table. 'If you're going there, I'm going to the Science Museum instead as a protest at your . . . dickery. Fliss, people dream of things happening to them like what's happened to you today. You've *got* to take it. Even if you decide to leave me to rot in the gutter while you stock up on diamonds.'

'I'm being serious.'

'So am I! Think of all the time you'll get to spend with Laurie, him helping you unofficially — hah!' She gurgles with laughter. 'It's so obvious you're in love with him.'

'It can't be, because I'm not,' I say firmly. Maybe it's not such a huge lie. If I'm aware of all the reasons why I shouldn't love Laurie, which I am, then that has to mean I don't, not wholly. At the very least, I'm halfway in and halfway out. If I'm in love with him, how come I can so perfectly inhabit the mindset of thinking he's a git and the bane of my life?

'You spend *hours* staring out of your window at his office, even when he's not in it.' Tamsin chuckles. 'I'm not going to waste my breath saying no good can come of it. Some good's already come of it — a hundred and forty grand a year for us to split between us.' She gives me a narrow-eyed grin to let me know she's been winding me up about the money. 'You've been rewarded for your good taste. Laurie might be a freak, but he's a shrewd freak. He's seen the way you babble like an idiot in front of him, crazed with lust. You're his perfect pawn: he gets to distance himself from the film in public while retaining control in private.'

'Why would he want to distance himself?' I say, determinedly ignoring everything else Tamsin's just said because if I allowed myself to take it in and believe it, I would have to devote the rest of my life to muffled sobbing. 'He's obsessed with it.'

'In case it goes tits up, which it might very well, now that Sarah's pulled out.'

'Sarah?'

'Jaggard. Oh, my God! Laurie hasn't told you, has he?'

My phone starts to ring. I snap it open. 'Hello?'

'Is that Fliss Benson?' a woman asks.

I tell her it is.

'This is Ray Hines.'

My heart leaps, like a horse over a fence. *Rachel Hines.* I have the oddest sensation: as if this moment was always going to come, and there was nothing I could have done to avert it.

She can't know how significant she is to me, how it makes me feel to hear her voice.

'Why is Laurie Nattrass leaving Binary Star?' She doesn't sound angry, or even put out. 'Does it have anything to do with Helen Yardley dying? I'm assuming she was murdered. I heard on the news that her death was "suspicious".'

'I don't know,' I say brusquely. 'You'll have to ask the police about that, and you'll have to ask Laurie why he's leaving. I'm nothing to do with anything.'

'Really? I got an email from Laurie saying you've taken over the documentary.'

'No. That's . . . a misunderstanding.'

Tamsin has found a pen in my bag and written 'Who?' on a beer mat. She shoves it towards me. I write 'Rachel Hines' beneath her question. She opens her mouth as wide as it'll go, flashing her tonsils at me, then scribbles furiously on the beer mat: 'Keep her talking!!!'

Even if I don't want to?

I heard two women on the tube discussing Rachel Hines, the day after she won her appeal. One said, 'I don't know about the others, but the Hines woman murdered her children, sure as I'm born. She's a drug addict and a liar. You know she abandoned her daughter when the poor mite was only days old? Stayed away for the best part of two weeks. What kind of mother does that? I can believe Helen Yardley was innocent all along, but not her.' I waited for her companion to disagree, but she said, 'It would have been better for the baby if she'd stayed away for good.' I remember thinking it was an odd way to put it: *Helen Yardley was innocent all along.* As if one could start out guilty and then become innocent of a crime.

'I rang to tell you what I'm sure Laurie neglected to mention: that I want nothing to do with the documentary. Evidently you feel the same way.' She sounds nothing like my idea of what a drug addict ought to sound like.

'You want nothing to do with it,' I repeat blankly.

'I've made it clear to Laurie from the start that he'll have to do without me, so I don't know why he keeps copying me in on information I don't need. Maybe he hopes I'll change my mind, but I won't.' She sounds calm, as if none of what she's saying matters to her; she's merely informing me of the facts.

'I'm in a similar situation,' I tell her, too angry about the way I've been treated to be tactful. How dare Laurie inflict her on me without giving me any choice in the matter? Tamsin's jiggling in her seat, desperate to know what's going on. 'Laurie can't take no for an answer,' I say. 'That's when he bothers to ask the question. This time he didn't. I had no idea he was sending out my details to everyone. I don't know why he assumed I'd take on the film without asking me if I wanted to.'

Tamsin rolls her eyes and shakes her head. 'What?' I mouth at her. I refuse to feel bad about any of this; it's Laurie's fault, not mine.

'Why don't you want to?' Rachel Hines asks, as if it's the most natural question in the world.

I imagine myself giving her an honest answer. How would I feel afterwards? Relieved to have it out in the open? It's irrelevant, since I'll never have the guts to put it to the test. 'I don't mean to be rude,

bother me. It's crazy to put wet laundry in a wardrobe, and I'm not going to start acting like a crazy person before anything's even happened.

I shudder. *Nothing is going to happen,* I tell myself. *Get a grip.*

I put the clothes back on the rack, stand it in the middle of my bedroom and close the door on it. Then I run to the kitchen, which I left in a state this morning: plates and magazines strewn everywhere, toast crusts, milk-bottle tops, orange peel. The fat black bin bag that I should have taken out days ago has leaked oily orange sauce onto the lino.

I look at my watch. Nearly eleven. She said an hour to an hour and a half. That means she could arrive in five minutes. I need at least fifteen to sort out the kitchen. I yank open the dishwasher. It's packed with shiny clean cutlery and crockery. I swear loudly. Who said dishwashers make life easier? They're the devious bastards of the household appliance world. When you want a clean cup or plate, you get a stinking cavern full of curry stalactites dripping baked-bean juice. When you want the damn thing empty and ready to receive, that's the moment it picks to be full to bursting with an entire dinner service, gleaming and ponging of lemon.

I pile the clean stuff randomly into cupboards and drawers, chipping a couple of plates that were already chipped, as most of my stuff is. Then I load the dirty things without bothering to rinse them as I normally would, and wipe the surfaces with a cloth that's probably dirtier than the mess I'm using it to wipe up. I'm quite shallow when it comes to cleaning — tidy and bacteria-infested suits me fine, as long as it looks presentable to the untrained eye.

I take out the rubbish, mop up the oil on the floor and stand back to survey the kitchen. It looks better than it has for some time. The thought pops into my head before I can stop it: *maybe I ought to have murderers round more often.* In the lounge, to a soundtrack of loud bangs from my pogo-jumping upstairs neighbours — their getting-ready-for-bed noises — I pick up about twenty DVDs from the floor and shove them in a cloth shopping bag, which I stuff behind the door.

I don't want Rachel Hines to know what DVDs I own, or anything else about me. I cast my eyes over the bookshelf that fills one whole alcove of my lounge, the one nearest the window. I don't want her to know what books I read, but I haven't got a bag big enough to house them all temporarily, or time to take them off the shelves. I toy with the idea of rigging up some kind of curtain to hide them, then decide I'm being paranoid. It doesn't matter if she sees my books. It only matters if I make it matter.

I plump up the sofa cushions and the one on the chair, then look again at my watch. Five past eleven. I pull open the curtains I closed when I got in, and, looking up to street level, see a man and woman walking past. They're laughing. Her heels clip the pavement as she hurries along, and I have to restrain myself from pushing up my rattly sash window and shouting, 'Come back!'

I don't want to be alone with Rachel Hines.

In the hall, I scoop up all the letters, bills and bank statements that have piled up on the table and put them in the one drawer in my kitchen that opens properly, underneath the cutlery divider. I'm about to slam it shut when the corner of a thick cream-coloured envelope catches my eye, and I remember that I ran out of the flat this morning without opening the post.

That card someone sent me at work, the one with the numbers on it — that arrived in a thick cream-coloured envelope with the same ribbed effect.

So? It needn't mean anything. A co-incidence, that's all.

This one's also addressed to Fliss Benson. And the writing . . .

I rip it open. Inside, there's a card with only three numbers on it this time, in tiny handwriting at the bottom: 2 1 4. Or is it supposed to be two hundred and fourteen? The first three numbers on the other card, the one Laurie threw in the bin, were 2, 1 and 4.

There's no signature, no indication of who sent it. I turn the envelope upside down and shake it. Nothing. What do the numbers mean? Is it some kind of threat? Am I supposed to be scared? Whoever the sender is, he or she knows where I work, where I live . . .

I tell myself I'm being ridiculous, and force the tension out of my body, letting my shoulders drop. I concentrate on breathing slowly and steadily for a few seconds. Of course it's not a threat. If someone wants to threaten you, they use words you understand: *do x or I'll kill you.* Threats are threats and numbers are numbers — there's no overlap.

I tear both the card and the envelope into small pieces and take them outside to the bin, resolving to waste no more time on what must be some idiot's idea of a joke. Back inside, I pour myself a large glass of white wine and walk up and down, looking at my watch every three seconds until I can't bear it any longer. I pick up the phone and ring Tamsin's home number. Joe answers on the second ring. 'She's puking her guts up,' he tells me.

'Can I speak to her?'

'Well . . .' He sounds doubtful. 'You can listen to her spraying the toilet bowl with gin if you want.'

'I'm *fine!*' Tamsin shouts in the background. I hear a scuffle; more specifically, I hear Joe losing. 'Ignore Joseph. He likes to make heavy weather of things,' says Tamsin, with the crisp enunciation of someone determined to sound sober. 'Well? How did it go? What did she say?'

'She's not here yet.'

'Oh. Sorry, I've slightly lost time . . . *track* of time,' she corrects herself. 'I thought it was really late.'

'It is — too late to turn up on the doorstep of a complete stranger. Maybe she's seen sense and decided not to come.'

'Have you — gonna say this carefully, right? — *checked* your phone for *texts?*' It sounds like 'shrek-ed your phone for sex', but I know what she means.

101

'Yeah. Nothing.'

'Then she's coming.'

My watch says twenty past eleven. 'Even from Twickenham, she should be here by now.'

'Twickenham? That's virtually in Dorset. She could be hours. What's she doing in Twickenham?'

'Doesn't she live there?'

'No. Last I heard she was in a rented flat in Notting Hill, five minutes from her ex-husband and the former family home.'

All I know about Rachel Hines is that she was convicted, and later unconvicted, of killing her two children. *Good one, Fliss. Nothing like going into a situation well prepared.*

'Why did I agree to this?' I wail. 'It's your fault — you were nodding at me like a maniac as if yes was the only possible answer.' Even as I'm saying it, I know it's not true. I said yes because I'd just heard that the film might be about to fall apart. Once that's happened and Laurie's at Hammerhead, he'll have no leverage with Maya or Raffi. They'll be able to make me redundant: punish me for daring to think I was Creative Director material, even though I never did, and save themselves a hundred and forty grand a year. I agreed to see Rachel Hines in the absurd hope that somehow it might lead to my becoming indispensable at Binary Star, which is pretty embarrassing, even when I'm the only person I'm admitting it to.

Does that mean I want to make Laurie's film? No. No, no, no.

'I won't let her in,' I say, certain this is the best idea I've ever had.

'There's nothing to be scared of,' says Tamsin unhelpfully.

'Easy for you to say. When was the last time you were visited by a murderer in the middle of the night?' I'm not sure Rachel Hines killed her babies — how can I be? — but it makes me feel better to pretend that I am.

'She isn't a murderer any more,' says Tamsin. Automatically, I think of the woman I overheard on the tube: *I can believe Helen Yardley was innocent all along.* 'Even before she appealed and won, Justice Geilow made a point of saying she didn't think Ray Hines would ever pose a threat to anyone in the future. She as good as said in her sentencing remarks that, though murder carries a mandatory life sentence, she didn't feel it was appropriate, and implied that cases of this sort shouldn't be a matter for the criminal courts at all. It caused an uproar in legal circles. God, I feel sober. It's your fault.'

'Justice who?'

Tamsin sighs. 'Don't you ever read anything apart from *heat*? If you're making the film, you're going to need to familiarise yourself with —'

'I'm not making the film. I'm bolting my door and going to bed. First thing tomorrow morning I'm handing in my resignation.'

'Fine, do that. You'll never know what Ray Hines wanted to talk to you about.'

Good.

'One of her objections to the film was sharing it with the other two women,' says Tamsin. 'Now that Helen's dead and Sarah's pulled out, Ray could be the main focus. Her case. It's the most interesting of the three by far, though I once said that to Laurie and he almost had me hung, drawn and quartered for treason. Helen was always his favourite.'

Helen's case, or Helen the woman? I manage to stop myself from asking. I can't be jealous of a murder victim who lost all three of her children and spent nearly a decade in jail. Even if it turns out Laurie's spent years crying into his pillow on her account, jealousy is not an acceptable option, not if I want to be able to live with myself.

I hear a car pulling up outside. My hand tightens around the phone. 'I think she's here. I've got to go.' I hover uselessly by my front door, trying to contain myself until I hear the bell. When I can't stand it any longer, I open the door.

There's a black car outside my house, with its lights on and its engine running. I climb the five steps that lead from my basement flat up to the pavement, and see that it's a Jaguar. From her telephone voice, Rachel Hines sounded like the sort of person who might own one. I wonder how this fits in with her being a drug addict. Maybe she isn't one any more, or maybe she's a heaps-of-cocaine-off-platinum-edged-mirrors junkie, not your bog-standard shooting-up-in-a-dirty-squat smackhead. *God, if I was any more prejudiced . . .*

I plaster a non-threatening smile on my face and walk towards the car. It can't be her; she'd have got out by now. Suddenly, the engine and lights cut out and I see her clearly in the street-lamp's glow. Even knowing as little as I do about her case, she's totally familiar to me. Hers is a household face, like Helen Yardley's — one that's been on the news and in the papers so often that most people in Britain would recognise her. No wonder she didn't want to meet me in the pub.

I can't believe she wants to meet me at all.

Her face is slightly too long and her features too blunt, otherwise she'd be stunning. As it is, she's the sort of plain that has missed attractive by a hair's breadth. Her thick wavy hair makes me look again at her face, thinking she must be attractive; it's the sort of hair you'd expect to frame the face of a beauty: well cut, lustrous, golden blonde. She looks like somebody important; it's in her eyes and the way she holds herself. Nothing like Helen Yardley, whose absolute ordinariness and accessible friendly-neighbour smile made it easy for most people to believe in her innocence, once her convictions were quashed.

Rachel Hines opens her car door, but still doesn't get out. Tentatively, I approach the Jaguar. She slams the door shut. The engine starts up, and the headlights come back on, blinding me. 'What . . . ?' I start to say, but she's pulling away. As she draws level with me, she slows down, turns to face me. I see her look past me at the house and turn, in case there's someone behind me, though I know there isn't. *It'll be just the two of us, won't it?*

By the time I've turned back, she's halfway

down the road, speeding up as she drives away.

What did I do wrong? My mobile phone starts to ring in my pocket. 'You're not going to believe this,' I say, assuming it's Tamsin calling for an update. 'She was here about ten seconds ago, and she's just driven off without saying anything, without even getting out of the car.'

'It's me. Ray. I'm sorry about . . . what just happened.'

'Forget it,' I say, grudgingly. Why is it so unacceptable, if you're a decent human being, to say, 'Actually, it's not okay, even though you've apologised. I don't forgive you'? Why do I care what's socially acceptable, given who I'm dealing with? 'Can I go to bed now?'

'You'll have to come to me,' she says.

'What?'

'Not now. I've inconvenienced you enough for one day. Tell me a time and date that suit you.'

'No time, no date,' I say. 'Look, you caught me off-guard in the pub tonight. If you want to talk to someone at Binary Star, ring Maya Jacques and —'

'I didn't kill my daughter. Or my son.'

'Pardon?'

'I can tell you the name of the person who

did, if you want: Wendy Whitehead. Though it wasn't —'

'I don't want you to tell me anything,' I say, my heart pounding. 'I want you to leave me alone.' I press the 'end call' button hard. It's several seconds before I dare to breathe again.

Back in my flat, I lock and bolt the door, turn off my mobile phone and unplug the landline. Five minutes later I'm rigid and wide awake in bed, the name Wendy White-head going round and round in my brain.

From *Nothing But Love*
by Helen Yardley
with Gaynor Mundy

21 July 1995

On the twenty-first of July, when the police came, I knew straight away that this time was different from all the other times. It was three weeks to the day since Rowan had died, and I'd become an expert at reading the detectives' moods. I was usually able to tell from their faces whether the questioning on that particular day would be relentless or sympathetic. One detective who had always been kind to me was DS Giles Proust. He always looked uncomfortable when I was being interviewed and left most of the questions to his junior colleagues. On and on they would go: did I have a happy childhood? What was it like being the middle sibling? Did I ever feel jealous of my sisters? Am I close to my parents? Did I ever have babysitting jobs as a teenager? Did I love Morgan? Did I love Rowan? Did I welcome both pregnancies? I wanted to scream at them, 'Of course I bloody well did, and if you can't see that with your own eyes and ears then you don't deserve the title of detective!'

I always had the impression that Giles Proust alone among the police didn't merely believe that I was innocent of the murder of my babies, but *knew* it, in the way that I knew it and Paul knew it. He could see I was no baby-killer, and understood how much I'd loved my two precious boys. Now here he was at my door again, with a woman I didn't recognise, and I could see at once from his facial expression that this was going to be very bad. 'Just tell me,' I said, wanting to get it over with.

'This is DC Ursula Shearer from Child Protection,' said DS Proust. 'I'm sorry, Helen. I'm here to arrest you for the murders of Morgan and Rowan Yardley. I don't have any choice. I'm so sorry.'

His regret was absolutely genuine. I could see from his face that it was breaking him up to have to do this to me. At that moment, I think I hated his superior officers more for his sake than for my own. Hadn't they listened to him, all those times he must have told them they were hounding a grief-stricken mother who'd done nothing wrong? I was as much a victim of my boys' deaths as they were.

However terrible the moment of my arrest was for me, I can never think of it without also thinking of Giles Proust and how terrible it must have been for him. He must have felt as helpless as I did, powerless to make the people in charge see and hear the truth. Paul had urged me many times not to assume anybody official was on my side. He was scared I might be naïvely deluding myself, storing up more pain for the future. 'However decent Proust seems, he's a policeman, don't forget,' he would tell me. 'The sympathy could be a tactic. We've got to assume they're all against us.'

Although I didn't agree with Paul, I could understand his attitude. For him it was a way of staying strong. At first he didn't even trust our close families, our parents, brothers and sisters, to be fully on our side. 'They say they're sure you didn't do it,' he would say, 'but how do we know they're not just saying that because it's what's expected of them? What if some of them have doubts?' To this day I am convinced that none of my relatives or Paul's ever thought I could be guilty. They had all seen me with Morgan and Rowan and seen my passionate love for them.

Paul would face no criminal charges, we

were told, but he was allowed to come with me in the police car, which was a great comfort to me. He sat on one side of me, DS Proust sat on the other, and DC Shearer drove us to Spilling police station. I sobbed as I was forcibly taken away from my beloved house where I'd been so happy — first with Paul, then with Paul and Morgan, then again when Rowan came along. So many beautiful memories! How could they do this to me after what I'd suffered already? For a moment, I was consumed with hatred for everything and everyone. I had no use for a world that could inflict such terrible suffering. Then I felt an arm round my shoulder and DS Proust said, 'Helen, listen to me. I know you didn't kill Morgan or Rowan. Things are looking bleak for you now, but the truth will come out. If I can see the truth, others will too. Any fool can see you were a good, loving mother.'

DC Shearer muttered something sarcastic under her breath, from which I gathered that she disapproved of what DS Proust had said. Maybe she thought I was guilty, or that DS Proust had breached some sort of protocol by saying what he said to me, but I didn't care. Paul was smiling. He finally recognised Giles Proust for the ally that he was. 'Thank you,' he said. 'It means everything to us to have your support. Doesn't it, Helen?'

I nodded. DC Shearer made another snide remark under her breath. DS Proust could have left it at that, having made his point, but instead he said, 'If this goes as far as a trial, which I very much doubt it will, then I'll be called as a witness. By the time I step down from the box, the jury will be as convinced as I am that you're innocent.'

'What the hell are you doing?' DC Shearer snapped. Paul and I shrank down in our seats, taken aback by her harsh tone, but Giles Proust remained unfazed.

'I'm doing the right thing,' he said. 'Somebody has to.'

I became aware that I had stopped crying. A wave of what can only be described as utmost peace washed over me, and I stopped worrying obsessively about what would happen to me. It was like magic: I was no longer afraid. Whether Giles Proust was right or wrong about my chances of standing trial or what a hypothetical jury would think, it didn't matter. All that mattered was that as I looked out of the window of the police car and watched the post-boxes and trees and shops whizzing by, I loved the world I had hated only a few moments earlier. I felt part of something good and whole and light, something that Paul and Giles Proust and Morgan and Rowan were also part of. It's very hard to explain the feeling in words because it was so much stronger than words.

I didn't know, as we drove to the police station that day, how bad things were going to get for me and Paul, how much more agonising suffering lay in store for us. But as fate went on to rain down blow after blow upon us, even when my spirits were at their very lowest and there seemed no hope of any respite, that peaceful sensation that came over me in the police car on the day of my arrest never left me, even though there were times when I had to struggle to find it inside myself. It's the same positive energy that has spurred me on in the work I have done on behalf of other women in similar situations to mine, and that has been the driving force behind my contribution to JIPAC. DS Proust taught me a valuable lesson that day: that you can always, and easily, give somebody the gift of hope and faith, even in the midst of despair.

12 September 1996
The contact centre was a horrible, soulless place, an ugly grey one-storey prefab that looked lost and forlorn in a vast, mostly

empty car park. I hated it on sight. There weren't enough windows, and those there were seemed too small. I said to Paul, 'It looks like a building that's keeping lots of unpleasant secrets.' He knew exactly what I meant. I shuddered and said, 'I can't do it. I just can't. I can't go in there.' He told me I had to, because Paige was inside.

I wanted to see her more than anything but I was scared of the joy I would feel as soon as we were together, because I knew it was something that the social workers could and would take away from me. If I came here for two hours every weekday, which was the deal Ned and Gillian had negotiated for me, that meant I would have to endure some Social Services flunky taking Paige away from me five times each week until my trial, and who knew what would happen after that? Even if I was acquitted, as Giles Proust kept reassuring me I would be, Paul and I still might not be allowed to keep Paige. Ned had explained to me about the difference between the burden of proof in a criminal case, where guilt must be proven beyond reasonable doubt, and the courts that steal children from their parents behind closed doors and under a veil of secrecy. In the family courts, all that needs to happen is for the judge to decide that the child is better off without his or her parents *on the balance of probabilities,* which means nobody needs to prove anything. All it will take is for someone who doesn't know me from Adam or Eve to decide I'm *probably* a murderer, and I'll lose my daughter. 'I've never heard of anything so cruel and unfair in my life,' I told Ned. 'To lose Paige would be unbearable, and what if I go to prison, and Paul loses both me *and* her?' Ned looked me in the eye and said, 'I can't lie to you, Helen. That might happen.'

'Take me home,' I told Paul as we sat in the car park outside the contact centre. 'I've already suffered three terrible losses and I can't cope with any more.' That was how I truly felt. Paige was alive and well, but I lost her when she was wrenched from my arms an hour after her birth to be taken into care. 'I can't lose my daughter all over again every day this week, and next week, and for God knows how long. I won't let them do that to me, or to her.' Up until this point I had been timid and cooperative, and it had got me nowhere. Let them see exactly what they're doing, I thought: depriving a baby of her mother. Why should I turn up and make Social Services feel good about themselves for 'letting' me have contact with my own daughter? They were tearing apart what was left of my family and I wanted them to realise it.

The drive back to Bengeo Street was the most miserable journey of my life. Paul and I didn't speak a single word to one another. At home we made a pot of hot, strong tea. 'You should go back there,' I told him. 'You need to make sure that you get to keep Paige, no matter what happens to me. You'll have to lie, but it's a price worth paying.' Paul asked me what I meant and I spelled it out for him. 'You must pretend to doubt me. Act like you're as worried as the social workers are about me being alone with Paige. Convince them that if they let you keep her, you'll make sure she's never alone with me.'

No words can express how much I hated saying this to Paul. He was my absolute rock and had stood by me unswervingly throughout my ordeal. His loyalty was the main thing sustaining me, yet here I was asking him to pretend to be a worse man than he truly was — a disloyal husband instead of a wonderful brave one. But I knew it was the right thing to do. The only thing that mattered now was stopping those child-snatcher social workers from giving our beloved Paige to another family.

When I lost first Morgan and then Rowan,

I didn't think anything worse could ever happen to me, but to lose Paige in this way would be worse, because it would be somebody's fault. The injustice would destroy me, and I feared it might actually kill Paul, however melodramatic that sounds.

'Please,' I begged him. 'Drive back there and see Paige. Ring them now and tell them you're coming.'

'No,' he said flatly. 'I'm not lying to anyone and nor are you. That would make us as bad as them. We'll fight evil with good and lies with truth and we'll win. DS Proust says we'll win and I believe him.'

'Ned and Gillian say we might not,' I reminded him, my eyes full of tears. 'And even if I'm found not guilty in the criminal court, the family court's a different matter.'

'Shut up!' Paul yelled. 'I don't want to hear it.' It was the first time since tragedy had struck our lives that he'd raised his voice to me, and I'm ashamed to say that I took the opportunity to give back as good as I got and vent some of the misery and despair that had built up inside me. The two of us were still screaming at each other ten minutes later when the doorbell rang.

I threw myself into Giles Proust's arms, and must have absolutely terrified the poor man as I shrieked at him that he had to help me make Paul see sense. 'You're the one who needs to see sense, Helen, and quickly,' he said sternly. 'Why aren't you at the contact centre? You're supposed to be there now, but I've just had a call saying you didn't turn up.' I did my best to explain my reasons to him. 'Listen carefully, Helen,' he said. 'However hard it is, you've got to spend as much time as you can with Paige. Don't miss a single visit, or they'll use it against you. I understand what you're scared of, but do you really want to turn your worst fears into reality by giving them ammunition? How do you think it looks if you don't even bother to turn up for the few hours a week you're allowed to spend with Paige?'

'Please listen to him, Hel,' said Paul quietly. 'We've no way of knowing what's going to happen, but at least this way we'll know we did everything we could — we didn't lie or give up the fight. In ten or twenty years' time, whatever our circumstances at that point, we'll be able to look back and be proud of ourselves.'

How could I resist the two of them once they'd joined forces? They were so wise and loyal and strong, and I felt unworthy, like a total coward and a failure.

Giles Proust drove Paul and me back to

the contact centre. We'd missed most of our allotted time with Paige, but there was still half an hour left. The contact supervisor looked about twelve. I'll never forget her name: Leah Gould. 'Leah Ghoul, more like,' I said to Paul later. She refused to wait in the corridor and watch us through the window, despite DS Proust almost going down on his knees and begging her to allow us that small degree of privacy. She insisted on staying with us in the horrid, small, too brightly painted room that reeked of the misery of countless families forcibly separated by smiling, officially sanctioned torturers — at least that's how it seemed to me at that moment.

When Leah Gould placed Paige gently in my arms, my misery was sent packing, if only temporarily. A tiny baby is such a joyful, hopeful bundle that it's hard not to respond, and I was suffused with a rush of love for my beautiful daughter. Paul and I showered Paige with cuddles and kisses. The poor child's face was sopping wet within a few minutes, we'd slobbered over her so much! 'No one will take her away from us,' I thought. 'That would be too crazy, given how much we love her and how obvious that must be, even to someone as unemotional and blank-eyed as Leah Gould.' At that moment, I firmly believed the powers-that-be would see sense and Paul, Paige and I would be allowed to have a future together.

I don't really know what happened next but I know that it was one of the oddest moments of my life. Suddenly Leah Gould was standing in front of me, saying, 'Helen, hand the baby to me. Please hand Paige to me. Now, please.' I did as I was told, confused. Time couldn't be up yet; we'd only been in the room a few minutes. I could see from the expressions on Paul and DS Proust's faces that they were also mystified.

Leah Gould virtually ran from the room with Paige in her arms. 'What did I do?' I asked, bursting into tears. Neither Paul nor Giles Proust could answer the question any more than I could. I looked at my watch. I'd spent a total of eight minutes with my daughter.

The episode only made sense when I learned from Ned some time later that Leah Gould was going to give evidence at my trial and say that I had tried to smother Paige right in front of her, in the guise of giving her a cuddle. I remember I actually laughed when I heard this news. 'Let her say that if she wants to,' I said to Ned and Gillian. 'Paul and Giles Proust were in that room too. No jury will believe they'd fail to notice an attempted murder taking place right in front of their eyes! One of them's a detective sergeant, for heaven's sake!'

Maybe I was naïve. Maybe if Leah Gould's testimony was the only so-called 'proof' the prosecution had had at its disposal, I'd have walked free, and Paul and I would have been allowed to keep our daughter. But though I didn't know it yet, Leah Gould's utterly baseless lie would sound frighteningly convincing alongside the expert opinion of somebody far more mature, articulate and highly esteemed, someone the jury would take very seriously indeed. It's hard to believe, looking back now, that there was once a time when I'd never heard of Dr Judith Duffy, the woman who would play the leading role in the destruction of the rest of my life.

4
8/10/09

The first irritation was Charlie walking into the kitchen. *Her kitchen.* Simon had been living with her at her place for the past six months. Most of the time he preferred it, though the exceptions to this rule were frequent enough to make him certain he wasn't yet ready to put his own house on the market. The second irritation was Charlie yawning. No one who'd had several hours of sleep had any business yawning. 'Why didn't you give me a nudge when you got up?' she said. 'You're my alarm clock.'

'I didn't get up. Haven't been to bed.'

He was aware of her staring at him, then at the book that lay on the table in front of him. 'Ah, your reading homework: Helen Yardley's tear-jerker. Where are Proust's yellow markers?'

Simon said nothing. He'd told her last night, he'd rather saw off his own head than read the copy the Snowman had given him.

Did all women make you answer the same question twenty times over? Simon's mum did it to his dad; both his grans did it to both his grandads. It was a depressing thought.

'That can't be the copy you ordered yesterday from Amazon . . .'

'Word,' he said abruptly: a one-word answer, both in form and in content. Word on the Street was an independent bookshop in the town centre, far less trendy than its name suggested. Local history, gardening and cookery books competed for space in the window. Simon liked it because it had no café; he disapproved of bookshops selling coffee and cakes.

'They had an evening event on last night. I popped in on the off-chance on my way home from work, they had the book, so I thought I might as well buy it, read it overnight, speed things up a bit.' Simon was aware of his right heel drumming on the kitchen floor. He forced himself to keep still.

'Uh-huh,' said Charlie lightly. 'So when the Amazon one arrives, you'll have three copies. Or did you put the one the Snowman gave you through the shredder at work?'

He would have done if he could have

guaranteed Proust wouldn't catch him in the act.

'If you've still got it, I wouldn't mind having a look at it.'

Simon nodded at the table. 'There's the book, if you want to read it.'

'I want to see which bits Proust marked out for your special attention. I can't believe he did that! The man's ego knows no bounds.'

'The bits about him,' said Simon quietly. 'As if those are the only parts of her story that matter. She thought he was Martin Luther King, the Dalai Lama and Jesus Christ our saviour all rolled into one.'

'*What?*' Charlie picked up *Nothing But Love.* 'The opposite, right?'

'No. She rated him.'

'Then she's guilty of bad judgement at the very least. Do you think she killed her children?'

'Why, because she's full of praise for Proust?'

'No, because she was sent to prison for murdering them,' said Charlie with exaggerated patience.

'I've been told to look out for people like you. The Snowman wants names. Traitors' names.'

Charlie filled the kettle. 'Can I say something without you taking it the wrong way? And if I make you a cup of tea at the same time?'

'Say what you want. I'll take it how I take it.'

'How reassuring. I feel so much better now. All right, then: I think you've got a dangerous obsession brewing. Fully brewed, actually.'

Simon looked up, surprised. 'Why, because I stayed up all night? I couldn't sleep. Helen Yardley's no more important to me than any other —'

'I'm talking about Proust,' said Charlie gently. 'You're obsessed with hating him. The only reason you stayed up all night to read that book is because you knew there were references to him in it.'

Simon looked away. The idea that he'd be obsessed with another man was laughable. 'I've never had a murder victim who's written a book before,' he said. 'The sooner I read it, the sooner I find out if there's anything in it that can help me.'

'So why not read the copy Proust gave you? Instead, you go to Word — which isn't on your way home from work, so you weren't just passing. You went out of your way to go to a bookshop that might not even have been open last night, might not have had the book . . .'

'It was and it did.' Simon pushed past her and into the hall. 'Forget the tea. I've got to get washed and go to work. I'm not wasting time talking about things that never happened.'

'What if Word had been closed?' Charlie called up the stairs after him. More point-less hypotheticals. 'Would you have gone back to work and picked up the copy Proust gave you?'

He ignored her. In his world, if you shouted a question at someone from far away and they ignored it, you left it at that, maybe waited till later to try again. Not in Charlie's world. He heard her feet on the stairs.

'If you can't bring yourself to read a book you need to read just because he gave it to you, then you've got a problem.'

'She rated him,' Simon said again, staring at his exhausted face in the shaving mirror Charlie had bought for him and attached lopsidedly to the bathroom wall.

'So what?'

She was right. If he found the disagree-ment of a dead woman unacceptable, he was as bad as Proust and well on the way to tyranny. 'I suppose everyone's entitled to an opinion,' he said eventually. Maybe some of the Dalai Lama's colleagues thought he was an arrogant twat. Did people in flowing orange robes have colleagues? If they did, was that what they called them?

'How much of your time is taken up with hating him?' Charlie asked. 'Eighty per cent? Ninety? Isn't it bad enough that you have to work with him? Are you going to let him take over your mind as well?'

'No, I'll let you do that instead. Happy?'

'I would be if you meant it. I'd get straight on the phone to that five-star hotel in Malaysia.'

'Don't start that honeymoon shit again. We agreed.' Simon knew he wasn't being fair; unwilling to negotiate, he'd given Charlie no say in the matter, then tried to spin it so that it looked like a joint decision.

What was it the Snowman had said? *I know I can count on your support.*

Simon was dreading his and Charlie's honeymoon. Next July was only nine months away, getting closer all the time. He was afraid he'd be unable to perform, that she'd be disgusted by him. The only way to stop dreading it was to reveal the full extent of his inadequacy even sooner.

He brushed his teeth, threw some cold water on his face and headed downstairs.

'Simon?'

'What?'

'Helen Yardley's murder is about Helen Yardley, not Proust,' said Charlie. 'You won't find the right answer if you're asking the wrong question.'

Proust got out of his chair to open the door for Simon — something he'd never done before. 'Yes, Waterhouse?'

'I've read the book.' *Which is why I'm here, giving you another chance to be reasonable, instead of at Human Resources complaining about you.* Except it wasn't a real chance; Simon couldn't pretend there was anything generous-spirited about it. He wanted to prove Helen Yardley wrong. It was ridiculous; embarrassing. Didn't he know Proust well enough after years of working with him?

'It's a pity you never met Helen Yardley, Waterhouse. You might have learned a lot from her. She brought out the best in people.'

'What did she do with it once she'd brought it out?' Simon asked. 'Bury it somewhere and leave clues?' He couldn't believe he'd said it, couldn't believe he wasn't being ejected from the room.

'What's that?' Proust nodded at the sheet of paper in Simon's hand. Was he stifling his anger in order to deny Simon a sense of achievement?

'I think there's an angle we're neglecting, sir. I've made a list of names I think we ought to talk to. All those who had a vested interest in Helen Yardley being guilty, and others who —'

'She wasn't guilty.'

'There are people who need to cling to the belief that she was innocent,' said Simon neutrally, 'and people who need to cling to the belief that she did it because they can't live with themselves otherwise: the eleven jurors who voted guilty, the prosecuting lawyers, the social workers who —'

'Dr Judith Duffy,' the Snowman read aloud, having snatched the paper from Simon's hand. 'Even in my line of work, I haven't met many human beings I'd describe as out-and-out evil, but that woman . . .' He frowned. 'Who are all these others? I recognise a few: the Brownlees, Justice Wilson . . . Waterhouse, you're surely not suggesting Helen Yardley was murdered by a high court judge?'

'No, sir, of course not. I put him on the list for the sake of completeness.'

'Any more complete, it'd be a perishing telephone directory!'

'Justice Wilson played a part in sending Helen Yardley to prison. So did eleven jurors whose names are also on the list. Any of them might have reacted badly when her convictions were quashed. I'm thinking . . . well, maybe someone reacted very badly.' Simon didn't want to use the word 'vigilante'. 'That's why Sarah Jaggard and Rachel Hines are on the list too. Chances are anyone who thinks Helen Yardley escaped justice will think Jaggard and Hines did too. We need to talk to them both, find out if anyone's been bothering them, if they've been threatened or noticed anything out of the ordinary.'

'Make up your mind, Waterhouse. Is this a list of people who have a vested interest in Helen Yardley being guilty, or is it something else entirely?' Proust held the piece of paper between his thumb and forefinger, as if it hurt him to touch it. 'Because it seems to me that Sarah Jaggard and Rachel Hines might have a vested interest in her being *not* guilty, since they were the victims of similar miscarriages of justice, and Helen campaigned on their behalf.'

Helen. Helen and her friend Giles.

'Sarah Jaggard was acquitted,' Simon said.

Proust glared at him. 'You don't think being charged with murder when all you've done is look after your friend's child to the best of your ability constitutes a miscarriage

131

of justice? Then I feel sorry for you.'

As far as Simon knew, the Snowman had never met Sarah Jaggard. Did his outrage on behalf of Helen Yardley automatically extend to all women accused of the same crime? Or was it Helen Yardley's certainty that Jaggard was innocent that had convinced him? If Proust had been an approachable sort of person, Simon might have asked these questions. 'You're right: not all the names on the list have a vested interest in Helen Yardley's guilt. They're all people we ought to talk to, though.'

'Justice Geilow gave Rachel Hines two life sentences for murder,' said Proust. 'She's nothing to do with Helen Yardley. Why's she on the list?'

'You said it yourself: the similarities between the Yardley and Hines cases are startling. Obsessions can spread. Obviously it's unlikely that Justice Geilow shot Helen Yardley, but . . .'

'She's an even less plausible murderer than Mr Justice Wilson, if such a thing is possible,' said Proust impatiently.

'I've also included the names of the twelve jurors who found Rachel Hines guilty,' said Simon. 'Unlike high court judges, jurors can be anyone. Isn't it possible one of the eleven who sent Helen Yardley to prison spent the nine years she was there thinking of himself as a good guy who helped put away a child murderer, and then couldn't take it when he heard she wasn't guilty after all? Nine years, sir.' Simon allowed himself the luxury of talking as he would to someone who was really listening. 'Think how hard it'd be to change the story after that long, the one you've been going round telling everyone you know, about who you are and what you did. After nine years it's a central part of your self-image. Maybe, that's all I'm saying,' he added for the sake of caution.

Proust sighed. 'I know I'm going to regret asking, but why are Rachel Hines' jurors on the list? You think one of them might have shot Helen Yardley? Wouldn't they be more likely to shoot Rachel Hines, according to your logic?'

Simon said nothing.

'I can read your mind, Waterhouse — always have been able to. Shall I tell you what you're thinking? This obsessed killer, if he's to be found on the Hines jury, might have shot Helen Yardley because she was instrumental in freeing Rachel Hines. Or he might have extended his retributive obsession to all three women and be planning to punish them all, as well as the appeal judges who overturned the murder convictions.

Perhaps our killer's a Hines juror who doesn't want to start with Rachel Hines in case that looks too obvious. How am I doing?'

Simon felt his face heat up. 'I think we should show the card with the sixteen numbers found on Helen Yardley's body to all the people on the list and ask if it means anything to them,' he said. 'This case isn't the simple either-or that we're usually faced with: a stranger killer versus someone close to the victim. Most of the people on this list didn't know Helen Yardley personally, but they're not random strangers either. They were as significant in her life as she was in theirs.'

'Laurie Nattrass.' Proust jabbed the list with his finger. 'He's already been interviewed and swabbed. You're not usually sloppy, Waterhouse. Fixated, deluded, yes, but not sloppy.'

'I'd like to talk to Nattrass again myself. I'd like to ask him about the sixteen numbers, ask if anyone he's come into contact with through JIPAC has threatened him or acted out of character, if anything's made him feel uncomfortable recently.'

'Like perishing what?' Proust pushed his chair back from his desk. 'A lumpy chaise longue? A boil on his backside?'

Simon stood his ground, didn't even blink at the volume. 'Those numbers mean something,' he said. 'I'm no psychological profiler, but I'm pretty sure one thing they mean is that this killer's going to kill again.'

'I warn you, Waterhouse . . .'

'He'll leave a similar card next time — either the same numbers or different ones. Either way, it'll mean something. Helen Yardley and Laurie Nattrass represented a lot of the same things to a lot of people. It's possible that whoever killed her might target him next. How about I interview Nattrass, Sarah Jaggard and Rachel Hines, and if none of them can move us forward, if they haven't been harassed recently, if the sixteen numbers mean nothing to any of them, we'll forget the rest of the names on the list and go back to the stranger killer theory.'

'And if Sarah Jaggard was shouted at in the street last week by some alcopop-swilling lowlife, what then?' Proust bellowed. 'We start swabbing Justices Geilow and Wilson for gunpowder residue? Where's the connection? Where's the logic?'

'Sir, I'm trying to be reasonable.'

'Then try, try and try again, Waterhouse!' The inspector's hand shot out as if to grab something. He clenched it into a fist and held it still for a moment, staring at it. *It's gone, knobhead.* Even the Snowman couldn't smash a mug twice.

'There's one person on this list to whom your obsession theory might apply,' Proust said with exaggerated weariness. 'Judith Duffy. She's made it her life's work to ruin innocent women's lives. That smacks of a level of obsession and . . . detachment from reality that ought to give us pause for thought, however professionally eminent she is, or has been. We should make it a priority to eliminate her, at least.' Proust rubbed his forehead. 'The truth is, I can hardly bear to utter the woman's name. You think I'm unaffected by all this? I'm not. I'm a person just like you, Waterhouse. You've read Helen Yardley's book. Put yourself in my place, if you can.'

Simon stared at the floor. He wasn't foolish enough to confuse an accusation of insensitivity with a confidence.

'There's a lot the book leaves out,' Proust went on. 'I could write a book of my own. I was at the hospital when Helen and Paul gave their consent for Rowan's life support to be switched off. Didn't know that, did you? Little Rowan was brain-dead. There was nothing that could be done for him, nothing at all. Do you know what I was doing there?'

I don't care. Tell someone else, someone who doesn't hate your guts.

'I was sent to collect the Yardleys, bring them in for questioning. Barrow's orders. A nurse from the baby unit had phoned us within an hour of them bringing Rowan in, accused Helen of attempted murder. Rowan had stopped breathing, not for the first time in his short life. When he was admitted to hospital, he had a Modified Glasgow Coma Score of 5. They put him on a drip and got it up to 14.' Proust glanced at Simon, as if suddenly remembering he was there. '15 is normal. For a while it looked as if he might be all right, but then he deteriorated. Helen and Paul weren't even in the room when his score started to drop again. Helen was too upset — Paul had to take her out. She wasn't even in the room,' he repeated slowly. 'If that's not reasonable doubt, I'd like to know what is.'

'Did the nurse have any proof Helen had tried to kill Rowan?' Simon asked. The only way he could deal with this was practically, by trying to fill in the gaps in the story, focusing on the Yardleys instead of on the Snowman. *He's not baring his soul, he's filling you in on the background. Relax.*

'Paul and Helen were known at the hospital,' said Proust. 'First Morgan and

137

then Rowan had several ALTEs — apparent life-threatening events. Both boys stopped breathing every now and then, for no reason that anyone could identify. Some sort of biological deficiency, I suppose — the most obvious explanation, but it didn't occur to the troublemaker who called the police. She called twice, the second time several hours after the first. Anonymously — no doubt she was ashamed of her despicable behaviour, and worried we'd taken no notice of her first attempt to spread poison.'

Whenever he heard the phrase 'no doubt', Simon doubted. Couldn't a baby's health go rapidly downhill as a result of damage previously inflicted by a parent, even if the parent wasn't present when the deterioration took place? He wanted to ask if there was anything else, apart from Morgan and Rowan Yardley's ALTEs, that had given the hospital staff cause to suspect their mother. Instead he said, 'Everyone working this murder ought to know all this.' A desperate attempt to block intimacy. Simon couldn't stand Proust telling him anything he wouldn't as readily have told Sam Kombothekra, or Sellers, or Gibbs. 'When we're not on shift, we should all be reading up on the background: Helen Yardley's trial, the appeal . . .'

'No.' Proust stood up. 'Not when there's no reason to assume her death is linked to any of it. It could have had as much to do with her physical appearance as with her imprisonment for murder. Judith Duffy, Sarah Jaggard, Rachel Hines, Laurie Nattrass — talk to those four, but no one else on your list, not yet. If we can avoid swabbing Elizabeth Geilow and Dennis Wilson for gunpowder residue, let's do that. Come to think of it, let's make it six: interview Grace and Sebastian Brownlee too. I've yet to come across a juror murderously obsessed with a case he heard thirteen years ago, but adoptive parents, paranoid their daughter might one day want to have a relationship with her biological mother, when the mother is someone as admirable and inspiring as Helen Yardley?' Proust nodded, as if making up his mind.

At what stage did he decide she was innocent? Simon wondered. The first time he met her? Before that, even? Was his staunch support of her a kind of contrariness, two fingers in the face of Superintendent Barrow's assumption that she was guilty? Could Proust have been in love with Helen Yardley? Simon flinched; the idea of the Snowman as an emotional being was repulsive. Simon preferred to think of him as a

139

problem-making machine, human in appearance but in no other respect.

He held out his hand for his list of names. If he left it in here, it would end up in the bin.

'First thing I did when I got to the hospital and saw what was happening, I rang Roger Barrow,' said Proust, settling back in his chair. He hadn't finished with Simon yet. 'He wasn't Superintendent then, and nor should he be now. I rang him, told him I couldn't bring Helen in for questioning. "She's just signed a consent form for her boy's life support to be switched off," I said. "She and her husband are about to watch their son die. They're in pieces." Helen was as innocent of murder as any person I'd ever met, and even if she wasn't . . .' The Snowman stopped, pulled in a deep breath. 'Bringing her in for questioning could wait until Rowan had passed on. Why couldn't it wait? What difference was an hour or two going to make?'

Simon was aware of his own breathing, the stillness in the room.

' "You want her brought in now, get someone else to do it," I said. "No, no," said Barrow. "You're quite right. Go and have something to eat, get yourself a pint, simmer down," he said. As if I'd lost on the horses or something — something trivial. "You're right, bringing the mother in can wait till later." He wanted me out of the way, that was all. When I got back to the hospital, the doctors told me Helen and Paul had been taken in for questioning by two bobbies, minutes after I'd left them — hauled out screaming, like some kind of . . .' Proust shook his head. 'And Rowan . . .'

'He was dead?' Simon blurted out, his discomfort starting to spin into panic. He needed light and air. He needed not to be hearing this, but couldn't find the right words to make it stop. It felt like an assault. Had Proust planned it? Had he watched Simon become hardened to his derision over the years, and decided that enforced intimacy was to be his new weapon?

'Rowan died with neither of his parents there,' said Proust. 'Alone. Doesn't that make you proud to be human, Waterhouse? Assuming you are.' A dismissive hand gesture indicated that he didn't expect an answer.

Simon exited as quickly as he could, giving no thought to where he was going. *The khazi;* his feet knew even if his brain didn't. He went in, headed for a cubicle and just had time to slide the lock across before a wave of nausea bent him double. He spent the next ten minutes spewing up black coffee and bile, thinking, *You make me sick. You make me fucking sick.*

5
THURSDAY 8 OCTOBER 2009

I'm in Laurie's office when I hear someone yelling my name. I think of Rachel Hines and freeze, as if by keeping still I can make myself invisible. Then there's more shouting and I recognise the voice: Tamsin.

I get to reception in time to catch the end of what looks like a strange dance. If I didn't know better, I might think Maya and Tamsin choreographed it together: each time Tamsin takes a step forward, Maya blocks her path or puts out an arm to stop her.

'Fliss, will you tell her I'm supposed to be here? I'm getting the imposter treatment.'

'Don't do this, Tam,' says Maya gravely. 'You're embarrassing all of us. We agreed yesterday would be your last day.'

'I asked her to come in,' I say. 'I need someone to get me up to speed on the film, quickly. There was no sign of Laurie when I came in this morning and I can't get hold of him on any of his phones, and anyway, he's . . .' I break off, wondering what I was about to say. He's leaving? He's crackers? 'I needed a reliable expert, so I rang Tamsin.'

'I'm offering my services for free,' Tamsin says cheerily. She's wearing a figure-hugging pink and orange dress that looks new and expensive. I wonder how to check, tactfully, that she's not planning to blow all her remaining money on luxury items as a prelude to driving off a cliff. I know Tamsin: she'll chicken out of the cliff part, but get as far as running up massive debts before latching on to her next faddy idea.

'Look, I've even brought my own refreshments,' she says. 'An old mineral water bottle from the days when I could afford it, full of nice cheap tap water. Yum.' She waves it in front of Maya's face. 'See? No concealed weapons.'

'Thanks *so* much, Fliss, for letting me know.' Maya twitches her nose like an offended rabbit, taking backward steps in the direction of her office. She's been arsey with me all morning. I keep giving her my best, most radiant 'hello's and getting only grunts in response. Binary Star is a different company today. Everybody's keeping themselves to themselves, trying not to meet anyone else's eye. It's like an office in mourning.

For Laurie.

I grab Tamsin's arm and drag her along the corridor to the room I need to start thinking of as my new condensation-free office, muttering, 'Thanks for your contribution.' I slam the door, lock it and put the chain across. If Laurie comes back and wants to get in, tough. He told me I could be him from Monday; all I'm doing is moving the new arrangement forward by two working days. Let him come back and catch me.

Let him come back.

'You're welcome.' Tamsin plonks herself down in Laurie's chair and puts her feet up on his model globe. Her face clouds over. 'You're being sarcastic, aren't you?'

'I could have done without the too-poor-for-mineral-water quip. I have to work here, Tam.'

'I thought you were handing in your notice first thing this morning.'

'I changed my mind.'

'How come?'

There's no reason not to tell her, though I'm not sure it'll make sense to anyone but me. 'I rang my mum this morning. I told her I was worried about being paid more than I'm realistically worth, Maya and Raffi resenting me, stuff like that.'

145

'She told you not to be an idiot?' Tamsin guesses.

'Not quite. She suggested I say to them that I wouldn't feel comfortable earning so much, and perhaps we could agree a salary that was somewhere between what I'm on now and what Laurie was on, something we could all feel happy with. I listened to her and I swear I could hear myself saying it, sounding ever so reasonable and timid — sounding like *her*, mousey and modest and unassuming and . . .' I shrug. 'Laurie was right. No one asks for less money. I don't care what Maya and Raffi think of me, but . . . I'd lose all respect for myself if I didn't try to make this work.' I feel obliged to add, 'Even though, secretly, I don't think I'm worth anywhere near a hundred and forty a year.'

'You're suffering from Reverse L'Oréal Syndrome,' says Tamsin. ' "Because I'm not worth it". So, you're going to make the film?'

'You don't think I can do it, do you?'

'If it can be done, you can do it,' she says matter-of-factly. 'Why wouldn't you be able to?'

I consider telling her what makes me different from her or Laurie or anyone else at Binary Star, why I can't hear the names

Yardley, Jaggard and Hines without feeling a cold dragging in the pit of my stomach.

I didn't tell my mother about Laurie's film. I mentioned the promotion and the pay-rise, but not what I'd be working on. Not that she'd have tried to stop me. Mum would be more likely to dance naked in the street than say anything that might lead to an argument.

Tamsin's the only person at work I've ever been tempted to tell. Trouble is, she's never silent for long enough. This time's no different. 'The question is, do you still have a film to make after Ray Hines left you stranded on the pavement? Have you spoken to Paul Yardley? Talked Sarah Jaggard back on board?'

'I haven't done anything yet.'

'Apart from spreading the contents of five box files randomly across the room,' says Tamsin dubiously, eyeing the papers on the floor and on every available surface.

'I was looking for something and I didn't find it. Does the name Wendy Whitehead ring any bells?'

'No.'

'What are the chances of it being buried somewhere in all this lot? I've skim-read as much as I've had time to, but —'

'Don't bother,' says Tamsin. 'Any name

that crops up even once, I'd know it. I know every expert witness, every health visitor, every solicitor . . .'

'What about just Wendy, then? She might have got married and changed her surname. Or divorced.'

Tamsin considers it. 'No,' she says eventually. 'No Wendys. Why?'

'She rang me last night.'

'Wendy Whitehead?'

'Rachel Hines.'

She rolls her eyes. 'I know. I was there, remember?'

'No, I mean later. After she'd driven away without getting out of the car. Almost immediately after. She apologised, said she still wanted to talk to me, but I'd have to come to her.'

'Did she say why she drove off?'

'No. I saw her looking behind me, sort of like . . . I don't know, it looked as if she was staring at somebody over my shoulder, but when I turned round there was no one there. I turned back and she'd driven away.'

'You think she saw something that scared her off?'

'What could she have seen? I'm telling you, there was nothing there. Just me. No one walking past, no neighbours looking out of their windows.'

Tamsin frowns. 'So who's Wendy Whitehead?'

I hesitate. 'This might be something you'd rather not know.'

'Is it bad?'

I don't know how to answer that without telling her.

'Is Joe shagging her behind my back?' Tamsin kicks the globe over. 'That'd be typical of my luck at the moment.'

I can't help smiling. Joe would never be unfaithful to Tamsin. His favourite hobby is making no effort whatsoever. You can almost see him looking at other women and thinking *Don't need to bother, already got one of those.* 'It's got nothing to do with your personal life,' I say. I can't stand the suspense, even though I'm the one with the information, not the one waiting to be told. 'Rachel Hines said Wendy Whitehead killed her daughter and son.'

Tamsin snorts and slumps back in Laurie's chair. *My chair.* 'No one was in the house when Marcella Hines died apart from her and Ray. Same with Nathaniel four years later — he was alone with his mother at home when he died. Wendy Whitehead certainly wasn't there, if she even exists. What's more interesting is why Ray Hines is lying, and why now.' I open my mouth

149

but I'm not quick enough. 'I know why,' Tamsin says. 'To reel you in.'

'So what do I do? Go and see her? Ring the police?' I spent most of last night asking myself these questions, unable to sleep for more than half an hour at a time.

'Go and see her for sure,' says Tamsin. 'I'm curious. I've always been curious about her — she's a strange woman. She's gone to great lengths to keep Laurie at a distance, but she can't seem to get enough of you.'

If there's even the tiniest chance that it's true, then I ought to tell the police. And if Wendy Whitehead turns out to be a real person, one who didn't murder Marcella and Nathaniel Hines? She might be interrogated or even arrested, and I'd have caused trouble for an innocent woman. I can't do that, not without finding out more. *Not without being sure it isn't exactly what Rachel Hines wants me to do.*

Why hasn't Laurie rung me back? I've left messages for him everywhere I can think of, saying I need urgent advice.

Marcella and Nathaniel. Now I know their names. I haven't thought much about having children, but if I did, I wouldn't give them names like that. They're the sort of names you choose if you think you're someone to be reckoned with. I wonder if this is my Reverse L'Oréal Syndrome kicking in again; what would I call my kids, Wayne and Tracey? *Because I'm not worth it.*

Wayne Jupiter Benson Nattrass. *Oh, for God's sake, Felicity, grow up!*

Why has Rachel Hines waited until now to mention Wendy Whitehead? Why would she go to prison rather than tell the truth?

'Tell me about her,' I say to Tamsin. 'Everything you know.'

'Ray? She drew the short straw when it came to husbands, that's for sure. Have you read the transcripts of Laurie's interviews with Angus Hines?'

'Not yet.'

'They're somewhere in all that lot.' Tamsin nods at the mess of papers. 'Dig them out, they're worth a read. You'll think Angus can't possibly have said those things until you come across the press cuttings in which he's quoted as saying the exact same things.' She shakes her head. 'Have you ever had that, where you hear something from a person's own mouth, something they'd have no reason to lie about, and you still can't believe it?'

'What does he do? What's his job?'

'He's some kind of editor at *London on Sunday.* He ditched Ray as soon as the verdict went against her. Paul Yardley and

151

Glen Jaggard couldn't have been more different. They were with their wives all the way, totally supportive. I reckon that's why Ray Hines is such an oddster. If you think about it, she suffered an extra trauma. Helen and Sarah were let down by the system, but not by the people closest to them. Their families never doubted their innocence. When you get a chance to read all the notes, you'll see that Helen and Sarah consistently refer to their husbands as their rocks, both of them. Never mind a rock, Angus Hines isn't even a pebble!'

'What about the drugs?' I ask.

Tamsin looks puzzled. 'Sorry, was I supposed to bring some?'

'Rachel Hines is a drug addict, right?'

She rolls her eyes. 'Who told you that?'

'I heard two women talking about her on the Tube once. She mentions it herself somewhere too . . .' I look around for the relevant bit of paper, but can't remember which corner of the office I dropped it in, or even what it was.

'Her interview with Laurie,' says Tamsin. 'Read it again — assuming you can find it among the debris of my once-immaculate filing system. She was being sarcastic, taking the piss out of the public's ridiculous perception of her. She's no more a . . .'

The door opens and Maya comes in carrying two mugs of something hot on a tray. 'Peace offering,' she says brightly. 'Green tea. Fliss, I need to speak to you as soon as poss, hon, so don't be too long. Tam, please say we're still friends. We can still have jolly nights out together, can't we?'

Tamsin and I take our cups, too stunned to speak.

'Oh, and I picked this up from reception by mistake, hon.' Maya pulls an envelope out of the waistband of her jeans and hands it to me. She flashes a sickly smile at us, waves the tray in the air and leaves.

A cream-coloured envelope. I recognise the handwriting; I've seen it on two other envelopes.

'Green tea?' Tamsin snaps. 'Slime is green. Snot is green. Tea's got no business being —'

'Tell me about Ray Hines not being a drug addict,' I say, tossing the envelope to one side. I know there will be numbers in it, and that I won't be able to work out what they mean, so I might as well forget them. It's someone's idea of a joke, and eventually they'll deliver their punchline. It's probably Raffi. He's the comedian around here. One of his favourite topics of conversation is funny things he said and how much everyone laughed at them. 'If she isn't or wasn't a druggie, why did anyone think she was?' I ask, trying to sound as if my mind's still on Rachel Hines.

Tamsin stands up. 'I've got to get out of here. You've been summoned, and if I stay, I'll end up killing somebody.'

'But . . .'

'Laurie wrote an article called "The Doctor Who Lied" — it's somewhere in all this mess. Everything you need to know about Ray Hines is in it.'

'What paper was it in?'

'It hasn't been published yet. The *British Journalism Review* are taking it, and the *Sunday Times* are publishing an abridged version, but both have to wait until Judith Duffy loses her GMC hearing.'

'What if she wins?'

Tamsin looks at me as if I've made the most idiotic suggestion she's ever heard. 'Read the article and you'll see why that's not going to happen.' She leaves the office with a parody of Maya's wave and a 'Bye, *hon*'.

I manage to restrain myself from begging her not to leave me. Once she's gone, I try and fail to persuade myself to put the cream envelope in the bin without opening it, but

I'm too nosey — nosier than I am fright-ened.

Don't be ridiculous. It's some stupid numbers on a card — only an idiot would be scared of that.

I tear open the envelope and see the top of what looks like a photograph. I pull it out, and feel a knot start to form in my stomach. It's a photo of a card with sixteen numbers on it, laid out in four rows of four. Someone's held the card close to the lens in order for the picture to be taken; there are fingers gripping it on both sides. They could be a man's or a woman's; I can't tell.

2	1	4	9
7	8	0	3
4	0	9	8
0	6	2	0

I look for a name or any writing, but there's nothing.

I stuff the photograph back into the envelope and put it in my bag. I'd like to throw it away, but if I do that I won't be able to compare the fingers holding the card to Raffi's fingers, or anyone else's.

Don't let it wind you up. Whoever's doing it, that's exactly what they want.

I sigh, and stare despondently at the papers on the floor. The envelope has made me feel worse about everything. I haven't got a hope in hell of making Laurie's film. I know it; everyone knows it. All these interviews and articles, the medical records, the legal jargon . . . it's too much. It'll take me months, if not years, to get on top of it. The idea that all this has become my responsibility makes me feel sick. I have to get out of the room, away from the piles of paper.

I close the door behind me and head for Maya's office, half hoping she'll fire me.

'You're a dark horse.' Maya folds her arms and looks me up and down as if searching for further evidence of my shady equestrian qualities.

'I'm really not,' I say. Then I take a deep breath. 'Maya, I'm not sure I'm the best person to —'

'Ray Hines rang me a few minutes ago, as I expect you already know.' Wisps of smoke are rising from her desk. Tamsin's bottom-drawer theory must be right.

'What . . . what did she want?' I ask.

'To sing your praises.'

'Me?'

'She's never rung me before, and never returned my calls. Funny that, isn't it? That she'd call me now. Apparently — though this is news to me — she had reservations about Laurie, ungrateful sloaney toff that she is.' Maya smiles. It's the sort of smile a waxwork might reject as being a little on the stiff side. 'Sorry, Fliss, hon, I don't mean to take my anger out on you, but, boy, does it make me mad. When I think how hard Laurie worked to get her out, and she has the nerve to say she never thought much of him . . . as if it's up to her to dish out judgements, as if Laurie's some jumped-up nobody from nowhere instead of the most garlanded investigative journalist in the country. She said he couldn't see the wood for the trees, except she's so stupid, she got it the wrong way round. Her exact words were "He can't see the trees for the wood". She'd still be in prison if it wasn't for him. Has she forgotten that?'

I give my best all-purpose nod. I want to know exactly what Rachel Hines said about me, but I'm too embarrassed to ask.

'Do you by any chance know where Laurie is?' says Maya.

'No idea. I've been trying all day to get hold of him.'

'He's bloody well left.' She sniffs and looks out of the window. 'You watch — we won't see him again. He was supposed to be in until Friday.' She bends down behind her desk. When she reappears, she's holding a well-stocked glass ashtray in one hand and an unambiguous, entirely visible cigarette in the other. 'Don't say a word,' she tries to joke, but it comes out more like a warning. 'I don't normally smoke in the office, but just this once . . .'

'I don't mind. Passive smoking reminds me of how much I used to enjoy the active version.' And makes me feel superior to the poor, weak fools who haven't given up yet, I don't add.

Maya takes a long drag. She's one of the oddest-looking women I've ever seen. In some ways she's attractive. Her figure's great, and she's got big eyes and full lips, but she's completely missing the chin-neck right-angle that most people have between their faces and their torsos. Maya's open-plan face/neck area looks like a flesh-coloured balloon that's been stuffed into the collar of her shirt. She wears her long dark hair in exactly the same style every day: straight at the top and elaborately curled at the bottom, held back by a red Alice band like a Victorian child's doll.

'Be honest with me, sugar,' she purrs. 'Did you ask Ray Hines to ring and talk you up?'

'No.' *No, I fucking didn't, you cheeky bitch.*

'She said she'd spoken to you several times yesterday.'

'She phoned me and said she wanted to talk. I'm going to ring later, set up a meeting.' I leave out the part about Wendy Whitehead, and, to be on the safe side, the story of last night's abortive rendezvous. Until I know what any of it means, I'm reluctant to hand it over.

'She's one step ahead of you.' Maya picks up a scrap of paper from her desk. 'Shall I read you your orders? Marchington House, Redlands Lane, Twickenham. She wants you there at nine tomorrow morning. Have you got a car yet?'

'No. I —'

'You passed your fourth driving test, though, right?'

'It was my second, and no, I didn't.'

'Oh, bad luck. You'll do it next time. Get a taxi, then. Twickenham by public transport's impossible — quicker to get to the North Pole. And keep me updated. I want to know what Ray's so eager to talk to you about.'

Wendy Whitehead. I hate knowing things that other people don't know. My heartbeat is picking up speed, like something walking faster and faster, unwilling to admit it wants to start running. Tamsin's right: Rachel Hines wants to reel me in, and she's afraid it isn't working. I didn't phone her back first thing this morning. It's mid-afternoon and I still haven't made contact. So she rings the MD, knowing I'll have to meet her if the order comes from Maya.

She's clever. Too clever to say, 'He can't see the trees for the wood' by mistake.

'Fliss?'

'Mm?'

'What I said about nobodies from nowhere . . . I didn't mean you, even if it sounded like I did.' Maya flashes me a poor-little-you smile. 'We all have to start somewhere, don't we?'

6
8/10/09

'How about if I buy the first drink tonight?' said Chris Gibbs, not seeing why he should have to.

'No.'

'How about I buy all the drinks?'

'Still no,' said Colin Sellers. They were in an unmarked police pool car, on their way to Bengeo Street. Sellers was driving. Gibbs had his feet up, the soles of his shoes against the door of the glove compartment, safe in the knowledge that it wasn't his to clean. He'd never have sat like this in his own car; Debbie would go ballistic.

'You'll do a better job than me,' he said. 'You've got the patience, the charm. Or is it smarm?'

'Thanks, but no.'

'You mean I haven't come up with the right incentive yet. Every man has his price.'

'She can't be that bad.'

'She's deaf as a fucking door knob. Last

time I was hoarse when I came out, from shouting so she could hear me.'

'You're a familiar face. She's more likely to —'

'You're better with old ladies than I am.'

'Ladies full stop,' Sellers quipped. He thought a lot of himself because he had two women on the go, one of whom he was married to and one he wasn't, though he'd had her so long he might as well be married to her; two women who reluctantly agreed to have sex with him in the vain hope that one day he might be less of a twat than he was now and always had been. Gibbs had only the one: his wife, Debbie.

'Ask her nicely, she might give you a hand-job. Used to be a piano teacher, so she'll be good with her hands.'

'You're sick,' said Sellers. 'She's like, what, eighty?'

'Eighty-three. What's your upper age limit, then? Seventy-five?'

'Pack it in, will you?'

' "All right, love, wipe yourself, your taxi's here. It's four in the morning, love, pay for yourself." ' Gibbs' impression of Sellers was as unpopular with its inspiration and target as it was popular with everyone else at the nick. Over the years, the Yorkshire accent had become considerably more pronounced than Sellers' real one, and quite a bit of heavy breathing had been added. Gibbs was considering a few more minor modifications, but he was worried about straying too far from the subtlety of the original. ' "All right, love, you roll over there into the wet spot, cover it up with your big fat arse." If you want me to stop, you know what you have to do.'

A few seconds of silence, then Sellers said, 'Sorry, was that last bit you? I thought you were still being me.'

Gibbs chuckled. ' "If you want me to stop, you know what you have to do"? You'd really say that, to an eighty-three-year-old grandmother?' He shook his head in mock disgust.

'Let's both do both,' said Sellers. He always caved in eventually. A couple more minutes and he'd be offering to interview both Beryl Murie and Stella White on his own while Gibbs had the afternoon off. It was like the end of a game of chess: Gibbs could see all the moves that lay ahead, all the way to check-mate.

'So you're willing to do Murie?' he said.

'With you, yeah.'

'Why do I have to be there?' said Gibbs indignantly. 'You take Murie, I'll take Stella White — a straight swap. That way we don't waste time. Unless you can't trust yourself alone with Grandma Murie.'

'If I say yes, will you shut the fuck up?' said Sellers.

'Done.' Gibbs grinned and held out his hand for Sellers to shake.

'I'm driving, dickhead.' Sellers shook his head. 'And we're wasting time however we do it. We've already taken statements from Murie and White.'

'They're all we've got. We need to push them for what they didn't think of the first time.'

'There's only one reason we're back here,' said Sellers. 'We've got nowhere else to go. Everyone close to Helen Yardley's got a solid alibi, none of them tested positive for gunpowder residue. We're looking for a stranger, to us and to her — every detective's worst nightmare. A killer with no link to his victim, some no-mark who saw her face on TV once too often and decided she was the one — someone we've no chance of finding. Proust knows it, he just won't admit it yet.'

Gibbs said nothing. He agreed with Simon Waterhouse: it wasn't as simple as someone close to the victim versus stranger murder, not in the case of a woman like Helen Yardley. Someone could have killed her because of what she stood for, someone who stood for the opposite. The way Gibbs saw it, Helen Yardley's murder convictions had started a war. She'd been killed by the other side, the child protection control freaks who assume parents want to kill their kids unless someone can prove otherwise. Gibbs kept this insight to himself because he didn't think he deserved the credit for it; as with all his best ideas, Simon Waterhouse had planted the seed. Gibbs' admiration for Waterhouse was his most closely guarded secret.

'He's really lost it this time.' Sellers was still talking about the Snowman. 'Telling us we aren't allowed to say or even think Helen Yardley might have been guilty. I wasn't thinking that — were you? If her conviction was unsafe, it was unsafe. But now he's put the idea into all our heads by telling us it's forbidden, and all of a sudden everyone's thinking, "Hang on a minute — what if there *is* no smoke without fire?", exactly what he's saying we mustn't think. All that does is make us think it's what he *thinks* we're going to think, which makes us ask ourselves why. Perhaps there's some reason we *ought* to be thinking it.'

'Everyone's thinking it,' said Gibbs. 'They have been from the start, they just haven't been saying it because they're not sure where anyone else stands. No one wants to be the first to say, "Oh, come on, course she did it — sod the court of appeal." Would you want to stand up and say that, when she's been shot in the head and we're all breaking our bollocks to find her killer?'

Sellers turned to look at him. The car swerved. 'You think she killed her babies?'

Gibbs resented having to explain. If Sellers had been listening . . . 'I can see what you're all thinking because I'm the only one *not* thinking it. What that Duffy woman said — it's crap.'

'Duffy who?'

'That doctor. When the prosecutor asked her if it was possible that Morgan and Rowan Yardley were both SIDS deaths, she said it was so unlikely, it bordered on impossible. SIDS is crib death — Sudden Infant Death Syndrome, where the death's natural but no reason can be found.'

'I know that much,' Sellers muttered.

'That was the quote: "so unlikely, it borders on impossible". She said it was overwhelmingly likely that there was an underlying cause, and that the cause was forensic, not medical. In other words, Helen Yardley murdered her babies. When the defence called her on it and asked if, in spite of what she'd said, it was possible for SIDS to strike two children from the same family, same household, she had to say yes, it was possible. But that wasn't the part that impressed the jury — eleven out of twelve of them, anyway. They only heard the "so unlikely, it borders on impossible" part. Turns out there's no statistical basis for that, it was just her talking shit — that's why she's up before the GMC next month for misconduct.'

'You're well informed.'

Gibbs was about to say, 'So should you be, so should everyone working the Yardley murder,' when he realised he would be quoting Waterhouse word for word. 'I reckon Helen Yardley would have walked if it hadn't been for Duffy,' he said. 'All the papers at the time printed the "so unlikely, it borders on impossible" quote. That's what springs to most people's minds when they hear the name Helen Yardley, never mind the successful appeal or Duffy being done for misconduct. And that's just regular people. Cops are even worse — we're programmed to imagine everyone on our radar's guilty and getting away with it: no smoke without fire, whatever legal technicalities might have got Helen Yardley out. I only know different because of Debbie's experience.'

'Your Debbie?'

Would he bother mentioning someone else's Debbie? What did he know about Debbies that weren't his? Sellers was an idiot. Gibbs wished he hadn't said anything now; at the same time, he was looking forward to flipping his trump card. This was his own original material, nothing to do with Waterhouse. 'She's had eleven miscarriages in the last three years, all at ten weeks. She can't get past that point, no matter what she does. She's tried aspirin, yoga, healthy eating, giving up work and lying on the sofa all day — you name it, she's done it. We've had all the tests, seen every doctor and every specialist, and no one can tell us anything. Can't find any problems, that's what they all say.' Gibbs shrugged. 'Doesn't mean nothing's wrong, though, does it? Obviously something is. Any doctor worth shit'll tell you medicine's always going to throw up mysteries no one can solve. How many miscarriages has Stacey had?'

'None,' said Sellers. 'How come you've never . . . ?'

'There you go — all the medical proof you need, and proof that Duffy's a cunt. If one woman can miscarry eleven pregnancies and another miscarry none, it stands to reason that one woman might lose two or even more babies to crib death, and others not lose any. Doesn't make it murder, any more than Debbie murdered all the foetuses she lost. Hardly takes a brain of Britain to work out that some medical issues might be there in one family and not in another, like big noses or a tendency to get varicose veins. Like having a microscopic dick's a problem in your family and not in mine.'

'Apparently there's a rare genetic condition that only affects men with dark curly hair and the initials CG,' Sellers said with a straight face. 'When they look at their own penises, their vision distorts and they see them as five times the size they really are. Sufferers also tend to have a problem with body odour.'

They'd arrived at Bengeo Street. It was a horseshoe-shaped cul-de-sac of 1950s red-brick semis with small front gardens, token patches of green. Many of the houses had extensions built on to their sides. It gave the street an overcrowded look, as if the buildings had over-eaten and were straining to fit into their plots. The Yardleys' house was one of the few on the street that hadn't been extended; no need, with no kids to fill it up, thought Gibbs. It was still cordoned off by police tape. Paul Yardley was staying with his parents, for which Gibbs was grateful. Dealing with Yardley was a nightmare. You'd tell him there was no news and he'd stand there and look at you as if he didn't recognise your answer and was waiting for the real one.

Gibbs looked at his watch: half past four. Stella White's red Renault Clio was parked outside number 16, which meant she was back from picking up her son from school. Sellers had rung Beryl Murie's bell and looked as taken aback as Gibbs had been two days ago to get, by way of a response, a wordless electronic version of *How Much is That Doggy in the Window?* that was audible across the street. 'Forgot to warn you about the deaf doorbell,' Gibbs called out.

Stella White opened her front door as he approached. She was holding a child's muddy football boots, a blue plastic alien toy and a toast crust. Her jeans and V-necked jumper hung off her thin frame, and there were dark circles under her eyes. If this was what life with children did to you, maybe he and Debbie were the lucky ones.

'DC Gibbs, Culver Valley CID.'

'I was expecting a DC Sellers,' Stella White said — upbeat, smiling, as if a DC Gibbs was some kind of bonus, or treat.

170

Sorry to disappoint you.

'Change of plan.' Gibbs showed her his ID, and allowed himself to be ushered into the front room. Television noise was coming from the next room, the one with the closed door: some sort of horse-racing commentary.

'Your husband watching the racing?' he asked. The room they were in looked as if it had had some money spent on it: thick swagged curtains, real wood floor, a slate and marble fireplace. Subtle colours that you couldn't easily describe, nothing as straightforward as red or blue or green. Debbie would have loved it, though she'd have been unwilling to live on Bengeo Street, however smart the house was inside; it was too close to the Winstanley estate, on the wrong side of town.

'I haven't got a husband,' said Stella. 'My son Dillon's got a thing about horses. At first I tried to stop him watching the racing, but . . .' She shrugged. 'He loves it so much, I decided it was mean to deprive him.'

Gibbs nodded. 'Any sort of interest's got to be good, hasn't it?' he said. 'When I was a kid I wasn't interested in anything. Nothing. I was bored out of my mind until I was old enough to drink and . . .' He stopped himself just in time, but Stella White was

171

grinning.

'Exactly,' she said. 'I'm just so glad he's passionate about something — it almost doesn't matter what. He studies form and everything. Get him on the subject of racing and you can't shut him up.'

'How old is he?'

'Four.' Seeing Gibbs' surprise, Stella said, 'I know. It can be a bit embarrassing. He's not a child prodigy or anything — just a normal kid who's crazy about horse-racing.'

'Next you'll tell me he speaks twelve languages and can cure cancer,' said Gibbs.

'I wish.' Stella's smile dimmed. 'I don't want to embarrass you by springing this on you, but I find it's easier if I do, and then it's out of the way. I've got cancer.'

'Right.' Gibbs cleared his throat. 'Sorry.'

'Don't worry, I'm used to it — the cancer, people's reactions to it. I've had it for years, and I've lived a better life because of it.'

Gibbs didn't know what else he could say apart from sorry. A better life? Who was she trying to kid? He was starting to wish he'd stuck with Beryl Murie.

'Please, have a seat,' said Stella. 'Can I get you anything to drink?'

'No, I'm good. I could do with Dillon joining us, if you can tear him away from the horses. I'd like to go over what you've already told us about the man you saw approaching Helen Yardley's front door, see if you remember anything new.'

Stella frowned. 'I doubt Dillon saw him. I was strapping him into his car seat — he sits in the back, so he'll have had a view of the back of the seat in front and not much else.'

'What about before you put him in the car? Presumably the man approached the house from the road. Might Dillon have seen him further down the street, before you strapped him into his chair?'

'He could have, I suppose, though I didn't notice him, not till he was right outside Helen's house. But to be honest, I don't think Dillon saw him at all. The detective who came last time talked to him, and it wasn't much use. Dillon said he'd seen a man, but that was pretty much it — he couldn't say when or even *where,* and by that point he already knew *I'd* seen a man . . . I think he was just saying it because he'd heard me say it.'

'If only the man had been a horse,' Gibbs attempted a joke.

'Oh, then he'd have remembered every detail.' Stella laughed. 'Dillon's quite good with detail usually, even when horses aren't involved, but he couldn't tell the detective anything: hair colour, height, clothes. Not that I was much better.' She looked apologetic. 'I *think* he had darkish hair and darkish clothes, I think he was tallish, regular build, and at the upper end of young or the lower end of middle-aged. I seem to remember he was wearing a coat, but who wouldn't have been? It's October.'

'Not carrying anything, as far as you remember?' Gibbs asked.

'No, but . . . he could have been, I suppose.'

'And you didn't notice if he had a car, or if there were any cars not usually parked on Bengeo Street that were there that morning?'

'I wouldn't know a Volvo from a Skoda,' said Stella. 'Sorry. I'm completely car-blind. There could have been twenty bright pink Rolls-Royces parked on the street and I wouldn't have noticed.'

'Not a problem,' said Gibbs. 'If I could have a quick chat with Dillon, though . . .' He produced his best smile. 'I'm not expecting him to tell me anything, but it's worth a shot. A lot of the blokes I know who are into the horses are also into cars.'

'Okay, but . . . if by any chance he starts to talk about Helen's death, could you . . .' Stella stopped. She looked embarrassed. 'I know this is going to sound weird, but could you try to be as positive about it as you can?'

Gibbs chewed his lip, stumped. Positive, about a woman who'd been fucked over by the legal system, robbed of her only surviving child and then shot in the head?

'This is going to sound very convenient from a woman with terminal cancer, I know, but I'm trying to bring up Dillon to believe what I believe: that there is no death, or there doesn't have to be. The spirit is what matters and that never dies. Everything else is trivial.'

Gibbs sat as still as a stone. He should have stuck with Beryl Murie, quit while he was ahead. 'What have you told Dillon about Helen Yardley's murder?'

'The truth. He knows she was a special person. Sometimes special people are chosen for soul challenges that most of us couldn't cope with, which is why Helen had a harder time than most, but now she's moved on to the next stage. I told him she'd be happy, if happiness is what her spirit needs, in her next life.'

Gibbs managed a non-commital nod. He looked again at the room he was in: fireplace with four framed photographs on the mantelpiece above it, two chairs, a two-seater sofa, bellows, a brass bucket for coal, a poker for the fire, two wooden coffee tables. No joss-sticks, nothing tasselled, no yin-yang symbols; Gibbs felt as if he'd been conned. 'What did you tell Dillon about the person who killed Helen?' he asked. Whoever he was, he was the one Gibbs wanted to move on to the next stage, the stage of being banged up for life and, ideally, beaten to mincemeat in some shithole of a prison.

'That was hard, obviously,' said Stella. 'I tried to explain to him that some people are afraid of experiencing their pain and try to redirect it to others. If you don't mind my saying so, you strike me as falling into that category.'

'Me?' Gibbs sat up straighter in his chair. *Get me the fuck out of here.*

'Not that I'm saying you'd do anything violent — of *course* you wouldn't.'

Gibbs wasn't so sure.

'It's just . . . I sense a lot of clouds close to the surface. Underneath those, there's a light burning brightly, but it's . . .' Stella laughed suddenly. 'I'm sorry. I'll shut up — I've got bigmouthitis as well as cancer, I'm afraid.'

'Can I have a word with Dillon?'

'I'll go and grab him.'

Left alone in the room, Gibbs exhaled slowly. What would Waterhouse think about a woman who saw perks where others saw tragedy, and violent death as a great opportunity, facilitating a soul's entry into a happier next life? What if you decided a friend of yours had suffered enough in her present incarnation and it was time for her soul to move up a level? Gibbs wondered if he ought to mention it.

Through the wall, he heard the sound of Dillon's muffled anger as the TV was switched off. He stood up and walked over to the display of photographs above the fireplace. One was of Dillon in his school uniform. He looked as if he was saying the 'ch' part of the word 'cheese'. There was a picture of Stella and Dillon together, and two of Stella alone, in running gear. In one she had a medal on a ribbon round her neck.

When she came into the room with Dillon, Gibbs said, 'Runner, are you?' It was something he'd considered taking up, before deciding he couldn't be bothered.

'Not any more,' said Stella. 'I haven't got the strength for it now. When I first got my diagnosis, I realised there was one thing I'd wanted to do all my life that I still hadn't done, so I trained and I did it: two or three marathons a year for about five years. I couldn't believe how much healthier it made me feel. Not only feel,' Stella corrected herself. 'I *was* healthier. The doctors gave me two years to live — I've managed to wangle an extra eight.'

'That's not bad.' Maybe thinking positive about death had its upside after all.

'I've raised pots of money for charity. Last time I ran the London Marathon, all the money I raised went to JIPAC — you know, Helen's organisation. I did a couple of triathlons, too, also for charity. Now I'm mostly doing public speaking — to cancer patients, doctors, Women's Institute, University of the Third Age — anyone who'll have me.' Stella smiled. 'If you're not careful, I'll show you my cardboard box full of press cuttings.'

'Can I watch telly?' Dillon asked impatiently. He was wearing a blue tracksuit with a school logo on the top. There were traces of chocolate round his mouth.

'Soon, love.' Stella stroked the top of his head. 'Once we've finished chatting to DC Gibbs, you can go back to your horses.'

'But I want to do what *I* want to do,' Dillon protested.

'Can you remember Monday morning?' Gibbs asked him.

'It's Thursday today.'

'That's right. So Monday was . . .'

'Before Thursday it was Wednesday, before Wednesday it was Tuesday, before Tuesday it was Monday. That day?'

'Right,' Gibbs agreed.

'We saw the man with the umbrella, beyond,' said Dillon.

'Umbrella?' Stella laughed. 'That's a new one. He didn't —'

'Beyond?' Gibbs knelt down in front of the boy. 'You mean ahead?'

'No. Beyond.'

'Did you see the man outside Helen Yardley's house on Monday morning?'

'I saw him and Mum saw him.'

'But he didn't have an umbrella, sweetpea,' said Stella gently.

'He did.'

'What colour was the umbrella?'

'Black and silver,' said Dillon, without missing a beat.

Stella was shaking her head in apparent amusement. She mouthed something at Gibbs that implied she'd explain later, once Dillon had been returned to the TV room.

'Did you see the man getting into or out of a car?'

Dillon shook his head.

'But you saw him outside the Yardleys' house, on the path.'

'And beyond.'

'You mean he went into the house?' Gibbs signalled to Stella not to interrupt.

She ignored him. 'Sorry, but . . . sweet-pea, you *didn't* see him go into Helen's house, did you?'

'Mrs White, please . . .'

'The more times he's asked, the more he'll invent,' said Stella. 'Sorry, I know I shouldn't leap in, but you don't know Dillon like I do. He's very, very sensitive. He can see that people want him to tell them things, and he doesn't want to disappoint them.'

'He was in the lounge,' said Dillon. 'I saw him in the lounge.'

'Dillon, you *didn't*. You're only trying to help, I know, but you didn't see the man in Helen's lounge, did you?' Stella turned to Gibbs. 'Believe me, if he'd had a black and silver umbrella with him, I'd have seen it. It wasn't even raining. It was bright, sunny and cold — what I call perfect Christmas Day weather, except in October. Most people want snow at Christmas, but I —'

'It wasn't bright,' said Dillon. 'There wasn't enough sun to make it bright. Can I watch the horses now?'

Gibbs made a mental note to look up last Sunday's weather forecasts for Monday. Someone cautious might have taken an umbrella with him even on a sunny morning, if rain had been predicted. *And if it hadn't?* Could the gun have been inside the closed umbrella?

'It *was* raining,' said Dillon, looking up at Gibbs with a hard-done-by expression on his face. 'The umbrella was wet. I *did* see the man in the lounge.'

Judith Duffy lived in a three-storey detached villa in Ealing, on a windy tree-lined street that felt neither like what Simon thought of as 'proper London' nor like anywhere else in particular. He decided he wouldn't like to live here. Not that he could have afforded to, so it was probably just as well. He rang the bell for the third time. *Nothing.*

He pushed open the gleaming brass letterbox and looked through it, saw a wooden coat stand, a herringbone parquet floor, Persian rugs, a black piano and red-cushioned stool. He took a step back when his view was blocked by purple material with a button attached to it.

The door opened. Knowing that Judith Duffy was fifty-four, Simon was shocked to see a woman who could easily have been seventy. Her straight iron-grey hair was tied back from her narrow, age-hollowed face. In the photograph of her that Simon had seen, the one the newspapers always used, Duffy had looked much rounder; there had been the hint of a double chin.

'I don't think I invited you to peer through my letterbox,' she said. It was the sort of phrase that begged, Simon thought, to be delivered with barely suppressed outrage, but Dr Duffy sounded as if she was merely stating a fact. 'Who are you?'

Simon identified himself. 'I've left you two messages,' he said.

'I didn't return your calls because I didn't want to waste your time,' said Duffy. 'This will be the shortest interview of your career. I won't talk to you or answer your questions, and I won't allow you to do whatever test it is that establishes whether or not I've fired a gun. Also, you can tell your colleague Fliss Benson to stop bothering me — I won't talk to her either. I'm sorry you've had a wasted journey.'

Colleague Fliss Benson? Simon had never heard of her.

Duffy started to close the door. He put out his hand to stop her. 'Everyone else we've asked has agreed to be swabbed, and cooperated with us in any way they can.'

'I'm not everybody. Please take your hand off my door.' She closed it in his face.

Simon pushed open the letterbox again

and saw purple. 'There's someone I can't find,' he addressed Duffy's cardigan, the only part of her he could see. 'Rachel Hines. I've spoken to her ex-husband, Angus. He said she's staying with friends somewhere in London, but he doesn't know where. I don't suppose you've got any idea?'

'You should ask Laurie Nattrass that question,' said Duffy.

'I'm planning to, soon as he rings me back.'

'So it's everyone minus one, then.'

'Pardon?'

'Cooperating. Laurie Nattrass can't be cooperating if he hasn't returned your calls.'

Do we have to have this conversation through a letterbox? 'Mr Nattrass has already been swabbed, alibied and eliminated, as you would be if you —'

'Goodbye, Mr Waterhouse.'

Simon heard the shuffle of her feet on the wood floor as she moved away. 'Help me out here,' he called after her. 'Between you and me, and I shouldn't be telling you this, I'm worried about Mrs Hines.' No matter what the Snowman said, no matter what Sam Kombothekra said, Simon's instincts told him he was looking for a serial killer, or a person with the potential to become one — someone who left cards bearing strange numerical codes in the pockets of his victims. Was Rachel Hines one of those victims? Or was Simon's imagination as out of control as Charlie was always telling him it was?

He let out a heavy sigh. As if in response, Judith Duffy took a few steps towards the front door. Now Simon could see her again, her shoulder and her arm. Not her face. 'I had lunch with Ray Hines on Monday,' she said. 'There, I've given you my alibi — and hers — so you can go away happy, and even if you aren't happy, you can go. Neither of us knew that it was the day someone would murder Helen Yardley. At that point it was just Monday 5 October, same as any other Monday. We met at a restaurant, spent the afternoon together.'

'Which restaurant?' Simon got out his pad and pen.

'Sardo Canale in Primrose Hill. Ray's choice.'

'Do you mind my asking . . . ?'

'Goodbye, Mr Waterhouse.'

This time, when Simon pressed the letter-box, he met with resistance. She was holding it shut from the inside.

He went back to his car and switched on his phone. He had two messages, one from a man he assumed was Laurie Nattrass whose message was a strange noise followed by the words 'Laurie Nattrass' and nothing more, and one from Charlie, saying that Lizzie Proust had rung to invite the two of them for dinner on Saturday night. Didn't Simon think it was weird, she wanted to know, given that they'd known the Prousts for years and no such invitation had been forthcoming until now, and what did he want her to say? Simon texted the word 'NO', in capitals, to her mobile phone, dropping his own twice in the process, in his eagerness to get the message sent. The Snowman, inviting him for dinner; the thought made Simon's throat close like a clenched fist. He forced his mind away from it, unwilling to deal with the violence of his reaction and the element of fear it contained.

He rang one of the three mobile numbers he had for Laurie Nattrass, and this time someone answered after the first ring. Simon heard breathing. 'Hello?' he said. 'Mr Nattrass?'

'Laurie Nattrass,' said a gruff voice, the same one that had left the message.

'Is that Mr Nattrass I'm speaking to?'

'Dunno.'

'Pardon?'

'I'm not where you are, so I can't see who

you're speaking to. If you're speaking to me, then yes, you're speaking to Mr Nattrass, Mr Laurie Nattrass. And I'm speaking to Detective Constable — and I'm spelling that with a "u" instead of an "o" and an extra "t" between the "n" and the "s" — Simon Waterhouse.' As he spoke, his words rose and fell in volume, as if someone was sticking pins in him and each new jab made him raise his voice. Was he insane? Pissed?

'When and where can we meet?' Simon asked. 'I'll come to you if you like.'

'Never. Nowhere, no-how.'

It was going to be like that, was it? One of those easy conversations. Could this man really be an Oxford- and Harvard-educated multi-award-winning investigative journalist? He didn't sound like one.

'Do you know where I might find Rachel Hines?'

'Twickenham,' said Nattrass. 'Why? Ray didn't kill Helen. Looking to fit her up again, are you? You can't step into the same river twice, but you can fit up the same innocent woman twice. If you're filth.' It wasn't only the volume that varied from word to word, Simon noticed — it was also the speed at which Nattrass spoke. Some sentences spurted out; others were delivered slowly, with an air of hesitation, as if his attention were elsewhere.

'Do you happen to have an address or contact — ?'

'Speak to Judith Duffy instead of wasting my time and Ray Hines'. Ask her what her two sons-in-law were doing on Monday.' It was an order rather than a suggestion.

Two sons-in-law. And, since these days the police looked at things from an equal opportunities perspective, two daughters. Were they worth checking out?

'Mr Nattrass, I need to ask you some questions,' Simon tried again. 'I'd prefer to do it in person, but . . .'

'Pretend your phone's a person. Pretend it's called Laurence Hugo St John Fleet Nattrass, and ask away.'

If this man was sane, Simon was a banana sandwich. Nattrass was certainly drunk. 'We're considering the possibility that Helen Yardley was murdered as a result of her work for JIPAC. As you're the . . .'

'. . . co-founder, you're wondering if anyone's tried to kill me. No. Next?'

'Has anyone threatened you? Anyone acting out of character, any strange emails or letters?'

'How's Giles Proust? Leader of the band now, isn't he? How can he be objective? It's a joke. He arrested Helen for murder. Have

187

you read her book?'

'Helen's . . . ?'

'*Nothing But Love.* Nothing but praise for dear old Giles. What do you think of him? Cunt, right?'

Simon started to say 'Yeah,' then turned it into a cough, his heart racing. He'd nearly said it. That would have been his job down the pan.

'If he thought Helen was innocent, why did he arrest her?' Nattrass demanded. 'Why didn't he resign? Morally colour-blind, is he?'

'In our job, if you're told to arrest someone, you arrest them,' said Simon. *Morally colour-blind.* If there was a better description of the Snowman, he had yet to hear it.

'Know what he did when she got out? Turned up on her doorstep with everything his henchmen had confiscated when they arrested her — Moses basket, crib, bouncy chair, Morgan and Rowan's clothes, the lot. Didn't even ring first to warn her, or ask if she wanted a van-load of reminders of her dead babies. Know how many times he visited her in prison? None.'

'I wanted to ask you about a card that was found in Helen Yardley's pocket after her death,' Simon said. 'It's been kept out of the press.'

'2,1,4,9 . . .'

'How do you know those numbers?' Simon didn't care if he sounded abrupt. Even at his rudest, he was no competition for Nattrass.

'Fliss had them. Felicity Benson, Happiness Benson. Except she's not very happy at the moment, not with me. She didn't know what the numbers meant. I chucked them in the bin. Do you know what they mean? Know who sent them?'

Felicity Benson. *Fliss.* Simon had no idea who she was, but she'd just leaped straight to the top of the list of people he wanted to speak to.

Angus Hines

Transcript of Interview 1, 16 February 2009

AH: Well? I assume you have questions you want to ask me and aren't here for the sole purpose of recording silence.

LN: I'm surprised you agreed to be interviewed, frankly.

AH: You mean that if you were me, you'd hide away in shame?

LN: I'm surprised you agreed to talk to me. You know where I stand. You know I'm making a film about —

AH: You mean I know whose side you're on?

LN: Yes.

(*Pause*)

AH: You think it's appropriate to take sides?

LN: Not appropriate. Essential.

AH: So, for the sake of clarity, whose side are you on?

LN: Ray's. And Helen Yardley's, and all

the other innocent women who've been locked up for killing children they didn't kill.

AH: How many altogether? Ever totted up the grand total?

LN: Too many. JIPAC's pressing for five cases to be reviewed at the moment, and there's at least another three that I know of — innocent women in the British prison system thanks to the lies of your friend Dr Judith Duffy.

AH: My friend? Oh, I see. So on one side we have you, my ex-wife and the scores of unjustly maligned mothers or baby-minders, victims of what I believe you've called a modern-day witch-hunt . . .

LN: Because it is one.

AH: . . . and on the other side there's me, Judith Duffy — anybody else?

LN: Plenty. Anyone who played a part in ruining the lives of Ray, Helen, Sarah Jaggard and other women like them.

AH: And in your righteous war, with its clearly defined armies, who's on the side of my children? Who's on the side of Marcella and Nathaniel?

LN: If you think —

AH: I am. I'm on their side. It's the only side I'm on. It's the only side I've ever been on. That's why I'm willing to be interviewed — by you, by anybody who asks me. You can try as hard as you like to cast me as a villain in your BBC documentary, but provided you represent me accurately, I believe the viewing public will see the truth behind your lies.

LN: Me? What have I lied about?

AH: Deliberately? Probably nothing. But going through life with blinkers on and spouting your prejudices at every opportunity is a form of lying.

LN: So I'm blinkered?

AH: You can't see the trees for the wood.

LN: The wood for the trees. The expression is 'You can't see the wood for the trees'.

AH: (*Laughs*) 'Oh! Let us never, never doubt/What nobody is sure about!'

LN: I see. So I'm blinkered because I've always believed in your wife's innocence? Unlike you, who betrayed her?

AH: I don't think I did betray her. And, for the record, I too now believe she's innocent. And I believe it all the more strongly for having once believed otherwise — something I wouldn't expect someone with your simplistic outlook to understand.

LN: Is that your way of saying sorry? Have you apologised to Ray for doubting her?

192

Have you even tried?

AH: I've nothing to be sorry for. All I've done is refuse, throughout, to insult anybody, my wife . . .

LN: Ex-wife

AH: . . . or my children, by lying. When the police first let it be known that they suspected Ray of murder, I doubted her innocence, yes. I also doubted her guilt. I was in no position to say for sure how Marcella and Nathaniel died, since I wasn't at home when it happened, on either occasion. The police were suspicious — I didn't see why they would be if there were no grounds for suspicion. They'd have had better things to do, surely? Two deaths for no apparent reason in the same family is unusual. Marcella and Nathaniel were perfectly well in the days before they died. There was nothing wrong with them.

LN: Are you a paediatrician? I'll have to amend my notes. It says 'photographer' here.

AH: Then you'd better make an amendment, as you say. I was promoted some time ago. I'm Pictures Desk Editor at *London on Sunday*. Someone else does the donkey work now. I get to sit at a desk eating chocolate biscuits and looking at

Big Ben out of my window. See how easily you can mistake an incorrect assumption for a fact? I don't make assumptions, unlike you. I made none about Ray. She loved the children — her love for them was genuine, I had no doubts on that front. At the same time, I was realistic enough to wonder whether certain psychological . . . conditions might exist in which love for one's child is compatible with doing it harm. Because of Ray's history.

LN: Oh, come on! She sits on a window ledge to smoke a cigarette — next thing she knows, the filth are out in full force, cordoning off the area around the house, standing in her bedroom where she can hear every word they're saying, on their mobiles to her GP asking about the percentage likelihood of her jumping.

AH: That's one version of the story, one of the many she's served up over the years: the 'all I wanted was some peace and quiet and a fag' remix. In court she tried to pass the whole thing off as an episode of postnatal madness, claiming she had no clear memory of either the window ledge or the cigarette.

LN: There's nothing wrong with Ray, psychologically or in any other way. She's a normal, healthy woman.

AH: Does it strike you as normal behaviour to climb out of a dangerously high window and sit on a small ledge, smoking? Not to mention that this happened on Ray's first day back after she'd inexplicably walked out on me and Marcella when Marcella was only two weeks old. Then, nine days later, she just as inexplicably walks back in, refusing to say a word about where she's been or why she left, and when pressed on the subject, she rushes upstairs and climbs out of the window. If that was your wife behaving like that and then she was accused of murdering your two children, you're telling me you'd have no doubts?

LN: If Ray was suffering from post-natal depression, whose fault was that? You snored your way through the first fourteen nights of Marcella's life while Ray was up every hour and a half breastfeeding. She'd endured two weeks of looking after a demanding baby with zero help from you, and she decided . . .

AH: . . . that if I didn't experience first-hand how hard it was, I'd never understand, so she took off and left me to my own devices. The 'my husband's a sexist bastard' feminist remix.

LN: You can call it that if you want. I call

it the truth.

AH: Nine days after her departure, Ray returned to find I hadn't coped on my own at all, as I'd been supposed to — I'd summoned my mother instantly, being an unreconstructed man. Since Ray's only desire had been to turn our home into a utopia of gender equality and me into Mary Poppins, she was furious with both me and Mum. She climbed out of the window to get away from us. You see? I'm as familiar with the lie as you are.

(*Pause*)

The fact is that from the moment I brought Ray and Marcella home from the hospital, I did my fair share of the child-care, if not more. If Marcella cried in the night, I was the one who got out of bed first. While Ray fed her, I made us both cups of tea, then sometimes we'd talk, or sometimes we'd listen to the radio. When we were bored of both, we'd open our bedroom curtains and try to look into neighbours' windows, see what was going on. Nothing much. Lucky bastards were sleeping.

(*Long pause*)

I was always the one who changed Marcella's nappy and settled her back to sleep. Not once or twice — every time. By the time I got back into bed, Ray would already be asleep. I did all the supermarket shopping, all the washing and ironing, cooked the evening meals . . .

LN: Then why did Ray walk out on you?

AH: Not only me. Me and Marcella. You don't ever wonder whether a woman who's capable of deserting her newborn baby might also be capable of killing that same baby a few weeks later?

LN: Never.

AH: A woman who has no qualms about lying under oath, implying in court that she was suffering from post-natal depression, then telling you later that it was all part of some feminist stand she'd decided to take?

LN: Not everyone who lies is a murderer.

AH: True. Ray certainly lied, but, as I said before, I no longer believe she harmed Marcella and Nathaniel.

LN: We all lie from time to time, but hardly any of us kill our own children. Most men might give their wives the benefit of the doubt. Paul Yardley did. Glen Jaggard did.

AH: You need first to have a doubt in order to give someone the benefit of it. Everything I've heard about Yardley and Jaggard suggests they never doubted. You were talking about normality before. Do you think that's normal? Natural?

(*Pause*)

I didn't think Ray was a murderer. All I knew was that our two babies were dead, four years apart, and some people thought Ray might have been responsible. I didn't think she was a murderer and I didn't think she wasn't a murderer. I didn't know.

LN: The result of your not knowing was that Ray had to spend the run-up to her trial living with a man who wasn't her loving husband any more but a sinister data-gathering stranger, watching her for signs of guilt or innocence. How do you think that must have been for her? And then when the verdict went against her, you gave an interview outside court saying you were glad your children's killer had been brought to justice and that you'd be starting divorce proceedings as soon as possible. Unless you were misquoted?

AH: No. That's what I said.

LN: You didn't even have the decency to speak to Ray in private first, before announcing your abandonment of her to a scrum of reporters and photographers. In fact, you didn't talk to Ray again until after her release, did you?

AH: I don't see this as being a loyalty issue. Is it disloyal to wonder if your wife
might have murdered your children when
that's the question everyone else in the
country is asking themselves? When you
hear her lie in court? She didn't only lie
about why she left home . . .

LN: Even without any creative editing on
my part, people are going to think you're
a cold-hearted monster. What if Ray had
been acquitted? How would you have felt
about her then?

AH: This isn't about feelings. I love Ray. I
always have and I always will, but I wanted
justice for Marcella and Nathaniel. I was
in a difficult situation. Since I knew I'd
never know for sure — and no one can
live with uncertainty for ever, especially
not me — I made a decision: whatever the
court's verdict, I would abide by it. If the
verdict had been not guilty, I would have
believed Ray was innocent.

LN: Let's have this absolutely clear: you're
saying that if it had gone the other way,
your doubts would have vanished just like
that?

AH: I would have seen to it that they did.
I'm not saying it wouldn't have taken
some self-discipline, but that was my decision. That's why we have a justice system,

isn't it? To make decisions that no man alone can be expected to make.

LN: I suppose you've never heard of the Birmingham Six?

AH: I've heard of them. And of the Guildford Four, and the Broadwater Farm Three, Winston Silcott and his cronies. And of the Chippenham Seven, the Penzance Nine, the Basingstoke Five, the Bath Spa Two . . .

LN: You're talking rubbish.

AH: How many fake examples will I have to invent before you take my point?
(*Pause*)

AH: You know, in a way it's quite comforting talking to you. You haven't got a hope in hell of understanding someone like me. Or Ray.

LN: How did you feel when Ray won her appeal and had her convictions overturned?

AH: I wondered whether it might mean she was innocent.

LN: Did you feel any guilt at that point?

AH: Me? I didn't kill my children, or lie in court, or arrive at an incorrect verdict. What did I have to feel guilty about?

LN: Do you regret divorcing your wife?

AH: No.

LN: But you no longer believe she's a

murderer?

AH: No. But I did when I divorced her, which means it was the right thing to do at the time, based on the information available to me then.

THE DOCTOR WHO LIED: THE STORY OF A MODERN-DAY WITCH-HUNT

Laurie Nattrass, March 2009
(Tamsin — this is for British Journalism Review *as soon as Duffy loses her GMC hearing)*

It's one of the staples of fiction: the doctor with the God complex, conceited enough to imagine he can draw a murder to the police's attention, explain how it was committed (injection of potassium between the toes) and still elude detection as the culprit. He never does, for that would deprive the lead sleuth of the opportunity to say, 'You've developed a God complex, doctor. You get a kick out of choosing who lives and who dies.'

In fiction, it makes for another predictable evening in front of the television. In real life, it's considerably more frightening. Harold Shipman, the GP who murdered hundreds of his patients, died without admitting his guilt or offering any explanation for his crimes. He was a contemporary bogeyman, an unassuming monster who moved among ordinary people undetected, passing himself off as one of them.

Following hot on his heels in the monster stakes is Dr Judith Duffy. Last week [adjust if necessary] Dr Duffy was struck off after a GMC hearing found her guilty of misconduct. Despite never having murdered anybody, Dr Duffy was responsible for ruining the lives of dozens of innocent women whose only crime was to be in the wrong place at the wrong time when a child died: Helen Yardley, Lorna Keast, Joanne Bew, Sarah Jaggard, Dorne Llewellyn . . . the list goes on and on.

Here's a horror story to rival the most terrifying tale any author of penny-dreadfuls could dream up. Dr Duffy doesn't make an appearance until later, but bear with me. In August 1998, Ray (Rachel) Hines, a middle-class physiotherapist from Notting Hill, London, gave birth to a baby girl, Marcella. Ray's husband Angus, who works for *London on Sunday,* saw no need to amend his lifestyle. He continued to work long hours and go out drinking with colleagues; meanwhile Ray, having temporarily given up the work she loved in order to stay at home with a baby who never slept for more than an hour at a time, became progressively more exhausted. So far, so familiar. Mothers everywhere will be nodding as they read this, muttering rude comments about men under their breath.

Most women believe themselves to be the equals of their male partners until the advent of the first baby, at which point most — even in this day and age, astonishingly — accept that the days of equality are over. The men continue to go out into the world, and come home insisting they need a good night's sleep in order to perform well the next day. The trouble is, there's a baby to be looked after, so someone has to put their career on hold, if not abandon it altogether. Someone has to summon up the energy, after a punishing day without a break, to cook, clean and iron. Someone must relinquish their freedom and identity for the greater good of the family unit. Those someones are invariably women.

This is what happened to Ray Hines,

but fortunately for Ray, or perhaps unfortunately, she is not most women. Having had the privilege of meeting her more than once, I can tell you that Ray is exceptional. Before tragedy and injustice devastated her life, Ray was one of the UK's most successful businesswomen, co-founder of the market-leading PhysioFit franchise. I once asked her to tell me how this came about. She said, 'I had a bad back as a teenager'. Referred to an incompetent physiotherapist who sat reading a magazine while Ray walked on a machine, Ray decided to do something about the standard of physiotherapy provision in the UK and made a career out of it. That's the sort of woman she is. Most of us would have asked our GPs to refer us to a better physiotherapist, and left it at that.

Ray decided she wasn't willing to be the sacrificial lamb of the family. When Marcella was two weeks old, Ray left home without telling Angus where she was going. For nine days, she stayed away, phoning home regularly but refusing to say where she was or when she'd be back. Her hope was that when she returned, Angus — who would presumably be struggling to cope alone —

would have realised the error of his ways, enabling the couple to go forward on a more equal footing.

No such luck. Ray came back to find Angus's mother living in her house, attending to all things domestic with great flair and enthusiasm. Angus would for ever after be able to say, 'My mum coped, so why can't you?' That's why Ray lied to Angus, initially, about the reason for her nine-day absence: she felt humiliated by her failed plan, and told him she had no idea why she'd walked out and couldn't remember where she'd been for the nine days she wasn't at home. Angus rejected that answer as unsatisfactory and wouldn't stop badgering her, so she ran up to their bedroom and locked the door. When Angus and his mother started to berate her through the door, she opened the window and climbed out onto a rather precarious ledge, to escape their harsh voices.

She lit a cigarette and thought about her options. She didn't think Angus would change for the better; if anything she thought he might get worse. She wondered, fleetingly, if she ought to disappear for good. Angus, his mother and Marcella would manage fine without her. She loved Marcella, but she wasn't prepared to live out the rest of her life as the family slave, and she wondered if this made her a bad mother, since most of her good-mother friends seemed to welcome slavery, or at least tolerate it with reasonably good humour. Not for one second did she think about jumping off that ledge.

Fast-forward three weeks. 12 November 1998, 9 p.m. Angus is out with friends from work. Ray has given Marcella her last feed of the day and settled her in her Moses basket. Life is, generally, better. Marcella is sleeping well and therefore so is Ray. Angus has suggested that Ray should go back to work as soon as possible, which is also what she wants, and they've agreed that Marcella will start at a local nursery when she's six months old. Angus regularly jokes that this will be brilliant for Marcella, and names the children of several of their friends who have been 'spoilt to the point of vileness' by having their mothers at their beck and call for the first five years of their lives.

Ray goes upstairs to her bedroom, and lets out a howl when she sees Marcella. Her face is blue and she's not breathing.

Ray summons an ambulance, which arrives three minutes later, but it's too late. Ray and Angus are distraught.

Enter one Judith Duffy, a perinatal and paediatric pathologist and Consultant Senior Lecturer in Infant Health and Developmental Physiology at the University of Westminster. Duffy performs the post-mortem on Marcella and finds nothing to suggest she did not die naturally. There is one fractured rib and some bruising, but Duffy says both were probably caused by attempts at resuscitation. The ambulance staff agree. Marcella is a victim of Sudden Infant Death Syndrome (SIDS), which means that no explanation for her death can be found.

Fast-forward four years. Ray and Angus have another baby, Nathaniel. One morning, when Nathaniel is twelve weeks old, Ray wakes to find Angus's side of the bed empty, and light streaming in through the curtains. She is terrified. Nathaniel always wakes her up before it's light, so something must be wrong. She runs to his Moses basket and the nightmare begins all over again: he is blue, not breathing. Ray calls an ambulance. Again, it's too late.

Again, the post-mortem is performed

by Dr Judith Duffy, who finds swollen brain tissue and evidence of subdural bleeding. She concludes that Nathaniel must have been shaken, even after consultation with an eminent colleague, Dr Russell Meredew, who disagrees. Crucially, Meredew points out that there is no tearing of the nerves in the brain, as there would have been if Nathaniel had been shaken. Dr Duffy tells Dr Meredew — OBE, incidentally, and winner of the Sir James Spence Medal for his contribution to extending paediatric knowledge — that he doesn't know what he's talking about. She says she has no doubt that Ray Hines shook Nathaniel to death, and smothered Marcella.

There is no alternative now but for the police to become involved, and in due course Ray is charged with the murders of her two children. Her trial begins in March 2004.

But wait a moment, I hear you say. Didn't Dr Duffy perform a post-mortem on Marcella and find nothing suspicious? Yes indeed. Her answer to this, in court, is that she examined the evidence again and revised her opinion. She argues that even if the fractured rib was caused by efforts to resuscitate Marcella, the bruising cannot have been, since Ray admits she was too scared to attempt any sort of resuscitation, and Marcella was already 'cyanosed' by the time the ambulance arrived. This means that there would not have been sufficient blood pressure to cause bruising when medics pressed down on Marcella's chest to try and get her heart beating again.

Again, Russell Meredew disagrees. He explains that it is possible for bruises to appear when blood pressure is almost down to nothing, or even — though this is rare — after death. He has seen many instances of the former and one or two of the latter. He also points out that Myocarditis, a viral inflammation of the heart muscle, is a more likely cause than shaking for Nathaniel's brain swelling and subdural haemorrhage.

It's almost impossible for any fair-minded person to comprehend what happened next, or rather what didn't happen. Without the death of Nathaniel, Dr Duffy would not have become suspicious about Marcella's death. Two things had made her think Nathaniel Hines hadn't died naturally: subdural bleeding and swollen brain tissue. Once Dr Meredew had explained that both could result from a naturally occurring virus, why wasn't that the end of the murder trial? Why didn't the prosecution realise their case had fallen apart? Why didn't Justice Elizabeth Geilow throw it out of court?

Inconceivable though it is, Russell Meredew — a man I'd trust to carry me across an enemy minefield — later confided to me that at the point when Dr Duffy told him she'd changed her mind about the cause of Marcella's death, she hadn't looked again at the file. 'She can't have reviewed the details — she'd come to me straight from Nathaniel's postmortem. It's hard not to conclude that she suspected foul play in the case of Nathaniel, and decided that meant Marcella couldn't have died naturally.' Meredew added that he didn't doubt that Dr Duffy had at some point dug out Marcella's file and had another look at it, but, as he brilliantly put it, 'If you go searching for flying pigs and there's a pale pink sky, what conclusion are you going to draw: a beautiful sunset or flying pigs as far as the eye can see?'

The jury, of course, would have been familiar with Dr Duffy's name. She was the expert who, at Helen Yardley's trial for the murder of her two sons in 1996, said that for crib death to strike the same family twice was 'so unlikely it borders on impossible' — a memorable soundbite indeed. I believe Ray Hines' jury remembered it, and thought that it meant Ray couldn't be innocent of murder, just as eleven out of twelve jurors in 1996 had concluded it meant Helen Yardley was guilty.

Russell Meredew did his best to save Ray. He called Dr Duffy's assertion that Marcella Hines was smothered and Nathaniel shaken to death 'a nonsense', explaining that smothering is 'covert homicide', whereas shaking is usually linked to losing one's temper. Smotherers are devious but controlled, so it's unlikely that any mother would smother one baby then shake the next, even assuming she were murderously inclined.

The court heard that there was an extended family history of similar tragedies in Angus Hines' family. Angus's nephew was stillborn, and his grandmother lost a baby to SIDS. His mother suffers from a disease called Lupus, where the body eats itself from within. Asked to explain what all this meant, Dr Meredew was unambiguous: 'It's highly probable that the defendant's husband's family contains a genetic auto-immune disorder. That would explain the still-birth, the SUDIs (sudden unexpected death in infancy), Lupus — all things you'd expect if there was an auto-immune malfunction.'

Was the jury listening? Or were they all thinking about 'so unlikely it borders on impossible'? Did they take against Ray because she wasn't a good witness? She contradicted herself several times, denied things she'd previously said to the police, and was accused by the prosecution of lying.

What no one knew was that Ray's lawyers had advised her to lie. She was betrayed by the very people whose job it was to protect her. Her defence team decided that the true story of why she left Angus and Marcella alone for nine days, and the smoking on the window ledge episode, would make her appear unsympathetic to the jury; they would think she was a feminist agitator. Instead, Ray was encouraged to pretend that she had been suffering from post-natal depression, didn't know why she'd left or where she'd gone when she was away, didn't know why she'd come back, had no memory of climbing out on to the window ledge. Not only was it illegal and immoral for Ray's lawyers to give her this advice (unsurprisingly, they now deny they did so), it was also a fatal miscalculation.

Ray was found guilty of two counts of murder and sentenced to life in prison. Her lawyers sought leave to appeal, citing Russell Meredew's claim that Dr Duffy couldn't have looked again at Marcella's medical notes at the point at which she'd told him she'd changed her mind and now suspected Marcella was murdered. But this was impossible to prove. It was Dr Meredew's word against Dr Duffy's. Leave to appeal was denied.

Then, in June 2004, two months after Ray was convicted, there was a breakthrough: a volunteer working for the organisation Helen Yardley and I set up together, JIPAC (Justice for Innocent Parents and Carers), spoke to somebody who worked with Dr Duffy — let's call him Dr Anonymous. He produced a copy of an email Dr Duffy had sent him in which she lamented her own idiocy in having allowed her arm to be twisted over Marcella Hines' post-mortem. Desmond Dearden, the coroner on whose desk Marcella's file landed, knew Angus Hines personally, and told Duffy they were a nice family. Astonishingly, he seems to have semi-blackmailed her into ignoring her suspicions and recording instead that Marcella Hines had died of natural causes. Here is an extract from Duffy's email to Dr Anonymous:

Why did I imagine even for a minute that Desmond knowing the family was any sort of guarantee? Why didn't I take umbrage at his not-so-subtle implication that if I didn't toe the line on this one then he wouldn't send any more coroner cases my way? The truth is, I wasn't sure about Marcella Hines. I was suspicious — aren't I always? — but I wasn't sure, as I have been in other cases — Helen Yardley, for example. I think I wanted to prove to myself that I'm not the terrible monster Laurie Nattrass thinks I am, and that, in a situation where I could think either the best or the worst of somebody, I'm capable of thinking the best. I know it sounds lame, but that's what must have been going on in my mind. And, yes, I'll admit it, I hated the thought of no more coroner cases coming my way. And now look what's happened! Another Hines baby is dead, and I'm under oath being asked why I 'changed my mind' about Marcella Hines' entirely natural death. If I could turn back the clock and give the cause of death as unascertained . . . but there's no point wishing, is there?

What happened next? Well, yours truly forwarded the email to Ray Hines' defence team, who forwarded it to the Criminal Cases Review Commission. Incredibly, leave to appeal was once again denied. The CCRC should have focused on Dr Duffy's lack of professional integrity and what that meant for a case in which she and her coterie, the hawks of child protection, were the only witnesses for the prosecution. Instead, they took in only that Duffy had harboured suspicions about Marcella Hines' death for longer than she had at first disclosed. Perhaps they imagined that this fact imbued those suspicions with greater validity. JIPAC has demanded to know why, as soon as this email came to light, Judith Duffy wasn't sacked and struck off, but so far we have received no satisfactory answer. Likewise, we have made enquiries as to why a coroner as corrupt as Desmond Dearden is still in post. The response is a deafening silence.

Hope finally came for Ray Hines when there was a breakthrough in Helen Yardley's case. A document came to light, courtesy of another Dr Anonymous, in which Dr Duffy consistently referred to Helen Yardley's son Rowan as 'she'. That's right: the expert who was so sure Rowan was murdered didn't even know what sex he was.

Next, the pathologist who had performed the post-mortem on Rowan Yardley came forward. After Rowan's death, she had contacted several people she regarded as expert and asked their opinion about the high level of salt she'd found in Rowan's blood. Judith Duffy, not knowing at that point that Rowan's brother Morgan had died, also with high blood-salt, three years previously, sent a reply in which she said that, 'the instability of blood chemistry after death renders it diagnostically immaterial. Dehydration is the most usual cause of high serum sodium'. Dr Duffy concluded by saying, 'Unless you're looking for a specific poison, blood results cannot and should not be relied upon.' A mere eighteen months later, Duffy had forgot-

ten that this was ever her view, and testified in court that Helen Yardley's sons
had died of deliberate salt poisoning.
She presented Morgan and Rowan's
high blood-salt levels as all the proof of
murder that anyone could need.

The CCRC finally saw sense. Helen
Yardley was granted leave to appeal. A
year later, so was Ray Hines. Some
unkind personage must have leaked
information to the press, because various accounts of Judith Duffy's disgrace-
ful behaviour appeared in national newspapers, and public opinion started to
turn against the woman who was once
lauded as a champion of children everywhere. Suddenly, Helen Yardley, JIPAC
and I were no longer the only voices calling for Duffy to be stopped.

In February 2005, Helen Yardley's
murder convictions were quashed. This
evidently gave Dr Duffy no pause for
thought, for in July 2005 she was back
in the witness box testifying against
Sarah Jaggard, the latest innocent
woman on trial for killing a child — Bea
Furniss, the daughter of a friend of hers.
Thankfully, the jury saw sense and
unanimously acquitted Sarah. They
listened to Bea's grief-stricken parents,

who were adamant that Sarah had adored Bea and would never have harmed her.

Did Dr Duffy listen? Had she listened when Paul Yardley and Glen Jaggard — two of the most solid, reliable men I've ever met — said over and over that their wives would never harm or kill a child? Did she listen to the scores of parents who had entrusted their sons and daughters to Helen Yardley's care, who said that Helen was incapable of violence or cruelty, that they would happily use her as a childminder in the future? Did Dr Duffy hear Sarah Jaggard's parents, two mild-mannered retired school teachers, or her sister — a midwife, no less — say that Sarah was loving and caring, that there was no way she would ever lose her temper and shake a defenceless baby?

The sad truth is that Dr Duffy listened to none of the real experts, none of the people who knew Helen or Sarah personally. Hers was the only opinion that mattered, and she would have stopped at nothing in her attempts to ruin the lives of innocent women, using her status as expert in the criminal and family courts to wreak further destruction on already ravaged families. Paige Yardley, the child Helen conceived and gave birth to while at home on bail awaiting trial, was forcibly taken from her birth family on the say-so of guess who? Dr Duffy told the court that Paige was 'at grievous risk of harm' and ought to be removed from her home 'without delay'.

Now Duffy's career and reputation lie in tatters, and not a moment too soon. It beggars belief that she was involved in the care arrangements for Paige Yardley when it was known she would appear for the prosecution at Helen's trial. It defies common sense, not to mention common decency, that she was allowed to give evidence as an expert witness at Sarah Jaggard's trial. Helen Yardley had been free for five months at that point, and the extent of Duffy's misconduct in connection with her case was well known. What better things had the GMC to do than take action against her, and why did it take them so long?

How time must have dragged for Ray Hines, who was not freed until December 2008. Unlike Helen Yardley and Sarah Jaggard, who had plentiful support from family and friends, Ray had been disowned and divorced by her husband Angus when she was found guilty. She had been reviled in the press as a 'drug addict', after Angus told a reporter she was a regular marijuana smoker. In fact, she only used the drug occasionally, when the bad back from which she has suffered all her life caused her so much agony that she'd have tried anything. She is as far from the stereotype of a grubby, sofa-surfing junkie as it's possible to be. She is a proud, spiky woman who holds her head high and refuses to cry for the cameras. She admitted in court that she can't think straight unless her home is tidy and that she believes it's bad for women to give up their careers and stay at home with their children. How Judith Duffy must have hooted with glee when she saw how easy it would be to take this remarkable woman and turn her into a murderous she-devil.

Even now, with Ray Hines free and Judith Duffy deservedly disgraced, JIPAC's work is far from done. 62-year-old Dorne Llewellyn of Port Talbot in South Wales is just one of the many women still behind bars for a crime she didn't commit: the murder, in 2000, of nine-month-old Benjamin Evans. Dr Duffy testified that Mrs Llewellyn must have shaken Benjamin, causing the brain haemorrhage that killed him, but couldn't answer when counsel for the defence asked how sure she was that the shaking episode, assuming there was one, had taken place while Benjamin was in Dorne Llewellyn's care. Interestingly, one of Dr Duffy's staunchest supporters is Benjamin's single mother, Rhiannon Evans, who was 15 when Benjamin was born. Now 23, she is a prostitute and well known to local police.

The case is currently under review by the CCRC. JIPAC is praying for a speedy and successful appeal. The only evidence against Mrs Llewellyn is the opinion of a doctor who's been struck off for misconduct, so how could any appeal judge uphold her conviction? Surely for our country's esteemed judicial system to make another heinous mistake in a child death case, having already made so many, is, to quote Dr Duffy, 'so unlikely it borders on impossible'?

second step?'

'You love him for the same reason everyone loves him: he's a mystery. You don't know what he is, and can't see any way to find out. That's kind of addictive, until you realise you'll never get the satisfaction you crave.'

If Tamsin knew the truth about me, would she change her mind about why I love Laurie? Would she say I'm deluding myself that by getting close to him, I can shake off the taint I've been carrying around with me? By loving the man who helped to free Helen Yardley and Rachel Hines, I can maybe . . .

Except I can't, not if he doesn't love me back. The more he treats me like his worthless skivvy, the more tainted I feel. What am I doing kidding myself that I can make Laurie's film, that I'll do such a brilliant job that he'll respect me and love me and I'll finally be able to move beyond the shame? I'll end up making something pallid and average because I feel guilty, then hiding its existence from my mum when it's broadcast, so that she won't be devastated.

Whatever I do, whether I make the film or not, I'm going to feel horribly guilty. That doesn't seem fair.

'I read Laurie's "Doctor Who Lied" rant,' I tell Tamsin.

'Fantastic, isn't it?' she says. 'If ever an article's going to make the entire legal system hang its head in shame, it's that one.'

'I thought it veered between pathetic and downright offensive.'

'Yeah.' She sniggers. 'Course you did.'

'I *did*,' I insist. It's true, isn't it? So why do I feel as petty as a jilted girlfriend sewing prawns into the linings of her ex's curtains?

I get rid of my helpful and not at all annoying friend, and leave the office, armed with Laurie's address. I stop the first taxi I see, praying the driver will be shy, unfriendly or a Trappist monk. My wish is not granted. I get a twenty-five minute lecture about the West being in decline because it doesn't produce anything any more, and a prediction that soon we Westerners will all be slaving away for a pittance on Korean assembly lines. I restrain myself from asking if, in exchange, a Korean person will come over here and be made to feel like shit by Laurie Nattrass.

How can he disapprove of what I'm doing? I haven't done anything yet, apart from contact the people whose names are in the files *he* left for me.

Laurie's house is one of a row of immaculate white stucco villas on a quiet, tree-lined street. The front door, glossy black-painted wood with two stained-glass panels, stands open. As with most things about Laurie, I have difficulty interpreting this. Does he want me to go straight in, or is he too busy and important to bother with mundane tasks like shutting doors properly?

I ring the bell and shout hello simultaneously. When nothing happens, I take a tentative step inside. 'Laurie?' I call out. In the hall there's a bike leaning against the wall, a grey and black canvas rucksack, a briefcase, a jacket scrunched up on the floor, a pair of black shoes. Above the radiator, four shelves run the length of one wall, housing a collection of neatly folded newspapers. Opposite these are two large framed photographs, both of what looks like an Oxbridge college. Where did Laurie go to university? Tamsin would know.

Between the two photos is a small square sticker that totally ruins the effect: a circle of gold stars against a navy background with a thick black line running diagonally through it. There's another sticker on a grandfather clock at the far end of the hall, stuck to the wood: 'Say No to the Euro'. It offends me, not because I give a toss about the euro one way or the other, but because the clock looks old and valuable, and shouldn't be used as a fly-posting site. It stands slightly wonky, as if it's too tired to straighten up.

The white-painted wooden steps directly in front of me are heaped with books and papers. Every step has a pile of something on one side, though not the same side in each case: anyone who wanted to go upstairs would have to zig-zag. I see JIPAC-headed paper, and several copies of *Nothing But Love:* one hardback and two paperbacks. I bet Helen Yardley didn't write any of it herself.

If I wrote a book, would Laurie read it?

I am not jealous of Helen Yardley. Helen Yardley lost all three of her children. Helen Yardley was murdered three days ago.

I pick up the hardback of *Nothing But Love* and turn it over. On the back cover, there's a photograph of Helen with her co-author, Gaynor Mundy. They've got their arms round each other to suggest deep friendship as well as a close professional relationship. Bound to have been the photographer's idea, I think cynically — the two women probably loathed each other.

I'm about to put the book down when I notice Helen Yardley's hand, draped over Gaynor Mundy's shoulder, and my mouth turns dry. Those fingers, the nails . . .

I drop the book and root in my handbag for the cream envelope. I try to feel pleased that I didn't bin it, but part of me wishes I had. If I'm right, I don't want to think about what it might mean.

Pulling out the photograph, I compare the fingers gripping the card in the picture to Helen Yardley's fingers on the cover of her book. They're the same: small square nails, neatly cut. Without stopping to think, I tear the photo and the envelope it came in into little pieces and drop them into my open bag like a handful of confetti. I notice that I'm shaking.

For God's sake, this is ridiculous. How many people must there be who have well-trimmed squarish fingernails? Millions. There is absolutely no reason to assume Helen Yardley is the person in the photograph I was sent, holding the card with the sixteen numbers on it — no reason whatsoever. There's no reason to think that because she was murdered . . .

I shiver, and force my attention away from my silly morbid fears. 'Laurie, are you there?' I call up the stairs.

Still no reply. I look in both downstairs rooms: a wet-room twice the size of my kitchen that contains a shower, basin, loo and more small square black tiles than I think I've ever seen before in my life, and a huge L-shaped kitchen-dining-lounging space; from its elegant finish in several different shades of nut and earth — brown and beige for posh people — I guess that it would prefer to be described as a space than a room. It looks as if it recently contained a party of eighteen who panicked mid-way through a slap-up meal and did a runner. Was Laurie one of them? How many of the twelve empty wine bottles did he drink, and who helped him? Did he host some kind of JIPAC shindig here last night?

I swan-neck my way up the stairs to the first floor, treading carefully, aware that one misplaced step could provoke a paper-quake and do irreparable damage to Laurie's filing system. I spot an envelope addressed to Mr L. H. S. F. Nattrass and a cardboard Nike shoebox with the word 'Accounts' scrawled on it in green-marker pen. L.H.S.F.: that's three middle names he's got, as well as all his awards, money and the world's admiration. I've only got one middle name and it's a terrible one: Margot. If I weren't so tired of psychoanalysing my romantic impulses, I'd wonder if my love for Laurie might be misinterpreted jealousy. Do I want to be his girlfriend, or do I wish, deep down, that I was him?

I come to a landing and a choice of four doors, one of which is ajar. As I move towards it, I see shapes in the gloom: the end of a bed and the lower part of a pair of legs. 'Laurie?'

I push open the door and there he is: Mr L. H. S. F. Nattrass, in a crumpled grey suit. The curtains are closed. Laurie's sprawled on a double bed that I assume is his, staring at a small TV on a chair in the corner of the room — an ancient one, by the look of it. There's a metal aerial balanced precariously on top that's almost as big as the TV itself. On the screen, a woman is crying in a man's arms, but there's no volume. Laurie stares at them as they mouth words at one another. Can he tell what they're saying? Does he care? A purple silk tie lies on the duvet beside him.

I turn on the light, but he still doesn't look at me, so I decide I won't look at him either. Instead, I take the opportunity to have a good nosey at his room, something I never thought I'd get to do. It's disappointingly similar to his office. *My office.* There are framed posters of constellations and planets on the walls, two globes, a telescope lying beside its case, a pair of binoculars, some weights, an exercise bike, three books: *The Nazi Doctors, Knowledge in a Social World*

231

and *Into That Silent Sea: Trailblazers of the Space Era, 1961–1965.* Wow, they sound like fun bedtime reading.

Poking out from under the bed is a dustpan and brush with a packet of disposable razors and a canister of shaving gel in the pan, as if they've been swept up off the carpet. Coins — silver, copper and gold — are scattered everywhere: on the bed, on the floor, on top of a chest of drawers. It makes me think of the bottom of a wishing well.

'What do the H, S and F stand for?' *Laurie Horrible Selfish Fucker Nattrass.*

'Hugo St John Fleet,' he says, as if these are perfectly normal names to have. No wonder he's a nutter.

'I love black and white films.' I nod at the screen.

'What about technicolour sentimental crap on a black and white TV — do you love that?'

'Why are you angry with me?'

'You leave a message for me saying you're trying to set up an interview with Judith Duffy and you need to ask why I'm angry?'

'I've set up interviews with lots of people,' I tell him. 'Judith Duffy's the one person so far who's refused to —'

'Judith Duffy ruins lives! Turn off that

drivel, for fuck's sake.'

Is he talking about *his* television, that *he* switched on when I wasn't even here?

'I'm not your servant, Laurie.' With feeling, I add, 'And I don't love black and white films — I only said it because it's . . . well, it's so hard to talk to you, and I have to say something. Come to think of it, people who bang on about how they love black and white movies really annoy me. It's blatant film racism. A film can be good or bad whatever its . . . colour scheme.'

Laurie examines me through narrowed eyes. 'Ring your GP. Tell him the antipsychotics aren't working.'

'Who's Wendy Whitehead?'

'Who?'

'Wendy Whitehead.'

'Never heard of her. Who is she?'

'If I knew, I wouldn't need to ask you, would I?' I make a show of looking at my watch. 'I've got things to do. Was there something you wanted to say to me?'

Laurie hauls himself off the bed, looks me up and down, then turns to pick up his tie. He drapes it round his neck and, holding it at both ends, pulls it back and forth so that it scratches against his shirt. 'Judith Duffy'd cut off her own legs sooner than talk to anyone from Binary Star,' he says.

'I thought of that. I didn't tell her where I worked, just my name.'

'Are you waiting for me to pat you on the head and tell you how clever you are?' he sneers. I'm glad he's being so rude and offensive; it's the best thing that could have happened. As of this moment, I officially don't love him any more. That deluded phase of my life is so over. 'You want me to make this film, don't you?' I say icily. 'How am I supposed to do that without —'

Laurie grabs my shoulders, pulls me towards him. His mouth collides with my lips. His teeth bang against mine. *A tooth for a tooth,* I think automatically. I taste blood and try to push him away, but he's stronger than I am, and makes a cage out of his arms to trap me. It takes me a few seconds to realise that what he thinks he's doing is kissing me.

I have just had sex with Laurie Nattrass. Laurie Nattrass just had sex with me. Oh, my God, oh, my God, oh, my God. Proper, complete sex, not the silly Bill Clinton kind. Or rather, not only the silly Bill Clinton kind. Which, of course, isn't at all silly as long as no one suggests it's an end in itself. Bad choice of words. What I mean is, it's no substitute for the real thing, the thing that

Laurie and I just . . . oh, my God.

It can't be true. It is true. It only doesn't seem true because he's now acting as if it didn't happen. He's staring at the TV screen and doing that thing with his tie round his neck again, as if his hands are having a tug of war. Would he notice if I discreetly reached for my bag, pulled out my phone and rang Tamsin? I could do with talking to someone impartial. Not about the sex itself — that would be crude, and I'd be too embarrassed to use any anatomical words — but about the weirdness that started when the sex finished. That's the part I'd really like to put under the microscope of gossipy analysis: the way Laurie managed to have all his clothes back on within three seconds, and what he said as he sat back down on the bed beside me, seeming not to notice that I was still naked: 'Stupid mistake. My fault.' At first I thought he was talking about us, but then he said, 'Her phone number was in the files I gave you. I should have taken it out. Thought you'd have more sense than to ring her, though.'

Can it have happened the way I remember it? Surely there was an organic, transitional phase I failed to notice, some word or gesture on his part that bridged the gap between intimacy and discussion of the film.

I wish I could check with Laurie that until a few minutes ago he was lying on top of me, but I'm getting the strong sense that he's moved on and wouldn't welcome a recap. Besides, how would I put it: 'Could you be so good as to confirm the following details?' Ridiculous. Obviously.

I don't need to check anything with anyone, for God's sake. I was here, wasn't I? The trouble is, it's too recent — maybe four minutes, maximum — since we . . . er, brought things to a conclusion. I've been mulling it over and I've decided that the temporal proximity of the event doesn't mean my memory's any more likely to be accurate than if it had happened five years ago. In five years' time, I hope to be able to be clinically objective about this afternoon, so that knowing what actually happened between me and Laurie won't be a problem then as it is now.

I wish I could talk to Tamsin.

If I lie still and don't put my clothes back on, will Laurie have sex with me again?

'Duffy won't ring you back,' he says. 'She'll assume you're an enemy. By now she thinks everyone's an enemy.' He seems pleased about this, as if it's what she deserves. I'm not convinced it does the world any good for any person to have only enemies, not to mention the individual involved, no matter what they've done, but I say nothing. 'Every detail of her personal and professional life has been judged by the tabloids and been found wanting,' says Laurie with relish. 'From her neglect of her own children when they were small in favour of her career, to the beefed-up qualifications on her first ever CV, to the two marriages she sabotaged by being a workaholic. By now the whole world knows what a bitch she is, and she knows it.'

'Mm-hmm,' I say brightly, this being the best I can do in the circumstances. As subtly as possible, I shuffle to the edge of the bed and pull on my knickers, bra, shirt and trousers. I can see my bag. It's not fully zipped up; I can see the edge of my phone poking out. Oh, what the hell. If Laurie can stare at the TV, mess about with his tie and talk about work . . .

I reach for my phone and switch it on. The message icon flashes on the screen, but I'm not interested in what anyone might have to say to me, only in the earth-shattering news I have to impart. I send Tamsin a text saying, 'Laurie pounced on me. We had sex. Immediately after, he dressed, acted like nothing had happened and started talking about Judith Duffy.

Good sign that he can be himself around me instead of putting on false romantic act?' I sign off with an F and two kisses, and send it. Then I turn my phone off again. Just because I was desperate to tell Tamsin doesn't mean I'm ready to deal with her reaction. I smile to myself. By deliberately including in the text a question that only a self-deceiving lovestruck fool would ask, I have inoculated myself against becoming that self-deceiving lovestruck fool. Tamsin will realise I was sending up the sort of girly women we hate, who never swear or burp in public and are much less canny than we are.

'I read the article you wrote,' I tell Laurie. ' "The Doctor Who Lied".'

There, see? Sex, love — they're just bodily functions as far as I'm concerned. I've forgotten all about both, in fact. They're trivialities, to be squeezed into the gaps between making brilliant, award-winning documentaries.

'Best thing I've ever written,' Laurie says.

'What? Oh, right: the article.' It's hard to concentrate when every inch of your skin is fizzing, and you feel as if you're lurching through space, high above the real world and the ordinary mortals who inhabit it. *Concentrate, Fliss. Be a grown-up.* 'I'm not sure you should publish it in its present form,' I say.

Laurie laughs. 'Thank you, Leo Tolstoy.'

'Seriously. At the moment it comes across as . . . well, biased. And nasty. As if you enjoy sticking the knife in. Doesn't that kind of . . . I don't know, weaken you? Undermine your argument? You present Judith Duffy as a hundred per cent evil and everyone who takes a stand against her as flawless: brilliant, trustworthy, heroic. I lost count of the enthusiastic adjectives you used to describe the people who agree with you. You talk about Dr Russell Meredew as if he's the second coming. It makes the whole thing sound too much like a fairy story, with handsome princes and boo-hiss villains. Wouldn't it be better to present the facts and let them speak for themselves?'

'Tell me you're not going to interview Judith Duffy,' Laurie barks at me.

I can't, so I carry on with my lecture. 'You say the friends and family of Helen Yardley and Sarah Jaggard are the "real experts", the people who actually knew them. You imply Judith Duffy ought to have taken notice when they said the women were innocent . . .'

'I more than *imply* it.'

'But that's crazy,' I say. 'No one wants to think that someone they love might be a killer. It reflects badly on them, doesn't it?

Their choice of best friend, or partner, or childminder. Surely their opinions are the least objective and reliable? And you can't have it both ways. If the nearest and dearest are the real experts, what about Angus Hines? He thought Ray was guilty, but you didn't let that sway you any more than Judith Duffy let Paul Yardley or Glen Jaggard's views sway her.'

Laurie stands up. 'Anything else, before you leave?'

He's kicking me out for having the wrong opinion. Or maybe he would have kicked me out anyway.

'Yes,' I say, determined to show I'm not intimidated by him. For an insane second, I consider telling him I'm speaking from personal experience, the worst experience of my life. No one can be objective about the culpability of a loved one. It's simply not possible. I have days when I think my dad must have been corrupt through and through — evil, almost — and days when I think he deserves no blame at all, and miss him so much I feel I might as well be dead too.

'I didn't like the bit in the article about Benjamin Evans' mum being a single mother and a prostitute,' I say eventually. 'You seemed to be suggesting that those two things made her more likely than Dorne Llewellyn to have shaken —'

'You read an out of date version,' Laurie cuts me off. 'Editor of the *British Journalism Review* agreed with you, so I took that bit out. I'll email you a copy of the sanitised version, in which I don't mention that Rhiannon Evans is a hooker who sings Judith Duffy's praises at every available opportunity and is keen for Dorne Llewellyn to stay in prison for the rest of her life.'

'Don't be angry with me, Laurie.'

He snorts dismissively. 'Do you know how easily your job could disappear? Carry on pursuing Judith Duffy and that's what'll happen. If you think I'm going to stand by and let you and her use my film as a vehicle for airing her distorted —'

'I'm not going to do anything like that,' I yell at him. 'I want to talk to her, that's all. I'm not saying you're wrong about her. She's the bad guy — fair enough. But I need to know what sort of bad guy she is if I'm making a documentary about the damage she's done. Is she well intentioned but prejudiced? Stupid? Is she an out-and-out liar?'

'Yes! Yes, she's an out-and-out fucking liar who destroys people. Will you stay away from her? This is the last time I'm going to ask you.'

Is he really so intolerant that he wants no point of view heard but his own? Is he worried about me? If so, might that mean he loves me?

Felicity Benson, how can you not despise yourself?

I didn't mean it. I've got a whole self-mockery thing going on here that's way more sophisticated than unrequited love.

I'd give anything to be able to tell Laurie what he wants to hear so that we could both be happy, but I can't bring myself to be a compliant idiot simply because it would please him. If I'm making this film, and it seems I am, I want to do it in the way I think it should be done.

'I've just worked it out,' I say. 'Why I love you. It's because we've got so much in common. We both treat me as if I don't matter, as if I'm nothing.' Not any more, I vow. From now on, I'm not nothing.

'*Love?*' says Laurie, in the way a normal, civilised person might say 'Genocide?' or 'Necrophilia?': shocked and appalled.

I pick up my bag and leave without another word.

Outside, I hail a taxi and take a while to remember my own address. Once I'm moving, and breathing again, I switch on my

242

phone and see that I have two new messages. The first is a text from Tamsin. 'You big, big, big, BIG eejit!' it says. The second is a voicemail message from a Detective Constable Simon Waterhouse.

8
8/10/09

Sam Kombothekra didn't like the way Grace and Sebastian Brownlee were holding hands. It wasn't suggestive of tenderness, but rather of taking a defiant stand against the enemy. They looked like two people about to charge into battle together.

'Gunpowder residue,' said Grace, her voice full of disbelief. Sam would have bet good money on this being the first time the phrase had been uttered beneath these high corniced ceilings. The Brownlees evidently believed that a period house ought to be filled with period furniture, and the sort of tastefully patterned wallpaper a bona fide Georgian might have chosen, as if the present era could be banished if one tried hard enough.

Paige Yardley's adoptive mother was a small slender woman with mid-brown hair cut in a neat bob. Her husband was tall and balding on top, with wild gingery-blond tufts above his ears that suggested he was unwilling to lose any more hair than he absolutely had to. He and his wife worked for the same law firm in Rawndesley, which was how they'd met, they'd told Sam. Sebastian Brownlee had mentioned twice so far that he'd had to finish work three hours earlier than he normally would in order to get home for this meeting. Both he and Grace were still wearing their work suits.

'You're not suspected of anything,' Sam reassured Grace. 'It's routine. We're asking everyone who knew Helen Yardley.'

'We didn't know her,' said Sebastian. 'We never met the woman.'

'I realise that, sir. Nevertheless, you and your wife are in a unique position in relation to her.'

'We consent,' said Grace in a clipped voice. 'Take your swabs, do whatever you need to, and get it over with. I'd rather not see you here again.' An odd way to put it, Sam thought. As if she might come down to breakfast one morning and find him sitting at her kitchen table. Come to think of it, the Brownlees seemed the type who might insist on taking all their meals in a formal dining room.

Sam had no reason to suspect them of anything. They had given him a full account of their movements on Monday. Together with their thirteen-year-old daughter, Hannah — the girl Sam couldn't help thinking of as Paige Yardley — they had left the house at 7 a.m. At 7.10, they had dropped Hannah off at the home of her best friend, whose mother gave the two girls breakfast and drove them to school on weekday mornings. Sebastian and Grace had then driven straight to their firm's office in Rawndesley, arriving there as always at about 7.50. After that, Sebastian had either been in the office or out at meetings with clients for the rest of the day. 'You're in luck,' he'd told Sam. 'Fee-earning solicitors like us have to make a note of how we spend every minute of our time, so that the right people can be billed.' He'd promised Sam copies of his and Grace's time-sheets for Monday, and contact numbers for all the people in whose company they had spent any of those individually itemised minutes.

Grace, who worked part time, had left the office at 2.30 p.m. and gone to pick up Hannah and her best friend from school, as she did every weekday. She and the two girls had then gone swimming at the private health club, Waterfront, to which both the Brownlees and the friend's family belonged. Grace had been able to give Sam the names and numbers of several acquaintances of hers who had seen her either in the swimming area or having a drink and a snack in Chompers café-bar with the girls afterwards. After leaving Waterfront, Grace drove Hannah's friend home, and she and Hannah got back to their house at 6.15 p.m. Sebastian Brownlee arrived home at 10, having eaten dinner with clients in Rawndesley.

Sam was certain everything the couple had told him would hold up. What was bothering him, then, if it wasn't that he thought they were lying? 'What time will Hannah be back?' he asked. There were framed photographs of her all over the living room wall. In Sam's experience, this many pictures of the same person in one room and no pictures of anyone or anything else could mean one of two things: a stalker with a dangerous obsession, or an adoring parent. *Or two adoring parents.*

Hannah Brownlee had glossy centre-parted brown hair, wide grey eyes and a small nose. She had Helen Yardley's face, only a younger version.

'You're not swabbing my daughter for gunpowder residue,' said Grace Brownlee angrily.

'That wasn't what I —' Sam began.

'I took her to my mother's house because

247

I knew you were coming. I didn't want her involved. Tell him, Sebastian,' she snapped. 'Let's not prolong the agony.'

'Hannah knows a local woman was murdered. People have been talking about it at school and it's been on the news, we could hardly keep it from her, but . . .' Sebastian glanced at his wife. She responded with a look that made it clear she wasn't going to help him out, so he turned back to Sam. 'Hannah has no idea Helen Yardley was her birth mother.'

'I've always been in favour of telling her,' Grace blurted out. 'I was overruled.'

'I wanted my daughter to have a regular, carefree childhood,' Sebastian explained. 'Not to grow up knowing she was the child of a murderer, someone who'd smothered two of her babies and would almost certainly have done the same to Hannah if Social Services hadn't stepped in. What father would place a burden like that on his daughter's shoulders, to be carried for *life?*' He aimed this last word at Grace.

'I take it you think Helen Yardley was guilty, then.' Nothing depressed Sam more than bigotry. What made Sebastian Brownlee so sure he knew better than three court of appeal judges?

'We know she was guilty,' said Grace. 'And

I agree with everything Seb's just said, except there's something he always fails to take into consideration.'

Sam wondered if it was therapeutic for the Brownlees to conduct this argument in front of him, a stranger. 'What's that?' he asked.

'A significant number of adopted children reach an age when it starts to matter to them to know where and who they come from. If I could guarantee Hannah would never be one of them, of course I wouldn't be in favour of telling her, but there are no such guarantees in this world. I wish her birth mother had been anyone but Helen Yardley — *anyone.* If I could, I'd bury my head, and Hannah's, deep in the sand and forget all about the truth, but I can't, or at least I can't be one hundred per cent certain that I'd get away with it, not for ever. If Hannah finds out when she's older, the shock'll be devastating. Whereas if we'd told her as soon as she was old enough to understand, if we even told her now . . .' Grace shot a pleading look at her husband.

'How old is old enough to understand that your natural mother wanted to kill you?' said Sebastian angrily. 'That she *did* kill your two brothers?'

'What have you told Hannah, then?' Sam

asked. 'About her birth parents.'

'Nothing,' said Grace. 'We told her *we* knew nothing, that we asked the social workers not to tell us. She knows she was adopted, but that's all.'

If Simon Waterhouse were here, would he be thinking that, since Hannah was absent, it was impossible to verify what she did or didn't know? What if she knew she was Helen Yardley's daughter, and Grace and Sebastian were lying because . . .

No. Impossible. Thirteen-year-old girls from Spilling didn't tool up with M9 Berettas and murder their mothers. Sam made a mental note to check that Hannah had been at school all day on Monday. 'What makes you so sure Helen Yardley was guilty?' he asked Grace.

Sebastian Brownlee touched his wife's arm: a sign that she shouldn't answer. 'We're busy people, Sergeant — as, I'm sure, are you,' he said. 'We'd like to go and collect our daughter, and you're not here to debate Helen Yardley's guilt. Shall we get on with what needs to be done?'

'I'd like an answer to my question,' said Sam. His throat was dry. The Brownlees hadn't offered him a drink.

Sebastian sighed heavily. 'How do we know she's guilty? All right, let's start with baby Morgan, the first son she murdered. Leaving aside the massive amounts of haemosiderin found in his lungs, all of different ages — not just one bleed, in other words, but several distinct bleeds, a clear indicator of repeated smotherings — leaving that aside, and the fact that four medical experts who testified for the prosecution said there was no way that much haemosiderin would be present if the death was natural, there was also the small matter of Morgan's serum sodium level, which was about five times what you'd expect for a child his age —'

'The level of salt in his blood,' Grace cut in with the explanation Sam needed. 'She used salt to poison him.'

Salt poisoning *and* smothering? Sam didn't believe Helen Yardley had deliberately harmed either of her sons, but even if she had, why would she simultaneously try to kill them in two different ways? In the interests of fairness, he had to admit you could easily turn that around: if you really want to hurt someone, maybe you attack them in any and every way you can think of.

'Morgan had been rushed to hospital more than once in his short life because he'd stopped breathing. Funny that, isn't it?' Sebastian Brownlee demanded. 'A perfectly healthy baby just stops breathing — how convenient. Each time he decided to perform his stopping-breathing-for-no-reason trick, it was the same time of day — between five and six in the evening, at the end of a long day of his mother being at home alone with him while his father was at work. You tell me why a baby would stop breathing, over and over again, at the same time of day.'

'Don't shout at him,' said Grace. Sam was about to tell her it was okay, but stopped himself.

'The defence's liar-for-hire doctors said maybe he had a respiratory disorder, maybe he was dehydrated, maybe he was suffering from nephrogenic diabetes insipidus — diabetes where your salt levels are up the pole instead of your sugars. They were making it up as they went along, and the jury knew it!' Sebastian let go of his wife's hand, stood up and started to pace. 'Let's move on to Rowan, baby number two. He also had too much salt in his blood. All the doctors agreed this was what killed him — the question was: had his mother poisoned him or did he have this rare form of diabetes? Or a faulty osmostat — that's the mechanism that regulates sodium in the blood. I suppose you could say there was no way of telling for sure, but the medical experts who testified for the prosecution thought it fitting to point out that the post-mortem had turned up a skull fracture and several healing fractures, of different ages, at the ends of Rowan's long bones. Metaphyseal fractures, they're called. Ask any paediatrician, or any social worker for that matter — they're the sort of fractures you get if you take a child by the wrist or the ankle and hurl it at the wall.'

Grace Brownlee flinched.

'The skull fracture was bi-lateral — also extremely rare for a non-inflicted injury,' Sebastian continued loudly, as if he was in court rather than in his own living room, addressing a larger audience than his wife and Sam. He paced up and down, his hands stuffed in his trouser pockets. 'Most skull fractures are simple and linear, confined to only one bone in the skull. Oh, the defence's doctors had a field day! One had the nerve to say that the skull fracture couldn't have caused Rowan's death because there was no brain swelling.'

'Seb, calm down,' said Grace in a resigned voice, as if she didn't expect him to take any notice.

'It might not have killed him, but it's still

a fucking skull fracture!' Having made this declaration, Sebastian sat down again, shaking his head. Was he done? Sam hoped so. His own fault for asking.

'One expert witness for the defence said the fractures could have been caused by something called Transient Osteogenesis Imperfecta, but there's no evidence that such a thing exists,' said Grace. 'OI's real enough, though rare, but Transient OI? No proof whatsoever — not so much as one recorded case. As Judith Duffy pointed out at the trial, OI has other symptoms, none of which applied to Rowan Yardley — blue sclera, wormian bones . . .'

'When Duffy said there was no such thing as Transient Osteogenesis Imperfecta, the defence QC tried to make her look arrogant by asking how she could possibly know that for sure,' Sebastian took over. 'Could she point to any research that proved OI could never take a transient form? Of course she couldn't. How do you prove that something doesn't exist?'

'I can't remember who's supposed to have said it, but it's true,' Grace muttered. ' "The greatest fool can ask a question that the wisest man cannot answer." '

'The defence tried everything. They even wheeled out the old chestnut of what-if-he-fell-off-the-sofa? I'm a lawyer,' Sebastian announced, as if Sam might not already be aware of his occupation, 'and if there's one thing I know, it's this: when you're running more than one defence, it's because you know you've got no single line of defence that's going to work.'

A loud sigh from Grace made him stop and look at her. 'None of this is how *I* know Helen Yardley was guilty,' she said. 'You can argue endlessly about medical evidence, but you can't argue with an eye-witness account from someone who had no reason to lie.'

'Leah Gould,' said her husband, taking her hand again as if to thank her for reminding him. 'The contact supervisor at the care centre where the Yardleys went to visit Hannah.'

Paige, thought Sam. Not Hannah; not then.

'Leah Gould saved our daughter's life,' said Sebastian.

'Helen tried to smother Hannah in front of her,' said Grace, her eyes filling with tears. 'Pressing her face against her chest so she couldn't breathe. Two other people saw it too — Paul Yardley and a detective sergeant called, of all things, Proust — but they lied in court.'

Sam did his best not to react. The Snowman, lie under oath about having witnessed an attempted murder? No. Whatever other bad things he was capable of, he wouldn't do that. Sam knew Helen Yardley had included her version of the incident in *Nothing But Love* — Simon Waterhouse had told him. Sam needed to read the book, however much he didn't want to.

'You'd expect her husband to lie,' said Sebastian bitterly. 'For better or for worse, even if you're married to a killer, but a police officer?' He shook his head. 'Unfortunately, at the trial, DS Proust's remembrance of things past was flawed to say the least. He testified that in his opinion Leah Gould had overreacted, that all Helen did was hug Hannah tightly, as any loving mother would if she thought she might be about to be separated from her daughter for years, if not for life. Eleven out of twelve jurors ignored him. They trusted Leah Gould not to have plucked an attempted murder out of thin air.'

'Though that's exactly what she herself ended up claiming to have done,' said Grace bitterly. 'That dreadful Nattrass man made so many waves in the media that everyone, even most of the original prosecution witnesses, ended up on the side of the convicted murderer against her victims. Nattrass made sure every tabloid scumbag got his very own Judith Duffy scoop, whether it was her promiscuity as a teenager, her callous childcare arrangements as a young mother, the job she'd been fired from as a student . . .'

'It wasn't about the evidence any more,' said Sebastian, clutching his wife's hand in a way that looked to Sam as if it might be painful for her. If it was, she said nothing. 'It had become political. Helen Yardley had to get out of jail free, and quickly; she was becoming an embarrassment to the system, even though all Nattrass had in his arsenal was a case against Dr Duffy, one prosecution witness among many. All right, her behaviour was questionable, but she was only a small part of the case. Except, suddenly, she wasn't. Some of the other doctors who'd testified against Helen Yardley changed their tune — none of them wanted to become Nattrass's next victim. The prosecution team didn't push for a retrial when they could and should have. Ivor Rudgard QC will have had it spelled out for him by someone from the Lord Chancellor's office as was: drop this or you'll never make red judge. So Rudgard dropped it.'

'Next thing you know, Laurie Nattrass interviews Leah Gould in the *Observer,* and she says she's no longer sure she saw Helen Yardley try to smother her daughter by pressing her face into her jumper. She now thinks it's likely she panicked for no reason, and she deeply regrets the part she played in convicting an innocent woman.' It was clear Grace could hardly bear to utter those words in connection with Helen Yardley.

'Of course she'd say that once Helen Yardley's free and everyone's talking about witch-hunts and the persecution of grieving mothers,' said Sebastian. 'It isn't easy to be the lone voice of dissent. More than ten years after the event, you can convince yourself that things were different from how they actually were, but the fact is that when she was in that room at the contact centre, Leah Gould pulled Hannah away from Helen Yardley and she believed that, in doing so, she saved Hannah's life.'

Sam was starting to feel sorry for the Brownlees. Their obsession was weighing them down, sucking the life out of them. He suspected they went over and over the story, feeling fresh outrage each time they reached the part where Helen Yardley was freed. 'How long have you lived in this house?' he asked.

'Since 1989,' said Grace. 'Why?'

'So before you adopted Hannah.'

'I'll ask again: why?'

'The Yardleys' house is on Bengeo Street, only about five minutes from here.'

'In terms of distance, perhaps,' said Sebastian. 'In all ways that matter, Bengeo Street is worlds away.'

'When you adopted Hannah, did you know where the Yardleys lived?'

'Yes. There were . . .' Grace stopped, closed her eyes. 'There were some letters forwarded to us by social services. From Helen and Paul Yardley to Hannah. Their address was on the letters.'

Needless to say, Hannah had never clapped eyes on them.

'Did you consider moving?' Sam asked. 'Once you decided not to tell Hannah who her birth parents were, didn't you think it might be a good idea to move out of Spilling — to Rawndesley, perhaps?'

'*Rawndesley?*' Sebastian reared in horror, as if Sam had suggested he move to the Congo.

'Of course we didn't,' said Grace. 'If you lived in this house, on this street, would you ever move?' She gestured around the room.

Did she want Sam to answer honestly? Had she really said that? Staring at her, wondering how to respond, he suddenly had it. He knew why he was suspicious of the

259

Brownlees, in spite of their solid alibis and middle-class respectability: it was something Grace had said as she'd let him in. He'd shown her his ID, explained that he was DS Sam Kombothekra from Culver Valley CID, but that there was nothing to worry about, his visit was a formality, nothing more. Grace's response had been almost exactly what you'd expect from a blameless woman. Almost, but not quite. She'd looked Sam in the eye and said, 'We did nothing wrong.'

It was dark by the time Simon got to Wolverhampton. Sarah and Glen Jaggard lived in a rented flat above a town-centre branch of Blockbusters on a busy main road. 'You can't miss it,' Glen had said. 'The sign's been vandalised and someone's scratched out the first "B", so now it's "Lockbusters". Talk about sending the wrong message,' he'd attempted a joke. 'No wonder we've been burgled twice since moving here.'

The Jaggards had been homeowners once, but had sold their house to cover Sarah's legal costs. Simon hadn't been convinced by Glen Jaggard's determined cheeriness on the phone. He detected in it the underlying fatigue of someone who feels he has no alternative, in the face of life's unremitting grimness, but to be upbeat all the time.

The flat looked as if it had an upstairs and a downstairs, judging from the windows. It was a decent size: probably about the same square footage as Simon's two-up two-down cottage, or Charlie's two-bed terrace. We ought to sell the pair of them and buy a bigger place together, thought Simon, though he knew he'd never suggest it and that, if Charlie did, his first reaction would be fear.

He remembered the Snowman jumping down his throat when he'd suggested Sarah Jaggard wasn't the victim of a miscarriage of justice. How could she be, when she'd been unanimously acquitted? Proust evidently thought that to be tried for manslaughter constituted miscarriage of justice enough, and Simon wondered if the woman he was about to meet agreed. Did she see herself as a victim, rather than someone who had triumphed over adversity? The shabby exterior of her home and the deafening traffic noise outside it made Simon think that she might, and he wouldn't blame her if she did.

Rusty wrought-iron steps led up to the flat, speckled with the black paint that must once have covered them. There was no doorbell. Simon knocked, then watched through the panel of cracked opaque glass as a large shape lumbered towards him along the hall. Glen Jaggard threw open the door, grabbed Simon's hand and shook it, simultaneously leaning forward to pat him on the back with his other hand, a manoeuvre that put the two men in awkward physical proximity. Simon took in Jaggard's checked shirt, jeans and walking boots. Was he planning on climbing a mountain later?

'You found Lockbusters, then?' Jaggard laughed. 'I couldn't believe it when our DVD player packed up about a week after we moved in. Talk about sod's law: you move to a flat above a DVD rental place and your DVD player packs in!'

Simon smiled politely.

'Go through to the lounge.' Jaggard pointed down the hall. 'There's tea and biscuits in there already. I'll get Sarah.' He took the stairs two at a time, calling out his wife's name.

Simon had been in many people's homes over the years, but this was a first: tea being made before he arrived. If he'd been late, would he have had to down it cold?

He was expecting the Jaggards' lounge to have nobody in it, since Glen and Sarah were both upstairs, and was surprised to find Paul Yardley there, looking terrible. His eyes were puffy, his skin waxy and greasy. *Like the congealed fat in a frying pan after you've cooked sausages.* The first time Simon had interviewed him after his wife's death, Yardley had said vehemently, 'Most people in my position would be thinking about topping themselves. Not me. I fought for justice for Helen once, and I'll do it again.'

Now, with equal intensity, he said, 'Don't worry, I'm not staying,' as if Simon had protested at his presence. 'I only came here to talk to Glen and Sarah about Laurie.'

'Laurie Nattrass?' On the wall behind Simon there was a framed newspaper photograph of Nattrass, Yardley and a tearfully smiling Helen, holding hands like a row of paper dolls. Taken on the steps of the court building after Helen's successful appeal, Simon guessed. It was the only picture the Jaggards had put up in the living room of their rented flat. Beneath the grainy black and white image was the headline 'JUSTICE AT LAST FOR HELEN'.

From the relative lack of furniture — two red chairs, one with a torn seat, a coffee table, a TV — and the bareness of the walls, Simon guessed that most of the Jaggards' possessions were in storage. *We won't be here long, no point filling the place with our stuff.* That's what Simon would tell himself, in their position. He wouldn't want to unpack anything that mattered to him and bring it to this dump with its damp-stained ceilings and cracked plaster. Did the Jaggards dream about buying a place soon, far away from the video shop with the damaged sign, so that they could put the past behind them once and for all?

Hadn't Sarah Jaggard also been photographed outside court after her acquittal? Simon was sure she had; he remembered seeing it on the news and in the papers. With Laurie Nattrass by her side, unless his memory was playing tricks on him. Why wasn't Sarah the one up on the living room wall?

'Do you know where Laurie is?' Paul Yardley asked. 'He's not returning our calls — not mine, not Glen's or Sarah's. He's never done that before.'

Nattrass had been eliminated; he'd been in meetings at the BBC all day Monday, so there was no reason to keep track of his movements. 'Sorry,' Simon said.

Paul Yardley stared at him for nearly ten seconds, waiting for a better answer. Then he said, 'He wouldn't ignore us. Do you know where he is?'

There was a creak of floorboards from

above, followed by the sound of very slow footsteps, as if a ninety-year-old was coming down the stairs. Yardley sprang out of his chair. 'Don't worry, I'm going,' he said, and was down the hall and out of the flat within seconds. Simon made no move to stop him or ask where he was going; he knew he'd feel bad about that later. Talking to a man who'd lost everything was no fun, but you had to make the effort.

He picked up one of the three chipped mugs on the coffee table and took a gulp of tea that was somewhere between hot and cold. He wanted a Bourbon biscuit as well, but didn't take one.

Glen Jaggard steered Sarah into the room with both hands. She was tall and thin with wispy brown hair, dressed in pink striped pyjamas and a white towelling dressing-gown. She looked at Simon briefly before averting her eyes.

'Sit down, love,' said her husband.

Sarah lowered herself into one of the red chairs. Everything she did — walking, sitting — had an air of awkward inexperience about it, as if she was doing it for the first time. She was nervous in her own home. *If that's how she thinks of it; if she doesn't think of her home as the place she had to sell to stay out of jail.*

Simon had familiarised himself with her case as best he could. She'd been charged with the manslaughter of Beatrice Furniss, a six-month-old for whom she had babysat regularly. Beatrice — or Bea, as she was known — was the child of Pinda Avari and Matt Furniss. Before she was arrested, Sarah was a hair stylist, and Pinda, an IT audit manager for a chain of bookmakers, was one of her longstanding clients as well as a friend. On the evening of 15 April 2004, Pinda and Matt went to a party, having dropped Bea off at the Jaggards' house. Sarah put on a Baby Mozart DVD for Bea, which they watched together. Glen Jaggard and three of his friends, who were also his colleagues at Packers Removals, were in the next room playing poker. Bea had never had a set bedtime, as Pinda and Matt were against imposed routines for babies, but at about nine o'clock she fell asleep on Sarah's knee.

Sarah put her down on the sofa and settled in to watch TV. An hour later, she glanced down at Bea beside her and noticed that the baby's skin had a blue-ish tinge and she thought, though couldn't be sure, that there was something funny about her breathing. She tried to rouse Bea, succeeded in waking her, but was frightened by how floppy she was. At one point Bea's eyes rolled back in her head and that was when Sarah feared something was seriously amiss. Carrying Bea gently, trying not to panic, she took her through to the kitchen to Glen and his friends. They took one look at Bea and told Sarah to phone an ambulance. By the time it arrived, Bea had stopped breathing. The crew was unable to resuscitate her.

The post-mortem found the cause of death to be extensive bleeding in the brain and eyes. The paediatrician who had performed it took the stand at Sarah's trial and said she believed Bea had died as a result of being shaken. Dr Judith Duffy, called as an expert witness, backed her up. Nothing, she agreed, would cause the sort of subdural and retinal haemorrhages Bea Furniss had suffered apart from violent shaking. The defence disagreed, and produced a research paper, published in the *British Medical Journal* and referred to in court and subsequently in the press as Pelham Dennison, to prove that the symptoms many doctors believed to be indicative of shaking could occur naturally. Even better, Sarah Jaggard's lawyers produced Pelham and Dennison in person to explain their research. Both doctors told the court that bleeding in the brain and eyes needn't be caused by inflicted trauma, and could as easily be the result of a non-induced hypoxic episode — in other words, a period during which a baby is deprived of oxygen owing to a breakdown of one of its internal systems.

Both Dr Pelham and Dr Dennison pointed to a history of heart arrhythmias in Bea's family; her maternal grandfather and her uncle had both died of a disease called Type 2 Long QT syndrome, which affects the heart. If Bea had also been a Long QT syndrome sufferer — and it was a genetic defect, so likely to be passed down through the generations — this might be sufficient to cause hypoxia, which might in turn cause death. Judith Duffy poured scorn on this hypothesis, pointing out that tests had conclusively proved Bea Furniss hadn't suffered from Type 2 Long QT, or from any of the six other identified variants of the disease. In response to the suggestions made by Pelham and Dennison that there might be other as-yet-unidentified forms of Long QT syndrome and that Bea Furniss might have suffered from one of those, Dr Duffy said that obviously she could not prove this was not the case, but that somebody ought to explain to the jury about the difficulties of proving a negative. Furthermore — and Dr Duffy took this to be the most significant point — there were clear stretching injuries to the nerve roots in Bea's neck, which were found at post-mortem to be swollen and torn. This damage could only have been done by shaking, said Dr Duffy.

The prosecution's theory was that Bea had been crying or screaming, and Sarah had shaken her in a fit of temper. Glen Jaggard and his three friends who had been in the house that night testified that Bea hadn't cried at all. The prosecution tried to claim first that the men might not have heard the crying over the combined noise of their poker game and the TV in the next room, and then that Glen Jaggard and his friends had a vested interest in protecting Sarah. One of the poker players, Tunde Adeyeye, took exception to this line of questioning and told the court in no uncertain terms that he had no interest in protecting people who killed babies, and that he was as certain as he could be that Sarah Jaggard had done nothing of the sort.

Pinda Avari and Matt Furniss, though 'visibly devastated by grief' according to one reporter who'd been in court, gave moving evidence in support of Sarah. Pinda said, 'If I believed somebody had killed my darling baby, I would want that person brought to justice more than anything and wouldn't rest until I made that happen, but I have no doubt whatsoever that Sarah loved Bea and would never have harmed her.' Matt Furniss said more or less the same thing.

The prosecution changed tack, and hypothesised that Sarah Jaggard had shaken Bea to death while she, Glen and the baby were alone in the house, before Glen's friends got there. That, argued counsel for the Crown, would explain why Tunde Adeyeye and the other two poker players had heard no noise from the baby. Did they make a point of assessing Bea's condition before commencing their game? Did they get a good look at her, before Sarah brought her into the kitchen in an apparent panic? All three men had to admit that they had called out hello to Sarah when they arrived but paid no attention to Bea, and couldn't swear that she hadn't died earlier, when they weren't present. Dr Judith Duffy seized on this when she was called back to the witness box, saying that the time window for Bea's death was consistent with this possibility; death could have occurred at any time between 7 and 10 p.m., and Glen Jaggard's friends had only arrived at 8. The defence argued that, since Pinda and Matt had only dropped Bea off at 7.45, it was highly unlikely that Sarah would have so quickly lost her temper with the baby. It was simply not credible, Sarah's barrister maintained, that a woman with Sarah's gentle and patient temperament, a woman with no history of violence whatsoever, would lose control of herself and become a baby-shaking monster within the space of fifteen minutes.

Dr Duffy wasn't a popular witness. More than once, the judge threatened to clear the courtroom if the heckling didn't stop. Laurie Nattrass was among the hecklers, and was quoted in one newspaper as saying he was happy to be held in contempt of any British court when those same courts were in the habit of making a mockery of justice.

After a trial that lasted six weeks, and during which Sarah Jaggard fainted several times, the jury returned a unanimous verdict of not guilty. On hearing this, Sarah fainted again. Simon knew he ought to feel sorry for her. He oughtn't to be thinking about the stretching injuries to Bea Furniss's neck that could only have been brought about by shaking. *According to Judith Duffy, who was about to go up before the GMC for misconduct.*

'I heard Paul Yardley asking you about Laurie,' said Sarah. If she wanted or ex-

271

pected Simon to respond, she showed no outward sign of it. 'I let him down. We all did. That's why he doesn't want anything to do with us.'

Simon found himself wishing Glen Jaggard hadn't left them alone. He could have done with a feeble Lockbusters quip round about now, to dilute the bleak, oppressive atmosphere Sarah had brought into the room with her. She seemed . . . Simon struggled to find the right word. *Hopeless.* Entirely without hope, as if her life was over and she didn't particularly care. 'How did you let Laurie down?'

'I told him I'd changed my mind about the documentary. About being in it, and . . . After Helen died, I begged him not to go ahead with it. So did Glen, so did Paul. We were all scared of drawing attention to ourselves, in case . . .' Sarah grabbed her mouth with her hand, as if to stop herself from crying, or from saying more.

'You didn't want a documentary linking you to Helen in case the killer made the same link and went for you next,' Simon guessed.

'I felt like such a traitor. I loved Helen like family, I *worshipped* her, but I was scared. There are people out there, sick people, who'd give anything to get their hands on women like us — me, Helen, Ray Hines. I've always known that. Helen never believed me. She said everyone knew we were innocent, Laurie had proved it — she was like him, she believed in good winning and evil being stamped out, but that's not the way the world works.'

'No,' said Simon. 'It isn't.'

'No,' Sarah echoed bitterly. 'And part of the reason it isn't is because of cowards like me.'

Simon could hear Glen Jaggard whistling in another room: the theme tune from *Match of the Day*. 'So Helen and Laurie are your heroes,' he deduced aloud, looking again at the framed photo on the wall.

'Laurie's not scared of anything or anyone. Neither was Helen. You can see their courage in their faces, can't you?' For the first time, Sarah sounded animated. 'That's why I love that picture, even though —' She grabbed her mouth again.

'Even though?'

'Nothing.'

'Even though what, Sarah?'

She sighed. 'Angus Hines took that photograph.'

'Ray's husband?' That didn't sound right. 'I thought he was a newspaper editor.'

'He is now, at *London on Sunday*. Before

that he was a press photographer. He hated Helen for being more loyal to his wife than he was. He visited her in prison once, to taunt her — no other reason. He wanted to torment her.'

Mentally, Simon added an item to his list: find out what Angus Hines was doing on Monday.

'Imagine what a shock it was for Helen to see him there, outside the court, when she'd just won her appeal. I'd have collapsed, but not Helen. She was determined not to let his presence spoil such an important moment. Look, you can see her determination.' Sarah nodded at the picture. 'I can't believe she's dead. Not that I wasn't scared before — I've always been scared — but it's so much worse without Helen, and now Laurie's not ringing . . .'

'You've got Glen,' Simon pointed out.

'I'm even scared of being swabbed, or whatever it is you're going to do to me.' Sarah ignored the mention of her husband. 'Isn't that crazy? I know I didn't kill Helen, but I'm scared the test'll come back positive anyway.'

'That won't happen,' Simon told her.

'Even before Helen was murdered I was frightened of Laurie's film and the effect it would have. The thought of being back in the limelight made me feel sick, but I didn't dare tell Laurie I wanted out. And then when Helen was killed . . .' Sarah let out a loud sob and buried her face in her hands. 'I was shattered, but I had the excuse I'd been waiting and hoping for. I thought I could persuade Laurie to give up on the film, I thought he'd understand my fears. Even if we never found out for sure that Helen was killed by some crazy child protection vigilante, if there was even a chance that was why . . . But Laurie sounded so cold when I tried to explain, so remote and distant. That was the last time I spoke to him. I don't suppose he cares what happens to me now.' Sarah sniffed. She picked up one of the mugs from the table, took a sip, then held it against her face as if it was a comfort blanket. Simon was on the point of steering the conversation away from Laurie Nattrass when she said, 'Now he's leaving Binary Star and someone else is making the film, some woman called Fliss. I don't understand it. Why would Laurie hand it over to someone else?'

Fliss Benson. Simon had left her a message and was still waiting for her to get back to him. So she was making the crib death documentary, was she? And she'd had a card with the same sixteen numbers on it,

Helen Yardley's sixteen numbers, if Laurie Nattrass's word could be relied upon. *Four rows of four. 2, 1, 4, 9 . . .*

Simon reached into his pocket for the small Ziploc bag he'd brought with him. He held it up in front of Sarah Jaggard's face so that she'd have no difficulty seeing it through her tears. 'Do these numbers mean anything to you?' he asked.

She dropped her tea in her lap and started to scream.

■ ■ ■ ■

PART II

■ ■ ■ ■

9
<u>FRIDAY 9 OCTOBER 2009</u>

'Cream coloured. Sort of ribbed,' I say, for what must be the tenth time. 'You know, a bit stripey, but not stripes of colour, more like . . . texture stripes.' I shrug. 'That's the best I can do, sorry.'

'And you don't remember the numbers?' DC Waterhouse asks. He's hunched awkwardly over his notebook in the middle of my sofa, dead centre, as if invisible people are squashing him in on either side. Every so often he looks up from his note-making and stares at me hard, as if I'm lying to him, which I am. When he asked me if I'd received any other unusual communications, anything that had worried me, I said no.

I should tell him about the second and third anonymous envelopes, but the prospect fills me with dread. *In case he tells me that three is so much worse than one, three constitutes a real risk.* He might look even more concerned than he does now, and the worry on his face is making me feel quite paranoid enough at its present level. Besides, there's no point saying anything — it's not as if I've still got the second card or the photograph to show him.

Yeah, right. The pieces of the picture are in your bag. How hard would it be for him to put them together and identify those fingers as belonging to Helen Yardley?

I wish I was better at self-deception. It's dispiriting, constantly listening to myself calling myself a liar.

'2, 1, 4, 9 — those were the first four numbers, the top row,' I say. 'I don't remember the others. Sorry.' I glance discreetly at my watch. 7.30 a.m. I need DC Waterhouse to leave, quickly, so that I can get to Rachel Hines on time.

He turns over a page in his notebook and passes it across to me. 'Could those have been the sixteen numbers?' he asks.

The sight of them makes me queasy; I want to push them away. 'Yes. I . . . I'm not sure, but I think . . . Yes, they could be.' Seeing him nod and open his mouth, I panic and blurt out, 'Don't tell me. I don't want to know.'

What the hell did I say that for? Now he'll think I'm scared of something.

He gives me a curious look. 'What don't

you want to know?'

I decide I might as well be honest, by way of a change. 'What the numbers are. What they mean. If it's got anything to do with —' I break off. I know better than to invite trouble by voicing my worst fear.

'If it's got anything to do with what?' DC Waterhouse asks.

'If I'm in danger, I'd rather not know.'

'You'd rather not know?'

'Are you going to repeat everything I say? Sorry. I don't mean to be rude, I just . . .'

'I haven't said you're in danger, Miss Benson, but let's suppose you were: you wouldn't want to know about it, so that you could protect yourself?'

This is what I dreaded; he's making it too real, threatening the sustainability of my denial. Now that he's put it like that, I have to ask. '*Am* I in danger?'

'There's no reason to assume that at this stage.'

Fantastic. That makes me feel heaps better.

Waterhouse watches me.

I open my ill-considered gob again, to break the uncomfortable silence. 'The way I see it, if someone's determined to . . . kill me, or whatever, then they're going to do it, aren't they?'

'Kill you?' He sounds surprised. 'Why

281

would anybody want to do that?'

I laugh. I'm glad I'm not the only one playing games here. He's told me he's from Culver Valley CID. He hasn't mentioned Helen Yardley, but he must know I know that she was killed in Spilling in the Culver Valley, and that his interest in the sixteen numbers must have something to do with her murder.

'I'm not saying someone wants to kill me,' I tell him. 'I'm saying that, if they did, they could do it easily. What am I supposed to do, hide in a bullet-proof bunker for the rest of my life?'

'You seem frightened,' says Waterhouse. 'There's no need to panic, and, as I said, no reason to assume —'

'I'm not panicking about being attacked or killed, I'm panicking about panicking,' I try to explain, fighting back the tears that are prickling my eyes. 'I'm scared of how scared I'll have to be if I find out why you're asking about the card and the numbers. I'll be in a whole new realm of fear — too terrified to get on with my life, too frightened to do anything but curl up into a ball and die of dreading what might happen to me. I'd rather not know, and let whatever's going to happen happen. Seriously.'

It might not make sense to anyone else,

but it makes perfect sense to me. I've always been phobic about hearing bad news. When I was a student, I had a drunken condomless one-night stand with a man I hardly knew, someone I met in a nightclub and never saw again. I spent the next ten years worrying about dying of AIDS, but there was no way I was getting tested. Who wants to spend the last few years of their life knowing they've got a terminal illness?

Waterhouse stands up, walks over to the window. Like everyone who's ever admired the view from my lounge — a greenish-stained light-well wall leading up to an uneven pavement — he makes no mention of the charming aspect.

'Try not to worry,' he says. 'Having said that, you need to take a few basic precautions. You live here alone?'

I nod.

'I'm going to try and organise for someone to keep an eye on you, but in the meantime, have you got a friend you can stay with? I'd like you to spend as little time as possible on your own until you hear different.'

Keep an eye on me? Would he say that if the threat to me wasn't serious?

This is getting ridiculous. Ask him what's going on. Make him tell you.

I can't bring myself to do it, even though

the truth might be an improvement on what I'm not quite allowing myself to imagine. Maybe I'd feel better if I heard it.

Yeah. Course you would.

'I'd also like you to halt all work on the crib death murders documentary for the time being, and broadcast the fact that that's what you're doing,' says Waterhouse. 'Contact everyone involved. Make sure they know it's postponed indefinitely.'

Resistance rears up inside me like a tidal wave. I don't know why I'm nodding mutely like an obedient sap when I have no intention of following his instructions. Either I'm lying again, or I'm agreeing with him because I know he's right in theory, I know that's what I ought to do.

I also know I can't. Can't give up on the film now, can't stop myself from going to Twickenham this morning. Despite the fear and the guilt, the pull inside me is too strong, like a current I have no hope of fighting. I have to talk to Rachel Hines, hear what she has to say about Wendy White-head, the woman she claims killed her children. I have to go deeper in.

It's nothing to do with truth or justice. It's me. If I don't see this through, all the way to the other side of whatever it leads to, I might go my whole life without ever fixing on who I am or how I feel — about myself, my family, my past. I'll be nothing — the nobody from nowhere, as Maya so graciously put it, trapped for ever, still tainted. I'll have missed my one chance. That terrifies me more than the idea of someone trying to kill me.

As if he's reading my mind, Waterhouse says, 'We're having trouble getting in touch with Rachel Hines. Do you have her contact details?'

The police must think the film is connected to Helen Yardley's murder.

'They're probably in a file somewhere. I think she rents a flat in Notting Hill, close to where she used to live with her family,' I parrot what Tamsin told me. Part of me would like to be helpful and give Waterhouse the Twickenham address, but if I do that, he'll make it his next stop, and I can't let that happen. I can't have him in my way. I'm the person Rachel Hines is going to speak to this morning; no one else.

'She doesn't seem to be staying there at the moment,' he says. 'You don't have any other address for her?'

'No,' I lie.

10
9/10/09

'Two new faces for you today.' Proust tapped the whiteboard with a pen. 'Or rather, one face and one police artist's best attempt at a likeness. The woman in the photograph is Sarah Jaggard. Some of you might have heard of her.'

About half and half, thought Simon. There were as many people nodding as looking blank.

'She was tried in 2005 for the manslaughter of Beatrice Furniss, the baby of a friend,' said the Snowman. 'She was acquitted. She has several links to Helen Yardley. One: Helen campaigned, under the auspices of JIPAC, on Mrs Jaggard's behalf. Two: Laurie Nattrass — I assume you've all heard of him — was until very recently making a documentary about three crib death murder cases, two of which were Helen and Sarah Jaggard. Three, and this is closely related to two: Dr Judith Duffy, regular star witness rified, and so convinced he was going to kill her if she didn't give him what he wanted, that she lied. She said "All right, I did shake her, I did kill her." '

Simon saw confusion on some of the faces around him, though a few people were shrugging as if to say, 'Anyone would say that, if someone had a knife to their throat.'

'Sarah Jaggard *did not* shake Beatrice Furniss, who died of natural causes,' said Proust, his metal-grey eyes raking the room for signs of dissent. 'She was being threatened by a madman. A madman who didn't know his own mind, as it turned out, because the minute she lied and said she'd shaken the baby to death, he started to tell her that she didn't. He said words to the effect of, "Don't lie. I told you, I want the truth. You didn't kill her, did you? You didn't shake her. You're lying." At which point Sarah Jaggard tried again to tell the truth: that she hadn't harmed baby Beatrice in any way, that she'd only said she had in fear of her life. The man got angry at this point — *angrier,* I should say — and said, "You're going to die now. Are you ready?"'

'Mrs Jaggard fainted in shock, but not before hearing a woman's raised voice. She was too frightened to make out what the voice was saying. When she came round to find herself flat on her back, her attacker was gone, and there was a woman standing over her, a Mrs Carolyn Finneran, who had come out of Boots and noticed a skirmish in the alleyway. Hers was the voice Mrs Jaggard heard before she fainted.' Proust paced the room as he spoke: his gang-plank walk, one foot slowly and carefully in front of the other. *If only there were an ocean for him to fall into.*

'If Mrs Finneran hadn't appeared when she did and scared our man away, it's reasonable to assume Sarah Jaggard might have died on 28 September,' said Proust. 'In any event, given the link between her and Helen Yardley, that this attack happened a week before Helen's murder is something we couldn't afford to ignore even if we didn't have something more concrete linking the two incidents. I won't keep you in suspense.'

The Snowman stopped in front of an enlarged copy of the card that had been found in Helen Yardley's pocket after her death: the sixteen numbers. 'Once Sarah Jaggard had been helped to her feet by Mrs Finneran, the first thing she did was reach into her jacket pocket for a tissue to wipe her face. She pulled out more than she bargained for: there was a card there, identical to the one you're all familiar with.' Proust held out his hand. Colin Sellers, standing behind him like a performing seal waiting for his cue, handed him two transparent plastic folders. Proust held them up so that everyone could see the cards inside. 'Same numbers, same handwriting — though that hasn't yet been officially confirmed by the people whose overpaid job it is to tell us what we already know. Exactly the same layout — the numbers divided into four rows of four horizontally and four columns of four vertically, and nothing else on the card except the numbers: 2,1,4,9, et cetera.'

An eruption of whispers and murmurs filled the room. Proust waited for it to subside before saying, 'Mrs Jaggard is adamant that this card was not on her person when she left home to go to the doctor's, and that there's no way it could have made its way into her pocket unless her attacker put it there. The numbers mean nothing to her, or so she told DC Waterhouse. She kept the card in the hope of working out what it meant, thinking it had to mean something. She informed neither her husband nor local police about the attack.' The Snowman raised his hand to halt the loud expressions of incredulity.

'Don't be so sure you would have behaved differently in her position. Her only experience of the law is a negative one. The thought of inviting the big boots of plod to re-enter her life when they'd crushed it once before was unappealing to say the least. She was also terrified that, if this man were caught, he would say she'd admitted to killing Beatrice Furniss. She decided a better way to deal with what had happened was never to leave the house again. Her husband Glen noticed a deterioration in her condition, but had no idea of the cause.'

'So we've got a serial, or an aspiring serial?' Klair Williamson asked.

'We don't use that word unless we have to,' said Proust. 'What we have is a strong interest in these sixteen numbers. No help so far from Bramshill or GCHQ, or from the Maths departments of the universities I contacted. I'm considering going to the press with it. If we need to wade through a thousand lunatics to find out what these numbers mean, then that's what we'll do. And, while I'm on the bad news, my request for a psychological profiler did not meet with a favourable response, I'm sorry to say. The usual excuse: lack of money. We're going to have to do our own profiling, at least until bust gives way to boom.'

'I thought boom and bust had been abolished,' someone called out.

'That was a lie told by a man every bit as criminal as the shaven-headed individual who held a knife to Sarah Jaggard's throat,' Proust snapped. 'A man . . .' — he tapped the police artist's image with his pen to make it clear who he was talking about — '. . . that Mrs Stella White, of 16 Bengeo Street, says *might* be the man she saw on Helen Yardley's driveway on Monday morning. He *might* have had a shaven head, even though in her original account, he had darkish hair. Her son Dillon says it's definitely not the same man, but then he also says it was raining on Monday, and that the man outside Helen Yardley's house had a wet umbrella with him. We know this is not true — there was no rain and none was forecast. Even if Helen Yardley's killer concealed his gun inside a fastened umbrella, that umbrella wouldn't have been wet. I think we're going to have to write off the Whites, mother and son, as being among the most unhelpful witnesses that have ever hindered our progress. Nevertheless, the cards in the pockets are a firm link between Baldy and Helen Yardley's murder, so at the moment he's our best bet.'

Baldy? thought Simon. Had the Snowman

293

looked in the mirror lately?

'Why would he use a gun for Helen Yardley and a knife for Sarah Jaggard?' a young DC from Silsford called out. 'And why attack one in her home and the other outside a shop? It doesn't fit in with the sixteen numbers in their pockets. That's typical serial, but the change of method and setting . . .'

'It's not the same man,' said Gibbs. 'Stella White said darkish hair, twice — to DS Kombothekra and then to me.'

'Shave your head tonight, DC Gibbs. We'll see if you've got enough hair by this time next week to be described as darkish.'

'You're not serious, sir?'

'Do I strike you as a frivolous sort of person?'

'No, sir.'

Simon raised his hand. 'If I can respond to the point about serial —'

'I don't know if you can, Waterhouse. Can you?'

'The attack on Sarah Jaggard wasn't a success. He was interrupted before he'd finished with her. With Helen Yardley, he decided to do it differently, better: in her house, husband safely out at work, gets her all to himself for a whole day, no one to disturb them, and shoots her at the end of be capable of rational thought,' said Klair Williamson. 'You wouldn't be calm enough to think, "Right, telling him what I think he wants to hear isn't working, so from now on I'll stick to the truth." '

Simon disagreed. 'If someone holds a gun to your head and keeps ordering you to tell the truth or else he'll kill you, eventually you're going to tell the truth. You've tried lying to please him — it's got you nowhere. Pretty soon your terror convinces you that he *knows* the truth, so you daren't lie any more.' Simon was pleased to see a few people nodding. 'We don't know much about this man, so we can't afford to ignore what he's told us himself, via Sarah Jaggard: all he wants is the truth. She said he kept saying that. If he's the same man who killed Helen Yardley — and I think he is — he spent the whole of Monday trying, literally, to scare the truth out of her.'

'And killed her at five o'clock because . . . ?' asked Rick Leckenby.

'He failed.' Simon shrugged. 'Maybe Helen refused to give him an answer. Maybe she said, "Go ahead, shoot me if you want to, but I'm not telling you anything." Or maybe she told him the truth and he didn't like it, so he killed her anyway.'

'I just can't see it going on like that for

eight and a half hours,' said Sam Kombothekra. 'Maybe one, or two . . .'

'Let's get back to work,' Proust said pointedly. 'Before Waterhouse is tempted to build
a leisurely lunch and siesta for the killer into
his fantasy. Felicity Benson, thirty-one years
old, single.' He tapped the name on the
whiteboard. 'Known as Fliss. She lives in
Kilburn in London and works for the TV
production company Binary Star. She's supposed to be taking over Laurie Nattrass's
documentary, the one about, among others,
Helen Yardley. On Wednesday — two days
ago — she opened an envelope addressed
to her at work and extracted from it a card
that made no sense to her, with our friends
the sixteen numbers on it. She showed it to
Mr Nattrass, who threw it in his office bin.
Sadly, it's well on its way to a landfill by
now; the chances of our finding it are zero.
Miss Benson is alive and well, and I've
asked for some resources to be devoted to
keeping her that way. The higher-ups are
stalling, as I knew they would. In the
meantime, Miss Benson has agreed to stay
with a friend and spend no time alone apart
from when answering a call of nature, at
which times the friend should remain close
at hand.'

Proust paused for breath. 'I believe this

young woman's in danger.'

No one disagreed.

'However, to play devil's advocate for a moment, there's clearly a variation here as well as a link,' he went on. 'The card is part of a pattern, but Miss Benson simultaneously breaks the pattern by having been neither attacked nor killed, which is why Superintendent Barrow isn't authorising protection. Strange logic on his part, since protection, as I understand it, is preventative and future-focused. Perhaps if Miss Benson were already dead, Superintendent Barrow would see fit to protect her.' The Snowman ran his hand over his shiny head. 'That's about it for now. Without neglecting any previously assigned tasks, we need to pursue the Wolverhampton angle — we might hit the jackpot and get Baldy on CCTV. We still need brands and suppliers for the card, the pen, the ink. Top priority is drafting something for the press. Oh, and we need a telegenic volunteer we can put in front of the cameras. That's you, Sergeant Kombothekra — your own fault for having clean hair and a winning smile.'

'What about the third woman featured in Nattrass's documentary?' Klair Williamson called out.

'Rachel Hines,' said someone.

'Has anyone contacted her to see if she's been sent the same numbers?' Williamson asked.

Proust packed up his files and headed for his office as if she hadn't spoken.

'One of you had better explain to me and explain fast about Laurie Nattrass and Rachel Hines, in a way that makes sense this time. Where are they?'

Clever, thought Simon. Making it their fault instead of his: the hurried account they'd given the Snowman was so garbled, he could hardly have presented it at the briefing. How could he have answered Klair Williamson's question, when he had so little information? And whose fault was that? The select few doubled as the scapegoats.

'I've told you everything I know,' Simon said. 'Nattrass told me Ray Hines was staying in Twickenham, Angus Hines said she was staying with friends, and Fliss Benson didn't know where she was. Since my first and only conversation with Nattrass, I've been unable to contact him. He's not at his house, at either of his offices . . .'

'He has more than one?' Proust's eyebrows shot up.

'Officially, today's his last day at Binary Star, but he's not there, and he seems to have started at another company already, Hammerhead,' said Colin Sellers. 'He's not there either, and he's not returning calls. Until we find him, we can't ask him about Ray Hines' Twickenham friends. Her ex-husband's given us a list of her friends, but none are in Twickenham.'

'We've eliminated Angus Hines for Helen Yardley's murder, sir,' said Sam Kombothekra.

'In one of his seven offices, was he?'

'He wasn't, sir. He had the day off on Monday. Between 3 p.m. and 7 p.m. he was in a pub called the Retreat in Bethnal Green with a Carl Chappell. I spoke to Chappell myself, sir — he's confirmed it.'

'While Judith Duffy was having lunch with Rachel Hines in Primrose Hill.' Proust sucked in his lips, stretching the flesh tighter on his face. 'Why would you have lunch with the person whose lies turned twelve jurors and one husband against you and deprived you of your freedom for four years? And why would Doctor Despicable wish to dine with a woman she believes is a child murderer? One of you, get her to talk. Maybe she knows something about the Twickenham contingent.'

'What about her two daughters and their husbands?' Simon asked.

'Is that premature? No, I don't think it is,' the Snowman answered his own question. 'I wouldn't put it past them to blame Helen Yardley and Sarah Jaggard for ruining their mother's life, or their mother-in-law's. Apart from anything else, we can't afford to ignore a suggestion made to us by Laurie Nattrass. If he turns out to be right, we'll never hear the end of it. You never know, one of the sons-in-law might be Baldy himself. Get on to it, one of you. With regard to tracking down Nattrass and Rachel Hines, pursue any link, however tenuous — her lawyers, people she met in prison, his friends and media contacts. Presumably they've both got relatives.'

'Yes, sir,' said Sam.

'If this is about revenge on the people responsible for Duffy's downfall, Laurie Nattrass and Rachel Hines would be on that list, along with Helen Yardley, Sarah Jaggard and Fliss Benson.' Proust frowned. 'Yet Nattrass told Waterhouse only that Benson had been sent the sixteen numbers, not that he'd had them himself.'

'Maybe the killer's only interested in women,' Sellers suggested. 'In which case, you'd expect Ray Hines to have been sent a card.'

'If we don't know where she is, maybe the

card-sender doesn't either,' said Sam. 'Which makes finding her all the more crucial, before he does.'

'It might be about a different sort of revenge,' said Gibbs, looking at Simon. 'Nothing to do with Duffy's downfall or with Duffy, but on baby-murderers and the people who side with them against their victims.'

'Baby-murderers, detective?' The Snowman stood up and walked round his desk. To Simon's left, Sam and Sellers were as still as the most ambitious participants in a game of musical statues. Simon made a point of shifting from one foot to the other and yawning, boycotting the fear-freeze.

'Baby-murderers?' Proust breathed in Gibbs' face.

'I meant from the killer's point of view. I don't think —'

'Are you the killer?'

'No.'

'Then speak from your own point of view. Say what *you* think: women slandered as baby-killers, women wrongly convicted as baby-murderers!'

'You mean say what *you* think,' Simon muttered, loud enough for Proust to hear. *You want trouble, I'll give you trouble. Come on, you tyrannical fuck. Don't waste your*

303

hostility on someone who's not going to make the most of it.

The inspector didn't take his eyes off Gibbs. 'All the right words are yours for the choosing, detective — all the words that make it clear you're on the side of good against evil.' Gibbs stared sullenly at the floor.

'You attack one woman, get interrupted, leave the numbers in her pocket,' said Proust conversationally, as if nothing unusual had happened. 'A week later, you shoot dead a second woman, leave the numbers in *her* pocket. The day after you kill the second woman, you send the numbers by snail mail to a third woman, whom you neither attack nor kill. Why? What's going on in your mind? Waterhouse?'

'My mind, sir? Or do you mean the killer's mind?' *All the right words are yours for the rejecting in favour of all the wrong ones, Baldy.*

'I don't want to give myself nightmares, so I'll plump for the latter.' The Snowman smiled, perching on the edge of his desk.

Why doesn't it matter what I say? How come Gibbs can make you angry and I can't? Simon couldn't work out if it was favouritism or a calculated neglect. He remembered Charlie's caution: *Helen Yardley's murder is about Helen Yardley, not Proust. You can't find the right answer if you're asking the wrong question.*

Knowing Charlie would be disappointed to see him behaving like a child, he forced his thoughts back into line. 'Fliss Benson's convinced Laurie Nattrass has gone into hiding because of her,' he said. 'It's probably too stupid to be worth a mention, but . . . they spent part of yesterday afternoon in bed together at his place.' He wondered if he should have said 'having sex' instead. Would that have sounded more natural? 'It had never happened before, and she thinks he regretted it straight away. Immediately afterwards, she says, he started acting distant and virtually threw her out. She's tried to ring him several times since, with no success, and he hasn't returned her calls.'

'He could return yours, though, couldn't he?' said Proust. 'He must know you don't want to speak to him about his intentions with regard to Miss Benson.'

'He wouldn't . . .' Sellers stopped, shook his head.

'Don't keep us in suspense, Detective. What would you do if you'd recently ejected a clingy woman from your bed and wanted to make sure she didn't find her way back into it?'

'Well, I might . . . I might switch off my mobile, go to the pub or to stay at a mate's house and kind of . . . forget to check my messages for a day or two. Just until things had died down. I mean, normally I wouldn't, normally I'd be happy to have any woman back who wanted more, but . . . she's tried to ring him several times since yesterday afternoon? That type's enough to spark off a spell of hibernation, sir — so much hassle, the sex isn't even worth it.'

'I don't think our inability to get hold of Nattrass has got anything to do with Fliss Benson, and I told her that,' said Simon. 'I thought we ought to consider it, that's all. More for what it says about Benson than anything else. She seems convinced it's all about her. I can imagine her being obsessive. She's kind of odd.'

'Takes one to know one, Waterhouse.'

'I asked her to halt all work on the documentary until further notice and she agreed, but . . . she struck me as one of those who'll agree to your face then do what she wants behind your back.'

'Women, you mean?' said Sellers. He was rewarded with a thin-lipped smile from the Snowman.

'I don't want to be told every time I turn up to interview someone that Benson and her camera crew have just left,' said Simon. 'I've looked into the possibility of getting an injunction, and been told there's no chance. Binary Star's documentary is about old cases, not Helen Yardley's murder, so there's no contempt issue.'

'We're going to have to rely on goodwill,' said Sam Kombothekra.

'Goodwill?' Proust eyed him coldly. 'I'd sooner place my trust in the tooth fairy.'

'What do you want us to do about Paul Yardley, sir?' Sam asked.

'Talk to him again, but go gently. Remember who he is and what he's been through. It's possible he forgot, which I suppose would be understandable in the circumstances, but we need him to tell us that he didn't ring emergency services straight after he found Helen's body. He first tried Laurie Nattrass's direct line at Binary Star, then his home number, then his mobile. Then he rang the police.'

'Would you forget phoning someone three times, however grieving and shocked you were, if the police were asking you to think back over your every movement?' asked Simon. 'Going gently's all well and good, but what Yardley's been through is irrelevant if he's lying to us and getting in the way of us —'

'Paul Yardley is not a suspect,' Proust cut him off. 'He was working when Helen died.'

'His alibi is one colleague, that's it — a mate he's worked with for years,' Simon stood his ground. Not only for the sake of disagreeing with Proust, though that was a fringe benefit. 'Yardley made three attempts to contact Laurie Nattrass before alerting us to his dead wife on the living room floor, and he didn't think to mention it to anyone? You can't tell me that's not a bad sign.'

'Paul Yardley isn't a liar!' Proust smacked the flat of his hand against the desk. 'Don't make me take you off this case, Waterhouse, because I need you on it!'

That's right: you want to yell at me, not have me round for dinner.

'I want to interview Stella and Dillon White myself,' said Simon. 'I don't think we can discount what Dillon said about the wet umbrella and the rain.'

'You never stop, do you? Sergeant Kombothekra, explain to DC Waterhouse why, in our job, we're sometimes obliged to discount things we know not to be the case, like rain on a sunny day, or the guilt of innocent people.'

'Have you read the transcript of Gibbs' interview with Dillon?' Simon asked Proust. 'What kind of four-year-old says, "I saw him beyond" about a man he saw across a narrow cul-de-sac?'

'He sounded like . . .' Gibbs screwed up his face. 'What's a soothsayer?'

'This meeting is over,' said the Snowman, with the sort of pronounced finality most people would hold in reserve in case they ever needed to announce the end of the world. 'I for one shan't mourn its passing.'

'Sir, if I can —'

'No, Waterhouse. No to all your suggestions and requests, now and for ever more.'

Simon wanted to punch the air in triumph. That had to be it now, surely: the end of Proust's sick special-friend campaign. There would be no more confidences, no more invitations; no flattery or favours asked. Traditional unvarnished hostility had been reinstated, and Simon felt lighter as a result, able to move and breathe more freely.

It didn't last long. 'Got your diary with you, Waterhouse?' the Snowman called after him as he was leaving the room. 'We need to sort out an evening for you and Sergeant Zailer to come to us for a bite to eat, since you can't do tomorrow night. Pity. Why don't the two of you talk it over and get back to me with some dates that'd work for you?'

11
<u>FRIDAY 9 OCTOBER 2009</u>

Marchington House is a mansion. Its size shocks me to a standstill. I crane my neck and gawp at the pillared entrance, the carved stone arch around the door, the rows and rows of windows, so many that I don't even try to count.

How can someone like me walk into a place like this? The house I grew up in is about half the size of the outbuilding I can see at the far end of the garden, beyond what looks like an enormous black eye-patch on the grass, a rectangular tarpaulin that I assume covers a swimming pool.

I nearly laugh, imagining how the owners of Marchington House would react if they were told they had to spend even one night in my flat in Kilburn. *I'd rather die, darling. Go to the east wing scullery and ask the maid for a vial of arsenic from the poison cabinet.* My hands tighten around the strap of my shoulder bag. I've brought with me everything I thought I would need, but I can see now that it's not enough. *I'm the wrong sort of person for this.* I might have a top-of-the-range digital recorder with me, but that doesn't mean I know what I'm doing here.

Why is Rachel Hines here? Does the house belong to her family? Friends?

Please can we make friends? As a kid I used to say that to my dad when I'd been naughty and he was cross with me. Pathetic as I know it is, I'd give anything to hear those words from Laurie. It would make a welcome change from hearing him say, 'This is Laurie Nattrass. Leave a message and I'll get back to you.'

I've resolved not to ring him or think about him at all today. I've got more important things to worry about. *Like the person who sent me a card with sixteen numbers on it, who might or might not want to kill me. Like the lies I told the police.*

I force my feet to move in the direction of Marchington House's front door. I'm about to press the bell when I notice the rings of stone around it, like ripples in water that have set. How many stonemasons were involved? One? A dozen? I take a deep breath. It's hard not to feel inferior when faced with a doorbell surround that looks as if it's had more time and care devoted to it

311

than all the places I've ever lived in put together.

This house is too good for a woman who . . . The thought surges up before I can stop it. I force myself to follow it through: a woman who killed her two children. Isn't that what I believe, or has reading Laurie's article changed my mind?

I expect to be waiting a while, but Rachel Hines opens the door within seconds of my ringing the bell. 'Fliss,' she says. 'Thanks for coming.' She holds out her hand and I shake it. She's wearing pale blue flared jeans and a white linen shirt with a strange, plum-coloured woollen thing over it, some kind of shawl, but with arms and a neck. Her feet are bare. *She feels at home here.*

'Would you like me to put some shoes on?' she asks.

I feel the heat rush to my face. How can she know what I was thinking? Was I staring?

'I've learned to read body language over the years.' She smiles. 'Call it a finely tuned survival instinct.'

'You must be less nervous than I am,' I say quickly, because I'd rather tell her than try to keep it to myself and fail. 'Bare feet means relaxed, or it does to me, anyway. But . . . I don't mind. Not that I'd have any right to mind.' *Shut up, you fool.* I realise I've been manipulated; my confession was entirely unnecessary.

'That's your interpretation of my bare feet? Interesting. The first thing I'd think would be "under-floor heating". And I'd be right. Take off your shoes and socks and you'll see — it's like having your feet caressed by warm sand.' Her voice is deep and soft.

'I'm fine,' I say stiffly. If I were paranoid, I might start to think that all her dealings with me so far have been designed to throw me off balance. I don't know why I'm using the conditional tense, come to think of it — that's exactly what I *do* think. 'Paranoid' is such a pejorative word; sensibly cautious is what I am.

Apart from when you lied to the police.

'Do you see how our minds are incapable of thinking freely?' she says. 'It matters to me that this house has under-floor heating, more than it would to most people. Your nervousness matters to you — maybe it makes you feel ineffective. In the space of about ten seconds, we've both used my bare feet to reinforce the patterns our minds are determined to follow.'

Is this conversation going to get easier? She's harder to talk to than Laurie.

You're not supposed to be thinking about him, remember?

She stands back to let me in. 'I'm less nervous than you are because I know for sure that you're not a murderer. You don't know that about me.'

I don't want to have to respond to that, so instead I look around. What I see takes my breath away: a large hall with a glossy pale stone floor and skirting boards made from the same polished stone, about three times the height of any I've seen before. Everywhere I look there's something beautiful: the figure-of-eight newel-post, top and bottom circles hollowed out in the middle like something Henry Moore or Barbara Hepworth might have made; the chandelier, a falling shower of blue and pink glass tears, nearly as wide as the ceiling; two large oil paintings side by side, taking up an entire wall, both of women seemingly falling through the air, with small pinched black mouths and their hair flying out behind them; two chairs that look like thrones, with ornate wooden backs and seats covered in shimmery material the colour of moonlight; the water-feature sculpture in the corner — a human figure, the body made of rough-edged pink stone, the head a perpetually rolling white marble ball with water sliding off it as it moves, like a sheet of clear hair. I'm most impressed by what can only be described as a sunken glass rug, a rectangle of clear glass unevenly flecked with silver and gold, set into the stone in the centre of the hall, with light glowing through from beneath.

For about two seconds, I try to kid myself that this trying-too-hard interior wouldn't suit me at all, that I find it vulgar and over-the-top. Then I give up and face the fact that I'd chop off my right arm to live in a house like this, or to have a friend or relative who did that I could stay with. Tonight, on police advice, I've arranged to stay at Tamsin and Joe's, on a hard futon in their cobwebby, rattly-windowed computer room. I hate myself for making the comparison. I am officially a horrible, shallow person.

'You don't know for sure that I'm not a murderer,' I say, to prove that Rachel Hines isn't the only one capable of unexpected pronouncements.

'I know that I'm not,' she says.

'Wendy Whitehead.' I hadn't been planning to mention her name so soon. I'm not sure I'm ready to know. That's how good a truth-hunter I am: *please don't tell me anything — I'm too scared.* 'Who is she?'

'I thought you might want a drink before —'

'Who is she?'

'A nurse. Well, she was. She's not any more.'

We stare at one another. Eventually I say, 'I'll have a drink, thanks.' If I'm about to become the only person apart from Rachel Hines who knows the truth about her children's deaths, I need to prepare myself.

This can't be happening.

I follow her into a kitchen that's more haphazard than the hall but still beautiful: oak floor, curved white work surfaces that look like a sort of spongy stone, a double Belfast sink, a stripe of pale green glass with water pulsing through it running all the way along the floor on one side, breaking up the wood. Against one wall there's a cream-coloured Aga, except it's three times longer than any I've seen before. It's only slightly shorter than a minibus, come to think of it. In the centre of the room there's a large battered pine table with eight chairs around it, and, behind that, one of those free-standing island things, shaped like a tear-drop, its curved sides painted pink and green.

Against the wall nearest to me, there's a purple backless sofa with a matching footstool pushed up against it. Both have been designed to within an inch of their lives. Together, they look like a wiggly exclamation mark. I notice a calendar on the wall: twelve months at a glance, with a tiny rectangle of space assigned to each day of the year. At the top it says 'Dairy Diary'. A Christmas present from the milkman? There's handwriting on it, but I'm not close enough to read it. Above the purple sofa are three paintings of stripes that warp when you look at them. I try to read the pencil signature at the bottom of the nearest one: Bridget something.

Above the minibus-Aga there's a framed photograph of two young men punting down a river. They're both good looking: one serious-faced and dark with a nice smile, the other blond and well aware of his sex appeal. A couple? Did they meet as students at Cambridge, hence the punt? If I was the sort of prejudiced person who leapt to conclusions about gay men and stunning interior design, I'd be concluding round about now that this might be their home.

'No family resemblance whatsoever, is there? You wouldn't believe three siblings could come out so different from one another.' Rachel Hines nods at the photograph and hands me a glass of something dark pink. 'Those two hogged all the good looks. And the charm.'

Not a gay couple, then. Of course. The sons of Marchington House would have studied at Cambridge. No sexed-up polytechnics for them. Rachel Hines probably went to Cambridge too, or Oxford. Any parents who install a strip of whooshy green glass in their kitchen floor would want all their children to get the very best education possible.

I wonder where those parents are. Out at work?

'It wasn't Wendy Whitehead's fault that Marcella and Nathaniel died. I tried to tell you that on the phone, but you cut me off. Please, have a seat.'

Not her fault? I realise how dry my mouth is, and take a sip of what turns out to be cranberry juice. 'You said she killed them.'

'She thought she was protecting them. So did I, which is why I let her do it.'

I wait for her to explain, trying to ignore the chill that's creeping up my back. For a second, as she stares at me, her poise seems to slip and she looks trapped, helpless. 'Can't you work it out? I've told you she's a nurse.'

'I've read Laurie's notes. There was no nurse at your house when . . . You were alone with both babies when they died.'

'Wendy gave Marcella and Nathaniel their first DTP jabs. You don't have children, do you?'

I shake my head. *Vaccination*. She's talking about vaccination. I remember reading something in a newspaper a while ago about crazy hippies who refuse to immunise their children and rely instead on ginseng and patchouli oil to ward off disease.

'They scream when you take them for their jabs. You have to hold them while the needle goes in, but you don't feel as if you're hurting them. You think you're doing your duty as a good mother. You make no comparisons or analogies, you don't think about the other circumstances in which people are injected against their will, all of them horrendous . . .'

I push her out of my way, walk over to the kitchen table and slam down my glass. I'm glad I didn't bother sitting. 'I'm going. I never should have come here in the first place.'

'Why?'

'*Why?* Isn't it obvious?' I can hardly contain my disappointment. 'You're making this up as you go along. Nothing was said at your trial about any DTP jabs.'

'Well spotted. You could ask me why.'

'Now you're making out that what happened to Marcella and Nathaniel was down to routine childhood vaccinations, trying to compare them to lethal injections on death row.'

'You don't know what I'm trying to say, because you didn't let me finish. Marcella was born two weeks early — did you know that?'

'What's that got to do with anything?'

'If you leave now, you'll never find out.'

I bend to pick up my bag. Now that I know I'm not going to be exec-ing a documentary about a murderer called Wendy Whitehead who nearly got away with it, I've no reason to stay. Rachel Hines must know that. What lie will she try next?

'Why are you so angry with me?' she asks.

'I don't like being messed around. Don't pretend you haven't been toying with me from the first phone call — insisting on coming to my house in the middle of the night, then driving away. Ringing me and saying Wendy Whitehead killed your children, conveniently forgetting to mention anything about vaccinations . . .'

'You hung up on me.'

'I lied to the police, thanks to you. They asked me if I had an address for you and I said no. I'm supposed to suspend all work

320

on the film until they give me the ɛ

shouldn't be here.' My bag slid ɛ

shoulder. I try to catch it and fail

to the floor. 'You sent me those ؛

the photograph, didn't you? It was

She looks puzzled, but puzzled

easy to fake. 'Cards?' she says.

'Sixteen numbers in a square. T

think whoever sent them might t

attack me or something. They did

but I can tell that's what they thir

'Slow down, Fliss. Let's talk ɛ

calmly. I promise you I didn't sen

—'

'No! I don't want to talk to you!

ing out of here now, and you're

to contact me again — I want you

that. Whatever game you've bee

with me is over. Say it! Tell me y

me alone.'

'You don't trust me, do you?'

'That's an understatement!' In

life, I have never spoken to any

ciously.

'My word's worthless, then.'

'Good point,' I say, heading fo

door. My lie to the police won't

correct it as soon as I can. I'l

Simon Waterhouse and tell hi

Hines is at Marchington House i

n and that I'm sure she's the person who
me those numbers. I don't know why it
n't occur to me before. I got the first
l in Wednesday morning's post. It was
Wednesday that she phoned me for the
time. Did she sit down on Tuesday and
ke a list? *Item one: abandon all other*
iects and devote all time henceforth to
ssing with Fliss Benson's head?

'liss!' She grabs my arm, pulling me back
ards her.

et go of me!' I feel dizzy, unsteady on
feet, as if by touching me she's injected
e, undiluted panic into my bloodstream.
ink of DC Waterhouse telling me not to
anywhere alone.

Do you think I killed them?' she asks. 'Do
think I murdered Marcella and Na-
niel? Tell me the truth.'

Maybe you did. I don't know. I'll *never*
ow — neither will anyone, apart from
. If I had to guess, based on what little I
ow of you, I'd say yes, I think you prob-
y did it.' There, I've said it, and fuck you,
rie, if you're telepathic and heard me
it and you're shaking your head in
gust. You never bothered to ask me what
ought about your protégées, did you?
len and Sarah and Rachel. My opinion
sn't matter. It matters as little as the sex

we had yesterday.

Without warning, I burst into tears. *Oh my God, oh my God, oh my God.* I try to regain control, but it's useless. I feel like someone who can't swim, powerless in the face of a gushing waterfall. It doesn't even feel as if the tears are coming from me and, for a few minutes, I'm too shocked by what my body is doing without permission to notice that someone is holding me tight, or to realise, because no one else is here, that that someone must be Rachel Hines.

'I'm not going to ask you. You probably don't want to talk about it.'

I shake my head. I'm sitting on the wiggly purple sofa in the kitchen, concentrating on drinking my cranberry juice, sip by sip. Perhaps by the time I finish it, I won't feel so horrendously embarrassed. Rachel's sitting at the table at the far end of the room, trying to keep a tactful distance. *As if either of us is likely to forget that she's just spent the last half hour mopping me up.*

'I didn't send you a card with numbers on it,' she says. 'Or any photographs. Did you ask the police why they thought the sender might attack you? If you're in danger, you've a right to know what's going on. Why don't you — ?'

'I don't need a life coach,' I mutter ungraciously.

'And if you did, you wouldn't recruit me,' she says, neatly summarising my views on the matter. 'I can explain why I drove away on Wednesday night, but it might offend you.'

I shrug. I'm already feeling unloveable, humiliated and terrified — offended might as well join the club.

'I didn't like your house.'

I look up, to check I've heard right. *'What?'*

'It looks dirty. The paint's flaking off the window frames . . .'

'I don't own it. I rent the basement flat, that's all.'

'Is it nice?'

I can't believe I'm having this conversation. 'My flat? No, it's not *nice.* It's about — ooh, let's see — five million times less nice than this house. It's small and damp and all I can afford.' I wonder if I ought to qualify this: *all I could afford, until recently.* Why bother? As soon as Maya hears Rachel Hines' revised opinion of me, not to mention Laurie's, I'll be unemployed and probably homeless. Even mouldy flats in Kilburn cost money.

'I looked at the outside of your house and I knew I wouldn't like the inside. I tried to tell myself it didn't matter, that I'd be okay, but I knew I wouldn't. I pictured us sitting and talking in a dingy lounge, with posters stuck to the plasterboard walls with drawing pins, and a throw over the sofa to hide the stains, and . . .' She sighs. 'I know how awful this sounds, but I want to be honest with you.'

'I can't complain, can I? I accused you of being a child-killer.'

'No, you didn't. You said you didn't know. There's a big difference.'

I look away, wishing I hadn't let her provoke me into expressing an opinion.

'Ever since prison, I've . . . I can't stand to be anywhere that isn't . . .'

'A stunning mansion?' I say sarcastically.

'The wrong physical environment, any kind of ugly surroundings — it makes me feel physically sick,' she says. 'It never used to. Prison changed me in lots of ways, but that was the first thing I noticed, the first night I was out. Angus and I had split up. I had no home to go to, so I went to a hotel.' She takes a deep breath, drawing in her chin.

Only three stars, was it? I don't say it. It's too easy to be cruel to her, and I know I'd enjoy it too much. *It's not her fault I started blubbing and made an exhibition of myself.*

325

'I didn't like the room they put me in, but I told myself it didn't matter — I'd only be there a few nights while I sorted out somewhere more permanent to live. I had this nauseous feeling that wouldn't go away, a bit like car sickness, but I tried to ignore it.'

'What was wrong with the room?' I asked. 'Was it dirty?'

'Probably. I don't know.' I hear impatience in her voice, as if she's been asked the same question countless times and still can't come up with an answer. 'It was mainly the curtains that bothered me.'

'Dirty?' I try again.

'I didn't get close enough to find out. They were too thin and too short. They stopped at the bottom of the window instead of going down to the floor. It was as if someone had pinned two handkerchiefs to the wall. And they were attached to one of those horrible plastic tracks with no pelmet or anything to cover it. You could see bits of string poking out behind the material at the top.' She shudders. 'They were disgusting. I wanted to run from the room screaming. I know it sounds crazy.'

Just a bit.

'There was a picture on the wall of a stone urn, with flowers strewn around its base. I didn't like that either. It was sort of washed-

understood if I'd said there was no difference between a hotel room and a cell at
Geddham Hall.'

'But . . . you'd split up. He thought
you'd . . .'

'Killed our children. Yes, he did.'

'Then why go to him? And why did he let
you in? *Did* he let you in?'

She nods. When I see her coming towards
me, I stiffen, but all she does is sit down at
the far end of the sofa, leaving a comfortable distance between us. 'I could tell you
why,' she says. 'Why I behaved as I did, why
Angus behaved as he did. But it wouldn't
make sense out of context. I'd like to tell
you the whole story, from the start — the
story I've never told anybody. The truth.'

I don't want to hear it.

'You can make your documentary,' she
says, with a new energy in her voice. I'm
not sure if she's begging or issuing an order.
'Not about Helen Yardley, or Sarah Jaggard
— about me. Me, Angus, Marcella and Nathaniel. The story of what happened to our
family. That's my one condition, Fliss. I
don't want to share the hour or two hours
or however long it is with anyone else,
however worthy their cause. I'm sorry if that
sounds selfish . . .'

'Why me?' I ask.

'Because you don't know what to think about me. I could hear it in your voice, the first time I spoke to you: the uncertainty, the doubt. I *need* your doubt — it'll make you listen to me, properly, because you want to find out, don't you? Hardly anyone really listens. Laurie Nattrass certainly doesn't. You'll be objective. The film you'll make won't portray me as a helpless victim or as a killer, because I'm neither one of those things. You'll show people who I really am, who Angus is, how much we both loved Marcella and Nathaniel.'

I stand up, repelled by the determination in her blazing eyes. I have to get out of here before she makes the choice for me. 'Sorry,' I say firmly. 'I'm not the right person.'

'Yes, you are.'

'I'm not. You wouldn't say that if you knew who my father was.' There, I've said it. I can't unsay it. 'Forget it,' I mutter, feeling dangerously close to tears again. *That's why I got upset: Dad, not Laurie.* Nothing to do with Laurie, and so slightly less pathetic. A tragically dead father is a better reason to cry than unrequited love for a complete arsehole. 'I'll go,' I say. 'I should never have come.' I grab my bag, like someone who really intends to leave. I stay where I am.

'It makes no difference to me who your

father was,' says Rachel. 'If he was the first on my jury to vote guilty, if he was the judge who gave me two life sentences . . . Though I think it's unlikely Justice Elizabeth Geilow's your dad.' She smiles. 'What's his name?'

'He's dead.' I sit down again. I can't stand up and talk about Dad at the same time. Not that I've ever tried. I've never even talked about it to Mum. How stupid is that? 'He committed suicide three years ago. His name was Melvyn Benson. You probably won't have heard of him.' *Though he'd heard of you.* 'He was Head of Children's Services for —'

'Jaycee Herridge.'

I flinch at the name, though I know it's ridiculous. Jaycee Herridge didn't kill my dad. She was only twenty months old. I feel trapped, as if something that's been gaping open has slammed shut. I shouldn't have said anything. After years of bottling it up, why tell Rachel Hines, of all people?

'Your dad was the disgraced social worker who killed himself?'

I nod.

'I remember hearing people talking about it in prison. I avoided the news and the papers as much as possible, but a lot of the girls couldn't get enough of other people's

331

misery — it was a distraction from their own.'

I swallow hard. The idea of Dad's suffering providing entertainment for the feral incarcerated masses is hard to take. I don't care if I'm prejudiced; if they can enjoy my father's downfall, I can think of them as scum who deserve to be behind bars. That way we're even.

'Fliss? Tell me.'

I have the oddest feeling: that I always knew, deep down, that this would happen. *That Rachel Hines is exactly the person I want to tell.*

Woodenly, I layout the facts. Jaycee Herridge was taken to hospital twenty-one times in the first year of her life, with injuries her parents claimed were accidental — bruises, cuts, swellings, burns. When she was fourteen months old, her mother took her to the doctor's surgery with what turned out to be two broken arms, saying she had climbed out of her pram and fallen on a concrete playground. The GP knew the medical history and didn't believe the story for a second. He alerted Social Services, wishing he'd done so several months earlier instead of allowing himself to be given cups of tea and lied to by Jaycee's parents, who always took great pains to reassure him when he visited them at home, cuddling Jaycee and making a fuss of her in his presence.

The social worker assigned to the case spent the next four months doing everything she could to remove Jaycee from the family home. She had the support of the police and of every health professional who had ever had contact with the family, but the council's legal services department decreed that there wasn't sufficient proof of abuse for Jaycee to be taken into care. This was a catastrophic error on the part of a junior legal executive who should have known that in the family courts, guilt did not have to be proven beyond reasonable doubt. All that was required was for a family court judge to decide that on the balance of probabilities, Jaycee would be safer in local authority care than with her parents, and, given the number and seriousness of her injuries, this would almost certainly have happened if the case had ever made it to court.

As Head of Children's Services, my father should have spotted this mistake, but he didn't. He was overworked and stressed, ground down by the tottering towers of files on his desk, and as soon as he saw the words 'unsafe to initiate care proceedings' and the signature of a legal executive beneath it, he probed no further. He would never have dreamed of trying to take a child from its parents against legal advice, and it wouldn't have occurred to him that a legal executive working in child protection could be so incompetent as to confuse criminal and civil standards of proof.

As a result of his misplaced trust and the legal executive's idiocy, Jaycee was left in the care of her parents, who finally murdered her in August 2005, when she was twenty months old. Her father pleaded guilty to kicking her to death and was sentenced to life in prison. Her mother was never charged with anything because it was impossible to prove she was involved in the violence against her daughter.

My father resigned. Jaycee's GP resigned. The legal executive refused to resign and was eventually fired. No one remembers their names now, and although everyone knows the name Jaycee Herridge, very few people would be able to tell you that her parents' names were Danielle Herridge and Oscar Kelly.

My father never forgave himself. In August 2006, a week before the anniversary of Jaycee's death, he washed down thirty sleeping tablets with a bottle of whisky and never woke up. He must have planned it well in advance. He'd encouraged Mum to spend the weekend at her sister's house, to make sure she didn't find him in time to save him.

I could tell Rachel Hines a lot more. I could tell her I spent the last year of Dad's life lying to him, pretending I didn't blame him for screwing up so horrendously when all the time a voice in my head was screaming *Why didn't you check? Why did you take someone else's word for it when a human life was at stake? What kind of useless cretin are you?* I've always wondered if Mum pretended too, or if she believed what she told him over and over: that it wasn't his fault, and no one could ever claim that it was. How could she believe that?

I drag myself back to the present. I need to finish explaining myself and get the hell out of here. 'What you don't know — because you can't — is that he talked to me about you not long before he killed himself.'

'Your father talked about *me?*'

'Not just you — all three of you. Helen Yardley, Sarah Jaggard . . .'

'All three of us.' Rachel smiles, as if I've said something funny. Then her smile disappears and she looks deadly serious. 'I don't care about Helen Yardley and Sarah Jaggard,' she says. 'What did your dad say about me?'

I feel like a sadist, but I can hardly refuse to answer her question, having got this far. 'We'd gone out for the day — me, him and Mum. One of the many trips Mum arranged to cheer him up after Jaycee died. The fact that they never worked and it was obvious he'd never be cheerful again didn't stop us trying. We were having lunch, me and Mum chatting brightly as if everything was fine. Dad was reading the paper. There was an article about you, your case. I think it must have said something about an appeal — that you were planning to appeal or that you might, I don't know.'

Laurie probably wrote it.

'Dad threw down the paper and said, "If Rachel Hines appeals and wins, there's no hope." '

Her lips twitch slightly. Apart from that, no reaction.

'He was shaking. He'd never mentioned your name before. Mum and I didn't know what to say. There was this horrible, tense atmosphere. We both knew . . .' I stop. I don't know how to say it without sounding awful.

'You knew that if he was thinking about me then he was thinking about dead babies.'

'Yes.'

'And that was a dangerous subject for him

336

to be thinking about.'

'He said, "If they let Rachel Hines out of prison, no parent who murders a child will ever be convicted in this country again. Everyone working in child protection might as well pack up and go home. More children like Jaycee Herridge will die and there'll be nothing anyone can do to stop it." He had this . . . ferocious look in his eyes, as if he'd seen some sort of vision of the future and . . .' *And it made him want out.* I can't bring myself to articulate this. I'm convinced — I've always been convinced — that Dad killed himself because he didn't want to be around if and when Rachel Hines was released.

'He had a point,' she says gently. 'If all the mothers convicted of killing their babies appeal and win, the message is clear: mothers don't and can't murder their children. Which we all know isn't true.'

'He started shouting in front of everybody.' I'm crying again, but this time I don't care. ' "Suddenly, they're all innocent — Yardley, Jaggard, Hines! All tried for murder, two of them convicted, but they're all innocent! How can that be?" He was yelling at me and Mum, as if it was our fault. Mum couldn't handle it, she ran out of the restaurant. I said, "Dad, no one's saying Rachel Hines is innocent. You don't know she's going to appeal, and even if she does, you don't know she'll win." '

'He was right.' Rachel stands up, starts to walk in no particular direction. She would hate my kitchen. It's too small for aimless walking. It would make her feel sick. 'My case effectively changed the law. Like your dad, the three judges who heard my appeal didn't see me as an individual. They saw me as number three, after Yardley and Jaggard. Everyone lumped us together — the three crib death killers.' She frowns. 'I don't know why we got to be the famous ones. Lots of women are in prison for killing children, their own and other people's.'

I think of Laurie's article. *Helen Yardley, Lorna Keast, Joanne Bew, Sarah Jaggard, Dorne Llewellyn . . . the list goes on and on.*

'Would I have had my convictions overturned if Helen Yardley hadn't set a precedent? She was the one who first piqued Laurie Nattrass's interest. It was her case that made him start questioning Judith Duffy's professionalism, which was what led to my being granted leave to appeal.' She turns to face me, angry. 'It was nothing to do with me. It was Helen Yardley, Laurie Nattrass and JIPAC. They turned it political. It wasn't about our specific cases any more — Sarah Jaggard's, mine. We weren't individuals, we were a national scandal: the victims of an evil doctor who wanted us locked up for ever. And her motive? Rampant malevolence, because we all know some doctors *are* evil. Oh, we're all suckers for a wicked doctor story, and Laurie Nattrass is a brilliant storyteller. That's why the prosecution rolled over and I was spared a retrial.'

'Because Laurie can't see the trees for the wood.'

'What? What did you say?' She's standing over me, leaning down.

'My boss, Maya — she said you said that about him. She thought you'd got the saying wrong, but you meant it the way you said it, didn't you? You meant to say that Laurie saw you as one of his wrongly accused victims, not as a person in your own right. That's why you want the documentary to be about you only — not Helen Yardley or Sarah Jaggard.'

Rachel kneels down on the sofa beside me. 'Never underestimate the differences between things, Fliss: your flat in a horrible terrace in Kilburn and this house; a beautiful painting and a soulless mass-produced image of an urn; people who are capable of seeing only their own narrow perspective,

339

and people who see the whole picture.'
She's pinching the skin on her neck again,
turning it red. Her eyes are sharp when she
turns to face me. 'I see the whole picture. I
think you do too.'

'There's another reason,' I say, my rapid
heartbeat alerting me to the inadvisability
of bringing this up. *Tough.* Now that I've
had the thought, I have to see her reaction.
'There's another reason you don't want to
be part of the same programme as Helen
Yardley and Sarah Jaggard. You think they're
both guilty.'

'You're wrong. I don't think that, not
about either of them.' When she speaks
again, her voice is thick with emotion.
'You're as wrong about me as I'm right
about you, but you're thinking — that's
what matters. If I wasn't convinced before,
I am now: it has to be you, Fliss. You have
to make this documentary. The story needs
to be told and it needs to be told now,
before . . .' She stops, shakes her head.

'You said your case changed the law,' I
say, trying to sound professional. 'What did
you mean?'

She snorts dismissively, rubbing the end
of her nose. 'My appeal judges concluded,
and wrote into their summary remarks so
that there would be no ambiguity, that when

a case relies solely on disputed medical evidence, that case should not be brought before a criminal court. Which means it's now pretty much impossible to convict a mother who waits till she's alone with her child and then smothers him. There isn't generally much other evidence in cases of smothering. The victim puts up no resistance, being only a baby, and there are no witnesses — you'd have to be pretty stupid to try to smother your baby in front of a witness.'

Or desperate, I think. So desperate you don't care who sees.

'Your father's prediction was spot on. My appeal judgement *has* made it easier for mothers to murder their babies and avoid prosecution. Not only mothers — fathers, childminders, anyone. Your dad was smart to see it coming. I didn't. I might not have appealed if I'd known that was the effect it would have. I'd lost everything already. What did it matter if I was in prison or out?'

'If you're innocent . . .'

'I am.'

'Then you deserve to be free.'

'Will you make the documentary?'

'I don't know if I can.' I hear the panic in my voice and despise myself. Will I be betraying Dad if I do? Betraying something more important if I don't?

'Your father's dead, Fliss. I'm alive.'

I owe her nothing. I don't say it out loud because I shouldn't have to. It should be obvious.

'I'm going back to Angus,' she says quietly. 'I can't hide away here for ever, with no one knowing where I am. I need to start living my life again. Angus loves me, whatever's happened between us in the past.'

'Does he want you back?'

'I think so, and even if he doesn't, he will when I . . .' She leaves the sentence unfinished.

'What?' I ask. 'When you what?'

'When I tell him that I'm pregnant,' she says, looking away.

DAILY TELEGRAPH, SATURDAY 10 OCTOBER 2009

Significant Lead in Helen Yardley Murder

Police investigating the murder of Helen Yardley, the wrongly convicted mother shot dead at her home in Spilling on Monday, confirmed yesterday that they have a lead. The police artist's image below is of a man West Midlands CID are keen to question in connection with a recent attack on Sarah Jaggard, the Wolverhampton hairdresser acquitted of the murder of six-month-old Beatrice Furniss in July 2005. Mrs Jaggard was threatened with a knife in a busy shopping area of Wolverhampton on Monday 28 September. DS Sam Kombothekra of Culver Valley CID said: 'We believe that the same man who attacked Mrs Jaggard may have shot Mrs Yardley. There is evidence that links the two incidents.' Helen Yardley spent nine years in prison for the murders of her two baby sons before having her convictions quashed on appeal in February

2005. A card with 16 numbers on it, reproduced below, was found in her pocket after her death. A similar card was left in Mrs Jaggard's pocket by her assailant.

DS Kombothekra has asked for anyone who recognises the man pictured below to contact him or a member of his team. He said: 'We can guarantee complete confidentiality, so there is no reason to fear coming forward, though we believe this man is dangerous and should not be approached under any circumstances by members of the public. We must find him as a matter of utmost urgency.' DS Kombothekra has also appealed for information about the 16 numbers on the card: 'They must mean something to somebody. If that someone is you, please contact Culver Valley CID.'

Asked to comment on motive, DS Kombothekra said: 'Both Mrs Yardley and Mrs Jaggard were accused of heinous crimes and found — though only after a terrible miscarriage of justice in Mrs Yardley's case — to be not guilty. We have to consider the possibility that the motive is a desire to punish both women based on the mistaken belief that they are guilty.'

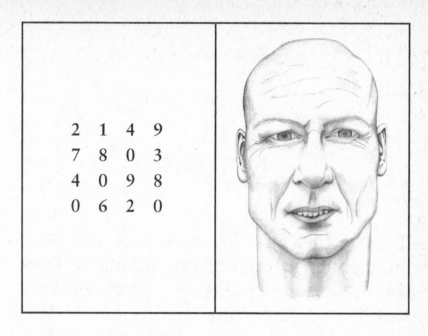

12
10/10/09

'I've no idea whether they were the same numbers or sixteen different numbers.' Tamsin Waddington pulled her chair forward and leaned across the small kitchen table that separated her from DC Colin Sellers. He could smell her hair, or whatever sweet substance she'd sprayed it with. Her whole flat smelled of it. He resisted the urge to grab the long ponytail she'd draped over her right shoulder, to see if it felt as silky as it looked. 'I don't even know that there were sixteen of them. All I know is, there were some numbers on a card, laid out in rows and columns — could have been sixteen, twelve, twenty . . .'

'But you're certain you saw the card on Mr Nattrass's desk on 2 September,' said Sellers. 'That's very precise, and more than a month ago. How can you — ?'

'2 September's my boyfriend's birthday. I was hanging around in Laurie's office try-

346

ing to pluck up the courage to ask him if I could leave early.'

'I thought you said he wasn't your boss.' Sellers stifled a sigh. He hated it when attractive women had boyfriends. He genuinely believed he'd do a better job, given the opportunity. Not knowing the boyfriends in question made no difference to the strength of his conviction. Like anyone with a vocation, Sellers felt frustrated whenever he was prevented from doing what he was put on this earth to do.

'He wasn't my boss as such. I was his researcher.'

'On the crib death film?'

'That's right.' She leaned in even closer, trying to read Sellers' notes. *Nosey cow.* If he stuck out his tongue now he could lick her hair. 'Laurie never seemed to want to go home, and I was embarrassed to admit that I did,' she said. 'Embarrassed to have made plans that didn't involve defeating injustice, plans Laurie wouldn't have given a toss about. I was hovering round his desk like an idiot, and I saw the card next to his BlackBerry. I asked him about it because it was easier than asking what I really wanted to ask.'

'This is important, Miss Waddington, so please be as accurate as you can.' *Can I play*

with your swishy hair while you suck my nads?
'What did you say to Mr Nattrass about the card, and what was his response?' For a moment, Sellers imagined he'd asked the wrong question, the X-rated one, but he couldn't have. She didn't look offended, wasn't running from the room.

'I picked it up. He didn't seem to notice. I said, "What's this?" He grunted at me.'

'Grunted?' This was torture. Couldn't she use more neutral words?

'Laurie grunts all the time — when he knows a response is required, but hasn't heard what you've said. It works with a lot of people, but I'm not easily fobbed off. I waved the card in front of his face and asked him again what it was. Typical Laurie, he blinked at me like a mole emerging into the light after a month underground and said, "What *is* that bloody thing? Did you send it to me? What do those numbers mean?" I told him I had no idea. He snatched the card out of my hand, tore it up, threw the pieces in the air, and turned back to his work.'

'You saw him tear it up?'

'Into at least eight pieces, which I picked up and chucked in the bin. Don't know why I bothered — Laurie didn't notice, or thank me, and when I finally got round to asking him if I could leave early he said, "No, you fucking can't." If I'd known the numbers were important, I'd have —' Tamsin broke off, tutted as if annoyed with herself. 'I have a vague memory of the first number being a two, but I wouldn't swear to it. I didn't think anything of it until Fliss turned up here in a state last night and told me about the card she'd been sent and an anonymous stalker who might or might not want to kill her.'

'Did Mr Nattrass say whether the card was sent to him at work or at home?'

'No, but if I had to guess I'd say work. I doubt he'd have bothered to bring it into the office if it had been sent to him at home. He seemed completely uninterested in it — it meant nothing to him.'

'Can you be sure of that?' Sellers asked. 'Anger might be one reason for ripping something to pieces.'

'Anger at having his time wasted, that's all. Honestly — I know Laurie. Which is why I wasn't surprised when Fliss told me he hadn't mentioned getting a similar card himself, when she showed him the one she'd been sent. Laurie doesn't waste words on anything he doesn't consider important.'

Sellers thought it was odd, nevertheless, that Nattrass hadn't mentioned it to Fliss

Benson. It would have been the most natural thing in the world for him to say, 'That's strange — someone sent me one of those a few weeks ago.' Why keep quiet about it, unless he was the person who'd sent the sixteen numbers to Benson — a second draft, after he'd torn up the first to put Tamsin off the scent?

What scent, dickhead? On 2 September, Helen Yardley was still alive. Nattrass can't be her killer — he's got an alibi, and looks nothing like the man Sarah Jaggard described.

Everyone had a sodding alibi. Judith Duffy, though she was still refusing to be interviewed, had left a message on Sam Kombothekra's voicemail detailing her whereabouts on Monday. She'd spent the morning with her lawyers, and the afternoon in a restaurant with Rachel Hines. Sellers couldn't begin to get his head round that, but there seemed to be no doubt about it — three waiters had confirmed that the two of them arrived at 1 p.m. and didn't leave until 5.

Duffy's two daughters and their husbands — Imogen and Spencer, Antonia and George — had been in the Maldives. They'd left the country before Sarah Jaggard was attacked and got back on Wednesday, two days after Helen Yardley was shot. Sellers had interviewed the four of them yesterday, and it had put him right off his traditional Friday night curry. He didn't usually let the job get to him, but he'd started to feel increasingly uncomfortable as he listened to them explain, one after another, that they didn't care if they never saw Duffy again. 'She's got no heart,' Imogen said. 'She ruined innocent women's lives to further her own career. You can't sink much lower than that.' Antonia wasn't quite so black and white about it. 'I'll never feel the same about Mum,' she said. 'I'm so angry with her, I can't bring myself to speak to her at the moment. Maybe one day.'

The two sons in law clearly regarded Duffy as an embarrassment. One went as far as to say he'd have thought twice about marrying her daughter if he'd known what would happen. 'My kids keep asking me why other kids at school are laughing at them, saying their granny's in all the papers,' he said angrily. 'They're only eight and six — they don't understand it. What am I supposed to say?'

Sellers hadn't been able to resist asking, though it had no bearing on the investigation, how healthy the relationship between Duffy and her daughters and sons-in-law had been before Laurie Nattrass had brought her lack of professional integrity to the public's attention. 'All right,' Imogen had said doubtfully. Antonia had nodded more enthusiastically. 'We were a normal family before this nightmare started.'

Sellers couldn't stand the thought of his own children one day saying similar things about him — that he had no heart, or they couldn't bring themselves to speak to him. Would Stacey try to make Harrison and Bethany hate him, if he left her?

Suki thought she would — the woman he'd been seeing behind Stacey's back for nearly ten years. She'd told him over and over, and he'd ended up believing her. She talked about Stacey as if she knew her better than Sellers did, even though they'd never met.

Suki didn't want Sellers full-time anyway. She had at one time, but not any more. 'This way you don't have to lose me or your kids,' she often said. Sellers was almost as bored of Suki as he was of Stacey. He'd tell them both where to stick it if in exchange he could have one night with Tamsin Waddington. Even one hour . . .

'Did you hear what I just said?'

'Sorry.'

'I know you're a man, but do you think you could pay attention?'

Sellers risked a grin. 'You'd make a good DCI,' he said.

'There's nothing suspicious about Laurie Nattrass failing to communicate efficiently,' said Tamsin. 'If he'd said to Fliss, "How interesting — I received a similar card myself, also with sixteen numbers on it, only a few weeks ago" — now *that* would have been suspicious. He once said to me, "Where's that coffee I asked for?" three seconds after I'd handed it to him. I pointed at the mug of coffee in his right hand, and he said, "Did you just give me this?" Then he dropped it and I had to make him another one.'

Sellers still wasn't convinced. Nattrass had failed to mention having been sent the sixteen numbers not only to Fliss Benson but also to Waterhouse, during their telephone conversation. He must have known at that point that the card was important, if a detective was asking about it. Waterhouse had asked him if he'd had any unusual emails or letters recently, and Nattrass had dodged the question. He'd described the card Fliss Benson had received and said nothing about being sent one himself. Was that the behaviour of an innocent man?

'I'm worried about Fliss.' Tamsin's haughty tone suggested Sellers had damn well better share her concern. 'I read the paper this morning — why do you think I called the police? I know a card like the ones Fliss and Laurie were sent was found on Helen Yardley's dead body. I know Sarah Jaggard was attacked and whoever did it left a card with sixteen numbers on it in her pocket. It doesn't make sense, though.' Her forehead creased.

'What doesn't?'

'With both Helen Yardley and Sarah Jaggard, the violent part came first, didn't it? He attacked them, then left the cards. Fliss and Laurie both got cards through the post, but they haven't been attacked. So maybe he *isn't* going to hurt them, because if he was, wouldn't he have done it already?'

Which is why Superintendent Barrow won't authorise protection. That and his loathing for the Snowman.

'Fliss isn't in good shape,' said Tamsin. 'I think she's really scared, though she insists she's not, and I'm almost certain there's something she's not telling me, something to do with the card. The numbers. She went off first thing this morning without telling me or Joe where she was going, and I've no idea where she is now. And . . .'

'And?' Sellers prompted.

'She promised a detective she spoke to

354

that she wouldn't work on the film, but she has been. There, I've shopped her,' said Tamsin proudly. 'I'm happy to be a grass if it keeps her safe. She met up with Ray Hines yesterday.'

'Where?'

'At her parents' house, I think.'

'Miss Benson's parents' house?'

'No, Ray Hines'.'

Sellers bit the inside of his lip. This was no good. Waterhouse would be furious.

'You did the right thing telling me.' He smiled. Tamsin smiled back.

All right, love, wipe yourself, your taxi's here. It's four in the morning, love, pay for yourself . . .

Fuck. The voice was back. Recently, Sellers had been finding it hard to banish Gibbs' impression of him from his mind when he was around a woman or women; it was doing nothing for his confidence. He'd heard it last Saturday night, just before he'd made a complete tit of himself. It had honestly been as if Gibbs was there with him, whispering in his ear. He could have sworn he *heard* it. Must have been the drink, since Gibbs was nowhere nearby. Thank God. Absolutely arseholed on a mixture of Timothy Taylor Landlord and Laphroaig, Sellers had tried to pick up a woman he'd seen through the window of a restaurant while walking home from the pub. He'd gone in and propositioned her, oblivious to her companions, a young man and a middle-aged couple. She'd been celebrating her twenty-first birthday with her boyfriend and parents, as she had repeatedly told him, but that hadn't stopped him. He'd continued to insist that she accompany him to a nearby hotel. Eventually the restaurant manager and a waiter had dragged him out on to the street, told him never to come back, and slammed the door in his face. He might have had more luck if he'd propositioned her mother, come to think of it.

'If either Mr Nattrass or Miss Benson contacts you . . .'

'Are you going to look for Fliss?' Tamsin asked. 'If I don't hear back from her soon, I'm really going to panic. Twickenham — that's where you want to start looking.'

'Why there?'

'I think that's where Ray Hines' parents live. And I'm pretty sure Fliss will have gone back there today.'

Sellers wrote 'Ray Hines — parents — Twickenham' in his notebook.

'She's next, isn't she?' said Tamsin.

'Sorry?'

'First Sarah Jaggard's nearly knifed, then Helen Yardley's shot. Ray Hines is number three, isn't she? She's bound to be next.'

This is the happiest I've ever been, thought Sergeant Charlie Zailer. She'd been in a state of deep joy all morning, but she'd been alone at home, and bliss — as she'd only recently discovered, never having experienced it or anything like it before — pulsed even more strongly through the veins, glowed all the more brightly under the skin, when you were around other people. Which was why she had wanted to throw her arms round Sam Kombothekra's neck and cover him with kisses — platonic ones — when he'd arrived to escort her to Proust's office, and why now, walking beside Sam along the corridor to the CID room, listening to his apologies and proclamations of innocence, she felt her happiness was reaching a peak. Here she was with her good friend, on this brilliant day, talking, breathing air. She didn't care about being taken away from her work, or the manner in which this had been effected. All that mattered to her was the scrap of paper in her pocket.

She hadn't been planning to tell anyone but her sister — it was private, after all — but she was still waiting for Liv to ring her back, and now here she was, strolling along with Sam . . . Well, *she* was strolling. He was marching, glancing back over his shoulder at her every few seconds, scared the Snowman would glaciate him if he took too long to round Charlie up. Who cared? And who cared what Proust wanted? Let him wait, let everything wait apart from the need to reveal that was surging inside her. She'd have preferred to tell Sam's wife, Kate — Kate would have been ideal, better than Liv, even — but Kate wasn't here.

'Simon wrote me a love letter this morning.'

Sam stopped, turned round. 'What?' He'd been too far ahead. It was hard to hear anyone clearly in the corridors in the oldest part of the police station; there was the constant sound of rushing water to contend with, something to do with the pipes. According to Simon, it had sounded exactly the same when he was a kid; the nick had been the local swimming baths in those days. Parts of the building still smelled of chlorine.

'Simon wrote me a love letter,' Charlie said again, grinning. 'I woke up and found it lying next to me in bed.'

Sam frowned. 'Is everything okay? You and

Simon haven't . . . broken up? He hasn't . . . ?'

Charlie giggled. 'Explain to me how you got that from what I just said. Everything is *fine*, Sam. Everything is perfect. He sent me a *love* letter. A proper one.'

'Oh. Right.' Sam looked perplexed.

'I'm not going to tell you what he wrote.'

'No, of course not.' If ever a man was happy to be let off the hook . . . 'Shall we?' Sam inclined his head in the direction of the Snowman's office. 'Whatever it is, let's get it over with.'

'What are you so nervous about? I'm used to this, Sam. Ever since I left CID, Proust's been in the habit of rubbing lamps and hoping I'll appear.'

'Why didn't he ring you? Why send me to fetch you?'

'I don't know. Does it matter?' Now that Charlie had told Sam about it, Simon's note felt more real. Perhaps she didn't need to tell Liv. Liv would demand to know exactly what it said. She'd pick holes in it, one big hole in particular: the word 'love' wasn't mentioned.

I do. I know I never say it, but I do.

Charlie appreciated the subtlety. She more than appreciated it; she adored it. Simon's note was perfect; those were the best eleven words he could have chosen. Only the crassest of drips would use the word 'love' in a love letter. I'm doing it again, she thought — arguing with Liv in my head.

Liv would ask if Simon had signed the letter, or put kisses at the bottom. No, and no. She'd ask about the paper. Charlie would have to tell her it was a corner of a page torn off the pad of lined yellow A4 she kept by the phone. She didn't care. Simon was a man — he was hardly going to use scented pink paper with a border of flowers. Liv would say, *Would it have killed him to use a whole sheet instead of tearing off a corner?* She'd say, *Big deal. You've been engaged for a year and a half and you still haven't had sex, nor is he any closer to explaining why he won't, but, hey, what does any of that matter now that he's written some words on a scrap of paper?*

Perhaps, after tonight, there would be no need for Simon to explain why he wouldn't. He'd left a message on Charlie's voicemail half an hour ago telling her he'd see her later, to try to get back as early as she could. He had to have written that note for a reason — he'd never done anything like it before. Maybe he'd decided it was time.

Charlie had torn a scrap from the pad herself before leaving for work. She'd writ-

360

ten, 'About the honeymoon: whatever you want is fine, even if it's a fortnight at the Beaumont Guest House.' That should make Simon laugh. The Beaumont was a bed and breakfast across the road from his parents' house. You could see it from their lounge window.

'He wants you at a disadvantage,' Sam was saying. 'That's why he's sent me to collect you. You're supposed to wonder if you're in trouble.'

'Sam, relax. I've done nothing wrong.'

'I'm only saying what Simon would say if he were here.'

Charlie laughed. 'Did you just snap at me? You did. You actually snapped. Are you okay?'

Sam's nickname, originally invented by Chris Gibbs, was Stepford, on account of his impeccable courteousness. He'd once admitted to Charlie that the part of his job he hated most was making arrests. She'd asked him why and he'd said, 'Putting handcuffs on someone seems so . . . . rude.'

He stopped walking and leaned against the wall, his body sagging as he sighed heavily. 'Do you ever feel as if you're turning into Simon? Too long spent in close proximity . . .'

'I still have no desire to read *Moby-Dick,*

let alone reread it twice a year, so I'd have to say no.'

'I interviewed the Brownlees the other day, the couple who adopted Helen Yardley's daughter. Both are alibied up to the eyebrows — I wasn't planning to spend any more time on them.'

'But?' Charlie prompted.

'When I told Grace Brownlee I was a detective, the first words out of her mouth were, "We did nothing wrong." '

'Exactly what I've just said.'

'No. That's the point. You said, "I've *done* nothing wrong." She said, "We *did* nothing wrong." They're basically the same, I know, but I also knew what Simon would have been thinking if he'd been there.'

So did Charlie. ' "We've done nothing wrong" means "I can think of nothing we've done that was wrong". "We *did* nothing wrong" means "That specific thing we did was entirely justified".'

'Exactly,' said Sam. 'I'm glad it's not just me.'

'Even the strongest mind can't withstand the Simon Waterhouse brainwash effect,' Charlie told him.

'I wanted to know what Grace Brownlee felt so defensive about, so I turned up unannounced at her house last night. Didn't take long to trick her into telling me by implying I already knew.'

'And?'

'How much do you know about adoption procedures?'

'You need to ask?' Charlie raised an eyebrow.

'Normally, if there's any chance a child in care might go back to its biological parents, that's the favoured option. While the case is being decided, the kid might go to foster parents. If the final family court decision goes against the birth mother, that's when Social Services start looking for an adoptive family. But some local authorities — and Culver Valley's one of them — have something called concurrent plan adoption that they use in a few select cases. It's massively controversial, which is why a lot of councils won't touch it with a bargepole. Some people say it violates the birth parents' human rights.'

'Let me guess,' said Charlie. 'Paige Yardley was one of those special cases.'

Sam nodded. 'You take a couple that you think would be ideal to parent a particular child, get them approved as *foster* parents, which is quicker and easier than getting them approved to adopt, and you place the child in their care as soon as possible. In theory, there was a chance Paige would go back to her birth family, but in reality everyone knew that wouldn't happen. Once it was official, once Helen and Paul Yardley had been told their daughter was no longer theirs — *then* the Brownlees were approved as adopters, and adopted the child who already lived with them, with whom they'd formed a stronger bond than you'd normally expect in a fostering situation, because, unofficially and off the record, the social workers had given them to understand that they were getting Paige for keeps.'

'Isn't that also a violation of the prospective adoptive parents' human rights?' said Charlie. 'There must be cases where the family court surprises everyone by deciding in favour of the birth mother. Presumably the social workers then have to say to the foster parents, "Oops, sorry, you can't adopt this child after all." '

'Grace Brownlee said they were told repeatedly that there were no guarantees, so in theory they knew things might not go their way — they wouldn't have been able to say they were misled, if it came down to it — but heavy hints were dropped that it *would* go their way, and that Paige would soon be their legal daughter. She was a high-profile baby, the only surviving child of a woman suspected of murder. Social Services were determined to do their very best for her, and they thought the Brown- lees would be ideal. Both lawyers — middle class, high-earning, nice big house . . .'

'Nose-rings? Serpent tattoos?' said Char- lie. Seeing Sam's puzzled expression, she said, 'I'm kidding. People are so predict- able, aren't they? Wouldn't it be fantastic, just once, to meet a respectable solicitor with a serpent tattoo?' She let out a yelp of a laugh. 'Ignore me, I'm in love.'

'The Brownlees were hand-picked,' said Sam. 'They were in the process of jumping through all the hoops would-be adopters have to jump through. One day they were invited to a meeting and told a baby girl was available for them — there were still formalities to be gone through, but that was all they were. But the good news, they were told, was that they didn't have to wait for the legal stuff to be signed off — all they had to do was apply to be foster parents and they could have their future daughter living with them within weeks. Sebastian Brownlee was keen but Grace had her doubts. She's less smug than her husband and more cautious. She hated the nudge- nudge-wink-wink element.'

'So that's what she meant by "We did

nothing wrong"?'

Sam nodded. 'Even once it was all done and dusted, court-approved and official, she was paranoid that one day Paige — Hannah, as she is now — might be taken away from them because of the underhand dealings at the beginning. Nothing her husband said to her could convince her it wasn't dodgy.'

'Was that likely? Paige being taken away, I mean.'

'Impossible. Concurrent plan adoption's not illegal. As you say, technically the verdict can still go in favour of the birth parents, and if it does, the prospective adopters have to lump it, which they know from the start.'

'In some ways, it's quite sensible,' said Charlie. 'I mean, from the kid's point of view, it has to be better to be placed with the adoptive parents as soon as possible.'

'It's barbaric,' said Sam vehemently. 'All the time the birth mother thinks she's in with a shot. Helen Yardley must have thought she and Paul stood a good chance of keeping Paige — they knew their sons had died naturally and they believed they'd be treated fairly. Some hope! All along, Social Services and Grace and Sebastian Brownlee — two strangers — knew that Paige was well on her way to her new family. Grace has felt guilty about that ever since, and I don't blame her. It's no way to treat people. It's not right, Charlie.'

'Maybe not, but lots of things aren't right, and a good proportion of those lots of things are stacked up in our in-trays. Why's this got to you?'

'I'd like to pretend my reasons for feeling like crap are noble and altruistic, but they're not,' said Sam. He closed his eyes and shook his head. 'I shouldn't have said anything to Simon. What was I thinking of?'

'You've lost me,' said Charlie.

'There was one thing I didn't understand: how could the social workers be so sure Paige Yardley wouldn't be returned to Helen and Paul? I mean, it was hardly your average care case. I can imagine a local authority knowing all about some unsavoury families' long histories of abusing and neglecting their children, saying they'll never do it again, then getting wrecked and doing more and worse. Those children being taken away from their mothers might seem like a done deal, but Helen Yardley was different. If she wasn't guilty of murder, then she was completely innocent. If her two sons were victims of crib death — which hadn't yet been decided in court, so no one could claim to know — well, then

Helen had done nothing wrong, had she? So why risk concurrent plan adoption? That was what I wondered.'

Sam exhaled slowly. 'Shows how naïve I am. So much for innocent until proven guilty. Grace told me the social workers all *knew* Helen had killed her babies, and they had friends at the hospital who *knew* it with as much certainty, who had been there when Helen had taken both boys into hospital, when they'd stopped breathing on several occasions. A social worker even said to Grace that she'd spoken to lots of doctors, one being Judith Duffy, all of whom had told her that Helen Yardley was, and I quote, "the classic Munchausen's by proxy mother".'

'Maybe she was,' said Charlie. 'Maybe she did murder them.'

'That's not fair, Charlie.' Sam started to walk away from her. She was about to follow him when he turned round and came back. 'Her convictions were overturned. There wasn't even enough evidence for a retrial. It should never have gone to court the first time. Is there anything more insane than making a woman stand trial when there's no solid evidence a crime's been committed? Never mind whether Helen Yardley committed it — I'm talking about a high chance that there was no "it" in the first place. I've seen the file that went to the CPS. Do you know how many doctors disagreed with Judith Duffy and said it was entirely possible Morgan and Rowan Yardley died of natural causes?'

'Sam, calm down.'

'Seven! Seven doctors. Finally, after nine years, Helen clears her name, then some bastard murders her, and there I am, supposedly investigating her murder, trying to get some kind of justice for her, for the sake of her family and her memory, and what am I doing? I'm listening to Grace Brownlee tell me about some contact centre care supervisor who claimed to see Helen try to smother Paige right in front of her.'

'Leah Gould,' said Charlie.

Sam stared at her blankly. 'How . . . ?'

'I'm reading *Nothing But Love*. Simon wanted me to, but he was too proud to ask. Luckily I can read his mind.'

'I'm supposed to read it too.' Sam looked guilty. 'Proust wasn't too proud to ask.'

'Not your cup of tea?'

'I try to avoid books that are going to make me want to top myself.'

'I think you'd be surprised,' said Charlie. 'It's full of brave, inspiring heroes: the Snowman, if you can believe it; Laurie Nattrass; Paul, the loyal rock of a husband. And that lawyer, her solicitor — I can't remember his name . . .'

'Ned Vento?'

'That's the one. Interestingly, he had a female colleague, Gillian somebody, who seems to have worked just as hard on Helen's behalf, but so far she hasn't once been described in heroic terms. I get the impression Helen Yardley was a man's woman.'

'Doesn't make her a murderer,' said Sam.

'I didn't say it did. I'm only saying, she seemed to lap up any attention that came her way from valiant male rescuers.' *A classic Munchausen's-by-proxy mother.* Wasn't Munchausen's all about getting attention?

Something else bothered Charlie about *Nothing But Love:* several times in the first third of the book, Helen Yardley had asserted that she hadn't murdered her two babies; rather, they had died of crib death. Unless Charlie had misunderstood, and she didn't think she had, crib death, or SIDS, meant an infant death for which no explanation could be found, so it was odd for Helen Yardley to say that was what her boys had died of, as if it were a firm medical diagnosis. It was as nonsensical as saying, 'My babies died of I don't know what they died of.' Wouldn't a mother who had lost two children to SIDS be more likely to search for a proper explanation, instead of presenting the absence of one as the solution rather than the mystery? Or was Charlie reading sinister undertones into *Nothing But Love* that weren't there?

'What shouldn't you have mentioned to Simon?' she asked Sam.

'Any of this. I was angry about Social Services stitching up the Yardleys and I was letting off steam, but it's got nothing to do with Helen's murder and I should have kept my mouth shut, especially about Leah Gould. Simon waved an *Observer* article in my face in which Gould was quoted as saying she'd made a mistake — hadn't witnessed an attempted smothering, had overreacted, was deeply sorry if she'd contributed to a miscarriage of justice . . .'

'Let me guess,' said Charlie. 'When you told Simon that Grace Brownlee was invoking Leah Gould's eye-witness account as proof of Helen Yardley's guilt, he decided that talking to her couldn't wait any longer.'

'If Proust finds out I covered for him, my life won't be worth living,' said Sam glumly. 'What am I supposed to do? I told Simon no, unequivocally no, and he ignored me. "I want Leah Gould to look me in the eye and tell me what she saw," he said. I should go

371

to Proust . . .'

'But you haven't.' Charlie smiled.

'I ought to. We're supposed to be investigating Helen Yardley's murder, not something that might or might not have happened in a Social Services' contact centre thirteen years ago. Simon's more interested in finding out if Helen Yardley was guilty of murder than he is in finding out who shot her. If Proust gets even a whiff of that, and he will, because he always does . . .'

'Sam, I'm not just sticking up for Simon because he's Simon, but . . . since when do you disregard the life story of a murder victim? Helen Yardley had a pretty dramatic past, in which Leah Gould played a crucial role, by the sound of it. Someone *should* talk to her. So what if it was thirteen years ago? The more you can find out about Helen Yardley the better, surely? About what she did or didn't do.'

'Proust's made it clear what our collective attitude has to be: that she's as innocent and undeserving of what happened to her as any murder victim,' said Sam, red in the face. 'For once, I agree with him, but it's not up to me, is it? It's *never* up to me. Simon flies around like a whirlwind doing whatever the hell he wants and I can't even pretend I've got a hope of controlling him.

All I can do is sit back and watch events slip further and further from my grasp.'

'There's something Simon cares about more than he cares whether or not Helen Yardley was a murderer, and more than he cares who shot her dead,' said Charlie, not sure she ought to be sharing this with Sam. 'Proust.'

'Proust?'

'He was at the contact centre that day too. Simon's only interested in what Leah Gould saw because he wants to know what the Snowman saw — if he witnessed an attempted child murder and lied about it in his eagerness to protect a woman he'd already decided was innocent. Proust's the one he's going after.' Charlie admitted to herself that she was scared of how far Simon might go. He was too obsessed to be rational. He'd been up most of last night, apoplectic with rage because Proust had tried again to invite them for dinner. He seemed convinced the Snowman was trying to torture him by forcing an invasive friendship on him, one he knew would be anathema to Simon. It had sounded far-fetched to Charlie, but her doubts, when she'd voiced them, had only inspired Simon to flesh out his paranoid fantasy even more: Proust had worked out a new genius way to humiliate him, rob him of his power. How can you fight back when all someone's doing is saying, 'Let's have dinner'?

Easily, Charlie had told him, desperate for sleep — you say, 'Sorry, I'd rather not have dinner with you. I don't like you, I never will, and I don't want to be your friend.'

Sam Kombothekra rubbed the bridge of his nose. 'This gets worse,' he said. 'If Simon's going after the Snowman, I'm going after a new job.'

'Where's Waterhouse?' was Proust's first question. He was arranging envelopes in a tower on his desk.

'He's gone to Wolverhampton to interview Sarah Jaggard again,' said Sam. One he'd prepared earlier, no doubt. Charlie tried not to smile. 'You didn't say you wanted to see Waterhouse, sir. You only mentioned Sergeant Zailer.'

'I don't want to see him. I want to know where he is. The two are different. I take it you're up to speed on our case, Seargent Zailer? You know who Judith Duffy is?' Proust flicked the envelope tower with his finger and thumb. It shifted but didn't fall. 'Formerly a respected child health expert, latterly a pariah, shortly to be struck off the medical register for misconduct — you know the basic facts?'

Charlie nodded.

'Sergeant Kombothekra and I would be grateful if you'd talk to Dr Duffy for us. One pariah to another.'

Charlie felt as if she'd swallowed a metal ball. A faint groan came from Sam. Proust heard it, but went on as if he hadn't. 'Rachel Hines could well be our killer's next target. She's vanished into the ether, and there's a chance Duffy knows where she is. The two of them met for lunch on Monday. I want to know why. Why would a bereaved mother have a nice cosy meal with the corrupt doctor whose fraudulent evidence put her behind bars?'

'I've no idea,' said Charlie. 'I agree, it's odd.'

'Conveniently, Duffy and Mrs Hines are each other's alibi for Helen Yardley's murder,' said Proust. 'Duffy won't talk to us, not willingly, and I was on the point of hauling her in unwillingly, but this strikes me as a better idea.' Proust leaned forward, drumming his fingers on his desk as if he were playing a piano. 'I think you could persuade her to talk to you, Sergeant. Establish a bond. If it works, she'll say more to you than she would to us. You know what it feels like to have your ignominy splashed all over the papers; so does she. You'd know exactly how to approach her, wouldn't you? You're good with people.'

What are you good with?

Pariah, ignominy — they were only words. They could have no power over Charlie unless she allowed them to. She didn't have to think about the events of 2006 if she didn't want to. Recently, she had been choosing not to, more and more.

'You don't have to do it, Charlie. We've no right to ask you to.'

'By "we", he means me,' said Proust. 'The disapproval of Sergeant Kombothekra rains down like an avalanche of tissue-paper, feather-light and easy to shake off.'

'I knew nothing about this,' said Sam, pink-faced. 'It's got nothing to do with me. You can't treat people like this, sir.'

Charlie thought of all the things she'd read about Judith Duffy: she'd cared more about the children of strangers than her own, both of whom had been sub-contracted out to nannies and au pairs so that she could work day and night; she'd tried to fleece her ex-husband when they got divorced, even though she earned a packet herself . . .

Charlie hadn't believed a word of it. She knew what trial-by-media did for a person's reputation, having been through it herself.

'I'll do it,' she said. The Snowman was right: she could persuade Judith Duffy to talk to her if she tried. She didn't know why she wanted to, but she did. She definitely did.

13
Saturday 10 October 2009

My mobile phone buzzes as I emerge from the underground. One message. A lifelong believer in sod's law, I expect it to be Julian Lance, Rachel Hines' solicitor, calling to cancel the meeting I've just travelled halfway across London to get to, but it's not. It's Laurie. I can tell straight away, because at first all I hear is breathing. Not heavy, not threatening — just the sound of him trying to remember which button he pressed, what he wanted to say and to whom. Eventually, his recorded voice says, 'I've got the latest version of my *British Journalism Review* article for you, the one on Duffy. Yeah.' There's a pause then, as if he's waiting for a response. 'Do you want to meet, or something? So I can give it to you?' Another pause. 'Fliss? Can you pick up the phone?' The sound of air being expelled through gritted teeth. 'Okay, then, I'll email it to you.'

Can I *pick up the phone?* No, you numb-skull, I can't, not once it's gone to voice-mail. How can Laurie Nattrass, recipient of every honour and plaudit the world can bestow upon an investigative journalist, not understand this basic fact of twenty-first-century telecommunications? Does he imagine I'm staring at my mobile disdain-fully while his voice blares out of it, wilfully ignoring him?

Is this his way of saying sorry for treating me so shoddily? It has to be. There's no point debating whether I ought to forgive him; I already have.

I listen to the message eight times before calling him back. To his voicemail prompt, I say, 'I'd love to meet or something so that you can give it to me.' Which might be the perfect casual-but-encouraging teaser, except I ruin it by giggling like a hyena. I panic and end the call, realising too late that if I'd only waited a few seconds, I'd have been given the option of re-recording the message. 'Shit,' I mutter, looking at my watch. I should have been at the Covent Garden Hotel five minutes ago. I pick up my pace, weaving in and out of the convoy of shoppers, glaring at the ones that have enormous bags fanning out from their sides like batwings, ready to smack me in the arm as I hurry past. It's doing me good to be out, busy, surrounded by people. It makes me feel ordinary — too ordinary for anything bad or newsworthy to happen to me.

I expect Julian Lance to be wearing a suit, but the man I see walking towards me as I open the door of the Covent Garden Hotel is wearing jeans, tasselled loafers and a zip-collared sweater over an open-necked striped shirt. He's got short white hair and a square, tanned face. He could be anything from fifty to a well-maintained sixty-five. 'Fliss Benson? I recognised you,' he says, smiling at my questioning look. 'You had your I'm-about-to-speak-to-Ray-Hines'-lawyer face on. Everyone does, the first time.'

'Thanks for seeing me on a Saturday.' We shake hands.

'Ray says you're the one. I'd have met you in the middle of the night, missed Sunday lunch — whatever it took.' Having made clear his commitment to his client, Lance proceeds to inspect me, his eyes taking a quick head-to-toe tour. For once, I'm not worried about looking a state. I dressed this morning as if for court, as if I was the one on trial.

I allow Julian Lance to steer me towards a table with two free chairs at the back of the room. The third chair is occupied by a woman with dyed red hair with lots of clips in it, and red-framed glasses. She's writing in a ring-bound notebook: big, loopy scrawl. I'm wondering whether I ought to suggest to Julian Lance that he and I sit elsewhere, somewhere more private, when the woman looks up and smiles at me. 'Hello, Fliss,' she says. 'I'm Wendy, Wendy Whitehead.'

'You know who she is?' Lance asks.

I nod, trying not to look flustered. *She's not a killer,* I remind myself.

'Ray said you wanted to talk vaccinations, and Wendy's the expert, so I thought I'd invite her along, give you two meetings for the price of one.'

'That's very helpful, thank you.'

I sit between the two of them, feeling totally out of my depth. Lance asks me what I'd like to drink. My mind is a complete blank; I can't think of any drinks, let alone one I might like. Luckily, he starts listing types of coffee and tea, which jolts my brain into action. I ask for Earl Grey. He goes off to order it, leaving me alone with Wendy Whitehead. 'So, Ray told you I gave Marcella and Nathaniel their first vaccinations?' she says.

'Yes.' *Their only vaccinations.*

She smiles. 'I know what she told you.

"Wendy Whitehead killed my children". She wanted to make you listen, that's all. When you're in the public eye in the way Ray was, nobody listens to you. You'd think it'd be the other way round, wouldn't you? Suddenly, you're a household name, you're all over the tabloids and the TV news — you'd think people would be hanging on your every word, eager to hear what you had to say. Instead, they leap to ill-informed conclusions, for and against, and start talking *about* you, telling more and more outlandish stories, whatever they need to say to liven up their boring suburban dinner parties: "I heard she did this, I heard she did that." And your poor little story, your *real* story — that's just a distraction, getting in the way of the fun they're all having. There's too much for it to compete with, so it gets lost.'

I ought to be recording what she's saying. Will she say it all again later, if I ask her nicely? Will she say it to camera? 'Rachel told me —'

'Call her Ray. She hates Rachel.'

'She told me vaccines killed her babies.'

'Vaccines administered by me.' Wendy Whitehead nods.

'Do you agree? Was that what killed Marcella and Nathaniel?'

'In my opinion? Yes. Obviously I didn't think so at the time — I'm not a baby-killer any more than Ray is. If I'd had the slightest idea . . .'

Julian Lance sits down, indicates that she should carry on. I have the sense that the two of them know each other well. They seem comfortable around one another. I'm the one who's uncomfortable.

'Anyway, I'm no longer a practice nurse. Many years have passed since I last injected a baby with neurotoxins. For the past four years I've worked as a researcher for a legal practice. Not Julian's,' she adds, seeing me glance at him. 'I work for a firm that specialises in vaccine damage compensation claims.'

'Marcella Hines was born two weeks prem,' says Julian Lance. 'Babies are supposed to have their first jabs at eight weeks, their second at sixteen . . .'

'It's changed now,' Wendy Whitehead tells him. 'They've accelerated the schedule again, to two, three and four months.' She turns to me and says, 'It used to be three, six and nine months, then two, four and six. The younger a baby is when it's vaccinated, the harder it is to prove it was destined to develop normally, if it has a bad reaction.'

'Biologically, Marcella was only six weeks

old when she had her first jabs,' says Lance. 'Ray rang up and asked for advice, and her GP told her to proceed as if Marcella were a normal eight-week-old baby, so Ray did. Immediately after the injections, Marcella took a turn for the worse.'

'Well, not immediately. It was about twenty minutes after. I saw it happen,' Wendy Whitehead takes over the story. 'We always asked parents to wait half an hour after any injection before taking their babies home, so that we could check all was well. Five minutes after she'd left my room, Ray burst back in with Marcella in her arms, insisting something was wrong — Marcella wasn't breathing normally. I wasn't sure what she meant. The baby was breathing, I couldn't see any problems, and I had some-one else in with me, another mother and baby. I asked Ray to wait, and when I'd finished with my other patient, I asked her and Marcella to come back in. I was about to examine Marcella again when she had a seizure. Ray and I watched helplessly as her little body bent and twisted . . . I'm sorry.' She presses her hand against her mouth.

'Less than five hours later, Marcella was dead,' says Lance. 'Ray and Angus were told definitively that the DTP-Hib vaccine couldn't have caused her death.'

'All the doctors they spoke to said, "We've no idea why your daughter died, Mr and Mrs Hines, but we know it wasn't the DTP-Hib jab that killed her." "How do you know?" "We just do — because our vaccines are safe, because they don't kill." '

'The timing had to be a coincidence, they were told,' says Lance.

'Rubbish,' Wendy Whitehead says vehemently. 'Even if Marcella hadn't been prem, even if there hadn't been a history in Angus Hines' family of auto-immune problems . . .'

'His mother suffers from Lupus, doesn't she?' I ask. I've got a vague memory of having read that somewhere, perhaps in Laurie's article.

'That's right. And there's a history of crib death in several branches of his family, which strongly suggests a genetic auto-immune disorder. Yes, these vaccines are mostly safe if you take babies with vulnerabilities out of the equation, but some babies *have* vulnerabilities. I wanted to yellow-card Marcella's death . . .'

'That means report it to the MHRA as a possible adverse reaction to a vaccine,' Lance explains. I have no idea what the MHRA is; I make a mental note to look it up later.

'. . . but my colleagues put pressure on

me not to. The practice manager hinted I'd be out of a job if I did. I listened to them all, and I shouldn't have. I suppose I wanted to believe them — if they were right, and Marcella dying five hours after having the jab was a coincidence, then it wasn't my fault, was it? It wasn't me that had done it to her. I did as I was told and tried to put it behind me. It sounds feeble and cowardly and it was, but . . . well, if everybody's telling you with great assurance that something's safe, you start to believe them. Over the next few weeks and months I vaccinated babies who reacted normally — screamed a bit but then were fine, and certainly didn't die — and I convinced myself that it wouldn't have done anyone any good if I'd yellow-carded Marcella's death. Ray and Angus would only have blamed themselves, and the last thing anyone wants is negative publicity for inoculations, in case it puts parents off. Herd immunity has to be preserved at all costs — that was what I thought at the time.

'When Ray rang me at work four years later, telling me she'd had another baby and asking my advice about whether to vaccinate him, I opened my mouth to tell her that DTP-Hib was perfectly safe, and I found I couldn't say it. I couldn't make the words come out. I told her it was her decision, that I didn't want to sway her one way or the other. She asked me if a tendency to react badly to vaccines could run in families.'

'Several studies have shown that it does,' Julian Lance leans his head towards me in a slow nod. Is he wondering why I'm not taking notes? Does he disapprove? Something about him makes me feel as if I'm doing something wrong. Come to think of it, I feel that way most of the time — maybe it's nothing to do with Lance.

Several studies have shown. Isn't that what people always say when, basically, they've got no evidence? Isn't it a bit like writing, 'It has been argued that . . .' in an A-level essay, when you're not sure who said what but you want to give the impression of substantial support for the point you're about to make?

'Ray was terrified of something happening to Nathaniel after what had happened to Marcella,' says Wendy. 'She wanted to do what was best for him, but she didn't know what that was. Should she give him the very same jab that she was certain had killed her daughter, even though dozens of professionals had assured her it couldn't have, or should she steer clear of it, and risk Na-

387

thaniel dying of diphtheria or tetanus? The chance of her son contracting either disease was extremely small, but she was understandably paranoid and semi-hysterical. I advised her to take plenty of time to make her decision, and speak to as many immunisation experts as she could. Privately, I hoped she'd decide not to give Nathaniel the jab — partly, selfishly, because I knew there was a good chance I'd be the one who'd have to give it to him. The ridiculous thing was, I'd still have said, if asked at that point, that the jabs were entirely safe, that all babies ought to have them at two, four and six months, just as the government advised — I'd have *said* that, but I didn't believe it, not deep down.'

A waiter arrives with a tray: my tea, and a coffee each for Lance and Wendy.

'In the end, Ray and Angus decided to immunise Nathaniel, but later,' Lance takes up the story. 'A doctor friend they trusted had told them that even a week could make a huge difference in terms of the strength of a baby's immune system. They're so much tougher every day, their systems so much better able to cope. That made sense to Ray and Angus, and seemed like a good compromise, so they waited until Nathaniel was eleven weeks old. He wasn't prem, and, although they were a little bit apprehensive, they trusted that he'd be fine. Their doctor friend had convinced them that to let a child go unvaccinated was dangerously irresponsible.'

Wendy Whitehead presses her hand against her mouth again.

'But Nathaniel wasn't fine,' I say.

'Twenty, twenty-five minutes after having the jab, his body convulsed, just like Marcella's,' she says, blinking away tears. 'Then he perked up a bit, and we thought, "Please, God", but he died a week later. Ray and I knew what had killed him, but we couldn't get anyone to back us up. I yellow-carded Nathaniel's death and was made redundant soon afterwards.' She lets out a bitter, throaty laugh. 'Even Angus wouldn't acknowledge that there was a clear cause of death for both his children — though he's big enough now to admit it was guilt that made him side with the doctors — for allowing both babies to have the jab, for the auto-immune problem that was on his side of the family . . .'

'You'll have heard that Angus didn't stand by Ray when she was convicted of murder,' says Lance. It's a question presented as a statement.

I nod.

'The trouble between them started long before she was convicted, or even accused. Angus was angry with her, and with Wendy, for insisting on a truth he wasn't ready to face up to.' Lance takes a sip of his coffee. 'By the time the police turned up at the door, he and Ray were close to splitting up.'

I wait. Politely at first, then, after a few seconds of silence, allowing my incredulity to show. Lance and Wendy are both looking as if that's it, end of story. 'I don't get it,' I say, in case it's a test and they're waiting for me to bring up the very obvious gaping hole in what they've told me. 'If there was a suspected cause of death for both babies, even if it was controversial — why wasn't it mentioned in court? I've looked through the trial transcript and there's nothing.'

'We tried,' says Lance. 'Wendy was ready to testify . . .'

'Ready, willing, eager,' she says, nodding.

'. . . but we were told in no uncertain terms not to refer to a possible adverse re-action to the DTP-Hib vaccine.'

'By whom?' I ask.

'By our four stellar defence witnesses.' Lance smiles. 'Four hugely respected medi-cal experts, all ready to say that there was no evidence of foul play in the case of either baby's death, no medical evidence that

390

couldn't just as easily be attributed to natural causes as to anything more sinister. Quite independently of one another, they each made it abundantly clear to me that if counsel for the defence so much as whispered the word "thiomersal", we'd have a fight on our hands. I couldn't risk it, couldn't let the jury hear our own witnesses calling our story a lie. That wouldn't have helped Ray at all.'

I can hardly believe what I'm hearing. I don't want to believe it; it's too horrendous. 'But . . .' *Ray Hines went to prison for murder. She was locked up for four years.*

'Yes,' says Wendy. 'That was how I felt too.'

'Surely there were other medical experts who'd —'

'I'm afraid not.' Lance frowns. 'I tried, believe me. Most doctors are terrified of speaking out about vaccine damage. Any who do tend to see their careers come crashing down around their ears.'

'If you've got a spare hour or two for Googling, you should read about what happened to Dr Andrew Wakefield and his colleagues,' says Wendy. Again, Lance leans forward and stares pointedly at the table in front of me, where I'm now certain he thinks my notebook ought to be. As if I'm going to forget any of this. I'll probably be able to recite what they're telling me word for word when I'm eighty.

'When Dr Wakefield dared to suggest that a possible link between the MMR vaccine, regressive autism and a particular kind of bowel disorder was worth investigating, a lot of powerful people made it their mission to destroy his credibility and his career. They literally hounded him out of the country,' says Wendy.

This is all very well, but I'm not making a documentary about Dr Andrew Wakefield. 'What's "thiomersal"?' I ask.

'Mercury, essentially,' says Lance. 'One of the most poisonous substances in the world, if you're thinking of injecting it into your bloodstream, and present in the DTP-Hib vaccines given to babies until 2004, when they phased it out.'

Present in the jab given to Marcella in 1998, and the one given to Nathaniel in 2002.

'Of course, they didn't phase it out because it was a highly reactogenic neurotoxin. No, it was completely safe — that was the official story most doctors stuck to. Then why were they phasing it out? They just were — nothing to do with it being dangerous.' Wendy's talking so fast, I'm struggling to keep up. 'Same with whole-cell pertussis — that's the "P" part of the DTP jab. They've phased that out too — the pertussis element is now strands, acellular — much less hazardous. And the polio vaccine, given orally at the same time as DTP-Hib — they now give the dead form instead of the live. But try getting anyone to admit any of these changes have been made because the old vaccines were too reactogenic and you come up against a brick wall.'

'Your tea's going cold,' Lance says to me.

Don't pick up the cup. I beat down my natural impulse to do as I'm told, and say, 'I like cold tea.'

'Why the change of tack, if you don't mind my asking? On the part of Binary Star?'

I don't know what he's talking about. It must be apparent from my expression.

'I spoke to your colleague Laurie Nattrass a few months ago and tried to tell him everything I've just told you, and he didn't want to know.'

'Laurie's working for a different company now. If I'm going to be making a documentary about Ray, I need to know everything.'

'It gladdens my heart to hear you say that,' says Lance. 'I'm sure you'll do an excellent job. Ray's a good judge of character. She was sensible to give Nattrass a wide berth.

Man's a coward, one who allies himself with fashionable causes. There's no risk to him in making a documentary about Judith Duffy, the doctor everyone loves to hate. He wants to destroy Duffy more than he wants to help Ray, and he made it clear he wouldn't touch with a bargepole an international health scandal involving governments, drug companies . . .'

'*You* didn't touch it with a bargepole when Ray was on trial,' I say. 'If Laurie's a coward, then so are you.'

For a second or two, as he stares down into his coffee, I think Lance is going to get up and walk out. He doesn't. 'It's slightly different,' he says coolly. 'If I took a risk and failed, that meant Ray getting two life sentences for murder.'

'That happened anyway,' I point out.

'True, but . . .'

'Women like Ray, Helen Yardley and Sarah Jaggard are only a fashionable cause, as you put it, because Laurie brought their predicament to people's attention. Judith Duffy wasn't the doctor everyone loved to hate until Laurie exposed her.'

Lance runs his tongue along the inside of his lower lip. 'I can't argue with that,' he says eventually.

'I read an article Laurie wrote about Ray's

case. He says you told Ray to pretend she was post-natally depressed and nearly threw herself off a window ledge, making her seem unstable to the jury.'

'That's wholly untrue.'

I wait for him to elaborate, but he doesn't.

'Did Laurie *say* he was scared of the vaccine issue?' I ask. I can't believe he would be, however many governments and drug companies were involved. Laurie would take on anyone. 'Or did he say he could only make one documentary at a time? You'd need about four hours to do justice to the whole jabs thing as well as tell three women's stories, and the story of how Judith Duffy shafted them. A documentary needs a focal point.'

'Your loyalty is touching, Fliss,' says Lance, 'but I remain convinced that Nattrass is a man who sees only what he wants to see. He had a troupe of doctors lined up to dish the dirt on Duffy. How do you think they'd have reacted if he'd introduced the vaccine issue? They'd have run a mile. Russell Meredew, the GMC's blue-eyed boy . . .' Lance laughs. 'He'd wet his pants at the mere suggestion, and Nattrass knows it.'

'Is Meredew on your radar?' Wendy White-head asks me.

'I'm going to be talking to him, yes.'

'Don't believe a word he says. He's probably the most unpopular paediatrician in the country. There's nothing he likes more than testifying against his colleagues at GMC hearings. He's the expert they've asked for an assessment of Duffy.'

'What?' That can't be right. Am I confusing Meredew with another doctor? No, I'm not. 'They both gave evidence at Ray's trial, didn't they? Her for the prosecution, him for the defence?'

'Yup.' Lance sounds resigned.

'But . . . the misconduct allegations against Duffy directly involve Ray's trial. Isn't that a conflict of interests?'

'Just a tad,' says Wendy. 'Funny, isn't it, that that hasn't occurred to the GMC, or to Meredew, who's happy to take their money.'

Russell Meredew — a man I'd trust to carry me across an enemy minefield. That's how he's described in Laurie's article.

'There's something I should probably tell you, if Ray hasn't already,' Lance says. 'She and Judith Duffy have become friends. Unlikely though it sounds, the two of them are a great source of support to one another.'

Friends. Ray Hines and Judith Duffy. I bury my face in my teacup to buy myself

396

some time. 'Just like Ray and Angus are now good friends, if not a bit more than that,' I say eventually.

'Ray's clever enough to know that forgiveness, of oneself and others, is the only happy way forward,' says Lance.

I can't prove it, but I have a sense he knows about the baby. Ray corrected me when I called it that. 'I'm only eight weeks pregnant,' she said. 'It's not a baby yet. A lot of pregnancies miscarry before twelve weeks and if this one does, I don't want to think I've lost another child.'

'Don't judge Ray, Fliss,' says Wendy. 'I'm sure you think that in her shoes, you'd want nothing to do with the husband who'd betrayed you, but you never know — you might surprise yourself.'

I'd have wax effigies of Angus Hines, Judith Duffy and everyone who'd ever said vaccines were a good thing lined up on my mantelpiece, with pins sticking out of them that I'd have made the effort to marinade in cyanide. I decide not to share this with Lance and Wendy.

'Ray doesn't blame Duffy for her guilty verdicts,' says Lance. 'She blames herself, which is fair.'

Did he really say that?

Whose side is anybody on here?

'The window ledge incident you referred to earlier, the one Laurie Nattrass used as an opportunity to lie about me in some article . . .'

'Laurie might have his faults, but he doesn't lie.'

Julian Lance inclines his head and stares at me from beneath his white eyebrows as if I'm the biggest fool who's ever sat across a table from him. 'I didn't tell Ray to change her story. Until we got to court, I'd only ever heard one version: that she'd stayed away from home for nine days because Angus was taking her for granted, expecting her to do everything for Marcella, and all the housework. Then she came back, found his mum in her house, and climbed out onto the window ledge to escape her overbearing mother-in-law. Also, she wanted to smoke, and didn't want Marcella to inhale the fumes.' Lance signals to the waiter to bring him the bill. 'I was worried about how that story would be received by a jury, but there was no way round it — we knew the prosecution were going to bring it up. I nearly had a heart attack when Ray stood in the witness box and started telling an entirely different story about post-natal trances and losses of memory. Not only was it a lie, it was a lie that made her sound exactly like

398

the sort of woman who might murder two babies.'

'How do you know it was a lie?' I ask. 'What if the first version was the lie? It sounds like one.' Why didn't this occur to me when I first read Laurie's article? Would a loving mother really abandon her baby daughter for nine days in order to make a point about equal distribution of housework and childcare?

Julian Lance and Wendy Whitehead exchange a look. 'I know Angus Hines,' says Lance. 'So does Wendy. He would have done his fair share. He *says* he did his fair share, that Ray had nothing to complain about.'

'Then . . . ?'

'That wasn't all she lied about,' says Wendy. 'She'd told the police and Julian that she'd phoned an ambulance straight away when she found Marcella not breathing, but in court she said she'd phoned Angus first, then phoned emergency services. Trouble is, there was no record of her call to Angus.'

'She never made it,' Lance underlines the point. I get it. How stupid does he think I am? I'm going to have to read the trial transcript properly. So far I've only skimmed it.

'She lied about Nathaniel, too,' says Wendy. 'The health visitor arrived just after Ray found him and called an ambulance — we're talking *seconds* after, not minutes — and Ray wouldn't let her in, just stared at her blankly through the window. Apart from the health visitor having no reason to lie, there were witnesses: neighbours who heard the poor woman pleading to be let in and asking Ray if she was all right.'

'In court, Ray said she let the health visitor in immediately,' Lance takes over. 'We know that's not true. It was between ten and fifteen minutes before she opened the door.'

I can feel their eyes on me. 'I don't understand,' I say, looking up from my tea.

'Neither do we.' Wendy smiles.

'There's a story here, a story Ray won't tell either of us,' says Lance. 'Part of that story is the reason why she lied so obviously and often in court. She's come close to admitting it once or twice.'

'She's told nobody why,' says Wendy. 'Not Judith Duffy, not me or Julian, not her family. I don't think she's even told Angus, even now. I'd resigned myself to never knowing. We all had.'

'I think she wants to tell you, Fliss,' says Lance. There's no mistaking the seriousness of his tone. 'You're the one she's chosen to hear the truth, the whole truth and nothing but the truth. I hope you're prepared for it. I'm not sure I am.'

It's only when he sees me coming and waves that I realise the man standing outside my flat is waiting for me. My first thought is that he must be police. Two detectives from Culver Valley CID left messages for me while I was speaking to Lance and Wendy: a DS Sam Kombothekra and a DC Colin Sellers. Both demanded I contact them immediately, and DS Kombothekra told me to speak to nobody and do nothing in connection with the documentary: two orders for the price of one. Tamsin also left a message, instructing me to ring her as soon as I could and before I did anything else. I ignored all three of them. I don't want to speak to anyone who's going to try to stop me doing what I need to do.

I slow down as the man walks towards me, combing my mind for a few basic facts about my rights. Can he force me to stop working if I want to work? Can he make me go to the police station with him? Detain me against my will? Laurie would know. *So might you, if you ever read anything that wasn't* heat *magazine* — that's what Tamsin would say. Come to think of it, it's easy to predict what most people are going to say most of the time. That's why I love Laurie. There's plenty wrong with him, but at least he's unpredictable. Not like Maya, who is always going to say, 'What smell? Smoke? Someone must be burning something outside.' Or Raffi: 'I know, I know — a dehumidifier. I'll look into it, Fliss, I promise.'

That's why I mustn't be stopped before I get a chance to speak to Ray Hines again: I don't know what she's going to say and I want to find out. Yes, I'm in danger, but not in the way the police think, from some cards and a photograph. I'm in danger of never being part of anything important, of having my whole bland life go by without anyone noticing or caring. Now I've got a chance to make sure that doesn't happen.

As I get closer, the man's face starts to look familiar. I work out who he is a few seconds before he introduces himself: Angus Hines. I recognise him from pictures in Laurie's files. 'I was wondering how long I was going to have to camp on your doorstep,' he says. He's almost good-looking, but his head could do with being a bit more three-dimensional. He's got a flat, square face that makes me think of a ventriloquist's dummy. When he opens his mouth again, I half expect it to make a clacking sound. 'Ray said you were meeting Julian Lance. How did it go? Was he helpful?' It doesn't occur to him to introduce himself. He clearly thinks I ought to know who he is, how much his opinions matter.

I want to turn and walk away, and not only because of what I know about him already, nothing to do with any ideas I might have entertained about making a wax effigy of him and sticking pins in it. He's talking as if he's in charge of me, brisk and presumptuous.

Seeing that I have no intention of answering him, he says, 'Fliss, I'll be honest. I'm not entirely happy with your . . . involvement in Ray's life, so I'm going to tell you what I told her: this documentary isn't only about her. It's about me, my family. It really matters to me, and to Ray — the first public account of our lives, to be watched by millions of people all over the country — all over the world, maybe. Laurie Nattrass might be the wrong man to make it, but that doesn't mean you're the right one. It worries me that my wife trusts you when she's spoken to you a grand total of once.'

'I'm not a man, and she's your *ex*-wife.'

'It worries me even more to hear her describe you as "objective". Because you're anything but, aren't you? Ray told me about your father.'

A conciliatory approach might work. Or it might be undermined by virulent secret loathing.

'Do you have someone else in mind to make the film?' I ask.

'No. That's not the point. And none of this is your fault. Ray shouldn't have —'

'It's precisely because of my father that I'll be more objective than anyone else would be,' I tell him.

'How so?'

I don't want to talk about this on the street, but the alternative would be to invite Angus Hines into my flat, and I definitely don't want to do that. 'My father made a careless professional mistake that cost a child her life. It ended up costing him his life too, ruining my mum's, and it didn't exactly enhance mine. If I find myself working on a film that involves child deaths, don't you think I'll do everything I can to get the facts right?'

'No, I don't,' says Hines, apparently not at all worried about upsetting me. 'The trouble with that sort of pop psychology is that you can twist it any way you want. Your

404

father didn't want Ray to appeal — he thought if she got out, baby-murderers everywhere would do their worst and get away with it. But Ray did appeal, and she won. She was vindicated, while he died in disgrace. You're telling me that doesn't make you want to find Ray guilty all over again in your documentary?'

'That's what I'm telling you, yes.'

'Come on, Fliss.' He smiles sadly, as if he cares about me and fears for my sanity. It freaks me out. 'You might think you're objective, but . . .'

'You think you know me better than I know myself?'

What else can I say in my defence? That's what it is: a defence. I'm being attacked in broad daylight outside my home. Just because he's only using words doesn't mean he's not attacking me. Mustering what confidence I have left, I say, 'I don't want to be like my father. When he said what he did about Ray, I hated him. He wanted her to stay in prison because of the effect her release would have on other people — nothing to do with Ray herself.' I'm cold. I want to be inside. I feel as if all my neighbours are listening through their walls, nodding to themselves because they've always thought I looked as if I had something to be ashamed of, and now they know what it is. 'He said nothing about whether he thought she was guilty or innocent — I don't think he knew the first thing about either of her . . . either of your babies' deaths. It was the same mistake he made with Jaycee Herridge — making assumptions and neglecting the details. If I make this documentary, the details are *all* I'm going to care about, whatever they might be, whatever picture they add up to, because I'm *better* than my father. I need to prove to myself that I'm nothing like him, and I don't care if that sounds disloyal!'

'A lot of people think loyalty means suspending your critical faculties and ceasing to think for yourself,' says Angus Hines. He pulls a handkerchief out of his coat pocket and offers it to me.

Am I crying? Yes, it seems I am. *Great.* 'No, thanks,' I say. *I'd rather let my face drip-dry in the wind than take anything from you.*

'You said a few minutes ago that you *found yourself* working on a documentary involving child deaths. Wasn't it your choice?'

'No, not at first. I didn't want anything to do with it. Laurie Nattrass called me into his office on Monday, told me he was resigning and dumped his crib death film on me without asking me what I wanted.'

Angus Hines stuffs his hanky back in his pocket, shaking his head. 'I don't know if you're deluding yourself or deliberately lying to me, but that's not how it happened. It can't be.'

How dare he speak to me like this? 'What? I'm not . . .'

'Your father killed himself in 2006. You started working for Binary Star in early 2007.' He flashes a smug smile at me. 'I work for a newspaper. I'm good at finding things out.'

Anyone would think he was whatever-his-name-is who uncovered the Watergate scandal. I'm not entirely sure what the Watergate scandal was, apart from something shocking involving Richard Nixon, so I'd better not mention it. 'I thought you were only a photographer,' I say, stressing the 'only'. I have nothing against photographers, and I know Hines is something more senior at *London on Sunday,* but at this point I'm willing to say anything that'll make him feel bad.

He pulls out his wallet and hands me a business card. 'Since you're so keen on details, get mine right.' Pictures Desk Editor. Big deal. 'You knew Laurie Nattrass was on the board at Binary Star — you must have known about his connection to Helen

Yardley, JIPAC, my wife. You didn't end up working with him by accident, did you?'

I can't deal with this. I push past him and head for my flat, fumbling in my bag for my keys. I let myself in and turn to close the door. Angus Hines is right behind me, so close we're almost touching.

'This conversation's over,' I tell him. How dare he walk into my home uninvited? I try to use the door to propel him out, but he's too heavy. 'Fine,' I say, gesturing for him to go on ahead of me. He smiles again, rewarding me for finally seeing sense.

He heads for the lounge, stopping on the way to look at what I've put up on the walls in the hall. As quietly as I can, I step outside, close the front door and morticelock it.

I run towards the main road faster than I've ever run before. I flag down a cab and tell the driver my work address. I need access to a computer, and the one at the office will do just as well as the one at home. It's Saturday, so hopefully no one will be in.

Oh my God, oh my God, ohmyGod. I've just locked the pictures desk editor of a major newspaper in my flat.

In the rear-view mirror, the taxi-driver eyes me hopefully. All I can see of him are his eyes, but that's enough. As a non-driver,

I spend a lot of time in cabs, and my instincts are razor-sharp. I'm getting a strong sense that this man has something pressing to tell me about an excellent biography of the Kray twins he's reading. I've already heard all about the bloke who had his smile extended by a knife from several other London cabbies; I don't need to hear it again. As a preventative measure, I pull out my phone and ring Tamsin.

'Fliss?' She sounds as if she'd given up all hope of ever hearing from me again. 'Where are you?'

I'm tempted to say 'Somalia'. 'On my way to the office. Relax. I'm fine.'

'You might be fine now, but the longer you —'

'I need you to do something for me,' I cut her off. 'You're not busy, are you?'

'Depends what you mean by busy. I've just downloaded a test thingie from MI6's website.'

'What?'

'I'm going to take it in a minute, under exam conditions. If I pass, I'll be one step closer to getting a job as an operations officer for cases — that's the official job title.'

'You mean a spy?' I can't help laughing, and once I start, I can't stop. *I've got a pictures desk editor locked in my flat and my best friend wants to be a spy.*

'Keep it to yourself, all right? It says on the website that you can't tell anyone.' She makes a dismissive noise. 'Seems a bit unrealistic, doesn't it? They can't mean *any-one* anyone.'

'No. I'm sure they mean you can tell whoever you like as long as they're not wearing an Al-Qaeda T-shirt.'

'Are you crying?'

'I think I'm laughing, but there's not much in it.'

'I'm deadly serious about this, Fliss. I spoke to a detective who said I'd make a good chief inspector, and it started me thinking . . .'

'Why were you talking to a detective?'

Tamsin groans. 'I know it's against your principles, but will you please buy a news-paper and read it? And when you've done that, come here so that I can not let you out of my sight.'

'Tam, I need you to go to mine. Have you still got the set of keys I gave you?'

'Somewhere. Why?'

'Just . . . go to my flat and unlock the door. Let Angus Hines out, lock up again — that's it, then you're done. It won't take you long. I'll pay any expenses — petrol, cab fare, tube fare, whatever — and there's

410

a slap-up meal in it too, at a restaurant of your choice. Just please, say you'll do it.'

'Can we rewind to the "Let Angus Hines out" part? What's Angus Hines doing in your flat?'

'He came in, I didn't want him there, I couldn't get him to leave, so I went out. I had to lock him in or he'd have followed me and I didn't want to speak to him. He's a horrible, self-righteous bully. He gave me the creeps.'

'You *locked* Angus Hines in your flat? Oh, my God! Isn't that . . . false imprisonment or something? Kidnap? Fliss, you can go to jail for incarcerating people against their will. What's wrong with you?'

I press the 'end call' button and switch off my phone. If she wants to let him out, she can go and let him out. If not, they can both stay where they are and have fun disapproving of me.

Maybe I ought to ask my taxi-driver if the Kray twins ever locked a pictures desk editor in their flat, and if so, what happened to them as a result. Except that he's now involved in a phone conversation of his own, which leaves me with no choice but to think.

Yes, I knew Laurie worked at Binary Star when I applied for the job. Yes, I knew about his links to Helen Yardley and JIPAC. I knew

411

he was trying to get Ray Hines out of prison. No, I didn't for a minute think I'd end up being coerced by him into taking on a film about miscarriages of justice involving crib death mothers. If I had, I'd have run a mile; Dad was dead by the time I started at Binary Star, but Mum wasn't.

She still isn't. It will break her heart if I make a documentary that portrays Ray Hines as innocent. Even if Dad was wrong to say what he said about her that day in the restaurant, that's not how Mum will see it. She'll be devastated.

That used to be enough to make me certain I didn't want to do it.

Then why go and work for Binary Star, alongside Laurie Nattrass?

Could I have been hoping, as early as January 2007, to find myself in the position I'm in now?

If I ring my home number and say all this to Angus Hines, will he finally be satisfied and let me make the documentary? I bury my face in my hands. *Oh, God. What have I done?* I should tell the taxi-driver to turn round and go back to Kilburn, but I can't face it. I don't want to go anywhere near Angus Hines ever again.

The cab pulls up outside Binary Star's offices. I pay and get out. The outer door's unlocked, so somebody must be in. I push through the double glass doors and slam straight into Raffi. 'A Felicity on a Saturday?' he says, hands on hips, mock disbelief all over his face. 'I must be seeing things.'

'Do . . . do you normally work on Saturdays?'

'Yup.' He leans forward and whispers in my ear, 'Sometimes I even work on the Lord's Day of Rest. Don't tell Him.' I wonder if there's something Raffi's scared of, something he's trying to convince himself is nothing. Why else would a person spend the weekend in the office? I decide I'm probably projecting; Raffi looks fine.

'I'm going to be working most weekends from now on,' I tell him, trying to sound busy and professional. He purses his lips at me. *I should think so too, the amount we're about to start paying you.* Is he beaming the words into my brain, or am I being paranoid? Either way, I feel as if I might as well be twirling a pistol in each hand, wearing a T-shirt with 'Stand and deliver' emblazoned across it.

'There's a surprise for you in your office,' says Raffi. 'Come to think of it, there were a couple of surprises for you in Maya's office, last time I looked.' Before I have a chance to ask what he means, he's gone, the doors banging behind him.

Maya's office door is shut, her 'Meeting in Progress' sign hanging from the handle. I can hear her and several other people talking over one another. Workaholic freaks, the lot of them. Don't they know what Saturdays are for? Why aren't they curled up on their sofas in their pyjamas, watching repeats of *A Place In The Sun: Home Or Away?*

Someone with a loud voice says, 'I appreciate that.' I wonder what the 'that' is. Fag smoke? Is this a secret meeting of the Nicotine in the Workplace Appreciation Society? I decide that whatever surprises Maya has for me can wait until later.

In the office that's either mine, Laurie's or nobody's, depending on your point of view, I find what looks like a small silver robot standing in the middle of the floor. It takes a few seconds for me to read the label that's stuck to it and work out what it is: a dehumidifier. My heart sinks to somewhere in the sub-gut region. A week ago I'd have been delighted, but not now. The timing says it all. Raffi knows this is supposed to be my new office, and he knows it doesn't have a condensation problem. Is the dehumidifier his way of letting me know I'll soon

414

be back in my damp old room where I belong?

I lock the door and turn on my computer. Laurie's sent me an email that says, 'Revised article attached', and, beneath that, 'Sent from my BlackBerry Wireless device'. The BlackBerry has contributed more words to the message than Laurie has, and it's never even had sex with me. If I weren't so on edge, I might find this funny.

There is no article attached to the message. Luckily Laurie has sent another email — from his laptop, presumably, once he realised he couldn't append the relevant file to his BlackBerry — this time consisting of no words, only the attachment. I open the article and click on 'print'. Then I root around in my bag for Angus Hines' business card. I send him an email, answering the last question he asked me as honestly and fully as possible, and explain that I ran away because I would have found it too hard to answer face to face. I tell him how painful it is for me to think about my dad, and that I tend to do anything I can to avoid it. I don't apologise for locking him in my flat, or ask if he's still there or has managed to get out.

Apart from the two from Laurie, the only interesting message in my inbox is from Dr

Russell Meredew. 'Fliss, hi,' it begins. What kind of greeting is that? Isn't this man an OBE? I check the files: yes, he is. It could be worse, I suppose: *Yo, Fliss, what up?* I read the rest of his email. 'I've spoken to Laurie, who tells me you intend to include interviews with Judith Duffy in the film. He thinks this is a bad idea, as do I. If you want to give me a ring, I'll explain why. I'm not trying to tell you how to do your job — please don't think that — but there's a danger in trying to be even-handed when it's a case of a bird in the hand being worth a pathological liar in the bush, if you get my drift. I think perhaps we should talk on the phone before proceeding with the interview we put in the diary the other day. My willingness to be involved in your project partly depends on what sort of project it turns out to be, as I'm sure you appreciate. Very best, Russell Meredew'.

In other words, don't listen to my enemy's point of view — just take my word for it that she's evil.

I press the 'delete' button, making a gargoyle face at the computer, then ring Judith Duffy's home number again and virtually beg her for a meeting. I tell her I'm neither for nor against her — I simply want to hear whatever she might have to say.

I'm about to grab the new version of Laurie's article and leave the office when I hear voices in the corridor that sound as if they're coming closer.

'. . . either of them gets in touch, please impress on them how important it is that they contact us.'

'I will.' That's Maya.

'For their own safety, they need to understand that all activity around this documentary film stops until further notice. It won't be for ever.'

'And if you find the Twickenham address Rachel Hines gave you . . .'

'I've told you, I haven't got it,' says Maya. 'I gave it to Fliss.'

'. . . or if you remember it . . .'

'I'm unlikely to remember it, since I never knew it. I was probably thinking about something else when I scribbled it down, and I handed it over without looking at it. Bring me a list of all the streets in Twickenham if you want, and I'll see if any of the names ring a bell, but, aside from that . . .'

'All right,' says the louder of the two men, in a strong Yorkshire accent. I recognise his voice from the message he left me: DC Colin Sellers. 'So if we could have a quick look round Fliss Benson's office before we go?'

'Which one?'

'She's got more than one?'

'She's kind of moved into Laurie's old office, but I'm not sure she's finished moving all her stuff yet. And Laurie's not been in to collect his things.'

'We need to see both.'

'Laurie's old office is just along here. Follow me.'

What about a warrant? I want to scream. I leap out of my chair and duck down behind the desk, remembering only when I see its four wooden legs that its bulk doesn't go all the way to the floor. *I knew that. Shit, shit, shit.*

The footsteps are getting closer. I spring up, lunge across the room at the dehumidifier and knock it over. I pick it up, turn it so that the broadest side is facing the office door, and sit with my back pressed against it, pulling my knees up to my chin and putting my arms round my legs, refusing to listen to the voice in my head that's saying, *What's the point? So they won't see you when they look through the glass in the door — so what? In a minute Maya's going to let them in, and they're going to find you, very obviously hiding from them.*

Is there any way I can pretend I'm sitting like this because I'm feeling particularly humid today? I'm sweating buckets; maybe that'll help make the lie convincing.

I hear the quieter of the two male voices say, 'What's that? An electric heater?'

'Never seen one as big as that,' says Sellers.

I tuck my chin into my chest. I had no idea I could do this: make a ball of my body while still sitting up. Maybe I ought to take up yoga. *What are you going to say when they unlock the door, walk in and see you?*

'Sorry, guys, do you want to start with Fliss's old office? It might take me a while to track down one of the spare keys for Laurie's. He was always forgetting his, using the spares, then putting them back in odd places.'

Thank God. My relief lasts about half a second, until it occurs to me that the only good thing about my old room was the view of Laurie's office, across the courtyard. I could lie on the floor beneath the window and not be seen by the police, but then if Maya walks past, she'll see me through the glass in the door. With much panicky swearing through gritted teeth, I shunt the dehumidifier round, so that its widest side now faces the window, and pull it a metre or so across the room. Will the detectives notice it's been moved, or will they assume all four

419

sides are the same?

This is the only place I can sit and not be visible from either vantage point. I assume the tucked-in-ball position again, and wait for what seems like years, listening out for the sound of the police coming back in this direction. *And when I hear them, my plan is to do what, exactly?* Questions flit round my brain: too many moths around a lightbulb, clustering blackly around the source of light, making it dark. Why am I bothering to pretend I might get away with this, and what's the point anyway? Why did Tamsin tell me to read a newspaper? Why do I love Laurie so much when I shouldn't even like him? Why can't I bear the thought of being told by DC Sellers that I can't speak to Ray again until he says I can? Why are the police looking for her? Do they think she killed Helen Yardley?

Is that the story she wants to tell me?

Footsteps. And DC Sellers' boom-box voice again, faint but getting closer. I scramble across the floor to the window and try to prise it open. It feels as if it's been painted shut. Have I ever seen Laurie with his window open? Did I ever notice anything apart from every detail of the man himself — the hairs on his arms, his ankles in black socks — in all the hours I spent gazing across the courtyard at him? *Silly question.*

I push and shove, leaning my whole weight into the window, muttering, 'Yes, thank you, thank you,' as if it's already given way — a little trick that's sometimes worked for me in other situations. There's a creak, then — glory and hallelujah — it opens. I climb out, and am about to lie down next to the wall when I remember my bag. *Shit.*

I push myself through the window again. Why is it such a tight squeeze? I can't have got fatter since three seconds ago. I'm surprised I haven't lost half my body weight, the amount I'm sweating. Back in the room, I freeze, panic rollercoastering through my veins. The police and Maya are right outside; seconds away. I hear a metallic jangling: a bunch of keys. I grab my bag, and half fall, half wriggle through the window. There's a loud tearing sound as I hit the courtyard's paving stones. Christ, that hurt. I kneel up and detach a swatch of material that used to be part of my shirt from a jagged shard of wood protruding from the window frame.

I hear the key turn in the lock. *No more time.* I push the wood that's come free back into the frame and give the window a shove. It almost shuts. There's no way I can close the catch, not from outside and not with

421

Maya and the two detectives walking into the room, so I do the only thing I can do: lie flat on my side, pressing my sore body against the wall under the window. I scan the rooms on the opposite side of the courtyard. I'm safe — they're all empty.

'It's a dehumidifier, Sarge,' DC Sellers says. So the quieter man's in charge.

'What do you reckon to Maya Jacques?' he asks.

Maya's not with them any more? What the hell's she doing, letting two cops loose in my office unsupervised?

'Good body, good hair, bad face,' says Sellers. Bad personality, I'm tempted to call out, from what I'm trying, euphemistically, to think of as my courtyard retreat. There are weeds sprouting up between the flagstones. One is almost touching my nose. Its leaves are sprinkled with soil and white powder: paint dust from the window. I'm already cold; soon I'll be freezing.

'I think she knows the Twickenham address. She protested a bit too much.'

'Why wouldn't she tell us?'

'Laurie Nattrass has nothing but contempt for the police — he says as much in a broadsheet at least twice a week. Do you think he'd tell us where Ray Hines is staying?'

'Probably not,' says Sellers.

'He wouldn't. He'd protect her — that's how he'd see it, anyway. I think we'd better assume everyone at Binary Star feels the same way. Here, look at this.'

What? What are they looking at?

'New message from Angus Hines.'

No, no, no. I nearly wail out loud. I left my email inbox up on the screen. This is the part where the police find out I locked a man in my flat. This is the beginning of me going to jail.

'Interesting.'

'Have you opened it, Sarge? Living dangerously, aren't you? Interception of Communications Act, and all that.'

'I must have leaned on the mouse by mistake. "Dear Fliss, here are two lists you might find interesting. One is of all the women, and a few men, against whom Judith Duffy has given evidence at criminal trials. The other is of all the people she's testified against in the family courts. All, on both lists, were accused of physically injuring and in many cases killing a child or children. You might also be interested to know that in another twenty-three cases, Dr Duffy testified in support of a parent or parents and said that, in her opinion, no abuse had taken place." '

'And?'

'That's it. "Best wishes, Angus Hines".'

That's it? No mention of illegal imprisonment in my basement flat? I swallow a sigh. It would be a basement flat, wouldn't it? I hadn't thought of that before. Locking up other human beings is never ideal, but when there's any sort of cellar involved, you know you're dealing with a monster. *Wonderful. Just wonderful.*

'Thirty-two on the criminal list, fifty-seven in the family courts,' says Sellers. I hear a whistle that I think means, 'That's a lot of people'.

'Family court proceedings are confidential. Where's he got these names from?'

A good question, but not the main one in my mind. Why has he emailed me the two lists, with no explanation? Is it his way of saying he wants me to make the documentary? Perhaps by locking him in my flat, I proved to him that I have flair and initiative. *Yeah, right.*

He could have got the names from Judith Duffy. She might well keep a record of everyone she's given evidence against in court. She and Ray are now friends, Ray and Angus are more than friends . . . I press my eyes shut, frustrated. I'm accumulating information, but making no progress. Each new thing I find out is like a thread that leads nowhere.

'Holy crap,' says Sellers.

What? *What?*

'New mail icon just flashed up again. I clicked on it . . .'

'You mean you leaned on the mouse by mistake. And?'

'Look at this photo.'

'Is that . . . ?'

'It's Helen Yardley's hand. Those are her wedding and engagement rings.'

'Holding a card with the sixteen numbers on, and . . . what's behind the card? A book?'

I can feel my heartbeat throbbing in my ears and throat. I'm glad they found it, not me. I hope they delete it, so that I don't have to see it.

'*Nothing But Love,*' says Sellers. 'Her own book. Seen the sender's address? hilairious@yahoo.co.uk. He's spelled "hilarious" wrong.'

'Forward it to your own email and close it.'

'Think it's him, Sarge?'

'I do,' the quieter one says. 'That picture was taken in Helen Yardley's living room — see the wallpaper in the background? I think he took it on Monday, before he shot her. Whoever he is, he wants Fliss Benson to know what he did. It's as if he's . . . I don't know, boasting or something.'

I can't decide if I'm relieved or disgusted. The idea that a killer has me on his mind and has contacted me four times makes me want to climb into a boiling hot shower and stay there for a long time. But if he's boasting to me, if I'm his audience, perhaps he's less likely to harm me. I desperately want to believe this.

I hear papers being shuffled. My files.

'Sarge, these are full of stuff about Yardley, Jaggard and Hines. We need to take all this away, and Benson's computer. And Nattrass's, even if we have to break into his house to get it.'

'You read my mind. I'll speak to Proust.'

I assume they're not talking about the dead French novelist.

'We need warrants, soon as possible. I don't see how any judge could knock us back. Helen Yardley's dead, Sarah Jaggard's been attacked, and Ray Hines is missing — presumed at risk until we track her down. The main thing linking the three women is the documentary.'

'Do we know where Benson was on Monday?'

Monday? A chill sweeps through me that has nothing to do with the weather as I re-

426

alise what they must mean. Helen Yardley was murdered on Monday. It's all I can do to stop myself from leaping up and yelling, 'I was here, in the office. I was here all day.'

'Leave those files as you found them,' says the quiet sergeant. 'I'll tell Maya Jacques to keep the office locked and make sure no one touches anything in here.'

Finally, they go. A few minutes later, I hear the thock-thock of Maya's heels and the sound of the key turning in the door. That's it. Everyone has finished with my office for the time being — everyone but me. I stay where I am and force myself to count to a hundred before moving. Then I climb back inside and close the window behind me. That's as close as I ever hope to get to a camping holiday, I think to myself as I brush the crumbs of dirt and dust off my clothes.

My hand shaking, I delete the email from 'hilairious' without opening it; the police have taken ownership of it, which is fine by me. I print out Angus Hines' email and put it in my bag, along with Laurie's revised article. Stupidly, forgetting the key sound I heard, I try to open the office door and find I can't. How ironic: I've been locked in. Isn't there something called locked-in syndrome? That's what I'm suffering from, me and Angus Hines. I guess all those irritating people who say 'What goes around comes around' must be right.

I unlock the door, then close and lock it behind me. I take the scenic route out of the office, the one that doesn't involve going anywhere near Maya, and hail another taxi. I give the driver my home address. If I see a strange car camped outside that might belong to the police, I'll tell the cab to drive past, but if I don't, I'd quite like to check my flat's still in one piece — no broken windows or piles of glass on the carpet, no scratch marks on the walls. *No irate Tamsin sitting on the sofa, waiting to deliver a stern lecture.*

Tomorrow I'll have to go back to the office and make copies of everything in those box files before the police take them away. Maya won't be in — Sunday's her manicure and pedicure day. Raffi might be around on the Lord's Day of Rest, as he called it, but the chances of him taking an interest in my activities are slim. If I'm efficient, I should be able to photocopy the lot in five or six hours. The thought makes me feel weak with exhaustion.

And once you've copied it all, where are you going to take it? Where are you going to hide? Tamsin and Joe's flat? Mine? Both are places the police are bound to come back to, if they're as keen to find me as they seem to be.

I think I probably made the decision a while ago, but it's only now that I allow myself to acknowledge it. Marchington House. That's where I'll go. Ray won't mind. I've known her less than a week, but I know she won't mind. There must be spare rooms there, plenty of space for me and the contents of several large box files. Plenty of time for me to plough through all the paperwork Laurie and Tamsin generated, looking for . . . what? Something Laurie missed because he couldn't see the trees for the wood?

I feel utterly drained, but I'm too wired to sleep, or even to stare out of the window. I need to do something productive. I pull Laurie's article out of my bag and start to read it. I stop when I get to a sentence that doesn't sound right:

Despite never having murdered anybody, Dr Duffy was responsible for ruining the lives of dozens of innocent women whose only crime was to be in the wrong place at the wrong time when a child or children died: Helen Yardley, Sarah Jaggard,

Dorne Llewellyn . . . the list goes on and on.

Three names isn't a long list. Why didn't Laurie include more, to prove his point? There *were* more in the original draft, I'm sure of it. I turn to the last page. Laurie has also, wisely — or perhaps because the journal editors gave him no choice — deleted his insinuation that Rhiannon Evans must have murdered her son Benjamin because she's a working-class prostitute and that's the sort of thing they do. It makes sense to cut that out, but why strike names off the list of Judith Duffy's victims — a list that's supposed to go on and on?

I rummage in my bag for the original article, but it's not there. I must have left it at home. I have another idea: Angus Hines' email. I pull it out and start to skim through the names. Two leap out at me: Lorna Keast and Joanne Bew. There's no other way I could know those names. They mean nothing to me. The first time I saw them was in Laurie's article, alongside the names Helen Yardley and Sarah Jaggard. I *did* see them; I'm not imagining it.

In the first draft, Lorna Keast and Joanne Bew were part of that list. So why aren't they now?

From *Nothing But Love*
by Helen Yardley
with Gaynor Mundy

5 November 1996

I didn't enjoy any of the days of my trial, but the worst was 5 November. That was when I came face to face with Dr Judith Duffy for the first time, when she gave her evidence in chief, which means in response to prosecuting counsel's questions. Unbelievably, I had never met or seen her before, even though she claimed to know so much about me and my family. But I knew what sort of person she was. Ned and Gillian had warned me. She's the sort of woman who is happy to say that a grief-stricken mother committed two murders without even bothering to speak to her or get to know her first. In contrast, Dr Russell Meredew, one of the many heroes of this story and the main expert witness for the defence, had spent days with Paul and me, interviewed us both at length, and painstakingly compiled what he called his 'dossier'. We joked that by the time he'd finished it was as thick as an encyclopaedia! Incidentally, Dr Meredew tried to present the dossier to Justice Wilson in court, and Wilson's shocking response was, 'You don't expect me to read all that, do you?'

I watched Dr Duffy closely as she took the stand and felt real, heart-shaking terror for the first time since the trial had begun. There was something about her that chilled me. Until that moment, I had assumed I would be going home with Paul at the end of this ridiculous charade. We would get Paige back and live happily ever after. I had no doubts about this because I was innocent. I knew it, Paul knew it, and the jury would know it too. Ned had assured me that once Russell Meredew had explained to them, in his gentle but authoritative way, that it was entirely possible both Morgan and Rowan died of natural causes, there was no way in the world I would be convicted of murder.

But when Judith Duffy's eyes met mine for the first time, I felt as if I'd been punched in the stomach. I saw no compassion whatsoever. Her bearing was haughty and arrogant. She looked exactly like the sort of person who would try to send me to prison for the rest of my life simply because she could, to prove that she was right. I didn't know at the time, but I found out later that Paul had felt exactly the same way about her, and so had Ned and Gillian.

I honestly felt as if I was being tortured as I sat there, helpless, listening to her describe what I must have done to my precious Morgan and Rowan in order to cause the injuries she claimed they'd sustained. I heard her tell the jury, many of whom were in tears, that I had poisoned my children using salt, that I had smothered them repeatedly, with the aim of taking them to the hospital and getting lots of attention for myself. I'd never heard anything so ridiculous in my life. If I'd wanted attention, I thought, I'd have walked down the street in a Minnie Mouse costume, done the cancan naked in my front garden — something funny and harmless. I would *never, never* have murdered my babies.

When I heard Dr Duffy say that Rowan's skull had been fractured, I wanted to scream, 'You're lying! I never hurt my babies! I adored them, I had nothing but love for them!'

I will never forget the way Dr Duffy's examination-in-chief ended. It's painfully etched on my mind for ever. When I checked the trial transcript, it corresponded almost word for word with what I remembered:

Rudgard: Mrs Yardley believes both Morgan and Rowan were victims of crib death, or SIDS.
What do you say to that?

Duffy: Leaving aside the fact that it's highly unusual for there to be two instances of SIDS in one household —

Rudgard: Forgive me for interrupting, Doctor — I wish to concentrate on the Yardley family, not other families you've encountered in your professional life. Let's not get into the statistics game. We all know how notoriously unreliable statistics are when applied to a specific case — they're meaningless. Is it possible, in your view, that Morgan and Rowan were both victims of crib death?

Duffy: I'd say that's so unlikely, it borders on impossible. What's overwhelmingly likely is that there was a common underlying cause of both deaths, and that the cause was forensic, not medical.

Rudgard: Then, in your opinion, both Morgan and Rowan Yardley were murdered?

Duffy: My opinion is that both babies died of non-accidental injuries, yes.

■ ■ ■ ■

I dissolved in tears as Judith Duffy calmly told these lies about me, but, although I was distraught, neither Paul nor I had any idea how much damage had been done by her use of the phrase 'so unlikely, it borders on impossible'. Ned, however, with all his years of trial expertise, knew exactly how dangerous it was for the jury to hear those words. It didn't matter that a few seconds earlier, they'd heard the great Ivor Rudgard QC say that statistics can't be relied upon in cases like mine — that wasn't the part that would stick in their minds. It wasn't as memorable or impressive as Dr Duffy's magic formula for finding guilt where there is none: 'so unlikely, it borders on impossible'.

When Reuben Merrills rose to cross-examine Dr Duffy, Ned flashed one of his brilliant ray-of-hope smiles at me: *Don't worry, Merrills is the best defence barrister in the land — he'll demolish her.* He certainly did his best:

Merrills: Let's be clear: is your contention that it's not possible for more than one baby born to the same two parents and

435

into the same household to die of natural causes?

Duffy: I didn't say —

Merrills: Because I could cite to you several cases of families that have suffered more than one crib death, with no hint of induced injury.

Duffy: Your terminology's confused. Natural causes and crib death aren't synonymous with one another. In a family that contains the haemophilia gene, it's obviously quite probable that more than one member will die a haemophilia-related death — that's natural causes. Crib death is what we call it when no explanation for death can be found.

Merrills: Very well, then, say crib death. Is it possible, in your view, for there to be more than one crib death in one family?

Duffy: Of course it is.

Merrills: To clarify: you're saying that *of course* it's possible for more than one child in the same family to be a victim of SIDS.

Duffy: It's possible, yes.

Merrills: Yet a short while ago, you said the opposite, didn't you?

Duffy: No, I didn't. I said that —

Merrills: You said that for Morgan and Rowan Yardley both to have suffered crib

436

deaths was 'so unlikely, it borders on impossible'.

Duffy: I meant that —

Merrills: You said, and the jury remembers you saying, that for there to have been two SIDS deaths in the Yardley family was 'so unlikely it borders on impossible.'

Duffy: No, I did not say that.

Merrills: Well, Dr Duffy, I'm sure the jury are as baffled as I am, because we all heard you say it. No further questions.

My heart was pounding like the hooves of an excited horse as I listened to this. Thank goodness, I thought. Now the jury will understand what a monstrous liar Judith Duffy is. How could anyone take her opinion seriously now that Reuben Merrills had caught her out in such a blatant lie? But my spirits clouded over when I looked at Paul and Ned and saw that they were both frowning. I found out later that they were seriously worried about the effect of repetition on the jury. Even though Merrills had made short work of proving that Duffy was a flat-out liar, he had twice repeated her original assertion that for Morgan and Rowan both to have died of SIDS was so unlikely it bordered on impossible. Ned told me later that repeating something over and over again is a highly effective way of getting people to believe it. 'The context of the repetition matters less than the repetition itself,' he said. He's right. I was being naïve. Time after time during my trial, the jury heard that phrase: 'so unlikely, it borders on impossible.' I didn't know it on 5 November, but I was going to spend nine years of my life in prison as a result of those six words uttered by Dr Duffy, a woman who had never heard me say so much as a single word.

24 October 2004
On 24 October, a journalist from the *Daily Telegraph* came to interview me in prison. Paul joked that I could barely fit in his visits now that I was a celebrity. That's what the prison staff called me too: 'our resident celebrity'. Everybody at Geddham Hall was wonderfully supportive. They all knew I was innocent, which was a welcome change from Durham, where I was hated and attacked. I knew I had Laurie to thank for people's change of attitude. He'd mounted such a wonderful campaign on my behalf, and even my lovely cautious Ned had been heard to mutter that my appeal next February might just succeed. Laurie had been do-

ing wonders out there in the outside world, and JIPAC was going from strength to strength.

I felt so frustrated, because there was only so much I could do from inside, but Laurie was heroically reassuring, and kept telling me that everyone knew JIPAC was my baby as much as his. I couldn't wait to get out and do more to help women in terrible situations like mine, women the justice system had betrayed and abandoned. There were so many of them and I felt so much love and pity for all of them. I'd heard that Rachel Hines was coming to Geddham soon. Her case was almost identical to mine: an innocent mother wrongly convicted of killing her two children. She'd recently been denied leave to appeal, and my heart broke for her.

One thing I could do in prison was write, and I found I loved it. At first I agreed to keep a diary only because Laurie asked me to, but once I started, I couldn't have managed without it. I told the journalist from the *Telegraph* that one day I hoped to publish a book about my life and everything I'd been through. She nodded, as if this was a perfectly natural thing to want, and only to be expected. I wasn't sure she understood how much it meant to me. She must have had to write all the time for her job, but I hadn't written anything since leaving school. She seemed nice, so I let her have a look at my work in progress. 'I bet my writing style's terrible, isn't it?' I joked.

'This poem's brilliant,' she said. 'Really, really good.' I had to laugh. She might as well have said, 'Yes, Helen, your writing style is terrible.' The poem, the only part of what I'd written that she'd praised, was the only thing in the notebook that wasn't by me! It was a poem I found in an anthology in Geddham's library, and I thought it was beautiful, so I wrote it down at the front of my notebook, to inspire me. It's by a woman called Fiona Sampson, and it's called 'Anchorage':

Those fasting women in their cells
drained a honeycomb brain
of every sugar drop of sense;
they made the skull a silvered shell
where love could live, cuckoo-like —

Would any question what she did
to distance her from how we live,
outside such dedication? — Shedding
the various world, so as to fit
in ways a jealous lover likes?

What flutters still is a bird: blown in
by accident, or wild design
of grace, a taste of something sweet —
The emptied self a room swept white.

I wasn't entirely sure what the poem meant,
but I knew that from the moment I first
read it, it meant the world to me and
became one of my treasured possessions. I
almost felt as if it must have been written
with me in mind! It was about women in
cells, which I was — for the time being at
least. I particularly loved the last verse
because it seemed to me to be so full of
hope. I thought that was what the writer
was trying to say: that even when you're
locked up and everything's been taken away
from you, you still have hope. Hope is the
bird that still flutters, 'blown in by accident,
or wild design of grace, a taste of something
sweet'. And because you've lost everything,
in your empty life that is now 'a room swept
white', a hope that might otherwise be so
tiny and fragile suddenly seems huge and
sweet and powerful, because it's the only
thing there.

Every night in my cell, I lay in my bed
crying for my lost babies and imagining
those wings of hope fluttering and flapping
in the darkness beside me.

14
10/10/09

'My being struck off is a foregone conclusion,' said Judith Duffy. 'It will happen even if I defend myself, and since I won't . . .'

'Nothing? Not even someone to speak on your behalf?' Charlie made sure to sound curious rather than disapproving. She'd only been talking to Duffy for ten minutes or so, but already it had made her aware of how judgemental she normally was, often entertaining herself while others were speaking by gleefully mocking their clothes, mannerisms, stupidity — all in the privacy of her own mind, of course, and so probably harmless, except she was finding now that she had shamefully little experience of listening to another person in what must (she assumed) be the ideal way — without the secret hope that within seconds her bitchy streak would have something to get its teeth into.

Talking of clothes, Judith Duffy's were a little odd. Individually, each garment was okay, but the ensemble didn't work: a lacy white blouse, a shapeless purple cardy, a grey knee-length skirt that might have been half of a suit, black tights, and flat black shoes with large bows on them that looked as if they would suit a younger woman better. Charlie couldn't work out if Duffy had tried to dress smartly or casually this morning; either way, she hadn't got the look quite right.

Charlie had talked her way into Duffy's house by appealing to what they had in common. It had taken more honesty than she'd thought it would, and she'd ended up almost convincing herself that she and this plain, prim-looking doctor were some kind of outcast soulmates, to the point that to condemn Duffy now for anything would feel like condemning herself, and Charlie was bored of doing that. She'd given it up roughly a year ago.

'Much to my lawyer's consternation, no — no defence at all,' said Duffy. 'And no appeal. I don't want to argue with anyone about anything — not the GMC, not Russell Meredew. Certainly not Laurie Nattrass. That man's appetite for being proved right is insatiable. Anyone who locks horns with

443

him is likely to find themselves still there twenty years later.' She smiled. She and Charlie were sitting on cushionless wicker chairs in her green-tiled, green-walled conservatory. From what Charlie had seen of the house, it was assorted shades of green throughout. The view at the back was of a long, neat, entirely plant-free garden — just lawn and empty beds — and, beyond a low wooden fence, a garden of the same proportions but with shrubs and flowers, leading to a conservatory that looked like an exact replica of Duffy's.

'When I first became unpopular, I used to plead my case to anyone who would listen. It took me more than two years to notice that standing up for myself made me feel worse rather than better.'

'There's something soul-destroying about trying to persuade people you aren't as bad as they think you are,' Charlie agreed. 'My natural inclination has always been to say, "Fuck you all — I'm even worse." ' She didn't apologise for her language. If being a pensioner netted you a free bus pass, outcast status surely earned you the right to swear.

'I'm as bad as I am and as good as I am.' Duffy wrapped her cardigan around herself. 'So is everybody else. We all feel pain, we all relieve pain, we all unwittingly cause pain

444

to others. Most of us at some point in our lives deliberately cause pain, of varying degrees.'

'At the risk of sounding like a smart-arse . . . You could fight for your job and your reputation at the GMC hearing and all that would still be true.'

'A GMC verdict doesn't change who I am, and neither does public opinion,' said Duffy. 'Nor does unhappiness, which is why I've given it up.'

'So you no longer care what people think of you?'

Duffy looked up at the glass above her head. 'If I say I don't, it sounds as if I'm dismissive of my fellow human beings, which isn't true at all. But . . . most people are incapable of forming a meaningful opinion about me. They can't see beyond the things I'm famous for having said and done.'

'Isn't that who a person is?' Charlie asked. 'The sum total of everything he or she says and does?'

'You don't really believe that, do you?' Judith Duffy sounded very much the concerned doctor. Charlie half expected her to produce a pad and pen, prescribe a powerful mind-changing drug. *For your own good, dear.*

'To be honest, I'm way too shallow to have given it any thought, so I won't pretend to have an answer.'

'What's the best thing you've ever done?'

'Last year I . . . well, I suppose I sort of saved the lives of three people.'

'I'll ignore the "sort of", which is you being modest,' said Duffy briskly. 'You saved three lives.'

'I should probably qualify that.' Charlie sighed. It wasn't a memory she enjoyed revisiting. 'A colleague and I saved *two* people's lives, though the person who was going to kill them ended up killing —'

'Don't qualify it.' Duffy smiled. 'You saved lives.'

'I suppose so.'

'I have too, dozens of them. I don't know the exact number, but there are plenty of children who wouldn't have lived to see adulthood if I hadn't persuaded a court to take them away from families that would have killed them. What greater gift can you give than the gift of continued life, when someone's threatened with extinction? None. You and I have both given that gift, more than once. Does that make us two of the greatest people who ever lived?'

'God, I hope not.' Charlie laughed. 'If I'm the best the world has to offer, I might have to resort to space tourism.'

'We aren't defined by our achievements any more than we're defined by our mistakes,' said Duffy. 'We're just who we are, and who really knows what that amounts to?'

'You could say that about Helen Yardley. You thought she murdered her children.'

'I still do.'

'But that wasn't *her,* was it, according to your theory? It was the worst thing she did, but it wasn't who she was.'

'No, it wasn't.' Duffy's voice took on a new energy. 'And I wish more people understood that. Mothers who murder their babies aren't evil, they aren't monsters. Mostly, they're trapped in little hells of the mind — hells they can't escape from and can't talk about to anyone. Often they conceal those hells so expertly, they convince the world they're happy and normal, even those closest to them.' She shifted in her chair. 'I don't suppose you've read Helen Yardley's autobiography, *Nothing But Love*?'

'I'm in the middle of it.'

'Have you noticed how many people she writes off as blind and stupid for not taking one look at her and *knowing* she didn't kill her two boys, because she was so distraught and grief-stricken, as surely no baby-killer would be? Because it ought to have been obvious to everybody how much she loved her children?'

Charlie nodded. She hadn't been impressed even the first time the point had been made. *You could have been pretending to be distraught, though, couldn't you?* was the retort that sprang to mind.

'Mothers who smother their babies usually do love them — deeply, as deeply as any mother who'd never dream of harming her child, though I know that's a hard idea to get your head round. Typically, they *are* distraught — quite genuinely. They're heartbroken, their lives are in pieces — exactly the same as an innocent mother who loses a baby to meningitis. Forget the controversial cases — I'm talking about the many women I've met in the course of my work who admit to having felt so desperate that they put a pillow over baby's face, or threw him under a train, or off the balcony. With the very odd exception, these women are devastated by the loss of the child. They want to die afterwards, they can't think of a reason to go on living.'

'But . . .' Was Charlie missing something? 'They caused that loss themselves.'

'Which, if anything, makes it worse.'

'But . . . Why didn't they just not do it, then? Do they think they want the child to die, and only realise too late that they don't?'

Judith Duffy smiled sadly. 'You're attributing a level of rationality to these women that simply isn't there. They do it because they're suffering terribly and don't know what else to do. That behaviour *came out* of them, out of their pain, and they didn't have the inner resources to stop it. When you're mentally ill, it's not always possible to think, "If I do this, then that will happen." Mentally ill isn't the same as mad, incidentally.'

'No,' said Charlie, not wanting to seem unsophisticated. Privately, she was thinking, *Sometimes they're the same. Both can mean going to the shops with no clothes on and shouting when you get there about aliens making off with your vital organs.*

'Mothers who kill their babies deserve our compassion in exactly the same way that mothers whose babies die of natural causes do,' said Duffy. 'I felt like cheering when Justice Elizabeth Geilow questioned, in her summary remarks, whether women like Ray Hines and Helen Yardley belong in the criminal system at all. In my view, they don't. What they're crying out for is empathy and help.'

'Yet you testify against them. You're a crucial part of the successful prosecutions that send them to prison,' said Charlie.

'I didn't testify *against* Ray, or Helen, or any of them,' Duffy corrected. 'As an expert witness in a criminal trial, I'm asked for my opinion about what caused children to die. If I think parent- or carer-inflicted violence is the cause of death, I say so, but I'm not *against* anybody when I say it. By telling the truth as I see it, I'm trying to do the best for everyone. Lies benefit nobody. I'm on every accused woman's side just as I'm on every endangered or murdered child's side.'

'I'm not sure the women would see it that way,' said Charlie tetchily. *Talk about trying to have it both ways.*

'Of course they wouldn't.' Duffy tucked her iron-grey hair behind her ears. 'But I also have to think about the children — defenceless and equally deserving of compassion.'

'You wouldn't say *more* deserving?'

'No. Though if you ask me what I think I'm here for, it's to save and protect children. That's my number one priority. However much compassion I feel for a woman like Helen Yardley, I'm going to make sure she doesn't kill a third child if at all possible.'

450

'Paige?'

Duffy stood up. 'Why do I feel as if I'm defending myself?'

'I'm sorry, I didn't mean to . . .'

'No, it's not you. Do you want another cup of tea?'

Charlie didn't, but she sensed the doctor needed some space to clear her head, so she nodded. Had she sounded too harsh? Simon would have laughed and said, 'Don't you always?'

While Duffy was pottering about in the kitchen, Charlie looked at the books on the small shelf in the corner of the conservatory. A biography of Daphne Du Maurier, a few Iris Murdochs, nine or ten books by someone called Jill McGown that Charlie hadn't heard of, lots of Russian classics, three vegetarian recipe books, *Forever . . .* No, surely not. Charlie crept across the room to check she wasn't seeing things. She wasn't. Judith Duffy had a copy of *Forever in my Heart* by Jade Goody. Talk about eclectic tastes.

'The Yardleys' inventiveness with names is one of the many reasons I'm in trouble,' said Duffy, returning with a mug of tea each for her and Charlie. 'I referred to their younger son Rowan as "she" in a report I wrote. I've only known of two other Rowans and both were female, so I assumed Helen's Rowan was too. Laurie Nattrass has made much of that, just as he's made much of my lack of personal involvement with the Yardley family, in contrast to Russell Meredew, who practically moved in with them at one point. I never spoke to Helen or Paul, never interviewed them.'

'Do you regret that?' Charlie asked.

'I regret not having time for the personal touch, but the reality is that . . .' Duffy stopped. 'I'm defending myself again.'

'You can't be. I'm not attacking you.'

The doctor's lips flattened into a line. 'The reality is,' she said less stridently, 'that I was the most sought-after expert witness in the country before Laurie Nattrass declared me the root of all evil, and I didn't have time to get to know every family. I had to leave that to others I hoped were properly trained to give parents like the Yardleys and the Hineses the help they needed. My job as an expert witness wasn't to meet and get to know the family — it was to look at samples under a microscope, look at the slides I was given, and make sense of what I saw. In the case of Rowan Yardley, I was looking at lung tissue and a fractured skull — that was what the paediatric pathologist who performed the post-mortem passed on to me. I wasn't asked to inspect the child's genitalia, hence the mistake about his sex.'

Duffy pushed her hair away from her face. 'I should have known he was a boy. I should have checked, and I deeply regret that I didn't, but . . .' She shrugged. 'Sadly, that doesn't cancel out what I saw through the microscope: clear evidence that in the course of his short life, Rowan Yardley had been subjected to repeated smothering attempts. No amount of sitting in the Yardleys' kitchen and chatting to them would have made the evidence of non-natural airway obstruction disappear. Or the skull fracture.'

Charlie sipped her tea, wondering if there was an analogy to be found in policing terms. If she was walking through the Winstanley estate, and saw a teenager in a hooded top knock an old woman to the ground, verbally abuse her and run off with her bag, unambiguous eye-witness evidence that a crime had been committed . . . Was that how certain Judith Duffy was about Helen Yardley? Were the doctors who testified in Yardley's defence saying the equivalent of, 'He wasn't mugging her, he was rehearsing for his part in a school play about thieves?'

'For what it's worth — and since I never

spoke to the woman, you might say it's not worth much — I believe Helen Yardley escaped from her little hell before she died,' Duffy said. 'What she went through gave her a purpose. Her campaigning work on behalf of other women — it was genuine, I think. She believed passionately in their innocence — Sarah Jaggard, Ray Hines, all of them. She suited being a celebrity, the perfect martyr-turned-heroine. It gave her something she needed: attention, recognition. I think she really wanted to do good. That's why she was so effective as a figurehead for JIPAC.'

Charlie heard pride and admiration in the doctor's voice; it made her feel uncomfortable.

'It's always difficult to untangle a person's motivations,' said Duffy, 'but if I had to guess, I'd say Helen's wish to be innocent herself would have fuelled her determination to believe other women were, others like her. The irony is that even if every last one of them were guilty, Helen's support would have been incredibly beneficial to them. By believing in their essential goodness, she probably helped them to forgive themselves for what they'd done.'

'Are you saying . . . ?'

'They're all guilty? No. What I'm saying,

and what people like Laurie Nattrass seem unwilling to take on board, is that the chances of an unexplained and unexpected child death being murder are far greater now than they used to be, proportionally. Fifty years ago there were 3,000 crib deaths a year in the UK. Gradually, as housing conditions improved, that went down to 1,000 a year. Then with more houses becoming smoke-free, less co-sleeping, and the 'Back to Sleep' campaign — persuading parents it was dangerous to put a baby down to sleep on its front — the SIDS rate came down to 400 a year. But those little hells of the mind . . .' Duffy glanced towards her kitchen, as if her own private hell was somewhere in that direction. 'Presumably there are as many of those now as there ever were, if not more — which means as many adults driven to harm children.'

'So the non-natural deaths are a bigger proportion of the total number,' said Charlie. That made sense.

'I would say so, yes. Though, because I'm not a statistician, I'm not sure whether that's the same thing or slightly different from saying that a reported crib death is more *likely* to be a homicide now than fifty years ago. Statistics might be helpful when you're looking at populations, but they can

455

be horribly distorting if you try to apply them to individual cases. I'm very precise when I talk about these things, which is why it's frustrating when fools misrepresent me.' Duffy sounded more resigned than angry. 'You'll have heard my famous quote: "so unlikely, it borders on impossible"?'

Charlie nodded.

'It's that more than anything else that's going to seal my fate at the GMC,' said Duffy. 'How could I say something so inaccurate and prejudicial about the odds of two siblings being crib deaths, without having firm statistical evidence to back it up? Simple: I didn't say it. I tried to explain what I'd meant, but Helen Yardley's barrister wouldn't let me speak. The exact question put to me was, "Is it possible that Morgan and Rowan were both victims of crib death?" It was *that* question to which I replied with the words I'm now universally hated for, but I wasn't talking about the two-crib-deaths-in-one-household aspect of the situation. On that, I'd have said that for two babies from the same family to be SIDS deaths would be uncommon, but quite possible if there was a medical condition in the family — a genetic predisposition, a history of heart arrhythmias.'

Judith Duffy leaned forward in her chair.

'When I said "so unlikely, it borders on impossible", I meant *given what I'd seen through the microscope* — nothing to do with number of crib deaths per family. I'd studied both boys' files in detail and found what I regarded as incontrovertible evidence of non-natural death in both cases — repeated attempts at smothering, salt poisoning, a bilateral skull fracture . . . Russell Meredew claims a baby can fracture its skull by falling off a sofa; I beg to differ. For Morgan and Rowan Yardley to have sustained the damage I saw and for it not to have been inflicted . . .' She frowned and laughed simultaneously, as if trying to work it out all over again. 'It's as likely as someone with a bone poking out through the skin of their arm not having a broken arm — so unlikely that, yes, it borders on impossible.'

Automatically, Charlie wondered if there was any weird syndrome that might make an arm-bone protrude from the skin without being broken. Acute skin shrinkage? Hole-in-the-flesh disorder?

'Being certain doesn't necessarily make me right, of course,' Duffy added. 'Humility's as important as compassion in my line of work. I made some bad mistakes: I originally said, in the case of Rowan Yardley, that blood results shouldn't be relied upon. Then later, when I found out about Morgan, who also had unbelievably high blood salt, and when I looked at the whole symptom picture, I changed my mind. Taken in isolation, perhaps, high serum sodium could possibly be explained away, but . . . Also, I didn't know, when I said it, quite how high Rowan's blood salt levels were. Another mistake I made was to allow a coroner friend of mine to tell me Marcella Hines' death had to have been natural causes, because he knew Angus Hines and the Hineses were "a lovely family".'

Charlie noticed that Duffy seemed more at ease talking about the things she'd done wrong than about wrongs done to her.

'When Nathaniel Hines turned up on my autopsy table four years later, I panicked. Had I relaxed my usual vigilance and taken Desmond . . . the coroner's word for something when I shouldn't have, and had another baby now been murdered as a result of my giving both Ray Hines and Desmond the benefit of the doubt? It was my worst fear, and I suppose that made me more likely to believe it was exactly what had happened. I went into over-protective, over-cautious mode, and as a result . . .' She tailed off, staring past Charlie into space.

'As a result?' Charlie prompted gently.

'I made a dreadful error in Ray's case. She didn't murder either of her children, but I told the court she did. My defensiveness was partly to blame.' Duffy smiled. 'I used to be very defensive. By the time Nathaniel Hines died, Laurie Nattrass's media onslaught against me had been raging for some time. I was determined not to be cowed by him. To say Nathaniel Hines was a crib death when I had doubts would have felt like a defeat. I suppose I wanted to show the world that mothers can be a very real danger to babies, and it's not just something I invented out of wickedness and because I enjoy ruining people's lives. And I *did* have doubts — I was told on good authority that Ray had suffered from post-natal depression and nearly jumped off a window ledge. What if I'd said natural causes, and the Hineses had had another baby and it had ended up dead too?'

'You and Ray had lunch together on Monday,' said Charlie. Seeing Duffy's surprise, she added, 'That's one of the reasons I'm here. The DI who's SIO on Helen Yardley's murder thinks it's odd that the two of you would spend time together.'

'It's only odd if you look at the world in a limited and limiting way,' said Duffy.

'Yup, that would be our DI.'

'Believe it or not, Ray and I are now good friends. I contacted her when she got out of prison, via her solicitor.'

'Why?' Charlie asked.

'To apologise. To admit that I'd been less than objective in her case. She was the one who suggested meeting. She wanted to tell me the truth about what had killed her babies. She believed it was the DTP-Hib vaccine, in both cases. After listening to her for half an hour, I was inclined to think so too.'

'But . . .'

'Her lawyers didn't bring it up at the trial because all their expert witnesses threatened to deny it, and, with no medical expert to say it was a possible cause of death, they'd have looked stupid. Ironically, if they'd come to me, I'd instantly have thought twice about Marcella and Nathaniel's deaths being murder. At least I hope I would,' Duffy amended. 'I like to think I would have woken up at that point.'

'But Ray's lawyers didn't go to you, because you were the bad guy, giving evidence for the other side.'

Duffy nodded. 'Angus Hines' mother has Lupus. There's a history of crib death in his extended family. That suggests a hereditary auto-immune problem. Plus, a reliable witness saw both Marcella and Nathaniel have a seizure almost straight after they were vaccinated. Vaccine damage — fitting, in particular — would account for all the things I saw: brain swelling, bleeding in the brain . . .'

'That ought to have come out in court. Even if they thought all the doctors would disagree with it.'

'Oh, I'm sure Julian Lance was right about that — that's Ray's lawyer. Everyone admits in theory that a small percentage of babies will react badly to a vaccine and in some cases die — there's even a body called the Vaccine Damage Payment Unit — but when it actually happens, in my experience, everyone closes ranks and says, "It wasn't the vaccine — that's perfectly safe, trialled and tested." '

Duffy smiles suddenly. 'You know, the first time I met Ray after she was released, she thanked me for caring enough about her children not to bow to the pressure I was under — Laurie Nattrass's pressure — and say they died naturally when it wasn't what I believed. That's what she said, even though she ended up going to prison because of my testimony.'

'Do you know where Ray's staying at the moment?' Charlie asked.

461

'Not the address,' said Duffy. She patted her knees. For a second, Charlie mistook it for an invitation to sit on her lap. Then Duffy said, 'I feel as if I've been talking about myself for an awfully long time. I'd like to hear about you.'

'I've told you about my fall from grace.'

'I'm sorry you had to yell the details through my letterbox,' said Duffy. 'Do you want to talk about it? *Have* you ever talked about it? I don't mean the bare bones of what happened, I mean the emotional impact —'

'No,' Charlie cut her off.

'You should.'

'Even if I don't want to?'

'Especially then.' Duffy looked alarmed, as if a reluctance to discuss past traumas was a symptom of a fatal illness. 'Keeping any kind of emotional damage locked inside you is a big mistake. Pain has to be expressed and really *felt* before it can dissolve.' Duffy half rose from her chair and moved it closer to Charlie's before sitting again. 'It was two years before I could bring myself to talk about Sarah Jaggard's trial,' she said. 'I had to be taken to court in an armoured van and escorted in through a back entrance. I knew then that there was no way she'd be convicted. By 2005, Laurie Nattrass had made me a household name, and not in a good way. My presence as an expert witness for the prosecution was enough to secure an acquittal for Jaggard. People screamed abuse at me in court, the jury stared at me as if they wanted me dead . . .'

A loud ringing sound interrupted her: the doorbell.

'I'll leave it. I'm not expecting anyone. I'd rather talk to you, and listen to you.'

Charlie hesitated. Could she tell this virtual stranger how she'd spent most of the past three years feeling? Should she? 'No, get it,' she said.

Duffy looked disappointed, but she didn't argue. Once she'd gone, Charlie stood up and put on her jacket quickly, before she could change her mind. She grabbed her bag and made her way towards the kitchen. She heard Duffy in the hall, sounding polite but firm, saying, 'No, thanks,' and 'Really, I'm sure. Thank you.'

Charlie stepped out into the hall at exactly the same moment as she heard the shot, saw the gun, and saw Duffy fall backwards, her head cracking on the uncarpeted stairs.

The man in the doorway turned and pointed his gun at Charlie. 'Get on the floor! Don't move!'

■ ■ ■ ■

'I can't have seen it, can I? She was innocent all along.' Leah Gould raised her voice to make herself heard above the noise in the café. She'd told Simon to meet her here — across the road from her office. Gould hadn't worked for Social Services for seven years. She'd taken maternity leave, then, when her daughter went to school, she'd got a job as a receptionist for a timber company, where she still worked.

'Only you know what you saw,' said Simon.

'But why would she have tried to smother her daughter if she didn't kill her two boys? She wouldn't, would she? Either she's a killer or she's not, and she wouldn't have had her convictions cancelled or whatever if she was guilty.'

'Why do you say that?'

Leah Gould took a bite of her cheese and onion toastie as she considered the question. Simon was starving. Soon as he was alone, he'd get himself something to eat. He hated eating in front of strangers.

'It's like Laurie Nattrass says: the courts'll do anything to avoid saying they made a mistake. They only admit they're wrong when they're forced to, when it's such a bad mistake that they can't deny it.'

'So because Helen Yardley won her appeal, she must have been innocent?'

Leah Gould nodded.

'Before the appeal — what did you think then?'

'Oh, I thought she'd done it. Definitely.'

'How come?'

'Because of what I saw her do.' More chomping on the toastie.

'What you *didn't* see her do, you mean?'

'Yeah. But I thought I did. It was only later I realised I couldn't have.'

Simon's hunger was making him more impatient than he would have been otherwise. 'Do you know anything about any of the three judges that heard Helen's appeal?'

Leah Gould looked at him as if he was crazy. 'Why would I know about any judges?'

'Do you even know their names?'

'Why would I?'

'Yet you trust them more than you trust your own eyes.'

Leah Gould blinked at him. 'What do you mean?'

Simon would have liked to prise the toastie from her fingers and kick it across the room. 'Helen Yardley's convictions were overturned because they were deemed unsafe. It's not the same thing as saying she's innocent. The appeal judges didn't necessarily think she was innocent of murder, though they might have done. One might have done, or two, or all three — they could have had the same opinion or different opinions.' This was useless. 'I'm interested in what *you* believe, based on what you saw.'

'I think she must have been giving her baby a cuddle, like she said.'

Something was missing here. Leah Gould had expressed no regret whatsoever. 'The evidence you gave in court was a big part of the prosecution's case,' said Simon. 'You claimed you saw Helen Yardley try to smother her daughter. You were asked if it could have been a cuddle — a mother in turmoil at being separated from her only surviving child, clinging on to that child — you said no.'

'Because that was what I thought at the time.'

Was guilt an emotion that only intelligent people felt?

'It wasn't just me. There was a policeman there. He saw it too.'

'Giles Proust?'

'I can't remember his name.'

'His name was Giles Proust. He disagreed with you in court. He described what he witnessed that day as an ordinary cuddle.'

Leah Gould shook her head. 'I was looking at him, not at Helen Yardley. He was watching her with Paige. That's when I first knew something was wrong. I saw his eyes change, and he looked at me, like he couldn't do anything and wanted me to stop it. That's when I looked at Helen and the baby and . . . saw what I saw. And I did stop it.'

'You stopped an attempted smothering? By taking Paige Yardley away from her mother?'

Leah Gould's lips thinned in disapproval. 'Are you winding me up? I've told you, I don't think that *now.* I'm telling you what I thought *then.*'

'And you thought, *then,* that DS Proust saw what you saw?'

'Yeah.'

'Then why did he say the opposite in court? Why say he saw only a cuddle?'

'You'd have to ask him.' No curiosity in her expression; not even a flicker of interest.

'I suppose if you could be wrong about what you saw Helen Yardley do, you could equally be wrong about Giles Proust. Maybe you misinterpreted the look he gave you;

467

maybe he was thinking about what he was going to have for his tea that night.'

'No, because he looked petrified. I thought: what kind of policeman can he be if he gets the willies so easily?' She shook her head, her mouth assuming the shape of disapproval once again. 'I mean, he should have stopped it, really. He shouldn't have relied on me.'

'Though now you believe there was no "it" to stop,' Simon reminded her.

'No,' she agreed, looking uncertain for a second. She pushed the last corner of the toastie into her mouth.

'In that case, what would have made Proust look so scared?'

'You'd have to ask him that.' *Chew, chew, chew.*

Simon thanked her and left, couldn't wait to get away. He turned on his mobile. Sam Kombothekra had left a message. Simon rang him back from the car. 'What happened with Leah Gould?' Sam asked.

'She's a bovine waste of space.'

'Nothing useful, then?'

'Not really,' Simon lied. He felt as if a huge weight had been lifted. He'd got exactly what he'd been hoping for. Leah Gould had changed her mind because it was no longer fashionable to believe Helen Yard-

468

ley was a murderer — simple as that. Simon was certain Gould *had* seen Helen try to smother Paige, and that Proust had seen it too.

Proust must have fallen for Helen's grieving mother act at the first time of exposure, fallen for *her.* He believed she was innocent, and he was always right — that was the one fact he knew about himself, above all others. And he had to *stay* right, even when he witnessed the attempted murder of Helen's third child. His preconceived ideas made it impossible for him to take the action that needed to be taken; he was powerless — as powerless as he'd been making everyone around him feel ever since. With one frantic look, he put the responsibility for saving Paige Yardley's life onto Leah Gould, then resumed the pretence: Helen's innocence, his rightness. He lied at the trial, but told himself he was doing the opposite.

In his heart, he must have known the truth. If he hadn't once visited Helen in prison, as Laurie Nattrass claimed . . .

Deep down, the Snowman had to know how grievously wrong he'd been. Was he afraid of it happening again, in as serious a situation? Was that why he needed everyone to pretend his judgement was flawless?

Knowing all this — knowing the Snowman didn't know he knew — had shifted the balance of power between them in Simon's mind. He no longer felt sullied and threatened by the dinner invitation. Charlie was right: he could easily say he didn't want to have dinner with Proust. Or he could accept, turn up with a bottle of wine and tell Lizzie Proust the truth about the man she'd married.

He had the power now — ammunition. It didn't matter that he couldn't prove it; he knew he could destroy the Snowman any time he wanted to.

'You on your way back, then?' Sam asked, pulling Simon out of his victory trance.

'After I've grabbed a sarnie, yeah.'

'Gibbs spoke to Paul Yardley.'

'Poor sod.'

'Gibbs?'

'Yardley. First he loses three kids, then someone offs his wife, then Gibbs engages him in conversation.'

'He's now admitting he rang Laurie Nattrass before he rang an ambulance. Apparently Nattrass told him to say he rang the ambulance first.'

'Did he, now?' said Simon thoughtfully.

'Not ringing the ambulance straight away looks bad, he said. He told Yardley we'd do everything we could to pin Helen's murder on him. "The filth always frame the husband if they can, and in your case they'll be especially keen to." '

'For fuck's sake!'

'Gibbs thought Yardley was telling the truth,' said Sam. 'Nattrass isn't stupid — he must have known we'd do a telephony check on the Yardleys' line.'

'You think he told Paul Yardley to lie because he wanted us to suspect him? He says to Yardley, "Say this and they won't suspect you", while secretly thinking, "Say this and they *will* suspect you"?'

'I don't know.' Sam sounded worn out. 'What I *do* know is that in the course of their conversation, Yardley told Nattrass about the strange card he'd found on Helen's body, sticking out of her pocket. And wait till you hear this: Sellers spoke to Tamsin Waddington, Fliss Benson's friend, who told him Nattrass had been sent the sixteen numbers too — she saw the card on his desk on 2 September, a month before Helen Yardley was shot. He said he had no idea who'd sent it to him.'

'What?' Simon leaned forward in his car seat, sounding the horn by mistake. He mouthed, 'Sorry,' at two women who turned to glare at him. 'So when Paul Yardley rang Nattrass and told him about the card in his

471

dead wife's pocket . . . ?'

'Nattrass should have been straight on the phone to us, scared of being the killer's next victim, yes. Even if he wasn't afraid for himself, when he found out Fliss Benson had been sent a similar card, he should have . . .'

'I spoke to Benson about the card,' said Simon. 'She took it into Nattrass's office and showed it to him, asked him what he thought it meant. He can't have told her about the card Paul Yardley found on Helen's body — Benson didn't mention it to me, and I think she would have. Come to think of it, Nattrass can't have told her about the card *he'd* been sent — she'd have mentioned that too.'

'Would she?' said Sam dejectedly. 'Fliss Benson's agenda in all this is starting to worry me. We can't find her, we can't alibi her for Monday . . .'

'If Benson's a killer, I'm Barack Obama.'

'Sellers and I were in her office this morning. She'd left her email inbox up on the screen. While we were there, someone emailed her a photo of Helen Yardley's hand, holding a card like the others — same numbers, same layout — and a copy of *Nothing But Love.*'

'What?' First a card, then a photograph of

472

a card . . .

'You said Benson was odd,' said Sam. 'Do you think there's a chance she could be sending these things to herself?'

Simon thought about it. 'No.'

'I've just got off the phone with Tamsin Waddington,' Sam told him. 'She's worried Benson's losing her grip on reality — that's how she put it. Benson rang her with a story about having locked Angus Hines in her flat, and could Tamsin go round with the spare key and let him out. When Tamsin got there half an hour later, the flat was empty — no Angus Hines in sight, no broken windows, everything the same as always. Hines couldn't have opened a window and climbed out — Tamsin found them all closed and locked, which could only be done from inside. Benson also apparently claimed she'd been to Rachel Hines' parents' house in Twickenham.'

'Did she lock them in too?'

'Rachel Hines' parents don't live in Twickenham, never have. I've just spoken to them. They live in Winchester.'

'So Laurie Nattrass and Fliss Benson join a police artist's drawing of a skinhead with bad teeth at the top of our "most wanted" list. Are we stepping up our efforts to track them down?'

'*I* am.'

'There's one more thing I need to do, then I'm straight back,' Simon told him.

'A sandwich, right?' Sam sounded suspicious. 'Please tell me you're talking about buying a sandwich.'

'Two more things,' said Simon, and pressed the 'end call' button.

Ten minutes later, he was sitting on a sofa made out of beanbags at number 16 Bengeo Street, drinking bitty yellow lemonade and watching horse-racing with four-year-old Dillon White. So far his attempts at conversation had been unsuccessful; the boy hadn't uttered a word. It occurred to Simon that one thing he hadn't tried was talking about horses. 'You've seen this race before, then?' he asked. Dillon nodded. His mother had mentioned that it was a recording, Dillon's favourite of a large collection. 'Because his favourite horse always wins,' she'd added, laughing.

'I wonder who's going to win,' Simon said.

'Definite Article.'

'Do you think? He might not.'

'He always does in this one.'

'It might be different this time.'

The boy shook his head. He wasn't interested in Simon and his strange ideas, didn't take his eyes off the screen.

'What do you like about Definite Article, then?' What was it Proust had said? *Try, try and try again, Waterhouse.* 'Why's he your favourite?'

'He's a vegetarian.'

Simon didn't know what answer he'd been expecting, but it wasn't that. 'Are you a vegetarian?'

Dillon White shook his head, eyes still on the screen. 'I'm plain.'

Plain as in unattractive? No, he couldn't mean that. Wouldn't all racehorses have pretty much the same diet? Weren't they all herbivores?

Stella White appeared with a large cardboard box, which she placed at Simon's feet. 'Here's my box of fame,' she said. 'There's quite a bit about JIPAC and Helen in there — hope it helps. Sweet-pea, I've told you, you're not plain — that's the wrong word. You're white. Or pink, if you want to be pedantic about it.'

'He said Definite Article was a vegetarian,' Simon whispered to her over her son's head, feeling like a grass.

Stella rolled her eyes. She sank down to her knees so that she was the same height as Dillon. 'Sweet-pea? What does vegetarian mean? You know what it means, don't you?'

'Black skin.'

'No, it doesn't. Remember, Mummy told you? Vegetarian means you don't eat meat.'

'Ejike's a vegetarian and he's got black skin,' said Dillon tonelessly.

'He's got very dark brown skin, and yes, he's a vegetarian — he doesn't eat meat — but that doesn't mean all brown-skinned people don't eat meat.' Stella looked at Simon. 'If it's not about horses he doesn't listen,' she said, standing up. 'I'll leave you to it, if you don't mind. Give me a shout if you need an interpreter.'

Simon decided to give the boy a break, let him watch his racing in peace for a few minutes. He took a handful of newspaper cuttings from the box Stella had given him and started to look through them. It didn't take him long to piece together her story: she'd been diagnosed with terminal cancer at the age of twenty-eight. Instead of feeling sorry for herself and waiting to die, she'd immediately set about turning herself into a world-class athlete. She'd sought out marathons, treks, triathlons; set herself physical challenge after physical challenge; raised hundreds of thousands of pounds for charities, including JIPAC.

Halfway down the pile, Simon found an article about Stella's relationship with Helen

Yardley: how they'd met, how much they relied on one another's friendship. There was a picture of the two of them together: Helen was sitting on the floor at Stella's feet and Stella was leaning in over her shoulder. The headline was 'Two extraordinary women'. Beneath the photograph, a quote from Helen had been isolated and put in a box, separate from the main text: 'Knowing Stella won't be here for ever makes me appreciate her more. I know she'll always be with me, even once she's gone.' There was also a quote from Stella in a box, further down the page: 'I've learned so much about love and courage from Helen. I feel as if my spirit will live on through hers.'

Except that Stella White wasn't the one who died. Helen Yardley was.

'So you like Definite Article because he's got black skin?' Simon asked Dillon.

'I like black skin. I wish I had black skin.'

'What about the man you saw outside Helen's house on Monday, when you were on your way to school? Do you remember?'

'The man with the magic umbrella?' Dillon asked, still watching the horses.

So now it was magic. 'What's an umbrella, Dillon?' If vegetarians were people with brown skin, and white people were plain . . .

'You hold it over your head to keep the

rain off you.'

'Did the man with the magic umbrella have black skin?'

'No. Plain.'

'You saw him outside Helen Yardley's house on Monday morning?'

Dillon nodded. 'And beyond. In the lounge.'

Simon leaned forward. 'What does beyond mean?'

'Bigger than infinity,' said Dillon, without hesitation. 'One, two, three, four, five, six, seven, eight, nine, ten, eleven, twelve, thirteen, fourteen, fifteen, sixteen, seventeen, eighteen, nineteen, ninety-nine, a hundred, a thousand, infinity, beyond. To infinity and beyond!' The last part had to be a quote; Dillon sounded as if he was mimicking someone.

'What's infinity?' Simon asked.

'The biggest number in the world.'

'And beyond?'

'The even biggest number of days.'

Days.

'Definite Article's going to win.' Dillon's face lit up. 'Watch.'

Simon did as he was told. When the race was over, Dillon reached for the remote control. 'We can watch it again from the beginning,' he said.

'Dillon? When did Definite Article win the race we've just watched? Did he win it today?'

'No. Beyond.'

'You mean a long time ago?' said Simon. He was sorry Dillon was only four; he'd have liked to buy him a pint. Gently, he took the remote control from the boy's hand. For the first time since Simon had arrived, Dillon looked at him. 'The man you saw outside Helen Yardley's house on Monday morning — it wasn't the first time you'd seen him at Helen's house, was it? You saw him before, a long time ago. Beyond. The first time you saw him it was raining, wasn't it? That was when he had his magic umbrella. Not on Monday.'

Dillon jerked his head up and down: clear agreement.

'You saw him in the lounge. Was anyone else there, in the lounge?'

More affirmative head-jerking.

'Who?'

'Auntie Helen.'

'That's good, Dillon, that's really helpful. You're doing brilliantly. You're doing as well as Definite Article did when he won that race.'

The boy's face lit up, and he beamed. 'I love Definite Article. When I grow up, I'm going to live with him.'

'Was it just Auntie Helen and the man, in the lounge?'

'No.'

'Who else was there?'

'Uncle Paul. The other man. And a lady. And Mummy and me.'

'How many people altogether?'

'All of us.' Dillon nodded solemnly.

Simon looked around the room, hoping to see something that might help him. Then he had an idea. 'One: Auntie Helen,' he said. 'Two: the man with the umbrella . . .'

'Three: the other man,' Dillon took over, speaking quickly. 'He had an umbrella too, but it wasn't magic so he left it outside. Four: Uncle Paul, five: the lady, six: Mummy, seven: me.'

'The other man and the lady — can you tell me anything about them, what they looked like?'

'They were plain.'

'What was magic about the magic umbrella? In what way was it magic?'

'Because it came from outer space and if you opened it you could make a wish and that wish would definitely come true. And when the rain dripped off it onto the carpet, it turned it into a magic carpet and you could use it to fly to space whenever you want and come back whenever you want.'

'Is that what the man told you?'

Dillon nodded.

'This man, did he . . . did he have hair on his head?'

'Vegetarian.'

'Brown hair? Did he have funny teeth?'

Dillon started to nod, then stopped and shook his head.

'You can say no if no's the right answer,' Simon told him.

'I want to watch the race again.'

Simon gave him back the remote control, and went in search of Stella. He found her in a small utility room at the back of the house, ironing and singing under her breath. She looked thin, but not unwell — not like someone with terminal cancer. 'Do you remember taking Dillon round to the Yardleys' house a while back?' he asked her. 'Helen and Paul were there, you and Dillon, two other men and one other woman. It was raining. The two men both had umbrellas.'

'We went round there all the time.' Stella frowned. 'The place was always full of people. Everyone wanted to be around Helen. People flocked to her.'

'All the time?'

'At least twice a week, she'd have us

481

round, usually with other people — her family, friends, other neighbours. Anyone, really. It was more or less open house.'

Simon tried not to look disappointed. He'd assumed that the occasion Dillon had described would stand out in Stella's memory; he should have realised not everyone was as unsociable as he was. Simon had never had seven people in his living room at the same time, not once. The most he'd had was three: him and his parents. The prospect of a neighbour crossing his threshold would unsettle him to the point of sleepless nights, he suspected. He had no problem with meeting people in the pub; that was different. 'Can you remember anyone you ever met at Helen's house telling Dillon his umbrella was magic?'

'No,' said Stella. 'I wouldn't put it past Dillon to have made that up. It sounds like the invention of a four-year-old to me — not something a grown man would say.'

'He didn't make it up,' said Simon impatiently. 'A man said it to him, the same man you saw outside Helen's house on Monday morning, the same man who killed Helen. I need you to put down that iron and start making a list of everyone you can remember meeting at the Yardleys' house — anyone at all, even if you only caught their first name, even the vaguest physical description.'

'In the last . . . how long?' Stella asked.

How many days ago was beyond?

'Ever,' Simon told her.

Charlie didn't know how long she'd been lying face down on Judith Duffy's kitchen floor. It could have been ten minutes, thirty, an hour. When she tried to speculate about time, it seemed to warp, loop back on itself. Duffy's murderer sat cross-legged beside her, holding the gun against her head. She was all right — she kept telling herself that — not injured, not dead. If he was going to shoot her he'd have done it by now. All she had to do was not look at him. That was the only thing he'd said to her: 'Don't look at me. Keep your head down if you want to stay alive.'

He hadn't told her she couldn't speak. Charlie wondered if she ought to risk it.

She heard a series of beeps. He was ringing somebody. She waited for him to start talking.

Nothing. Then the beeps again. 'Fucking answer,' he muttered. A smashing sound told Charlie he'd hurled his phone at the wall. She saw it in her peripheral vision: it had fallen and landed by the skirting board. She heard him start to cry, and the knot in her stomach tightened. If he lost control, that was bad news for her — he was more likely to kill her, deliberately or by accident.

'Stay calm,' she said, as gently as she could. She was on the point of losing control herself. How long would this go on for? How long had it gone on already?

'I shouldn't have done what I did,' he said. A Cockney accent. 'She didn't deserve it.'

'Judith Duffy didn't deserve to be shot?' He could have been talking about Helen Yardley. *Check.* Simon would say check.

'You get too far in and then you can't get out,' he said, sniffing. 'She did her best. So did you.'

Charlie's stomach turned over. When had she done her best? She didn't understand, and she needed to — understanding might save her life.

He murmured an apology. Charlie swallowed a mouthful of bile, thinking this was it, this was when he was going to shoot her.

He didn't. He stood up, walked away. Charlie raised her head and saw him sitting on the stairs next to Judith Duffy's body. Apart from his shaved head, he looked only a little like the police artist's sketch she'd seen in the paper — his face was a different shape. Charlie was sure it was him, though.

'Head down,' he said without feeling. His

mind wasn't on Charlie. She had the sense that he didn't care any more what she did. Lowering her head only a fraction, she watched as he pulled a card out of his jeans pocket and placed it on Judith Duffy's face.

The numbers.

Seeing him coming towards her again, she twisted away from him, but all he wanted was his phone. Once he had it, he headed for the front door. Charlie pressed her eyes shut. Being so close to free and safe was hard to bear. If it went wrong now, if he came back . . .

The front door slammed. She looked up and he was gone.

PART III

15
MONDAY 12 OCTOBER 2009

'If I'd known Marcella was going to die when she was eight weeks old, I'd never have left her, not for a second,' says Ray. 'I thought I'd have her for the rest of my life, years and years to spend together. Instead, I only had her for eight weeks. Fifty-six days — it sounds even shorter when you say it like that. For nine of those days I wasn't even there. I walked out on my own daughter when she was only two weeks old. For years that made me hate myself. Sorry, should I look at you or at the camera?'

'The camera,' I tell her.

She inspects her fingernails. 'You can always find a reason to hate yourself if you're that way inclined. I thought I was getting better at forgiving myself, but . . . I hated myself yesterday, when I found out what had happened to Judith. I'm not overly fond of myself today.' She tries to smile.

'Did you kill Judith Duffy?' I ask. 'Because

if you didn't, then it's not your fault that she's dead.'

'Isn't it? People hated her because of me. Not only me, true, but . . . I contributed, didn't I?'

'No. Tell me about walking out on Marcella.' I sense she's trying to put it off; talking about Judith Duffy is easier.

She sighs. 'I'm scared you'll judge me. Isn't that ridiculous? It didn't upset me at all when we first met and you told me you thought I'd probably killed my children.'

'Because you knew you hadn't, so my judgement didn't apply to you. But now you're going to tell me about something you did do.'

'I used to have a business: PhysioFit. It was extremely successful. Still is, even though I'm no longer part of it. As well as individual clients, we provided physio-therapy for businesses. Let's use your company as an example — Binary Star. Let's say your boss decides that you all spend too long sitting hunched over your computers. She can see your posture dete-riorating, you're all complaining of back pain, the office is a breeding ground for vertebral occlusions. Boss decides to intro-duce routine physiotherapy provision for all Binary Star employees. First thing she does

490

is invite several companies to tender for the contract.'

'Like PhysioFit?'

'Exactly. Assuming this is years ago, when I was still involved, what would happen is that my colleague Fiona and I would go to Binary Star's offices and give a presentation that would last two or three hours. Fiona would talk about the business side of things, contract terms — all the stuff that I'm not particularly interested in. Then when she'd done her bit, it would be my turn to talk about the physiotherapy itself: what it involves, what conditions it's particularly useful for, how it's not only a last resort for chronic pain but something that can be preventative as well. I'd talk about postural training and cranial osteopathy — that was my specialism — and about the foolishness of believing, as some people do, that a machine can provide physiotherapeutic services as efficiently as a human being. Of course it can't. When I put my hands on someone's neck, I can feel —'

She breaks off, giving me a sheepish smile. 'Sorry. I nearly forgot I wasn't actually tendering for your business.' She turns back to the camera. 'You get the idea, I'm sure.'

'You sound passionate about it,' I tell her. 'I'd employ you.'

'I loved my work. I didn't see why having children meant I had to give it up. When I found out I was pregnant with Marcella, the first thing I did was put her name down for a good local nursery. She was going to start when she was six . . . months. Sorry.'

'It's okay. Take your time.'

Ray makes a tunnel out of her hands, breathes through it. 'That seemed a good compromise to me: six months at home with my baby, then back to the clinic.' She turns to look at me again. 'Lots of women go back to work when their babies are six months old.'

I point to the camera.

'The day after I had Marcella, Fiona came to visit me in the hospital. She brought a box of duck-shaped biscuits with pink icing on them, and some good news from Phys-ioFit: we'd been asked to give a presentation to the bosses of a Swiss company with offices all over the world, several in the UK. It was a massive contract, one that would enable us to make the leap from national to international, and we really wanted it. We got it, too. They chose us over the competition. Sorry, I'm jumping ahead.'

'No problem. I'm going to edit all this, so don't worry about chronology.'

'I want to see the finished version before

it's aired,' Ray says immediately.

'Of course.'

She seems to relax. 'The company's headquarters were in Geneva. That's where Fiona was going, to meet and impress the bosses. "It's such a shame you're on maternity leave," she said. "I've heard you do your spiel a thousand times, and I can recite it word-for-word, but it won't be the same as having you there." She was right. It wouldn't have been the same without me. Of the two of us, I was better with people, and this was such an important presentation for PhysioFit. I couldn't bear the thought of not being there. I couldn't convince myself that my presence might not make the difference between success and failure.'

I think I know what's coming. She went. Obviously she went. But why the lies? Why not tell the story she's telling me to Julian Lance? In court?

'I asked Fiona when the meeting was scheduled for. She told me the date. It was three weeks away. Marcella wouldn't even be a month old when Fiona set off for Switzerland. I . . . this is the part you might not understand. You'll think I should have been straightforward about what I wanted to do, said "Sorry, everyone, I know I've just had a baby, but I simply must jet off on a business trip — toodlepip, see you all soon." '

'Angus would have been unhappy about it?'

Would he have been as unhappy as I was when I worked out how he'd escaped from my flat? I got back to find a note from Tamsin stuck to my fridge: 'No Angus Hines anywhere on the premises, unless you've got a hidden room I don't know about. RING ME!'

I didn't. I couldn't bring myself to contact Angus, either, and ask him how he managed to escape without breaking glass or drilling through a wall. I got my answer this morning when I snuck back home for some things I needed, and bumped into Irina, my cleaner, who is also a PhD student at King's. 'How can you lock your friend in the flat?' she demanded. 'Not nice, Fleece. He was so embarrassed to ring me to say what had happened.'

I ran to the drawer where I keep business cards, spare lightbulbs, takeaway menus and tea towels (there's not much space in my flat, so things have to double up). Irina's card was there — 'The Done and Dusted Cleaning Company' — on top of a neat pile that hadn't been quite so neat last time I'd opened the drawer.

I rang Angus and left a message saying I needed to speak to him as soon as possible. When he called me back, I yelled at him for rummaging in my kitchen drawers and demanded to know why he'd lied to Irina. Why did he tell her I'd forgotten all about him and locked the door behind me by mistake? Why hadn't he smashed a window and climbed out, like anyone normal would have? He said he didn't want to embarrass me by giving my cleaner the impression that I was the sort of person who would lock a man in her flat. 'I don't know what you're so angry about,' he said. 'I was trying to be considerate. I assumed you'd rather not have a broken window.' I told him that wasn't the point, resenting his implication that Irina would have abandoned me in a flash if he hadn't gallantly concealed my true nature from her. The whole conversation made me feel twitchy and paranoid. I tried not to imagine him methodically going through my business cards, putting each one to the back of the pile until he found Irina's.

I haven't told Ray any of this. I don't think Angus has either.

'My plan, at first, was to be straightforward,' she says to the camera. 'It wasn't even a plan — it was simply the obvious thing to do. That night, Marcella and I left hospital and went home. I opened my mouth to tell Angus a dozen times, but the words wouldn't come out. He would have been horrified. Not that he wasn't supportive of my work — he was. He was all in favour of me going back when Marcella was six months old, but going to Switzerland when she was three *weeks* old was completely different. I knew exactly what he'd have said. "Ray, we've just had a child. I've taken a month's unpaid leave because I want to spend time with her. I thought you did too." Then there were all the things he *wouldn't* have said but that I'd have heard anyway: "What's wrong with you? What sort of heartless wife and mother are you that you'd sacrifice precious family time to go on a business trip? Don't you think you ought to get your priorities right?" '

Ray sighed. 'Over and over, I had the argument in my head: "But this is so important, Angus." "And my work, that I'm taking a month off from, that's not important, I suppose?" "No, but if we miss out on this contract, it'll be a disaster." "Let Fiona take care of it — she's perfectly capable of handling it on her own. And it wouldn't be a disaster. PhysioFit's thriving — there'll be other clients. Why does this one matter so much?" "Because it *does,* and I'm determined to go, even though I can't justify it." "And if another equally crucial business opportunity presents itself the week after, and the week after that? You'll be equally determined to go, won't you?" '

'Was he right?' I ask.

She nods. 'I was obsessed with PhysioFit. That's why it was so successful, because every detail mattered to me so much. My drive and passion were so relentless that the company had to do well — it had no other option. Angus doesn't understand what that feels like. He's never had his own business. Yes, he took a month off when Marcella was born, but so what? Were fewer people going to buy the newspaper because Angus's photographs weren't in it? Of course they weren't. I don't know, maybe they were,' she contradicts herself. 'The difference is that for Angus, work's something he does to earn money. He doesn't live and breathe his job the way I did. His passion in life was me. And Marcella and Nathaniel.' She falls silent.

'So you never told him about Switzerland? But you went, didn't you?'

'Yes. I rang Fiona the following day and told her I was going with her, but not to say a word to anyone. She laughed at me, called me a loony. Maybe she was right.'

I think about myself, hiding from the police in order to make sure I can do my work uninterrupted.

'It wasn't only Angus I was frightened of telling. There was also my mum and his mum, both of whom were being super-helpful devoted grannies. If I'd been honest about my plans, I'd have had to have the same argument with them, too. The thought of their concerned faces, the earfuls I'd have got about what I should and shouldn't do — it made me want to curl up under my duvet and never come out. I wanted to enjoy Marcella, not waste time being told how wrong and stupid I was, and having to defend myself. My mum and Angus's mum are both lovely, but they're also rather fond of knowing what's good for everybody they care about. When they join forces, it's a nightmare.'

I try not to notice how lonely this story is making me feel. My mum goes to great lengths to avoid commenting on anything I do, terrified she might offend me. I can ask her what she fancies watching on TV, and she'll jerk like a rabbit that's heard a gunshot and squeak, 'Whatever you want, you decide,' as if I'm a fascist dictator who might chop off her head if she says *Taggart* instead of *Come Dine with Me.*

'As the days went by, I realised I had to make a plan, quickly,' Ray tells the camera. 'Fiona had booked my plane tickets. I'd already lied to everyone about how painful I found breastfeeding. It was a doddle, for me and Marcella, but I pretended it was agony so that I could get her onto formula milk, knowing I was going away. I needed a story to get me out of the house for three days without any hassle. I racked my brains but could think of literally nothing, until one day I realised that was it: nothing was the answer.'

I wait. It's crazy, but I'm tempted to turn to the camera and ask its opinion. *How can nothing be the answer? Do you know what she's talking about?*

'Want to hear my brilliant plan?' says Ray. 'Step one: start acting vacant and dazed. Get everyone speculating about what might be wrong with you. Step two: pack a bag suddenly and, when asked where you're going, keep repeating, "I'm sorry, I have to go. I can't explain it — I just have to go." Step three: go. Go to a hotel near Fiona's flat, because Fiona's flat is obviously the first place Angus will look, so you can't stay there. Stay at the hotel for a few nights, phoning home regularly to reassure everyone you're okay. When they ask you where you are, refuse to tell them. Say you can't come back yet. Step . . . I can't remember what step I'm on.'

'Four.'

'Step four: go to Geneva. Do the presentation with Fiona. Get the contract. Step five: go back to London, this time to a different hotel. Ring home, say you're starting to feel better. Instead of being monosyllabic, engage with your husband. Ask after Marcella. Say you're missing her, you can't wait to see her again. It's true; you can't. You'd rush back straight away if you could, but it has to be gradual. Everyone would be suspicious if you were suddenly normal again — well, as normal as you ever were, which, come to think of it . . .' She smiles sadly.

'Step six: after a night or two — a gradual recovery — go back home. Say you don't want to talk about why you left or where you've been. All you want is to be with your family and get on with your life. Step seven: when your mother-in-law harangues you mercilessly for what she calls "a proper explanation", climb out of your bedroom window and smoke a fag in mid-air, enjoying the knowledge that you're not scared of anything any more. You've proved to yourself that you're free, and from now on you'll do what you want.' Ray looks at me. 'Self-ish, or what? But I *was* selfish when Marcella was born — I don't know if it was the hormones, but I was suddenly much more selfish and self-obsessed than I'd ever been before. It felt like . . . like an *emergency*, like I had to do what *I* wanted, look after me, or I'd be taken over, somehow.'

'If you really felt you needed to go to Switzerland, Angus should have let you go,' I say.

'Step eight: after a policeman's pulled you in through the open window, imagining he's saved your life, and once a shrink has told your mother and your mother-in-law to leave you alone for the sake of your mental health, here's your chance to improve by leaps and bounds. Another day or so and you're happy, full of energy. You got away with it. You've calmed down a bit, the post-natal panic has faded, and now all you want is to have a lovely time with your husband and your beautiful, sweet daughter. Your husband's thrilled — he was so worried about you; he thought he'd lost you. And now here you are: home again, his. Let the celebrations begin.' She looks anything but joyous.

'Wouldn't it have been easier to tell the truth and take the flak?'

501

Ray shakes her head. 'You'd think so, wouldn't you? But it wasn't. It was easier to do what I did, much easier. It must have been, because I was able to do it, having been *un*able to force myself to tell the truth.' She chews the inside of her lip. 'The way I did it, I avoided responsibility. A zombie who doesn't know what she's doing attracts pity, whereas a successful businesswoman who casts aside her newborn baby to empire-build attracts only condemnation. Angus understands. It's funny, he wouldn't have done then, but he does now.'

'He knows?'

Ray nods.

Interesting. He doesn't know she's staying at Marchington House and he still doesn't know about the pregnancy, but she's told him about her eight-step plan to drive him half-mad with worry. What kind of relationship is theirs, exactly?

'I miss Fiona,' Ray says quietly. 'She's still running PhysioFit. She's got another business partner now. Before my trial I wrote to her and begged her not to say anything about Switzerland to anyone, and she never did. She thought I'd done it, though — thought I was guilty like everyone else did.'

'When did you tell Angus about Switzerland?' I ask.

'Remember the hotel I told you about, where I stayed when I left prison?'

'The one with the urn pictures in every room?'

'When I couldn't stand it there any longer, I went to Angus, to our house in Notting Hill. That was when we sorted everything out. I'd . . . I'd like Angus to be here when I tell you about that,' she says. 'I'd like us to tell it together, because that's when everything came to a head and things finally started to get better between us.'

I try to look pleased for her.

'Don't be cross with him for giving you a hard time, Fliss. He's very protective of me, and he doesn't always treat people fairly.' Ray's tone suggests this is a legitimate lifestyle choice rather than a character defect. 'Neither do I, I suppose. We all do what we have to do, don't we? I lied to my lawyers, lied to Laurie Nattrass, lied in court — was that fair?'

'Why did you? Why did you tell two different lies about those nine days you were away? Why did you lie about how long it took you to let the health visitor in, and about who you phoned first, Angus or the ambulance?'

My phone buzzes. A message. I grab my bag, as sure as I can be that it won't be

Laurie. Having ignored twenty calls from me in the past two days, he's unlikely to have decided twenty-one's my lucky number. *Please don't let it be him.*

'I lied in court because —' Ray begins.

'I have to go,' I tell her, staring at my mobile. There on the tiny screen is all the proof I need. I've no idea what to do with it. One press of a button would delete it, but only from my phone. Not from my mind.

'Someone important, by the look of it,' says Ray.

'Laurie Nattrass,' I say neutrally, in the way I might say any old name.

16
12/10/09

They had a profiler.

They also had seven detectives from London's Major Investigation Team 17, none of whom looked as if they'd appreciated being relocated to Spilling. Simon felt uneasy having them around; his only experience of detectives from the Met, last year, had been a wholly negative one.

The profiler — Tina Ramsden BSc MSc PhD and most of the rest of the alphabet after that — was petite, muscular and tanned, with shoulder-length blonde hair. Simon thought she looked like a professional tennis player. She seemed nervous, her smile veering towards the apologetic. Was she about to confess that she hadn't the foggiest? Simon had a few ideas if she didn't.

'I always introduce my profiles by saying there are no easy answers,' she began. 'In this case it needs saying all the more emphatically.' She turned to Proust, who was leaning against the closed door of the packed CID room looking as displaced as a disadvantaged character from the Goldilocks story: *Who's been standing in my spot?* 'I'll apologise in advance, because I'm not sure how much help I can be with the externals that might enable you track this person down. I wouldn't want to commit myself to age group, marital status, ethnicity, social and educational background, occupation . . .'

'Let me commit to some of them on your behalf,' said Proust. 'Baldy's been seen by two eye-witnesses: Sarah Jaggard and our very own Sergeant Zailer. We know he's between thirty and forty-five, white and shaven-headed. We know he has a Cockney accent. There's some disagreement over the shape of his face . . .'

'I discounted the two eye-witness statements,' Ramsden told him. 'A profile's useless if you create it around any givens. You look at the crimes — nothing else.'

'*Could* he be a thirty-nine-year-old white Cockney skinhead?' Proust asked her.

'On age, race, job, qualifications, whether he's single or in a long-term relationship — all the externals, as I said — I wouldn't want to commit,' said Ramsden. 'Character-wise, he could be a loner, or very sociable on the face of it.'

'It isn't particularly helpful to hear that he could be anyone, Dr Ramsden,' said the Snowman. 'We've had more than three hundred names suggested since Baldy's ugly mug desecrated the papers on Saturday, and another hundred or so wild theories about the sixteen numbers, each more preposterous than its predecessor.'

'You want to know what I'm able to tell you about this man? The most striking thing about him is the cards he sends and leaves at the scenes of his crimes. Sixteen numbers, the same ones in the same order in each instance, arranged in four rows of four.' Ramsden turned and pointed to the board behind her. 'If we look at the ones retrieved from the bodies of Helen Yardley and Judith Duffy, and the one Sarah Jaggard found in her pocket after she was attacked, we see that our man likes to be neat and consistent. Wherever the number four occurs, for example, it's written in exactly the same way. Same with the number seven, same with all the numbers. The distances between the digits are also highly regular — they look as if they've been measured with a ruler to get them exactly the same. The rows-and-columns layout tells us that he values order and organisation. He hates the idea of doing anything in a haphazard way, and he's proud of the workmanship that goes into his cards — that's why the card he uses is thick, high-quality, expensive. Though, unfortunately for you, widely available.'

A few groans from the poor sods who'd spent days establishing precisely how wide that availability was.

'Obsessed with order could mean military,' Chris Gibbs suggested. 'Bearing in mind he's killing with a US army-issue gun.'

'It could mean military,' Ramsden agreed. 'It could also mean jail, boarding school, any institution. Or you could be looking for someone who grew up in a chaotic, unstable family and reacted against it by becoming highly controlled. That's not unusual — the child whose bedroom's unbelievably tidy, but outside his bedroom door, the place is a tip: crockery flying, parents screaming at each other . . . But, as I said, I don't want to talk about the externals because I'm not sure about them. The only thing I want to get specific about is the mindset, at this stage.'

'You say he's highly controlled,' Simon called out from the back of the room. 'Assuming he's got family and friends, won't they have noticed that about him? Sometimes mindset spills over into externals.'

'Aha! Thank you, Detective . . . ?'

'Waterhouse.' Simon disliked many things, but high up on the list was having to say his name in front of large groups of people. His only consolation was that no one knew how hard he found it.

'I didn't say he was highly controlled,' said Ramsden, looking pleased with herself. 'I said he might have come from a family that was both practically and emotionally messy.'

'And he might have reacted against it by becoming highly controlled.' Simon knew what he'd heard.

'Yes,' she said, giving him what he took to be some kind of waiting signal with her hand. 'I'd say it's likely that *at some point,* this man was a control freak who ordered his life successfully. But his control's slipping. That's the most interesting thing about him. He's doing everything he can to stay on top of things, he's clinging to the illusion that he's in control, but he isn't. He's losing his grip on the real world, on his own position within it — possibly on his sanity. The same cards that reveal his meticulousness and love of order simultaneously reveal his irrationality and inconsistency. Think about it: he shoots Judith Duffy and Helen Yardley dead and leaves cards on their bodies. He attacks Sarah Jaggard with a knife, not a gun, in broad daylight on a busy street, not in her home, *doesn't* kill her, and places a card in her pocket. He also sends cards to two television producers, whom he neither attacks nor kills, and then, to one of the producers, he goes on to send a photograph of Helen Yardley's hand holding a card as well as a copy of her own book.'

Ramsden surveyed the room to check they were all taking her point. 'He thinks he's got a carefully thought-out plan, but *we* can see that he's all over the place, flailing around without a clue what he's doing, imagining everything's under control when in fact it's accelerating all the time in the direction of uncontrollability. His mental trajectory is like a shopping trolley sliding down a steep slope, picking up speed as it goes, the wheels twisting this way and that — you know what the wheels on shopping trolleys are like, how hard they are to steer.'

A few people laughed. Simon didn't. He wasn't about to take Tina Ramsden's conclusions on trust just because she could demonstrate that she'd been to the supermarket.

'He thinks he's clever coming up with this square of numbers that seems to defy interpretation,' she went on, 'but they could be entirely meaningless. He could be mad, or just plain stupid. Possibly he's got a nihilistic streak: he wants to waste police time by getting you all to chase a meaning he knows isn't there. Or — and I know this isn't very helpful, I know it sounds like I'm saying anything's possible — he might be highly intelligent, and the sequence of numbers could be meaningful, containing a clue either to his purpose or his identity.' Ramsden paused to take a breath. 'But even if that's the case, his choice of card recipients tends to suggest that the part of his brain that knows what it's about is in the process of being swamped by the trolley-rolling-downhill part.'

Simon opened his mouth, but she was in full flow. 'Sarah Jaggard and Helen Yardley — okay, a clear link. Both were tried for child murder. Judith Duffy? Not only does she have nothing in common with Jaggard and Yardley, she's their polar opposite: their opponent in an extremely high-profile controversy. Can't your man decide what side he's on? Laurie Nattrass and Felicity Benson — they're linked to all three women via their work, but otherwise there's no common ground. Nattrass and Benson aren't personally involved in any child death cases.'

511

'Let me stop you there,' said Proust. 'It transpires that Miss Benson is personally involved. We found out this morning that her father lost his job over a Social Services cock-up that led to a child death. He committed suicide.'

'Oh.' Ramsden looked a little flustered. 'Well, all right, so Benson's linked to child deaths via her work *and* her personal life. In a way, that proves my point even more. Basically, there's no pattern. These people have nothing in common.'

'Are you serious?' said Simon. 'I can describe the pattern in a sentence: he's sending cards to people connected to the Binary Star documentary and the three cases featured in it: Yardley, Jaggard, Hines.'

'Well, yes, obviously in one sense you're right,' Ramsden conceded. 'Those cases loom large in his mind — I wouldn't deny that. In fact, I'd say he's likely to be someone who's suffered a severe emotional trauma in connection with this issue. He could have lost a child himself, or a sibling, or a grandchild, to crib death perhaps, which might have led to an obsession with people like Helen Yardley and Judith Duffy. But to kill both of them when, as I said, they're polar opposites in terms of what they stand for — there's no sense or rationale to it. And the most worrying thing about the trolley-rolling-downhill type of killer is that he tends to accelerate before he smashes himself to smithereens.'

'Sorry to interrupt, but . . .' Simon waited to see if the Snowman would silence him. He didn't. 'You're talking as if the killer's link to the Binary Star film might be purely thematic — he's a bereaved parent and that's why he's become obsessed with the three cases.'

'I only said he *might* . . .'

'The connection has to be stronger and closer than that,' said Simon. 'I don't know how thoroughly or how recently you were briefed, but Laurie Nattrass sent out an email on Tuesday to everyone connected to the documentary — doctors, nurses, lawyers, police, the women and their families, people at the BBC, JIPAC people. At 3 p.m. on Tuesday, nearly a hundred people got Nattrass's email saying Fliss Benson would be taking over as executive producer on the film. Until that moment, she had no connection whatsoever to these cases. One of the people who received the email must be the card-sender. He or she read Nattrass's message, immediately prepared a card for Benson and went out to post it to her at Binary Star, where she received it on

Wednesday morning.'

'Dr Ramsden, all those on the receiving end of Nattrass's email have alibis for one or both of the murders,' said Proust. He might as well have waved his arms in the air and yelled, 'Listen to me, don't listen to him'. 'Without exception. And unless DC Waterhouse thinks Sarah Jaggard and Sergeant Zailer are conspiring to mislead us — which I won't be so naïve as to rule out, for he has a penchant for wrong-headed thinking — then we don't need to bother with "he or she". We know Baldy's a man.'

'Yes,' said Simon, 'and we know he killed Duffy and attacked Jaggard, but we don't know he's the card-sender, and we don't know he's our shooter for Yardley.'

'We're assuming he is, though, right?' said DS Klair Williamson.

'Yes,' said Proust firmly.

'I'm not,' Simon told her. 'Dillon White took one look at the police artist's image and said no, he wasn't the man with —'

'Warning: DC Waterhouse is about to refer to a magic umbrella,' the Snowman snapped.

'There are two people involved in these killings,' Simon presented his theory as if it were fact. He'd worry about maybe being wrong later. 'One's Baldy. The other could be a man or a woman, but let's say "he" to make it easier. That's who's in charge, that's the brain behind the operation: clever, controlling and *in* control. That's who sends the cards, knows what the sixteen numbers mean and is challenging us — letting us know we'll only catch him if we can prove we're as smart as he is.'

'So we've got Baldy and Brainy.' Colin Sellers laughed.

'The Brain could be paying Baldy to do his bidding,' said Simon. 'Or maybe Baldy's loyal to him for some reason, owes him favours. When Baldy said, "You get too far in and then you can't get out," he was talking about the hold the Brain has over him. The Brain, the card-writer and sender, is the person Baldy tried to phone from Judith Duffy's house, after he'd shot Duffy. He wanted instructions about what to do with Charlie, whether to kill her or not.'

'If you're right, then alibis or no alibis, anyone who received Laurie Nattrass's email on Tuesday could be the card-sender,' said Sam Kombothekra. 'Or anyone at Binary Star, anyone either Nattrass or Benson told about Benson taking over as executive producer.'

'I'd expect the Brain to have a firm alibi for Saturday, when Duffy was killed, but not for Monday,' said Simon. 'I think, after Baldy messed up with Sarah Jaggard and got interrupted by a passer-by, the Brain decided he'd take care of Helen Yardley himself. Then, with Duffy, he gave Baldy another chance. Maybe he'd given him a bit more training in the interim.'

'I apologise unreservedly for DC Waterhouse,' said Proust. Tina Ramsden started to shake her head, and opened her mouth to speak, but the Snowman drowned her out as he warmed to his favourite theme: Simon's worthlessness. 'You have absolutely no reason for thinking two people are involved in these attacks. A four-year-old boy who talks nonsense and the fact that Baldy tried to ring somebody? He could have been phoning his girlfriend to tell her he wanted toad-in-the-hole for his supper. He could have been phoning anyone for any reason. Well, Dr Ramsden? Couldn't he?'

Ramsden nodded. 'When people find themselves in threatening situations, seeking reassurance is a common impulse.'

'What, so he's there in Judith Duffy's hall with a dead body in front of him, holding Charlie at gunpoint, and he suddenly takes a break to ring a mate because he wants the comfort of a familiar voice?' Simon laughed. 'Come on, you're not serious?'

'I'm not convinced there's any loss of control or irrationality involved,' said Chris Gibbs, standing up. 'Whether there's two of them or only one, how do you know everything that's happened so far isn't part of a plan? Just because Helen Yardley and Judith Duffy have both been killed . . .'

'Which strongly suggests the killer doesn't know which side he's on, or maybe he's reached the point where he can only remember names now, and not which side *they're* on,' said Tina Ramsden. Simon approved of her willingness to muck in. She gave as good as she got on the interruption front, and didn't seem to take offence if people disagreed with her.

'It doesn't necessarily suggest that,' Gibbs looked around for support. 'Let's say the killer's Paul Yardley . . .'

'Would that be the same Paul Yardley who has alibis for Monday and Saturday, no Cockney accent and a full head of hair?' Proust asked. 'Talking of full heads of hair, Gibbs, you appear still to have one. Didn't I tell you to shave it off?'

Simon willed Gibbs to go on with his theory, and he did. 'Let's say Yardley's belief in Helen's innocence wasn't as rock solid as he made out it was — maybe he *did* have his doubts, even if he never expressed them.

Most men in his position — let's face it, you wouldn't *know*, would you? Not for sure. All Yardley knows is that his life's been ruined — first he lost his two sons, then his wife was sent to prison, then he lost his daughter to Social Services. Getting out of bed in the morning must have been a struggle for him, but while Helen's still in prison, he's got a purpose, and that's to get her out. Once she's out, there's nothing more to aim for. She's busy with Laurie Nattrass and JIPAC. What's Yardley thinking about, day after day, while he fixes people's roofs?'

'Facias and sofits?' Sellers suggested with a chuckle.

'Make your point, Gibbs,' said the Snowman wearily.

'What if Yardley's the type for brooding? What if he starts thinking someone ought to pay for all the shi— all the suffering he's been through? Whose fault was it? Helen's, perhaps, if she killed his sons. Duffy's? Thanks to her, Yardley lost his wife for nine years.'

'What about Sarah Jaggard?' Simon asked.

'Sarah Jaggard wasn't killed,' said Gibbs. 'She wasn't even hurt. Maybe she was never supposed to be. Maybe she was supposed to mislead us, to broaden the focus out, from Helen Yardley's case to other similar cases.'

'Let me get this straight,' said Proust, smoothing down the lapels of his jacket. 'You're saying Paul Yardley killed his wife and Judith Duffy because he wanted to punish someone for wrecking his life and, of the two of them, he wasn't sure which was to blame?'

Gibbs nodded. 'Possibly, yeah. Or there's another way it could work: not as an either-or, but he blames them both equally: Helen for the loss of his two boys, and Duffy for the loss of Helen and his daughter.'

Simon thought both these possibilities stretched credulity somewhat, but he was pleased Gibbs had put them forward. At least one of his colleagues had an imagination.

Tina Ramsden was smiling. 'You seem to have a whole team full of psychological profilers,' she said to Proust. 'Are you sure you want me to stick around? I have to say, I can't agree about there being two people involved.' She looked at Simon and shrugged apologetically. 'And I'm as certain as I can be about the escalating irrationality. The card-sender as the rational, controlled one doesn't work because the way he distributes the cards isn't regular — sometimes he posts them, with no violence, or emails them in photographic form; other times he leaves them in the pockets of murder victims.'

'The numbers, if we knew what they meant, would lead to us identifying him,' said Simon. 'It's a challenge. He's sending cards to people he sees as his intellectual equals, people he thinks ought to be clever enough to crack his code.' Seeing Sellers open his mouth, Simon raised a hand to stop him. 'Were you about to say that Helen Yardley was a childminder, and Sarah Jaggard's a hairdresser — not great intellects, as the Brain would see it, and yet they got a card each?'

Sellers nodded.

'No. They didn't. Helen Yardley and Sarah Jaggard *did not* get a card each. Judith Duffy *did not* get a card.' Simon listened as the sound of confusion filled the room. 'Yardley, Jaggard and Duffy weren't the intended recipients of those three cards. Anyway, Duffy was dead by the time she got hers. Those three cards were for us: the police. Our job is to work out what's going on, right? Laurie Nattrass and Fliss Benson's work consists of trying to unearth the truth that lies behind three miscarriages of justice.'

He had everyone's full attention. 'We need to start looking at the two things separately, the violence and the cards. In the first category, two women were murdered and one threatened at knifepoint, all three connected with crib death murder cases. In the other category, five cards were sent, three to the police, however indirectly, and two to documentary-makers — all five to people the Brain thinks might be intelligent enough to make sense of his code. There's nothing irrational about any of it,' Simon addressed Tina Ramsden. 'It makes perfect sense, and it means that Fliss Benson and Laurie Nattrass aren't at risk of attack, any more than we all are.

'The choice of victims for the violent behaviour also makes sense: Helen Yardley and Sarah Jaggard were picked for a reason, though not the most obvious one. The Brain wanted to show us that we'd underestimated him. That's why Judith Duffy was the next victim, not Ray Hines.' Simon was sure he was right about this. 'We forced his hand. On Saturday, Sam here was quoted in every national newspaper as saying that our working assumption was that the killer was a self-appointed punisher, attacking guilty women he thinks have got away with their crimes. But that's *not* his motivation, and later that same day he proved it to us by killing Judith Duffy — I'm using "he" as shorthand for "he or she", remember.'

'Sexist,' a female voice mumbled.

'He may have had no reason to kill Duffy whatsoever, other than to demonstrate to us that we were wrong about his motivation,' said Simon. 'Just as he's meticulous — writing his number fours and number sevens the same every time — he's also objective, or so he thinks: fair and clear-thinking. He wants us to notice that about him. He's probably someone who associates vigilantism with extreme stupidity — unwashed, tabloid-reading hang-em-and-flog-em proles. He wouldn't like the symbolism of that, because he's clever, and if I had to guess, I'd say he's middle-class. He wants us to realise that any justice doled out by him, or by Baldy on his orders, is exactly that: noble justice, not grubby revenge. By murdering the leaders of the two warring armies — Helen Yardley and Judith Duffy — he's showing us he's fair and impartial.'

Everyone stared. No one wanted to be the first to react. Proust stood with his arms folded, staring up at the ceiling, his neck almost at a ninety-degree angle. Was he meditating?

'Well, if no one else wants to jump in, I

will,' said Tina Ramsden, after nearly ten seconds of silence. She held up her notes so that everyone could see them, and tore them in half, then in half again. 'You have no idea how annoying it is to have to do this, after I sat up most of last night cobbling all this together, but I'm no use to you if I'm not honest,' she said. 'I defer to DC Waterhouse's superior analysis.'

'His what?' Proust turned on her.

Ramsden looked at Simon. 'I prefer your profile to mine,' she said.

'So you think his plan was to sweep you up in his arms and give you a good rogering?' said Olivia Zailer enthusiastically. She'd dropped everything and come to Spilling to take care of her sister after her ordeal, having first checked Charlie had no injuries that would necessitate any heavy lifting or staunching of bodily fluids.

'No idea,' said Charlie. 'All I know is, he sent me a love letter — well, a love scrap of paper — and told me to get back as early as I could on Saturday.'

'But then, when he next saw you, he didn't make a move.' Olivia wrinkled her nose in disappointment.

'The next time he saw me was just after I'd had a gun held to my head by Judith

Duffy's killer. I was too shaken up even to remember that sex might have been on the cards, and Simon was more interested in interrogating me about the man they're calling Baldy.'

Liv snorted. 'His work-life balance is like a seesaw with a concrete rhinoceros strapped to one end. Still, at least he sent you a sweet letter — that's a big step forward, isn't it?'

Charlie nodded. She and Olivia were sitting at her kitchen table, drinking tea, though Liv had brought a bottle of pink champagne. 'To celebrate you not getting shot,' she'd explained.

The sun was shining as if it couldn't tell the difference between summer and winter; Charlie had had to lower her kitchen blind. Since Simon had sent her those eleven words, the sun had shone almost constantly, even though whenever she caught the local news there were big grey clouds covering the Culver Valley. Charlie trusted her own senses; the TV people had got it wrong.

'I nearly didn't tell you about the love letter,' she said.

'*What?*' Nothing horrified Olivia Zailer more than the thought of not being told something.

'I thought you'd think it was pathetic —

not even a proper sheet of paper, the word "love" missing . . .'

'Please! How hard-hearted do you think I am?'

'We're having a bit of a feud over the honeymoon,' Charlie told her. Was she so used to scrapping with Olivia that she had to find something for her sister to attack, so that she could assume her customary defensive position? 'Simon's parents are scared of flying, so he started off saying we had to go somewhere in the UK.'

'Please tell me Simon's parents aren't going with you on your honeymoon.'

'Joking, aren't you? They get palpitations if they go as far as the bottom of the garden. No, they're scared of *Simon* flying. His mum told him she wouldn't sleep or eat for a fortnight if she knew he was going to be "going on those aeroplanes", as she calls it.'

'Stupid mad bint,' said Olivia crossly.

'Trouble is, she means it. Simon knows she *wouldn't* eat or sleep until he was safely back, and knowing he'd return to find a withered death's head where his mother used to be would spoil his fun. Though the difference, it has to be said, would be marginal.' Charlie stopped to check her guilt level: zero. 'I didn't want to spend my honeymoon in the Rawndesley Premier Inn, which is a suggestion my future father-in-law made in all seriousness . . .'

'Unbelievable!'

'. . . so we compromised. Simon agreed to go anywhere that's less than three hours' flight time, and I agreed to lie to his parents and pretend we're going to Torquay — close enough to sound safe, but far enough away that Simon can legitimately tell his mum he can't pop back for Sunday lunch.'

'I assume Kathleen and Michael know cars sometimes crash,' said Liv.

'Ah, but we're going to Torquay by train.' Charlie couldn't help laughing. 'Because people die on motorways. It's so ridiculous — Simon's in his car every day, but because this time he'd be venturing out of his mum's comfort zone . . .'

'People die in train crashes,' Olivia pointed out.

'Please don't tell Kathleen that, or we'll be forced to spend our honeymoon fortnight in her front room.'

'So where are you going?'

'Marbella — flight time just under three hours. Two hours and fifty-five minutes.'

'But . . .' Olivia's eyes narrowed. 'If you're lying to Kathleen and Michael, you could go anywhere: Mauritius, St Lucia . . .'

'I said all that to Simon, and do you know

what he said? Go on, have a guess.'

Liv closed her eyes and bunched her hands into fists, muttering, 'Hang on, don't tell me, don't tell me . . .' She looked about six years old. Charlie envied her sister's uncomplicated enjoyment of all life had to offer. 'He'd be too far away if his mum got ill and he suddenly had to fly back? I wouldn't put that sort of ruse past her, you know.'

'Good guess, but the truth is even madder: the less time Simon spends in the air, the less chance there is of him dying in a plane crash and being caught out in a lie by his parents.'

'Which would obviously be the worst thing about dying in a plane crash.' Liv giggled.

'Obviously. Without having referred to any statistics, and completely ignoring the fact that most plane crashes happen on take-off or landing, Simon's decided short-haul flights are less lethal than long-haul.'

'Can't you try to persuade him? I mean, *Marbella?*'

'I've found this amazing villa on the internet. It's —'

'But you'll have to fly to Malaga. The plane'll be full of people with "love" and "hate" tattooed on their knuckles, singing

"Oggie, oggie, oggie".' Liv shuddered. 'If it has to be less than three hours, what about the Italian lakes? You'd fly to Milan . . .'

'Is that better?'

'God, yes,' said Liv. 'No tattoos, lots of linen.'

Charlie had forgotten to factor in her sister's colossal snobbishness. 'I thought you'd disapprove of the lying, not the destination,' she said. 'Part of me's tempted to sack it and make the lie true. I do love Torquay, and I don't want there to be anything negative or complicated connected with our honeymoon. In an ideal world, I'd like to be able to tell the truth about it.'

'You can, to everyone but Kathleen and Michael. It's not as if they ever meet or speak to anyone.' Olivia unzipped her bag and pulled out four books with creased spines. 'I brought you these. I hope you're grateful, because they've bent my new Orla Kiely handbag out of shape.' She poked the bag's side with her index finger. 'I wasn't sure how long you'd be off work, but I brought enough . . .'

'I'm going back tomorrow.' Seeing her sister's crestfallen expression, Charlie said quickly, 'I'll have them anyway, though. Thanks. I'll read them in Marbella.'

Olivia adopted her strict schoolmistress

expression. 'You're not planning to read a novel until next July?'

'Are they good? Are they ones you've reviewed?' Charlie asked. She picked one up. The cover picture was of a frightened-looking woman running away from a dark unidentifiable blur behind her. Liv tended to bring her novels about women who ended up leaving the useless and frequently psychotic men they'd been wasting their lives on, and going off into the sunset with better men.

'I've got a book I want you to read,' said Charlie. She nodded at the copy of *Nothing But Love* on the table.

'A misery memoir?' Olivia slid it towards her, then made a show of wiping her fingers on her trousers. 'Did you buy it shortly after booking your flight to Malaga?'

'You can't say no,' Charlie told her. 'I've just been nearly killed — you have to be nice to me. I'd be interested to know how you think Helen Yardley comes across — as a genuine miscarriage-of-justice victim or as someone playing a part.'

'Why, do you think she might have killed her kids after all? I thought it turned out that she hadn't.'

Turned out. Liv had trouble distinguishing between real life and fiction. She opened the book at a random point in the middle and held it up close to her face. The optical effect was surreal, as if she was wearing the back cover of *Nothing But Love* as a mask. *Hello, my name's Olivia, and I've come to this party dressed as a misery memoir.*

'There are exclamation marks in it — not inside quotation marks, in the narrative,' she said, horrified. She turned another page. 'Do I really have to —'

Charlie grabbed the book. Her hands trembled, then the shakes spread to the rest of her body. 'Oh, my God. I don't believe this.' She flicked through the pages as quickly as she could. 'Come on, come on,' she muttered under her breath.

'I was reading that,' Liv protested.

The adrenaline pumping through Charlie's body made her fingers too stiff and too wobbly at the same time. She couldn't get them to work properly, and ended up turning too many pages. She flicked back and finally found the page she was looking for. This was it. It had to be.

She stood up, knocking her chair over. Yelling, 'Sorry,' over her shoulder, she grabbed her car keys and ran out of the house. As she slammed the door behind her, it occurred to her that she must look like the frightened running woman on the cover of the novel Liv had brought her, the one whose title she had already forgotten. Her brain only had room for one book's name at the moment.

Nothing But Love. Nothing But Love. Nothing But Love.

17
MONDAY 12 OCTOBER 2009

An hour and a half after leaving Marchington House, I'm standing outside the Planetarium, as instructed. I'm not sure if Laurie's late or if he's thought better of meeting me and not bothered to inform me of his change of mind; all I know is he isn't here. After twenty minutes, I start to wonder if he might have intended for us to meet inside. I check the text he sent me, which is full of his usual warmth and intimacy: 'Planetarium 2 p.m. LN.'

I'm about to go and look for him inside when I spot him walking towards me, head down, hands in his pockets. He doesn't look up until he has to. 'Sorry,' he mumbles.

'For being late, or for ignoring my calls?'

'Both.'

He's wearing a pink shirt that looks new. As far as I know, Laurie has never worn pink before. I want to bury my face in his neck and smell his skin, but that's not what

I'm here for. 'Where have you been?' I ask him.

'Around and about. Let's walk.' He nods at the road ahead, then sets off.

I follow him. 'Around and about isn't an answer.' I harden my heart, and my voice. 'I rang the JIPAC office this morning — no one there's heard from you for days. I've been to your house more than five times — you're never there. Where are you staying?'

'Where are *you* staying?' he fires back. 'Not at home.'

'You've been to my flat?' *Don't dare to cave in, Felicity. This has to be done.* 'I'm staying with Ray Hines in Twickenham, at her parents' place.'

Laurie snorts dismissively. 'Is that what she told you? Ray's parents live in Winchester.'

I think back over our conversations. I assumed Marchington House belonged to her parents because of the photo in the kitchen, of her two brothers punting down a river. Maybe the house belongs to one of the brothers.

'I'm camped out at Maya's place,' says Laurie.

'Maya?' I'm not the only one lying to the police, then. She neglected to mention that Laurie had moved in with her, when they

533

asked her if she knew where he was.

Maya's keen on pink.

'Is something going on between you?' I ask before I can stop myself.

'Is this what was so urgent that you had to talk to me immediately?' Laurie stops walking and turns on me. 'Look, I don't owe you anything, Fliss. I gave you an opportunity at work because I thought you deserved it. End of story. We had a fuck the other day, but do we have to make a meal of it?'

'Of the sex? No, we don't. There are a couple of things we do have to make a meal of, though. Three things, to be precise — three meals. Think of them as breakfast, lunch and dinner.'

'What things?'

'Let's walk,' I say, setting off in the direction of Regent's Park. I know what this means: I'll never be able to go there again after today. 'Have you been reading the papers?' I ask Laurie. 'Turns out that card someone sent me — remember the one I showed you, with the numbers on it? Whoever killed Helen Yardley and Judith Duffy put cards exactly like it on their bodies. I've spoken to Tamsin. I know you got one of those cards too. She saw it on your desk long before Helen Yardley was killed.'

'So?'

'Why didn't you mention that, when I showed you the card I'd been sent and asked you what it could mean? Why didn't you say "Someone sent me one of those too"?'

'I don't know,' Laurie says impatiently.

'I do. You knew about the card found on Helen's body, didn't you? You must have done — it's the only thing that makes sense. I don't know how you knew, but you did. My guess is that Paul Yardley told you, and you were scared. You worked out that whoever was sending the cards had moved on to killing. If they'd killed Helen, maybe you'd be next. You and Helen and JIPAC have your loyal supporters, but you've also got enemies. I found several anti-JIPAC websites yesterday, all of which claim you've created a climate of fear for doctors and paediatricians. Most of them are terrified to testify in suspected abuse cases, in case you set out to destroy them the way you did Judith Duffy.'

Laurie says nothing, just walks alongside me, head down. I'm glad I can't see his face.

'You panicked. There was no way you were going to continue with your quest for justice if it meant there might be some actual consequences for you personally, like someone trying to kill you. All that matters to you is you, right? You needed to distance yourself from the crib death murders controversy quickly, so you announced that you were leaving Binary Star, going to Hammerhead. Incidentally, I've been chatting to people at Hammerhead about you. I know when they first made you that offer you couldn't refuse: more than a year ago. Funny how you suddenly decided to accept, the day after Helen Yardley was murdered.'

I stop, so that he can confirm or deny it. He says nothing.

'You emailed everyone telling them I was taking over the film. You chose me because, if you're right and whoever ends up making that film *is* going to be a killer's next target, better that it should be someone disposable like me, someone who's never going to amount to anything anyway.'

I pick up my pace, full of furious energy. Who'd have thought anger would have aerobic benefits?

'Course, you could have gone to the police, couldn't you? Told them about the card you'd been sent, how it was the same as the one found on Helen's body. And when I showed you my card, you could have alerted me to the danger I was in. It's pretty obvious why you did neither. You couldn't risk anyone putting two and two together: your being on a killer's mailing list, and your suddenly dropping the crib death film like a hot brick. People might have concluded you were scared. The great Laurie Nattrass — scared! Imagine if that had leaked out to the press. That was why Tamsin had to go. She was the only person who knew you'd been sent those numbers; she'd seen the card on your desk.'

'Tamsin's redundancy wasn't down to me,' Laurie snaps, making me wonder if this is the first thing he's heard that he disagrees with. 'Raffi said we were overstretched, we had to make some savings . . .'

'And you suggested Tamsin as the sacrifice,' I finish the sentence for him. 'My best friend.'

We're in Regent's Park. I'd probably think it was beautiful if Laurie and I weren't having the most wretched conversation in the world.

'I had a best friend,' he says tonelessly. 'Her name was Helen Yardley. And I didn't choose you to take over the film because I thought you were disposable and wouldn't amount to anything — that's your paranoia.'

I chose you because I love you. I chose you because the film is important to me, and so are you.

'I thought you'd be easy to control. The film mattered to me, and I thought I could get you to make it the way I wanted it made.'

Oh. Right.

'You've got an inferiority complex.' He makes it sound like a disgusting medical condition, something I should be ashamed of. Surely it's a good thing that some of us are riddled with self-doubt. Don't the people like me balance out the people like Laurie?

'How could you not tell me?' I say. 'When I showed you that card, how could you not say . . .'

'I didn't want to worry you.'

'*You* were worried, enough to —'

'Do we have to analyse everything to death?' he cuts me off. 'You've done what you came to do, staked out the moral high ground.'

I reach into my bag and pull out the second draft of his *British Journalism Review* article. 'I've read this.' I thrust it at him. He doesn't take it. The pages fall to the ground. Neither of us bends to pick them up. 'I thought it was better than the first version. Scrapping those names from the list was a good move.'

Laurie frowns. 'What list?'

'The one that goes on and on.'

538

'Fuck are you talking about?'

' "Dr Duffy was responsible for ruining the lives of dozens of innocent women whose only crime was to be in the wrong place at the wrong time when a child or children died: Helen Yardley, Lorna Keast, Joanne Bew, Sarah Jaggard, Dorne Llewellyn . . . the list goes on and on." Ring any bells?'

Laurie turns away.

'One problem. In this latest draft' — I bend to retrieve the pages — 'the list doesn't go on and on. In this draft, the list is only three names long: Helen Yardley, Sarah Jaggard, Dorne Llewellyn. I'm no editor, but I think the original version's better. If you want to invoke the dozens of innocent women whose lives were ruined by Duffy, five names works better than three. So what happened? Was it a word-limit thing?'

Laurie is walking away, heading towards the boating lake. 'Why ask if you already know?' The wind brings his words back to me.

I run to catch him up. 'You deleted Lorna Keast and Joanne Bew. Keast was a single mother from Carlisle with a borderline personality. She smothered her son Thomas in 1997, and her son George in 1999. Judith Duffy testified against her, and she was found guilty in 2001. By the time Helen Yardley's convictions were quashed, you'd managed to kick up such a stink about Duffy that the CCRC was forced to act: it started to re-examine similar cases. In March this year — I'm guessing just after you wrote the first draft of your 'Doctor Who Lied' article — Lorna Keast was granted leave to appeal, which had previously been denied. Obviously the honest side of her personality was to the fore that day — she was devastated when her lawyers told her she might be in with a chance of getting out. She'd always protested her innocence up until that point, but when she heard she might soon be freed, she confessed to having smothered both her sons. She said she wanted to stay in prison, wanted to be punished for what she'd done. She wouldn't hear of having the charge changed to infanticide, which was a possibility once she'd confessed, and would have carried a lighter sentence — she wanted to be punished as a murderer.'

'What your Google searches won't have told you is that, as well as being barking mad, Lorna Keast is one of the thickest women ever to drag her knuckles along the surface of this planet,' says Laurie. 'Even if she was innocent, being found guilty and sent to prison might have been enough to convince her she was a murderer and deserved to be behind bars.' He flashes a contemptuous look in my direction. 'Or maybe she preferred the safety of prison life to having to fend for her brainless self on the out.'

'Or maybe she was guilty,' I say.

'So what if she was? Does that make Judith Duffy any less dangerous? Of course I knocked Keast's name off the list — I don't want people reading the article and thinking that if Duffy was right about her then she might have been right about all the others. She *wasn't* right about Helen, Sarah Jaggard, Ray Hines, Dorne Llewellyn . . .' Laurie grabs my arm and swings me round to face him. 'Someone had to stop her, Fliss.'

I shake off his hand. 'What about Joanne Bew?'

'Bew was granted leave to appeal.'

'Whoa, let's rewind a bit. What was she in prison for?'

Laurie's mouth flattens into a thin line.

'Why don't I tell us the story? Joanne Bew murdered her son Brandon . . .'

'Let's fast-forward a bit,' Laurie parodies me. 'There was a retrial and she was acquitted.'

'Then why delete her name from the article? Surely she's your best illustration of the harm irresponsible experts can do: first she's convicted, all because of a doctor's flawed testimony against her, then she's retried and acquitted once that same doctor's been exposed by the wonderful Laurie Nattrass. Come on, she's JIPAC's perfect poster girl, isn't she? No? Why not, Laurie?'

He's staring at the boating lake as if it's the most fascinating expanse of water in the world.

'Joanne Bew, former landlady of what's now the Retreat pub in Bethnal Green, murdered her son Brandon in January 2000,' I say. 'She was blind drunk and at a party when she did it. There was a witness: Carl Chappell, also very drunk. Chappell was on his way to the loo, and he passed the door of the bedroom where Joanne had put six-week-old Brandon down to sleep. He happened to look into the room, and he saw Joanne kneeling on the bed with a cigarette in one hand and her other hand pressed over Brandon's nose and mouth. He saw her hold her hand there for a good five minutes. He saw her press down.'

'As you say, he was smashed. Had form too: GBH, ABH . . .'

'At Joanne's first trial in April 2001, Judith Duffy gave evidence for the prosecution. She said there were clear signs of smothering.'

'Which is the only reason the jury believed Chappell,' says Laurie. 'His eye-witness account tallied with a respected doctor's expert opinion.'

'Lots of other people also testified against Joanne. Friends and acquaintances said she never referred to Brandon by his name — she called him 'The Mistake'. Warren Gruff, Joanne's boyfriend and Brandon's father, said she mistreated the baby from day one — sometimes when he was screaming with hunger, she'd refuse to give him milk and try to feed him chips or chicken nuggets instead.'

'She was a bad mother.' Laurie shrugs and starts to walk. 'Doesn't make her a murderer.'

'True.' I catch him up, keep pace with him. I imagine myself linking my arm through his and nearly laugh. He'd regard that as such an affront; I'd love to see his reaction. I'm tempted to do it, just to prove to myself I have the nerve. 'Bew was already a convicted killer, though, wasn't she?' I say instead. There's no surprise on Laurie's face. He knew I knew, and he thinks that's it, that's my trump card. That's why he's not worried. 'She and Warren Gruff had both served time for the manslaughter of Bew's sister, Zena. They punched and kicked her to death in the kitchen of Gruff's flat after a family row, and each blamed the other. At Bew's first trial in 2001, Zena's death wasn't mentioned — someone must have thought it might prejudice the jury. I can't think why, can you? I mean, just because a woman punches and kicks her sister to death, and is a bad mother — as you say, it doesn't mean she must have murdered her baby. Though, as it happened, and even without the inconvenient Zena anecdote, all twelve jurors *did* believe Joanne Bew was a murderer.'

'You ever watched a criminal trial?' says Laurie scornfully.

'You know I haven't.'

'You should try it some time. Watch the jurors being sworn in. Most of them can't read the oath without stumbling over the words. Some can't read it at all.'

'What about the jury that acquitted Joanne Bew second time round, in May 2006? How stupid were they? They *were* told that Bew had served time for the manslaughter of her sister. What they didn't know was that she'd previously been convicted of murdering Brandon. They didn't know it was a retrial.'

'That's —'

'Standard. I know.' I walk as close to Laurie's side as I can without touching him. He moves away, widening the gap between us. 'Judith Duffy didn't testify against Bew the second time,' I continue with my story. 'By May 2006, you'd made sure no prosecutor in need of an expert would touch her with a bargepole. I wonder if the jury would have believed Carl Chappell, though, if he'd testified again that he watched Bew smother Brandon?'

'They didn't get a chance to believe or disbelieve him,' says Laurie. 'Chappell updated his statement to the effect that he was so drunk that night, he wouldn't have known his own name, let alone what he did or didn't see.'

'You can tell he's a drinker, can't you?' I'm nearly there, nearly at the end of this protracted worst moment of my life. 'The bulbous nose and the broken veins. He's a prime candidate for one of those makeover shows, don't you think? *10 Years Younger.*'

Laurie stops walking.

I carry on, talking to myself. I don't care if he can hear me or not. 'I can't watch that programme now Nicky Hambleton-Jones doesn't present it any more, can you? It's not the same without her.'

'You've met Chappell?' Laurie's by my side again. 'When?'

'Yesterday. I'd found an article on the internet that suggested he used to be a regular at the Retreat, or the Dog and Partridge as was, so I paid a visit there and asked if anyone knew him. Quite a few people did, and one told me which betting shop he'd be in first thing this morning. That was where I found him. Is that how you found him too, when you needed to track him down and offer him two thousand pounds in exchange for a revised statement, a statement full of lies that would secure a not-guilty verdict for Joanne Bew and another point to you in the battle against Judith Duffy?'

'Look, whatever —'

'Chappell wasn't there when you popped in, so you left a note for him with someone who said they'd pass it on. And they did.'

'You can't prove any of this,' Laurie says. 'You think Carl Chappell keeps notes from years back, just in case the British Library wants to acquire his archive one day?' He laughs, pleased with his own joke. I remember Tamsin telling me a few months ago that the British Library had paid some obscene amount of money for Laurie's papers. I wonder how much they'd pay for a long letter to him from me, detailing exactly what I think of him. Maybe I should get in touch with them and ask.

'Chappell didn't keep the note,' I say, 'but he remembers what happened, and he remembers where you told him to meet you. If only you'd picked Madame Tussauds, or the National Portrait Gallery, or here in Regent's Park, by the boating lake.'

Laurie must think I'm enjoying this. I'm hating every second of it.

'What message did you leave for him, exactly? Was it a bit like the one you sent me?' I pull my phone out of my bag and hold it up in front of his face. 'Was it "Planetarium 2 p.m., LN."? "Dear Mr Chappell, Meet me outside the Planetarium — there's two thousand quid in it for you"?'

'You think I gave him the two grand to *lie*? You really think I'd do that — pay a man to pretend he didn't witness a murder when he did?'

'I really think you'd do that,' I tell him. 'I think you did what you had to, to make it look as if Joanne Bew was yet another innocent woman in prison thanks to Judith Duffy.'

'Cheers for the vote of confidence,' says Laurie. 'The truth, if you're interested, is that Carl Chappell witnessed nothing whatsoever the night Brandon died. He was a mate of Warren Gruff's, Brandon's dad. Gruff put him up to lying at Joanne Bew's first trial. He'd made it clear he expected Chappell to lie again at the retrial, which was what Chappell, who can't think for himself, was planning to do. I paid him to tell the truth.'

I try to remember what exactly Carl Chappell told me. *He gave me two big ones to say I hadn't seen nothing.* Have I misjudged Laurie? Have I just done to him what I'm accusing him of doing to Judith Duffy: invented whatever story I needed to in order to condemn him?

'The two grand took care of Chappell's gambling needs, but it did nothing to alleviate his fear of Gruff, who's a thug,' says Laurie. 'You ought to track him down, ask him how much I paid him, out of my own pocket, for a promise not to beat Chappell to death if he gave a new statement.'

'How much?' I ask.

Laurie beckons me to come closer. I take a step towards him. He reaches for my hand, closes his fingers around my phone. I try to hang on to it. I fail.

'What good's that going to do you?' I ask. He can delete the text he sent me, but not my memory of it. I can tell anyone I want to that Laurie told me to meet him at the Planetarium, just as he told Carl Chappell, and probably Warren Gruff too.

'No good,' he says. 'No good at all.' Running towards the lake like a fast-bowler, he bowls my phone into the water.

18
12/10/09

'Olivia was holding the book up, spread open.' Charlie demonstrated for Proust's benefit. Simon and Sam watched too, though they'd already heard the quicker version of the story. 'I was sitting across the table from her — my eyes must have been on the back cover. I wasn't aware of looking at it — one minute I was daydreaming, the next I was thinking, "Hang on a minute, those look familiar." '

'Every published book has a thirteen-digit ISBN number printed on its back cover and title page,' Simon took over. 'The ISBN for Helen Yardley's *Nothing But Love* is 9780340980620, the last thirteen numbers of our number square. As well as a card, the book was in the photograph emailed to Fliss Benson, to help her make the connection.'

'The first three numbers on the cards — 2, 1 and 4 — we think that's a page number,' Sam told Proust.

'It has to be,' Charlie agreed. 'What else can it mean?' She placed *Nothing But Love* on the desk, open at page 214.

The Snowman jerked his head back, as if someone had put a plate of slugs in front of him. 'It's a poem,' he said.

'Read it,' said Simon. 'And the paragraphs above and below it. Read the whole page.' How much time did they waste, on each case, getting Proust up to speed? His rigidity was the problem: he liked to be told things in a certain way — formally and in stages, with each logical progression clearly highlighted. No wonder Charlie hadn't wanted to be part of the delivery committee on this one. 'Can't you tell him?' she'd groaned. 'Whenever I try to explain something to him, I feel like I'm auditioning to present *Jackanory.*'

Simon watched the Snowman as he read: a study of forehead compression in slow motion, with the frown lines becoming more and more pronounced. Within seconds, the inspector's face had lost several centimetres in length. ' "What flutters still is a bird: blown in/by accident, or wild design/of grace, a taste of something sweet — The emptied self a room swept white." Would someone like to tell me what it means?'

'I'm not sure the meaning matters, from

our point of view,' said Charlie. 'On the same page, there's a reference to a journalist from the *Daily Telegraph* who went to Geddham Hall to interview Helen Yardley. We think that's the significant —'

'Track him or her down,' said Proust.

'We already have, sir,' said Sam. 'Geddham Hall keep a record of —'

'You have? Then why not tell me so, Sergeant? What's the point of a perishing update if you fail to update me?'

'The journalist was a Rahila Yunis, sir. She still works for the *Telegraph*. I spoke to her on the phone, read her page 214 of *Nothing But Love*. At first she was very reluctant to comment. When I pressed her, she said Helen Yardley's recollection of their interview at Geddham Hall wasn't correct. Helen did have a favourite poem written in her notebook, or journal, or whatever it was, but Rahila Yunis said it wasn't that "room swept white" poem. She's going to check her old files, but she thinks the poem Helen Yardley copied into her notebook and claimed to be fond of was called "The Microbe".'

'We could only find one poem with that title,' said Charlie. 'It's by Hilaire Belloc.'

'Hilaire spelled h-i-l-a-i-r-e,' said Simon. 'As in hilairious@yahoo.co.uk.'

'Are you going to make me read another poem?' Proust asked.

'I'll read it to you,' said Charlie.

' "The Microbe is so very small
You cannot make him out at all,
But many sanguine people hope
To see him through a microscope.
His jointed tongue that lies beneath
A hundred curious rows of teeth;
His seven tufted tails with lots
Of lovely pink and purple spots,
On each of which a pattern stands,
Composed of forty separate bands;
His eyebrows of a tender green;
All these have never yet been seen —
But scientists, who ought to know,
Assure us that they must be so . . .
Oh! Let us never, never doubt
What nobody is sure about!" '

Simon was trying hard not to laugh. Charlie had read the poem as one might to a five-year-old. The Snowman looked startled. 'Give me that,' he said.

Charlie handed him the sheet of paper. As he stared at it, his lips silently formed the words, 'never, never doubt'. Eventually he said, 'I like it.' He sounded surprised.

'So did Helen Yardley, according to Rahila

Yunis,' said Sam. 'It's not hard to see why. For "scientists", read "doctors". She must have had Judith Duffy in mind. Duffy can't have been sure Morgan and Rowan were murdered, because they weren't. And yet she never, never doubted.'

'I like it.' Proust nodded and handed the poem back to Charlie. 'It's a proper poem. The other one isn't.'

'I disagree,' said Simon. 'But that's not the point. The point is, why was Rahila Yunis so unwilling to talk at first? Why not say, as soon as Sam had read her the extract, that Helen Yardley had lied? And why *did* Yardley lie, in the book? Why did she pretend that it was "Anchorage" by Fiona Sampson that meant so much to her, and that she'd talked to Rahila Yunis about, when it was Hilaire Belloc's "The Microbe"?'

No reply from Proust. He was mouthing silently again: *never, never doubt.*

'Why aren't we in there?' Colin Sellers had been trying to lip-read what Simon, Sam, Charlie and Proust were saying.

'Because we're out here,' said Chris Gibbs.

'Only Waterhouse'd get away with bringing his girlfriend.'

Gibbs snorted. 'Why, do you want to take

554

all your girlfriends to visit the Snowman? His office isn't big enough to squeeze them all in.'

'How's it going on the name-that-Baldy front?' Sellers asked, not expecting to get away with changing the subject quite so soon.

'Not bad,' said Gibbs. 'Of all the names that have come in so far, only two have come up more than twenty times each.' He stood up. 'I'm off to 131 Valingers Road in Bethnal Green to interview one of them: Warren Gruff, ex-army. I said all along, didn't I? British military.'

'What about the other one?'

'Other one?'

'The other name that's come up more than twenty times,' said Sellers impatiently.

'Oh, that one.' Gibbs grinned. 'Matter of fact, the second one's come up more often than Warren Gruff's — thirty-six mentions, next to Gruff's twenty-three.'

'Then why . . . ?'

'Why aren't I going after the second name first? Because it's got no surname or address attached to it. It's just a first name: Billy. Thirty-six people rang in to say they know Baldy as Billy, but don't know anything else about him.'

'Does the sarge know? We need to —'

'Track Billy down?' Gibbs cut Sellers off again. 'I will be doing — at 131 Valingers Road, Bethnal Green.' He laughed at Sellers' confusion. 'Warren Gruff; Billy. You really can't see it? Think along the lines of nicknames. You're supposed to be a detective, for fuck's sake.'

Finally, Sellers made the connection. 'Billy Goat Gruff,' he said.

19
MONDAY 12 OCTOBER 2009

'Ray?' The problem with Marchington House is that it's so big, there's no point calling out anybody's name. I'd be better off ringing her on her mobile, except that mine has been thrown into a boating lake, and without it, I don't know her number.

I check the lounge, family room, kitchen, snug, utility room, both studies, the games room, the music room and the den, but there's no sign of her. I head for the stairs. Distributed over the top three floors of the house are fourteen bedrooms and ten bathrooms. I start with Ray's room on the first floor. She's not in there, but Angus's jacket is, the one he was wearing when he accosted me outside my flat. There's also a bulging black canvas bag on the bed with *London on Sunday'* printed on it in small white letters.

I wrestle with my conscience for about half a second, then unzip the bag. Oh, God, look at all this: pyjamas, toothbrush, electric razor, dental floss, at least four balled-up pairs of socks, boxer shorts . . . Quickly, I pull the zip closed. Words can't express how much I do not want to look at Angus Hines' boxer shorts.

Great. My prisoner has come to stay — the man I yelled at for being decent enough not to smash my window. I'm going to have to see him again and die of shame. This must be how the purveyors of apartheid felt when all that truth and reconciliation stuff started and they had to spend hours telling Nelson Mandela what rubbish human beings they were. I think that's what happened, anyway. I'm considering giving up *heat* magazine and subscribing to something more serious instead, to boost my general knowledge: *The Economist* or *National Geographic.*

I unzip the side pocket of Angus's suitcase, having decided it's bound to be underwear-free: he wouldn't divide his boxer shorts equally between the compartments. I'm surprised to find two DVDs in there, both of Binary Star programmes I produced: *Hate After Death* and *Cutting Myself.* So Angus's investigation of my credentials is ongoing. Actually, *Hate After Death* is the best work I've ever done, so I hope he's watched it. It was a six-parter about families in which a feud between one branch and another had spanned several generations. In some cases, parents on their deathbeds had extracted promises from their children not to let their enmities die with them, to hate on their behalf even after their deaths, to hate their enemies' children, and the children of those children.

Sick. Sick to want to pass on your anger and resentment to others, sick to hang on to those feelings yourself.

I'm not angry with Laurie any more. I don't hate him, or wish him harm. What I wish is that . . . I don't allow myself to think it. There's no point.

As I'm putting the DVDs back in Angus's bag, I hear footsteps. They seem to be coming from the landing above me, but when I go and investigate, I can't find anyone. 'Hello?' I call out. I check all the bedrooms on the second and third floors, but there's no sign of life. I must have imagined it. I decide to go to my room, get into bed and have the protracted pillow-thumping cry I've been looking forward to since Regent's Park.

I open the door and scream when I see a man standing next to my bed. He doesn't seem at all startled. He smiles as if I ought to have known I'd find him there.

'Who are you? What are you doing in my room?' I know who he is: Ray's brother, the dark one from the punting photo in the kitchen. He's wearing a white V-necked cricket jumper and trousers that are more zips than material. I've never understood that: why would you want to shorten and extend your trousers at various points during the day? Who's the target audience: people whose calves only work part-time?

'You've got that the wrong way round,' says Ray's brother, still grinning. 'You're in my room.'

'Ray said this was a guest room.'

'It is. It's my guest room. This is my house.'

'Marchington House belongs to you?' I remember what Laurie said about Ray's parents living in Winchester. 'But . . .'

'You know different?'

'Sorry, I just . . . You're so young. You look about my age.'

'Which is?'

'Thirty-one.'

'In that case I'm younger than you. I'm twenty-nine.'

I feel a fit of tactlessness coming on. 'When did you fit in getting rich enough to buy a house like this? At school, between double Latin and croquet? Or did you make constructive use of a detention?' I'm talking nonsense, still freaked out by having found him in my room. Why was he lying in wait for me? How dare he own Marchington House? Did he open my suitcase? Was he looking at my underwear, while I was looking at Angus Hines'?

'Croquet and Latin?' He laughs. 'Is that what you learned at your school?'

'No, we learned gang warfare and apathy,' I snap. 'I went to an inner city comprehensive.'

'Me too.'

'Really?'

'Really. And I'm not rich, apart from this house. I inherited it last year from my grandfather. I run a window-cleaning business. This isn't where I live — I'm still in my rented flat in Streatham. This place is way too big for me, and the décor's too . . . womanly. My gran was an interior designer.'

'Just you?' I say. 'You inherited this whole house?'

'All six of the grandchildren inherited a property,' he says, looking sheepish. 'My grandfather was very wealthy. Something to do with diamonds.'

'Oh, right,' I say. 'I'm lucky: both my grandads are still alive. One's something to

do with an allotment and the other's something to do with sitting in a chair waiting to
cark it. Look, Ray said I could stay here,
and —'

'You want me to get out of your room?
My room? Our room?'

That's it: he's definitely been rooting
through my knickers. That was an unambiguous innuendo.

'I'm supposed to kick you out,' he says.

'Kick me *out?*'

'That's right. Don't worry, I'm not going
to. I don't see why I should do his lordship's
bidding, do you?'

His lordship . . . Angus Hines. I might have
known.

Is that why he and Ray aren't here? Too
scared to do their own dirty work? Did they
watch *Hate After Death,* think it was hopeless and lose all faith in me?

'Do you come from a rich family, if you
don't mind my asking?'

I do mind, but I've no right to, after what
I asked him. 'No. Poor. Well, ordinary,
which effectively means poor.'

'How so?'

'What's the point in having a *bit* of
money?' I say crossly.

'You're a strange woman, Fliss Benson.
Has anyone ever told you that?'

'No.'

'I hated school, actually,' he says, as if it's the obvious next thing to say. 'My parents could have afforded to send all of us to Eton, no problem. We could have lived the croquet-and-Latin dream, but instead we went to Cottham Chase and had to spend every day fighting to attain the dubious title of cock of the school.'

'Did you succeed?' Eton's a boys' school. Ray couldn't have gone to Eton.

'No. Which was a huge relief. The cock's responsibilities were onerous: you were expected to kick the crap out of literally everybody that crossed your path. I'd have had no free time.'

'Why didn't your parents send you somewhere better if they could afford it?'

'They thought that sending us to the local dump was sure to bring about global equality.' He smiles at me again, as if we're best friends. 'You know the type.'

I haven't a clue what he's talking about. 'Look, about you booting me out . . .'

'I've already told you: I'm not going to.'

'Why don't you evict them instead?' I blurt out. 'I'm not the one causing the trouble. If there were a public vote, like on *Big Brother,* I'm sure I'd get to stay in.'

'Them?' He looks surprised.

'Ray and Angus.'

'You want me to ask Ray to leave?'

'I want you to ask Angus to leave.'

'Is Angus her ex-husband?'

Never trust a man with too many zips on his trousers, that's my motto. 'Don't pretend you don't know the name of your own sister's ex,' I say crossly. 'Though I'm not sure how ex he is any more.'

'My sister?' He laughs. 'Sorry, do you mean Ray Hines?'

I stare at him in disbelief. Who else could I mean?

'Ray isn't my sister. Where did you get that idea? Ray is someone I'm temporarily allowing to stay in an empty house I own.'

This is making no sense. 'There's a photo of you up in the kitchen, punting down a river.'

'The River Cam, yes. With my brother — my nice brother, not the stupid one who uses and discards beautiful women he really ought to treat better.'

What's he talking about? 'I was looking at the photo, and Ray said, "Not much of a family resemblance, is there? Those two got all the good looks." Or words to that effect. But if you're not Ray's brother . . .'

For the first time since we started talking, he looks angry. 'Then who am I?' he says, completing my question. 'If I tell you, you'll hate me on the spot, and it'll be *his* fault, like everything always is.'

Before I have a chance to respond, he's gone. I run after him, shouting 'Wait!' and 'Stop!' and all the other stupid pointless things you shout at people who turn their backs and leave you behind at great speed. I get down the last flight of stairs just in time to hear the front door slam. Through the window, I see him drive away in a car with a cloth roof, probably unzippable, like the bottoms of his trousers.

I storm into the kitchen and pull the punting photograph off the wall to get a better look at it, as if it might be able to tell me what's going on. My fingers touch a flap of paper on the back of the frame, and I turn it over. There's a label on the back; one corner has come loose and curled up. On it, someone has handwritten, 'Hugo and St John take a punt! Cambridge, 1999.' My heart does its best impersonation of a bouncy ball. *Hugo. St John.*

Laurence Hugo St John Fleet Nattrass. His lordship.

I run round the house like a demented person, pulling drawers open, panting loudly. I don't care how long it takes — I'm going to find something, something better

565

than what I've got, something that proves to me what I already know.

I find it in a sideboard in the den. Or rather, I find *them:* photograph albums. On the first page there's a picture of a jowly middle-aged man smoking a pipe. I pull it out and turn it over. 'Fleet, 1973' is all that's written on the back. *Laurie's dad.* Next, I select a photograph of a smiling baby sitting in what looks like the lotus position in front of a chair. I turn it over and read the tiny handwriting: 'St John Hugo Laurence Fleet Nattrass, eight months old, 1971'. This must be the blond brother from the punting photograph, younger than Laurie and older than . . . Zip-man must be Hugo.

Did Fleet Nattrass only know three boys' names apart from his own? Is it a posh family thing, giving all your children the same names in a different order?

Not much of a resemblance, is there? Ray thought I knew she was staying at Laurie's brother's house. She assumed he'd told me.

The person who wants me evicted isn't Angus Hines. It's Laurie.

The house phone rings. I crawl over to the table on my hands and knees and pick it up, hoping it might be Ray.

It's Maya. 'Fliss,' she says. She sounds

caught out, as if she wishes I hadn't answered. I don't need to ask her how she knew where to find me. I hear a drawing in of breath.

'Let me save you the trouble,' I say. 'You're afraid you're going to have to let me go. That about right?'

'Close enough,' she says, and hangs up.

I'm sitting cross-legged on the floor in the hall when the front door opens and Ray and Angus walk in. Distractedly, Angus says, 'Hello, Fliss.' He doesn't look as if he's thinking about me locking him in my flat. If he's surprised to find me at his feet, he shows no sign of it. He squeezes Ray's arm and says, 'I'll be down shortly,' then heads for the stairs as if he has something important to attend to.

'Did you tell him you're pregnant?' I ask Ray. His suitcase upstairs can only mean one thing. Not long ago, he didn't even know where she was staying. 'Is he happy about it?'

'Happy's difficult for both of us, but . . . yes, he's pleased.'

'Are you back together, then? Are you moving back to Notting Hill?' Childishly, I want her to say she's moving out because I know I'll have to. I can't stay in Laurie's brother's house. *What did you think, idiot? That someone like you can live in a place like this for ever?* 'Is Angus coming to live here, too?'

Ray's smile vanishes, and I notice how tired she looks. 'No. We're not going to be living together.'

'Why not?'

'Let's get set up for the camera,' she says. 'It's all part of the same story.'

'Did you tell Angus the baby might be Laurie's and not his?' I ask, making no effort to lower my voice. I'm guessing that at some point Ray and Laurie slept together. Why wouldn't he try it on with her? He slept with me in an attempt to persuade me not to interview Judith Duffy for the film; he shacked up with Maya to avoid me and the police, or maybe so that the card-sender wouldn't know where to find him. No doubt bedding Ray was part of his campaign to persuade her to be involved in the film: first he offered his body, then Marchington House as a refuge. He must have been furious when neither did the trick.

From Ray's point of view, why wouldn't she have sex with Laurie? At forty-two she could still have another child. If she has Laurie's baby rather than Angus's, there will be no genetic auto-immune issue to worry about.

She takes my arm and leads me into the den. Closing the door behind us, she says, 'Please don't call it a baby. It isn't one, not yet. And there's no "might" about it. It's Laurie's. Angus had a vasectomy while I was in prison. He wanted to make sure he'd never go through the pain of losing another child.'

'But . . .'

'I told him the truth,' says Ray. 'Don't you think I'm sick of lies by now? Do you really think I'd try to start my new life, and Angus's, based on a lie?'

'So you're going to tell Laurie?'

'Laurie Nattrass is nothing to me, Fliss. Personally, I mean.'

Lucky you.

'I can withhold information from him and it won't be living a lie, not in the way it would be if I lied to my husband.' She looks caught out. 'Angus and I are getting remarried,' she says.

But you're not going to be living together? 'Will he be able to feel the same about Laurie's baby as he would about his own?' I ask.

'He doesn't know,' says Ray. 'Neither do I. But we don't have the option of "his own". This is all we have, our only chance of being . . . well, I suppose a family, though an unusual one. Are you going to tell Laurie?'

'No.' I'm not going to tell him about Ray's pregnancy, and I'm not going to tell anybody about him bribing Carl Chappell and Warren Gruff. With regard to Laurie, I'm going to do nothing. I don't want to destroy anybody's life — not Laurie's, not Ray's, not Angus's.

'Can I ask you one more favour?' says Ray.

'What?' I haven't granted any so far, unless my memory's letting me down.

'Don't tell Angus you know. It would make it harder for him if he thought anyone else knew.'

What happened to no more lies? I don't say it because it's a ridiculous thing to say, or even think. If no one ever told a lie again, life would quickly become impossible.

Ray nods at the camera. 'Shall we get started?'

'I need to make a phone call first,' I tell her. 'Why don't you sort us out with drinks?'

Once she's gone, I use the antique phone on the table in the corner to ring Tamsin. She doesn't sound pleased to hear from me. 'Just to remind you of the etiquette: you're supposed to drop your friends when you've got a new man, not when you've lost your marbles,' she says. 'In the event of a loss of marbles, you're allowed to spend as much time with your friends as you ever did, as long as you remember to look confused and call them by the names of people who've been dead for years.'

'Please tell me you haven't got a new job yet,' I say.

'Job?' She sounds as if she's forgotten what one is.

'How hard would it be for you and I to set up on our own?'

'As what?'

'As what we are: people who make TV programmes.'

'You mean our own production company? I've no idea.'

'Find out.'

I hear a long, gusty yawn. 'I'm not sure how I'd go about finding out, to be honest.'

'Find a way,' I say, and then I cut her off to show her I mean business. I'm sure that's how MI6 would handle her lazy, uncooperative streak. It'll all work out, I persuade myself. It has to work out.

Now all I have to do is tell Ray and Angus that it's not going to be Binary Star making the film after all.

20
12/10/09

'So we're sure Warren Gruff's Baldy?' Simon asked Sellers.

'I am.' Charlie stared at the grainy photograph on the computer screen. 'That's the man I saw.'

'I am too,' said Sellers. 'Gruff's ex-army, went to Iraq first time round. And look at this.' He leaned across the desk, reaching for an article he'd printed out, and knocked over his can of Diet Coke. 'Fuck,' he muttered as the liquid fizzed over the keyboard.

'I never thought I'd see the day,' said Charlie. 'Colin Sellers on a diet.'

'This was in the *Sun,* June 2006,' said Sellers. 'What diet?'

Simon took the article and started to read. 'Heard of Joanne Bew?' he asked Charlie.

'No. Who is she?'

'She was convicted of murdering her son, Brandon, then retried and acquitted. Gruff was her boyfriend, Brandon's father. He was none too happy about her acquittal. Far as he's concerned, she smothered his son, and he doesn't care if she sues him for saying it. She mistreated Brandon from the day he was born, by the sound of it.' Simon winced and dropped the article on the desk. 'I can do without the depressing details.'

'Are you saying I need to lose weight?' Sellers asked Charlie, covering his gut with a protective hand. 'It's all muscle, this. Used to be, anyway.'

'Sorry. I just assumed, because of the Diet Coke . . .'

'Diet was all the machine had left,' he told her. 'It tastes like shit.'

'His girlfriend killed his kid and got away with it,' said Simon, more to himself than to Sellers and Charlie. 'He's ex-military — maybe he's killed before. Probably has. How easy would it be for the card-sender, the Brain, to get him on side? Easy enough when Sarah Jaggard and Helen Yardley are the targets, women who — like Joanne Bew, as Gruff would see it — murdered kids and got away with it. But what about when the Brain decides Judith Duffy's the next victim? Duffy testified against Joanne Bew at her first trial — it says so in the article. Gruff'd be favourably disposed towards Duffy . . .'

'Which explains what he said to me,' Charlie finished his sentence for him. 'That Duffy didn't deserve to die, that she'd done her best. He meant she did her best to put Joanne Bew behind bars, didn't he?'

'He also said you did your best,' Simon reminded her. 'He meant the collective "you" — the police.'

'So the Brain had some kind of hold over him?' said Charlie. 'If Gruff didn't want to kill Duffy, but did it anyway.'

'Gruff had attacked Sarah Jaggard, provided the gun for the murder of Helen Yardley. What he said to you was spot on: he was in it up to his eyebrows and couldn't back out at that point — the Brain would have made sure . . .' Simon stopped mid-sentence, seeing Sam Kombothekra heading their way.

'Just because I'm drinking Diet Coke and I'm not skinny like you doesn't mean I'm on a diet,' Sellers muttered to Charlie. He tilted his head, inspecting his belly from a different angle.

'I think we've got a solid lead on Ray Hines' whereabouts.' Sam sounded excited. 'Laurie Nattrass has a brother, Hugo, who owns a house in Twickenham. He doesn't live there — he lives in Streatham — which is why it's taken this long to unearth it, but . . . Simon?'

Charlie clicked her fingers in front of his face. 'Wake up. Sam's trying to tell you something.'

Simon turned to Sellers. 'What did you just say? About the Diet Coke. Whatever you said, say it again.'

Sellers gave up trying to pull in his stomach muscles. He sighed. 'Just because I'm drinking Diet Coke and I'm a bit on the heavy side doesn't mean I'm on a diet.'

'That's it.' Simon spun round to face Charlie. He stared at her as if he'd forgotten Sellers and Sam were there. 'That's *it*. A thin person with a diet drink might just like the taste of it, but a fat person with a diet drink . . .'

'Fat?' Sellers sounded outraged.

'So the alibi's bullshit.'

'What alibi?' Sam asked.

'I need to talk to Dillon White again.' Simon's words tumbled out as his thought process speeded up. 'And Rahila Yunis.'

'The journalist who interviewed Helen Yardley in prison?' asked Charlie.

'I need her to tell me why she withheld the most important part of the story about her visit to Geddham Hall. I know why, but I want to hear it from her. Sam, I need photographs: Laurie Nattrass, Angus Hines,

Glen Jaggard, Paul Yardley, Sebastian Brownlee.'

Sam nodded. He could have pointed out that, as skipper, he was the one who ought to have been assigning the tasks; he was wise enough not to.

'*Whose* alibi's bullshit?' Charlie asked, knowing the chances of getting an answer at this point were considerably slimmer than Colin Sellers.

'Sellers, you check out the Twickenham address,' said Simon, his eyes darting back and forth as he pieced together the story in his mind. 'If you find Ray Hines there, don't let her out of your sight.'

21
MONDAY 12 OCTOBER 2009

'He suspected me from the first time the police came to the house,' Ray says to the camera. I nod, willing her to carry on, to tell me as much as she can before Angus joins us. I'm afraid she won't be quite so open once he's listening. 'He changed towards me, became horribly cold and remote, but at the same time he wouldn't let me out of his sight. He moved into one of the many spare rooms we'd at one point hoped to fill with children . . .' She stops. 'You know we wanted to have lots?'

'No.'

'Angus is one of six. We wanted at least four.' She falls silent.

'He wouldn't let you out of his sight,' I say, prompting her.

'He . . . monitored me. It was as if someone had asked him to spy on my every move and report back. In my most paranoid moments, I wondered if that might be the case.

It wasn't, of course. The police would have assumed — did assume, in fact — that Angus and I would stick together. He was watching me closely for his own purposes, no one else's. He was trying to gather evidence of my guilt or innocence.'

'He didn't believe Marcella and Nathaniel reacted badly to the vaccine?'

Ray shakes her head. 'I don't blame him. All the experts tell you vaccines are safe, and he wasn't there when both children had fits. Only Wendy and I saw what happened. For all Angus knew, I was a murderer who'd persuaded Wendy to lie.'

'You were his wife,' I remind her. 'He should have known you wouldn't kill your children.'

'Maybe he would have, if it hadn't been for the zombie-like depression I faked in order to go to Switzerland with Fiona. That made him doubt everything he thought he knew about me. I can't blame him for that — it was my fault. I didn't blame him even then, but —' She breaks off, eyeing the ceiling as if afraid he might burst through it at any moment. *She can't be frightened of him, not if she's planning to marry him again.*

'I quickly became terrified of him,' she says. 'He wouldn't talk to me — that was the scariest thing. I kept asking if he thought

I'd killed Marcella and Nathaniel, and he wouldn't answer. All he ever said was, "Only you know what you've done, Ray." He was so blank, so horrendously . . . *calm.* I couldn't believe how composed he was when our lives were falling apart — me charged with murder, maybe going to prison. Looking back, I think he had a breakdown. I'm *sure* it was that. People never tell you it's possible to go mad in a quiet, orderly way, but it is. That's what happened to Angus. He didn't think he'd broken down with grief, he thought he was in full possession of his faculties and responding in the only rational way: I'm accused of murder, so it's his job to watch me and record my behaviour in order to ascertain whether there's any factual basis to the accusation — that's how he'd have put it to himself, I'm sure.'

'When you say "record" . . . You mean he wrote it down?'

'Eventually I got desperate, when he point blank refused to communicate with me. I searched the room he was sleeping in and found all this . . . terrible stuff in one of the drawers: a notebook describing my behaviour, reams and reams of articles he'd downloaded from the internet about the importance of vaccination and the corrupt self-publicists who claim the jabs are dangerous . . .'

'What did he write about you in the notebook?' I ask.

'Oh, nothing interesting. "Breakfast 8 a.m.: one weetabix. Sits on sofa crying, one hour." That sort of thing. I didn't do anything much at that point in my life, apart from cry, answer the police's endless questions and try to talk to Angus. One day, when I couldn't take his staring silence any more, I said to him, "If a jury finds me innocent, will that convince you I'm telling the truth?" He laughed so horribly . . .' She shudders. 'I'll never forget that laugh.'

And yet you're willing to marry him for a second time.

'He said, "You seriously expect me to base my opinion on the views of twelve strangers, most of whom probably aren't educated? Do you think Marcella and Nathaniel meant that little to me?" I completely lost it, then. I screamed at him that he'd never know, in that case, if he wouldn't believe me and wouldn't believe a jury. He very calmly told me I was wrong. One day, he said, he would know. "How?" I asked, but he wouldn't tell me. He walked away. Every time I asked him that question, he turned his back on me.' Ray pinches the top of her

580

nose, then moves her hand as if she's suddenly remembered the camera. 'That's why I lied in court,' she tells it. 'That's why I started being as inconsistent as I could, contradicting myself whenever I could. I didn't know what Angus's plan was, but I knew he had one, and that I had to escape from him and . . . whatever he intended to do to me.'

I nod. I know all about needing to escape from Angus Hines. *Turning round, finding him right behind me in the doorway of my flat . . .*

Where is he? What's he doing upstairs that's taking so long?

'I couldn't bear another day with him,' says Ray. 'He'd become this terrifying . . . *thing,* not my husband at all, not the man I loved. Prison would be nothing compared to the horror of living with *that* any longer — at least in prison no one would try to kill me, and that's what I became increasingly certain Angus would do. That was how insane he seemed.'

'You lied so that the jury would think you were untrustworthy.'

'So that they'd dismiss me as a liar, yes. I knew that once they thought that, a guilty verdict was a done deal. You have to understand, I didn't care where I lived. I'd already lost everything: my husband, my two children. And my home — it was worse than hell. I couldn't breathe there, couldn't sleep, couldn't eat. Prison would be a welcome relief, I thought. And it was. It really was. I wasn't scared all the time, or under surveillance. I was able to spend my time doing the only thing I wanted to do: thinking about Marcella and Nathaniel in peace. Missing them in peace.'

'But you made the world believe you'd murdered them. Didn't that bother you?'

Ray gives me an odd look, as if I've made a freakish suggestion. 'Why would it? I knew the truth. And the only three people whose opinions would have mattered to me were gone. Marcella and Nathaniel were dead, and the Angus I loved . . . I felt as if he'd died with them.'

'So after you found Nathaniel, when you said you let the health visitor in immediately . . .'

'I knew perfectly well that I didn't. I made her wait on the doorstep for at least ten minutes, exactly as she said in court.'

'Why?'

She doesn't answer straight away. When she speaks, it's a whisper, 'Nathaniel was dead. I knew the health visitor would see that as soon as she came in. I knew she'd say it out loud. I didn't want him to be dead. The longer she waited outside, the longer I could pretend.'

'Do you want to take a break?' I ask.

'No. Thanks, but I'll carry on.' She leans into the camera. 'Angus will be down in a minute. I'm hoping that talking about what happened will be the beginning of his recovery. I had therapy in prison, but Angus has never opened up to anyone. He's never been ready before, but he is now. That's why this documentary's so important — not only as a way of telling and explaining . . .' She covers her stomach with her hands.

The baby. That's who Ray wants to talk to — not me, not the viewing public. Her child. The film is her gift to the baby: the family story.

'Angus lied, too,' says Ray. 'When I was found guilty, he told the press that he'd made a decision before the verdict came in: he would believe the jury whatever they said, guilty or innocent. I knew that was a lie, and Angus knew I knew it. He was mocking me from a distance, reminding me of his scorn for the inadequately educated jury and his promise that one day he would find out if I was guilty or not through his own efforts. He knew I'd understand the hidden message behind his official words. For as long as I stayed in prison, though, he couldn't get to me.'

'Did he visit you?'

'I refused to see him. I was so scared of him that when Laurie Nattrass and Helen Yardley first took an interest in me, I wished they'd leave me alone. It took a lot of therapy to persuade me that since I wasn't a murderer, I probably shouldn't be in jail.'

'If you wanted to guarantee you'd go to prison and stay there, why didn't you plead guilty?'

'Because I was innocent.' She sighs. 'As long as I said clearly that I hadn't killed Marcella and Nathaniel, I wasn't letting them down. People had the option of believing me. If I'd said I'd done it, I would have been betraying their memories by pretending there had been a moment when I'd wanted each of them to die. I didn't mind lying about other things, but I couldn't have stood in court and said under oath that I'd wanted my beloved children dead. Besides, a guilty plea would have been counterproductive. It would have netted me a lighter sentence, maybe even a lesser charge — manslaughter instead of murder. I might have been out in five years — less, for all I know — and then I'd have had to face Angus.'

'But when you did get out, after you'd left

the urn picture hotel, you went back to him, to Notting Hill. Weren't you still scared of him?'

She nods. 'But I was more frightened of living the rest of my life in terror. Whatever Angus had in store for me, I wanted it over with. When he opened the door to let me in, I honestly thought I might never leave that house alive again.'

'You thought he'd kill you, and you still went to him?'

'I loved him.' She shrugs. 'Or rather, I *had* loved him, and I still loved the person he used to be. And he needed me. He'd gone mad, so mad that he didn't realise how much he needed me, but I knew. I'm the only person in the world who loved Marcella and Nathaniel as much as Angus did — how could he not need me? But, yes, I thought he might kill me. What he'd said to me kept going round in my head: that one day he would find out whether I was guilty or not. How could he find out, if he wouldn't believe me or a jury? The only thing I could think of was that he would let me know I was about to die, that there was no way out. Maybe then I'd finally confess, if there was anything to confess to. Maybe he planned to torture me, or . . .' She shakes her head. 'You think all sorts of terrible things, but I had to find out. I had to know what he was planning to do.'

'And? Did he try to kill you?'

The door opens. 'No, I didn't,' says Angus.

'He didn't,' Ray echoes. 'Which was lucky for me, because if he'd tried, he'd have succeeded.'

No. That's the wrong answer. He did try to kill her. He must have, because . . . Something clicks in my mind: the cards. The sixteen numbers. And the photographs, Helen Yardley's hand . . .

I turn to Angus. 'Sit next to Ray and look at the camera when you're talking, not at me,' I tell him. 'Why did you email me those lists — all the people Judith Duffy testified against in the criminal and family courts?'

He frowns, unhappy with the leap from one subject to another. 'I thought we were talking about what happened when Ray came home?'

'We will, but first I want you to explain why you sent me those lists. To the camera, please.'

He looks at Ray, who nods. I see that she's right: he does need her. 'I thought you'd find it useful to see how many people Judith Duffy had accused of deliberately harming or killing children,' he says.

'Why? Why would that be useful to me?'

Angus stares at the camera.

'You don't want to tell me. You think I ought to be capable of working it out. Well, I'm sorry, but I'm not capable.'

'Isn't it obvious?' he asks.

'No.'

'Tell her, Angus.'

'I assume you know the catchphrase Judith Duffy was famous for: "so unlikely, it borders on impossible"?'

I tell him I do.

'Do you know what she was talking about when she said it?'

'The odds of there being two crib deaths in one family.'

'No, that's a popular misconception.' He looks pleased to be able to contradict me. My heart's thudding so hard, I'm surprised the camera's not shaking. 'That's what people think she meant, but she told Ray otherwise. She wasn't talking about general principles, but about two specific cases — Morgan and Rowan Yardley — and the likelihood that they died naturally, given the physical evidence in both cases.'

'Are you going to tell me why you sent me those lists?' I ask.

'I've got my own likelihood principle, which I'll happily explain to you,' says An-

587

gus. 'If Judith Duffy testifies that Ray's a murderer, and Ray denies it, what are the odds of Duffy being right?'

I think about this. 'I've no idea,' I say honestly. 'Assuming Duffy's an unbiased expert, and that Ray might have a strong motivation to say she was innocent even if she wasn't . . .'

'No, leave that out of it,' says Angus impatiently. 'Don't think about motivation, impartiality, expertise — none of those things can be scientifically measured. I'm talking about pure probability. In fact, let's not use Ray and Duffy — let's make it more abstract. A doctor accuses a woman of smothering her baby. The woman says she didn't do it. There are no witnesses. What are the odds of the doctor being right?'

'Fifty-fifty?' I guess.

'Right. So the doctor, in that scenario, might be totally and completely correct in her judgement, or she might be totally, utterly wrong. She can't be a bit right and a bit wrong, can she?'

'No,' I say. 'The woman either did or didn't murder her child.'

'Good.' Angus nods. 'Now, let's up the numbers a bit. A doctor — the same doctor — accuses three women of murdering babies. All three women say they're innocent.'

Ray, Helen Yardley and Sarah Jaggard.

'What are the odds of all three of them being guilty? Still fifty-fifty?'

God, I hated Maths at school. I remember rolling my eyes when we did quadratic equations: *Yeah, like we're really going to need* this *skill in later life.* My teacher, Mrs Gilpin, said, 'Numerical agility will help you in ways you can't possibly imagine, Felicity.' Looks like she was right. 'If, in each case, the probability of the doctor being right is fifty-fifty, then the chance of her being right in all three cases would . . . still be fifty-fifty, wouldn't it?'

'No,' says Angus, as if he can't believe my stupidity. 'There's only a one in eight chance of the doctor being right, or wrong, in all three cases.' Ray and I watch as he pulls a crumpled receipt and a pen out of his jacket pocket and starts to write, leaning on his knee. 'G stands for guilty, I for innocent,' he says, handing me the receipt once he's finished.

I look at what he's written.

Woman 1:	G	G	G	G	I	I	I	I
Woman 2:	G	G	I	I	I	I	G	G
Woman 3:	G	I	G	I	I	G	I	G

'You see?' he says. 'There's a one in eight chance of the doctor being right in all three cases, and a one in eight chance of her being wrong in all three cases. Now, imagine there are a thousand such cases . . .'

'I see what you're getting at,' I say. 'The more cases there are of Judith Duffy saying women are guilty and them protesting their innocence, the more likely she is to be right sometimes and wrong sometimes.' *That's why, in your email, you also made sure to tell me that on twenty-three occasions, Judith Duffy testified in favour of a parent. Sometimes she's for, sometimes she's against — that was your point. Sometimes she's right, sometimes she's wrong.* In other words, Laurie's portrayal of her as a persecutor of innocent mothers is a flat-out lie.

'Precisely.' Angus rewards me with a smile. 'The more wrongly accused innocent women Laurie Nattrass pulls out of his hat, so-called victims of Duffy's alleged desire to ruin lives, the more likely at least some of them are to be guilty. I have no trouble believing in a miscarriage of justice, or that a doctor can get it wrong. But to expect people to believe in an endless string of miscarriage-of-justice victims, in a doctor who gets it wrong every single time . . .'

'And I was supposed to work that out,

from those lists you sent me?'

'Hines' Theorem of Probability, I call it: one woman accused of murder by Judith Duffy might be guilty or innocent. A hundred women accused of murder by Judith Duffy must be guilty *and* innocent. *Lots* of them are likely to be guilty, just as lots of them are likely to be innocent.'

'And you wanted to make sure I knew this, because Laurie didn't seem to,' I say quietly. 'He seemed to think *all* the women Duffy accused of child murder had to be innocent. He couldn't see that there must be guilty ones too, hiding among the blameless.'

'He couldn't see the trees for the wood,' says Ray, nodding.

The doorbell rings.

'Do you want me to get it?' she asks.

'No, I'll go. Whoever it is, I'll get rid of them.' I force myself to smile and say, 'Stay put, I'll be back in a second.'

In the hall, I panic and freeze halfway to the door, unable to take the next step. Judith Duffy opened her front door and someone shot her, a man with shaved hair.

The letterbox opens and I see brown eyes, part of a nose. 'Fliss?' I recognise the voice: it's Laurie's zippy-trousered brother. Hugo. Why did he ring the bell? It's his house, for

God's sake.

I open the door. 'What do you want?' Without authorisation from my brain, my hand starts performing a winding-up gesture: *come on, get on with it.*

'I wanted to apologise for the way I —'

'Never mind about that,' I say, lowering my voice. 'I need you to do something for me.' I pull him inside and into the room nearest to the door, the music room. I point at the piano stool and he sits down obediently. 'Wait here,' I whisper. 'Just sit, don't do anything apart from sitting. In silence. Turn your mobile off, and pretend you're not here. Don't play the piano, not even one note. Not even "Chopsticks".'

'I can't play "Chopsticks".'

'Really?' I thought everyone could play 'Chopsticks'.

'I can, however, just sit and do nothing apart from sitting. That's a talent of mine that's often been remarked upon by those close to me.'

'Good,' I say. 'Wait here, and don't leave. Promise you won't leave.'

'I promise. Do you mind if I ask — ?'

'Yes.'

'But what — ?'

'I might need you to drive me somewhere,' I tell him.

'Where's your car?' he asks, also in a whisper.

'Still in the Rolls-Royce showroom, waiting for me to win the lottery or find a rich husband. Now sit quietly until I come back.' I turn to go back to the den.

'Fliss?'

'I've got to go. What?'

'How about me as the rich husband?'

I flinch. 'Don't be stupid. I've had sex with your brother.'

'Would that be a problem for you?'

'I don't know why you're using the conditional tense,' I hiss at him. 'It *is* a problem for me, a huge one.'

'It's a huge problem for me too,' says Hugo Nattrass, beaming like an idiot. 'Do you think that counts as us having quite a lot in common?'

Simon passed his phone back to Charlie. 'I don't suppose you're going to tell me who that was or what they said,' she predicted.

'When I'm ready.' He was having one of his workouts, as Charlie liked to call them. Unlike other people's workouts, they didn't involve treadmills or rowing machines; they involved nothing but Simon and his brain. Anyone who tried to join the party was quickly shown how irrelevant they were.

'That's the third secret call you've taken since we set off. Are there going to be more?'

No answer.

'It's a safety issue apart from anything else,' said Charlie tetchily. 'If you weren't so keen to keep me in the dark, you could put your phone on speaker-phone and drive with both hands.'

'Just because you've got a can of Diet Coke and you're fat, doesn't mean you're on a diet,' said Simon, as they turned into

Bengeo Street.

'Oh, not this again!' Charlie banged her head on the passenger window.

'You've got an umbrella with you, and it's raining. Doesn't necessarily mean you've got an umbrella with you *because* it's raining.'

'Meaning?'

Simon parked outside Stella White's house. 'Dillon White told Gibbs he saw the man with the umbrella in Helen Yardley's lounge. At first we didn't take it seriously, because it didn't rain on Monday, nor had rain been forecast, and Stella White, our only other witness, saw no umbrella. She also said there was no way her son could have seen the man in the Yardleys' lounge that morning. Subsequently, we find out Dillon saw the man on a previous occasion — in Helen's lounge, where he, Dillon, was too. So were Stella, Helen and Paul Yardley, and another man and woman Dillon couldn't name. That day it *was* raining, and rain from the man's umbrella was dripping on the carpet.' A long pause. Then Simon said, 'Anything you want to ask me?'

'Yes,' said Charlie. 'Will you please tell me what it is you think you know?'

'You don't want to ask me if the Yardleys have a hall?'

'Not especially.'

'Well, you ought to. They *do* have a hall, with a wood-laminate floor. Leading through to the lounge. Why would you take a sopping wet umbrella into a carpeted lounge? Why not leave it in the hall, especially if the hall isn't carpeted?'

'Because you're inconsiderate?' Charlie suggested. 'Busy thinking about other things?'

'What if you're not inconsiderate?' said Simon. 'What if you're thoughtful enough to make up an entertaining story for a little boy, about space travel and magic? And yet you deliberately take your umbrella into the lounge and let it drip on the carpet. Why would you do that?'

'Is the umbrella a crucial prop in the magic story?'

Simon shook his head. He had the nerve to look disappointed that she hadn't worked it out yet. Had he forgotten it wasn't her case? She wasn't supposed to be in a car with him on the way to Bengeo Street; she was supposed to be getting on with her own work.

'Dillon said the other man who was there, the one who wasn't Paul Yardley or Magic Umbrella man — he had an umbrella too, but it wasn't magic so he left it outside.'

Simon took his eyes off the road and looked at Charlie. 'When Stella told Gibbs that last Monday was a sunny, bright day, Dillon said, "It wasn't bright. There wasn't enough sun to make it bright." That's what he'd heard the man say — he was parroting word for word.'

'He didn't mean last Monday,' said Charlie. 'He was talking about the "beyond" day a long time ago, when it was raining and presumably overcast.'

'When *there wasn't enough sun to make it bright,*' Simon emphasised.

'Tell me in the next five seconds, or I'll tell your mother that you're involved in a conspiracy to lie to her about the honeymoon,' Charlie threatened.

'In a way, the man was right about the magic. The umbrella had at least one special power: to create light. That's what it was: a photographer's light umbrella, black on the outside, shiny silver stuff on the inside. It belonged to Angus Hines. He's Pictures Desk Editor at *London on Sunday* now, but he wasn't always. He used to be a photographer, worked for various papers, including one that featured an article about two extraordinary women — Helen Yardley and Stella White.'

'So the other man and woman Dillon

mentioned . . .'

'I'm guessing a reporter from the paper and a make-up person,' said Simon.

'How often do we see those things at press conferences, where there's never *any* natural light, let alone enough?' said Charlie, cross that she hadn't guessed. How many photographers' light umbrellas had illuminated her unhappy face in 2006, when all the papers had wanted pictures of the disgraced detective, and the Chief Constable had told her she had to agree if she wanted to keep her job?

'Angus Hines had no choice but to drip rain on the Yardleys' lounge carpet,' said Simon. 'It was the most photogenic room in the house, and he wanted to take his photos in it. When Stella White gave me a list of everyone she remembered meeting at Helen Yardley's house, of course Hines' name wasn't on it. Stella's been photographed for the papers hundreds of times — the marathon runner determined to defeat cancer. She's not going to remember the names of individual photographers, is she? When I asked her about Dillon seeing the man with the magic umbrella, she didn't make the connection with a light umbrella because I'd already told her it was raining that day — in asking the question, I gave her the reason for the umbrella to be there, so she didn't bother thinking beyond that.'

'But . . . Helen Yardley was part of JIPAC,' said Charlie, frowning. 'She lobbied for Ray Hines' release, didn't she? She must have known who Angus was when he turned up at her house, and if Stella White was there with her . . .'

'Helen behaved as if she didn't know Hines from Adam, greeted him as you would a stranger,' said Simon. 'The first of the three phone calls I've just taken was Sam. He's spoken to Paul Yardley. Yardley remembers the "beyond" day only too well. Angus Hines is one of the bad guys as far as Yardley's concerned — he didn't stand by his wife the way Yardley stood by Helen, the way Glen Jaggard stood by Sarah. When a reporter turned up at the Yardleys' house with Angus Hines in tow to take the photos, Yardley expected his wife to kick up a stink and throw him out.'

'She didn't?' Charlie guessed.

'According to Yardley, Helen didn't want to give Hines the satisfaction of knowing he'd riled her. Yardley could tell she hated having Hines in the house, but she shook his hand and said, "Nice to meet you." ' Simon chewed his bottom lip. 'As if she'd never met him before. And he went along with the pretence.'

'Which is why Hines made no impression whatsoever on Stella White,' Charlie reasoned aloud. 'Because Helen treated him as if he were any old press photographer.'

'Exactly.' Simon nodded.

'And then, last Monday, he turned up at her house a second time, and Dillon White caught a glimpse of him and recognised him from the "beyond" day,' Charlie spelled out what she assumed was Simon's hypothesis. 'He stayed all day and ended up shooting Helen dead. Hang on, didn't you tell me Angus Hines had an alibi?'

Simon smiled. 'He does, or rather, he did: a man called Carl Chappell who said he was drinking with Hines at the Retreat pub in Bethnal Green last Monday between 3 and 7 p.m. When Sellers showed us that article from the *Sun* about Warren Gruff, Bethnal Green rang a bell. Gruff lives there, his ex-girlfriend Joanne Bew murdered his son Brandon there . . . but I couldn't think where else I'd come across Bethnal Green recently. Then I remembered: Angus Hines' alibi. Before we set off, I asked Sam to probe a bit further. Didn't take him long to find out that Brandon Bew was murdered in a flat above a pub in Bethnal Green that used to be the Dog and Partridge, that's

600

now called the Retreat . . .'

'Unbelievable,' Charlie muttered.

'. . . and that Carl Chappell testified for the prosecution at Joanne Bew's first trial, claimed he witnessed her smothering Brandon. Sam spoke to Chappell — Angus Hines had given him Chappell's mobile number when he'd offered up Chappell as his alibi. Chappell was drunk enough and stupid enough, when Sam leaned on his story about being with Hines last Monday, to boast about how lucky he was with money, said Angus Hines had paid him a grand in cash for the false alibi. He also said that someone else — a man he'd seen on telly a few times, a man he described as big and fair-haired with a big neck — had paid him two grand not to testify at Joanne's retrial, to say he hadn't seen anything the night Brandon died — he'd been too drunk.'

'Laurie Nattrass?' Charlie wondered out loud. Who else could it be?

'Yeah. Nattrass.' Simon sounded angry. 'Mr Justice-For-All. He must have wanted Joanne Bew to be acquitted second time because he knew it'd look bad for Duffy — yet another innocent woman she'd testified against. And Chappell wasn't the only person Nattrass bribed — he also paid off Warren Gruff, to stop Gruff breaking Chappell's arms and legs when Chappell said he wouldn't testify against Joanne.'

'How the hell do you know that?' Charlie asked.

'Second phone call was Gibbs,' said Simon. 'Gruff's confessed to attacking Jaggard and killing Duffy. He's in custody, and talking — up to a point, at least. I thought the Brain — Angus Hines, that is — I thought he had some kind of hold over Gruff, but from what Gibbs says, it's more a case of misguided loyalty. Gruff thought Hines was the only person who truly understood him — Hines had lost two children, he'd lost one. Hines had been vilified in the press by Nattrass and various other commentators for saying he believed his wife was guilty, but he stuck to his guns. Gruff looks up to him. Which is why he killed Duffy — the woman who did her best to bring his son's killer to justice — even though it was the last thing he wanted to do, because it was part of Hines' great plan. Gruff admired Duffy, but Hines is his hero. He would have done whatever Hines told him — his role was to be the helper. That photograph Sellers showed us of Gruff, on the computer? It was taken by Angus Hines for the *Daily Express,* after Joanne Bew's retrial, when Gruff was briefly newsworthy again. That was how Hines and Gruff met. Hines might have had some genuine sympathy for Gruff, who knows? Either way, he certainly knew how to manipulate him.'

'You said "Hines' great plan",' Charlie talked over him. 'What was it?'

'Gibbs says Gruff won't say, claims he's not clever enough to explain it properly. Says Hines'd never forgive him if he spoke on his behalf. Hines is the one who has to explain — it's his plan.'

Charlie hated the thought that Gruff had admired Duffy but killed her anyway, when he could so easily have come to his senses at that point, listened to his instincts and said no. Why hadn't his hero-worship of Angus Hines ended the instant Hines had asked him to kill someone he didn't think deserved to die?

Charlie hadn't told Simon that Duffy hadn't wanted to answer the door to Gruff, that she, Charlie, had insisted, because she'd been too embarrassed to have the heart-to-heart the doctor seemed to want.

I'll leave it.

No, get it.

Charlie had expected to feel guilty about Duffy's death, but, oddly, she didn't. She could imagine what Duffy herself would have said. *The life you failed to save doesn't make you a bad person, any more than the lives you saved make you a good one.* Something like that, anyway.

'Know why Angus Hines chose Carl Chappell to bribe for an alibi?' Simon asked, glancing out of the car window at Stella White's house. 'Because he knew Nattrass had bribed Chappell.'

'How did he find that out?' Charlie asked.

'Chappell told him himself. Hines tracked Chappell down, told him he'd been researching child-death cases that involved Judith Duffy as an expert witness. He wanted to know why the eye-witness to the murder of Brandon Bew had changed his story. For the price of a bottle of whisky, he got his answer. Chappell was pissed out of his head when he was trying to reconstruct what Hines said to him, but from what Sam managed to piece together, it seems Angus Hines had the idea of using the very same people Nattrass had used, but in the opposite direction — in a direction Nattrass would have hated if he'd known about it. It was one of his little power games — proving he was the one in charge of all the players on the board, not Nattrass. He said to Chappell, "I'm the one paying you now — remember that." I reckon he picked Gruff as his killer-helper for the same reason: Nattrass had controlled Gruff previously, so Hines needed to show that he could control him even more effectively. Up to a point, that is.'

'You keep saying that,' Charlie told him. 'Warren Gruff is talking *up to a point,* Angus Hines was controlling Gruff *up to a point . . .*'

'Yeah,' said Simon defensively. 'Up to the point that as soon as we hint that we're on to them, both Warren Gruff and Carl Chappell give up Angus Hines. Hines is smart: he knew that'd happen, knew he couldn't rely on Gruff and Chappell to keep their mouths shut. He doesn't care. He wants us to know it's him — always has, right from the start. Hence the cards. He wanted to draw our attention to page 214 of *Nothing But Love* because he knew it would lead us to him, assuming we picked up on his clues, which we didn't at first. As I say, he's clever. As a nickname for him, I was spot on with "the Brain". He's got a master plan and he's looking forward to bragging about it — I only wish I knew what the fuck it is, and whether it involves killing Ray. If Sellers doesn't get to Twickenham in time, or if Hines has taken Ray somewhere else . . .'

'Sellers will get there in time,' said Charlie automatically. She had no idea whether he would or not.

Simon shifted in his seat, rubbing the small of his back. 'Hines must have guessed that Gruff and/or Chappell would give up not only him but Laurie Nattrass. I reckon he likes the idea of Nattrass getting done for perverting the course of justice — the irony would appeal to him. Nattrass supported Ray when Hines didn't, he attacked Hines publicly for his failure to support her.'

'It'd be his word against Gruff's and Chappell's, though, wouldn't it?' said Charlie. 'It's a non-starter. Laurie Nattrass'll be just fine — his sort always land on their feet.' There was something niggling at the back of her mind. She was about to give up trying to pin it down when it suddenly came into sharp focus. 'How does page 214 of *Nothing But Love* lead back to Angus Hines?' she asked.

'The third phone call was from Klair Williamson,' said Simon.

'Who?'

'She's one of the detectives on the Yardley–Duffy murders. I asked her to speak to Rahila Yunis, the journalist who interviewed Helen Yardley at Geddham Hall prison and says Yardley lied about the poem.'

'Didn't Sam say Yunis seemed reluctant to talk at first?'

'Right.' Simon nodded. 'Well, now we

know why: Yunis was withholding the most important part of the story. Angus Hines was there that day too, at Geddham Hall. He wasn't supposed to be. The rules said no photographers, but Laurie Nattrass and Helen Yardley had briefed Yunis and Hines on how to break those rules, who to talk to at the prison to make it happen. A lot of the guards liked Helen and believed she was innocent, so they bent the rules for her — Hines and his camera were allowed in. The powers-that-be at the *Telegraph* were worried about Hines being the photographer on this particular job, given that he was famous at the time for denouncing his wife as guilty and Helen was equally famous for proclaiming Ray Hines' innocence.'

'Understandable,' said Charlie.

'Yeah. Except, according to Yunis via Klair Williamson, Helen Yardley only agreed to the interview on the condition that there'd be a photographer present. A particular photographer — none other than Angus Hines. Hines was equally enthusiastic. He and Helen Yardley were keen to encounter one another, it seems. When they did, each seemed so focused on the other that they barely noticed Yunis was there, according to her. For nearly half an hour she couldn't get a word in edgeways.'

'What were they talking about?' Charlie asked.

'Ray Hines. Helen accused Hines of disloyalty and tried to convince him of the error of his ways. Hines accused Helen of supporting Ray only as a way of furthering her own cause and underlining her own innocence, using Ray as a symbol for herself, or words to that effect.'

'Interesting,' said Charlie. 'How do the two poems come into it, "The Microbe" and the "room swept white" poem?'

'When Helen presented "The Microbe" as her favourite poem, Hines burst out laughing and accused her of being stupid. "But scientists, who ought to know, / Assure us that they must be so . . . / Oh! Let us never, never doubt / What nobody is sure about!" ' Simon recited. 'For Helen, the poem was about Judith Duffy's arrogance in thinking her guilty, but Angus Hines pointed out that it could equally apply to Russell Meredew and the other doctors who testified in Helen's favour. They were as convinced of their monopoly on the truth as Duffy was. The experts on *both* sides told the jury never, never to doubt what nobody was sure about. According to Rahila Yunis, Hines thanked Helen for introducing him to "The Microbe" and told her it was now also his favourite poem, because it validated all the doubts he'd ever had about Ray, Helen, Sarah Jaggard — all the women who cried crib death when accused of murder. Yunis told Klair Williamson that Helen was visibly disturbed when Hines said this, though until that point none of his comments seemed to have bothered her at all. Shortly after he mocked her choice of poem, she put an end to the interview. A couple of hours later, Laurie Nattrass was on the phone to Yunis, saying: "I don't know what Angus Hines said to Helen because she won't tell me, but I've never seen her so angry." All Helen had told Nattrass, apparently, was that Hines had made a fool of her, humiliated her. There was no feature in the *Telegraph* — Nattrass told Yunis to pull it, or she'd very quickly find herself out of a job. She believed he meant it, so she did as she was told. She doesn't like talking about it because Nattrass humiliated *her* — terrorised her into dropping a good story.'

'So Helen lied in her book about the poem that was supposedly so important to her,' said Charlie thoughtfully.

'She didn't only lie,' said Simon. 'She stole. Well, sort of. "Room Swept White" is Rahila Yunis's favourite poem. She told Helen that, before Angus Hines chipped in and pointed out that "The Microbe" didn't mean what Helen thought it meant. Shit.' Stella White had appeared on the doorstep of number 16 and was staring at them, a quizzical expression on her face. 'She must be wondering why we're parked outside and not coming in,' said Simon. 'Have you got the photos?'

'Yep.' Charlie climbed out of the car and stretched. Her knees creaked, as if she hadn't moved for years. She was heading for Stella's house when Simon pulled her back. 'Once we're finished here, you and I are going home,' he said. 'Straight home.'

'Okay. Mind if I ask why?'

'Yes.' He turned away from her, shouted a hello to Stella.

'Is it anything bad?' Charlie called after him.

'Hopefully not that bad,' he said over his shoulder.

And then he was in the house and she couldn't ask him anything else, not without being overheard.

Dillon sat hunched on the sofa, kicking it with his heels. 'I dragged him away from his horse-racing,' said Stella. 'I thought you deserved his full attention for a change.' Her son looked as if he thought otherwise, but he said nothing.

'You look very well,' Simon told Stella. 'Better than when I last saw you.'

'I'm in remission,' she said. 'Just found out today. Can't quite believe it, but there you go.'

'Well done.' Charlie beamed at her. *Straight home:* it could only mean one thing . . .

'Hi, Dillon,' said Simon awkwardly.

'Hello,' the boy replied in a monotone. Charlie wasn't sure which of them was winning on the social skills front.

Simon held out his hand for the photos and she gave them to him. 'I'm going to show you some photographs,' he told Dillon. 'I'd like you to tell me who they are.'

Dillon nodded. One by one, Simon showed him the pictures, starting with Glen Jaggard. 'Don't know,' he said. Sebastian Brownlee also got a 'Don't know.'

'What about this one?' Simon held up a picture of Paul Yardley.

'Uncle Paul.'

'And this one?' Laurie Nattrass.

'I've seen him,' said Dillon, suddenly animated. 'He went to Auntie Helen's house lots of times. Once I was playing outside and he told me to look where I was going and he said a very rude word to me.'

'And this one?'

Dillon's eyes lit up. 'That's him,' he said, smiling up at Simon. 'That's the man with the magic umbrella.'

The photograph was of Angus Hines.

23
Monday 12 October 2009

'When Ray turned up on my doorstep after she'd been released —'

'It was my doorstep too,' she cuts in.

'Our doorstep,' Angus corrects himself. 'When she turned up, I was happy to let her in. While she was in prison, I'd devised the perfect test. Hines' Test of Guilt, I call it.' Ray's eyes are pleading with me: *listen to him, give him a chance. However awful this sounds, don't walk away.*

I remind myself that Hugo is in the next room. That's not as close as it would be in most houses, but it's close enough. If I screamed, he'd hear me. Any time I can't stand this any more, he'll drive me away from here and from Angus, who I'm now certain is a murderer.

Angus Hines: maker of probability tables, arranger of numbers in squares. He sent me the cards. I was supposed to guess what they meant, just as I was supposed to guess his meaning when he sent me the list of people Judith Duffy had testified against in the criminal and family courts. He sent me the two photographs of Helen Yardley's hands. Did he take them just before he shot her?

I had a bad feeling about him from the moment I met him: so bad I locked him up. My instincts must have been screaming at me that he was dangerous. Ray was scared of him too, at one time. Why isn't she still?

'I took Ray up to what had once been our bedroom,' he says. 'The room where years before she'd climbed out of the window and smoked a cigarette sitting on the ledge. I opened the window, grabbed her and dragged her over to it. I pushed her head out, and the top half of her body, and I held her there: half out, half in. She knew I could easily have pushed her out if I'd wanted to. There's no way she'd have survived the fall.'

'You told me you didn't try to kill her,' I say, keeping my voice steady.

'I didn't. As Ray said, if I'd tried I'd have succeeded. What I tried to do was make her believe I'd kill her if she didn't tell me the truth. And I would have done.'

'And then you asked her if she'd killed Marcella and Nathaniel.'

'Hines' Test of Guilt: put a woman who might or might not be guilty of murdering her children in a life-threatening situation. Convince her you'll kill her if she doesn't tell the truth, but that you'll let her live if she does. Whatever the truth is, you'll let her live — tell her that. Then ask her if she committed the murders. Whatever her first answer is, don't accept it. Keep ordering her to tell you the truth, as if you don't believe what she's said. If she changes her answer, do it again. Keep doing it — keep ordering her to tell you the truth, and eventually she'll be so scared and so unable to work out what the right answer is, you'll get the truth out of her. At that point, she'll stop chopping and changing: she'll stick to her story, and that story will be the true version of events. If she continues to chop and change in a way that makes it impossible for you to identify the truth, kill her as you threatened to.'

Don't interrupt him. Don't argue with him.

'Ray passed with flying colours.' Angus smiles at her, as if this is all perfectly normal. Ray keeps her eyes fixed on the camera. 'She didn't chop and change, not at all. She really believed I was going to kill her, yet not once did she say she was guilty. That's what proved to me that I'd been wrong about her.'

'I couldn't have said I'd killed my babies

615

when I hadn't,' says Ray quietly. 'Not for anyone or anything. Not even if Angus was going to kill me if I didn't.'

'Did you tell the police what Angus did to you?'

'No. It'll be difficult for you to understand, but . . . I knew it wasn't Angus who opened the window and . . . It wasn't him. It was his pain and his grief that did it, not the real Angus, the one that existed before the grief. I also . . . You won't understand this either, but I respected him for doubting my innocence. His duty as a father was to do his absolute best for Marcella and Nathaniel, even after they were gone. *Especially* once they were gone. If so many intelligent people thought I'd killed them, how could he not take that seriously? He'd have been letting them down. And . . .'

'What?'

'I understood exactly how he felt about me, because it was how I felt about all the other women: Helen Yardley, Sarah Jaggard . . .'

'I asked you before if you thought Helen was guilty. You said no.'

'I never thought she *was* guilty.' Ray leans forward. 'I thought she *might be* guilty. Same with Sarah Jaggard. There's a big difference. I agree with Angus: the more of

616

these supposed miscarriage-of-justice victims there are, the more guilty ones there must be among them, using innocent women like me as their camouflage.'

Hines' Theorem of Probability. I think of Joanne Bew. Lorna Keast.

'I didn't want anything to do with Helen or Sarah, inside or outside of a TV documentary, because I didn't know if they were murderers,' says Ray.

Yet you know Angus is a murderer, and you're planning to marry him.

'You wanted to find out, didn't you?' I ask him. 'Your Test of Guilt had worked on Ray, so you decided to try it on Helen.'

'Ray had nothing to do with it,' says Angus. 'I discussed my Theorem of Probability with her, but I didn't tell her what I intended to do.'

'You wanted to make someone pay for your pain and suffering, but Ray was innocent, so she couldn't pay. And even if by then you were convinced your children had died from a vaccine, who could you punish for that? Wendy Whitehead? No, she was on Ray's side, *against* the vaccine. It would have been hard to settle on an individual or individuals to blame. Much easier to use your test of guilt to find a baby-killer: Helen Yardley, or Sarah Jaggard. They might be

617

guilty even if Ray wasn't — you could make *them* pay.'

'I delegated Sarah Jaggard to somebody else,' says Angus. 'He made a hash of it — did it in broad daylight in a public place and was interrupted. That's why I did the Test on Helen myself, though I probably would have anyway. Sarah Jaggard killed — or didn't kill — a child that wasn't her own. I was less interested in her.'

'You murdered Helen Yardley,' I say, feeling sick. 'You shot her in the head.'

'I did, yes.' *He said it. He confessed to the camera.*

'And you killed Judith Duffy.'

'Yes. The police seemed determined to mistake me for a pro-Duffy vigilante. I had to set them straight. They needed a lesson in truth and fairness. Impartiality. Unless you're impartial, how can you judge? Duffy made some bad mistakes — she was the first to admit it.'

Next to him, Ray is crying.

'Why didn't you go to the police?' I ask her. 'You must have known as soon as Helen died . . .'

'I had no proof.'

'You knew what he'd done to you.'

'His word against mine.' She wipes her eyes. 'He could have accused me of lying, and . . . I didn't want to hurt him or damage him any more than he's already been damaged. *This* is what I wanted: for him to tell his own story. I knew he couldn't be allowed to carry on, but . . . I wanted it to end in the right way, and I thought I could persuade him.'

'Marriage and a new baby in exchange for a confession and no more killing?' I say. *Laurie Nattrass's baby.*

Ray winces, hearing me put it so starkly.

'Ray's right,' says Angus, taking her hand. She leans into him. *She still loves him.* 'This way's better. I needed to be ready to tell the story.'

Is that what he was doing upstairs, all the time Ray and I were talking? Readying himself?

'Judith Duffy died while you waited for him to be ready,' I tell her.

'I know that, Fliss. How do you think that makes me feel?'

'Judith wouldn't have minded,' Angus says.

I stare at him in utter disbelief. 'Wouldn't have minded being murdered?'

'No. Her children had disowned her, she'd lost her professional credibility — she was about to be struck off, in all probability. She had nothing to live for apart from what she'd always lived for: protecting children, bringing their killers to justice. I think she'd have approved of Hines' Test of Guilt.'

'Fliss, listen,' says Ray. I hear desperation in her voice. 'I know what you're thinking, but everything's going to be okay now. It's finished. Angus's . . . test, it's over. He knows that; he accepts it. I know you think I ought to abandon him and hate him, but I can't, because *this isn't him.*'

'Do you agree with that?' I ask him.

'Yes,' he says without hesitation. 'I didn't used to be like this. I used to be Angus Hines. Now I'm . . . something else, I don't know what.'

A chill runs all the way through me. How terrifying to turn into something you recognise as not yourself — something uncontrollable and horrifying — and yet not be able to define that thing or feel the horror.

'Angus will go to prison, but he won't be alone in the world,' says Ray. 'He'll be punished as he should be for what he's done, but he'll have hope too, and a reason to carry on — a new child to love, me. Even though we won't be together maybe for years, I can write to him, visit him, take our baby . . .'

'What do the sixteen numbers mean?' I ask.

'They mean that Helen Yardley was a liar,' says Angus. 'If she could be a liar, so could Sarah Jaggard. So could any of them. Once Laurie Nattrass worked that out, I hoped he'd be a bit more selective in choosing who to champion. I hoped the same about you, once I heard you were taking over the film. As for the police, they can't say I didn't play fair. Every time I killed, I left a card. All they had to do was use their brains and they'd have worked out that the person most likely to draw those sixteen numbers to their attention was me. I gave them all the information they needed to find me.' He smiles.

He's mad.

But this isn't him. This is his pain and grief, not the real Angus Hines, the one Ray loves and wants to help.

'What's the connection between the numbers and you?' I ask him.

'If you're clever, you'll work it out,' he says.

'It doesn't matter,' Ray whispers. 'All that matters is that it's over, Fliss, and you're going to make a programme that tells the whole truth of what happened. You will do that for us, won't you? For us, and our child, for . . . for the record?'

'Yes. Yes, I will.'

There's one more question I have to ask Angus Hines. I've put it off for as long as I can, because I don't want to hear the answer. 'When you did the Test of Guilt on Helen, what did she say?'

He smiles at me.

'There's no point,' says Ray. 'He won't tell you.'

'Did she confess to murdering her children? Did she insist throughout the ordeal *you* inflicted on her that she was innocent, like Ray?'

'You'd like to know, wouldn't you?'

'Do *you* know?' I ask Ray.

She shakes her head.

'Tell me about Monday 5 October,' I say to Angus, as if it's a different question from the one I've already asked twice. 'Tell me about doing your Test on Helen. Don't pretend you don't want to talk about it. You want me to understand how clever you are.'

'All right, then,' he says easily. 'I'll tell you.'

Just like that?

The doorbell rings. 'No prizes for guessing who,' says Angus. 'Whoever rang the bell before, you told them to go to the police.'

'I didn't, actually.' I hear footsteps, the front door being opened. *No. Not now.*

'Is there someone else in the house?' Ray looks worried.

'It's okay,' I tell her. 'We're going to carry on filming.'

The door of the den inches open and a large sweaty man with messy blond hair appears, with stupid, disobedient Hugo Nattrass behind him. Since when did sitting in silence and doing nothing include letting strangers into the house?

'Wait in the other room,' I snap at them.

'I'm DC Colin Sel—'

'I don't care who you are. Go outside, close the door and wait,' I say quickly, before my resolve has a chance to weaken. 'We're busy here.' Sellers must see something in my eyes that convinces him, because he retreats without another word.

'Thank you,' says Ray, once he's gone.

I move the camera closer to Angus so that his face fills the frame. 'Whenever you're ready,' I tell him.

The Times, Tuesday 29 June 2010

WRONGLY CONVICTED BABY-KILLER ACQUITTED

Dorne Llewellyn, 63, from Port Talbot, walked free from Cardiff Crown Court yesterday after being found not guilty at a retrial for the murder in 2000 of nine-month-old Benjamin Evans. The vote for acquittal was unanimous, as was the guilty verdict at Mrs Llewellyn's original trial. In April 2001, in the same courtroom, the prosecution persuaded 12 jurors that Mrs Llewellyn shook Benjamin to death while babysitting for him. She spent nearly nine years in prison.

Mrs Llewellyn was one of many women convicted on expert evidence provided by Dr Judith Duffy, who was murdered in October last year. At the time of her death, Dr Duffy was being investigated for misconduct. She alleged that Benjamin must have been shaken because he had suffered bleeding in the brain, but did not mention that there was also evidence of older bleeds. The second jury to hear the case was persuaded by the five independently appointed medical experts that there was no basis on which to convict Mrs Llewellyn of murder, as she had babysat for Benjamin only once, and there was clear evidence of brain bleeds dating back to before that occasion. Mrs Llewellyn and her friends and family wept on the steps of the court after hearing the 'not guilty' verdict.

JIPAC chairman Laurie Nattrass said on Mrs Llewellyn's behalf: 'The jury demonstrated its utter scorn for this insane and unsubstantiated murder charge by taking a superlative 40 minutes to return a unanimous 'not guilty' verdict. We should celebrate this triumph of justice over its enemies.' Mr Nattrass added: 'Currently the most dangerous of those enemies is the criminally idiotic Tom Astrow.' Professor Astrow, chairman of the Criminal Cases Review Commission, has proposed that in certain cases where possible child abuse is an issue, the jury and all reporters ought to be made to leave the courtroom while the judge examines the complex medical evidence with two experts. Professor Astrow told *The Times* on Monday: 'A layperson jury is simply not able to process the incredibly complex disagreements between experts on the finer points of medical opinion.'

Mr Nattrass disagrees: 'Astrow's proposal is, by any definition, craziness of the worst kind, yet another terrifying by-product of the rash of false accusations sparked off by Judith Duffy and her paranoid cohort of guilt-seeking paediatricians. To exclude jurors based on the assumption that they're too stupid to understand the medical evidence is patently immoral, as well as incorrect. Dr Russell Meredew OBE, author of some of the most brilliant papers ever written on unexpected child deaths, describes Judith Duffy's testimony at Dorne Llewellyn's first trial as "crap". Even a layperson can understand that. Instead of dismissing jurors as stupid and excluding them, why not exclude experts who are biased, devious and arrogant? What kind of judicial system is it where jurors are expected to reach a verdict after being protected from any evidence regarded as too contentious in case it confuses them? As for banning reporters from the courtroom, I can scarcely believe someone in Astrow's position in the twenty-first century would advocate such a move from light towards darkness. JIPAC will put its full weight behind ensuring that Astrow's proposals are seen for the disasters they are and rejected out of hand.' Professor Astrow was unavailable for comment.

A Room Swept White:
A Family's Tragedy
By Felicity Benson

This book is dedicated to the memory of my father, Melvyn Benson.

ACKNOWLEDGEMENTS
Thank you to Ray and Angus Hines for allowing me to tell their story.

Thank you to all the police officers from Culver Valley CID, especially DS Sam Kombothekra, whose generosity and patience have been quite staggering.

Thank you to Julian Lance, Wendy Whitehead, Jackie Fletcher and the JABS contingent, Paul Yardley, Glen and Sarah Jaggard, Ned Vento, Gillian Howard, Dr Russell Meredew, Dr Phil Dennison, Dr Jack Pelham, Rahila Yunis, Gaynor Mundy, Leah Gould, Stella White, Beryl Murie, Fiona Sharp, Antonia Duffy, Grace and Hannah Brownlee.

Thank you to Laurie for giving me the chance.

Thank you to Tamsin and the gang at Better Brother Productions.

Last but not least, thank you, Hugo, for your unwavering support, and for your foresight in predicting that I would one day love you more than I love your house. I do, but only just.

INTRODUCTION

On Monday 5 October 2009, Angus Hines got up at 6 a.m. and drove a hired car from his home in London's Notting Hill to Spilling in the Culver Valley. His destination was number 9 Bengeo Street, the home of Helen Yardley. As he drove, he listened to the *Today* programme on BBC Radio 4. Helen's husband Paul had already left for work, so Helen was alone in the house when Angus arrived at 8.20 a.m. It was a bright, sunny winter day, clear skies, not a cloud in sight.

He must have rung the doorbell. Helen must have let him in, though they were not on friendly terms and the last time they had met they had argued. Angus spent the whole day alone with Helen in her house. At some point during the hours they spent together, Angus produced a gun that he'd obtained from an acquaintance, an M9 Beretta 9 millimetre. At five o'clock in the afternoon, he used that gun to shoot Helen dead because, according to him, she had failed a test he'd devised for her — or, rather, not specifically for her, but for all women accused of murdering babies who claim to be innocent of the crime — women like Sarah Jaggard, Dorne Llewellyn, and of course Angus's wife, Ray. It was Angus's own personal connection to a case of this sort that led him to formulate the test that he calls, without any irony, 'Hines' Test of Guilt', though he has twice asked me if I think he ought to change its name to 'Hines' Test of Truth'. Here's how he explained its rules to me:

'Put a woman who might or might not be guilty of murdering her children in a life-threatening situation. Convince her you'll kill her if she doesn't tell the truth, but that you'll let her live if she does. Whatever the truth is, you'll let her live — tell her that. Then ask her if she committed the murders. Whatever her first answer is, don't accept it. Keep ordering her to tell you the truth, as if you don't believe what she's said. If she changes her answer, do it again. Keep doing it — keep ordering her to tell you the truth, and eventually she'll be so scared and so unable to work out what the right answer is, you'll get the truth out of her. At that point, she'll stop chopping and changing: she'll stick to her story, and that story will be the true version of events. If she continues to chop and change in a way that makes it impossible for you to identify the truth, kill her as you threatened to.'

The first two times I asked Angus what happened when he subjected Helen Yardley to his Test of Guilt, he wouldn't tell me. He taunted me by saying, 'You'd like to know, wouldn't you?' and seemed to relish his superior knowledge and my frustrated ignorance. Then, suddenly and for no apparent reason, he changed his mind and announced that he was willing to tell me the story of what happened at Helen's house on Monday 5 October. The telling process took nearly three hours from start to finish. I will summarise what Angus told me very briefly, and spare you the more chilling aspects of his account; I wish I could have been spared them myself.

Angus told me that Helen spent very little

time — less than half an hour — changing her story from innocence to guilt and back again before finally admitting to having smothered both her sons. That's why he shot her, he said: to punish her, because she was a murderer. But, he told me, before he shot her, he spent several hours listening to her long and comprehensive confession: what she'd done, why she'd done it, and how she felt about it.

This book is the story of the Hines family — Ray, Angus, Marcella and Nathaniel — and of the police investigation into the murders of Helen Yardley and Judith Duffy. Angus Hines' murder of Helen Yardley isn't how the story begins. Insofar as you can pinpoint the origin of any story, I think this one started in 1998, when Angus and Ray Hines had their first baby, Marcella. I've started with this much later incident, Angus's shooting of Helen Yardley in October 2009, not because it's violent and shocking and attention-grabbing — though it is, all those things — but because I want to set it apart from the rest of the book, because I believe Angus's account of it, and therefore my account of it, to be a lie. That's another reason why I have condensed and summarised what Angus told me about what happened between him and Helen that day: I don't want to devote any more space than I must to a story I'm sure isn't true.

By the end of this book, you'll have formed an opinion of Angus, and you'll be able to decide for yourself if he's the sort of man who would ignore the terms and conditions of his own Test of Guilt/Truth, according to which only lying is punishable by death, and shoot Helen Yardley even after she had told him the truth about her guilt. Maybe you'll decide he couldn't risk leaving her alive because she'd seen him and would have gone to the police. My impression, for what it's worth, is that Angus was never afraid of being found out — he freely distributed what he regarded as clear clues to his guilt, as you will see later in the book.

Angus's respect for the law is limited to a handful of detectives: DC Simon Waterhouse and Sergeant Charlotte Zailer chief among them, for reasons that will become clear. In general, however, he has little respect for the police or the legal system, and my theory — though I must stress it is only a theory — is that he doesn't think anybody but him deserves to know the truth about what happened on Monday 5 October 2009 between him and Helen Yardley. I think he feels that, as the sole inventor of the Test of Guilt/Truth, only he is entitled to know its results.

Is that why he shot Helen, so that she wouldn't be able to tell anybody her version of what happened that day? To ensure that he would always be the sole owner of that information? Given his delight in his knowledge, and the power it gives him in the face of others' ignorance, does that mean the story he told me is the opposite of what really happened? Might he get a kick out of misleading me as much as possible, and if so, does that mean his Test in fact proved Helen to be innocent? I believe that's unlikely too, because the fact remains that he shot her dead; Angus's rules clearly state that if you tell the truth, you're allowed to live.

Perhaps Helen didn't waver once but consistently protested her innocence, and perhaps in spite of this Angus didn't believe her — in which case his Test would have been revealed to him as a comprehensive failure. Would that have been enough to make him shoot her? I believe it might. I also believe, given the history between Helen and Angus — a history you will read about — that she might well have refused to say anything at all. Was she determined to resist him, even though he had a gun?

Silence from her would have constituted a defeat for him, and she would have known that. Or did she keep 'chopping and changing' her story, to use Angus's terminology? Did she keep saying different things, hoping to stumble on the one that would make him put away the gun and leave? Did he kill her because he simply couldn't ascertain what the truth was?

If Angus didn't discover on that day that his Test was flawed, did he perhaps discover a flaw within himself, an inability to stick to the terms and conditions he'd laid down for himself? Before he was a killer, Angus was a devoted father who lost two children and then his wife when she was wrongly accused of their murders. Did Helen confess to smothering her two babies, and was Angus so overcome by anger and disgust that he couldn't resist pulling the trigger? If that is what happened, he might never tell anybody — he prides himself on being a planner, always in control and thinking ahead. He would never admit to being so swayed by emotion that he went against his own plan.

I am hoping, and Paul Yardley and Hannah Brownlee are hoping, that one day Angus will tell us what really happened at 9 Bengeo Street on Monday 5 October. It's a slow process, but I'm doing my best to chip away at his image of himself as super-rational and in control. I have tried to explain to him that his Test is useless: people do not behave predictably when threatened with imminent execution. Ordered to tell the truth about the most traumatic event in their lives, some might choose the story they wish to believe about themselves — let's say, for the sake of argument, a lie — and stick to it, on the grounds that their lives wouldn't be worth living anyway if they acknowledged the painful truth. Some might tell the truth and stick to it; some might waver, changing back and forth from one version to another. Angus has no way of proving how either a guilty or an innocent person would respond to being tortured. To me this is an undeniable fact, but he insists I'm wrong.

He clams up completely when I point out to him the main flaw of his Test: that it involves judging, condemning and execut-ing other human beings — three things no one should ever do. If what you're about to read proves anything conclusively, it's the necessity for compassion and humility, as well as the undeniable fact that if people could learn to be more forgiving, of them-selves and others, there would be less to forgive all round. If attempts to understand

and help could replace judgement and condemnation, even when heinous crimes have been committed — *especially* when heinous crimes have been committed — then there would be fewer heinous crimes committed in the future. A popular misconception is the idea that to understand and help a criminal means to let him or her 'get away with it'; this is not the case, as I hope this story will prove. Personally I believe that, irrespective of whatever legal action might or might not be taken, nobody ever 'gets away with' anything: what we do has an effect on us from which we can't escape.

Before handing in the final version of this book to my editor, I went to visit Angus in prison and took the manuscript with me. I made him read this introduction. When I asked him if there was any aspect of it he objected to, he shook his head and handed it back to me. 'Publish it,' he said.

ACKNOWLEDGEMENTS

I am very grateful to the following people, all of whom helped substantially with the writing of this book: Mark Fletcher, Sarah Shaper, Jackie Fletcher, Mark and Cal Pannone, Guy Martland, Dan, Phoebe and Guy Jones, Jenny, Adele and Norman Geras, Ken and Sue Hind, Anne Grey, Hannah Pescod, Ian Daley, Paula Cuddy, Clova McCallum, Peter Bean, David Allen, Dan Oxtoby (who, without meaning to, inspired a plot twist) and Judith Gribble.

Several medical experts helped me to make sense of many of the controversial issues surrounding crib death: chiefly Dr Mike Green and two other people who would prefer not to be named. All three, and several others, were enormously generous with their time and knowledge, for which I am hugely grateful.

Thank you to Fiona Sampson, author of

the brilliant poem 'Anchorage' — which is reprinted in the novel and from which the novel's British title is a quote — and to Carcanet Press for allowing me to use the poem. Thanks also to The Estate of Hilaire Belloc and PFD for allowing me to use 'The Microbe' in this book.

Thank you to Val McDermid, who invented Reverse L'Oréal Syndrome.

Massive thanks to my inspirational agent Peter Straus, to the wonderful Jenny Hewson, and to my superb publishers Hodder & Stoughton, especially Carolyn Mays, Karen Geary and Francesca Best.

I wouldn't have been able to write this novel if I hadn't read three books: *Unexpected Death in Childhood* edited by Peter Sidebotham and Peter Fleming, *Cherished* by Angela Cannings and Megan Lloyd Davies, and *Stolen Innocence: the Sally Clark Story* by John Batt. The experiences of women such as Sally Clark, Angela Cannings and Trupti Patel were part of the inspiration for *A Room Swept White,* though none of the characters or cases in my novel are based on real people or cases.

ABOUT THE AUTHOR

Sophie Hannah is the author of the international bestsellers *Little Face, The Wrong Mother,* and *The Dead Lie Down.* In 2004 she won the Daphne Du Maurier Prize for suspense fiction, and she is also an award-winning poet. She lives in Cambridge, England, with her husband and two children.

The employees of Thorndike Press hope you have enjoyed this Large Print book. All our Thorndike, Wheeler, and Kennebec Large Print titles are designed for easy reading, and all our books are made to last. Other Thorndike Press Large Print books are available at your library, through selected bookstores, or directly from us.

For information about titles, please call:
  (800) 223-1244

or visit our Web site at:
  http://gale.cengage.com/thorndike

To share your comments, please write:
  Publisher
  Thorndike Press
  10 Water St., Suite 310
  Waterville, ME 04901

1-1-1996

Charmed Circle

Also by Barbara Whitnell

The Song of the Rainbird
Crosscurrents

Charmed Circle

Barbara Whitnell

St. Martin's Press
New York

Library of Congress Cataloging-in-Publication Data

Whitnell, Barbara.
    Charmed circle / Barbara Whitnell.
       p.   cm.
    "A Thomas Dunne book."
    ISBN 0-312-10438-3
    1. Man-woman relationships—England—Fiction.   2. Family—
England—Fiction.   I. Title.
    PR6073.H653C43   1994
    823'.914—dc20   93-33527
                                                CIP

First published in Great Britain by Hodder and Stoughton Ltd.

First U.S. Edition: January 1994
10 9 8 7 6 5 4 3 2 1

To Brenda
best of sisters, best of friends

Charmed Circle

1

Suppose Barney had come on any other day? Suppose it had been one of those awful days when a teething Tess had kept her up all night and her head felt as if it were stuffed with cotton wool, not an original idea in sight? Could she then have presented him with quite such a brave and independent front?

Probably not, Rachel thought; but it so happened she was walking on air that day, despite the fact that it had proved one of those maddening mornings that had, for once, begun with the promise of real summer, only to collapse limply under a blanket of cloud, like some pathetic convalescent testing his strength too far.

Ignoring all warning signs, she had spurned Nancy's prudent urging towards cardigans and umbrellas, and had left home in her one decent dress of navy-blue linen with a red and white dotted silk scarf at the neck, the knotting of which had caused her considerable time and trouble. For once she had felt pleased with the overall effect. It was a day, she told Nancy, for ermine and pearls. And bathing in ass's milk. What it was emphatically *not* was a cardigan sort of day.

"You'll be sor–ry," Nancy had sung out as she left home; but though she was undeniably cold, she wasn't sorry. Nothing could spoil this marvellous day – not the weather, or the crowds, or even the drabness of the London streets, still showing signs of wartime austerity even though the war itself had been over for more than a year.

Better times were coming – for her, for the country. Never mind the goose pimples, she said to herself as she strode up Piccadilly towards Green Park tube station with her head up, biting her lip

1

to hide the exultant grin she was powerless to subdue altogether. Never mind the fact that a casual glimpse at her reflection in a shop window had shown her that the scarf had taken on a life of its own and was now sticking up in two points like rabbits' ears in a wholly unsuitable position somewhere below her left ear. She was above such petty considerations. Indomitable, that's what she was. Capable. Self-sufficient.

Had one small success really achieved all this? One swallow doesn't make a summer, she warned herself, rather as Grandma might have done – Grandma who could never bring herself to forswear the pleasure of pricking her bubble of happiness. Or anyone else's, for that matter.

Oh, *pooh* to Grandma! She had a right to exult. This, after all, was the day when all her childhood dreams had become reality. This was the day when she had signed the contract that had turned her into a real, live author. No frog, transformed by a kiss into a handsome prince, could possibly have felt more elated.

There had, after all, been disappointments in plenty. Times when, sunk in despondency, she had been quite certain that she had no talent at all, no fresh ideas, nothing to offer; days, in short, when the future was too frightening to contemplate. No doubt there would be more, but at this moment she was undismayed by the thought of them. This was the day that hope was born; no, not hope. Certainty. They would be all right, she and Tess. As people said with irritating frequency during the war, they could take it.

Thus it was in buoyant mood that she hurried along, oblivious of the rain that, having threatened for the past few hours, was now beginning in earnest. What did getting wet matter? Or being jostled by the milling throng in the station? She had intended to come home earlier, but had found much to talk about with Graham, her newly appointed agent, and now had struck the beginning of the rush hour.

Anxiously she looked at her watch. Tess was all right with Nancy, she knew that, and there was a bottle made up for her, but she had promised to be back for the six o'clock feed. The last thing she wanted was to appear to be taking Nancy's good nature for granted; heaven alone knew she did enough! She paid an acceptable amount of rent for her room, but because she worked odd hours at the BBC was often free and always willing to look after Tess in an emergency. In addition, she nearly always cooked the evening meal. She enjoyed cooking, she said, and it was more satisfying to cook for two than for one – not to mention the advantage gained by having two lots of rations to play with. And because she had a talent for making a little go an appetisingly long way, Rachel could see the force of her argument. Nevertheless, she was aware of the need to tread carefully.

It was still drizzling when she left the train at Hammersmith, but fortunately Inverness Street was no more than a five minutes' dash from the station. Number 14, which Rachel had bought with the money left to her by her grandmother, was in the middle of a yellow-brick terrace, bay windows to the ground and first floors. Identical houses stretched to the right and left, as far as the eye could see, except for a gap towards the end of the street caused by a doodlebug. You could still see the remains of pink nursery paper on an exposed wall and the place where a staircase was once fixed to it.

Rachel never walked past that gap unless she couldn't possibly avoid it. Bomb damage was still everywhere in London, grown over for the most part with rosebay willowherb. She had learned not to notice it, but somehow this was different; perhaps it was the wallpaper, and the fact that it was so near home.

As she opened the door the savoury smell from the kitchen wafted towards her and her stomach churned with hunger. There was no sound from Tess; no sound, even, from Nancy, which was unusual. She was given to singing about the house: opera, music-hall ditties, the latest hits – anything. But now there was only silence.

"Hallo, I'm home," Rachel called, as she squeezed past the pram that occupied most of the hall space. "And you were absolutely right about the weather. I'm freezing!"

She followed the smell through to the kitchen. Nancy was stirring something on the stove. She turned as Rachel came in, and at once it became clear that something unusual and of great import had occurred. Nancy had one of those sort of faces. Her joys were more joyful; her tragedies soul-searing; her laughter the very essence of amusement. Now she was registering suppressed excitement and an all-consuming curiosity, her small, sallow-skinned face positively vibrating with the momentousness of the situation.

She cut short Rachel's apology for her late arrival with a wave of the cooking spoon.

"There's someone to see you," she hissed. "A man!"

"Man?" Rachel was startled, almost as if Nancy had mentioned a hitherto unknown species. She glanced down the hall towards the front room, to where her visitor presumably sat in cheerless isolation. "Who, for heaven's sake?"

Nancy opened her dark eyes wide and sucked in her cheeks. "Guess!" she said.

"*Who?*"

At the sight of her face, Nancy relented. "Barney Rossiter," she mouthed, in an exaggerated, lip-stretching way. "I didn't know what to do with him," she went on, only slightly more audibly. "I didn't want to bring him in here because of all the nappies drying. He might have guessed – "

"What do you suppose he thought when he saw the pram in the hall?" For a moment Rachel looked panic-stricken; then she shrugged her shoulders. "Oh, who cares! Let him think what he likes, he's getting nothing out of me. Where is Tess, anyway?"

"Still asleep. I thought it better to leave her. The later the last feed, the longer she'll sleep tonight and the more peace you'll have. I'll see to her when she wakes up. Go on," Nancy added, making a shooing motion with the cooking spoon as Rachel still clung to the doorpost as if in need of support.

Barney. Here.

The best of the bunch, certainly. But she hadn't wanted to see him again. What should she say? How should she handle it? She wasn't ready. She needed more time.

"At least you've got some good news to tell him," Nancy added, turning back to the pan on the stove.

Yes, of course. The book! She had good news. You're strong, she reminded herself. Successful. Indomitable. She stood a little straighter.

There was no mirror downstairs. Well, it didn't matter. She didn't care what Barney thought, did she? Still, she fluffed out her hair with her fingers, smoothed her skirt and tugged at the scarf before taking a deep breath and making for the front room.

He was not, after all, sitting. He stood by the bookcase, studying the titles on the shelves, his back towards the door. The sound of her entrance was masked by that of a car revving up in the street outside. She looked at him silently for a moment, gathering her resources. It was going to be even more difficult than she had imagined.

The best of the lot, she thought again. There had always been a bond between them. She'd even fooled herself into believing that she could love him once, a long time ago. Perhaps she could have done. Perhaps she might yet. Seeing his familiar blond head, the way the hair grew on the nape of his neck, she was conscious of a deep well of affection for him. They might have been happy. If only –

4

But he'd *known*! Remembrance and pain and common sense came rushing in like shock troops to save her from vain regrets. He'd known – or at least suspected – and said nothing! How could she ever forget that, or forget where his loyalties would lie if ever there was another show-down? Besides, there was Tess. If ever anyone was off limits, then Barney Rossiter was the one.

But when, sensing her presence, he swung round to look at her and she caught the full force of those blazing blue eyes, she reached out blindly to hold the back of a chair, so desperately did she need something to cling to.

"Hallo, Rachel," he said softly. His small, fine-boned face with the high-bridged nose and thin mouth was just as she remembered, but his smile seemed more tentative. "Should I have thrown my hat in first?" he went on as she continued to stare at him blankly.

With an effort she pulled herself together.

"Barney! What a surprise! It's wonderful to see you."

"You're sure?"

"Of course. Why shouldn't it be?"

He gave a brief, incredulous laugh. "I don't need to tell you – "

"It wasn't really your fault."

"You've forgiven me, then?"

Suddenly the awkwardness was gone and there was only delight. She crossed the room towards him, hands outstretched. "Oh Barney, of course I have! You were on my side. I knew that, really, and it's so good to see you – it's been ages – "

"And whose fault is that? I thought you were lost and gone for ever. Sunk without trace! No one's heard a word from you since – since heaven knows when. How are you, Rachel?"

"Fine! And you? Are you out of the Army?"

"Oh, for three months now."

They stood with hands joined, smiling at each other. Was he as conscious as she of the overwhelming weight of all that had happened, she wondered? What could she say? Where did they begin?

She turned from him, struck suddenly by the unwelcoming atmosphere of the largely unused room. It never caught the sun at the best of times. Now, with the rain pattering against the windowpane it seemed utterly cheerless.

"August!" she said bitterly. "Summers used not to be like this – "

"When you were a gel?" Barney laughed. "You sound like Ma. She says it's the bomb that's upset the weather."

"Maybe she's right." Awkwardness again. Rachel hugged herself against the cold. "To hell with austerity, I'm going to light the fire," she said. "Dammit, no matches – " Without a word he proffered his cigarette lighter, an amused twist to his mouth as if such unpreparedness was no more than he might have expected. As if it brought back memories.

"What are you doing with a lighter, anyway?" she said as she crouched down. "You used not to smoke."

"Well, I do now."

He would have changed in other ways as well. Foolish to think that he wouldn't.

"There, that's better," she said, standing up straight and smiling at him once again. "Do sit down, Barney. I ought to get you something. Tea? I'd offer something stronger if I had it – "

"Do shut up," he said, not sitting down. Rachel was aware suddenly of the pounding of her heart. He looked at her, those startling eyes unreadable. "Are you really glad to see me?" he asked her.

"Of course!" She reached out towards him once more and suddenly was in his arms and they were hugging each other just as if nothing had happened and there were no shadows between them. Just as if there were no Tess, no Gavin, no Diana.

But that was an illusion, Rachel reminded herself. There were shadows in plenty. And Tess was more than a shadow. Tess was a three-dimensional reality, and the most important thing in her life. Gently she extricated herself from Barney's embrace. The danger signals in her head were flashing too insistently to be ignored.

"You might as well sit," she said.

He settled himself into the chair she indicated and crossed his knees, still regarding her thoughtfully. By the time she had arranged herself in the chair opposite, she had achieved a degree of calmness. Friendly but uninvolved delight was the order of the day, she warned herself.

"Now tell me how you tracked me down," she said.

"Your aunt told me," he said. "Mrs Courtney, isn't it? Sylvia Courtney. She came to Warnfield last week."

"Why would she do that? She hardly ever came when Grandma was alive. Oh, of course – I remember now. She asked your mother to keep some things from The Laurels for her, didn't she?"

"That's right. She wrote to Ma when The Laurels was sold and asked us to keep those blue ceramic pots for her, the ones that were in the porch, and a couple of prints. She said she'd collect them

6

later. That's why she came last week. She stayed for tea and told us about you."

"Dear Sylvia!"

"She said she only found out herself that you were in London a couple of weeks back."

"I know. I ran into her in Jermyn Street outside the cheese shop. I was on my way to the London Library."

"*Why*, Rachel?"

"I wanted to check some facts about Women's Suffrage – "

"Don't be an idiot! I mean why the secrecy?"

As if on cue, Tess began to cry – great, whooping yells which meant that she had woken, she was hungry, and furthermore thoroughly outraged that six o'clock was upon her and not a bottle in sight.

Rachel was fully aware that having a baby who slept from three to six most days seemed, to most people, not only eccentric but possibly immoral as well; but it was a routine that suited her way of life perfectly – and since it was Tess herself who had imposed it, she could only assume it suited her, too. It meant that she would be awake and lively until Rachel went to bed, when she would then – teething apart – sleep soundly all night until well after eight in the morning. As Rachel had little social life and worked as much as possible during the day, the evenings she spent with her small daughter were precious to her, and unbroken nights equally so.

There was a loud and reassuring cry from Nancy and the thump of footsteps running up the stairs.

"Coming, my darling. Hush, my sweetheart – "

"Who is that woman?" Barney asked.

"That's Nancy. A friend. She rents a room upstairs."

He pulled a face. "Bit of a bind, surely, having a tenant with a kid? Odd-looking woman. She's awfully dark, isn't she? Touch of the tarbrush, I imagine."

Rachel welcomed the spurt of anger this caused. She didn't want to remember the good things about him – would rather think of his arrogance. It proved he was still a Rossiter, still felt superior to the rest of the world, still judged people by crude, Rossiter standards.

"I've always considered that such an offensive figure of speech," she said coldly.

"Sorry!" He lifted his hands as if in supplication and raised his eyes to heaven. "I didn't mean anything derogatory."

And if you believe that, Rachel thought silently, you'll believe anything.

"Nancy's a friend in a million," she said.

She didn't elaborate. How could she begin to describe the times that Nancy had been her rock and anchor and guiding star? She it was who had comforted her in bad times and rejoiced in the good. She had visited her in the maternity ward at Tess's birth, and taken her share of walking the floor in those early days when feeding problems had reduced Rachel to a worn-out wreck. Together they had laughed and cried; but mostly they had laughed, for Nancy was blissfully, delightfully, irrepressibly funny.

"Is there a husband?" Barney asked. "Oh dear," he went on, as Rachel shook her head. "A Fallen Woman! Ma was very involved in Fallen Women at one time, when we were very small. Lannie and I used to imagine them littering the High Street."

Rachel's smile was barely discernible, and Barney grimaced once more.

"Sorry," he said. "There I go, putting my big foot in it again. But don't you mind having a yelling kid in the house? She's damn lucky to find someone so amenable."

"I don't mind. She doesn't yell much." Rachel looked away from him and smiled vaguely in the direction of the popping fire.

She had told no one from her old life about Tess, and she was certainly not going to begin with Barney Rossiter. Only Nancy knew all the facts. She hadn't told Sylvia, her father's only sister, when she had run into her in Jermyn Street. She hadn't even told her parents who were far away in Africa, where they had been throughout the entire war.

They would have to know one day, of course. They would be home on leave before too long, as soon as passages became available, but until then it had seemed utterly pointless to agitate them by announcing the arrival of an illegitimate grandchild, or run the risk of their total rejection.

Undoubtedly, had they been in the country, they would have urged adoption – but now, by the time they knew of the matter, Tess would be far too old for there to be any question of such a thing. And if, in fact, they did reject her –

No. She still didn't want to think about that.

So she had kept her secret, and bought the house. Nancy and she had been good friends during the war, on a bleak RAF station in Scotland. It had seemed heaven-sent when Nancy was offered a translator's job by the BBC, and let it be known that she was looking for accommodation in London. Barney's guess had been right, even though she had disliked his turn of phrase. Nancy's maternal grandfather originated from Ceylon and had made sure

8

that she spoke Tamil, even though she had lived in England all her life.

Freelance writing had kept the wolf from Rachel's door. She had attended a local clinic, pretending not to notice the sneering glances at her ringless fingers, and had written chatty, superficial letters to her mother and father; and not once had she mentioned Tess.

"Barney, you'll never guess – such a wonderful thing has happened to me." She turned to him now, full of eagerness. "I've written a novel and it's been accepted. There! What do you think of that? I signed the contract this very day – not a bad advance, either. It'll keep me until I finish the next one. Isn't it terrific? Didn't I always say I would?"

She leaned forward, vivacious and beguiling, reminding herself of nothing more than the bird who trails a broken wing to distract the predator away from her brood. She was trailing her excitement, her small success, and it had the desired result. The baby upstairs was forgotten.

"Rachel, that's *wonderful!*" He looked genuinely delighted on her behalf. His smile, the way his face lit up, was as appealing as ever and she was surprised by a sudden pang of longing. She had been lonely, it seemed in that moment, for a long, long time. It would be so easy to turn to him, to capitulate. But she mustn't – she mustn't!

He reached for her hands and held them tightly in his.

"I knew you'd make it! This calls for a celebration. You'll have dinner with me, won't you?"

Rachel withdrew her hands and smiled at him nervously.

"I can't, Barney."

"Why on earth not?"

"I have to work."

"Oh, come on, now – "

"Besides, Nancy's cooked supper and she'd die if it went to waste. I'd ask you to stay, but – "

"I wouldn't dream of it."

He was hurt; and who could blame him? Somehow she and Nancy could have made the meal go round, if the will had been there. Fleetingly she remembered the lavish, casual hospitality of the Rossiters before the war and wondered if rationing had affected them in the same way as everyone else. It was hard to imagine, somehow.

Barney didn't argue any more, but looked at her, faintly puzzled.

9

"Tell me about you," she said hastily. "What are you doing with yourself?"

He gave a small, self-deprecating laugh.

"Not very much," he said. "Casting around, mostly."

"Are you going back to Art School?"

He laughed again.

"No, I'm not. You know damned well I was never any good. I only went because Ma wanted it so much. Somehow she managed to convince me I had some talent, but it was wishful thinking, nothing more. She was so desperate for one of us to take after her."

"You did some good things. I loved that picture you painted for me. I've still got it somewhere."

"Kid's stuff! No, I never had what it takes."

"So what are you going to do?"

He sighed. "Remember Guy Seamark? He's really keen on antiques. His house was always stuffed with them – I suppose he grew up knowing a fake Chippendale or Hepplewhite or whatever from the genuine article. Anyway, he wants to open a shop – "

"In Warnfield?"

"No, no. In Yorkshire. He got married during the war to a girl from Huddersfield. A nice kid, really. She was a Wren. Very pretty. But – well, his parents didn't go for it at all. I suppose you can understand it. Her accent's pretty ghastly. They gave him an ultimatum – her or them. He chose her, so they've sort of cut him off."

Rachel stared at him, disbelieving.

"Go on," she said.

"Well, Guy wants me to go in with him. I mean, I may not be much of an artist but I know a bit about painters – "

"It sounds as if it might be fun, Barney."

He sighed again.

"Ma's dead agin it. She says Guy's unreliable – "

"Unreliable? What about all those years of dogged devotion to Diana?"

"Yes, well, that's different, I suppose. She says his judgment can't be relied on – I mean, marrying a girl like that."

"With a Yorkshire accent? Is that really all they've got against her?"

"She simply isn't their sort, Rachel. Her father's a platelayer on the railway and her mother works in a textile factory. She left school at fourteen. Honestly, the war's got a lot to answer for."

"D'you know," Rachel said, after a short pause. "I didn't vote

Labour at the last election because I was so pro-Churchill; but you make me feel I wish I had."

"Oh, God!" Barney laughed and ran his fingers through his hair. "Don't get on your political high horse again. You know what sort of trouble that gets us into."

There was a second's pause as they both remembered.

"Anyway," Barney said, hurrying on to cover the awkward moment, "whatever the rights or wrongs of it, Guy's living up in a place called Holmfirth which he says is lovely, and he wants me to go up there too and put my little bit of gratuity in with his. Neither of us have got much. His people won't lift a finger, even though they could, and mine have never had a lot to spare. Of course," he went on, "it's the going so far away that Ma doesn't like, just as much as the precariousness of the whole thing. She's got me an interview with a shipping firm in the city. That's why I'm here. I've been there today."

"And?" she prompted.

"Well, I think the job is mine if I want it. It's not wildly exciting, but it's got good prospects. And of course, I could live at home until I'm able to afford something else."

"Lovely," Rachel said ironically. "You could wear a bowler hat and striped trousers and catch the 8.15 from Warnfield with all the other zombies. My grandfather did it for years."

"Well, it's a living. A good one, actually. We can't all be creative, you know."

"Talking of which," Rachel said. "How's Alannah?"

"Fine. She's finished her stint with ENSA, and she's at home at the moment. Resting, they call it. Actually, she's not resting at all, but dashing around the place trying to get a job in some new scheme for taking theatre to the masses. Diana's getting married in a couple of months. A doctor. A brilliant chap, a wonderful GP. Ma saw him first and kind of homed in on him."

"He can't have stood a chance."

"He didn't need much encouragement, once he saw Di. He dotes on her."

"How nice."

"Oh, come on, Rachel," he said awkwardly. "Forgive and forget. He's asked me to be his best man and Alannah's to be bridesmaid. You must come – well, perhaps not," he finished, seeing her expression.

"Thanks for the thought, at least, but I don't think so, do you? What about your love life?" Rachel asked recklessly, "Are you married or engaged or anything?"

11

"No, not anything. At least – " His smile was tentative, his eyes watchful. He leaned towards her. "Rachel – "

"I've just remembered," she interrupted, jumping to her feet. "We do have about two inches of sherry left in the kitchen. We really ought to drink a toast."

To what? she asked herself as she bustled out to the kitchen for bottle and glasses. Nancy raised questioning eyebrows almost to her hairline, giving every evidence of a curiosity beyond bearing, but Rachel merely wrinkled her nose teasingly and kissed Tess's cheek in passing.

What kind of a toast would be appropriate? To the past? To the future? But there was no future. No Barney-and-Rachel future, anyway, though judging from the look in Barney's eyes, he still cherished hopes. Unbelievably.

"You ought to find a nice girl," she said on her return to the front room, dividing the sherry between the two glasses.

"Don't be so bloody patronising!"

"Nothing like the love of a good woman to steady a man." Relentlessly jolly, she held out the two glasses towards him. "There – I pour, you choose." It was an echo of childish days – days of ginger pop and lemonade and Tizer. He grinned in recognition of it.

"Rachel – " he began again.

"Cheers!" She lifted her glass towards him. "Here's to my future as a bestselling author and yours as a successful entrepreneur, and may we both prosper mightily. Tell me, what happened to Daphne? Daphne Baker?"

"Daphne?" He looked a little taken aback. "She's still around. "As a matter of fact – " he paused, embarrassed.

"As a matter of fact what?"

"I'm taking her to some Municipal dance thing next Saturday. Ma's throwing a sort of party first, so there'll be a crowd of us going."

"Well, that's good." Rachel smiled at him widely. "You could do a lot worse than Daphne Baker. She always had a soft spot for you, you know."

"Dammit, I'm only taking her to a dance!"

"She's a nice girl. Pretty, too. Do you remember that time when she and Alannah – "

"Rachel, forgive me, but I didn't come here to talk about Daphne Baker. I couldn't give a damn about Daphne Baker. I wanted to see you, to find out how you are and what you're doing with yourself and to ask you out to dinner. If you won't come out with me tonight, we can surely make a date for some other time, can't we? Warnfield isn't so far away. And if I do take this shipping job, I'll be here every day. Hey – I've just had an idea! You could chuck out the Fallen Woman and let her room to me."

"You've got a hope! She's a marvellous cook."

"Well, OK, forget that bit – but please, I really would like to see you again."

"Oh, I don't know, Barney. I don't think so." Rachel looked down into her drink. Some rather strange foreign bodies were drifting about down at the bottom and she tried hard to fish them out, pretending that this concern was the only thing on her mind. "I say, have you got these black things in your sherry, too?"

He didn't answer her and when she looked up she found his eyes on her, his lip caught between his teeth.

"Rachel, I know how hurt you were – how we hurt you," he said softly. "I couldn't regret it more. It was a rotten, lousy business, but it's all in the past now. I've always felt – you bloody know how I've always felt! About you, I mean. I've often thought about those few weeks at the beginning of the war, and Shawcross Street, and how happy we were. How happy I was, anyway. Remember that day on Box Hill?"

Too well, Rachel thought regretfully. Barney had seemed then much as he seemed now: the best and most attractive option open to her. Which wasn't fair on either of them. She abandoned the foreign bodies and put the glass down on the table beside her.

"Barney – " she began, and fell silent as she saw the intensity of his blue, blue gaze.

Just one word, she thought. That's all it would take. One word, one gesture of encouragement, and he would leap at the chance to take her back into the world she had vowed never to enter again.

Never mind the past. Never mind Daphne, or any other girl Barney might take home to be charmed by his father, baffled by his mother and condescended to by his sisters. Never mind the fact that she had long consigned the entire Rossiter family to perdition. Barney was, after all, the best of the lot, the one who had first shown her friendship, the one who had always been on her side. Well, almost always.

She wasn't in love with him; had never been in love with him. Yet affection was there and – amazingly – a touch of magic. Rossiter magic. Surely, surely, she wasn't still in thrall? Impatient with herself, she got up and went to the window, fidgeting with the catch as if unsure whether to open it.

13

One word, and her loneliness and insecurity would be a thing of the past. Barney loved her. She'd always known it. He might even love her enough to accept Tess; and even though there was no passion on her part, there was affection. There were, surely, worse grounds for a marriage?

But it was out of the question. No matter in what direction she turned, she could see nothing but danger and the certainty of grief. Even if Mrs Rossiter did another of her amazing U-turns, and welcomed her back into the fold – as she might do, Rachel recognised, if it meant that by so doing she would keep Barney in Warnfield – the whole idea was impossible.

She had danced too often to the Rossiters' tune and she would have no more of it – not now, not with success within her grasp, and certainly not now that she had Tess.

The lock of fair hair had fallen over Barney's brow, just as it had always done. It gave him a vulnerable look, at odds with the arrogance in those deep blue eyes.

"Go in with Guy, Barney," she said suddenly. "Do what feels right to you."

He pushed the lock of hair away in the gesture she remembered so well.

"I don't know," he said. "Ma's right, really. Guy's a bit of a scatterbrain – "

"He could have grown up."

As Barney hadn't, she realised suddenly. There was a fatal weakness in his character, perhaps more apparent now than it had been before. Dunkirk, Tobruk, years in the Eighth Army. Promotion, certainly. Medals, perhaps. Who knew what had happened to him during all that time?

Whatever it was, it hadn't changed him significantly. He still toed the family line. He was a Rossiter, through and through.

"It's been so good to see you, Barney," she said, a note of finality in her voice. "Do remember me to everyone."

"Is that it, then? Aren't we going to meet again?"

"Oh, of course! Why shouldn't we? I can't say exactly when, I'm afraid. I may be going away. My plans are very uncertain."

"Well, let me know."

"I will, I will!"

"You'd better tell me the name of your book."

"It's called *With This Ring* – "

"A love story?"

"Well – " she hesitated. "Sort of. Love and hate. Life, you might say. It's supposed to be quite funny."

"*With This Ring*." He took a notebook from an inside pocket and repeated the title slowly as he wrote it down. It suddenly sounded, Rachel thought, as silly a title as she had ever heard, but he said that everyone would be thrilled to hear about it, especially Alannah. She would be the most thrilled of all and would certainly want to get in touch now that Rachel was found again. And Rachel nodded and smiled and assented to everything, certain that he would be proved wrong.

He left, finally, walking out into a blue and gold evening that suddenly seemed to have remembered, after all, the morning's promise. Rachel closed the door behind him and leant against the wall in the passage for a moment.

Illogically, she felt bereft. Had she done the right thing? It might have been all right . . .

Fool, fool, fool, she berated herself. Of course it wouldn't have been all right. Never, never was Tess going to be subjected to the Rossiters. It was madness to have let the thought even cross her mind, and equally crazy to think that she could find happiness within a hundred miles of them, taking into account all that had happened.

It was then that it dawned on her that neither she nor Barney had actually mentioned Gavin by name, and she knew then that she hadn't been wrong. The past was something she had to put behind her.

"He's gone," she said to Nancy, who was sitting in the old wheel-back chair Rachel had found in a junk shop in the Goldhawk Road, giving Tess her bottle.

Rachel crouched down beside them, looking at her daughter with love, all her ambivalent feelings for Barney receding. Tess relinquished the teat for a moment to give her mother a wide, milky grin before suddenly coming to her senses, realising she was wasting good feeding time and sucking with renewed earnestness and concentration.

Nothing else matters, Rachel thought. Only Tess.

"Shall I take her?" she asked Nancy.

"OK. I'll see to the vegetables." To the accompaniment of rumbles of discontent from Tess, Rachel took Nancy's place in the chair, placating her hungry child by making all the foolish sounds and grimaces that mothers make, until once more the teat was in place and the contented sucking could continue. "I just hope you know what you're doing," Nancy said, pursuing the subject as with great vigour she mashed the potatoes. "That family have got off altogether too lightly."

15

"Maybe. I only know I must keep away from them if I want to save my sanity."

"I have to admit that he was rather charming, though, your Barney Rossiter."

"They're all rather charming. Always were, every man jack of them."

They had certainly charmed her. They had caught her young, put their mark on her, and Barney's visit had only proved that it was there still. They were stamped all through her, she thought, like the letters in seaside rock.

With the bottle finished, she stood up and sat Tess in her high chair.

"It's a beautiful evening," she said. "Why don't we take her out for a stroll to the park after supper?"

Nancy was instantly agreeable.

"Good idea. Supper's ready now."

"I could push the boat out and stand you a half of shandy at the Green Man by way of celebration. We could sit outside."

"Why not?"

Nancy, putting plates on the table, turned to smile at her, but there was something in Rachel's face that caused the smile to fade a little.

"Put it all behind you, Rachel," she said softly. "You don't need them. Forget them."

"I'm going to," Rachel said. "I have already." But she sighed as she spoke, and hearing it, Nancy gave a small, sceptical laugh.

"That'll be the day," she said.

2

"*A*re you spying on us?"

At the sound of the boy's voice Rachel was gripped by a chilling paralysis. She had often read of blood freezing in the veins; now she was experiencing this phenomenon for herself. She had been found out, revealed as that worst of creatures – a sneak, a peeping Tom. The shame of it was unendurable. She felt quite sick, unable to breathe or move. She wanted to die – quickly, that minute, no hanging about.

She had immediately recognised the voice that had challenged her. It belonged to the younger boy, the one they called Barney, which wasn't quite as bad as if she had been discovered by his sister Diana, or Gavin, the big boy; but even so it was something she had dreaded ever since finding the loose brick in the wall that, once removed, had provided such an enchanting window on life next door. Perhaps, she thought, if she kept very, very still . . .

"I say, *you*! You in the spotty dress. Don't think I can't see you. You'd better come out and explain yourself. We Rossiters don't like being spied on."

Rachel's cheeks were burning as after a few more minutes of immobility she wriggled out backwards from the shrubbery where the lilac tree cascaded over the wall from the adjoining garden. Ineffectually she tried to pull the twigs and leaves out of her hair, at the same time tugging at the skirt of her outgrown cotton dress which Grandma considered quite good enough for playing in the garden. Bad enough to be caught redhanded in her shameful activity without giving this arrogant, accusatory male a glimpse of navy-blue school knickers.

He was sitting on the wall that divided the two gardens,

subjecting her to an unfriendly stare. Even his nose seemed intimidating, being bony and high-bridged, and as for his eyes, she felt as if they must be able to look right through her. She had never seen anything like their colour or their clarity. His grey flannel shorts were dirty in a long-standing way and his shirt was torn. His socks were wrinkled and shoe-laces flopped, untied, from disreputable plimsolls; yet, in spite of all, he looked, well – *posh*! There was no other way to describe it; not, at least, one that sprang readily to Rachel's twelve-year-old mind despite her insatiable appetite for the written word.

She felt at a considerable disadvantage, having to look up to meet that gaze.

"I – I wasn't exactly spying," she said miserably, rubbing at the side of her face where a twig had scratched her. He remained implacably hostile.

"What would you call it, then?"

Helplessly she searched for the words that would exonerate her, scuffing the gravel on the path with her sandal in a way that would have earned a sharp rebuke from Grandma.

"Well?" He was as stern and inflexible as any schoolmaster facing an errant pupil.

"It's just that – " nervously she hesitated. What on earth could she say? 'Just that watching you is like watching a play?' 'Just that life over the wall at Kimberley Lodge is a hundred, thousand times more fun than life at The Laurels'?

"Just that there's no one here but me," she said at last.

Nervousness made her voice quaver, and even in her own ears the explanation sounded pathetically weak. She forced herself to meet those extraordinary eyes and saw that Barney was subjecting her to an unwavering scrutiny, biting the inside of his cheek as if in thought. His blond hair hung carelessly over his brow and stuck up in a tuft at the back of his head. If it were not for the eyes, she told herself, he would look quite ordinary – not like the other boy. Gavin. No one would ever consider him ordinary.

He frowned and nodded slowly once or twice as if he had considered the crime, weighed the evidence, and found that, after all, there might just possibly be a few mitigating circumstances.

"Well." He paused, as if unsure what to say next, then seemed to make up his mind. "Have a humbug?" he offered, pulling a crumpled paper bag from his pocket.

The clutch of fear Rachel had felt at the first sound of his voice loosened its hold a little, and she accepted this substitute for an olive branch with humble gratitude.

"I say, thanks. I – I don't think I can reach it, though."

"Can you catch?"

Not very well, would have been the honest answer. She had no eye for a ball – a lack which had served her ill at St Ursula's, the boarding school to which her parents had despatched her from Uganda. St Ursula's was the kind of school where an inability to put balls into nets was rated as only slightly less heinous than compulsive arson.

It would not, therefore, have surprised her in the least if the humbug had evaded her inept grasp and landed on the gravel at her feet, but by some miracle she managed to hang on to it.

"Thanks," she said again. She put it in her mouth and licked the palm where it had left a residue of stickiness. Still regarding her thoughtfully, the boy put a sweet into his own mouth and for a few moments conversation languished.

"What's your name?" he asked at last.

"Rachel." The reply was indistinct, hampered by the humbug. "Rachel Bond."

"I'm Barney Rossiter."

"I know."

"Yes, I suppose you would." He appeared to retreat a little from his former tentative friendliness. "I suppose there's not much about us you *don't* know."

"I don't know all that much," Rachel said defensively, as if by minimising the extent of her knowledge she would make the crime that much less.

She knew a great deal, though. She knew that the Rossiters seemed to laugh a lot and that their quarrels, heated though they could be, were soon over. She knew that Mrs Rossiter painted pictures and worked tapestries, and was blonde and smiling and serene, making nothing of misdemeanours that would have sent Grandma into hysterics and would even have raised objections from her own mother – things like eating buns out of a bag or pouring milk direct from a bottle into a teacup. They seemed, in some indefinable way, above such things as doileys and paper napkins. The fine summer weather had meant that the family seemed almost to live in the garden, and Rachel had therefore experienced ample opportunity to observe their eating habits.

She knew that they had a big, buxom, slow-moving maid they called Pommy, whose name was really Mrs Pomeroy, so Doreen said. She came in daily and could be seen walking to and from Kimberley Lodge night and morning with a curious rolling gait, a shopping bag made of oilcloth banging against her ample thighs.

She knew, too, that the children went to local schools – the boys to King Edward's College and the girls to Brookfield House – and had friends who came and went in a casual manner. She knew that Mr Rossiter laughed every bit as much as his children, teasing them and being teased in return. She knew that they were all keen on games and caught and threw balls with enviable grace and expertise. She knew that Diana played the piano and that Gavin was as handsome as any film star and that Barney liked to go off on solitary, unexplained exploits of his own, which often annoyed Alannah. Only that day Rachel had heard her complaining to her mother on the subject.

"Don't whine, dear," Mrs Rossiter had said equably. "It's frightfully unattractive as well as unproductive."

Her voice was melodious and measured, matched by the way her needle went in and out of the canvas in an unbroken, hypnotic rhythm.

No matter how Alannah complained, no matter how any of them argued and plotted, Rachel knew that they were an entity, a corporate force, united against all outsiders. As she watched through the wall, envious of the fun and the jokes and the easygoing camaraderie, even of the sudden squalls, it was this unity that struck her more than anything else.

"I don't know anything at all, really," she said now, hoping Barney would believe her.

He remained silent for a moment, sucking his sweet reflectively. Then, quite carelessly, as if they were of little importance, he said the magic words she had sometimes dreamed of hearing without ever believing the dream would come true.

"Do you want to come over? As you're on your own."

She almost choked on the humbug.

"I'll have to ask my grandmother," she said.

"Tell you what." He had swung his legs back to his side of the wall and was speaking to her over his shoulder. "I'll get Ma to come round and issue an official invitation if you like. Your grandmother can't refuse that, can she?"

"Would your mother really do that?" It seemed too miraculous to be true.

"She will if I ask her."

He sounded sure of himself, but as he prepared to leap down from the wall and out of her sight Rachel felt a sudden shaft of fear that such a marvellous thing would never – *could* never – come to pass.

"When?" she asked urgently.

20

Barney looked back at her, frowning.

"Well, *now* of course."

What a hope, she thought as he disappeared. Surely he must know that grown-ups didn't behave in that way. They were always busy and required notice, and they had to make up their faces and put on their hats and gloves before paying calls. 'Presently', Rachel's mother always said, not meaning it in its literal sense at all, but rather 'tomorrow' or 'next week' or 'some unspecified time when I'm in the mood'.

But perhaps Mrs Rossiter was different in this, as well as in other ways. Rachel's sightings of her had, naturally, been subject to certain limitations, but she had seen her in the garden often enough to know that she was as unlike her own mother as it was possible for anyone to be. Her mother was called Kitty, and Rachel had always thought it an exceptionally suitable name. She was sleek and beautiful and very slim, with long, mysterious green eyes that were much admired by the young Colonial officers in Entebbe. No one could believe that she was old enough to have a daughter of Rachel's age. When the mood took her she could be lively and skittish, the best of companions. In those moods, Rachel adored her, and even she could see that she was very young, both in looks and ways, to be a mother. She guarded her complexion jealously against the hot sun of Uganda and it was pale and smooth as a lily – whereas Mrs Rossiter bloomed and billowed rather like one of the peonies that flamed in Kimberley Lodge's wild and magical garden.

Would Grandma let her go to Kimberley Lodge? Oh, she had to – she *had* to! Rachel bit her thumbnail in agitation, unable to guess what reaction Grandma would have to the invitation. She had already divined that, when it came to the family next door, her grandmother found herself in something of a dilemma.

The Rossiters were well thought of in the town. Although this summer holiday was Rachel's first experience of Warnfield and she had been at The Laurels no more than two weeks, she had learned that much from Grandma's conversation with her cronies over the teacups. Mr Rossiter was an architect – *the* municipal architect, employed by the Town Council, and had been responsible for the design of the new Town Hall, generally agreed to add a great deal of distinction to an otherwise lacklustre High Street. And Mrs Rossiter was a well-known local artist whose paintings were often exhibited at the library. Gavin and Diana, for their part, were the leading lights of the Tennis Club, and had distinguished themselves by winning the Mixed Doubles two years in succession.

21

Set against this was the undeniable fact that they played loud music and entertained visitors who banged car doors late at night. And the grass verge in front of their house remained unmown, a lush island of untrammelled growth in a sea of green velvet. The Rossiters were, Mrs Bond said, a law unto themselves, caring nothing for the opinion or the convenience of their neighbours. It was some time before Rachel cottoned on to the fact that they felt themselves superior to such things, and many years before she fully appreciated the seriousness of this charge in her grandmother's eyes. She, Rachel was later to realise, dedicated her entire life to the pursuit of genteel conventionality.

"But what can you expect," she had heard Grandma demand of Grandpa, "of a mother as *arty* as Mrs Rossiter? If you can call those pictures she paints 'art'! I certainly can't! They're nothing but great splodges of colour simply flung at the canvas! And as for her clothes – why, there are times when she looks like a gypsy."

Mr Rossiter was no better. An architect was, after all, a professional man and it was surely up to him to dress the part, not wear those dreadful hairy tweeds and – would you believe it? – *golf* stockings to work. What was wrong, Grandma would like to know and frequently demanded, with black coat and striped trousers, wing collar and bowler hat, as worn by every other decent man in civilised society? She thanked God that she had no trouble of that kind with Grandpa, a senior bank manager of subdued and amenable disposition who saw to it that the garden was neat and the verge mown, and was often heard to say that he had nothing left to strive for now and was content to 'bat quietly until retirement'.

But then again – oh, poor Mrs Bond! It really was a dilemma of immense proportions – Kimberley Lodge was bigger and more imposing than The Laurels. And Lady Garfield-Ponsonby, herself a pillar of the Art Society, as well as being a respected member of St Ethelburga's where Mrs Bond herself worshipped Sunday by Sunday, was a frequent visitor.

The house stood on the corner of Ranelagh Gardens and Parkside Avenue and had a turret and two huge bay windows, no less impressive for being half-hidden behind a tangled shrubbery. As well as painting, Mrs Rossiter sat on committees (in company with Lady Garfield-Ponsonby, yet again, as well as other crowned heads of Warnfield) and was a leading light in the Women's Institute, giving talks and judging competitions. Such things, after all, carried weight.

When would Mrs Rossiter come? Rachel didn't for one moment

be gazing with wrapt attention at the picture of highland cattle which hung over the fireplace and was smiling faintly, her chin resting on her hand. The wide sleeve of her jacket had fallen back to reveal a plump arm, creamy and smooth. By contrast, Grandma reminded Rachel more than ever of a plucked chicken. She was fingering her pearls, which was always a bad sign, indicative of some inner turmoil; but she too was smiling, even if the smile was only a small and half-hearted effort.

"Ah, Rachel," she said as her granddaughter entered the room. "I don't believe you have met Mrs Rossiter who lives at Kimberley Lodge next door. Say 'how do you do', nicely."

One day, Rachel thought – *one day* – she would say 'how-do-you-do-nicely' just to *show* Grandma, but this wasn't the day to make any such gesture of defiance.

"How do you do, Mrs Rossiter," she said, and bobbed a little curtsey, as insisted upon at school when greeting the headmistress or any important visitor.

"My, my – such pretty manners!" Mrs Rossiter beamed at her. "It's to be hoped you have a civilising effect upon my gang of ruffians." Later Rachel was to become aware that the deprecatory way Mrs Rossiter referred to her family was no more than an affectation; at that moment, however, she was conscious of a twinge of apprehension. Surely they weren't really ruffians? How would they treat her? What would Grandma think? "You will come and play with them, won't you?" Mrs Rossiter continued. "They're simply longing to meet you."

Rachel knew perfectly well that this was untrue. Barney had taken pity on her, nothing more. They were so self-sufficient as a family that the others probably knew nothing of her existence. Well, they'd know about her now, all right. Barney no doubt had told them about the circumstances in which he had discovered her, and she felt she would be lucky if they even spoke to her, never mind 'longing' to meet her. Still, it was kind of Mrs Rossiter to be so polite.

"I'd love to," she said breathlessly.

"Then run along and make yourself tidy," Grandma said. "Your hair is a disgrace. Give it a good brush."

Mrs Rossiter laughed.

"Oh really, there's no need," she said. "Compared to my brood, Rachel is already tidiness itself."

She might as well have saved her breath. Grandma didn't stop smiling, but the smile seemed to tighten and harden and her eyes took on the kind of determined glint that Rachel had early learned not to disobey. There was an added edge to her voice when she spoke.

"Run along, dear."

Rachel did not hesitate but turned and ran from the room. Grandma had a sort of fixation about hair; nothing angered her more than seeing it falling over her granddaughter's face. Her own hair was shingled at the back, but on either side of her face were rigid iron-grey waves, protected at night with a salmon-pink net which she tied under her chin. She wore plain dresses in muddy colours which she considered suitable for her age, her only adornment the single string of pearls and a modesty vest edged with lace which filled in the V-necks favoured by her dressmaker.

Rachel was back in a few moments, breathless with haste and excitement. Mrs Rossiter and Grandma rose to their feet immediately, as if thankful that their meeting need not be prolonged any further.

"We lunch at twelve thirty," Grandma said.

"I shall see she is back in good time."

"It's very kind of you – "

"Not at all. The children will be delighted."

On a flood of polite phrases Mrs Rossiter wafted out of The Laurels. She smiled at Rachel in a kindly way as they progressed side by side down the path and out of the gate. Anxiously Rachel smiled back, worried about her reception next door, the word 'ruffians' returning to haunt her. Would the girls hate her? She couldn't see any reason why not.

She was so nervous that it was hard to concentrate on Mrs Rossiter's questions, still less answer them, and was thankful that the lack seemed to pass unnoticed since Mrs Rossiter mostly supplied the answers herself.

"Do you enjoy boarding school?" she asked. (*Enjoy* boarding school! How could anyone do that?) "Yes, of course you do! Such fun to have your friends with you all the time. And do they feed you well? For we are what we eat, my dear, no one can deny it. Nutrition is of such importance. The mind *is* the body."

Rachel was silent as she contemplated the heavy puddings, the lumpy custard, the thick shiny gravy that was the daily lot at St Ursula's. There seemed no way to express adequately their repellent nature, but she was saved the necessity of trying to do so as Mrs Rossiter continued her monologue.

"We thought of it for the boys," she went on. "My husband was anxious for them to go to his old school, but I

26

couldn't bear the thought of parting with them. Perhaps I was selfish – "

"Oh, *no*," Rachel assured her, as her voice appeared to trail away uncertainly. "It's much better at home."

Mrs Rossiter smiled faintly, but said nothing. Nor did Rachel, for they were already entering the gate of Kimberley Lodge and the panic which swamped her drove everything else from her mind. She found herself wishing suddenly that she had never left The Laurels, where little was expected of her except to be quiet and tidy and make no trouble. It might be boring, but it was at least safe. It was, however, too late to change her mind now. Here she was, on the other side of the wall, in the area of garden that was so familiar to her.

There was no sign of the big one – Gavin. She was thankful for that, for it was quite unnerving enough meeting the girls. Diana was swinging indolently in a hammock reading a book. She had thick, corn-coloured hair pulled back in a single heavy plait with tendrils escaping to curl around her face. Her mouth was full, rather sulky in repose, but she smiled as she said hallo, and her eyes were amused. She knows, Rachel thought, shame engulfing her again. They all know. I can't bear it. Shall I turn and run?

"Were you really spying on us?" Alannah, the younger one, asked. She had straight, short, slippery fair hair caught back with a tortoiseshell slide that looked as if it was about to fall out. She was wearing a pair of boys' khaki shorts, fastened at the waist by a belt with a snake buckle.

"Shut up, Lannie. I told you not to say anything about that," Barney said severely. "She's all on her own."

Alannah continued to look at Rachel curiously, neither welcoming nor hostile. "How old are you?" she asked, getting down to essentials. "I'm eleven and three-quarters and Barney's thirteen. Diana's fifteen."

"Sixteen next month," Diana corrected her, not lifting her eyes from the page.

"I'm twelve and a half," Rachel said.

"Gosh, you don't look it. Does she, Barney? I'd have said *much* younger." Rachel thought she detected a scornful note. "Are you living next door for ever, or just for the holidays?"

"Just for the holidays. I'm at boarding school."

"*Gosh!*" The note had subtly changed. Now Alannah sounded intrigued – even admiring. "Is it awful, or is it absolutely super, like in books? Do you have midnight feasts and things, and lots of fun in the dorm after lights out?"

27

Rachel struggled for honesty, knowing that a denial would diminish her in Alannah's eyes.

"Well," she said at last. "Not very often."

Not ever, if she were to be truthful. An image of the dormitory flashed on her inward eye, cold and austere. Iron bedsteads in two rows, separated by a line of washstands bearing chipped bowls and ewers. She saw the granite face of Miss Simkins, the housemistress, as she stood with one hand on the light-switch, her eyes travelling from one bed to the next as if suspecting all manner of nameless crimes would be perpetrated the moment the room was plunged in darkness. She heard the stifled sobs of Alice Jamieson in the next bed, whose parents were in Singapore and who suffered the pangs of homesickness less stoically than most. Poor Alice lost all control of her emotions once lights were out; as Rachel did herself, were she to be honest. The only difference between her and Alice Jamieson was that she made no sound, but lay with the tears trickling silently across her cheeks and into her ears, longing painfully for everything that she had left behind in Africa.

Resolutely she turned her thoughts away from St Ursula's. There were still six weeks of the holiday left, and they seemed to stretch all the way to infinity.

"I always thought school stories were daft," Alannah said.

"No you did not." Barney crowed with laughter. "Look how you lap up those dopey Dimsie books – "

"Only 'cos they're *hilarious!*"

"Shut up, you two." Diana's voice was weary. "Rachel didn't come here to listen to you arguing. You'll make her wish she'd stayed on her side of the wall."

"Are the girls nice? Have you got lots of friends?"

"Well – " again Rachel hesitated. "Not lots," she said at last. "Just one or two."

There was Alice, of course, who regarded her as an ally. And Julia Dodd, who slept in the bed on the other side of her. She was the daughter of a country clergyman – a dreamy, peaceful girl who read as avidly as Rachel herself and was equally useless at games. She had attained St Ursula's on the strength of a scholarship awarded to promising offspring of the clergy, which made her the object of wariness and some distrust on the part of the other girls, who tended to despise her clothes and her possessions and her general lack of push. Recognising each other as misfits, the two girls had gravitated together, finding, much to the relief of each, great affinity.

28

"Why are you at boarding school, anyway?" Alannah asked. "And why are you staying with the old – with Mrs Bond?"

"She's my grandmother. My parents are in Africa – Uganda, actually. That's where I was born."

"Gosh, *Africa!*" No doubt about it Rachel thought, cheering up a little, she had succeeded in impressing Alannah. "Do you live in the jungle, in a mud hut?"

Rachel laughed at that.

"Heavens, no! My father works for the Government and we live in Entebbe. That's a township by Lake Victoria. And our house is made of stone."

"Sounds as if you might just as well live in Warnfield. Are there any wild animals?"

"Crocodiles in the lake, and hippos too. They come at night and eat the vegetables in the garden."

"What about savages?"

Rachel thought of Melika, the warm, comforting, uncritical presence who stayed with her at nights when her parents were at the Club or out to dinner with friends. Who, with whispers and giggles, got her up and gave her breakfast the next morning, very quietly so that Mummy shouldn't be disturbed. Daddy was always off at the crack of dawn, no matter how late he had been up the night before.

"We have black servants," she said. "But they're not exactly savages."

"Aren't you afraid of ending up in a cooking pot?"

"Oh, *do* shut up, Lannie." Barney sounded disgusted by his sister's ignorance. "You really do talk utter rubbish."

"You shut up. I want to find out about Rachel." She turned to her again. "Were your parents sad when you had to leave? Ours would be *devastated!*"

"They'd pay to get rid of you," Diana murmured into her book. No one took any notice of her.

"Of course they were sad," Barney said, more irritated than ever. "*Honestly*, Lannie! You're such an idiot. Come on, let's do something. Let's play cricket. You can bat first, Rachel. Diana, move yourself – come and make up the side."

"Not on your life." Unmoving, Diana continued to read.

Rachel prayed that she wouldn't weaken and that Barney would abandon his idea. One ball, and the small amount of status she had acquired in Alannah's eyes would melt away and they would all realise how utterly unworthy she was to receive their friendship. But Barney, grumbling, was already fetching the equipment from a shed and hammering stumps into place.

"Don't be a spoilsport, Di," he urged as he laboured. "We can't have much of a game with three of us. You'll ruin everything if you don't play."

"Too bad." Diana's voice was a study in indifference.

A new voice made itself heard.

"Do you want me to make up the side? I'll bowl if you like."

Gavin. The big one. Rachel's humiliation, then, was to be total.

She turned to see him leaning casually against the open french window, tall and elegant, a striped silk scarf knotted at the open neck of his shirt. She knew she had never seen anyone more beautiful in her whole life. His hair was a reddish gold and seemed to gleam in the sun and his eyes were as blue as Barney's; bluer, if anything. His smile revealed perfect teeth. With a movement of his shoulders he pushed himself away from the window and sauntered across the grass, setting Diana's hammock in motion as he passed.

"Whom have we here?" he asked, smiling in Rachel's direction.

"This is Rachel – Rachel Bond from next door. Mrs Bond's granddaughter."

This last piece of information was heavy with meaning. Rachel could tell at once that Grandma was a joke with the Rossiters and that Barney was warning Gavin to watch his words.

"She comes from *Africa* and goes to *boarding school*." When Alannah spoke you could almost see the italics.

"Well, well – such grandeur! Welcome, Rachel-Bond-from-next-door."

Rachel was too overwhelmed to reply. He was still smiling at her, but all she could manage in reply was a small, apologetic smirk, and when he actually proffered his hand, her taking of it was no more than a reflex action.

"Cold little paw," he remarked loftily. "Well, Barney-me-lad, what about this game of cricket, then? I have to be in town by eleven thirty, but if you want me on the team until then, I'm your man. Who's in first?"

"Rachel," Barney said.

She thought briefly of fainting dead away. It seemed the only way out.

"I've changed my mind," Diana said, tipping herself out of the hammock. "Bags I bat first."

30

"But I promised Rachel – "

"I don't mind a bit," Rachel said quickly. "I'll field if you like."

"OK. You're a good sport, Rachel. Go over by the apple tree. A bit further. *There*, that's fine." Barney was as authoritative as if he were captaining England. "Look, you and Gavin better be against the rest of us because he's so good. Everyone ready?"

Gavin, tossing the ball from one hand to the other with his back to Rachel, turned and smiled at her over his shoulder.

"We'll show them, won't we?" he said.

Her heart seemed to turn a somersault and suddenly it was difficult to breathe. She felt hollow inside, as if she really were going to faint, and at once she knew the reason for it. Hadn't she read about such feelings a dozen times in Doreen's magazines?

She, Rachel Bond aged twelve and a half, had, on the twenty-seventh day of July, 1933, fallen hopelessly, irredeemably in love. There could be no doubt of it.

"You must ask your new friends to tea," Grandma said, after Rachel had been paying daily visits to Kimberley Lodge for over a week. "One must return hospitality." However distasteful such a duty might be, she could have added, if the expression on her face was anything to go by. The fact that her granddaughter had apparently been welcomed next door did not, it seemed, go any way towards crystallising her ambivalent feelings towards the Rossiters.

The whole idea of issuing such an invitation filled Rachel with horror. Teatime was an informal affair at the Rossiters. If there was cake, then they ate cake, with no nonsense about the need to eat bread and butter first, and during this spell of warm weather they helped themselves in the kitchen and brought a laden plate out into the garden, tea or lemonade slopping from thick mugs.

Rachel knew from experience that tea at The Laurels would be a very different affair, with fish-paste sandwiches and eggshell china, and Grandma presiding behind the silver teapot, questioning the Rossiters about their lives and their parents' activities in that relentless, probing way of hers, pretending she was doing nothing more than make polite conversation. They would be on to her in a flash, Rachel knew, and she wouldn't put it past Diana to make up shocking stories of life next door out of sheer devilment. Rachel had learned quickly that Diana liked to shock, and instinct told her that if by so doing she could make life difficult for the newcomer to the family circle, then she would find it all the more amusing.

Diana, while not positively unfriendly, wasn't an easy person to know. She was pleased with herself – well, hadn't she the right to be, looking the way she did? Rachel couldn't blame her. And she seemed to be good at everything. She'd won a special prize at school, Alannah told her, for French, and was the only girl *ever* to have got a hundred per cent for Maths. In addition, she moved with easy, athletic grace, and had won cups for hockey and the high jump, as well as tennis.

"It's simply frightful for me! She's absolutely always top," Alannah complained – but proudly. She liked to bathe in her sister's reflected glory, even though it irritated her when teachers at school held her up as an example. "It just isn't fair! And it'll be worse next year when she's in the Sixth Form. I bet she's made a Prefect right away."

Rachel couldn't argue with that. Diana was one of life's natural prefects. She didn't know how she could bear it, sitting at tea, attempting to toy with a sandwich, knowing that this glittering, superior creature was shrieking with laughter behind what would undoubtedly appear to be a demure exterior.

At least she didn't have to worry about Gavin because she was perfectly certain he wouldn't come even if invited – in itself unlikely since it was Gavin that Grandma objected to most of all. It was his friends who banged car doors late at night, calling out over-enthusiastic goodnights and last-minute witticisms. And it was Gavin (or so Grandma believed) who was responsible for playing 'that dreadful jazz' which could sometimes be heard floating from an open window. Rachel had not seen fit to tell her that Mr Rossiter was equally responsible, for her opinion of him stood low enough without adding anything so damning. 'Negro music' she called it, considering it both infantile and decadent. That any responsible adult could actually enjoy it was simply beyond belief.

No, Gavin wouldn't come, Rachel felt sure. He lived a life apart – a life which only Diana was privileged to share, except for occasions such as that first day in the garden when he had deigned to bestow the honour of his presence, briefly but with such devastating results. Rachel continued to worship him humbly from afar. Shy and unsure of herself with all of them, the very sight of Gavin was sufficient to turn her into a blushing imbecile, incapable of speech, with all such moments lived and relived with increasing embarrassment once she was on her own again.

His particular friend was called Guy Seagrave, the son of a

wealthy businessman who resided in Warnfield but owned a string of small department stores to the north of London.

Guy had the unbelievable distinction of owning a sports car, and together, bathed in glamour, he and Gavin dashed here and there, playing tennis in the park, drinking coffee at the Moo Cow Milk Bar, sauntering through the High Street in their striped blazers and straw boaters like two young princes.

Perhaps, Rachel thought, if she ignored Grandma's suggestion for long enough the whole thing would be forgotten. She should have known better than that. Grandma was like a dog worrying at a bone when an idea took root in her head. Usually it was Grandpa who suffered; he was always being badgered about fixing the days for their holiday (one week in a rather superior private hotel in Hove), or having the house painted, or mowing the verge. Now it was Rachel's turn.

"I think Thursday," Grandma said reflectively at breakfast one day. "I shall send round a written invitation – "

"Oh, you don't have to do that," Rachel said hastily, worried that after all Grandma might invite Gavin by name and that he might feel obliged to accept. "I can quite easily ask them."

"I trust I know how to behave." Grandma's voice was icy and her thin nostrils dilated gently.

In the event, and much to Rachel's relief, only Alannah came. By great good fortune, Grandma had picked a time when Barney was away spending a few nights with a friend who lived on a farm outside Warnfield. He was due back that very day, but Mrs Rossiter considered his time of arrival too chancy to allow her to accept on his behalf. Diana pleaded a headache at the last moment – best cured, she considered, by exercise and fresh air; i.e. by going to the open-air swimming pool in the park with Gavin and Guy. Rachel happened to see her driving off, perched on the folded-back canvas roof of Guy's car, and felt nothing but relief.

The occasion was as stiff and formal as she had feared, but Alannah – clad unfamiliarly in a pink-and-white checked dress with a smocked yoke – handled it superlatively, carrying on a conversation with Grandma about local matters with aplomb and apparent enjoyment, coping with admirable efficiency with the sandwiches and the Worcester china. Alannah, Rachel knew by this time, liked nothing better than to act a role, adopting different voices and manners with astonishing ease. This afternoon she was Being a Lady Out to Tea, and was being it to considerable effect; though Rachel's appreciation of her performance was diminished by the sure knowledge that it would be enacted all over again for her family's amusement once she was home again.

"The child has good manners, I'll say that for her," Grandma said with some surprise after she had gone.

"They all do, Grandma."

Grandma shook her head in bewilderment, defeated, as always, by the contradictions presented to her by the Rossiters.

"Really, it's quite beyond my comprehension," she said, and declined to explain when Rachel questioned her. Not that any explanations were necessary, for Rachel knew exactly what she meant. Was not her grandmother's reaction precisely the same as her own had been, when, on that first morning, she had discerned Barney's essential poshness despite his disreputable garb?

"It's a great pity," Mrs Bond said with a sigh – meaning, Rachel presumed, all the noise and the laughter and the flamboyance. "I do hope dear Ivor would approve of my letting you play with them." Her eyes strayed to the photograph on the mantelpiece which showed Rachel's father in his Colonial Officer's uniform, staring straight ahead in a solemn, resolute, responsible kind of way. She sighed. "It's a heavier duty than you appreciate, Rachel, to be a proxy parent, especially at my age. I had thought that your Aunt Sylvia . . ." She neglected to finish her sentence, but she did not need to. Aunt Sylvia couldn't be bothered with her, Rachel knew that. She wasn't sure what her aunt did with herself in London, but she had made it abundantly clear that beyond the occasional meeting of a train and tea at Fullers', no more could be asked of her. Her life, it seemed, was too much of a social whirl for her to welcome the complication of an unwanted niece.

"I do appreciate it, Grandma, and I'm sure Mummy and Daddy would approve of the Rossiters. They'd want me to enjoy myself."

"Be that as it may . . ." Clearly Mrs Bond remained unconvinced.

"Mummy would like them, I know." Unwisely Rachel pursued the subject, and Grandma smiled thinly.

"Perhaps Mummy would," she said, faintly ironic. Mummy's standards, her tone implied, left much to be desired. Rachel was not supposed to know how strained the atmosphere was between the two women closest to her father, but she was not that much of a fool. She had once overheard Grandma describing her mother as a 'flibbertigibbet', and there were times when she sighed and referred vaguely to 'poor Ivor'. Rachel said no more, but took up a book that Alannah had lent her – a book that was supposed to portray boarding-school life but to her seemed as far from the truth as some fantasy by Jules Verne.

"I think bath and bed," Grandma said, as eventually the clock on the mantelpiece chimed eight.

Automatically Rachel protested.

"But Grandma, it's not nearly dark yet – and Grandpa's not home. He said we'd have a game of chess."

"My dear child, these Lodge Meetings go on until all hours. I'm not expecting him for a long time, and chess is certainly out of the question. Now off you go, there's a good girl. Goodnight and sleep well."

Resignedly Rachel kissed the cold cheek that was offered to her, thinking that it didn't matter, she could just as easily read in bed – yet vaguely aware that there ought to be something more, that though the sun had faded and the shadows were long it was not yet time to close the door on the day. Upstairs in the bathroom at the back of the house she opened the window and leaned out.

Music and laughter floated towards her on the still evening air. There they all were, all the Rossiters, hidden from her by the shrubbery and the wall and the trees, but clearly audible just the same. She could hear Mr Rossiter's voice and a shout of laughter from Barney, now home from his visit. Diana was playing the piano, the sound of a Chopin nocturne floating through the open french windows. She would slow down in a minute, maybe play a wrong note or two. It was a hard bit, she said. *There*, that was it.

Gavin was in the garden – she heard Mrs Rossiter call his name from inside the house, and the sound of it made her feel weak with love for him – for all of them. Rachel longed with every nerve, every pore, every fibre of her being to be with them, not here in this chill, aseptic bathroom with its pungent aroma of Wright's Coal Tar soap.

There, in that moment, she knew a greater loneliness than she had ever experienced in her life before. All warmth, all colour seemed to be concentrated in that garden beyond the wall and she saw herself, small-faced and pale, standing bleakly apart, destined always to be outside the charmed circle.

For a little while she stood there, not seeing the beauty of the summer evening, not seeing anything except the desirable world that was closed to her. Then quietly, matter-of-factly – because what else was there to do? – she closed the window and ran her bath.

35

3

It was a week after Barney's visit to Inverness Street that the
letter came from Sylvia asking Rachel to lunch with her in
Kensington.

"How antisocial of you not to have a telephone," she wrote
plaintively. "Still, you can always phone me. If I hear nothing
from you I shall assume that you will come on Wednesday at
12.30, when I shall look forward to a really good chat!!"

Rachel's own feelings about a really good chat, particularly of
the type that merited two exclamation marks, were definitely
mixed. On the one hand, she admitted to herself that she yearned,
in the absence of any other relatives to brag to, to tell Sylvia about
the book. On the other, was she to come clean about Tess, or
continue to conceal her baby's existence?

Until Jermyn Street, she had not seen Sylvia since before the
war. They had never been close; in fact the opposite had been the
case. She had always known that as far as Sylvia was concerned,
she was nothing but a nuisance. The summer of 1936 when, much
to the dismay of both of them, she had been forced to spend several
weeks under her aunt's roof, was still something she remembered,
if not with horror, then with desolation. Certainly the small
amount of train-meeting and escort duty that had routinely been
required of Sylvia was carried out only under sufferance. Rex
Courtney, her husband, was something quite high up in the Civil
Service, though Rachel had always been vague about his precise
function.

Soon after the outbreak of war he moved to the Foreign Office
– an appointment that was greeted with a certain amount of awe
in the family. Rex's new job, it was generally believed, was

hush-hush and of great national importance. Churchill, Mrs Bond frequently told her friends, would have been lost without him.

Whatever it was, the job kept him in London throughout the blitz and the buzz bombs and all the quiet period in between; and though, no doubt, it had its stressful moments, there were times when he was able to relax and enjoy himself, as was proved when Rachel happened to see him once at the theatre on one of her rare visits to London during the war. She had pretended not to, however, because he was with a predatory-looking blonde in ATS uniform.

Sylvia evacuated herself to the West Country. Rex's family had come from Cornwall and he had inherited a cottage in the village of St Bethan, at the mouth of the river Pol, not long before the war. The Courtneys had spent several holidays there prior to 1939 and Rachel had heard much regarding St Bethan's charms.

"You really must come down," Rachel clearly remembered Sylvia saying with casual insincerity on several occasions.

"I'd love to," she had invariably replied; untruthfully, of course, for after the summer of 1936 she would have preferred to enter a corrective institution rather than submit herself to any further holiday with Sylvia. No definite invitation had ever materialised, however, which came as a great relief.

Her grandmother had made the journey once, just after her husband died in 1942. She had reported that St Bethan was like a picture on a calendar, but even so she had not liked the place. She had mistrusted the drains, it seemed, and complained that the seagulls shrieked incessantly, making sleep impossible. However, she further told Rachel, Sylvia had found some bridge-playing cronies who lived within reach, and was apparently enjoying herself.

Rachel had been shocked, feeling it immoral that an able-bodied woman in her forties should pass a war playing bridge; and as she held Sylvia's letter in her hands and wondered what she should do, she reflected that it explained why Sylvia, almost alone among the population of London, should look quite unchanged by the past five years. She had always been, if undeniably on the plump side, a stylish woman; beautifully coiffed and well made-up, nails painted and earrings in place. One was, Rachel thought, more than usually conscious of face powder in her presence, its scent and texture. She was always velvety with it, like a bee dusted with pollen.

Nothing had ever ruffled the surface of her self-satisfaction and certainly five years of war had left no mark. If there were now a few silver threads among the gold, it seemed likely her hairdresser had dealt with them competently – and no doubt expensively – for none were visible. She'd had no son or daughter in the forces to cause her concern; no bombs or fire-watching duties to disturb her rest. Looking at her, one could not imagine she had worried about Rex in London or her parents in Warnfield, or had ever gone short of the little luxuries that everyone else had learned to live without.

Well, good luck to her Rachel thought now, less censorious than she once had been. Who could blame Sylvia for finding a comfortable little niche? At least she had relieved Rex of the necessity of worrying about her while he was getting on with his important job at Churchill's right hand, which perhaps was a more valuable contribution to the war effort than donning a uniform to perform duties that she was, as like as not, totally unsuited for.

Yes, she would go to lunch, Rachel decided, but she wouldn't take Tess. Nancy was at home that day and readily agreed to look after her. She *liked* looking after her, she maintained stoutly. Nothing would be easier than to give her some lunch and put her down for a sleep.

Rachel was suitably grateful. She might, she said, take advantage of the really good chat to confide all to Sylvia – or at least, as much as she intended to confide to anyone.

The flat had suffered some bomb damage, Sylvia had told her when they met, but it was not immediately obvious. It looked to Rachel just as she remembered it – not large, admittedly, but cosily affluent, like a satin-lined casket. The blue ceramic pots from The Laurels were in evidence in the entrance hall, one on each side of the front door, containing spectacular and exotic greenery.

Sylvia greeted her warmly, clasping her to her soft, cashmere-clad, pearl-decked bosom in a way she certainly would not have done when Rachel was a child.

"My dear, it's lovely to see you," she cried. "I'm simply bursting to tell you my news. Rex has been posted to Washington! Isn't it wonderful? We're off quite soon, and I must say I can hardly *wait*! Just imagine – no rationing and no austerity and no beastly Socialists! Won't it be perfect bliss?"

Rachel was duly congratulatory.

"That's marvellous," she enthused.

"We'll have a sherry to celebrate, and you must tell me all your news," Sylvia went on; following which she reverted, without pause, to the subject of Washington: the house she would be justified in expecting, the entertaining, the clothes. Quite understandable, as Rachel reminded herself, for who would not be excited at such a prospect? "My dear, forgive me," Sylvia said at last. "Now it's your turn. Tell me what you've been up to."

"Well, actually – " Rachel began.

"More sherry, dear? You're sure? The man at the corner shop is such a poppet, he always keeps this brand for me. He's one of the old school, not like most of them. You should have heard them in Peter Jones the other day! Simply take it or leave it! Life is never going to be the same again, you do realise that, of course? These people have us where they want us now, and well they know it." She fell silent, regarding her niece thoughtfully. "Just think!" she mused. "I could have a daughter your age myself if things had been different. It might have been fun, choosing clothes and so on. Well, no use crying over spilt milk. When do you expect Ivor and Kitty to come home?"

"When they can get berths. In the spring, they hope."

Tess would be fourteen months old by March. No one would expect Rachel to give her up, not then. She'd be safe by March. Oh, what a fool she was! She was safe now. She wasn't a child to be ordered to do this or that. She was an adult, a mother, and she'd go to the stake rather than give up Tess.

She took a deep breath.

"Sylvia – "

"Rachel, my dear, you did say when we met in the street that you kept busy with your little stories and articles?"

"That's right. And you'll never guess – "

"They do pay you, these magazines?"

"Yes. And Sylvia – "

"Then, my dear, I hope you'll forgive me for saying it but I do advise a really good haircut. I know just the man. In Grafton Street. Look on it as an investment. It's the same with dress, quality never dates. Remember how pleased you were with my choice of clothes, that time you stayed with me before the war?"

That at least was true, and Rachel opened her mouth to acknowledge the fact; but even in this she was thwarted.

"Ah, here's *dear* Mrs Morrissey to tell us that lunch is ready," Sylvia said, rising to her feet. "You're quite sure you won't have another sherry? Well, I'll just top up my glass . . ."

She was nothing more than an audience, Rachel realised. Sylvia had no interest in her affairs; how she had passed the war, how she spent her time now. Well, she thought, as she tucked into her steak and onions, mashed potatoes and cauliflower, at least she was getting a damned good feed out of it.

"How is Rex? Is he pleased about this move to Washington?" she asked, when Sylvia drew breath for a moment.

"My dear, of course! It is promotion, after all." Sylvia looked, Rachel thought, like a large contented pussy-cat as smilingly she contemplated her husband's successes. "Oh, I must tell you, Rachel," she went on, changing the subject as yet another random thought occurred to her. "I was up in Warnfield recently and saw Mrs Rossiter. You hadn't been in touch with any of them, she said. What a funny little person you are! She seemed most concerned about you. The girl was home – the pretty one. Diana. The one that was on all those recruitment posters during the war. She's engaged – getting married fairly soon, I understand. I gave them your address, so I expect you'll get an invitation."

"I doubt it," Rachel said. "I wouldn't accept it, anyway."

"Why on earth – ?" Sylvia stopped masticating a moment to stare at Rachel in astonishment, then, quite unabashed, resumed her meal. "Well, I can see it might be embarrassing for you – "

"You could say that."

"Well, whoever was at fault, it's all water under the bridge now. They don't appear to bear a grudge."

"I should think not!" Rachel gasped with amused outrage. "If any grudges are to be borne, then I'm the one to bear them. Not that I do, believe me. I just don't want to have any more to do with them."

"Well, I think you're very foolish. Barney came in while I was there. He's matured very nicely, *and* it seems he's in the running for a good position with a shipping firm. Of course, it's all who you know these days, isn't it? Mrs Rossiter managed to get an interview for him through Lady something or other in Warnfield." She paused for a moment, glimmering knowingly. "He's an attractive creature, and *most* interested to hear about you. How old are you now? Twenty-five? Time you settled down and found yourself a nice husband. Don't be surprised if Barney comes looking for you."

"He already has."

"There, now – what did I tell you?" Sylvia looked delighted with her prescience. "Did he take you out?"

"No." Rachel went on cutting up her meat, avoiding her curious gaze. "He did ask me but I was busy that night."

Her aunt stared at her.

"You must be out of your mind! Is there someone else? Is that it?"

"No, it's not that," Rachel assured her. "It wouldn't do, Sylvia –

you surely must see that! Besides, I have other things on my mind at the moment."

Perhaps if Sylvia had pursued the subject of just what was on her mind, Rachel thought afterwards, she might have force-fed her the news about the acceptance of the novel; even told her about Tess. But she reverted once more to the joys she might expect to await her in Washington and the moment was gone.

Clearly, Rachel thought, her aunt wasn't interested in her affairs, and it would, under those circumstances, be pointless to parade her little triumph before her, still less to tell her of Tess's existence. With any luck, Sylvia would go to Washington and stay there for a considerable time. Rachel had an idea that Harrods, or possibly Sloane Square in view of the mention of Peter Jones, represented the end of the known world to her, so that even visits home to London would be unlikely to include a side trip to Hammersmith.

This, then, was likely to be the last time she saw Sylvia for a very long time. So she ate her lunch, listened to her aunt with a polite smile on her face, admired her photographs of Cornwall (you had to hand it to her – who but Sylvia would contrive to pass five years of war in such an idyllic situation?) and left at ten to three, thanking her for the lunch, and wishing her good luck in Washington.

Out on the street once more, Rachel was conscious of a feeling of depression. She had wanted to like Sylvia; wanted to be assured that blood was thicker than water and that, after all, they could communicate with each other now that she was an adult and not an importunate child.

It hadn't worked like that. Somehow the meeting had only served to underline the fact that she had no one but herself to depend upon.

She had Nancy, of course – but one could hardly expect her to be around for ever. She'd been seeing a lot of George lately. Whether that meant anything or nothing, Rachel wasn't sure, but it certainly gave her pause for thought.

Gone was the euphoric feeling of self-confidence that she had experienced on the day that Barney had appeared at her door. Now, suddenly, she was worried about the next book. She had managed to write one acceptable novel, but there was no assurance of continued success – no absolute guarantee that she could pull off the same trick a second time.

It was only later, when she was in bed, that she associated this mood with the Rossiters. It seemed as if they were reaching out their hands from the past to denude her of all her confidence, stripping off, piece by piece, the tough outer shell she had grown over the years to reveal the quivering, raw flesh beneath. And even when she slept the fantasy continued, only now she could see their faces quite clearly, all of them except Gavin. Where was he? In her dream she seemed to think he was hiding nearby. She was desperate to tell him about her book, but though she searched for him she couldn't find him. Nevertheless, she knew he was there somewhere, quite close, and to the accompaniment of Rossiter laughter she searched on, ever more frantically.

The dream was confused, the events without logical sequence, but suddenly he was present in the room, and everything was just as it had been once upon a time when Rachel was young and innocent and believed in happy-ever-after. He put his arms around her and she was warmed and comforted, so that it was with a rush of gladness that she woke to the sound of a bird singing in the ornamental cherry outside her bedroom and the little gurgling noises that meant that Tess was greeting the day in her own particular way.

It took a full five seconds before she realised the truth – that there was no happy-ever-after, and that she was alone. A wave of sadness swept over her, followed by one of sheer panic. She closed her eyes and willed herself to overcome it, as she had done so many times before when her loneliness and responsibilities seemed too much to bear. She was strong, she reminded herself. Indomitable. Remember?

"What on earth's the matter with you?" Nancy asked her at breakfast. "You look ghastly!"

"Well, gee, thanks. Nothing like the odd compliment to boost the old ego."

"You're not worrying about you-know-who, are you? I thought you were going to put the past behind you."

"So I am." Rachel sighed gustily. "I had the most ghastly dream, that's all. I can't seem to shake it off."

"Oh, dreams." Nancy shrugged hopelessly. "What can you do about dreams? I don't know which sort are the worst. I dreamed that I was being chased over a Scottish moor by that rather nice redheaded RAF doctor – d'you remember him?"

"Yes," Rachel said dryly. "He was the one who sounded your chest no matter what was wrong with you. Ingrowing toenail, earache – "

"Well, he caught me, and I was just waiting for him to have

his wicked way with me when he stuck a thermometer in my mouth."

Rachel, spooning Farex into Tess who sat pink and placid in her high chair, smacking her lips as if she were savouring some gastronomic delight, looked up and grinned.

"Oh, frightfully Freudian," she said, and was grateful. Trust Nancy to put things in perspective, she thought.

"Oh, by the way," Nancy went on, "is it all right if I invite George to supper tonight?"

"Yes, of course. You don't have to ask, you know that. I like him."

"Do you? Honestly? You don't think he's a few bob short of a pound? He has some crazy ideas, you know. My God, is that the time?"

The pips heralding the nine o'clock news had caught her unawares. Without waiting for an answer, she gulped her coffee, grabbed her mackintosh (unlike Rachel, she was constitutionally unable to trust the morning's promises, no matter how cloudless the sky) and rushed from the house.

It was a warm, still day; a day for the country, not London. Rachel dressed Tess in a beautifully embroidered frock of pink lawn that Nancy had made for her, and with much difficulty added a pink and white cotton sunbonnet.

Several old ladies stopped and clucked at Tess during the excursion down the sunlit street. She looked (Rachel thought in her totally unprejudiced way) more than usually fetching with her fair quiff peeping out from her sunbonnet.

"Little love," they said, and, "Bet her Daddy's proud of her," and, as always, "What lovely blue eyes she's got!"

All the better to enslave me, Rachel thought. And all the better to betray my secret. She smiled at them, giving no hint of the chill of fear their words engendered. She was suddenly conscious again of panic – a dark, jagged threat on the horizon of this golden day. She slowed her steps, dawdling towards the park, silent now, all her fears rushing back. She hated the thought that she was once more within the Rossiters' orbit, her whereabouts known. The nightmare was only a sympton. Was she now to be haunted by them?

No, of course not! She sat down on a park bench and idly rocked the pram, lifting her face to the sun, forcing herself to be calm. She had rebuffed Barney. He was hardly likely to seek her out again, whatever he had said at the time and whatever torch he had carried over the years.

But suppose he did? Suppose this time he caught sight of Tess? What then? Oh, *damn* Sylvia! It had been the worst possible luck bumping into her like that just before her visit to Warnfield.

It was impossible to relax, to enjoy the sun and the flowers and the expanse of grass. Restlessly she got up and pushed the pram back the way she had come.

As if catching her mood, Tess began to whimper and rub her nose with her fist – a sure sign that she was tired or bored or wanted a drink. Perhaps all three.

Rachel quickened her steps, anxious now to be home. And not only for Tess's sake, either. The urge to close the door on the outside world was irresistible. Once home, she tried to swamp her unease in a frenzied attack on the household chores. Tess, in high spirits now having had her drink of juice, crowed with delight as she hurled small toys to the floor.

This was a new game. Was she encouraging bad habits, Rachel wondered, as patiently she retrieved them? Was she spoiling Tess?

Maybe, but somehow she doubted it. She found it hard to believe that there could ever be too much kindness displayed towards children. Or warmth, or approval, or understanding.

She remembered too well how she had longed for it – how once she imagined that she could find it in the Rossiter household, how she warmed her hands at their fire.

Though the sun shone that summer of 1933 there was little warmth at The Laurels. After an early supper, Grandma usually settled down to some knitting, while Grandpa would either potter gently in the garden or sit and read *The Times*. Occasionally he would challenge Rachel to a game of chess or Halma, but not often.

No one spoke very much. Mr Bond distrusted Ramsay MacDonald but on the whole supported the National government, relying on the good sense of Stanley Baldwin to keep the Labour riff-raff in order. These, however, were thoughts he kept to himself. Though he was sometimes inspired to give grunts of approval or snorts of derision as he rustled the pages of his paper, he seldom gave voice to anything that made sense to Rachel.

Not that she minded. The world of politics and governments and foreign affairs was something for adults, something so far outside her experience that though she might, if pressed, have been able to supply the name of the Prime Minister, she knew of no other politician and was happy in her ignorance; until, that is, she entered the Rossiter household.

There, things were very different – though even among the Rossiters, politics was clearly a masculine preserve for it was only Gavin and Mr Rossiter who chose to speak of them; and not only speak, but argue forcibly, since each took his stance on an opposite side of the fence.

Gavin supported the Labour Party. He was an ardent pacifist and tended to shout his views about the inequity of means testing and the need for class struggle and a new order, while his father regarded Neville Chamberlain's financial policies with approval, was in favour of free enterprise and assured all who would listen that the spendthrift policies of the Socialists would bring the country to its knees.

"Look at Russia," he instructed Gavin several times a week. "Is that the kind of society you want here?"

"Why not, if we can't get rid of the stinking, rotten cesspit of capitalism any other way. Who starts wars? The capitalists, that's who – the fat cats at the top who don't give a damn about the workers. Our class-ridden society is evil. The game's up, Dad – "

"*God*, you're a bore, Gavin!" That was Diana, reaching for something to throw at him. "And such a hypocrite! You love your comforts and privileges as much as anyone."

"Not at the expense of everyone else. Yes, of course I like my comforts, but in a perfect world everyone should have them! There should be a levelling up, not a levelling down – "

"Ha! You mean like Russia? Tell that to the peasants in the glorious Soviet Union!"

"Children, children!" Mrs Rossiter was always smiling, pacific, her needle going in and out. She never shouted or became angry; and though she sometimes shook her head at Gavin's more extravagant excesses Rachel quite rapidly discerned that while she was proud of all her children, for Gavin she reserved a very special pride. And who could blame her? Certainly not Rachel.

Though he and his father argued constantly, the arguments sometimes spilling over into exasperation, even rage, there was little animosity in it. Mr Rossiter was, in Rachel's eyes, a quite remarkable father.

He was, for one thing, a great joker. At first Rachel was wary of him, not knowing how to take him. She was not accustomed to a father who performed a soft-shoe-shuffle into the dining room, hat and cane in his hand; or one who delighted in singing comic songs round the piano with his family.

He loved to play games, and he played to win. Not like Grandpa when he played chess, always leaving himself open so that Rachel could take the game – a ploy which annoyed her more than she could ever express. Mr Rossiter liked nothing better than a family game of cricket or rounders; but if wet weather should keep them indoors, then with equal enthusiasm he would join in Racing Demon or charades or – Rachel's absolutely least favourite thing – a game called Adverbs, of which all the Rossiters seemed inordinately fond. It called upon one member of the party to leave the room, returning to guess what word had been chosen in his or her absence by demanding certain actions to be performed 'in the manner of the adverb'.

Her baptism of fire as far as this game was concerned came quite quickly after her introduction to the Rossiters.

Had they chosen things like 'quickly' or 'dreamily' or 'hesitantly', Rachel thought, going over and over the day as she always did once she was in bed, it wouldn't have been nearly so bad; or simple actions like – well, like setting a table or combing one's hair. She was still smarting, and did for many days, about her failure to act convincingly the catching, killing and plucking of a chicken 'perfectly'. It had been *awful*! She hadn't known where to start and had just stood there, head bent, pleating her skirt between her fingers.

Only the kindness and the tact of Mr Rossiter had saved her. Oh, he was such a kind man, she thought. If she wasn't already in love with Gavin, then she might quite easily be in love with him. If he hadn't been so old, of course. He must, surely, be all of forty – but still handsome, for all his great age, with glossy, chestnut-coloured hair and those sparkling blue eyes, and his air of enjoying everything so much.

"It's only a game," Diana had said to her amusedly after the Adverbs debacle. "There really wasn't any need to get upset. You really are a goose, Rachel." She was smiling at her in a lofty, head-girl kind of way.

"No, she's not!" Alannah, in those early days, was always passionate in defence of her, as if Rachel was her particular responsibility. "You shouldn't have given her such a hard thing to do. You know what Mummy said – we've got to be kind to Rachel. We should *pity* her, being so far away from her own home and having to live with old Mrs – with her grandmother."

"Pity," Diana said, "is only another form of self-indulgence. It's patronising to pity people."

"How can you say that? What about the starving children in

46

India?" Alannah was clearly intent on widening the argument. "What about the men who pull rickshaws in China?"

"When I see Rachel pulling a rickshaw," Diana said, arranging herself in the hammock, "then I might pity her."

It was a disquieting thought, that the Rossiters were under orders to be nice to her. Rachel had hoped – it was only a little hope, but it had undoubtedly been growing – that she was making a place for herself in the family. She wasn't any good at cricket, or even at Adverbs as she had so obviously demonstrated, but Limericks was another matter altogether. This was a game where she felt she had come into her own, a game where each player supplied the line of a limerick. She was inventive at rhyming, quick-witted when it came to the amusing twist at the end. Her most satisfying moment, the most wonderful moment of her entire life, had been when Gavin had laughed and commended her, just the other day.

And there was another thing. She and Alannah were collaborating on writing a book. It was, naturally, a school story, about which Alannah was far more of an authority than Rachel.

"It'll be the school story to end all school stories," Alannah said. "We'll have a madcap of the fourth, and a school sneak, and a *marvellous* hockey captain called Pamela, and a Head Girl who's *odiously* calm and wise – "

"Helena?" Rachel suggested.

"Perfect! And the sneak will be called Ethel Craddock – gosh, can't you *see* her, all poky and pointy-faced? What'll we call the Madcap of the Fourth?"

"Daphne?" offered Rachel, but Alannah looked unconvinced. "Pauline? Pat?" Still Alannah shook her head. "Dymphna?"

"*Dymphna*! Oh, that's it! Oh, clever you, Rachel! Dymphna it is. Hurrah for Dymphna!"

It became a catch-phrase in the family, a kind of battle cry. Making a catch at cricket, Mr Rossiter would throw his panama hat in the air and shout it in triumph; or the whole family would roar it in unison when Mrs Rossiter came from the kitchen bearing a cake for tea.

There were numerous things that they roared in unison. Apparently when Alannah was a little girl, she had asked someone to 'do her a flavour'. "Certainly, madam," Gavin had replied smartly. "Chocolate or strawberry?" Nowadays, no one asked for a 'favour', always a 'flavour'; and the reply always came back 'chocolate or strawberry'. In unison, of course. It was, Rachel thought, the most enormous fun, and she was proud that Dymphna had achieved the same status.

47

"One day," she said dreamily, lying on her back in the grass one summer's afternoon after a satifactorily productive writing session, conscious of the scent of the honeysuckle hedge, feeling happy and at peace with herself, "I'm going to write a proper book."

Alannah was beside her, lying on her stomach. She was chewing a pencil, an exercise book open in front of her.

"This *is* a proper book!"

"Oh, you know what I mean. A book that people will buy. A book that will go in libraries."

Alannah's silence was heavy with doubt.

"Oh well," she said after a moment, obviously making a great effort to carry out her mother's instructions regarding kindness towards their less fortunate neighbour and speaking with a patently false note of encouragement. "Perhaps you can do it. Anyway, it's good to have ambition."

"I mean it, Lannie." Rachel opened her eyes and looked at her determinedly. She saw that Alannah was regarding her with concentrated compassion.

"I know you do, Rachel. It's just that it must be awfully hard to write a proper book. I wouldn't want you to be disappointed." Her voice was full of concern for her friend. "I mean, it seems to me that you have to be quite clever to write a book."

"I'm good at English. It's my only thing, really."

Alannah said nothing, but her expression implied doubt.

"I expect Di could do it," she said after a moment. "She's so clever, she can do anything. No, I wouldn't be a bit surprised if Di wrote a book one of these days. But I'm not sure about you, Rachel. You can *try*, of course – "

"I intend to," Rachel said huffily, not at peace any more.

"Oh, don't be offended! Please, please don't be offended! You're my best friend, you know that, but I have to be honest."

Rachel was offended, in spite of this. I *will* do it, she thought, gritting her teeth with determination, but saying no more; and later, before she went to sleep that night, she indulged in a highly entertaining fantasy wherein she was signing copies of her books in a huge London store, besieged by a throng of people all anxious to buy, among their number the entire Rossiter family.

She wouldn't let them pay for her book, she decided, but would rise to her feet, and would graciously present them each with a copy, for which they would be suitably thankful.

"We knew Miss Bond before she was famous, you see," Mrs Rossiter would explain to others in the crowd. "We are so proud of her."

One day, she thought. One day.

The Rossiters had other friends who often dropped in from time to time. Sometimes they stayed for meals, quite without arrangement, and there always seemed enough to go round, no matter how many sat at the table. At first this had astonished Rachel – and even more astonishing was the casual way these friends used the telephone to let their parents know they wouldn't be coming home. It was, she thought, like being in a different world. Just imagine Grandma – well, one couldn't, and it was hopeless even to try. She would have had fifty fits to have her hospitality taken for granted in this way.

Guy Seagrave was a frequent visitor because not only was he Gavin's friend, but he was madly in love with Diana. At the beginning of the summer, when Rachel had first got to know the Rossiters, his devotion had been welcomed by the object of it – even encouraged. He was reasonably nice-looking – not as handsome as Gavin, of course, but just as tall, with black hair and brown eyes, and of course there was the car. Such a possession was enough to increase any young man's sex appeal, even in the eyes of someone as self-sufficient as Diana, and even if he did have spots.

Alannah didn't care for him at all – mainly, Rachel suspected, because he didn't take any notice of her.

"He's so wet," she said to Rachel scornfully. "He doesn't have a word to say for himself when Di's about."

"He must be awfully in love with her." Rachel knew the feeling and was sympathetic.

"Well, I hope no one's ever in love with me, if all it does is make them so soppy. Di says he's the strong and silent sort, and she's not wrong there. He doesn't say a word. He just *gawps*!"

"I expect he's just shy when she's about."

"It won't last you know," Alannah prophesied sagely. "I've seen it all before. She likes boys to fall for her, but once they do, she can't be bothered."

"What about Gavin?" Rachel had longed to ask since that first day, but had been afraid to do so. "Is he in love with anyone?"

Alannah pursed her lips and wrinkled her nose.

"Don't think so. There are lots of girls who like *him*, of course, and he took Polly Roberts out for a while. They were always going to the pictures and dances and things, but he went off her – which didn't surprise me one bit! She's got the most terrible laugh I ever heard, just like a braying donkey."

"You don't think he likes Marjorie Newton?"

49

Alannah thought for a while before answering, her head on one side, while Rachel went on turning the pages of the *Girls' Own Paper*, trying hard to look as if the question was of no importance. She was distinctly worried about Marjorie, who had started coming to the house with great frequency. She was a friend of Diana's, a thin, rather intense girl with red hair and green eyes who became highly animated the moment Gavin appeared, tossing her spectacular locks and flashing those sparkling eyes. She was clever, Diana said. Rachel thought her prickly and even more unpredictable than Diana herself, but she did have a certain kind of distinction.

"He might," Alannah admitted. "She makes him laugh."

"Who makes who laugh?" Barney asked, joining them without warning. He, alone among the children, spent as much time with friends outside the confines of Kimberley Lodge and its garden as he did within them. No one knew quite what he did with himself. His mother encouraged him to take a sketch-book out into the country with him, but he was always reluctant to show what he had done.

"Marjorie Newton makes Gavin laugh. Rachel wanted to know if I thought he liked her – "

"I was just *asking*!" Embarrassed, Rachel was blushing scarlet.

"I think he does," Barney said. "He's put her photograph on his chest of drawers in the bedroom."

"Well that proves it, then," Alannah agreed. "Di won't think much of it, will she?"

Rachel stared at her.

"Why not? I mean, Marjorie is her friend – "

"Bet she won't be for long. Di doesn't like her friends to fall for Gavin."

It seemed incomprehensible; but then, much of what went on in Diana's and Gavin's world was beyond Rachel's understanding. Brother and sister were very close, and would often remove themselves out of earshot of the others to sit and talk and talk and talk, always very quietly, as if they were exchanging secrets. About what? Marjorie? Guy? Other friends? Politics? Rachel had no idea.

But equally there were other occasions when a quarrel would flare up, and this Rachel hated more than anything. It was always quite different in nature from the brief spats between the other children which were usually about the ownership of certain articles, or the division of labour. There was a frightening intensity about the way the insults flew between Diana and Gavin

50

– a tense, unbearable whiteness, a feeling that nerves were at breaking point and that anything might be said, anything done.

"I hate you, I hate you, I hate you," Diana had screamed one day, a fight erupting out of one of their sotto voce conversations, this time in the corner of the living room. Rachel, alone with them since Alannah had temporarily removed herself to get lemonade from the kitchen and Barney was out on his own concerns, felt her stomach constrict with panic. She watched in horror as Diana flung herself on the carpet and pounded it with her clenched fists. Aghast, Rachel looked on, biting her fingers, close to tears, seeing the end of Rossiter family harmony for all time. "I could kill you, Gavin Rossiter! I wish you were dead!"

"So do I," Gavin spat in return. His face was a greenish white, his lips drawn back in a snarl. No sign now of the debonair charmer whom Rachel had adored on sight. "Because then I'd never have to speak to you again. In fact if I ever *see* you again, that'll be too soon for me."

"Beast, beast!" Diana leapt up from the floor and, like one demented, threw herself on him, flailing at him with her fists. Gavin grabbed hold of them and twisted her arms behind her back until she screamed with pain. Wildly Rachel rushed out to find Alannah.

"It's awful in there," she gasped. "I think they're going to kill each other – "

"Just ignore them," Alannah said calmly, filling two glasses with lemonade from a large jug.

"It's all you can do," Pommy said, shaking her head as she rolled pastry, as if she had long given up any hope of understanding either Gavin or Diana. "It'll all be over in five minutes, mark my words."

"Pommy's right," Alannah assured her. "They'll be back to normal before long. Di's awfully baggy lately because of waiting for her School Cert. results. Mum says we've got to make allowances."

"But she said she hated Gavin! She said she wished he was dead."

"She always says that. She doesn't mean it."

Alannah hadn't seen Diana's face, Rachel thought, disbelieving her. Or Gavin's, come to that. Surely it meant something, all that blanched, furious hatred?

"We'll just leave them alone," Alannah said. "Let's go up to the old nursery."

It was a day of brief spells of sunshine interspersed with

prolonged squally rain; just the day for concentrating on the book – *Hurrah for Dymphna*, as it was now officially titled. But somehow Rachel could find little joy in it. She kept thinking of those frightening scenes down below. It was like a fire or a shipwreck, she thought. Even when the shouting was over, the damage would still be there. For once, time seemed to hang heavily, and long before her normal time of departure she made an excuse to go back home.

In the front hall she encountered Diana and Gavin, just emerging from the sitting room, amicably making plans for the afternoon.

"Just off, then?" Gavin remarked to her in his normal pleasant manner.

"Oh Gavin, your talent for stating the obvious almost amounts to genius," Diana said, sounding affectionately amused.

Rachel, shaken by the fierceness of the quarrel, was now equally amazed by the absence of any trace of it. Diana was calm and smiling, more beautiful than ever, as if the rage that had possessed her had been cathartic, leaving a radiant tranquillity in its wake.

That's the Rossiters for you, Rachel thought, as, totally baffled by them, she made her way next door. She'd never understand them. Never.

4

'**M**r and Mrs Hugh Rossiter request the pleasure of the company of Miss Rachel Bond at the wedding of their daughter, Diana Marguerite, to Dr Thomas Penrose, MD, DSO, at 11.30 a.m. on 20th October 1946 at St Mary's Church – '

Rachel stared at the invitation in disbelief. She had recognised Mrs Rossiter's bold, flamboyant hand the moment she saw it adorning the square envelope on the mat in the hall, and had guessed what it must contain. That she should even dream of sending such a thing surely demonstrated an insensitivity that beggared belief, Rachel thought, even though she held the irrefutable evidence of it in her two hands.

There was a little note included with the invitation.

'Dear Rachel,' it said. 'We were so glad to discover where you have been hiding yourself all these years. I do hope you can come to Diana's wedding! You were so much one of the family in the old days and it would be lovely to see you again. I am coming to town shortly to look for something to wear for the occasion. Perhaps we could meet?'

It was signed: 'With love, as always, Carina Rossiter'.

As always? Rachel couldn't help feeling a touch of sardonic amusement at that, but though she smiled she was conscious of a twist of fear. Her instinct hadn't been at fault, then. The net seemed to be closing. They were moving in on her.

It was a day for Beattie Jenks from next door to look after Tess during the morning. Three times a week she came in, Mondays, Wednesdays and Fridays, from ten o'clock to twelve thirty, and Rachel had developed the habit of being poised for flight the moment she came in through the door. Otherwise she found herself pinned to the kitchen wall while Beattie regaled her with the latest in the long-running saga involving various members of her colourful family and acquaintances.

On this particular Wednesday morning Rachel was caught unawares, the invitation still in her hand. Beattie spotted the unmistakable gold lettering and the wedding bells with entwined ribbons almost before she was inside the door, and was thrilled and excited on her behalf, wondering aloud what Rachel would wear.

"You'll have to buy a new outfit," she said. "When is it? October? Ooh, I love an autumn wedding! It'll be all chrysanths and dahlias. I wonder what the weather will be like? It could be chilly by then. A nice fine tweed suit would be the thing. I can see you in a sort of beigy colour with tan etceteras. Suit you a treat, it would, honest. I'll get you the coupons, easy."

Rachel shook her head, managing at length to break in on Beattie's speculations.

"I'm not going," she said. Beattie's mouth fell open.

"What? Oh, that's a shame, that is! You don't get out much. If it's Tess that's the problem – "

"No, no, nothing like that," Rachel assured her. "Nancy would have her for the day, I'm sure, but I simply don't want to go."

Beattie looked astonished and seemed inclined to debate the point, but Tess provided a welcome diversion by starting to wail and was borne off upstairs for a nappy change.

Rachel took the opportunity to escape into the dining room which doubled as her study. She was working on an article about holidays for children, commissioned by a magazine – the kind of thing that had been her bread and butter for the past eighteen months and as such was not to be despised – but somehow, much to her fury, the words remained elusive. It was all because of the Rossiters, she thought angrily. Foolish though it might be to think it, they had re-entered her life and they posed a threat.

George Collins came to supper that evening. It was impossible, in spite of Nancy's apparent doubts on the matter, not to like George. He had the face of an engaging monkey, boyish and mischievous, as if his sins, cheerfully admitted by him to be many, were no more than lovable idiosyncrasies. Rachel doubted if he were capable of fidelity to any woman, yet he was the sort of man that a woman could forgive and forgive and forgive again.

And Nancy loved him. Looking at them across the table that night Rachel was suddenly sure of it, and was guilty of a sinking of the heart. She was only too aware that anyone not blinded

54

by George's charms would realise that marriage to him would be more of a roller-coaster ride than a bed of roses. What she, personally, would do without Nancy to buttress and cheer her, she could hardly bear to think.

He was, she saw as she came back into the kitchen after putting Tess to bed, in a particularly elevated mood.

"Tell Rachel your news," Nancy urged him.

"Sure." He poured more wine, and, his face alive with excitement and confidence and the kind of vitality that made him the man he was, he lifted his glass towards her.

"Pray raise your glass to Collins Air Services. God bless them and all who fly with them. You may well look amazed! I'm in business, Rachel my love! How about that?"

He and an ex-RAF engineer had somehow managed to buy an old Lancaster bomber, he told her, which they were going to convert to fly freight from an airfield in Norfolk. Air freight was the coming thing. Between them they had the know-how, the enthusiasm, the capacity for hard work. They couldn't fail!

"But planes can," Rachel pointed out. "Parts can. You'll need massive capital, George."

"We've raised a loan. We've got enough, believe me." His eyes as he leaned across the table were bright with excitement. "All we need is this little bundle of efficiency here to run the office and do the hustling for freight – " He turned and smiled at Nancy, putting his arm around her shoulders. "Imagine what her contacts on the Indian sub-continent can do for us!"

"George, you know quite well I haven't agreed," Nancy said. But she would, Rachel saw with resignation, wishing she could feel happier about it.

Afterwards, when George had gone, Nancy came slowly back into the kitchen where Rachel had started washing the dishes.

"You don't approve, do you?" she asked. "What we didn't mention, but is rather germane to the entire thing as far as I'm concerned, is that he's asked me to marry him."

"Oh, Nancy – "

"You've got to have faith, Rachel."

"And hope," Rachel admitted. "And love. And the greatest of these is love."

"I hate the thought of leaving you in the lurch."

"You won't be, Nance. You've seen me through the worst. I want you to do whatever makes you happy. Honestly."

It was true, she assured herself. It was, it was! But the panic that seized her once she had gone to bed was purely selfish. She had relied so much on Nancy – her presence, her practical help, her common sense. From the beginning they had fitted in with each other without strain. How could she manage without her? Nancy had been her family these past two years.

She'd have to find a new lodger. Oh, what an awful, awful thought! She didn't want a new lodger; couldn't bear the thought of a stranger in the house. An advertisement in the newspaper might produce anyone, anyone at all – a homicidal maniac, or a child molester. How could you tell?

It was as if, while she slept, her mind had been methodically examining her options, for the moment she opened her eyes in the morning she knew exactly what to do. Later, while on a visit to the shops, she parked the pram outside the telephone kiosk and dialled Sylvia's number.

"It's Rachel," she said, when she heard her aunt's voice. "I've been wondering – the cottage in St Bethan. Is it occupied at the moment?"

"My dear, *such* a worry," Sylvia replied, maddeningly avoiding a direct answer. "I want to sell the place, but Rex won't hear of it. I had enough of it during the war without wanting to spend any more holidays there, and now there's this Washington posting which means we won't be in a position to use it for ages even if we wanted to, but Rex says – "

"Is it occupied?" Rachel asked again, more urgently. Tess had been sound asleep when left outside the telephone box, but through the glass Rachel could see she had pulled herself up and now sat grasping the sides of the pram, her mouth pulled down into the crying position.

"Well, no. Were you wanting a holiday? The thing is, Rex was thinking of a long let – "

"That's what I want," Rachel said. "A long let."

"Oh!" Sylvia sounded surprised, and a little dismayed. "We'd have to charge rent, you know."

"Well, of course! I'm not asking for any favours. I want to get out of London and thought I might let my own house and rent yours, if it happened to be available."

"But what on earth would you want to do that for? My dear, what an extraordinary idea! What about your work?"

"I could do it better there. Look – can I come and talk to you about it? Say, tomorrow morning?" Beattie would be on duty once again, which meant she could leave Tess for an hour or so.

"Very well." Sylvia still sounded bewildered. "You'd better

come at ten. I have a hair appointment at eleven. I can't promise anything, though. I'm not at all sure that Rex – "

"I'd be a good tenant, Sylvia, I swear. There'd be no trouble about the rent, and I'm quite house-trained these days, I promise."

"Rex was thinking more of a family. Someone settled."

"I'm settled! Or at least I can be until you want the house yourself. There might be advantages in having someone known to you, who'll look after your interests, don't you think? Look, Sylvia, I have to dash – " Tess was definitely crying now, unhappy at her abandonment. "I'll see you at ten tomorrow. And you will put in a good word with Rex about me, won't you?"

"I can't make any promises," Sylvia said again. "I believe Rex has already written to a house agent in Truro."

However, the following day when Rachel presented herself at the flat, she was smiling in a conspiratorial way.

"I managed to talk Rex round," she said. "He didn't think much of the idea at first, but I put it to him that blood is thicker than water and that Ivor would want us to help you if we possibly can."

"I'm sure he'd be grateful – "

"We discussed everything last night. All the arrangements. Rent, and so on."

The sum mentioned seemed, to Rachel, exorbitant.

"Of course, for a stranger we'd charge more," Sylvia went on, seeing her shock. "Empty properties are like gold dust at the moment. No doubt you'll be able to get an equal amount for your house."

"My house," Rachel pointed out, "has three good bedrooms and one tiny one, and is five minutes from a tube station. But never mind. If that's the going rate, then I'm happy to pay it. Please thank Rex for his generosity," she added sardonically – and then wished she hadn't. She wanted the cottage no matter what rent was demanded. Alienating the owners was hardly the best way to go about the matter.

She need not have worried, for Sylvia had noticed nothing amiss.

"There's a Mrs Hoskings who looks after the place," she said. "Let me know when you intend to move and I'll drop her a note and tell her you're coming. I still can't imagine what you think you'll find to do down there! It nearly killed me, I can tell you."

"Well you see, there's this book," Rachel began. "I've written one that's coming out next year, and the publishers want another – "

This glorious fact had, she realised, been obscured by Barney's visit and her ensuing obsession with the Rossiters, plus Nancy's coming departure, now an established fact. Now, suddenly, it was the only thing that mattered. Relief and joy flooded through her and she grinned hugely at her aunt.

"It's rather marvellous, isn't it?" she said.

"Why, my dear, yes, of course. How very exciting! I *do* hope it has a happy ending. I can't abide these nasty modern novels that purport to show life as it is, can you? Not, of course, that I pretend to be much of a reader. However, let me know when it comes out and I'll put it on my list at Harrods. They're awfully good about getting absolutely anything! Well, keep in touch. I must fly now."

Yes, of course – the hair appointment, Rachel reminded herself. She would have to leave. And she *still* hadn't mentioned a word about Tess!

No time now. Anyway, it didn't matter. Rex, apparently, had preferred to let his cottage to a family rather than a single person. Well, she was a family! She hadn't, after all, lied about anything; just neglected to tell the whole truth.

Back in Inverness Street, Beattie reported that Tess had been good as gold the whole morning.

"But not a wink of sleep," she said. "She should go down the minute she's had her din-dins, bless her."

"This," Rachel later said to Tess, spooning strained carrots into her mouth after Beattie had gone, "is *dinner*."

At which information Tess smiled seraphically, made a grab at the spoon and smeared carrot over bib, face and hair.

"And you are a little monster," smiled her mother, adoringly.

Loving mother though she was, she was pleased when Beattie's prediction came true and Tess went to sleep the moment she was tucked up in her cot. It meant that Rachel could work for an hour or so, and maybe get the article finished.

Meantime the invitation to Diana's wedding lay beside her typewriter, demanding an answer. She wrote a formal refusal – 'Miss Rachel Bond regrets – ' and hesitated for some time about the necessity of replying to Mrs Rossiter's letter. In the end, she wrote a few lines saying that she was sure Mrs Rossiter would understand that she felt unable to attend, though she wished Diana and her fiancé well. She added that she was leaving London shortly so was unlikely to be able to meet her. Anyone normal, she reflected, would get the message; but she had no real conviction that this applied to a monumental ego such as Mrs Rossiter's.

How sad it was, that things should come to this! It was hardly believable, when one considered how much she had revered them all and longed for their approval.

Now she wanted nothing more than to get as far away from them as possible. She would, she resolved, set about letting the house the very next morning. Nancy might know someone suitable at the BBC.

And then – Cornwall! A new place, a new beginning. It would be a challenge, she thought, not getting on with the article, but instead staring into space. She'd be on her own again. Well, that was nothing new; hadn't she always been on her own when it came down to it? She was happiest that way.

Which was strange, really, when you considered how she had longed, when young, to belong. To be part of a family. One of the Rossiters.

"They sound an awfully jolly crowd," Julia said when she had returned to school after that first summer holiday in Warnfield. "You must have had wonderful hols, Rachel."

"Didn't you, then?" Rachel couldn't miss the touch of wistfulness in Julia's voice. "I thought you were going to Margate."

"Cliftonville, actually. Well, we did go there, but it was a bit dull. It was a special guesthouse, you see, for clergymen and their families, only the trouble was that there was no one of my age there. The other children were just toddlers – quite sweet, most of them, but not what you'd call kindred spirits, exactly."

"Oh, bad luck!"

How unbelievably satisfying it was, Rachel thought smugly, just to be able to say 'bad luck' to someone else, when, at the beginning of the holiday, she herself had been so sunk in gloom; and how wonderful it was to have so much to tell Julia and Alice! All about the games and the laughter and the songs around the piano; and the picnic they all had on Chuffington Common when the news came through about Diana's marvellous School Certificate results.

Well, perhaps not quite all. Rachel didn't mention how the thought of Adverbs was enough, still, to engulf her in shame, or how dull it was at Grandma's house, and somehow cold, even on the warmest day. Or how Diana and Gavin had one of their awful rows on Chuffington Common and nearly ruined the whole occasion. She had, in fact, almost forgotten such things herself, so enchanted was she by her retrospective look at the holidays.

"I think Barney sounds nicest," said Alice.

"Barney's all right," she admitted. "So's Alannah. We're writing a book."

Oh, there was so much to tell that it quite overcame the awfulness of going back to school; and in fact, even this wasn't the horror that Rachel had anticipated because although Miss Scrimgeour, the fearsome headmistress, was still in evidence, Miss Simkins had left and her place had been taken by Miss Rayner, who was much younger, with a thin, eager face and an Eton crop. No one knew why and the whole school buzzed with speculation. Milly Danvers-King said she thought Miss Simkins had been taken ill.

"Nothing trivial, I trust," Rachel said, which is what Diana had said when Guy Seagrave had gone down with some stomach complaint just before the end of the holidays, long after she had grown tired of him. This witticism had a gratifying response, raising quite a laugh. Rachel even heard Janet Fanning repeating it to Morag Blunt, who had been out of the room, and it was all she could do to keep the smile of delight from her own face. No one, last term, had taken the smallest notice of anything she said.

"Maybe English lessons will be better from now on," remarked Janet when they were unpacking in the dormitory; and Rachel, only half listening, her mind back in Warnfield with the Rossiters, was suddenly brought back to the present with a rush of joy. For English was her *thing*, as she had said to Alannah, and having Miss Simkins to teach her had removed any pleasure she might have taken in it. Now, surely, it would all be different.

"Don't you hate being back?" Alice Jamieson whispered, her homesickness for Singapore as intense as ever. But Rachel grinned at her, unsympathetic.

"Could be worse," she said. "Cheer up, Alice."

Alice looked betrayed. She had known about Rachel's nocturnal tears, even if they were silent, and had regarded her as an ally. But now it seemed she had no one.

"You've changed," she said accusingly to Rachel.

"Oh, rubbish! Here, have a sweet." They were humbugs, pressed upon her as a leaving present by Barney. He *was* nice, Alice was right – none of the others had given her anything. Nice but, well, ordinary. Not like Gavin. Alice took a sweet, but repeated the accusation.

"You have changed, you know."

60

Rachel didn't deny it again. Alice, she thought, was probably right. Just *being* with the Rossiters must have had some effect, surely? Maybe some of their Rossiter-ness had rubbed off on her. And if so, then she was jolly glad.

'Dear Mrs Rossiter,' she wrote after a few days back at school. 'I hope you and Mr Rossiter are well and happy. I am writing to thank you for being so kind to me during the school holidays. I enjoyed the times I spent at Kimberley Lodge very much and hope I wasn't a nuisance. It was the best holiday I have ever had.

'I have heard from my parents that they are coming home on six months' leave soon, and will be here by Christmas, so I might not be at Grandma's house next holidays. We may take a flat in London, my mother says, but it's not decided. Perhaps it won't happen. I hope not, anyway.

'We have a new English mistress who is very nice. Being back at school isn't as bad as I thought.

'Well, that is all the news so I will say goodbye.

'Love from Rachel.'

The possibility of the flat in London for the period of her parents' leave – information so lightly dropped in a letter from her mother – had shaken Rachel to the core. She could see no possible reason for it. There was, after all, plenty of room at The Laurels.

May be it wouldn't happen. Sometimes her mother was inclined to get ideas – expensive ideas – and though her father didn't actually oppose them openly they somehow failed to come to anything. The question of the flat seemed, to Rachel, to be just one of those kind of ideas. How she hoped so! She couldn't bear to miss Christmas with the Rossiters.

"We always do a pantomime and have a big party, with dancing and everything," Alannah had told her. "Everybody comes. I expect we'll even ask your grandma and grandpa if you're here."

"Your grandmother can take the short cut, Rachel," Diana had said, with mock sweetness. "She can fly over the wall on her broomstick."

Traitorously, Rachel had smirked at this, but Barney had kicked Diana under the table and told her to shut up.

Alannah had sworn she would write once Rachel had gone back to school, and indeed one long letter did arrive early in the term. It told her that Diana was now a Prefect, just as she had foretold; and it contained a rambling and totally confusing account of Alannah

61

being caught writing *Hurrah for Dymphna* when she ought to have been doing her French prep, and how she was sent to the Head and had an awful wigging, and how abso–bally–lutely awful it was to be the sister of a Prefect, constantly asked why she wasn't as clever as Di all the time, as if she could help it!

> 'If only I could be sent to St Ursula's!' Alannah wrote longingly. 'I've been *begging* Mummy and Daddy to send me but they won't hear of it. I've told them that if your parents can stand it, then they jolly well ought to be able to, but it isn't any good, they won't listen. If you have a midnight feast or anything please take notes because we may be able to use it for the book. I'm not doing any more of it now because there's so much prep I'm getting writer's cramp and anyway it's not the same without you. I hope your parents decide to stay in Warnfield for the Christmas hols, or what shall we do?'

Rachel was touched and pleased by these last remarks and wrote back at length and at once; but she heard no more from Alannah who, it seemed, had exhausted her writing capacity by this one initial effort. Or perhaps the amount of prep had swamped her altogether. It was left to Mrs Rossiter, answering Rachel's previous letter, to give her the news from Warnfield.

> 'Thank you for your charming letter. You were a most welcome visitor during the holidays and I am sure I speak for us all when I say we shall be glad to see you back in Warnfield again, whenever that might be. I happened to see your grandmother in town only yesterday, and she assured me that you and your parents would be spending Christmas at The Laurels and, indeed, that they would be staying there for the period of their leave, so perhaps the latest news is that they have decided against the London flat.'

The letter continued with news of Diana's elevation to the position of Prefect, and Gavin's achievements on the Rugby field; of details of a children's art competition in which Barney had won a prize and had several pictures on display in the Public Library, ('Such a thrill', Mrs Rossiter wrote, 'that one of my sons is following in my own footsteps. I cannot express to you my emotion as I stood in that room and gazed at them!'); and of the role that Alannah had secured in the school play, Barrie's *Dear Brutus*:

62

'Because although she is, perhaps, a little young, there is no doubt she is talented above the ordinary. Needless to say, she is quite delighted at the honour – even, perhaps, a little nervous – but I know that she will cover herself with glory and make me very proud of her, as indeed I am of all my children.

'As for you, my dear, I can only wish you an enjoyable and successful term and thank you once again for writing. I may say that, by the time you left us to go back to school, we had grown very accustomed to seeing you on this side of the wall! You were quite one of the family, almost a Rossiter.'

Almost a Rossiter! Rachel's heart swelled with pride as she read these words, and she hugged the thought close to her all the day long, and at night, too, until she went to sleep. Alice was right, then, she thought. She *had* changed! She was almost a Rossiter! She wondered if her mother and father would notice it.

"A fire in the bedroom," said Grandma, "is nothing short of extravagance, and downright unhealthy, if you ask my opinion. Except in case of illness, of course."

"You must remember, mother, that we left Uganda in November when it was beginning to get quite hot. Kitty simply isn't used to this climate."

Ivor Bond's voice was the same one he used when settling disputes among the natives: calm, pleasant, utterly reasonable, yet at the same time firm. Keeping the peace between his mother and his wife, he reflected, had much in common with his duties among the litigious Baganda, the only difference being that in Africa he wielded more power. Here in Warnfield no one took a great deal of notice of him, least of all Kitty. And they had been at The Laurels less than a week!

"Then she should wear warmer clothes!" Underwear, Mrs Bond meant, but she could not demean herself by discussing such a matter with her son. She had been shocked to the core by the sight (in the wash, naturally) of the sketchy garments worn by her daughter-in-law, who surely should be old enough to have enough sense to know that winter in England demanded good, long, winceyette knickers and wool-next-the-skin. Now, *they* would have been a sensible use of poor Ivor's salary, instead of that coat and hat which must have cost a fortune in Bond Street! Kitty must have dragged him to the West End the moment her foot had stepped on dry land! She'd had a good look at the labels and knew quite well where they had been purchased. That was an unnecessary extravagance if ever she saw one, for had not she, personally, kept in mothballs the coat worn by Kitty on her last leave? Good warm velour with still a great deal of wear in it. But not good enough for my lady, oh dear me, no!

At least she'd been able to scotch her daughter-in-law's ridiculous plan to rent a flat in London. What a dreadful waste of money that would have been, when Ivor had a perfectly good home to come to! Not to mention the chaos that would have ensued. Why, Kitty had no more idea of running a home than a child – and Mrs Bond didn't hesitate to say so on all possible occasions.

"I'm sure I don't know how you'd get on, my dear, having to think of providing meals without the help of servants," she said, as Kitty made a late appearance for lunch. "Good dinners don't cook themselves, you know." And:

"I'm so happy to have you staying here. Flats in London cost a great deal of money. Someone, after all, has to think of poor Ivor's pocket." And:

"What a good thing you have such a large bedroom, my dear, bearing in mind the way your things seem to get scattered about! Flats in town are so small and poky, aren't they? So inconvenient – and, after all, not at all what Ivor is used to."

Kitty said nothing to all of this, but Rachel saw her little, three-cornered, kitten's smile and knew that underneath the surface her mother was boiling with rage. She was conscious, too, of the sound of her mother's voice haranguing her father, once they were alone in their bedroom at night. Grandma and Grandpa couldn't hear the low, insistent whisper because they were at the front of the house; but Rachel, from the adjoining room, could hear it, rising and falling, on and on. She couldn't distinguish words, but didn't need to. Her mother, she knew, was not happy with the situation. Who could be?

Rachel had gone next door to Kimberley Lodge the day after she had arrived back from school. Alannah had greeted her warmly and Barney, too, had grinned at her in a friendly way and asked her if she'd made the First Hockey XI yet, which was his idea of a joke. Neither Gavin nor Diana had been at home. They were out doing their Christmas shopping, Alannah said, and she and Barney were busy doing their lists, and what did Rachel think? Would Gavin like a volume of W.H. Auden's poetry, or a cigarette lighter? A cheap one, she added gratuitously.

"I didn't know Gavin liked poetry," Rachel said, in some surprise.

64

"Well, he likes Auden – at least, he says he does. Auden's all the thing, isn't he, because he's one of the young intellectual revolutionaries? That's what Di says, anyway. And Gavin does like being all the thing. But on the other hand, he's just started smoking a pipe, so I'm a bit torn. I'm going to buy Di the music of *The Gay Divorcee*. She's mad about it! I say, do you want to be in our pantomime?"

"Can I be?" Rachel's delight lit up her face.

"You could be an ugly sister. We were having to make do with just me, but there really ought to be two. Di's Cinderella, of course, and Gavin's Prince Charming, and Barney is Buttons – "

"Who's the Fairy Godmother?"

"Well, that's *it*, you see. That's the whole joke. We haven't got one, but Dad's going to be Father Christmas instead. He's written it so that he comes down the chimney on Christmas Eve and instead of finding the whole house asleep, he finds Cinders still cleaning up the fire and getting in his way and at first he gets really cross. He's so funny! When we did the read-through, we were laughing so much that we couldn't go on for ages and Mummy banged on the door and said if it was as funny as all that, then she was going to come and listen too, but we wouldn't let her because it would spoil the surprise."

And she, Rachel Bond, was going to be part of it! It was just too marvellous for words. This was going to be the best Christmas ever. Mrs Rossiter said that of course the whole household from The Laurels must be invited, she was longing to meet Rachel's parents. She would write a little note that very minute, asking them to the pantomime and party on Christmas night.

"What's this?" Grandma said suspiciously, when Rachel handed her Mrs Rossiter's letter.

"It's an invitation," Rachel explained. "The Rossiters want us all to go over. They're doing a pantomime, and Alannah wants me to be an Ugly Sister – "

"Well, I hope you told her it was out of the question," Grandma said. "We don't go out on Christmas Day. It's a family time, I always think."

"But Grandma, they *need* me! I'm an Ugly Sister! And there's a party afterwards with games and dancing, and lots of people are going. All their friends and neighbours and relations. Mr Rossiter's parents are staying for Christmas, so you'd have other older people to talk to, and Mrs Rossiter said particularly how much she wanted to meet Mummy and Daddy – "

"Then surely it would be the height of rudeness to refuse,

mother-in-law?" Kitty smiled but her voice reminded Rachel of icicles, cold and clear and hard. "I, for one, should hate to offend your neighbours and Rachel's good friends, so pray don't turn down the invitation on our account."

She left the room without saying any more, but the speaking look she gave her husband as she passed him on her way to the door told him what she expected him to do, and uncomfortably he cleared his throat.

"I think, perhaps, Kitty is right on this occasion, Mother – "

"Well, I can't agree! Christmas is being together with one's family in one's own home – "

"We can be together in our own home on Boxing Day, Grandma," Rachel pointed out.

"It seems typical of the Rossiters to turn the whole thing into a – a *jamboree*! Have they forgotten the meaning of Christmas? Why, the vicar was only saying last Sunday that the forces of commercialism are taking over – "

"The Rossiters aren't going to charge us," Rachel said, in the kind of voice that Diana would have used had she been present. Both her father and grandmother looked at her in astonishment.

"Well! I think we can do without that kind of rudeness, Rachel."

"Please don't use that tone to your grandmother, Rachel," her father said sternly.

"I didn't mean to be rude, Grandma, honestly." Rachel had been as surprised as the others at her own temerity, and hastened to make amends. "It's just that I do want to go so much, and be in the pantomime and everything, and it really will be awfully jolly. I'm sure you and Grandpa will enjoy it just as much as everyone else."

"I doubt that!"

"Mother, I think Rachel has a point." Ivor cleared his throat again, gearing himself up for opposition – never a stance that came easily to him. "It's not as if Sylvia and Rex are going to be here with us to make it a real family gathering, is it?" This matter was a sore point with his mother, and it was bold of him to raise it at this juncture. "We shall no doubt all enjoy it, and Kitty and I are certainly keen to meet Rachel's new friends. Why don't you give me the letter and let me reply on your behalf?"

"Well, I can hardly insist that you stay at home, I suppose, if you are determined not to."

She was, however, far from mollified, and Rachel heard her complaining bitterly, sotto voce, to Grandpa after he came back from the bank, about the lengths that poor dear Ivor would go to just to please Kitty.

"I swear I'd have walked out of the house then and there if she'd insisted on refusing that invitation," Kitty said with unusual frankness when she came into the bedroom for a cosy chat before Rachel went to sleep. "But your father knows I'm just about at the end of my tether! Can you imagine how awful it would be, sitting here looking at each other in dead silence, knowing that a party was raging next door? You're a poor little puss, having to put up with her every holiday."

"It's not so bad, really; not now that I know the Rossiters."

"You're very fond of them, aren't you? Your letters were full of them. I must say I'm dying to meet them, though Mrs Rossiter sounds – " she broke off, smiling, her lip caught between her teeth. "I'm sure she's really quite charming," she said.

"Oh, she is, Mummy. You'll like her, I promise – and Mr Rossiter, too. He's awfully nice, and terribly funny."

"And the boys? Are they funny?"

"Yes. Well, sometimes."

"And handsome?"

"Mm. 'Specially Gavin."

"I believe you have a soft spot for him!"

Rachel knew she was blushing and hoped the bedside light was too dim for her mother to see.

"He's got loads of girlfriends."

"And Mr Rossiter? Is he handsome?"

"Oh, yes. Terribly."

Kitty gave a small crinkly smile indicating complicity, and gently pressed her forefinger on the tip of Rachel's nose.

"I can't wait to meet them all. Now, go to sleep, darling. Tomorrow we'll go shopping and buy presents for them, since they've been so good to you. And for everybody else, too – though what to get Grandma I can't imagine."

"She could do with a new broomstick," Rachel said pertly, quoting Diana but making no acknowledgements, and was delighted to see her mother's eyes brim with laughter.

"Oh, wicked!" she said, not in the least angry. "You're as bad as your naughty mother! Go to sleep and wake up a better girl."

The town was crowded when they went to do their shopping next day. All the shops were decorated and there was a Father Christmas outside Drake's Department Stores.

"This is fun, poppet, isn't it?" Enlivened by the festive atmosphere, Kitty Bond's cheeks and eyes were bright with a sudden access of good spirits. "When we've finished with everyone else, I'm going to buy myself a gorgeous dress. Come on, let's go and spend some of Daddy's hard-earned. What on earth shall we buy for Grandma – seriously, now! No more funny suggestions."

They settled on a handbag, and a pure silk tie for Grandpa. Presents for the Rossiters took a little longer, but at last they decided on a puzzle for Alannah and a hand-painted bracelet for Diana, and a new sketch-book for Barney.

"We could buy a really expensive cigar for Mr Rossiter," Rachel suggested.

"He smokes cigars, does he? Mmm – I do love the smell of cigars!" Kitty narrowed her eyes as if in ecstasy at the very thought. "Now Gavin! What shall we get for him?"

"I don't know about Gavin," Rachel said.

"And Mrs Rossiter?"

"I don't know about her, either."

"Soap? Or talcum powder? I haven't met the lady, but I imagine she would like something pretty and flowery and thoroughly wholesome, don't you? Parma violet, perhaps."

Rachel darted a quick glance at her mother. There was something in her voice – but no, she looked serious enough.

"That would be lovely," she said. "Soap, I think."

"Which only leaves Gavin. Any ideas?"

Rachel bit her lip in perplexity. She wanted to get something special – something that would impress him with her thoughtfulness and understanding, that he would want to keep. A book, perhaps? Something other than Auden? Who was the poet that Miss Rayner had recommended so highly?

She browsed in the bookshop while her mother disappeared in search of a dress, and it was there that her eye fell on a book of Stephen Spender's poems. That was it – that was the name!

She picked up the book, and turning the pages found the verses she was looking for, the poem that Miss Rayner had read to them one morning just before the end of term. She had been thinking of dinner at the time, obsessed by hunger, but in no time she had forgotten all such mundane considerations. Now, reading it again, she felt the same strange prickling at the back of her neck, the excitement in the pit of her stomach that she had felt then.

> Through corridors of light where the hours are suns
> Endless and singing. Whose lovely ambition
> Was that their lips, still touched with fire,
> Should tell of the Spirit clothed from head to foot in song.

It was wonderful, wonderful! What it meant, she didn't know – but it didn't matter! It was the sound and the shape of it that she loved; and reading further, she came to 'streamers of white cloud/And whispers of wind in the listening sky'.

How she loved 'listening sky'! Oh, there was no doubt about it, this is what she would buy for Gavin, but she would read all the poems in the book before she wrapped it up and would try to make sense of them. And when she got back to school she would tell Miss Rayner how much she liked them. That particular poem, anyway.

When she arrived at the shop, her mother was pirouetting in a black satin dress with a low scooped neckline, no back at all, and a hem that flared in zigzag lines.

"What do you think, darling?" she asked Rachel, peering over her own shoulder to see her back view in the pier glass. "It's rather gorgeous, isn't it? And not all that expensive, really. Grandmama will disapprove, of course, but then she'll do that anyway, and I'm desperately in need of something to wear at the Rossiters'."

"You look lovely," Rachel said, truthfully. "But – "

"But me no buts, darling." Kitty's mind, it seemed, was made up. "Daddy won't grudge me a new dress at Christmas, I'm quite certain."

Rachel smiled and shrugged her thin shoulders. Her mother was probably right, she thought. And it really was a super dress. Everyone would surely admire it. Even the Rossiters.

5

Kimberley Lodge seemed to vibrate with music and laughter and winking lights, which were strung not only on the Christmas tree inside the drawing room but in the trees outside the house as well. There were coloured paper chains everywhere and great swags of holly over pictures and mirrors and on top of the grandfather clock.

Rachel had arrived before the rest of her party, as there was to be a last, quick run-through of the pantomime before they changed into their costumes. The rehearsal seemed to go quite well. She didn't have much to say, being very much the junior Ugly Sister. Her contribution was largely confined to shrieks of rage and astonishment, and a brandishing of fists. It was given to Alannah to do most of the clowning, which she did with supreme self-confidence.

The performance was to take place in the hall where rows of chairs had already been arranged, full use being made of the stairs and the half-landing in a way that had been perfected over the years. This was the eighth year in succession that Mr Rossiter had produced a pantomime. Christmas wouldn't seem the same without it, people said.

The girls changed and made up in Alannah's bedroom, amid much excited mirth – at least on the part of the Ugly Sisters. Diana was a little more contained.

"I'm not sure," she said, combing her hair down over her shoulders for the opening scenes, "that I'm not getting just a bit beyond all this. It's all rather childish, don't you think?"

"Oh, rubbish, Di!" Alannah wasn't having any of that. "If Daddy can do it, then you can."

70

"Dad's just an infant at heart. Gavin says he feels a real idiot in his tights. *He* says it's positively the last year for him." She peered closer at her face in the mirror, smoothing her eye-shadow with a delicate finger. "Maybe next year we could put on something a little more sophisticated. Noel Coward, or something."

"Rats," muttered Alannah. "Who wants to be sophisticated at Christmas? Besides, we'd have to learn lots of lines if we did that. In a pantomime we can say what we want to, more or less."

"Ad lib," said Diana. "That's what they call it in the real theatre."

"I know!" Alannah tossed her head, already embellished with her Ugly Sister's wig, made with loving care by Mrs Rossiter. Rachel, a very recent member of the cast, had to make do with a highly improbable and vastly inferior cotton-wool-over-cardboard edifice, but she knew it didn't matter. No one would be taking much notice of her.

"It's a pity about Rachel's wig," Diana said, as if she could divine her thoughts. "I'm afraid it was a bit last-minute. Mummy said she didn't have the time, so I would have to do it. But I didn't have much time either – "

"It's all right," Rachel said. "I'm supposed to look ridiculous."

"There's ridiculous and ridiculous," murmured Diana obscurely.

Rachel's feeling of pleasurable excitement ebbed considerably, its place taken by one of anxiety. She might have guessed that she would look ridiculous in quite the wrong kind of way. Why on earth had she wanted to be in this wretched pantomime anyway? She could have been down below with her mother and father and grandparents – they'd surely have arrived by now – waiting with all the other guests to be entertained; preparing to laugh, preparing to enjoy herself. She was going to make a hash of it, she felt it in her bones. She was going to be nothing but a disgrace to herself and her parents, and no one would ever speak to her again –

"Come on, girls," called Mr Rossiter, banging on the door. "Are you decent in there? It's time to start."

The show opened with the Ugly Sisters sweeping arrogantly down the stairs. The audience crammed the hall, some sitting on chairs, some on the floor at the very front, many standing at the back and around the edges. Paper hats were on heads, glasses in hands, and there was laughter and applause as Alannah and Rachel made their entrance.

Rachel felt a little better. She saw her parents at once and couldn't resist grinning at them. Even a quick glance showed that her mother looked outstanding in the new black dress, and that, alone among the company, Grandma, like Queen Victoria, was plainly not amused by the sight of the Ugly Sisters.

It didn't matter. Everyone else was laughing and barracking as, at the entrance of Cinders, the sisters displayed their utter, utter beastliness. Rachel's confidence grew and she found she was beginning to enjoy herself after all. Maybe she wasn't going to make a hash of it. She could see her mother smiling, clapping her hands with delight as Cinderella and Buttons performed their dance. Diana, it had to be admitted, was wooden as an actress when compared with her younger sister, but she moved so gracefully and looked so charming that the delivery of her words was unimportant.

And then came Mr Rossiter in the guise of a petulant, over-worked Santa Claus, his comic irritability causing much amusement. Oh, but he was *good*! Rachel thought, peeping through the kitchen door which roughly served as the wings. Everyone was enjoying it. She could see her mother joining in the singing of 'Ain't it Grand to be Blooming Well Dead' which somehow Mr Rossiter had contrived to include in the plot, and even her father, who was inclined to remain on his dignity, was smiling and nodding his head in time to the music.

Old hands said afterwards that it was the best pantomime ever.

"Aren't you glad you came, mother-in-law?" Kitty demanded of Mrs Bond.

"Very clever, most droll," Mrs Bond said, giving a wintry smile. "Such a pity it all has to be so *noisy*!"

"Mr Rossiter is to be congratulated," her husband said, with unaccustomed firmness. "And our little Rachel did very well, very well indeed."

"How handsome the elder son is!" remarked Kitty appreciatively.

"Handsome is as handsome does." Mrs Bond's dour reply was entirely predictable, and Kitty gave a small, suppressed smile.

"Let's mingle," she said, putting her arm through Ivor's. "I believe Mrs Rossiter is trying to get us all into the drawing room so that the hall can be cleared for dancing."

Ivor responded with alacrity. Having been in Colonial Administration for a considerable number of years, he knew full well that a hostess's every whim must be obeyed – and in any case, he had rather taken to Mrs Rossiter. She had welcomed them on their arrival with a charming little speech and a kindly smile. She was, he thought, a truly motherly woman. He liked her luscious curves and the old-fashioned modesty of her un-bobbed hair that she wore in a heavy knot at the nape of her neck.

So far he and Kitty had not met Mr Rossiter, who had been busy preparing for the pantomime when they arrived. As their small party moved off into the drawing room, however, their host made his appearance, still in costume, to a chorus of greetings and congratulations from the assembled guests. Kitty was calling out with the best of them, even though she hadn't been introduced.

"How Kitty does love a party," Mrs Bond remarked in her falsely mild kind of way.

"Well done, well done, Mr Rossiter," Kitty was crying, just as if she had known him for years; she was clapping her hands and smiling as he approached the spot where they were standing. "Oh, how we enjoyed it all!"

Impulsively, charmingly, she held out her hand to him and, equally charmingly, he bestowed a whiskery kiss upon it.

"You must be Rachel's delightful mother," he said. "How lovely to meet you, Mrs Bond. And Mr Bond. Such a pleasure to welcome you here – and the senior Bonds, of course. The Bearer Bonds, as you might say!"

Kitty squealed with laughter. "Oh, *Bearer* Bonds! Did you hear that, Ivor?"

Ivor smiled politely. Rachel, had she been present, would have recognised that smile. She had seen it often on other occasions. It meant that he was glad that his wife was enjoying herself, but was worried, too. Sometimes, it had to be admitted, Kitty went too far. It was greatly to be hoped that she would refrain from any excesses on this occasion.

For her part, Kitty bloomed and blossomed at each introduction, sensing the admiration, almost purring with delight, not caring a bit that her mother-in-law's disapproval seemed to grow with every smile she bestowed. Already the gramophone in the corner was playing a tango – 'Goodnight Vienna', one of her favourites – but she knew it would never occur to Ivor to ask her. He didn't like dancing, never had. She tapped her foot and twitched her shoulders in time to the beat, catching Hugh Rossiter's eye. Smilingly he came to her side.

"Have you ever danced with Santa Claus before?"

"Never! But there's always a first time."

Rachel and Alannah, coming downstairs together, saw them dancing together in the hall. For a moment they stood and watched as with exaggerated swoops and turns, making a mockery of the graceful dance and laughing gaily as they did so, the couple covered the floor.

"You're not like her, are you?" Alannah commented, and Rachel shook her head.

"I'm supposed to be like Daddy," she said.

Alannah continued her scrutiny.

"She's very – " she began, and paused while Rachel waited, suddenly a little anxious, for her to finish the sentence.

"Very what?"

"Well – " for a second Alannah hesitated, seemingly at a loss to describe Kitty. She shrugged after a moment, apparently unable to find words tactful enough. "Well, flashy, I suppose," she said at last. "I wouldn't think she was my mother's sort." Clearly this was in no way a compliment, for she added after a short silence: "If you'll forgive me saying so. She uses an awful lot of makeup, doesn't she?"

Rachel was speechless with anger. How *dared* Alannah be so critical? Honestly, she could be awful sometimes! Anyone would think that only Rossiters were any good – that anyone who was the slightest bit different was beyond consideration.

For a moment she continued standing next to Alannah, lips pressed close together in rage, her breathing ragged.

"I don't care what you think," she said at last in a furious whisper. "My mother's a lot prettier than yours, so there!"

Not looking where she was going, she turned and ran upstairs, away from Alannah. Blind with rage, she ran round the corner on the upstairs landing and went smack into Gavin who was just emerging from his room, having changed out of costume and into evening dress. The sight of him in his dinner jacket was sufficient to drive all else momentarily from her mind. Never had he looked so grown-up, so handsome, so altogether wonderful. Laughing, he held her by the shoulders.

"Hi, steady on! Where are you rushing to in such a hurry? What's wrong?"

"Nothing. I left something in the bedroom – "

Gavin looked at her searchingly, but appeared to take her word for it.

"Well, I'm glad you did because I wanted to say 'thank you' again. I loved my book and I feel terrible that I didn't get you anything."

"That's all right. I didn't expect it – I mean, I just wanted to say thank you to all of you because I'm always here – "

"Thank you for having me!" He was teasing her. They always

teased her about insisting on saying 'Thank-you-for-having-me' every time she said goodbye to Mrs Rossiter, but on this occasion she didn't mind it at all. Her heart was banging in her rib-cage with nervousness, and with what remained of her anger with Alannah, but she managed to smile back at him.

"That's right! I hope you like Stephen Spender."

"I certainly do. He's got the right ideas."

"Like Auden?" Alannah had decided on the cigarette lighter, Rachel knew, but it seemed a good opportunity to air the name.

"Mm." He looked surprised. "You're well informed, aren't you?"

"I like poetry. There's one poem in the book I gave you – "

"Hey, Gavin! Gav–in!" From along the passage came Diana's voice, demanding and insistent. Rachel felt his hands tighten a little on her shoulders as he gave her a little shake of farewell.

"I must away. Thanks again." He raised his voice, looking down the passage in the direction of Diana's room. "All right, all right, keep your hair on, Di! I'm coming."

Biting her lip in disappointment, Rachel watched him go. She'd wanted so much to tell him about 'whispers of wind in the listening sky' – to let him know how much she loved it. It would, she thought, have been like giving him another present.

"What are you doing, mooching about here?"

Barney's voice took her by surprise and she turned round quickly, embarrassed that he should have found her staring at nothing.

"I'm not mooching!"

"Well, it looked jolly like it to me. What's up?"

"Nothing." She turned to go.

"Hey, wait a sec. I've got something for you." Barney dived back into his bedroom. "Here! I'm sorry it's not wrapped, or anything, but I didn't finish it until last night, and today has just been one big rush. I hope you like it." He held out a picture in a plain wooden frame.

"You did this for me?" Surprised, Rachel smiled at him.

"I said so, didn't I? Well, take it, silly."

It was a picture of the back garden in summer, just as it had been when she had first seen it. There were flowers, and leaves on the trees, and the high stone wall, and a figure in the hammock, with yellow hair. Diana, of course. And there was Mr Rossiter with his panama hat tipped over his eyes sitting in a deckchair, and Mrs Rossiter sewing her tapestry, and Gavin dressed for tennis, holding a racquet, and two distant figures huddled over a book.

75

"See?" Barney said. "That's you and Lannie doing *Hurrah for Dymphna.*"

"Oh Barney, it's lovely." The fact that she had quarrelled with Alannah – that probably she wouldn't be welcome in this house ever again – seemed to give the gift an added poignancy. "Thank you. I'll keep it for ever and ever. But where are you?"

"I'm drawing it, you dope!"

"You should have put yourself in it, just to make it complete. But I really love it," she added hastily. "It's awfully good."

"It's not really. I had to do Ma hundreds of times, and she still hasn't come out right."

"But I can see who it's supposed to be. Thanks *tons*, Barney."

"Is there somewhere you can have it at school?"

"Yes. Miss Rayner lets us have pictures over our beds. She's terrific – "

"You haven't got a crush on her!" Barney's nose wrinkled in disgust.

"No, of course not." Rachel refuted this indignantly. "It's just that she's nice, that's all. Miss Simkins wouldn't let us do anything."

"So school's not so bad now? I'm glad of that. I didn't like to think of you being unhappy."

"I'm not," Rachel assured him, her anger with Alannah almost gone at this revelation. It had not occurred to her that her happiness, or lack of it, was something that had ever crossed any of the Rossiters' minds, once she had left Warnfield.

"Shall I keep the picture until tomorrow?" Barney asked her. "You won't want to be bothered with it at the party."

He held out his hand, but grinned with embarrassed pleasure when she refused to be parted from it.

"I'll put it with my coat," she said.

Downstairs, all except the elderly guests seemed to be dancing, laughing heartily as the gramophone wound down and the music grew slower and slower.

"To the rescue!" cried Gavin, swooping across the floor to wind it up. The tempo picked up and dancers quickened their steps. Barney and Rachel stood on the stairs, looking down at them.

"I say," breathed Barney. "Your Ma's jolly good, isn't she?"

Rachel could have hugged him.

"She loves dancing. Daddy doesn't, much. She says he can't tell a waltz from an eightsome reel."

Diana was two-stepping with Guy, but neither looked happy.

They weren't talking to each other and Diana was wearing what Rachel had come to think of as her snooty look.

"Is Di being beastly to Guy again?" she asked.

Barney sighed and shook his head as if defeated by his sister's moods.

"All their crowd went to a party over at Jean's place last night. I think he managed to upset her there, somehow. Don't know how."

"Who's Jean?"

"Haven't you met her? She's Gavin's new girl. Her family had loads of visitors so they couldn't come tonight, but you're bound to see her before long. He's absolutely soppy about her."

"Oh!"

She didn't mind; of course she didn't mind. It was enough to worship Gavin from afar. After all, he was nearly eighteen – a man, really – and she was only twelve. Well, thirteen next month, but even so, far too young for Gavin to notice.

Soppy he might be about the unknown Jean, but he appeared to be making do quite happily with a bouncy little dark-haired girl whom Rachel didn't recognise. How strange it was to think of life going on here in Warnfield – people meeting and getting to know each other, falling in love and falling out again, when all the time she was in that other world of St Ursula's.

"Whatever happened to Marjorie Newton?" she asked Barney. "Gavin was all over her last holidays."

Barney shrugged his shoulders.

"It sort of fizzled out," he said vaguely. "Things do, don't they?"

"I suppose they do."

Maybe, Rachel thought, things would go on fizzling out until she was old enough for Gavin to notice her. Surreptitiously she counted on her fingers, pressing them against the pink silk of her party frock. In another few years – say by Christmas 1937, she would be almost seventeen herself. Was that old enough? Or would Gavin, at twenty two, still think of her as a child?

"I say," Barney breathed, "Just look at your Ma!"

The music had changed to the Charleston. The dance had been out of fashion for years, but this record had long been lurking in Mr Rossiter's record collection and had been deemed suitable for inclusion on this occasion.

It was, Rachel knew, her mother's *pièce de résistance*. She had seen her perform it at parties before this, but never with quite so much verve. This was a parody of the original dance, with the kicks, the shrugs, the vo-de-o-do hand movements, the facial expressions, all exaggerated for the maximum comic effect.

Kitty had been dancing with Mr Rossiter's brother Kenneth; but now the floor cleared around her and while certain elements of the guests were clapping in time to the music and cheering her on, Rachel was horribly aware of strained smiles on the faces of others, notably other ladies.

Hearing the clapping, the more elderly among the guests who had been engaged in quiet conversation in the drawing room were enticed from their chairs and came out to the hall to see what all the commotion was about.

Rachel, standing on the stairs beside Barney, clutched the newel post and prayed that Grandma would not be among their number. She could see her father standing a little to the left of the door leading to the drawing room. He had been conversing with Mr Seagrove, who was now among those who applauded.

"What's going on?" asked Mr Rossiter's amused voice behind her. "Is someone putting on a floor show?"

She turned to see that he had been upstairs to abandon his Santa Claus costume in favour of a dinner jacket, a sprig of misletoe pinned to its lapel.

"My mother's dancing," she said, inadequately.

"Why, so she is! How absolutely tophole! Quite a girl, your mother." Mr Rossiter was smiling broadly, clearly delighted at the turn the party had taken. "Why isn't anyone partnering her?"

He didn't wait for a reply, but leapt down the remaining stairs and pushed his way through the crowd. Kitty blew him a provocative kiss and kept on dancing, spurred to even greater efforts now that her host was beside her. Her kicks became even higher, her movements more extreme, Hugh Rossiter matching her every move. Gavin, laughing like a maniac, wound the gramophone and began the record all over again.

Rachel stared at them, mesmerised. They looked – well, wonderful, really. Somehow Mummy and Mr Rossiter *went* together. They both looked more alive, more colourful than most other people, but at the same time it was horribly embarrassing to have her mother so much in the limelight, attracting all this attention, and she felt quite certain that nothing but trouble would come of it.

Anxiously she flicked a glance towards the door where her father stood. He was smiling that strained, sick-looking smile she had seen before. And oh Lord – both Mrs Rossiter and her grandmother were standing there together. Mrs Rossiter was smiling faintly in a way that was reminiscent of Diana at her most superior; but her grandmother's expression was one of utter disgust, as if all her darkest suspicions regarding her daughter-in-law had been confirmed. Rachel was so worried by the look on her face that she didn't notice that Mrs Rossiter, not generally given to swift movement, had made a sudden dive for the gramophone.

All at once the music stopped. The clapping continued for a moment but died away raggedly when it was perceived there was now no beat to accompany. Similarly, Kitty and Mr Rossiter stood still and looked towards the gramophone, bewildered at the silence.

Mrs Rossiter, it became obvious, had lifted the arm of the gramophone in mid-record, and now stood with it still held almost distastefully between finger and thumb.

"Supper is served in the dining room," she announced in her calm, mellifluous voice. "Please come and help yourselves, everybody. Mrs Bond, you must be simply exhausted! Heaven knows, it was exhausting enough just watching you."

She smiled sweetly in Kitty's direction but moved away at once, almost as if fearful that Kitty would choose to join her; and, once she had turned away, she smiled no longer.

In a gesture of loyalty, Rachel ran down the stairs and slipped through the knots of people who stood between her and her mother.

"Come and have some supper with me, Mummy," she said, attempting to take her arm.

"Hallo, darling."

Rachel saw that her mother and Mr Rossiter were still glowing, still smiling at each other, and the glance she received in answer to her plea was unfocused and very brief. She tugged at Kitty's arm, earning a quick frown.

"Oh darling, don't be a little pest! Run along with Daddy and Grandma."

"I want you to come."

"That," Kitty said to Mr Rossiter, taking no notice of Rachel, "was the most fun I've had for ages."

"We make a good team. We must – "

Kitty was never to know what future plans Hugh Rossiter might be forming, for Ivor appeared at her elbow in that moment and grasping her arm firmly, bore her off to the dining room.

From then on, Rachel thought, it was downhill all the way. Grandma kept saying they never should have come and that as soon as supper was over, she intended to leave. Daddy was silent and worried-looking, trying to pacify his mother at the same time as keeping an eye on Mummy's glass, which kept, somehow, being filled up when he wasn't looking.

And Alannah cut her dead. There was no mistaking it. She walked right past the Bonds on her way to join the group around Diana and Gavin; and Rachel, seeking escape from the tensions surrounding her family group, had made as if to join her. Alannah had seen her, had tossed her head and, looking away, had kept on walking.

It's all over, Rachel thought, sick with loss. She still felt angry with Alannah, but the feeling of bereavement was even stronger. She heard Diana give a burst of laughter. At her mother's expense? Very likely! If Alannah thought her showy before, she would undoubtedly have more to say about her now. Well, let her. She was jealous, that was all. She couldn't bear anyone else to enjoy any of the limelight. What was so wrong about dancing?

But it wasn't just the dancing, Rachel had understood that perfectly well. It was the way they'd looked together, her mother and Mr Rossiter. That was why Daddy was looking so frozen-faced; why he had spoken quite sharply at supper when Mr Rossiter had come round with the wine.

"Kitty, *no!*" he had said, as if she were a naughty child. Mummy had been furious!

"For the love of heaven, aren't I allowed one night to enjoy myself?" she'd demanded, quite loud enough to make others nearby turn round to look at her. "I've had ten days of total boredom under your mother's roof. Ten days of criticism and pointed remarks. My God, it feels more like ten years! I'm not sure I can stand much more of it."

There was no doubt that it was not only people nearby who were looking at them now; or else studiously not looking, which was almost as bad. Rachel got up, hoping that Grandma was too busy being shocked by her daughter-in-law to notice that her granddaughter had left a large proportion of food on her plate. To take food and not eat it was, in Grandma's book, one of the most heinous crimes imaginable.

She collected up a few plates and glasses and made a rapid escape with them to the kitchen where, much to her relief, she found Barney looking neither more nor less aloof than usual, sitting on the kitchen table, swinging his legs, and drinking ginger beer.

"Enjoying yourself?" he asked her.

"Yes, thanks." Rachel avoided his eye as she found a place to dump the plates. "The food was lovely."

"There's trifle to come, and fruit salad and stuff. And then Dad says we can play Murder in the Dark."

"Oh." Rachel's response was markedly lacking in enthusiasm.

"What's the matter? It's jolly good fun."

"Come along Barney – do your bit in the dining room. I haven't got Pommy to help me today!" Mrs Rossiter bustled into the kitchen carrying glasses, effectively preventing the need for Rachel to reply. "There are dirty plates to be cleared away, you know."

"I'll help." Rachel badly wanted to redeem herself, without knowing, quite, what her crime had been.

"Thank you, dear," said Mrs Rossiter. The words were kind enough, but Rachel, looking up to smile at her in a placatory sort of way, saw that her eyes were cold, her full lips pursed. Was she, then, no longer 'nearly a Rossiter'? "I believe, however, that your parents are preparing to leave – "

"Oh, they can't be! Not yet!" Barney, tray in hand, paused on his way to the kitchen door. "We haven't played Murder or done Sir Roger or anything! They haven't even had any pud! Rachel can stay, can't she?"

"Better not," Mrs Rossiter said, still in that pleasant, impersonal way. "Rachel must do as her parents say."

"Well, it's jolly hard cheese, I must say."

Barney banged out of the kitchen, leaving Rachel with Mrs Rossiter. For a moment, she hovered, silent and uncertain, while Mrs Rossiter stacked plates and upended cutlery into a jug.

"Such a pity you have to leave, Rachel dear," she said at last. "But I suppose needs must."

"Yes." Still Rachel hovered, not knowing how to get out of the room. She couldn't just go, not without saying something. But what could she say? She couldn't say 'Mummy isn't bad, she just loves parties and dancing.' Or 'Mummy and Daddy don't usually quarrel.' Or 'living with Grandma just makes everything worse.'

"I think you ought to run along," Mrs Rossiter said, with another of those meaningless little smiles. "Your parents will be wondering where you are."

"Yes," Rachel said again. She looked at Mrs Rossiter and sighed. There really was nothing more to say, was there? Well, only one thing.

She stopped on her way out, her hand on the door knob.

"Thank you for having me," she said.

"This house is like a morgue," Kitty said more than once in the days that followed Christmas. "Thank heaven I have one friend."

"Who?" asked Rachel.

"Why, *you*, silly! You're my only friend in this place. Everyone else looks at me as if I were a scarlet woman – and why, in heaven's name? Because I enjoyed a dance! Is it possible, I ask myself?"

It was a miserable time. Rachel could still hardly believe that she had, in school parlance, broken friends with Alannah – and with Mrs Rossiter too, unless she had imagined all that coldness in the kitchen. Which she was sure she hadn't.

She tried to keep on feeling angry with Alannah, but, as the days went by, all she felt was a sense of unhappiness. Miserably she remembered all the hours they had spent together, giggling over *Hurrah for Dymphna*. Were those days really gone?

Perhaps if she apologised – but what for, she asked herself? For standing up for her mother? She certainly wasn't going to do that. She did, however, pluck up enough courage to call at the house once, several days after the party, to find that Alannah was out with the other children.

"I'll tell her you called," Mrs Rossiter promised; but there had been no answering call from Alannah and Rachel couldn't bring herself to try again.

"I'm sorry if I spoiled things for you, darling," her mother said one day, when they walked past Kimberley Lodge on their way to town where they planned to go to the cinema. "But honestly, what did I do, I ask you? I merely enjoyed myself, that's all. I thought that was the whole idea! The last thing I expected, after all you'd told me about them, was that Mrs Rossiter would look at me as if I were something the cat had brought in."

"Mr Rossiter liked you," Rachel said comfortingly, and Kitty smiled.

"You know, I rather believe you're right," she said. "And I rather believe that *that* was the reason for Mrs Rossiter looking daggers at me for the entire evening – or at least, such of the evening I was allowed to spend there. The poor soul must have a somewhat cataclysmic life if she has hysterics every time that husband of hers looks at another woman. Any fool can see he has a roving eye – "

"*Mr Rossiter?*" Rachel was so shocked that she stood stock-still on the pavement for a moment. "Oh no, Mummy, I'm sure you're wrong. He and Mrs Rossiter are absolutely devoted to each other. He's always bringing her flowers and chocolates and things."

"Hmm. Maybe." Kitty smiled to herself, clearly unconvinced. "He's a handsome devil, though, isn't he, and she's really frightfully overweight. And not at all what one could call stylish, with all that hair and those strange clothes. One couldn't blame him for looking elsewhere."

"But – " Rachel was silent, not knowing how to express the admiration she had always felt for Mrs Rossiter – and still did despite her coldness at the end of the party. She had never noticed that she was particularly overweight and had always thought her clothes colourful and utterly right for her. "She reminds me of a rose," she said at last. "Sort of creamy and velvety."

"Full blown," said Kitty, laughing. "And past her best."

It seemed almost like blasphemy. Rachel made no reply, not knowing which way her loyalties should lie. She felt rather glad that another week would see her back at school, where life was at least uncomplicated.

Meantime, it was fun to be taken to the pictures so often, for Kitty was a great film fan and seemed anxious to make the most of her time in Warnfield by visiting as many cinemas as possible. Together they watched Greta Garbo and Charles Laughton and Jessie Matthews, laughing and crying by turns. They thrilled to the obligatory galloping hoofs of the 'B' feature and giggled when the organist rose from the depths, seated at what was billed as the Mighty Wurlitzer. The Mighty Wurtilizer, Doreen called it, to rhyme with fertiliser, which caused them much amusement.

Needless to say, Grandma was not amused, in fact she dismissed it all as 'American rubbish'.

"Filling the girl's head with nonsense," she grumbled to her son. "It shouldn't be allowed. I know *I* wouldn't allow it! You should put your foot down, Ivor."

It dawned on Ivor, very slowly because that was the way things always dawned upon him, that perhaps Kitty had some justification after all in wanting to live in a separate establishment, away from his mother. Perhaps a flat would, after all, not be a bad idea; and if it happened to be in London, then in the Easter holidays he would be able to take Rachel to museums and art galleries, classical concerts and so on. He would enjoy that, he thought. And Rachel would, too. Even Kitty. They could go about as a family, for once, as they hadn't seemed to do much in Uganda, and certainly didn't do here. Not since Christmas, anyway.

Perhaps it was time to forget Christmas, he thought. He was

growing tired of the continuing strife, of trying to please two women with such entirely different outlooks on life. It would be nice, he thought wistfully, to have a contented wife again; for though life with Kitty was never without its ups and downs and a certain amount of jealousy on his part had always been an integral part of it, he couldn't deny that when she was happy, then she was a very different woman indeed from the waspish creature she became under her mother-in-law's roof. She was a good wife, really; had always stood behind him, doing her duty by entertaining the right people, putting up with petty annoyances – the vagaries of native servants, the clouds of lake flies.

London, then, it would be.

"*London!*" Alannah said, as if it was the last place on earth that anyone would want to live. "Gosh, how terrible."

It was over a week now since the party, and at last Rachel had steeled herself to make one more foray into Rossiter territory. Alannah had looked up from a jigsaw puzzle without surprise as Rachel had gone into the old nursery.

"Hallo," she had said, as if nothing had happened between them. "What on earth have you been doing with yourself? Haven't seen you for ages. I say, do come and help me with all this sky, it's an absolute beast."

Rachel helped her, and throughout the morning there was no mention of Christmas. Now that all the decorations were down, the festivities did, indeed, seem to have happened a long time ago. At Rachel's announcement that she would be spending the Easter holidays in London, Alannah seemed dismayed.

"What are we going to do about *Dymphna*?" she asked.

"Let's have a look at it now," said Rachel.

The notebooks were produced and Alannah read a page or two. Neither of them laughed. After a while Alannah stopped reading and looked at Rachel.

"It doesn't seem so funny now, does it? Gosh, when I think how we hooted when we wrote it! If you ask me," she went on, slapping the notebook down on the table, "I think it's time we gave dear Dymphna a decent burial."

"No," Rachel said, reaching out for the book and for the other which lay on the table unread. "I'd like to keep it, if you don't mind."

In spite of her undoubted relief that relations between herself and Alannah had apparently been restored, with no ill-feeling, she couldn't help feeling a curious sentimental sadness about the

Dymphna project as she looked down at the shiny red covers of the two books. The story had seemed so good at the time.

"*Sic transit gloria*," she said solemnly, wondering if it would always be like this – if it would ever be remotely possible for her to achieve something that was not, in the end, disappointing.

"Begging yours?" said Alannah, employing a phrase deplored by both Mrs Rossiter and Rachel's grandmother, for once in harmony.

"'The glory has departed'," Rachel translated. But Alannah had lost interest in the matter.

"Come on, let's play a game," she said. "Let's find Barney and make him play Consequences – "

"Or Limericks," suggested Rachel.

"Or Battleships, or Racing Demon. *Something*, anyway. Gosh, poor you, *London*," she added, remembering. "What on earth will you do with yourself?"

"Cornwall!" Nancy said, to the adult Rachel. "What will you do with yourself?"

"I shall write, of course. That's the whole idea."

"But here you have Beattie to look after Tess."

"I know, I know. I suppose it all seems crazy to you, but I have the feeling I must go. Don't you ever feel that things are 'meant'? That's the way I feel about this."

A city girl from birth, Nancy looked dubious.

"Are you sure you won't die of boredom?"

"Rubbish, of course I won't! It's a beautiful place that'll inspire me. You and George will have to come and stay."

"George and I," Nancy said, "aren't going to be able to afford to stop working until about the year 2000, at a modest estimate."

They could, indeed, hardly spare time for a wedding. Now that the decision was made, it seemed no time at all before George procured a special licence and they were married at Caxton Hall with just a few friends in attendance, all of whom came back to Inverness Street afterwards. It was a wild, noisy party which no one, least of all the bridal pair, dreamed of leaving before the small hours. Rachel, left contemplating the debris – the cigarettes squashed into half-eaten sandwiches, the half-empty glasses and bottles, the dirty coffee cups – collapsed into a chair and stared at it dumbly. At least, she thought, they'd had a good send-off.

"Please God, let it work," she prayed earnestly. "And let it work out for me, too.

She felt quite sure it would. Only sometimes, in the still watches of the night, did she think that Nancy might be right, that she might be bored so far from London. Most of the time she felt excited, as if something new and glorious awaited her – as if this idea of living in the country was something that had been buried in her subconscious for a long, long time, awaiting its moment.

6

To Rachel's delight, the advent of Miss Rayner had indeed brought the joy back into English lessons. Her enlightened attitude had its effect out of school hours, too. Her room became a place where the girls felt able to air grievances or discuss affairs of the day, and she cast a new and more compassionate light on such social phenomena as the hunger marches and the miners' strikes which were proving to be such a feature of the thirties. Ghandi's campaign of civil disobedience, President Roosevelt's New Deal, the rise of the Nazi party in Germany – all were subjects to be examined and discussed.

Janet Fanning said she was no better than a Communist and that she had a good mind to tell her father, but she was squashed by the others who were thoroughly enjoying the new regime. However, when Miss Rayner lent Julia Dodd an old copy of *Travels with a Donkey* which she had owned at school, they noted gleefully that her Christian name was Rosemary – and from then on she was known as Red Rosie.

Rachel drank in all Red Rosie's views as if they were Holy Writ, so well did they chime with those that Gavin expressed so forcefully in arguments with his father; and it was to Red Rosie's room that she went for comfort after the Christmas holidays, downcast by the thought that she would be going to London and not to Warnfield when term ended.

"Make the most of it," Miss Rayner urged her. "There's so much to see and do there."

Rather to her surprise she found that Red Rosie was right. The holiday in London proved to be a success, despite the absence of the Rossiters. Her parents were different away from Warnfield

87

and Grandma's disruptive barbs, though Kitty involved Rachel in little private jokes at her husband's expense, largely concerning his meticulous planning of expeditions.

"We muster at 9.10 precisely to catch train at 9.25. Mackintoshes will be worn," Kitty would say, with a wink at Rachel. There seemed no rancour in it, however, and Ivor suffered it with good humour. Rachel prayed that such harmony would last. There had been times when those insistent, low voices through the bedroom wall had made her fearful. People did get divorced, after all. There was a girl at school whose mother had gone off with another man and everyone knew about it and pitied her.

Back at school, knowing it would be at least three years until she saw them again, she felt bereft and miserable. Only Alice understood, for she had been through the same thing herself; and Red Rosie, of course, for she understood everything.

"I hate it here," Rachel wept, her longing for all the warmth and colour her parents would find in Africa having impelled her towards Red Rosie's study where she felt free to unburden herself. "Next time I'll go with them and I'll never come back."

"And what will you do in Uganda?" Red Rosie asked gently. "Wait for a handsome Colonial Officer to sweep you off your feet? Is that what you want?"

Rachel sniffed and scrubbed at her eyes. The Uganda dream really didn't tie in with the Gavin dream at all. It was very confusing.

"In my opinion, you ought to set your sights on University Entrance," Red Rosie went on, causing Rachel to forget her tears altogether.

"Gosh! I don't think I'm brainy enough."

"Nonsense!" Miss Rayner roundly dismissed such humility. "It's well within your grasp if you work hard. We'll take one step at a time."

It induced a secret glow, knowing that Miss Rayner considered her University material. It meant she was as good as Diana, Rachel thought; then laughed at herself, because she knew that she wasn't, and never could be. But she was pretty good all the same. Miss Rayner had said so. In her dreams she envisaged herself mixing with the Rossiters on equal terms, her assurance greater than it had been before.

Only occasionally did she think of Mrs Rossiter's coolness to her after the Christmas party. Friendly relations had been restored all round before she left Warnfield to return to school; but she still burned a little with indignation when she considered the matter, for after all, *she* had done nothing to incur displeasure. She couldn't help feeling let down. Mrs Rossiter had been on something of a pedestal – the perfect mother, an ideal of womanhood. Now she knew she was capable of less than perfect behaviour.

But such thoughts were swept away and the pedestal restored when a rare letter arrived from Alannah. Would Rachel, she asked, like to come on holiday with them to Clearwater-on-Sea for two weeks in August? Her mother had been on to Rachel's grandmother and had persuaded her to agree to the idea.

"We'll have fun," Alannah wrote. "Do say you'll come!"

Diana wouldn't be with them. She was going to France, as guest of a French family.

"It'll improve her French, I suppose," Alannah said, "but why she wants to bother, I can't imagine. She's terribly good already."

The boys weren't going to be there, either – or at least, only intermittently. They were camping somewhere in the New Forest, but had promised to drop in from time to time, since Clearwater was relatively easy to reach on bicycles. And Mr Rossiter couldn't get away from the office. He, it was explained, would come down for the two weekends.

"So it's only you and me," Alannah explained to Rachel. "That's why we asked you, really. None of my friends here were able to come, you see. I mean, we're jolly glad to have you and all that, but the idea is that you should keep me company so that Ma can go off and do her painting. It's not that she doesn't want to be bothered with me, exactly, but just that I do get rather tiring because I want to be doing things all the time."

"Oh," said Rachel.

It was a little deflating, somehow, to realise that she was merely a substitute for Diana and the boys and other, closer friends; and even more deflating to realise that Gavin wouldn't be there – at least, not all the time. She had indulged in many a daydream about him; little fantasies in which, with the rest of the family miraculously disposed of, the two of them strolled along the shore discussing poems and politics and life in general. Ever since she'd known about the holiday she had paid even more attention to Miss Rayner's views on current events, and followed her directions towards the latest trend in both novels and poetry – swotting up, as it were, in case the opportunity to air her knowledge to Gavin should arise.

The house rented by the Rossiters stood on its own at the end of a narrow concrete strip bordered by tussocky grass which led along the cliff in the direction of the main beach and the town of Clearwater. 'Sea View', as, with conspicuous lack of imagination, the house had been called, was quite new, with white walls and a green roof and wrap-around windows of the kind that was very fashionable. Mr Rossiter maintained that, architecturally, it was quite grotesque, but Alannah and Rachel were enraptured by its modernity, particularly by the tubular steel furniture in the sitting room and the curtains with their black and orange zigzags.

"Well, at least we have the sea to look at," Mr Rossiter said resignedly, averting his eyes from the interior and gazing appreciatively out of the window. "Let us thank the good Lord for that."

And indeed, Rachel did thank the good Lord, for from the moment she opened her eyes in the morning, she was overwhelmingly conscious of the sea; first the sound of it as it threw itself on the rocks of the cove just below Sea View, then – with a never diminishing thrill of pleasure – the sight of it as she sat up in bed and saw it blinking placidly in the early sun.

She loved the freedom they enjoyed, too, though she vowed never to mention it to Grandma who had been gloomy and full of dire warnings on this very question. Though exaggerated, Rachel admitted to herself that her fears were by no means unfounded. She and Alannah were able to amuse themselves pretty much as they liked.

Mr Rossiter caught the train back to town on Monday morning, and from then on, Mrs Rossiter was engrossed in her painting, leaving the two girls to enjoy the pleasures of town and beach, of which there were many. You could rent things called Whoopee Boats, or watch Punch and Judy or sing jolly hymns with a red-faced, fat little parson with gleaming spectacles who smiled and smiled beneath his panama hat.

There were donkey rides, and a strange, swarthy man who made pictures in the sand. Passers-by were supposed to show their appreciation by throwing pennies down. Alannah and Rachel gazed at his creations in wonder but retained their pennies, preferring to spend them on entry to the pier which to them was the source of all delight.

Here there were machines that told your fortune, analysed your handwriting, guessed your weight. Machines that simulated football matches, showed them What the Butler Saw, sent silver balls spinning round with the chance of turning a ha'penny into a shower of coppers should they fall into the right hole. There were little cranes in glass cases that for a mere penny could be directed over glittering prizes nestling in a sea of noxious-looking green sweets. Breathlessly the girls watched their descent, desperately turning the wheels that were supposed to manœuvre them in the right direction; and always a cascade of green sweets was their only reward. Constantly disappointed, they were constantly hopeful. There was always next time.

For Alannah, the best thing of all was undoubtedly the Pier Pavilion and Uncle Frank's Follies. Uncle Frank was a strangely hairless man who, like the parson on the beach, smiled without ceasing. There were, however, no other similarities. Uncle Frank wore a bright sky-blue suit with silver lapels and a silver stripe down the outside of his trousers, and a silver top hat with a curly brim that he flourished a good deal. He told jokes, few of which made any sense to the girls, though the adults present laughed uneasily.

His small team of artistes consisted of two blonde girls billed as the Singing Shubettes; Tony Tonetti, who was pale and willowy and appeared to model himself on Jack Buchanan; a seedy, foxy-faced older man, known as Wally who acted as Uncle Frank's straight man; and a woman of uncertain age, ample proportions and improbable auburn hair who was invariably introduced as 'Your Own, Your Very Own, Gloria Dawn'.

Gloria Dawn, dressed in a flowing gown and carrying a long chiffon handkerchief, was clearly intended to add a little culture to the programme. While the Singing Shubettes dressed as Teddy Bears to sing and dance to 'The Teddy Bears' Picnic', or Cowgirls ('Home on the Range') or Guardsmen ('Something about a Soldier'), and while Tony Tonetti crooned into the microphone popular songs of the day, Gloria Dawn's repertoire consisted of tear-jerking ballads of the kind sung in Victorian drawing rooms to the accompaniment of soulful glances. In fact, it might be said that soulful glances were her forte.

Rachel and Alannah thought her exquisitely funny. Away from the show they rolled around in helpless mirth as they invented more and more outrageous songs for her to sing, more and more exaggerated gestures. And at the show itself, they could hardly control themselves as Uncle Frank came on to the stage, his face rearranged into the serious expression he considered suitable for the introduction. If Rachel glanced sideways to see Alannah biting her lips, she was undone. If Alannah heard so much as a stifled sob from Rachel, an explosion was inevitable.

"We ought not to go any more," Rachel said. "I think Uncle

Frank's getting mad." Indeed, this was true. Uncle Frank had turned a particularly murderous look upon them that afternoon when their giggles had proved impossible to control.

Alannah would not countenance staying away from the show, however, for there was one part of it she wouldn't miss for anything. This was the moment when children were invited up to the stage to give their own performance, the act attracting the most applause being rewarded with the princely sum of half a crown.

Uncle Frank disliked children who recited. He liked those who sang or danced – preferably both. In particular, he liked a diminutive, bubble-haired, cute little girl who sang 'Keep Your Sunny Side Up', off-key and with a slight lisp.

In spite of his outrageously partisan approach to the whole matter, however, Alannah still succeeded in winning the prize on several days. Kipling was her speciality. With one or two well-chosen 'Barrack Room Ballads', delivered in a cockney accent and with a great deal of pathos, she had the audience, many of whom remembered the Great War and had developed a somewhat cynical approach to it, in the hollow of her hand.

"Well, that's it!" Uncle Frank said, handing over the half-crown to her for the third time. "Three times only, that's the rule. And no more recitations for the rest of the week. Give the singers a chance, I say. And the dancers. Fair dos for all."

"No one ever said anything about that before," Alannah said furiously as they walked home along the cliff. "He made it up on the spot. He hates me!"

"Why?"

"Because he knows we laugh at Our Own, Our Very Own Gloria Dawn, I suppose. And also he's a snob. Yes he is," she went on as Rachel laughed. "Inverted snobbery, it's called. Diana told me about it. He doesn't like me because I'm not working-class. I expect I make him feel inferior – for one very good reason! He *is* inferior! And he hates kids who recite. Did you see his face when that boy said he was going to do 'The Charge of the Light Brigade'? Oh, *spit*! I was counting on earning a bit more money this week. It's Ma's birthday on Saturday and I wanted to buy her something nice. Oh well, it'll have to be flowers as usual."

"'Only a Rose'," carolled Rachel, throwing back her head and striking a pose in the manner of Gloria Dawn. Alannah stood still.

"You know," she said, "*you* haven't got a bad voice. You could do it."

"Do what? Oh – " as realisation dawned "– you mean, I could sing? Oh, I couldn't, really I couldn't, Lannie."

"Yes, you could. What do you know the words of, all the way through?"

"Nothing. Honestly. Oh, I couldn't – "

Afterwards, Rachel couldn't explain why she gave in. Perhaps it was the idea of having money with which to buy a present for Mrs Rossiter. Perhaps, secretly, she had longed to be up there on the stage, proving herself just as good as Alannah, not merely 'almost a Rossiter' but one of their number. For whatever reason, she allowed herself to be coached in the words of 'Bye-bye Blackbird', even though she protested constantly, assuring Alannah she'd never have the nerve to respond to Uncle Frank's call.

"Nonsense," Alannah said briskly. "You're miles better than that disgusting little curly-haired creature. All you need is to put a bit more expression in it. At least you're in tune!"

But she wasn't cute. Rachel, staring at herself in the mirror, could see that quite clearly. Her face was too thin, her hair too straight. Even so, Friday afternoon found her getting up, rather like a sleep-walker, and going towards the stage when Uncle Frank announced the contest. She didn't even need Alannah to push her, which assistance had been promised should she delay in answering the call. She went quite of her own free will – a matter which was, afterwards, no consolation at all.

Her heart was thumping madly, reverberating throughout her whole body, and her knees were trembling so much that she stumbled as she went up the steps to the stage. She tried to smile at Uncle Frank as he asked her the usual questions – her name and age and where she came from, but managed no more than a nervous twitch of the lips.

"So you're going to sing 'Bye-bye Blackbird', eh? Well, don't look so scared. No blackbird's going to peck off your nose, not while you're in my capable hands!" Uncle Frank leered towards the audience as he spoke, and there were a few sycophantic sniggers in response.

Wally, who played the piano as well as acting as straight man, began the introduction, and for the first time Rachel looked directly out over the audience.

It was a full house, for it had rained earlier and the weather was still too unsettled to attract many to the beach. The sea of faces seemed to shimmer before her – old ones, young ones, hatted, bareheaded, their eyes all directed towards her. Her mouth was dry and she couldn't swallow, couldn't seem to breathe; and then, suddenly, her vision cleared, her attention caught by the sight of two familiar figures in the back row. Her jaw dropped in disbelief. It just couldn't be true, she thought, amazed and horrified. It just couldn't be. But alas, it was. There, to her utter astonishment, sat Barney and Gavin, grinning hugely.

They had been expected that weekend, but not here, not now. Why had they come? It was like a bad dream, a nightmare. She was paralysed, the words of the song completely gone from her mind, conscious of nothing but total panic.

"Well, between you and me, I reckon she'd rather be waving bye-bye to you lot than a wagon-load of blackbirds. You've scared her to death," Uncle Frank said to the audience, inviting them to laugh at her. "Come along, dear, no one's going to eat you. Once more from the top, Wally, if you please."

Wally played the introduction again, and still there was silence from Rachel, a silence that seemed to go on for several centuries. She wanted to die – or at the very least, to run away and hide. But she was incapable of movement, her feet apparently glued to the stage. Uncle Frank was doing his best to attract her attention, mouthing the words at her, beating time, but though she darted a look in his direction her eyes were drawn back to the sight of the audience and to Gavin and Barney.

With a sudden sob, she turned and bolted, down the steps from the stage, along the gangway at the side of the theatre. Someone – Barney? – tried to grab her arm in passing, but she shook him off.

Outside the shameful tears felt cool on her cheeks. She hurried back down the pier, towards the entrance, sensing that people were turning to look at her, certain that all of them knew of her humiliation. How could she have been such a fool? What on earth would the Rossiters think of her now? It was worse than Adverbs. Worse than anything. Oh, *why* had she ever agreed to attempt such a thing? They'd despise her more than ever, that was certain.

The tide was out and it was shadowy under the pier, with seaweed festooned on the rusty supports and girders. There was a rank, unpleasant smell and the damp sand was dark and discoloured.

Rachel didn't care. She knew she deserved no better. She sat down with her back against a broad wooden post, laid her head down on her bent knees, and sobbed, sure that her world had, finally, come to an end.

★

It was some time before she became aware of Barney. When she did, she would not look at him.

"Leave me alone," she said, ungraciously.

"You're being daft. Honestly, what the hell does it matter?" He squatted down beside her and began prodding the sand with a small piece of driftwood. "Coo, this place stinks. I bet all the sewers of Clearwater empty out here."

"I don't care." Rachel gulped and sniffed. "I don't seem to have a hankie."

"I have. Here, take it. It's not very clean," he added. He was right, but she was in no position to be fussy. "I bet it's really unhygienic here," Barney went on. "What a stink! Maybe we'll get sick."

"Go away, then. I don't care if I die."

"You're being daft," he said again. "Look, what does a potty show like that matter? You got stage fright, that's all it amounts to. Lots of people get it."

"I made a fool of myself!"

"Well, all right, maybe you did, but it doesn't matter. You'll remember it longer than anyone else."

"You and Gavin were laughing. I could see you."

"No, we weren't. Oh, we may have done when you first went up, but not afterwards. I knew how you were feeling."

"You couldn't have! Anyway, what were you doing there?"

"We arrived earlier than we thought, and Ma said you and Lanny were here so we thought we'd come too, just for fun. But it had started by the time we got there, so we just slipped in the back. Gosh, that man's a slimy toad, isn't he? And that awful Gloria woman!"

"Oh, Barney!"

Rachel put her head down and wept again, her tears coming to an abrupt halt when, to her total astonishment, she felt his arm around her. It was unexpected and embarrassing, especially when he landed a kiss somewhere close to her left ear.

The embrace, if such it could be called for Rachel's role was one of shocked immobility, lasted no more than a few moments. Sniffing and dabbing at her eyes, she drew away from him. There was silence between them and they did not look at each other.

"It'll be all right, Rachel, honestly," he said.

"You'll all despise me even more than you do already," she muttered, not admitting that it was Gavin's opinion that mattered above everything. To think that she'd made such a fool of herself in front of *him*! How could she bear it?

"Nobody despises you, idiot." He got to his feet and prodded with his toe at a half-buried bottle. "We like you."

This was so unexpected that Rachel stared at him directly, forgetting the embarrassment of the kiss.

"*Do* you? Honestly?"

"Of course. Why wouldn't we?"

She sniffed mournfully. "You're just being nice because you're sorry for me."

"Don't be so wet, Rachel. You're talking a load of rot." This was so much more the Barney she was familiar with that she began to feel that there was, perhaps, life after Uncle Frank. "Come on," he went on, stretching out a hand to pull her to her feet. "Let's have a go at that football machine on the pier. Bet I beat you."

Rachel gave her eyes one last wipe on his unsavoury handkerchief.

"I bet you do, too," she said, resignedly. But, as she followed him over rocks and pools and bits of driftwood, she felt almost cheerful.

They liked her! Barney himself even liked her enough to kiss her – and seemed to prove it further not only by paying for her to re-enter the pier but by buying a threepenny stick of Clearwater rock which he presented to her with a flourish.

And after all, she comforted herself as together they made their way home to Sea View, it could have been worse. Diana could have been there.

It was, however, too much to hope for that she wouldn't be teased about the incident. Gavin said that Uncle Frank was trying to book her for the entire season and that she was from now on to be known as 'Our Own, Our Very Own Rachel Bond'. Though she still burned inside, she knew how important it was to appear a good sport, so she laughed at the jokes and pretended not to care; but she was even quieter than usual during the evening and disappeared early to her bedroom, longing for solitude.

It was Mrs Rossiter who eventually came looking for her. Rachel, who had been lying in bed gazing at the ceiling, reliving every ignominious moment, sat up hastily.

"My dear child," said Mrs Rossiter, her voice honeyed with sympathy. "Are you still upset about that silly incident at the theatre? Alannah told me about it – oh, not to laugh at you, I promise, but just to explain. Really, you mustn't mind a little teasing! We all have to put up with it in this family."

"I made such an ass of myself," Rachel said, not looking at her and picking at the cotton bedspread, with her head bent and her hair hanging like two curtains on each side of her face.

"But from the best of intentions! I gather it was to make some money to buy me a birthday present. I think that's very sweet, and so do the others."

"Any of them could have done it without thinking twice. Oh, it was awful, Mrs Rossiter! I just *stood* there!"

Mrs Rossiter sat on the bed beside her, and taking Rachel's two hands in hers pulled her round to face her. Her expression, Rachel saw, was one of great sweetness.

"Now listen," she said gently. "You are our dear, timid little Rachel! We can't be all the same! Alannah and the others are life's fortunate ones. Not everyone has their showy kind of gifts – the ability to amuse, to be noticed. Just as important are the Marthas of this world, the steadfast workers. Your gifts are just as valuable, even if less obvious, so cheer up and don't make yourself miserable by longing to be different."

Tears threatened to overwhelm Rachel once more.

"You're awfully kind," she said humbly. But she couldn't help sighing to herself when Mrs Rossiter had gone. Being a Martha didn't sound nearly as much fun as being a Rossiter – or even *almost* a Rossiter.

Back in Warnfield, she found that Alannah was spending more and more time at the Tennis Club, following in Diana's footsteps and winning much commendation. Rachel became a loyal and enthusiastic spectator but, feeling she had learned her lesson at Clearwater, declined to join in. There was one definite advantage to this interest in tennis: it was often possible to watch Gavin playing, either singles or with Diana. He usually won, and win or lose, he was always something to behold in his tennis gear. As indeed was Diana. Both had their admirers but, to Rachel's secret relief, there seemed no girl that Gavin favoured more than another. Jean, as so many others, had in her turn fizzled out.

Life at The Laurels was as dull and colourless as it had ever been, but at least her grandfather no longer allowed her to win every chess game, which was a relief. Rather to Rachel's amazement, since her grandmother did nothing but complain about her, Doreen still worked in the kitchen – less happily now, since Molly from Magnolia House had only this week left domestic service for more congenial work as an usherette at the Gaumont.

"S'all right for you," Doreen said, slumped over the sink

scraping potatoes. "You can go off next door whenever you feel like it. Go off to your precious Rossiters." Her shoulders heaved in what Rachel recognised as excessive mirth. "Makes me laugh, she does, that Lady Paint Pot of yours, what thinks so much of 'erself. All those colours and flowers on her hat and what-not, floating along like she was Queen of the May. If she knew what I knew – "

"What do you know?" Rachel couldn't resist rising to the bait. Doreen gave a malicious leer in her direction.

"That husband of hers. Mr Hugh Rossiter. No better than he should be, Molly told me. And *she* knows because her brother's wife works up the Town Hall and hears what goes on."

What on earth could she mean? Rachel stared at her in bewilderment.

"Rot! You don't know what you're talking about!"

"Oho, don't I? All right, I won't say no more, then."

"You better hadn't." Rachel was very much on her dignity. "The Rossiters are friends of mine."

"Huh! Fine friends, I must say." For a moment or two Doreen scraped and said nothing, but she couldn't maintain her silence for long. "A roving eye, that's what your friend Mr Rossiter has got," she said. "Molly'll tell you. Can't keep his hands off the typists, Molly says."

"Then she's lying."

"He's got a special lady friend."

"Shut up," Rachel snapped rudely.

None of it was true – if she was ever sure of anything, then she was quite sure of that. She forgot the shared film magazines, the times when, in desperation, she had sought Doreen's company. Now, seeing her lumpy figure in its shapeless overall, the cap with the elastic at the back and the upturned brim at the front pulled low over her brow, Rachel felt nothing but hatred for the girl. What did she know?

"You can finish these yourself," she said rudely, and banging a half-empty pea-pod down on the table, slammed out of the kitchen.

Doreen's allegations were so outrageous, so patently untrue, that she forgot them almost immediately. When, back at school, Julia asked her about the holidays, there was a multitude of other matters that were far more worth remembering, like the celebration when Gavin heard of his place at Christ Church, and when they all went to the zoo.

She felt sorry for anyone who didn't have the Rossiters living next door, though the last week of the holiday hadn't been entirely free from strife. There had been one of those mysterious conflicts of will between Gavin and Diana that had upset the whole household before it was just as mysteriously resolved; and a whole series of arguments between Gavin and his father. One, witnessed by Rachel, had concerned the rise of Fascism.

Mr Rossiter was inclined to dismiss it as a minor, foreign kind of peccadillo that would soon pass – and as for Mosley, well, he wasn't preaching much beyond patriotism and devotion to the Royal Family, surely?

Gavin had exploded.

"God, you're complacent!" he'd raged. "You and all your lot! Don't you know what's happening in Germany – the persecution and the book-burning? And the rearming?"

Mr Rossiter had remained calm, his faith in the League of Nations unshaken despite Germany's decision to withdraw. It wasn't any of Britain's business, he said – and he seemed amused at Gavin's apparent change of heart. Last year, he pointed out, Gavin had been a pacifist. This year he was sounding positively warlike. What, he wondered, would next year bring forth?

His smiling tolerance seemed to infuriate Gavin more than any argument; but later, from the bathroom window, Rachel had heard them all laughing heartily together in the garden so she knew that no lasting harm had been done.

"Tell me about the holiday in Clearwater," Julia begged. "Was it absolutely super?"

"Super-duper," Rachel assured her. She went on to recount some of their more amusing doings. She even described Your Own, Your Very Own Gloria Dawn. But she said nothing about her own excursion into show business.

Though the memory of that experience recurred at intervals when she least expected it, flooding her once again with a feeling of unbearable, disintegrating shame, there were other abiding memories of Clearwater that lasted equally long.

The sight of the sea from the bedroom window, for one, and the little curling waves that threw themselves against the sand. Maybe she'd live by the sea, when she grew up. Yes, that's what she'd do – she'd live by the sea and write books.

With Gavin? In Africa? After she'd been to Oxford? (If Gavin was there, then clearly no other University was worth striving for.)

She wasn't quite sure where this dream fitted in with all her others, but it didn't really matter. That was what was so good about dreams. You could have everything.

"Look," Rachel said, standing at the living-room window and holding Tess up at shoulder level. "I always wanted to live by the sea and now here we are. There it is, in all its glory."

Tess, unimpressed, crowed and gurgled and made an attempt to grab a handful of hair which Rachel skilfully foiled. She allowed Tess to slip down to one hip and continued to gaze, entranced.

It was a cool, cloudy day and the sea was slate grey with touches of silver in the ripples that shirred the surface. It looked magnificent, Rachel thought, but formidable, unfriendly – not at all the same sort of sea in which she had frolicked at Clearwater all those years ago. But even as she watched, the sun came from behind a cloud like a spotlight bringing a stage set to life.

She found it fascinating, this early and brief lesson in the sea's changing moods. It seemed to promise so much and demand so little. It was all there, for her enjoyment.

The journey from Paddington had seemed endless and the autumn afternoon was darkening when the taxi finally deposited her in the street where six stone steps led up to Gull Cottage. Rachel had emerged gingerly from the ancient vehicle, feeling shell-shocked and decidedly the worse for wear, for the drive had taken place at breakneck speed through narrow lanes where at any moment she had expected to come face to face with another car – or a cow at the very least.

The driver – no impetuous youth as one might have imagined by his mode of driving, but a hefty, red-faced man with a bull neck and a check cap worn on the back of his head – had enlivened the journey by shouting disjointed and totally incomprehensible comments in an impenetrable accent over his left shoulder. In return she had made what she trusted were suitable noises, representing interest, disbelief or amusement by turns; and apparently she hadn't erred too badly for he was geniality itself at their journey's end, carrying her cases up to the front door without being asked, and then returning just as cheerfully for the folding pram.

To Rachel's intense relief the cottage felt reasonably warm. She supposed Mrs Hoskings must be responsible for that, and was thankful. Tess, who had behaved impeccably for the entire journey, was now tired and hungry, and feeding her had been Rachel's first priority. Afterwards, she prowled around, Tess in her arms, exploring her new territory.

She liked what she saw. The front door opened directly into a room with a fireplace at one side and a door to the kitchen in the far wall. Beside the fireplace were two wing chairs, covered in faded chintz. They were deep and comfortable, she found. Trust Sylvia! Though, as she looked around, she thought that probably it was Rex's unknown forebears who had been responsible for the furnishings, since they were decidedly Victorian. There had been a gilt mirror just like that over the fireplace at The Laurels, and a gate-legged table too, just like the one in the window. A telephone stood on a small drop-leaf bureau. Though she couldn't imagine who would want to call her, she was glad to see it; it made her feel that at least she was in touch with the known world.

There were two smaller armchairs, covered in some dark green material; heavy oil paintings of ships in stormy waters; shelves stacked, not with books but with china ornaments.

The ornaments would have to be packed away, she decided, if she were to find places for the books she had brought with her. It was all she could do not to get down to the task right away. Her spirits rose. With her books around her, this would be a lovely room.

By this time, darkness had fallen and she drew the curtains across the window – chintz, to match the chairs; but not before she had looked out to see the lights of Polvear spilling down the hillside across the river. It was not until the following morning, however, that the full glory of the view was revealed.

Gull Cottage was built on a kind of small plateau roughly halfway up the hill which led from St Bethan quay. From the front window she was high enough to look over the rooftops of houses lower down. To the right she could look up-river, where hills, covered with trees in all their autumnal glory, folded down to creeks and inlets, where boats both large and small went about their business.

Below her the river was at its widest, with the small port of Polvear almost directly opposite, just as Rex had described it. Larger than St Bethan, its grey stone church tower protruded from the cottages that surrounded it, while other houses clustered higgledy-piggledy down the hill, and lined the river's edge. There were warehouses and boatyards beside the water, too, and there in the centre was the quay and a small square of larger buildings.

To the left was the mouth of the river, guarded by two magnificent headlands, and beyond it the open sea.

"Just look, Tess," she whispered delightedly. "It's ours – all ours!" The thought that it was there to be looked at whenever she chose seemed, for the moment, totally unbelievable.

A knock at the door brought her back to more practical matters. A woman stood at the front door, smiling and friendly. She introduced herself as Mrs Hoskings.

"I'm your neighbour," she said, in an accent which immediately entranced Rachel. "Your auntie will have told you about me. She left me a key, so's I could keep an eye on the place. I've brought ee a pasty and a few home-made buns, just to say welcome, like."

"How very kind of you! Thank you so much. Won't you come in?"

"Oh, just look at that liddle maid," Mrs Hoskings said as she came into the room, tickling Tess under the chin. "She's some lovely, dear of her. Your auntie never said."

"Didn't she?" Rachel smiled sunnily. "This is Tess. I'm so grateful to you for making the house so nice and warm for us last night. Tess appreciated it, and so did I."

"Well, it struck cold, like, when I come in for a quick dust round. You'll be wanting to light the boiler today, I 'spose."

"Will I?"

"You won't get no hot water, else."

"Is it hard to light?" It looked it, Rachel thought. The stove had a malevolent, bad-tempered look about it.

"Bless you, no," Mrs Hoskings said. "I'll do it for ee."

Rachel breathed a sigh of relief as Mrs Hoskings removed her coat revealing a serviceable wrap-around apron beneath, and tackled the stove's mysteries, soon coaxing it into life. When that was done she helped Rachel upstairs with Tess's cot which, together with the packing cases, had been delivered a day or two before and left in the outhouse. She then carried an odd table into the main bedroom upstairs so that Rachel could set up her typewriter there, established a friendly relationship with Tess, and gave invaluable information regarding milk deliveries, the whereabouts of the Food Office, and the best sources of meat and groceries.

A busybody? Well, maybe. Over a cup of tea and one of Mrs Hoskings' own yeast buns, Rachel took stock of her. She was sixtyish, she supposed, and rotund. Rather like a cottage loaf, Rachel thought. Her hair was grey and skewered with hairpins into a knot at the back of her head; but she had fine dark eyebrows and eyes that were a clear, peaty brown. She must have been quite a looker in her day.

"Now don't ee forget, my dear," she said as she put her coat on before she left. "I'm down the steps and to your left, no distance away if you want me. 'Tidn't that I want to interfere, like, but I'm ready to help if needed. I could give ee one morning a week seeing you're busy with your writing. I go up the school other days."

"I'd love that," Rachel said warmly. "To have the place cleaned through just once a week would be wonderful. Of course, what I really need is a girl to look after Tess a few mornings a week."

Mrs Hoskings pursed her lips and nodded thoughtfully.

"Well, I'll look out for ee. 'Tis hard, being on your own with a baby. Will your husband be coming soon?"

For a moment, Rachel hesitated. Nancy had suggested that, in a small place like St Bethan, she might consider buying herself a wedding ring and passing herself off as a war widow – of which, as she rightly said, there were plenty about.

At the time Rachel had rejected the suggestion out of hand. There were too many difficulties, she said; ration books, for one, and the fact that one lie would undoubtedly lead to another, and as one who was bad at lying, she would be bound to entrap herself sooner or later. Besides – why should she lie? If the villagers of St Bethan rejected her, then they would have to get on with it.

Now, however, faced with Mrs Hoskings, she was conscious of a great need to be liked and accepted, and she wavered a little. Then, slowly, she let out her breath.

"There isn't a husband," she said. "I'm not married."

"Not married?" Mrs Hoskings stared at her. "You and that dear little maid, you'm on your own?"

Rachel nodded.

"That's right."

"I see." There was an instant cooling of the atmosphere, like a cold wind suddenly blowing over them. Mrs Hoskings looked embarrassed, as if she hardly knew how to react to this revelation. "Oh, well," she said awkardly at last. "It takes all sorts. You're not the first and you won't be the last, I daresay."

The coolness remained, however.

"Will you still want to come and work here one morning a week?" Rachel asked.

For a moment Mrs Hoskings considered the matter, her eyes narrowed. Then she nodded.

"I'll come," she said. "I don't know what they'll say up chapel, but I'll come."

"Perhaps," Rachel said, forcing a smile, "they'll say, 'let them that are without sin cast the first stone'."

Mrs Hoskings looked sceptical.

"What they'll say," she said, with some asperity, "is that the war's got a lot to answer for. A lady like you! Mrs Courtney's niece! 'Tis awful, that's what 'tis." She sighed heavily. "Well, I'll see you Thursday, Mrs – pardon – Miss Bond."

"Thursday, Mrs Hoskins," Rachel said. "Thank you for the buns and the pasty." She closed the back door, and for a moment rested against it, lost in thought.

Was this going to work? Clearly, it wasn't going to be easy – but then, what had she expected? Commendation? Hardly! After all, it wasn't so very many years since women in her situation had been consigned to mental institutions, accused of moral instability.

She would have to be tough, self-reliant. She wouldn't be accepted at once, that much was clear. She'd have to work her passage, prove herself, show that she was, after all, a reasonably worthy member of the human race. She closed her eyes, suddenly weary and a little afraid; then she pushed herself away from the door with sudden determination. She'd make it work, she thought. She would have to make it work. Somehow.

Later, with most of her unpacking done and a need to buy some provisions, she took advantage of a comparatively settled spell of sunshine to push Tess down the hill towards the quay and the few small shops.

Those she met in the street wished her good morning pleasantly enough, but she was conscious of curious glances. They would soon know, she thought. The word would spread. Well, let it! She was thankful she had told Mrs Hoskings the truth, glad beyond words that she would not be called upon to remember a pack of lies.

The sun went behind a cloud and the light drained from the day. There was an autumnal chill in the air, and the grey stone cottages seemed to huddle for comfort around the tiny quay where, as she watched, the open boat that was the Polvear ferry unloaded its few passengers.

She could hear the slapping of the water against the dock, and leaning over, saw a frond of seaweed waving this way and that, just below the surface.

That's like me, drifting hither and thither, she thought, fighting depression. She lifted her head, and for a moment she watched the people leaving the boat, walking away from the quay, up the hill, back to their homes. The village seemed to absorb them, enfold them, welcome them, as if knowing they belonged. Could she ever hope to feel like that?

Give it time, she thought. And as she continued to look, the sheer beauty of the place brought its own peace.

It'll be all right, she thought, suddenly calm. Then she, too, turned for home.

7

*F*ifth-formers were awarded the coveted privilege of a room to themselves. Rachel joyfully celebrated her liberation from the hated dormitories by hanging Barney's picture on one wall and a reproduction of Constable's *Hay Wain* on another. With her books and family photographs on the shelves, she was delighted with her own small domain.

She had seen little of Gavin during the recent summer holiday for he had spent much of the time travelling on the continent with a group of student friends. A constant stream of picture postcards had arrived from various places in Austria, France, Belgium, Holland and Germany. They told his family little, except that he was still alive and still on the move, but Mrs Rossiter kept every one of them on the mantelpiece and examined them constantly as if searching for clues concerning his activities.

"Montmartre," she said fondly, gazing at the one he had sent from Paris. "Oh, what memories! I was a student there, you know. I'm so delighted that Gavin's seen it. Such an experience for him! Such an education – "

"Such wine, such girls!" Diana added scornfully. She, alone among them, affected total indifference regarding Gavin's where-abouts, openly despising his friends whom she dismissed as long-haired poseurs. Even so, she had spent a week with him in Paris and had apparently enjoyed it.

"It's not fair," Alannah grumbled to Rachel. "I wasn't allowed to go. Gosh, I can't *wait* to be as old as they are."

It was a sentiment with which Rachel could only agree. By next summer, she thought with satisfaction, she would be nearly sixteen. Well, fifteen and a half, anyway. Maybe her skin would have cleared up by then, people said it often did. Alannah said so, anyway, though what she knew about it Rachel couldn't imagine. No one in the Rossiter family seemed to suffer from pimples or any other such unattractive adolescent manifestation, not even Barney who was one on his own when it came to looks.

Diana, now eighteen, had left school bearing a vast number of prizes and scrolls of honour. Various universities, it was said, were competing for her favour, but to her scornful astonishment Oxford was not among them. Lady Margaret Hall had failed to offer her a place.

"They must be mad," Alannah said loyally.

It did not seem, to Rachel, quite so extraordinary. Despite the fact that, according to Alannah, half the junior school swooned at the sound of Diana's name, it seemed quite feasible that others might find her as unattractively cold and supercilious as she, personally, had always done.

January, February; inexorably the year passed. Rachel's Oxford dream was now in the ascendancy, and two more years at school in the sixth form a virtual certainty. An unworthy thought spurred her on. What heaven it would be if she could achieve a place where Diana had failed!

Such prospective glory was still years ahead, however. If only all subjects were as enjoyable as Eng. Lit! Rachel didn't care how many hours she spent reading set books or how often she picked over the bones with Red Rosie when homework was done. Her happiest moments were spent in the housemistress's room with Julia and Alice. Together with a few of the sixth-form girls they spent hours drinking cocoa and arguing about such things as whether Portia would have been a suffragette and should *The Merchant of Venice* be produced at all, now that people were more aware of the evils of anti-Semitism, as practised in Nazi Germany.

Miss Rayner's views on that and other matters were widely aired. Italy's brutal invasion of poor, defenceless Abyssinia was bitterly deplored; and nearer home, she still agonised over the squalor that existed in northern cities and the inhumanity of the Means Test. The Industrial Revolution had abolished responsibility, she said. Human beings were a secondary consideration; dividends were all important. Didn't they agree, she asked them, that men had a right to work or maintenance?

At least rearmament would give employment, suggested Vera Meadows, one of the sixth-form girls. There was a touch of defiance in her manner, for Red Rosie's views on this matter were well known. She, it went without saying, was a passionate believer in disarmament and the League of Nations.

"If you ask me," Janet Fanning said after one such discussion when the girls were on their own again, "Red Rosie's asking for trouble, sounding off the way she does. Scrimgeour doesn't like it. She told my father so."

"What on earth would we do if Rosie got the sack?" Rachel asked Julia, uneasy that Miss Rayner was the subject of conversation between Miss Scrimgeour and Mr Fanning – and who knew how many other parents?

"There's no chance of that," Julia replied reassuringly. "Rosie's a wonderful teacher, and Scrimgeour knows it."

Rachel hoped she was right, but couldn't help worrying about it – until, that is, the beginning of March when, with the Easter holidays just over the horizon, she was presented with a more immediate cause for concern. A letter arrived from her grandmother saying that a troublesome gall-bladder meant an operation and long convalescence and that she would be unable, therefore, to have Rachel for the holidays as planned. Other arrangements would have to be made.

"She means Aunty Sylvia," Rachel groaned. "I can't bear it! What am I to do?"

"Come to us." Julia knew all about Aunty Sylvia. "Oh, *do*, Rachel! It would be fun. Mum won't mind a bit."

Rachel hugged her friend, genuinely grateful. Going to Julia's house was bound to be a million times better than going to Aunty Sylvia. But how could she bear not to see Gavin?

In fact, she bore it quite well, thanks to the kindness of the Dodds. The rain fell almost daily and the rectory echoed to the sound of the ping-ping of raindrops as they fell into receptacles placed strategically all over the house. Wet though it was, however, the atmosphere was one of warmth and acceptance, of gentle humour and dry, scholarly wit. Mr and Mrs Dodd seemed old to Rachel, a generation removed from her own parents, but from the beginning she had felt at home with them, parting from them at the end of the holiday with real affection.

"My dear, you must be sure to come again," Mrs Dodd said. "Not, alas, next holidays since we are to undergo a prolonged visit from my niece and her husband and young family, home on furlough from China. But soon. We've enjoyed having you."

"I've had a lovely time," Rachel assured her with perfect honesty.

Back at school, the exams were now looming large; but beyond them, so sweet that Rachel could hardly bear to think of it, lay the summer holidays. Her friendship with Julia had grown and deepened during the weeks they had spent together, but nothing and nobody could quite compete with the Rossiters. With Gavin, anyway. Her grandmother reported a good recovery – adding gloomily, however, that at her age one never could tell. More cheeringly, Alannah wrote to wish her luck just before the exams began.

'Let's hope your grandmother is fit by next hols,' she went on. 'From what you tell me about your Aunty Sylvia, it would be a fate worse than death to have to go there. Can you beat it? Barney's going to some camp in Switzerland this summer, but I'm *still* considered too young to go anywhere! Never mind. I think Gavin and Di are going to be here most of the time, so it should be fairly lively at home. Bet you'll be glad to be here, with all the exams a thing of the past!'

Would she *not*! Rachel felt a tremor of excitement at the very thought, and inspected her chin closely for incipient pimples. She truly believed they were fading away. Another month might make all the difference.

The exams were spread over two weeks, and it was a relief when the long-awaited ordeal at last began. Geography, History, French, English – all went well. Rachel congratulated herself on having swotted the right things; fate, she thought, was being kind. But she was brought back to earth when, halfway through the second week, the post brought another letter from Grandma. It was her grandfather who was ill this time, struck down with shingles and suffering frightful pain and distress. Absolute quiet was essential, and devoted nursing – all the more exhausting, Grandma wrote, since she herself was not after all fully recovered. This time Rachel would have to go to Aunty Sylvia. Arrangements were already made.

"If only I could go to the Dodds' again!" Rachel said miserably to Red Rosie. "Julia wants me to, but they're full up with Mrs Dodd's niece and thousands of children, home from China."

"What about your other friends – the Rossiters?"

For a moment Rachel hesitated, biting her lips. She could feel the tears, hot and swelling, behind her eyes.

Why hadn't they asked her? They must know the situation. Maybe they would offer a last-minute reprieve, she thought, hopeful to the end. No word came from them, however.

It was an unsmiling Sylvia who met her at the station.

"Do drop the 'Aunty'," she said as the taxi took them back to the flat. "It makes me feel old. Whatever made you bring that enormous trunk? There's simply no room for it at the flat."

"But we have to bring everything – "

"I've no idea where we're going to put it. Schools really are the bitter end. I wonder who on earth designs those hideous uniforms? You must change into something more civilised the instant you get to the flat. I've a friend coming to tea."

In her narrow slit of a room, Rachel changed into a cotton dress, badly in need of pressing, and looked dolefully at herself in the mirror. Gosh, it was going to be awful staying here! Eight whole weeks. How could she possibly stand it?

"Tea's ready, Rachel," Sylvia called. Her voice was different now, trilling and sweet. "Come and meet Clarissa."

As Rachel emerged into the sitting room, she was aware of the slight frown on Sylvia's face as she took in the creased dress and the school shoes that she had forgotten to change. She saw the two women exchange glances, raise eyes to heaven.

Clarissa, platinum blonde and fashion-plate thin with orange lips and nails, extended a limp hand.

"So you're the niece," she said, unanswerably.

"How do you do?" Rachel said politely.

"I do frightfully well, thank you." Clarissa screwed up her eyes in a smile that failed to alter the shape of her painted mouth in any way. She turned to Sylvia. "Too old for the zoo and too young for civilised society. What on earth does one do with a child of this age?"

"There's no need to do anything," Rachel said coldly. "I'm not a child and I can look after myself."

"I'm rather banking on it, my dear." Sylvia smiled at her winningly. "Beginning with tonight. Rex and I have had tickets for *No, No Nanette* for simply ages – I'm dying to see it, couldn't bear to miss it. It seems too bad to leave you on your first night – "

"It's all right," Rachel said stiffly.

"I'll leave supper for you, of course, and you can always listen to the wireless. Let's see what's on. Oh look, there's a discussion on modern poetry. You like poetry, don't you?" Sylvia turned to Clarissa. "*Quite* the little bluestocking, our Rachel! Never with her nose out of a book."

"Well, she doesn't inherit that from you, darling!"

"What do you mean? I read *The Murder of Roger Ackroyd*!"

"Only because it was all the rage."

"Is there a library near?" Rachel asked abruptly. Both women turned and looked at her, then looked at each other.

110

"There's Boots, in Ken High Street," Sylvia said.

"Or Harrods," Clarissa offered. "That's quite near."

"I mean free ones."

"Oh, there's bound to be." Sylvia sounded vague.

Tea was brought in and handed round. Rachel, hungry by this time despite her misery, munched stolidly through several slices of sponge cake. She neither spoke nor was spoken to, and to the accompaniment of what she considered quite the most boring conversation she had ever heard, almost exclusively concerned with other people's infidelities, she made a survival plan.

From the time she had stayed in London with her parents, the capital had exercised a strong fascination for her. Miss Rayner, on that occasion, had assured her that there was a multitude of things to see and do there, and Rachel had proved the truth of this for herself.

All right, she thought now. It was clear that Aunty Sylvia (*Sylvia*, she must remember) would like it if she made herself as scarce as possible. She would, therefore, buy a map, find out about buses, and go *everywhere*! Museums, galleries – everything. Hampstead Heath, Soho, Kew – that wasn't far from London, was it? It said so in Noyes's poem.

And she'd buy a new, stiff-covered exercise book and write a daily report – a diary of everything she had seen and done. And she'd find a library – lots of libraries. She loved libraries and could spend hours in them, just browsing and looking up things.

She became aware, suddenly, that Sylvia and Clarissa were looking at her as if expecting her to say something. She licked a piece of icing sugar from her lip.

"Sorry?" she said.

"We were talking about the Rossiters," Sylvia said. "You'd think they might have invited you to stay with them."

"I expect they were busy."

"Thoughtless, more like. Mrs Rossiter sounds frightfully odd."

"She's not odd, she's lovely!" Rachel spoke vehemently, the colour flooding her face.

"Hm!" Sylvia raised her eyebrows sceptically. "Your mother had a different tale to tell. Wasn't there some stupid rift that Christmas they were home? She's a real earth-mother type," she went on, turning to Clarissa. "Weaves her own skirts and knits her own stockings, by the sound of it. I thought she sounded a total yawn! Though of course," she added, "it seems she does have her cross to bear. Kitty told me that Mr Rossiter is well-known the length and breadth of Warnfield as something of a ladies' man."

"That's rubbish! He's just nice to everybody," Rachel said, stung to anger. "It isn't fair, the way everyone says horrible things about him, when he's just being friendly and jolly." She got up from her chair. "I think I'll go and unpack properly, if that's all right, Aunty Sylvia." She laid particular emphasis on the 'Aunty', just to pay Sylvia out.

"Quite all right," Sylvia said silkily, and Rachel heard both women laugh as she left the room.

"Well!" Clarissa sounded amused. "This provincial Romeo has one fan, at least. Of course – " Outside the door, Rachel paused to hear the rest. "She's just the age for a *grande passion*, isn't she? Oh my dear, *what* a trial for you!"

And for me, Rachel thought mutinously, depressed at the thought of the long, lonely evening ahead of her. But as the holiday progressed, she found the lonely evenings, of which there were many, almost more preferable to the ones when friends came for drinks or dinner when invariably she felt awkward and out of place. But at least these parties had one positive and highly satisfactory outcome.

From the moment of her arrival, Sylvia had openly and vocally regretted everything about her appearance – her clothes, her hair, her deportment. A certain amount of money had been deposited with her for Rachel's pocket money and essential replacements, and finally, unable to stand the shame any longer, Sylvia marched her niece round to Barkers in order to rectify all that could be rectified.

For the first time, Rachel warmed towards her and was grateful. Clothes were Sylvia's passion and she chose wisely. Looking at herself once they were home, Rachel could only marvel at the unrecognisable image she could see in the mirror. Dressed in the full blue and white skirt that emphasised her waist and the pretty white blouse with the butterfly sleeves, her hair thinned and shaped and held back with a blue band, she looked almost pretty and certainly more grown up than she had ever looked before.

Hanging in the wardrobe was a printed silk dress for better wear, another new blouse, and a little dark-blue jacket that Sylvia had donated from her own wardrobe. There were sandals, too – not the flat regulation things that Rachel had worn ever since she could remember, but pretty ones with a bow on the front.

"We mustn't buy anything else," Rachel said to Sylvia guiltily, remembering the new skirt she would need next year in the Sixth Form. "There can't be much money left."

"I'll wire to your father and tell him to send some more," said Sylvia gaily; but Rachel, mindful of Grandma's comments regarding poor Ivor's pocket, looked worried.

"I don't think you ought – "

"Oh, nonsense! I refuse to have you mooching about the house looking like a scarecrow."

Something of Rachel's pleasure in her fine feathers evaporated; but she rallied again when, next evening, she appeared at one of Sylvia's little drinks parties, dressed in the printed silk. Gordon Boothby, Clarissa's husband, was a bulky, thick-lipped, red-faced man with a loud laugh; she had disliked him on sight, but even so it was impossible not to feel just a little gratified, if embarrassed, by the compliments he paid her.

Sylvia had no idea what she did with herself during the day, for Rachel – knowing instinctively that her aunt would object to long and solitary excursions on the tube to areas of London she considered undesirable – usually said she had been to the library or to the Science Museum or the V & A. There had, it was true, been some disturbing encounters: a seedy and persistent man who had followed her from St Pauls, and another, coming to sit close to her in a railway carriage suddenly vacated by other passengers.

Neither had bothered her unduly. She felt perfectly capable of dealing with such pests, and said nothing when she got home, for her rambles about London were the only things that kept her sane. She delighted in her discoveries; the sweep of Regency crescents, the grandeur of St Pauls and, by contrast, Wren's small, city churches. She loved the squares and the parks and the markets.

It was after a river trip to Greenwich that she returned to find that Sylvia had been speaking to Grandma on the phone.

"She says you can go there for the last two weeks," Sylvia said, and smiled a bitter little smile at Rachel's exclamation of delight. "Has it been so awful?" she asked.

"No, of course not." Rachel knew she sounded stilted and insincere, and tried to remedy matters. "You've been very kind," she said.

"Well, it hasn't been altogether easy for us," Sylvia said. "We're just not used to having young people about the place. It might have been different if I'd had children of my own."

"I know." Rachel smiled at her a little awkwardly. "I'm grateful, really."

There was a moment's silence. Rachel hovered indecisively as Sylvia, on the point of going out, picked up her handbag and searched through it. She was conscious that something more ought to be said; that perhaps, after all, there was the chance of some sort of communication with her aunt, some possibility of *rapprochement*. Then Sylvia snapped her bag shut.

"Well, now we'll be able to go to Biarritz with Clarissa and Gordon," she said. "I was afraid we'd have to cancel."

The moment had gone, and Rachel went to her room.

One more week in London – then Warnfield!

Rachel had heard nothing from Alannah in response to the letter telling her of her holiday plans; still, she felt certain that nothing would have changed, once they were together again. Communication between them had always been like that. There had been long silences between them, even quarrels, but it never mattered, they always seemed to pick up the friendship again.

They were all like that, all the Rossiters. Barney would look up and grin at her as if she'd only been away for a day or two. Gavin would make a joke and maybe tweak her hair. Mrs Rossiter would enfold her in an embrace. Mr Rossiter would give her a quick hug and kiss the top of her head. Diana would – well, Diana would greet her with total indifference, but then that was normal, too. She'd probably lift her eyebrows and say 'Look what the cat's dragged in', but Rachel wouldn't mind that. Gone were the days when she'd agonise over such remarks. Now she would just pull a face, or throw a cushion, or something.

Would they notice her new clothes, see that she'd changed? Her shape had, anyway. Her chest had got bigger, it seemed to her, even since she'd been in London. You could almost call it a bust. Would Gavin be aware that she was very nearly a woman?

Sitting on top of the bus that was taking her from Trafalgar Square where she had been visiting the National Gallery up the Haymarket towards Piccadilly, she pondered such things, making plans. This was the last day she would wear the new skirt before washing it, she thought. Then she would iron it and keep it for making an entrance at Kimberley Lodge. Maybe she ought to buy another blouse.

There was a small gathering of taxis outside Swan & Edgar in Piccadilly, forcing the bus to a halt. Rachel looked idly out of the window in the direction of Eros where today, in the sunshine, there were people sitting around the base of the statue. Tourists from all over the place, she thought, feeling proud because now she felt that this was *her* city. And as she looked, she saw a backview that seemed suddenly familiar; a backview that made her gasp with astonishment and delight.

Gavin! Surely it was? She'd know the shape of his head

anywhere, from any angle. Oh, why didn't he turn round? He was sitting on the steps talking to another young man. The bus would go on in a second. He *had* to turn round!

And he did – and it was Gavin! Her heart was leaping like a wild thing as she pushed past the woman in the seat next to hers and stumbled along the now moving bus.

"'Ere, 'ere, steady as you go, ducks," called out the conductor, punching tickets at the rear of the bus; but she took no notice, clinging to the rail beside the stairs as they swung into Regent Street, remembering too late that she hadn't paid and dismissing the thought without a qualm, not caring if the entire Metropolitan Police Force pursued her and thrust her into Holloway for the crime. Gavin was *there*, in Piccadilly, and she had to get to him before he went off somewhere else.

She lurched down the stairs and stood on the platform, leaping off the moment the bus came to a halt a little way up Regent Street. Regardless of other pedestrians, she ran back the way they had come. People looked at her over their shoulders, but she was unaware of them, for Gavin was her only thought. Suppose he had gone when she got back to the Circus? She wouldn't have a hope of finding him in these crowded streets.

But he hadn't gone. He was still sitting on the base of the statue, one knee drawn up, an elbow resting on it, smiling a little as he watched the passing show.

A taxi hooted as she darted across the road and a motor bike swerved dangerously, its driver shouting a startled insult. She was unaware of both of them.

"Gavin!" she shouted, and as he turned to look in her direction she saw his smile widen in delighted recognition. She flew towards him, and though he had never embraced her before, he held out his arms to her and she rushed into them.

"If it isn't our Rachel," he said, swaying from side to side, still holding her tight. "And all grown up, too. Who'd have thought it! Just look at you, girl!" He held her at arm's length, grinning widely. "You've cleaned up a proper treat!"

Thank heaven she was wearing the new skirt and the hairband and everything! Rachel couldn't believe her luck. Yesterday she'd gone out in the awful, outgrown printed cotton that she couldn't bear the sight of. Just imagine if she'd seen him then!

"What – what are you doing here?" she managed to stutter at last.

"Just seeing life," Gavin said. "Here – meet Peter." He turned to the brown-haired young man who was still sitting on the steps, regarding them with a smile. He stood up when his name was mentioned and proffered a hand.

"Peter Merrick," he said, politely.

"Rachel Bond," Rachel said, shaking his hand and instantly forgetting him.

She felt quite sure she must be dreaming. Nothing seemed quite real and when, a little while later, she found herself sitting opposite Gavin at a table for two in Lyons' Corner House, she could hardly remember how they had got there.

Gavin ordered egg and chips and a pot of tea, and she said she'd have the same, even though she'd had tea and a doughnut only half an hour before. She demanded news of Warnfield and the family, but this Gavin was unable to give her. He'd been staying with Peter, he told her. In Gloucestershire, he added.

She looked at him curiously. There was something about the way he spoke that made her think he was hiding something. Maybe there was a girl, she thought resignedly. Maybe he hadn't been staying with Peter at all. She pushed the unwelcome thought away.

"How long are you here for?" she asked.

"Just for two nights. We're going to see *The Seagull* tonight – Edith Evans and Peggy Ashcroft."

"Oh, lucky you! It's wonderful!"

"You've seen it?"

"No, only heard about it." Everyone had been talking about it at Sylvia's last drinks party, but afterwards Sylvia had said it didn't really sound her sort of thing. Rachel thought she was probably right.

Gavin frowned as he shovelled a forkful of chips into his mouth.

"It seems a pretty rotten thing, doing something so enjoyable when all hell is let loose in Spain."

Yes, Spain, Rachel thought. People had been talking about Spain too, but current affairs weren't discussed very much in Sylvia's household and she had no idea what was going on. There'd been something on a newsreel, though, when she last went to the pictures. Something about Franco bombing British ships at Gibraltar. Honesty, she felt, was the best policy.

"I don't really understand it," she said humbly.

Gavin explained. There was the legally elected government on one side, he told her, and General Franco on the other, fighting to bring it down. How, he asked her, could anyone defend that? It was contrary to all democratic beliefs, made a nonsense of all human rights. General Franco pretended the fight was about Catholicism against Communism – but clearly he had no more regard for religion than the man in the moon. Less, in Gavin's humble opinion. The fight was about Left against Right – a legally elected Communist government against filthy Fascists. And what did the British Government do? They drew up their skirts like the collection of puritanical old women that they were and refused to intervene, said it wasn't their quarrel; and what was worse, they were persuading other countries to follow their example. They should, Gavin assured her, be tarred and feathered. And then shot.

"But – " Rachel began.

"It's good against evil, Rachel old girl – as simple as that."

"War is evil. Rearmament is evil." Miss Rayner said so, didn't she?

"Well, maybe we have to make a choice between two evils. Look what old Musso has done in Abyssinia! Horrible things are happening, Rachel."

"I know."

"I was in Germany last year. It's frightening. Hitler's a madman. Believe me, he's not wasting time while the British draw back from rearming! He'll help the Fascists in Spain. He *wants* a world war, and he'll provoke one if he can."

"Gosh," breathed Rachel. He knew such a lot! She loved his fire and enthusiasm, the way his eyes flashed. Even eating egg and chips, he looked magnificent. She poured the tea, scarcely taking her eyes off him.

Finishing his food, he sat back in his chair and smiled at her.

"I know what you're thinking," he said. "That I'm nothing but a windbag, spouting a lot of hot air. That's what Di thinks, anyway."

"Oh, I don't!" Rachel assured him. "I just wish – well, it seems awful not being able to *do* anything, doesn't it?"

Gavin glinted a smile at her as he stirred his tea.

"Shall I tell you a secret?" he asked her. "Can you keep mum?" Could she! Eyes shining, Rachel nodded vigorously. "Well," he went on, leaning towards her confidentially, "don't tell a soul, but I've joined the University Air Squadron. I'm learning to fly. It means when the balloon goes up, as I'm quite convinced it will, I'll be ready for it. Ma would go mad if she knew – in fact she and Dad positively forbade it, but I forged Dad's signature."

"Gosh," Rachel said again.

"Ma was dead against it. She had a brother, you see, who was a flyer, and he was killed in the last war. She simply can't bear any talk of another one. Well, nobody welcomes the prospect, of course, but she's practically psychopathic about it. She almost had hysterics when the subject was raised about my learning to fly, and Dad said I wasn't to mention it again. Di had hysterics, too. She went into one of her spitting rages."

"You haven't told Diana?"

"I haven't told anyone except you."

Oh, the pleasure this gave her! She felt as if her heart would burst.

"You know last year, when I was supposed to be abroad?" Rachel nodded. "Well, part of the time I was, but for three weeks I was at camp near Oxford. Same this year."

"But all those cards – !"

"Oh, I wrote them in advance. I had friends who posted them for me wherever they happened to be. This year I'm supposed to be staying with Peter."

"They'll surely have to know eventually."

"Sufficient unto the day."

"Is it fun?"

"Flying? I love it!"

"You're not frightened?" He laughed at that.

"We learn on Avros – they're the safest things in the world. It's safer than riding a bicycle. This year I've been learning to fly on instruments."

He'd be the best one in the whole Squadron, Rachel was quite sure of that. Her eyes shone as she looked at him. Just imagine – she was the only one he had chosen to tell – the only one in the whole world!

"London's great, isn't it?" he said, grinning over his teacup. "Have you enjoyed yourself?"

"Well, sort of. I've been exploring – "

"Sounds fun." He looked at his watch. "I mustn't be too long. I've got to meet Pete and some others around six thirty, to make plans for tomorrow."

"What's happening tomorrow?"

"Didn't I tell you? We're joining an anti-Means Test March. There's a whole crowd of us from the camp. The thing's a disgrace, an obscenity."

"Oh, I agree." Rachel, on more familiar ground, spoke earnestly. She knew all about the Means Test. "It's entirely wrong for people who are prevented from earning their living to be subjected to that kind of – "

"Must go, love." Gavin cut her short, reaching out to squeeze her arm. "It's been absolutely great to see you."

"I'm coming to Warnfield next week."

"Wonderful! You'll be in time for Di's birthday party. I've sworn to be back for that, on pain of death. There's going to be a dance."

"Gavin – "

About to rise from his seat, both hands grasping the table, he looked at her.

"What is it?"

"Oh, never mind." She had wanted to ask if she could come on the March, too, but knew he wouldn't be keen on the idea. It didn't matter. She would be seeing him in no time.

On the way home, she hugged herself in her delight. What luck, what incredible, marvellous, stupendous luck it had been, to pass through Piccadilly at just that moment – and in her new clothes, too. What on earth would she wear at Diana's dance? She couldn't, just *couldn't* wear her old party dress, which was much too short and too tight and too juvenile for words.

Poor Ivor's pocket, she thought with a sigh. Sad as it might be, she was going to have to make still more inroads upon it.

Through the trees she could see the bulky shape of The Laurels. She could even see the bathroom window where, more than once, she had stood and listened to the Rossiters enjoying themselves in their garden on a summer's evening. Now she was on the right side of the fence.

A wooden platform, just a few inches high, had been put over the grass for dancing. Alannah said that her father had borrowed it from the Council; it was the one, she said, that they'd used in the park at the Silver Jubilee celebrations.

There were lights strung in the trees, and a three-piece band that played quicksteps and foxtrots and waltzes – all of which Rachel could do quite well, thanks to dancing classes at school and Julia's willingness to take the man's part.

In floating pale blue georgette over blue satin, with a wide satin sash (approved by Sylvia and bought in C & A's summer sale, drastically reduced) she felt transformed; but only Mr Rossiter and Barney had asked her to dance.

Barney had seemed shy and abrupt at first, rather as if she were a stranger. Was he remembering that kiss at Clearwater? Surely he didn't imagine that she had attached any importance to it?

She did her best to put him at his ease – which seemed odd,

when she remembered that first day when he had sat on the wall and looked down on her, like some lord of creation.

"You seem a bit peculiar," she said, when he settled down next to her at the supper interval. They were sitting on the low wall that edged the rose bed, with a fine disregard for Rachel's new dress, and were eating ice-cream. "Have I changed, or something?" She wasn't exactly fishing for compliments, she told herself; not really. Still, it would be nice to hear that she did, indeed, look different.

He turned and looked at her, his mouth twisted as if in thought.

"Well, I thought so at first," he said with a grin. "You looked so much more grown-up. But as soon as I saw you with a dollop of ice-cream on your nose, I knew you hadn't changed at all."

"Oh, no!" Hastily Rachel felt her nose. "You beast! I've got no such thing!"

"Caught you, though, didn't I? Tell me what you've been doing with yourself."

"I've been exploring," Rachel told him, just as she had told Gavin. But Barney was interested, and asked questions; he even seemed to envy her.

"To be honest," she said, for somehow it was easy to be honest with Barney, "it was a bit lonely. Some days I didn't talk to a soul all day – not more than 'please pass the salt', anyway. You wouldn't have liked it really."

"It does sound a bit of a far cry from the Rossiter household. You never know, I might welcome a bit of peace."

"It's good to be back."

Why hadn't they invited her to stay? She hadn't asked Alannah, and Alannah hadn't told, but instead had prattled of the play she had been in at the end of term, and the tennis match she'd won, and a new friend she'd made – *American*, of all things – whose father had been over on some temporary assignment at Burnetts, the big electrical manufacturing plant on the edge of town, and of the marvellous party they'd given before they went back. She'd been glad to see Rachel, though. They had laughed as they had always laughed together, and it seemed, Rachel told herself, as if she had never been away.

But she knew she had, when she looked at Diana. This was Diana's nineteenth birthday party, and she was undoubtedly grown up now. Her skin was smooth and tanned and she wore her blonde hair cut close to her head – rather like a young Greek god, Rachel thought. Her eyebrows were plucked, thin and arched,

120

which did much to add to her air of sophistication. Her dress was very plain, sage-green satin with narrow gold shoulder straps. She looked, Rachel thought, quite devastating.

There were a number of her college friends at the party; but she still queened it over the old ones, too. Guy Seagrave was obviously as adoring as ever, and Gavin's friend, Peter Merrick, clearly had eyes for no one else.

Gavin was having a good time, but didn't seem to be dancing with any one girl in particular. Would he remember that they were special friends, now that she knew his secret? Would he ask her to dance before the evening was out?

Whenever the band began a new number, she couldn't resist a quick glance in his direction, just in case; then, finally, when she had almost given up hope, it actually happened. He came across to where she was sitting with Alannah, made a little, mocking, courtly bow, and led her to the floor.

She would never again, she knew quite well, hear 'These Foolish Things' without remembering this night. There was the scent of stocks in the air, and the stars were at last appearing, adding their own magic to the summer night. It was a dream come true, a fantasy. If her hands weren't otherwise engaged – one resting on his shoulder, the other clasped in his – she would pinch herself to make sure she was awake.

They didn't talk very much. It was all passing far too quickly, she thought with sudden panic – and her hand must have tightened on his shoulder, for he looked at her quizzically.

"What is it?" he asked her.

"Nothing."

"You will remember that what I told you in London is a secret, won't you?"

"Of course!"

"You won't tell Alannah? I know you and your girlish secrets! You're all the same – "

"We're not, and I won't say a word. If you don't trust me, you shouldn't have told me."

"I do trust you." He smiled into her eyes and she felt light-headed, as if she were going to faint.

The music stopped, but he didn't move away.

"How did the March go?" Rachel asked him. "I read about it in the paper."

He had no opportunity to answer, for Diana had approached from behind and had pulled him round to face her.

"Pray excuse me, little Miss Cinderella!" She smiled at Rachel over Gavin's shoulder, but it was there, that edge of derision that Rachel had always been aware of. "Time you went back to the nursery slopes."

"What a bossy-boots she's become in her old age," Gavin turned to smile at Rachel too, but he made no demur and together he and his sister drifted away to the strains of 'Smoke Gets in Your Eyes'.

Rachel stood for a moment watching them, feeling a strange twist of pain at her heart that was almost pleasurable.

They're so beautiful, she thought. Both of them – almost as if they were made of something more than the flesh and blood of ordinary mortals.

"They do me credit, don't you think?" said a voice beside her.

She turned to see that Mrs Rossiter had joined her. She nodded, smiling; and together, Mrs Rossiter's hand through the crook of her elbow, the two of them stood watching Gavin and Diana. When the older woman spoke again, her voice was no more than a whisper.

"What mother could help but be proud?" she demanded softly. "I ask you. What mother could help it?"

8

The journal that Rachel had begun while in London had become something of a habit. Back at school, enjoying the minor privileges of the sixth form, she continued, intermittently, to record her doings and her thoughts. For posterity? Hardly! Who, she thought, would be interested in her wild delight that she was now excused obligatory games – reprieved from the boredom, for so she saw it, of chasing a ball up and down a hockey pitch or leaping ineffectually around a netball court? And could anyone appreciate her overwhelming gratitude for the fact that sixth-formers were allocated studies, to be shared with two others?

She and Julia and Alice ('We three, we happy three, we band of duffers', as Julia put it, for all had failed to distinguish themselves in any sporting activity of any kind) had turned to each other quite naturally, and so far had cohabited in perfect harmony.

Alice was fair-haired, fresh-faced, and rather earnest. She worried constantly about being overweight, which in no way inhibited her intake of doughnuts, freshly made and sold every day at the tuck-shop. So determinedly tearful when she had first come to St Ursula's, she still tended to be over-sensitive and a little slow to see the point of any joke until it was explained to her very carefully. Julia and Rachel teased her, but only with the greatest affection.

"And she is improving," Julia said. "She actually made a joke herself yesterday. I had to think about it very hard, but there it was. Almost a wisecrack."

"She'll have us rolling in the aisles before too long," said Rachel.

They all knew they would never achieve sixth-form stardom. The positions of House Captain or Head Girl would, inevitably, go to those whose talents were more to Miss Scrimgeour's taste – *rounded* girls, as she was fond of saying, with team spirit as well as intelligence.

"I'm as rounded as they come," Alice grumbled, looking at herself in the mirror. She wasn't happy at the reflection she could see there, but was plainly delighted with herself for making a joke out of it.

"Ah, but rounded in which direction?" Rachel asked darkly. "And where, may I ask, is your team spirit? Do you lose one wink of sleep if St Ursula's fails to beat Norwood House? Are you on the sidelines, cheering your nicely rounded throat hoarse?"

"No, she's not," Julia said, answering on Alice's behalf. "She's sitting on her nicely rounded backside, sunk in decadence, reading *Gone with the Wind*."

The shiny-covered notebook that Rachel had bought to record her explorations in London was full, and she had bought another. It was on the first page of this that, long after lights had been dimmed in the dormitories – and indeed, long after even a sixth-former should have been asleep – sitting up in bed with the book resting on her knees, she inscribed the date.

18th November, 1936 – Today a European War moved a step nearer, according to Red Rosie, for Germany and Italy have recognised the government of General Franco and are providing him with assistance despite agreeing to non-intervention. This year has been a dreadful one, what with the activities of the Italians in Ethiopia, and now this terrible war in Spain. I have never seen R.R. so down. She has a friend (lover?) who has gone to Spain with the International Brigade and though she had a letter from him a few days ago, posted in Madrid, since he wrote Madrid has been under siege and there has been hand-to-hand fighting in the streets. Unimaginable! Think of it happening in London!

Had a long discussion tonight in R.R.'s room (me, Julia, Alice, Vera, Morag, Jill) about whether war can ever be justified. R.R. thinks not, but says in spite of herself she can't help being filled with admiration for the idealistic young men who have joined the I.B., because there is something splendid about those who are prepared to fight for what they see as a war of good against evil. We all knew she was thinking of her friend. How terribly torn she must be, between respecting his ideals and her own hatred of war.

Not all the talk was of Spain. We also talked about prayer, and holidays. Can't remember how we got from one to the other, but R.R. believes that though prayer is useless for altering physical things (i.e. like praying for fine weather if a depression is already forming over the Atlantic, or a safe journey if the car's brakes need attention), it's the manifestation of love for another and is a force which can be transmitted through the ether, creating a positive field of influence surrounding the person who is being prayed for. I'm almost sure she loves the man in Spain and was thinking of him. I shall go on praying for Gavin anyway, just in case. I think one should give God a chance.

Re holidays, R.R. loves France, especially Provence. She cheered up a lot while she was talking about it. She made us aware of the warmth and the colour of it – or was it just that it made me think of Uganda? No, I don't think so. The feel was quite different. She talked about sitting on the side of a mountain, drinking wine and eating nectarines and smelling the thyme, and somehow I could just see it all. She's clever like that, she can make you see the things she describes, and she looked so happy while she was speaking of it. I think she was there with The Lover, but she carefully avoided saying so. I wonder how old she is? About 35, I think, but is still very attractive in spite of her age. Not pretty, exactly, but good-looking. She reminds me of that line in Rupert Brooke's poem about the girl who 'tossed her brown, delightful head, amusedly among the ancient dead'. Being in the sixth form is so different! She always seemed more like a friend than a teacher, but now there is an even greater feeling of barriers being down. She *almost* admitted tonight that she didn't like Scrimgeour! Not quite, of course, because that would never do, but she did say they didn't always see eye to eye, which I imagine is putting it mildly!!

Letter from Mummy this morning. She and Daddy have been on safari in Kenya – not real safari, with guns and things, but travelling around quite a lot staying at up-country hotels. It sounded wonderful! Sometimes I *thirst* for Africa. We went once to Kenya before I came to England and reading Mummy's letter brought it all back to me. I remember how funny it was to feel cold in the evening and to sit in front of a roaring fire, when the days were so warm and the air

125

so very clear and still. Quite different from Entebbe. I stood on a hillside once and could hear the sound of a tractor below me in the valley. It looked like a toy, but I could hear it so plainly. Oh, when will I see it all again? Mummy still thinks I'm coming home after a year in the sixth form. They were pleased about my good exam results, of course, but it doesn't seem to occur to anyone that I might like to take a degree, and I haven't said a word, I don't know why. I suppose because I still can't really believe I'm good enough. I'll wait until I've done a year in the Sixth and then see how things go.

She chewed the end of her pencil, thinking about it, wondering why she found the subject so difficult to talk about. It was all right at school, of course, with Red Rosie, and with Alice and Julia. They all knew what she wanted to do, and didn't see anything particularly remarkable about it. Julia cherished similar ambitions, and her parents took it for granted that these would be fulfilled. Grandma, however, had a strange and almost scornful attitude towards higher education for women, and Mummy and Daddy seemed to think it irrelevant – a waste of time unless one was going to be a teacher. Even the Rossiters – who, Rachel felt, might have taken a different view since their own daughter was at London University – assumed that she had reached saturation point with School Certificate. Mrs Rossiter had urged her to take a shorthand and typing course – '*such* an advantage for any girl,' she had said, adding that Mr Rossiter always maintained that a good secretary was worth her weight in gold.

"And you would be an *excellent* one, Rachel, I'm certain of it," she had said earnestly. "You're such a dear, methodical, unobtrusive little creature."

"You make her sound like Mrs Tittlemouse," Barney said, sounding irritated on her behalf, and Rachel was grateful for his intervention. She hadn't followed up the conversation, though, or attempted to state her very different ambitions. Had she done so, she would have felt like Yeats:

I have spread my dreams under your feet;
Tread softly, for you tread on my dreams.

Yawning, suddenly overwhelmed with sleepiness, she put the book down on the table beside the bed, hopped out to turn off the light, and, with the room in darkness, went to the window to pull the curtain aside and look out at the night.

She was in a room high up in the east wing; a servant's room, no doubt, in the old days when the house had been occupied by landed gentry. It had been raining earlier in the evening, but now the sky was clear and the moon was shining. It shone on the handsome bulk of the school with its sweeping drive, glinting on the puddles, palely lighting the front porch. It would be shining on Gavin, too, wherever he was. She knew that to be no more than a cliché, well used by poets and lovers through the ages, but all the same she liked to think of it.

The school faced south – a feature made much of in its glossy brochure, which also spoke at length of its extensive, park-like grounds. Rachel had long ago worked out that Oxford lay vaguely to her left, and it was in this direction she looked now. Tightly she closed her eyes, summoning every bit of positive thought that she could muster, putting her last ounce of effort into a prayer for Gavin.

Afterwards, she continued to look out over the bleached gardens, the moon so bright that she could almost see the individual leaves on the trees. Had he felt it, she wondered? Had he felt surrounded by her love, just for that moment? Would he ever feel it?

Suddenly aware that her feet were cold on the bare lino, she scampered back to bed. She could, she thought, think of Gavin just as easily under the bedclothes.

There was no Rossiter pantomime at Christmas any more; but there was still a party at which they played charades and all the old-time favourites, or most of them. The game of Adverbs seemed to be forgotten, much to Rachel's relief, for she had never been able to come to terms with it.

It was during a game of Sardines that, as they huddled together in the airing cupboard, Barney kissed her again. She couldn't in all honesty say that it was an enjoyable experience, mainly because – as on the last occasion – she was utterly unprepared for it. Which shouldn't, she recognised, really make any difference. If it had been Gavin, she would have rallied from the shock in short order and would have given as good as she got. With Barney, however, it was like being kissed by a brother; not unpleasant, exactly, but rather pointless.

She made no comment, and nor did he, mainly because they were almost immediately joined by Alannah and her friend Daphne Baker who, amid many giggles, squeezed into the cupboard beside them.

Daphne had a crush on Barney, so Alannah had told her. What a pity it was, Rachel couldn't help reflecting, that it hadn't been Daphne who found Barney first. Maybe he would have kissed her instead, which would have given a lot more pleasure. Sometimes life could be so unsatisfactory.

Rachel, with a shelf jutting painfully into her back, began to think that perhaps Adverbs hadn't been so bad after all, and was heartily thankful when they were all discovered and were able to troop back to the drawing room where dancing was being organised by Gavin. He had a new girlfriend called Jacqueline who was not only extremely attractive but seemed nice as well. Try as she might, Rachel could see nothing to her detriment.

I ought to be used to it, she thought drearily. Heaven knows there have been enough girls over the years, and none of them last very long; but even so, she couldn't avoid feeling an aching desolation at the sight of them laughing together.

The dancing took place to the same gramophone and the same records, she realised, as on that Christmas Day three years before when Mummy and Mr Rossiter had danced together and caused such a lot of unnecessary fuss. Christmas 1936 passed without any such upset, but Rachel did wish Barney hadn't kissed her. It unsettled her. She didn't know what to make of it. And she did wish Jacqueline didn't have such pretty dark curls and such a flawless skin. That night, in yet another new journal, she wrote:

I have a horrible feeling that this might be *it*, for Gavin and Jacqueline looked so right together. I hope not. And what on earth does Barney mean by kissing me like that? Does he want me for his girl friend? Or is he just trying to get a bit of practice? If the former, I fail to see how it's possible he could be attracted to me when all I feel for him is mild affection.

She studied this for a moment, chewing her lip, then crossed out 'mild'. The affection she felt for Barney was more than that, she decided on reflection. But it was still only affection. She went on,

Actually, I feel that the second alternative is more likely. He's not a bit like Gavin – I bet he was twice as experienced as Barney when he was sixteen! I got the feeling that Barney is as green as I am, so if he's experimenting then it's just too bad for him! What I know about kissing (as he must recognise by now) you could write on the back of a postage stamp in block capitals and still have room left over for the Gettysburg Address. He didn't say one word when we were dancing – not about that, anyway, just went on and on about whether or not he should go to Art College. Mrs Rossiter is passionately keen that he should go, but he doesn't think he's good enough. I didn't know what to say, except that I supposed if his mother thought he was good enough, then he probably was. He's not happy about it, though.

You'd think, if he really liked me, that he'd have said *something* nice, just for once. It was Gavin who said I was looking pretty. I don't honestly think he meant it, but it was nice of him to say it. And you never know, he might have meant it, in spite of Jacqueline.

Jacqueline or no Jacqueline, it was good to be among them all again, part of the family. Even Diana seemed more friendly than in the past. One afternoon soon after Christmas, Rachel found herself involved in a brisk argument with her, regarding *Emma* – was she too bossy and too much of a prig to be a likeable heroine? Diana held that she was – that she was totally impossible and that Mr Knightley wouldn't have looked at her twice in real life, but Rachel argued that it was her faults that made her human.

"And after all, she's very honest about herself," she went on earnestly. "She does learn."

"But of all the interfering busybodies in fact or fiction, she takes the cake," Diana maintained.

Rachel was diverted afterwards to see that they had been talking, actually conversing, for over five minutes – and as equals, too. It must, she thought, be some kind of a record. Had the time come at last when Diana accepted her as one of them?

It seemed quite a possibility; and she certainly felt a true member of the family when, alone in the kitchen with Mrs Rossiter one morning, she was the recipient of certain confidences regarding the distant courtship of the Rossiter parents.

"My father never cared for Hugh," Mrs Rossiter said. "He was a rather austere man, you see, and he thought Hugh a lightweight, which was terribly unfair. Of course, he might give that impression, I can see how people might think it of him, but it's quite untrue. I knew right from the beginning that it was he I wanted as the father of my children."

"Really?"

Rachel was a little startled at this aspect of the relationship. In her book, people fell in love and they got married. Children, surely, hardly came into the picture at that stage.

"Oh yes!" Mrs Rossiter's eyes glowed with a reminiscent light as she paused in drying a milk jug. "He had such vigour and vitality, such a *glow* about him! 'I want sons like that,' I thought. Well, Barney is more like my father to look at than his own, except for the eyes, but Gavin, you'll agree, is the image of Hugh."

"Yes, I suppose he is. Taller, though."

"He gets that from my family. But he has all of his father's charm, don't you agree?"

"Oh, yes!" How could Rachel disagree with that?

"And such intelligence! It shows in his face, of course. There's a fineness there, a liveliness. And of course," she went on more matter-of-factly, resuming the drying briskly, "he's full of affection for his home and family. I know I'm lucky to have such a son. I suppose one day I shall have to share him with another woman, but not yet, not yet!"

"You don't think Jacqueline – " began Rachel, diffidently.

"Jacqueline? That little dark girl who came to the party? My dear Rachel, give Gavin credit for some taste! She's pretty enough, I grant you, but hardly his intellectual equal. Oh no, when Gavin chooses a girl it will be someone very special, I promise you. Well, well! I mustn't go on. You'll think me a doting mother, and no mistake. It's not that I don't think anyone good enough for him, you understand, or that I don't care for the other children. I'm proud of all of them, and with good reason. There's something about the first-born, though . . . Oh, I can't explain! You'll find out, in time."

Rachel smiled guardedly and said nothing. She – who better? – knew how easy it was to dote on Gavin, yet there was something in Mrs Rossiter's enthusiasm that caused a flicker of unease, as if she had revealed herself naked in the High Street. People just didn't go on like that, Rachel thought. They spoke of their children with detached affection, however proud they were of them underneath. She tried to imagine her own mother conversing in the same vein, and failed miserably.

But when later she was in the old nursery with all of them – Barney making toast in front of the fire, Alannah lying on her back on the floor with her legs upright, pressed against the wall (which she had read somewhere was recommended practice for anyone who required shapely ankles), Diana elegantly draped in a chair reading *This Gun for Hire*, Gavin sitting in the window seat with his profile turned towards them all, drumming his fingers as if lost in thought – she couldn't help thinking that Mrs Rossiter's fervour was understandable. They were a pretty impressive and unusual lot. Especially Gavin.

As she looked across at him, he turned from the window and looked straight into her eyes. She smiled a little nervously, feeling somehow caught out, but the smile he gave her in return was perfunctory, as if he was not really seeing her. With an exaggerated movement, lifting his hands before pressing them down on the window seat to lever himself upright, he stood for a moment, looking now not at her but at Diana who, blissfully unconscious, went on reading.

"I wish to make an announcement," he said abruptly.

"Is it worth getting my legs down for it?" Alannah asked, not moving.

He didn't reply. Diana looked up, but slowly, unwillingly, one finger keeping her place. Then, seeing his expression, she shut the book and put it to one side.

"It looks as if it might be," she said.

"Toast's ready!" Barney, his fair-skinned face reddened by the glow of the fire, was sitting back on his heels. "Who wants first bit?"

"Leave it!" Gavin's voice was curt, making Barney look up in astonishment.

"What on earth is it?" Alannah asked, now sitting the right way up.

"I'm going to Spain," Gavin said harshly, without any preamble. For a moment there was silence. Then Diana spoke.

"You surely couldn't be such a damned fool," she said coldly.

"I'm not going to fight. At least I don't think so. I've volunteered to drive a supply lorry out there, full of stretchers and blankets and clothes and primus stoves and so on. They're all badly needed. You can't object to that!"

"Why can't I? Have you seen today's paper? They're bombing Madrid, it says."

"Ma won't let you go," Alannah said fiercely. Gavin laughed briefly.

"She can't stop me! I shall be twenty-one in three months' time."

"Maybe you'll never be twenty-one." Diana's face was bone-white, drained of colour. "Have you thought what that would do to her?"

"Of course." Hands thrust in his pockets, he flung himself on the arm of the chair where Rachel sat. Because it was the nearest, she told herself, sitting very quietly. Not for any other reason. Still, it felt good having him so near. Maybe, instinctively, he had turned to her for the support he knew he wouldn't get from his own family. "I've thought about what it would do to me, as well. I've thought about it endlessly, but in the end it boils down to one thing. Have I the guts to do what I know to be right?"

"You idiot, it's not our fight," Diana said through clenched teeth, leaning towards him. "Even your precious Labour Party says that."

"I'm disgusted with the Labour Party! It's a collection of lily-livered time-servers. The Labour Party can only live when it leads. It'll die for certain if it continues to flounder around dodging the issue like it's doing at the moment."

"Better the Labour Party should die than you."

"Oh, shut up, Di! I've told you, I'm driving a lorry, not fighting."

"That's what you say now." Abruptly Diana jumped to her feet, her book falling to the floor. "I know you. You'll get into it if you can. You're just a stupid kid, that's all – a stupid kid who's spoiling for a fight. Well, go then!" Her voice rose. "Go then. Go and find your bloody corner of a bloody foreign field and see what comfort it is to you when you're dying, with your guts hanging out. And what about your degree? You're in your final year, for God's sake – "

"Di, listen – " He rose from beside Rachel and made a move to hold her, but she shrugged away from him.

"Don't touch me! You're a selfish, self-centered, self-deluding, utterly, utterly stupid *moron*, and I want nothing more to do with you." Her lips were drawn back, her face contorted as she pushed past her brother. "I said, don't touch me – and don't ever speak to me again, either! I tell you this, Gavin – " She paused on her way to the door and with hands clenched by her sides, turned to glare at him. "If you go, I never want to see you again, never, never – "

Turning, she slammed out of the room, leaving silence behind her.

"Toast, anyone?" Barney asked at last, in one of his funny voices. No one took any notice.

"Do you have to go, Gavin?" Alannah asked, more subdued than Rachel could ever have believed.

"Yes, I think so." Gavin sat down on the arm of Rachel's chair again.

"Do us a favour," Barney said. "Stick to driving the lorry, won't you? That I can understand. But fighting? We neither of us believe in that, do we?"

Rachel looked at him with interest. Barney was not one to parade his beliefs and it caused her some surprise to find that he had any.

"I'm not making any promises," Gavin said.

"Then you jolly well should!" Alannah was glaring at him from her position on the floor. "Don't you care anything for us? And surely it's mad to leave Oxford now."

"It'll be all right, Lannie. A number of us are involved. We'll get special dispensation, we hope."

"You *hope*?" Barney's voice soared with dismay, all thoughts of toast forgotten. "You must get that sorted out, surely? You can't waste the better part of three years. Are you sure you're doing the right thing, Gavin?"

"I'm sure," he said quietly.

"Well, I'm not!" Alannah's voice was tight with misery. "Di's right! You're just being selfish, not thinking of us at all."

"He's not selfish!" His nearness made Rachel brave and the words seemed to burst out of her. "I think it's perfectly splendid. Don't you know what's going on out in Spain? Aren't you proud that Gavin's standing up for what he believes in? I would be, if he were my brother. He's helping the cause of democracy – "

"Oh, do dry up, Rachel!" Alannah snapped the words, angry now. "What do you know about it? He's not your brother."

"I know it's a war between good and evil. I think it's marvellous that Gavin wants to stand up and be counted."

"Bless you!" Gavin turned, and putting an arm around her shoulders, leant to kiss her cheek. "Listen to Rachel, you lot! She's got the right of it. This is a fight I want to be part of."

"Fight? You said you were only going to drive a lorry," wailed Alannah.

"So I am. But if I should get a chance to fly a plane, then I will – "

"*Fly?*" Alannah and Barney chorused the word together.

"Yes, fly! I've been learning – haven't I, Rachel?" Still holding herself stiffly within the circle of his arm, Rachel nodded. "I'm part of the University Air Squadron – a pilot, and a damned good one, though I say it myself. Soon we'll be part of the RAF Reserve."

"Ma will die," Alannah said dramatically. "You know how she's always been about flying."

Gavin was more down to earth. "No she won't," he said. "She'll be upset but she'll get over it. A lot depends on your attitude. Why can't you see my point of view? Surely you can, Barney?"

"Maybe. Have you talked to Dad?"

"Not yet. I intend to tonight. I just wanted to tell all of you first – get you on my side, as it were. I seem to have failed dismally, with the exception of Rachel here." He hugged her again and she smiled at him tremulously, the smile fading as she caught sight of Alannah's expression.

"Rachel," Alannah said bitterly, "is not family. She never has been, she never will be."

"Rot!" Gavin was almost breezy again now that he had got his confession off his chest, at least to his siblings. "I always think of her as an honorary sister. Well – " he stood up and consulted his watch. "Dad should be arriving home any moment. I want to beard him and talk to him first."

"He'll kill you for what you're going to do to Ma," Alannah shouted after him as he left the room. "And as for you, Rachel Bond," she went on when he had gone, leaping to her feet and thrusting a twisted, enraged face close to Rachel, "you can just go home!"

"Hey, steady on, Lannie," protested Barney.

"She's nothing but a snake in the grass – taking Gavin's part against us! What does she know about it? They're bombing people out there and killing them with machine guns." A thought occurred to her and she turned back to Rachel again. "And what was that about flying? Why did you know about it when we didn't?"

"I told you I met Gavin in London, just by chance. He told me then."

"That was ages ago! Why didn't you tell us?"

"He told me not to. It was a secret."

"How *dare* you!" Alannah glared at Rachel, her face as white as Diana's had been. "Keeping a secret like that about *our* brother! Well, if he dies, it'll be your fault."

"Lannie, don't be so bloody silly," Barney said wearily. "Rachel, don't take any notice of her. She doesn't know what she's saying."

"Oh, yes I do! I never want to see you again, Rachel Bond. I never want to see your smug little face. When I *think* what we've done for you over the years – "

"Shut up, Lannie," Barney said again, more sharply. "If Gavin said it was a secret, than Rachel was right not to tell."

"Alannah – " began Rachel.

"Oh, go to hell," snapped Alannah. "You make me sick, both of you. I'm going to find Diana."

"I'd better go," Rachel said, when the door had slammed behind her.

"No, wait." Barney got up from his position on the hearth-rug and came close to her. "Don't let Lannie upset you, Rachel. You know what she's like – she makes a drama out of everything."

"Should I have told? I couldn't, could I, Barney? It was Gavin's secret."

"Of course you shouldn't. Anyway, what difference would it have made? Gavin does what he wants."

"I hope he's right about going to Spain." Suddenly Rachel was a prey to doubts. Even if the cause was a just one, maybe – just maybe – it was futile to risk dying for it.

"You sounded sure enough just now."

"Did I? Yes, I suppose I did. I don't honestly know what I think, really. It was just that everyone seemed so against Gavin . . ." her voice trailed away. Oh, why did everything have to be so mixed up?

"I almost felt like enlisting myself!"

"Oh no, don't, please!"

"Would you care?"

"Of course."

There was a look in his eyes that made her think he might attempt another kiss, and to forestall him she turned away towards the door.

"I must go," she said. "Tell Lannie – " she hesitated.

"What?"

"Tell her I didn't mean to upset anyone. Tell her I hope we're still friends."

"Oh, you know Lannie! She'll get over it."

"I wonder." Rachel went to the door and opened it, then looked back to where Barney still stood. "Do you think Gavin's right?" she asked. "Honestly?"

Barney gave a short, derisive laugh.

"I think he's a dope," he said.

It was during the course of the following morning that a note arrived from Mrs Rossiter asking Rachel to call and see her after lunch. It was a very formal letter with no hint of the close relationship that had marked their conversation in the kitchen only a day or two before, and Rachel's heart sank a little as she read it; however, it seemed so manifestly unfair that she should be blamed for Gavin's decision that she approached the interview with no more than mild uneasiness. She was totally unprepared for the sight that confronted her when a tight-lipped Diana ushered her through a strangely silent house into her mother's presence.

The interview took place in her bedroom – a large colourful room with a gilt, roccoco bedhead. At some distance from the bed there was an ornate bureau with its top down in the writing position, and here Mrs Rossiter sat, pen in hand. Rachel could see several pages of blue writing paper covered in her flowing hand.

Though it was afternoon, she was still wearing a loose wrapper and feathered mules, and her hair, usually caught up in a knot, was streaming down her back. Her eyes were swollen and red as if she had been crying without ceasing for hours on end, grief making her almost unrecognisable.

Rachel's nervousness had grown as she followed Diana up to the room, for it was clear that Diana was as angry as ever – and not only with Gavin. Now her anger appeared to encompass Rachel as well. However, in the face of Mrs Rossiter's misery, Rachel forgot her nervousness and hurried towards her.

"Oh, Mrs Rossiter, please, please don't be so upset!" she implored her. Mrs Rossiter turned tragic eyes upon her.

"You ask that of me?" Her voice was rough, as if it hurt her to speak. "*You!* If you'd spoken out earlier, we might have been able to knock this ridiculous scheme on the head. You've a lot to answer for, Rachel."

Taken aback, Rachel faltered for a moment, then rallied.

"Honestly, I don't see why," she said.

"You don't see why?" Diana, who had been hanging back, now entered the fray. "You encouraged Gavin in his stupid ideas. Oh yes, Alannah told us everything you said yesterday about it being grand and glorious for him to stand up for what he believes in. You little fool! What do you know? You're encouraging him to go to his death, you realise that?"

"No, no, that's not fair!" In desperation Rachel turned from one to the other. "His mind was made up. He doesn't take any notice of me."

"He told you about learning to fly," Diana said bitterly. At this Mrs Rossiter gave a low moan, and burying her face in her hands began to cry again.

"But he's only driving a lorry to Spain – "

"He'll fly, given half a chance. Permit me to know my brother a little better than you do. You should have told us."

"It was a secret!"

"Don't be so infantile. We had a right to know."

"That's enough, Diana." Mrs Rossiter made an effort to compose herself, wiping her eyes and straightening her back so that she looked directly at Rachel. Her lips were pressed together in a straight, uncompromising line. "I want to speak to Rachel myself."

"Oh, please Mrs Rossiter – " began Rachel, attempting to forestall her.

"Be silent and listen to me! I am distressed and hurt – very, very hurt by your attitude, Rachel." Her voice quavered and she bowed her head, gathering her resources. "Our family," she went on tremulously after a moment, "has shown you nothing but friendship and kindness over the years. I have done my best to treat you as one of my own." Emotion overcame her once more and she looked away from Rachel until she succeeded in composing herself again. "We have taken you on holiday, included you in family celebrations, and asked for nothing in return but your friendship and loyalty and love – "

"But you've had all of that, Mrs Rossiter. Always!"

Mrs Rossiter gestured feebly to silence her, a handkerchief clutched in her hand.

"I feel betrayed, Rachel," she went on brokenly. "Betrayed that you, *you* of all people, to whom we have never stinted our hospitality, should have been so grossly ungrateful as to behave in this way."

"But Mrs Rossiter, I haven't done anything!" Rachel fought back tears of unhappiness and frustration.

"You encouraged him. We know from Alannah that you yourself have political views quite different from our own – "

"No!" Desperately, Rachel denied it. "Well – " she amended. "It's true I agree with Gavin up to a point, and I can't help admiring anyone as brave as he is – "

"Exactly! You have encouraged my son to risk his life for some wild political ideal that neither of you understand."

"I don't know why you're blaming me – "

"You knew about his flying," Diana put in. "You can't deny that."

"It was a secret!" Rachel's voice emerged as a desperate wail. She felt as if she was on some mad roundabout, coming back each time to this same point. Surely they understood that she couldn't betray a confidence? It was like a nightmare, none of it making any sense. Gavin had always defended his beliefs strongly, they knew that. It was ludicrous to think that her opinions would have swayed him, one way or the other.

"There is no need to raise your voice," Mrs Rossiter said icily. "I want you to leave now. It will, I think, be a long time before I can bear to see you in my house again – "

"If ever," put in Diana.

"If ever," echoed Mrs Rossiter. "I feel our hospitality has been abused, our generosity set at nought. There is nothing more I wish to say."

"This isn't fair," whispered Rachel, tears now streaming down her face. "This isn't fair."

Emotion drove sensible argument from her mind. Later she would be able to think of all she ought to have said. Now, helplessly, she stumbled from the room.

The house was silent, with no sight or sound of Barney or Alannah. Then she heard the front door bang, and thinking it might be one or the other of them, she ran down the stairs; but, to her surprise, it was Mr Rossiter who stood in the hall, taking off his overcoat.

"Well, hallo," he said a little awkwardly, seeing her.

"Oh Mr Rossiter," she began, scrubbing at her eyes with her handkerchief. "Mrs Rossiter's so angry with me, and honestly I don't know what I've done – "

"Yes, well, there there!" He patted her shoulder in an embarrassed way, uncharacteristically subdued, as if there had been a death in the house. "You meant no harm, I'm sure. Carina tends to get upset sometimes. You must understand what a great shock Gavin's announcement was to her. She's not herself. That's why I've come home so early. I felt she might need me."

"I didn't mean any harm." In spite of her best efforts, Rachel began to cry again. "Oh, can't you talk to Mrs Rossiter?"

"Well – " Mr Rossiter, already edging up the stairs, shrugged his shoulders. "You have to realise, Rachel, that my wife – and the girls, too, are very fond of Gavin."

"Do they imagine I want him to be killed?"

"No, no, of course you don't! Look, Rachel my dear, please calm yourself. This will all blow over." He looked around the hall as if desperately seeking a way of escape. "Really, these upsets – " he paused, sighed, ran fingers through his hair and shook his head in desperation. "They're so damaging, so unpleasant for everyone. I simply can't bear having the house in such a turmoil. Carina is not, generally, an unreasonable woman, but where Gavin's concerned . . ." his voice trailed away and he stood looking at Rachel helplessly and with some exasperation as she wiped her eyes and nose. "It will blow over," he went on, almost as if he were trying to convince himself. "It always blows over. Eventually. Now run along home and – " he hesitated for a moment, not knowing what panacea to suggest. "And have a nice cup of tea," he finished lamely.

He gave her a bright and encouraging smile, and left her, marching rather self-consciously up the stairs towards his wife's room, as if he knew quite well that he had failed to help Rachel but was determined not to admit it. Halfway up, he turned to look back at her, saw her still standing there, and came down a step or two, looking more exasperated than ever.

"Do go home, Rachel," he said. "Look, I know that none of this was your fault, but you must try to forgive Carina. She has to find someone to blame, you see – "

"Why me?" Rachel asked tearfully. But he had said all he had to say, dispensed all the sympathy of which he was capable, and was proceeding up the stairs.

"Women!" she heard him say under his breath.

Grandma saw Rachel's grief and demanded explanations which, when received, filled her with a righteous and self-congratulatory fury. Hadn't she always said that the family next door were unstable, unreliable, unfeeling and generally undesirable? Hadn't she always deplored the fact of Rachel's friendship with them? Perhaps, she said, Rachel would in future take a little more notice of her knowledge of the world and of human nature.

Not that Rachel had told her everything, by any means. It was only slowly that the whole story emerged, but when it did the resentment of years coalesced to form a white-hot anger. She had to be persuaded not to march round to Kimberley Lodge there and then to give Mrs Rossiter a piece of her mind.

"It wouldn't do any good, Grandma," Rachel assured her hastily, knowing that this could only make a bad situation worse. "I don't feel I want any more to do with them."

"I should hope not! The woman sounds completely unbalanced. Mind you, I've always thought there was something very strange about her – haven't I said so a hundred times? It was a mistake for you to get so involved with them. I've a good mind, in spite of what you say, to go round there and tell her that she's behaved despicably."

"Grandma, no! Honestly, I just don't care any more."

She did care, though. She seemed to care more rather than less as the hours passed, for more and more of Mrs Rossiter's accusations, unregistered at the time, came back to haunt her.

Oh, why didn't Alannah call round to tell her it was all a mistake? Now that they'd had time to think about it, they'd surely see that nothing she had said would affect Gavin's actions. Should she write? Should she attempt to explain all over again? Maybe she should call at Kimberley Lodge herself; come to think of it, Alannah still had the copy of the *Diary of a Provincial Lady* that she'd lent her, and she had no intention of losing that! It surely would be in order for her to go and ask for it before she went back to school. It took her some time to pluck up her courage, but on her last afternoon she went next door and rang the bell.

It happened to be Alannah who answered the door. Rachel knew at once from her expression that nothing had changed, she was still unforgiven. She was invited to stand in the hall while Alannah went to find the book and, unsmilingly, handed it over.

"Alannah – " began Rachel appealingly. "We've been friends for a long – "

"Goodbye, Rachel," Alannah said, cutting her short, holding open the door.

"Oh, *Lannie* – " Rachel tried again, but stopped at the sight of the stony face that looked back at her. For a moment she hesitated. "Tell your mother," she went on resolutely, "that I have never been ungrateful. Not ever."

Alannah raised a supercilious eyebrow, a trick she had been practising for some time and had now, apparently, perfected. Her lips curved in a small derisory smile, but she said nothing. Rachel turned and left, hearing the door shut behind her.

Rain was falling and sodden laurels dripped on to the path. The whole world seemed utterly without hope, as if no one, ever, would smile again; but as she reached the gate she met Barney coming in, and he greeted her with welcome warmth.

"Rachel! I've been wanting to talk to you. I was coming to see you later on. Can I come back with you?"

"Grandma will be there." And would give them no privacy, Rachel knew – in fact she would undoubtedly relieve herself of the piece of her mind she had been threatening to give Mrs Rossiter for the past three days.

"I want to talk to you." Barney caught hold of her arm and looked around wildly. "Tell you what – let's go in the shed."

It smelt of wood and creosote; a summer smell, Rachel thought, associated with deckchairs, and games of cricket, and tea in the garden. They perched uncomfortably on a crate and looked at each other.

"I'm sorry I haven't seen you before this," Barney said. "I've been away. I drove Gavin to Oxford and stayed the night."

"He's really going, then?"

"'Fraid so. And guess what – he's engaged!"

"*Engaged?*" Rachel stared at him blankly.

"To Jacqueline. Well, I'm not surprised myself, but Ma and the girls are almost as upset over it as they are about his going to Spain!"

Rachel gave a brief and mirthless laugh.

"Well, at least they can't blame me for that!"

"Rachel – " He edged nearer to her and put his arm around her shoulders. "I'm sorry – I'm so terribly sorry for the way they've treated you. It's so unfair."

Rachel, who had managed all day so far without crying, suddenly felt the tears prick her eyes again and merely nodded in reply, biting her lip.

"You've got to understand that where Gav's concerned, they're not rational."

"I think I do understand," Rachel said. "I understand that I'm the scapegoat. Gavin can't be blamed for anything, so they've fixed on me – your father said as much. I wonder if *you* can understand how frightening it is when all you Rossiters close ranks! I feel as if I'm in some sort of outer darkness."

His arm tightened around her.

"Not all the Rossiters," he said. "I've stood up for you, honestly. They're behaving like idiots, and I've told them so."

"What does your father say?"

"Dad?" Barney shrugged. "He's angry with Gav, not you, but it's anything for a quiet life with Dad. He hates it when Ma gets into one of these states and he'll agree to anything, just so long as she calms down."

"Does she get in these states often? I've never seen it before."

"Not often, thank God, but sometimes. So does Di."

"I know about Di! I've never understood it."

"Who could?"

Barney sounded gloomy, and for a few moments they sat in silence. Rachel was conscious of his arm still around her and, for once, was grateful for it, for the comfort it gave her. She leaned her head against his shoulder and closed her eyes.

"Rachel – " Barney's voice was rough. "I'm not like the others. I still think an awful lot of you."

"Do you?"

"You know I do! I wouldn't hurt you for anything."

She twisted her head round to look at him. The lock of hair was over his forehead, just as it had been that first time. She was really awfully fond of him. Perhaps if she really tried, she thought, she might be able to fall in love with him. If that was what he wanted.

His arm tightened round her. He was going to kiss her again, she realised. She closed her eyes and tried very hard to persuade herself that she was enjoying it as he held his lips unyieldingly against hers. Maybe that's all kissing *was*! If so, it was a dreadful con.

"I – I think you're sweet," he said awkwardly. "Will you be here next holidays?"

"I don't know. I haven't thought that far." But now that he'd mentioned it, she had a sudden vision of the Rectory in Little Milbury, and she felt the first peace that she had felt for some time. The atmosphere there – the quiet, the gentle good-humour, seemed to her, at this point, the most desirable thing in the world. "I may go to my friend Julia's, if they'll have me," she said.

"Can I write, then?"

"Oh, please! I want to know what happens – whether Gavin is safe. And what you decide to do with yourself," she added hastily, realising that she had been somewhat deficient in tact.

"I shall miss you," he said.

For a moment they looked at each other without speaking. Then Rachel smiled.

"I was so scared of you that first time when you accused me of spying on you," she said. "You glared down at me from the top of the wall like some High Court judge."

Barney laughed. "That seems a long time ago."

"It can't all be over, can it?" The thought was so shocking that she felt sick.

He shook his head, then bending his head he kissed her again.

"It isn't over," he said softly. "It can't be."

Rachel sighed.

"Well, it feels as if it is," she said.

She had never been more glad to get back to school. The weight of misery around her heart seemed to ease a little as she went up the steps and through the front porch – a phenomenon that she would have found it hard to believe a year or two ago. Now she could hardly wait to see Julia and Alice and Red Rosie. Even the indescribable and unmistakable smell of polish and girls and the memory of thousands upon thousands of school meals, once so depressing, now seemed welcoming.

Girls called out to her as she made her way to her room.

"Hallo, Rachel. Good hols?"

In reply she smiled and nodded and asked the same of them.

"Seen Julia?" she added, as she went on her way. "Any sign of Alice?"

She was arranging books on the shelves in her room when Alice arrived looking distraught. She closed the door behind her and stood leaning against it, panting as if she had raced along the corridor to impart her news.

"Guess what," she said, without any preamble. "Red Rosie's left."

"*What?*" Aghast, Rachel seemed not to notice that one of the books she was holding had slipped to the floor. "She can't have! Who told you?"

"I've just seen Scrimgeour in the entrance hall. Honestly, there's no mistake. She introduced me to the new Housemistress – and oh Rachel, she's awful! All sort of mincy and scrunged up – I hated her on sight."

"She can't have left," Rachel repeated, refusing to believe it. "Maybe she's just ill, and this woman is temporary." Alice always looked on the dark side. It simply couldn't be true!

"No! Julia's ill with flu and won't be coming back for a few days – Scrimgeour told me that, too – but Rosie's resigned. Taken up an appointment in Wales, Scrimgeour said. I bet they had a fight, don't you?"

"I bet they did," Rachel said. "And I bet it was about Rosie's politics. Someone's made trouble for her." The desolation was complete. No Rossiters, no Miss Rayner. "How are we going to stand it?"

"I can't imagine. It's just awful, isn't it? Julia's going to be devastated."

"Aren't we all?" Slumped on the bed, all the spirit gone out of her, Rachel contemplated the future and could see no joy in it anywhere, nor any possibility of joy.

Alice sighed.

"I suppose I must go and unpack," she said. "Actually I feel like going straight home. Oh, by the way," she added, half out of the door. "Scrimgeour wants to see you after supper in her study. She asked me to tell you."

"What on earth for?" Rachel asked the question listlessly, not caring.

"She didn't say. Maybe she's going to make you a Prefect."

"Ha ha!" Rachel was grimly amused at such a far-fetched idea, but no alternative reason for the summons suggested itself and for the moment she dismissed it from her mind. The sight of Miss Spalding, Miss Rayner's replacement, was enough on its own to occupy her thoughts. Never had she seen anyone less attractive. Her long thin nose was reddened, her shoulders rounded, her teeth protruding, clearly she was devoid of all dress sense; and none of the girls, Rachel least of all, appreciated that her ingratiating manner was due entirely to a paralysing shyness. As a replacement for Red Rosie, Rachel considered, she was a total disaster. How Miss Scrimgeour could ever have thought otherwise it was impossible to imagine.

Alice had to remind Rachel that she was required to present herself to the headmistress. Hastily straightening her hair and her blouse, she knocked at the door. She found Miss Scrimgeour sitting at her desk, regarding her unsmilingly.

"Alice said you wanted to see me, Miss Scrimgeour," Rachel said politely.

"Indeed, I did." Miss Scrimgeour laced her fingers together in the steeple position and looked at Rachel over the top of them, a cold gleam in her pale eyes. For a moment she said nothing.

Rachel's own eyes alighted on an exercise book on the desk that separated them. How odd, she thought idly, that Miss Scrimgeour should have a book so like her own journal. Her gaze intensified and sharpened. Surely it *was* her own journal? There was the smear where she'd spilled cocoa, and the crease on the corner. There could be no doubt about it – it was one of the old ones she had left at school, for she'd taken only the current one to Warnfield.

"You recognise this?" Miss Scrimgeour asked her, holding the notebook up between finger and thumb as if it was something unsavoury she barely liked to touch.

"That's mine! It's private! Where did you get it?"

Miss Scrimgeour replaced the book on the desk and laced her fingers together again.

"You left it in the study, did you not?"

"It was locked in the cupboard. I'd never have left it if I'd thought anyone was going to go snooping about."

"No one," Miss Scrimgeour said icily, "was snooping about, as you so inelegantly put it. It is common practice to clean out the cupboards during the holidays – the same key fits all of them, as you must surely know, and we've found this necessary since even sixth-form girls tend to horde food and other perishables."

"There was no food in my cupboard. You had no right to read that."

144

"The first page was seen quite by chance, and quite rightly brought to me." Picking the book up again, she handed it over the desk to Rachel. "Read it," she ordered.

Rachel looked down at it. It was the entry for the 18th November where she had written of the discussion in Rosie's room about the Spanish Civil War, where she had said what she had parroted almost word for word at Kimberley Lodge – that there was something splendid about those who were prepared to fight for what they saw as a war of good against evil.

"I shan't read it to you," she said defiantly. "No one but me was meant to see it."

For a moment Miss Scrimgeour looked at her through eyes narrowed with anger.

"It is quite clear to me," she said at last, "that Miss Rayner has a very great deal to answer for. I had my suspicions all along that she was indoctrinating you senior girls with all manner of undesirable political ideas. This gives me proof of it – and not only of her suspect politics, but of immoral behaviour as well. All this talk of going to Provence with her lover. It's quite, quite disgusting! And in addition," she went on, holding up her hand as if to stem Rachel's protest, "I have received a letter from Mrs Rossiter, whom I know full well has been a good friend to you over the years. She told me what took place during the holidays – how disappointed she was in you."

Speechless now, Rachel stared at her.

"I have spoken to you now, like this, before the term begins in earnest, to give you due warning," Miss Scrimgeour continued. "I wish to hear no Communist nonsense from you – no left-wing political claptrap that could contaminate any of the younger girls – "

"It wasn't like that – "

"Enough!" Miss Scrimgeour banged the desk with the flat of her hand. "If it weren't for the fact that your parents are abroad, I'd very probably expel you. As it is, I shall give you one more chance to behave sensibly."

A burning desire to clear Miss Rayner's name gave Rachel more courage than she might otherwise have possessed.

"Please, Miss Scrimgeour, please try to understand," she begged, coming a step closer to the desk. "It truly wasn't like that. Miss Rayner didn't try to make us think one way or the other. We discussed different points of view, that's all. She made it seem interesting, all the things that were going on in the world. Don't you see – "

"That will do."

"Where is she?"

"That is no concern of yours."

"I'm not a child, Miss Scrimgeour. I want to write to her."

"I should not be doing my duty by your parents were I to allow any such thing. Kindly go, and see that you behave with more circumspection in future."

For a moment, still clutching the notebook in her hands, Rachel stared at the woman behind the desk, wanting to speak, longing to find the words that would make her see how mistaken she was. She looked at the narrow face, at the rigid, thin-lipped mouth, then hopelessly she shook her head. There was no talking to her, no way of explaining, no hope of understanding. Anyway, she thought with a flash of insight, it wasn't really anything to do with politics. That was just the excuse. Miss Scrimgeour had, for some reason, disliked and feared Red Rosie from the beginning. Jealousy? Perhaps. Rosie had seemed to command the love and respect of the girls almost effortlessly, which Miss Scrimgeour had never done. And now that she came to think of it, wasn't there something in that journal entry about the two of them not seeing eye to eye? Something about Rosie implying her dislike of Scrimgeour? Yes, it all added up. Without another word she left the room.

That night sleep eluded her for a long time. She stared dry-eyed into the darkness, conscious of an overwhelming weight of misery that seemed to be crushing her; and not only misery, but fear, too, as if, inexplicably, the worst was yet to come.

Which was, as she told herself, moving her head restlessly on her pillow, quite ridiculous. What more could happen? She'd lost Gavin, the entire Rossiter family, and Red Rosie, all in one fell swoop. That was enough, wasn't it? Nothing more could possibly go wrong – unless, of course, the unthinkable happened and Gavin was killed, just as his family feared. She felt cold and sick at the very thought.

Oh God, keep him safe, she prayed fervently. Please keep him safe. Jacqueline didn't matter. She'd manage, somehow, to cope with the idea of Jacqueline, just so long as he was safe.

Funny, she thought; she hadn't really cried for him yet, and for the end of all her dreams. It was as if all her tears had been shed before Barney had told her the news about his engagement. Or as if, even now, she couldn't really believe it. Yet she knew it to be true, knew that the Gavin dream was over. And what about the Oxford dream. Was that over too? Without Rosie, it just wasn't the same, somehow.

But that was ridiculous! She owed it to Rosie to keep on; owed it to herself to go as far as she could. Once Julia was back, she thought, she would feel better. Julia was such a dear – such a staunch, funny, rock of a friend who would never, not in a million years, treat her as Alannah had done. Exposed to a few doses of Julia's down-to-earth common sense, everything would look different. Calmed by the thought of her, and of her gentle parents who would, she felt certain, welcome her again to their home, she slept at last.

When both she and Alice were called once more to Miss Scrimgeour's study the next morning, she felt both angry and rebellious.

"What now?" she demanded of Alice as they made their way there. "What more can she possibly say? She said it all to me last night." She had an uneasy feeling, though, born of those irrational night-time fears, that there was something worse in store, and her heart was beating fast when together she and Alice went into the study.

Miss Scrimgeour's face was grave.

"Sit down, girls," she said, in a very different tone from the one she had used to Rachel the evening before. "I'm afraid I have some very bad news for you. I felt it only fair to tell you first before I make an announcement to the school."

She paused and looked at them and Rachel's heart seemed to shrivel with dread. With sudden, heart-stopping certainty, she guessed the truth.

"Julia?" she whispered.

"I received a telephone call this morning. I'm afraid she died yesterday of meningitis."

There was a sudden, strange sensation as if the room was tilting sideways. Tearless, Rachel stared at the carpet, concentrated on it, noting its red and blue lozenges and the squiggly pattern each contained. Squashed beetles, she thought. They had always reminded her of squashed beetles. There were girls' voices, happy voices, coming faintly from the corridor outside. Inside, Alice was giving small gasping sobs – Alice who had cried so much and for so long when she had first come to school, but never quite like this.

Looking up, Rachel saw Miss Scrimgeour's eyes upon her, saw the criticism in her face. She thinks I don't care, she thought. She thinks I'm unfeeling. And she's right, because somehow I can't seem to feel anything.

But the pain would come, she knew, and she feared its coming. Because she also knew that once she began to weep for Julia, she might never be able to stop.

9

Izzy Pollard, who ran the St Bethan Stores halfway down the hill that led to the small quay, was as free with her endearments as all the Cornish. 'My dear', 'my bird', 'my 'andsome', 'my lover' all fell trippingly from her lips, but Rachel, seeing her hard, snapping eyes and pinched mouth, knew they were not to be taken at face value.

"Oh, the dear liddle soul," she said now, bending down to look at Tess. She had come out from behind the counter to serve Rachel with vegetables. "Don't favour ee though, do un? She'm like her daddy, I s'pose."

Rachel said nothing but smiled noncommittally, glad to see that Tess showed enough perspicacity to favour the shopkeeper with an impassive stare even if she herself lacked the courage to do so. It didn't do to antagonise Izzy Pollard, for she it was who wielded power – if not over life and death, then certainly over such little luxuries as made life worth living. The odd extra egg, for example, or good quality marmalade. It paid to keep on the right side of Izzy Pollard, but even so, Rachel saw no need to pander to idle curiosity.

Izzy retreated behind her counter and, reaching beneath it, brought forth a tin of salmon with the air of a conjurer producing a rabbit from a hat.

"There," she said, lowering her voice to a conspiratorial hiss. "I'll let ee 'ave it for half a crown, never mind the points."

"Half a crown?" It seemed an exorbitant sum but even so Rachel wavered. It would be a change, she thought; and if she refused it, Mrs Pollard would undoubtedly be offended and offer her nothing more in future.

"No points!" Izzy glinted her sly little smile towards Rachel. "'Tis worth summat, that."

"Yes. Yes, all right." Rachel made up her mind. "Put it with the rations and the vegetables. They will be delivered this afternoon, won't they?"

"Soon's my Billy's home from school, Mrs Bond, you can rely on it."

Rachel opened her mouth to correct this form of address, then closed it again, convinced that Izzy Pollard knew the truth but merely wanted the satisfaction of hearing the malefactor confirm with her own lips that, despite the baby in the pram, she had no husband.

She had been in the village for three weeks now; ample time for the word to get around. She was not entirely sure if the curious glances and the muted response to her 'Good mornings' and 'Good afternoons' were the norm. Perhaps they were, and she was seeing slights where none were intended. Perhaps this arms-length treatment was no more than any stranger would have received.

She accepted it philosophically, thankful that at least Mrs Hoskings, having registered her disapproval, seemed now to have decided to overlook the matter. Or perhaps she was just naturally fond of children. For whatever reason, she seemed to have taken to Tess and had already knitted her a woolly bonnet ready for the cold winds of winter and had stated her intention of knitting matching mittens, if Rachel would provide the wool.

In spite of this strange and rather detached existence, Rachel found, somewhat to her surprise, that she was content. She was busy with proofs of *With This Ring* as well as the first draft of the new book, and she had no time to worry overmuch about the village's reaction to her presence.

She and Tess had settled into a way of life that seemed to suit them both. As if the River Tamar had proved to be some hitherto unremarked dateline, Tess had changed her habits from the moment she arrived in Cornwall and now slept for two hours in the afternoon, waking about three thirty and being once more ready for bed by seven. If only, Rachel thought, she could find a replacement for Beattie so that she had a few mornings free, she could ask little more of life.

From the room she had designated her study, she had a narrow, interrupted view of the river. More a glimpse than a view, as she wrote to Nancy, now living in a flat in Norwich and apparently thriving on marriage to George, despite a constant panic about the health of the aged Lancaster and a life spent hustling for freight.

'But from the living room, the view is – if you'll forgive the hackneyed phrase – breathtaking,' she wrote. 'Literally. Every morning, it's just as if I'm seeing it for the first time. You and George must come! Why not spend Easter here? You must surely be able to take a break at some time, though it certainly sounds as if you are frantically busy. I hadn't appreciated the problem of getting freight for the return journey as well as the outward one. It sounds enormously difficult. *What* a time George had in Nyasaland! Oh Nancy, dear Nancy, how I hope it works out! I'm keeping everything crossed – eyes, toes, the lot.

'You're going to need St Bethan by Easter. The ability to feast one's eyes so liberally has a therapeutic effect. I have found it makes for a feeling of serenity and contentment. Or is it just that I'm not worrying about the Rossiter factor any more? A bit of each, perhaps. Somehow, I can't imagine being angry or worried or frustrated, ever again.'

She would be, she knew. Perfect contentment was surely an unattainable state – which perhaps, for a writer, was no bad thing. A time would come when she needed the stone in the shoe, the unscratchable itch – stimulation, fresh people, a dash of culture. A man?

Her thoughts swerved away. One day, she thought. Maybe. But not yet.

Mrs Hosking's efforts to find a girl to look after Tess had proved so far unsuccessful, but one morning she came up with what appeared to be a sensible suggestion.

"Your best bet," she said to Rachel one day, "is to have a word with Teacher – Mrs Laity, that is." She paused, duster in hand, to add the customary potted biography. "She'm a lovely woman, Mrs Laity. A widow, she is, married a Polvear lad who died very young on a motor bike, poor soul. 'Tis likely she'll know a good girl leaving school soon. Maybe one whose mother wouldn't be too fussy, like."

Rachel ignored this throwaway line and welcomed the suggestion with enthusiasm.

"That sounds a good idea. Where do I find her?"

"She'm up at the schoolhouse. Master's house, it used to be, only we don't have no Master now, only Teacher for the big ones and a wisht little thing as comes over from Polvear every day for the Infants. Poor soul, pale as a whitewashed wall, she is, true as I'm 'ere."

Rachel, diverted by this graphic description, nevertheless resolved to follow up Mrs Hosking's suggestion as soon as possible. She thought of phoning, but decided instead that a personal approach would be better, and pushed Tess up to the schoolhouse that very afternoon at an hour when she guessed lessons would be finished for the day.

Mrs Laity welcomed her warmly, inviting her into the house at once, even though it was clear she had not long been home. She brushed aside all apologies for disturbing her peace after what, surely, must have been a tiring day.

"I'm pleased to see you, believe me," she said. "A cup of tea and a little adult conversation is most welcome after the undiluted company of the eights-to-fourteens. Come in, do. I know exactly who you are! You're Mrs Courtney's niece, and a famous author – "

Rachel laughed at that.

"Hardly! I've written one book that isn't published yet and I'm about one third of the way into another."

"Oh, do allow the village a little bit of excitement. It's an achievement any way you look at it. Congratulations!"

"Did you know my aunt?" Rachel asked.

"Only by sight." Mrs Laity looked faintly amused. "We moved in different circles. She's not the reason for this call, is she? I don't think she was aware of my existence."

"Oh, no! It was actually about the fourteen-year-olds I wanted to see you." Rachel, now settled with Tess on her lap in the comfortable, book-filled little sitting room, hoped very much that these different circles would not prejudice the schoolmistress against her, for she had taken to her on sight. Mrs Laity had a lively, interesting sort of face; rather like a bird, Rachel thought, with her bright eyes and the way she had of cocking her head on one side to listen attentively. "I wondered," she continued, "if there happened to be a potential mother's help among their number."

"Well – " Mrs Laity looked thoughtful and Rachel had the distinct and uncomfortable feeling that she was being assessed, weighed up, to see if she were a fit person to employ one of her girls. "There might be. Look, why don't you put Tess down on the carpet? We can corral her with the cushions – she can't do any harm. May she have a biscuit?"

"I don't want her to mess up your things."

"She won't. Not irretrievably, I'm sure. There – what a lovely baby! You must be very proud of her."

"I am. But – " Rachel paused and Mrs Laity tilted her head in enquiry.

"But what?"

"About the help I need," Rachel went on after a moment's hesitation, "I realise that it might be embarrassing for you – that – you might feel my home isn't a suitable place for any of your girls."

Mrs Laity, now pouring tea, shot her a mischievous look.

"Yes, I know all about that, too," she said. "Well, I suppose there are those who might hold those views, but your situation isn't exactly unique in St Bethan, you know. Many a bride is married with a distinct bulge under the white satin."

"But at least they've donned the white satin! They're regularising the situation."

"Hm. Some do, some don't. I daresay we have a few Yankee toddlers among us with fathers who delightedly embraced all the dangers of the Normandy landings as an alternative to facing their responsibilities here. Plus, of course, many little mistakes of the home-grown variety. Oh, there'll be those who hold up their hands in horror because it gives them the appearance of virtue – and they're the worst, in my experience. I could tell you a few things about some of those Holy Joes – but I won't! Believe me, I've had my share of malicious gossip. Teachers are supposed to live lives of blameless rectitude, attend chapel regularly, never darken the doors of the Ship Inn – "

"And do you?"

Mrs Laity laughed.

"I think 'mostly' is the answer to your question – but it's not always easy to conform and I've rather given up trying. As long as what I do feels right to me, then I'm afraid I can't worry too much about what St Bethan thinks. The important thing is that I'm devoted to the children. I think they know that."

"Have you been here a long time?"

"I was born in Polvear. My father was the Methodist minister and we lived there until I was about five. After that we moved about – Southampton, London, York – that's the way it is, in the Methodist church – but I always spent holidays here and vowed I'd return one day. Then I met and married Jim. His parents ran the big hotel you can see over the river, the one towards the end of the point. They were quite old, nearing retirement, and we were in the process of taking over when Jim had his accident – "

"I heard about it. I'm so sorry."

"All that was twenty years ago. I went back to teaching, my first love. I had no stomach for the hotel without Jim. I taught in Truro and then Penzance and then, during the war when women were given a somewhat better crack of the whip than ever before, I took over this place. Temporarily, it was said, but I can't think they'll demote me now, though one never knows. The ways of the County Council defy understanding sometimes."

"So I believe." Deftly Rachel fielded a piece of soggy biscuit and wiped clean Tess's hands and mouth. "About the girl – " she reminded Mrs Laity.

"Yes, the girl. There is one who'll be leaving after Christmas. She loves helping with the little ones. Marlene Pengelly, her name is – "

"Heavens!"

"Don't hold it against her. She's a good girl and I think she might be interested. I'll talk to her, if you like. Sound her out."

"Would you? I'd be awfully grateful. The only thing is that I couldn't afford to employ her full time."

"That might just possibly be an advantage. Mrs Pengelly does bed and breakfast in the season and needs Marlene's help. I'll send her down for a chat and you can talk to her yourself. You'd like her, I think."

"But would she like me?"

"Why not? She's had plenty of experience with babies. She's the middle one of seven – not all of which, I am reliably informed, are the guaranteed progeny of Mr Pengelly, so there aren't any stones to throw."

Tess, who had been happily engaged with her biscuit and the few toys that Rachel had brought with her, now embarked on more adventurous exploration, crawling over the cushions to pull herself up on the settee.

"I'd better take her home," Rachel said, raising her voice above the crows of delight that were beginning to make conversation difficult.

"She's an awfully good baby," Mrs Laity said. "But how on earth you manage to work, I can't imagine. Do you ever get out in the evening?"

Rachel shook her head as she got to her feet to gather up Tess and the toys. "That's when I work – when Tess is asleep. Anyway, I haven't anywhere to go out *to*."

"Then come here – please do!" Mrs Laity, seeing that Rachel was intent on leaving stood up too and began helping with the clearing-up process. "Leave the work, just for once. I'm having a few friends round for a meal next Saturday. You'd like them, I think. It won't be wildly exciting – just pleasant chat. Marlene would sit in for you, I'm sure. Do say you'll come!"

"I – I think I'd like that very much." Rachel spoke hesitantly, but with dawning pleasure. She had felt instantly drawn to the schoolmistress despite the age difference between them and was glad to think that she, too, was not averse to pursuing the friendship. "Yes, I'd love to come, if Marlene really will look after Tess for me. Thank you very much for asking me, Mrs Laity."

"The name's Emma," Mrs Laity said.

"And mine's Rachel."

Emma Laity laughed aloud.

"I know," she said.

She would, of course, Rachel thought as she went back down the hill towards Gull Cottage. St Bethan was like that, and there was nothing to be done but accept the fact.

She couldn't settle to her writing that evening; couldn't, somehow, think of the right words. Which was, she told herself, just plain daft when she knew, more or less, what she wanted to say. Surely it wasn't the prospect of a night out that had put her in such a turmoil? She swore and tore yet another page out of the typewriter. Why couldn't she write? Where now was all that tranquillity she had boasted about to Nancy?

She sighed and put her head between her two hands.

She knew perfectly well why all inspiration had deserted her. It was because of the letter she had received from her mother a couple of days before, redirected from London. She'd put it behind the clock on the mantelpiece, promising herself that she would reply to it as soon as she had a free moment. So far that moment hadn't arrived and meanwhile the sight of the letter seemed to accuse her more with every passing hour.

It had carried, understandably, a plaintive note.

'I know things go astray. Your father had a letter from his bank in London yesterday posted four months ago. Still, I can't help worrying. It really is such a long time since we heard – not since the marvellous news about your book. Daddy and I are so proud of you – I tell everyone about my daughter who is an author! I'm sure

155

you're busy, but we long for more up-to-date news. Please write soon.

'It seems now that we are unlikely to get home before March at the earliest. *Such* a long wait, but of course you know your father – everyone else has to go before he can get away! 'Twas ever thus. I can't tell you how I'm looking forward to seeing you again. Little did we know, when we said goodbye at Mombasa in 1939, that it would be 1947 before we were all together again! Such a long, long time. What a lot has happened to us and to the world.'

Indeed, indeed, thought Rachel, abandoning the book as a lost cause. She made up the fire with some driftwood she had found on the beach and sat beside it, staring into the flames with her chin in her hand.

She knew she would have to reply. It was sheer cowardice to dodge the issue like this – but oh, there was so much at stake! Should she string them along for a bit longer? Tell them that she had rented out her house in London and come to live in Sylvia's cottage to write her next book? Maybe that's what she'd do. Once they were here and could see Tess in the flesh, it would all be a great deal easier.

On the other hand, was it fair? Nancy had always urged her to tell – said it was wrong to hide the truth from them. If only she could be sure of their reaction!

They were proud of her, her mother had said. They boasted about her. Would they still be proud of her when they knew the truth?

Hardly! They'd be ashamed and disgusted. Her mother might say it was no more than she expected, given the perverse way Rachel had behaved in Uganda, the unsuitable friends she had insisted on associating with. Not for them the apportioning of blame elsewhere.

Not like the Rossiters.

"*Damn* the Rossiters! If it were not for them – " Abruptly she got up, went to the kitchen, made tea, then brought the cup back to the armchair beside the fire.

If only she knew for certain that her parents loved her, that they wouldn't turn their backs on her. What a complicated business it was, she thought miserably, this parent–child relationship! Surely, if there was one thing that was proved beyond doubt it was her strength and independence; she could never have got anywhere without it. Yet their love and their forgiveness mattered so much. She supposed it always would.

There were times in the past when she'd fought with her mother, times when they'd said unforgivable things to each other. On the surface they were forgotten, smoothed over; but had they left rancour behind them? Alannah had always said –

Damn Alannah! Why had Rachel let those sly little remarks get under her skin? They were only made to show the superiority of all things pertaining to the Rossiters. Why, knowing that, had they affected her so much, and still affected her? They don't love you, she'd said. How could they, when they send you away like this?

It wasn't true. She was certain it wasn't true. And yet – and yet –

Oh God, what was she to do?

The tea, forgotten, cooled on the table beside her.

Into her mind, suddenly, came the memory of that awful time; that long-ago September of 1937. She'd felt sure of her mother's love then. When she'd needed her more than she had ever done before in the whole of her life, her mother hadn't hesitated. She'd come flying halfway round the world to her rescue. She'd taken on Miss Scrimgeour and the whole of St Ursula's in a way that, even now, provoked amusement and admiration. She'd been on Rachel's side then, all right. Blood had proved thicker than water.

Dare she hope that it was still the same?

She couldn't think what her mother was doing there. This was school – the san, she realised dazedly, looking around at the white-walled room with the four beds, one in each corner. She'd been here twice before, once when she'd had flu, once when she'd broken her ankle. But this time? She couldn't remember being ill or hurting herself.

Gradually a picture emerged and she remembered. She remembered the uncontrollable weeping, and Miss Spalding's consternation. She remembered Miss Scrimgeour's flushed face and her unconvincing concern. She remembered faces, hundreds of faces, staring at her.

"You had a little breakdown," her mother said gently.

Rachel stared at her.

"You mean I went potty?"

"Not at all. The doctor explained it to me, and he'll explain it to you if you're well enough to take it in. There was just too much for you to bear all at once."

The Rossiters, Red Rosie, Julia. She remembered it all and was conscious of the dull weight of sadness, and of bewilderment, too.

"You came home because of me?" The thought was astonishing. Her mother had always seemed so far away, so unreachable.

"I flew! Just imagine! I came Imperial Airways – oh, such an adventure, I can't tell you, and so quick. Only five days, door to door – can you imagine it? Miss Scrimgeour phoned Grandma, and seemed in such a state about you that Grandma cabled us to tell us you were ill, and I couldn't bear not to come just as quickly as I could. Daddy's coming later by sea. We were due for leave anyway in four months."

"How long have I been ill?"

It had been almost three weeks, she learned with astonishment. More than sufficient for her mother to take an intense dislike to Miss Scrimgeour, Miss Spalding, Matron and everything pertaining to St Ursula's. Her intention, Rachel gleaned over the next few days, was to take her away from school at the earliest possible time sanctioned by the doctor.

"I'm not leaving you here with that woman," she said forcefully. "I've told her you're not coming back, and she can whistle for her next term's fees in lieu of notice. If she makes a song and dance about it, I'll report her to the Headmistress's Conference, or whatever it is, and write to *The Times*. I blame her entirely for what happened to you."

"Where are we going, then? Not Warnfield? Please not Warnfield!"

"Certainly not. We're going to rent a little place in the country somewhere. I'm arranging it with an agency – it's all in hand. Then we'll all go back the long way, round the Cape."

No Oxford, then. No university at all. Rachel felt too tired to argue, far too lethargic to do anything but accept the plans that others had made for her. And if the truth were to be told, she had no enthusiasm now for study. The thought of seeing Africa again seemed the first good thing that had happened for a long time; she craved it, hungered for it, could see it in her mind's eye as bright and as colourful as on the day she had left it and it called to her now like a comfortable, undemanding womb that she longed to re-enter. If anything could heal the hurt inside her, then it was the sight of Lake Victoria, gleaming blue in the sunlight. She felt quite sure of it.

"Oh, I'm so glad," she said, more enthusiastic than she had been about anything for some time past.

The place in the country where they spent the next eight months proved to be twenty miles distant from Warnfield, which Kitty Bond considered far enough from her mother-in-law to be well outside daily contact, yet not so far as to prevent Ivor getting over to see her fairly frequently, once he arrived in England. April Cottage, the house they rented in a village not far from Aylesbury, was damp and rather cold, but though Kitty complained, Rachel barely noticed it.

It was a strange time; a limbo sort of time. Her grief did not lessen, exactly, but it grew manageable, helped in part by a wonderful letter she received from Julia's mother, full of comfort, asking her to stay at the Rectory just as soon as she felt fit enough.

It was a letter that filled her with admiration and astonishment – how *could* people go on believing in a merciful God when such awful things happened? – and she replied with gratitude. She knew, however, that the invitation was one she would never accept. Julia belonged to the past, to the St Ursula's-Red Rosie-Rossiter time, and though she would never forget her, Rachel knew instinctively that she had to move on, somehow.

She felt herself to be distanced from humanity as if nothing had the power to affect her very much. Sometimes she shopped with her mother in Aylesbury, and together they went to the cinema. There was no dissension then. She was meek and docile, like a small child. Afterwards, she could never remember much about the films they saw. She took walks in the country, borrowed books from the library, helped in the house. She smiled and was agreeable, arguing with no one, even when her father made reactionary political statements that would once have had her quoting Red Rosie at her reddest. Now nothing seemed to matter enough to risk rocking the boat.

She knew no young people locally, and did not want to know them. Sometimes she would see a group of them at the bus stop or cycling along the road and would hear them talking to each other. It was as if they spoke a foreign language, meaning nothing to her. She felt sad, bereft, no longer young, as if part of life she had once enjoyed was dead to her. Summer turned into autumn, and though she acknowledged the beauty of the golden woodlands which surrounded the village, she did not thrill to it as once she would have done.

Then suddenly, one day in early November, towards the end of their tenancy of April Cottage, right in the middle of watching Ronald Colman in *Lost Horizon* at the Regal Cinema, she felt an inexplicable irradiation, as if a light had been switched on. She lost the thread of the story, impatient with it and with herself. It was as if a commanding voice had said to her: 'OK, that's it, the mourning's over. There's a life out there waiting to be lived.' The rest of the film passed over her head for she was too occupied in thinking about her future to take it in. Suddenly she was restless, even excited. There were plans to be made.

A few days later she enrolled for typing lessons. She'd need to learn to type, she told her parents, if she was ever to write.

"Good idea," her father agreed heartily. "And who knows, you might find it useful in Uganda. I daresay there'll be some little voluntary job crying out for a typist."

If Rachel thought of Red Rosie who had been so scornful of using her time in this way – or, indeed, of Mrs Rossiter who had promoted typing skills with a fervour equal to her father's – she gave no sign of it. In the event, she rather liked her typing class. She found it strangely calming to sit banging out meaningless phrases in time to a wind-up gramophone, and was pleased that she seemed to show an aptitude for it, progressing through the exercises with gratifying speed.

Though she made no close friends among the other girls, she was on good terms with them and found it fun to exchange notes and measure progress, to commiserate and to giggle; and when a boy she had noticed about the village drew her into conversation at the bus stop and asked her to go to the pictures with him, she found herself agreeing to do so. He was quite nice, she told Kitty afterwards, but no, she didn't think she would bother to see him again.

The truth was, she still couldn't get Gavin out of her mind. He had been there all along, she realised, even though for a long time she had refused to acknowledge it. She longed for news of him. Was he safe? Was he well? Was he married? It was agony, not knowing.

There had been a letter from Barney waiting for her when she recovered from her breakdown, but it had been written three weeks earlier and contained no fresh news. She had not, somehow, been able to muster the energy to reply to it at the time, and had not done so since. Somehow the longer she left it, the more difficult it seemed to write at all, as is the way of such things.

Now, in her new no-nonsense mood, she sat down and wrote to him, saying that she had been ill but was now better and was looking forward to going to Uganda just after Christmas. How was everyone? she asked. And what was the news of Gavin?

Her mother, hearing the sharp bark of laughter with which

Rachel greeted Barney's reply, looked up enquiringly from reading her own letter, spectacles on the end of her shapely nose.

"What's the joke?" she asked. For a moment Rachel made no reply; then she shook her head.

"It's nothing," she said. "Nothing at all. I must fly – I'm late for my class."

On the bus to Aylesbury and her typing lesson, she read the letter again.

Gavin, Barney had written, never got to Spain. He went down with mumps a few days before the lorry was due to leave and had been far too ill to drive. By the time he'd recovered, disillusioned members of the International Brigade were already trickling back with stories of maladministration and muddle, and he had thought better of the whole enterprise. He'd managed to get a good degree, and the engagement still seemed to be on, though Mrs Rossiter was much against it . . .

So it was all futile, all that upset. Seeing nothing of the countryside, Rachel stared out of the bus window. If she'd just kept her mouth shut, she thought bitterly, how differently things would have worked out. She would still have the Rossiters – but did she want them, now that she had seen them in their true colours? The sight of Mrs Rossiter, distraught and accusatory, deaf to reason, not kind any more, was almost as great a shock as any other she had sustained. Mr Rossiter, too, who had always seemed so warm and friendly, had proved a broken reed. He'd known she was innocent and had seen the distress she was suffering, but could only see things from his own point of view. It would have cost him so little, she thought now, to stand up for her.

And Alannah – how quick she had been to turn on her! Past friendship had appeared to mean nothing. She was better off without them.

She wouldn't write any more, she decided, now that she knew Gavin was safe and still engaged to Jacqueline. She would forget them, cut them out of her life, look forward instead of back. She tore the letter into small pieces and deposited it in a convenient litter bin in Aylesbury High Street.

There was the voyage to look forward to now. They were going round the Cape, so she'd see Table Mountain, and the beaches of Durban, and Lourenço Marques, and Dar es Salaam. Magical names, all leading home.

The Rossiter days were over, she said to herself. Africa was waiting.

10

The supper party at Emma Laity's house was a great success. Rachel, who agonised for some considerable time over what to wear, finally settling on a multi-coloured wool skirt and black sweater enlivened by Grandma's amber beads, realised from the moment of arrival that she needn't have worried unduly. Emma's friends were clearly a fairly motley assortment, characterised not by their style but by their entertainment value.

Conversation was lively. It encompassed the deeds of the Labour Government, which member of it one would least like to entertain for a long weekend, Jean-Paul Sartre, the magnificence of the St Bethan Male Voice Choir, the possibility of civil war in India and the awfulness of Izzy Pollard, among other things. There were strong opinions, much argument, and a great deal of laughter, and at the end of it Rachel felt as if a door had opened on a world she had all but forgotten.

It was in the middle of a conversation with a mild, bespectacled teacher from Truro called Derek on the subject of post-Butler education that she found her attention wandering. It wasn't that the topic was dull; far from it. It was simply that suddenly she wasn't enjoying herself any more.

Tess never woke at night unless she was ill or teething. But suppose, just this once, she did? Suppose she had a nightmare? After all, it was surely possible for a baby to have a nightmare. The world must be full of frightening things – buses and cars and aeroplanes. Well, not buses in St Bethan, perhaps, but other noisy things. Dogs. Seagulls. Seagulls could make the most terrifying noise when they put their minds to it.

She found herself unable to concentrate on Derek any more, though she presented a listening mask towards him.

Suppose Tess woke up and found only a stranger to comfort her? Marlene seemed a nice enough girl, bright and competent, but hardly more than a child herself. Would she know what to do in an emergency? Suppose the house burnt down?

"I think," she said to Derek – but gently, because he looked the kind of man who could be easily hurt – "I ought to go home now. I'm a bit worried about my baby."

"Oh?" He looked confused. "I hadn't realised – I mean, I didn't think you were – "

Married, he meant. Rachel smiled at him, but made no explanations. She would leave all that to Emma.

"I'm sure you're worrying unduly," Emma said as she escorted her to the door.

"I expect I am. I hope I am. Emma, it's been a lovely party. I had a wonderful evening."

"In spite of the untimely departure?"

"In spite of. Forgive me. I know I'm being a neurotic idiot."

"That's right," Emma said; but she laughed sympathetically as she spoke and Rachel knew she understood and that the dawning friendship had not suffered.

"Emma, come and see me, won't you?" she said.

"You can count on it."

In spite of her sudden panic, Rachel had indeed enjoyed the evening and could only agree with Emma, when she found Tess sound asleep in her cot, that her sudden flight had been unnecessary. She would have to be on her guard against being foolishly over-protective, she told herself, and a complete bore into the bargain.

It was therefore rather ironical that only the following day she should lay herself open to criticism regarding her care of Tess.

It happened in the afternoon. She had desperately needed a fresh supply of typing paper – a commodity unobtainable in St Bethan, but available, so she was told, from the newsagents in Polvear. Accordingly she put Tess in her pram immediately after lunch and went over the river on the ferry.

She had been in Polvear only twice before, and though it was a cold November afternoon, she enjoyed walking through the narrow streets, looking at the unfamiliar shops and the attractive architecture of the small port. Compared to St Bethan, it seemed a veritable metropolis.

Tess quickly fell asleep which meant that Rachel could browse in peace. She spent a happy half hour in the bookshop, bought some vegetables from the greengrocer which looked a great deal fresher than those offered by Izzy Pollard, and stood for a moment on the quay. A man was rowing, his oars gleaming silver as they rose and fell; and slowly, almost majestically, a cargo boat with an unfamiliar flag slid past the quay, on towards the loading dock a little further up-river. Throughout all, Tess slumbered peaceably, not even disturbed by the noise of the ferry when finally Rachel decided it was time they were getting back to St Bethan.

The village, seen from this perspective, seemed almost deserted, with only a few black match-stick figures standing about the quay waiting for the ferry to return to Polvear. There was no colour now. The river was slatey-grey, and grey, too, the cottages that looked as if they had hunkered down to wait for spring. A few lights had already appeared, piercing the gathering gloom of the afternoon.

Rachel thought of the busy London streets, the press of people on the tube, and regretted nothing. This was beginning to feel like home.

The man who ran the ferry helped her lift the pram out on to the quay; and still Tess slept. Rachel took a deep breath. The hill leading up to Gull Cottage was steep, particularly down here on its lower slopes, and it needed an effort to get under way. As she passed Izzy Pollard's shop she paused. The rations weren't due until the following day, but they might be in stock already. If so, and she could pick them up now, then it would save a trip tomorrow.

There were two steps up to the shop – always difficult with the pram. She wouldn't be more than a minute, she thought, and Tess would be perfectly safe outside.

She was less than that, for the rations were not in stock. Impossible not to think that Izzy Pollard took delight in saying so, she thought, turning back towards the door.

To her horror, she saw that the pram was moving downhill. With a cry she leapt for the door, only to run full tilt into a woman who was already on the step.

"The pram! My baby!" Almost incoherent, she pushed the woman aside and rushed out into the street where already the pram was gathering momentum on its short, steep journey towards the quay.

She had never run so fast, never felt such panic. There seemed no one about to halt its progress; only the ferry, now leaving the quay, the faces of its passengers, like circles of white paper, turned towards the land and the flying pram.

Then suddenly, out of nowhere, a tall thin figure materialised, grabbed the pram and brought it to a halt. Still Rachel ran.

"Oh, thank God!" she sobbed. "Thank God."

The man who held the pram watched her approach. He was breathing hard, and his face, she saw as she came close to him, seemed contorted by extreme emotion, his teeth clenched as if in anger. She'd seen him about the village before, she realised, but had no idea who he was. She had thought him odd, different, with his pale, thin, unsmiling face. He was always alone, always dressed in an old Navy-surplus donkey jacket.

"Thank you," she said, reaching out to take the handle of the pram. "Thank God you were there!"

"What is it you think of?" His words, uttered in broken English, seemed to be flung at her like a handful of pebbles. He was shaking, she saw; as she was herself. "Are you mad woman? Why do you not take care of your child?"

"The brake was on. I don't know what happened."

"Is not on now! You have no right to have baby. Perhaps your child drown, if I am not here!"

Tess had begun to cry. Rachel lifted her out of the pram and held her close.

"You think I don't know that?" Angry herself now, and still shocked at the near-accident, Rachel was close to tears. "If you don't mind letting go of the pram," she said, her voice trembling, "I'll take my baby home now. Thank you again."

Without a word the man swung round and strode off across the quay, in the direction of a small shipyard that had recently re-opened after being closed throughout the war.

Others had collected now, and all were sympathetic, ready with words of comfort.

"Don't take no notice of ee, the bloody foreigner! 'Tis they brakes," said a man whom Rachel recognised as a fisherman, always about the quay. "They'm not like the pre-war ones. Proper ramshackle, they are."

"'Twasn't your fault, my 'andsome," said a woman who had come out of one of the nearby cottages. "The very same thing happened to me when my Jackie was a tacker. Is the little maid all right?"

"Right as rain," Rachel said. "Better than I am, I think. She was startled by the shouting, that's all."

She refused the kindly woman's offer of a cup of tea on the grounds that she wanted to get Tess home as soon as possible; and more shaken by the strange man's anger than she cared to admit, she once more pushed the pram up the hill towards home, the mood of well-being that she had experienced on the ferry now thoroughly dissipated.

She made up the fire and sat before it, rocking Tess against her shoulder, a prey to agonies of guilt. Not fit to be a mother, she thought. The wretched man was right! But she had put the brake on, she *had*, she was sure of it!

Tess, quite recovered, gurgled contentedly, and slowly Rachel's fears subsided. She couldn't get the stranger's words out of her mind, however, and at intervals – throughout Tess's bath time, giving her a bottle, tucking her into her cot – they continued to accuse her.

Not fit to be a mother. And, with that letter still unwritten, not fit to be a daughter, either. All in all, it had been some time since she had felt so low in her own estimation.

Emma called the next afternoon.

"Are you all right? I heard about what happened. Betty Pearce told me."

"Who? Oh!" Of course, Rachel thought. Betty Pearce was the wisht little soul, pale as a whitewashed wall according to Mrs Hoskings, who had been one of the passengers waiting for the ferry as she left it, and therefore one of those on the boat who had looked so helplessly towards the near-disaster. "Yes, we're fine," she assured Emma. "Tess was all right in no time, but I seem to have taken a bit longer. Do come in! I couldn't be more pleased to see anyone."

She made tea, recounting the event as she did so for Emma's benefit.

"Who is that man?" she asked as they both settled down by the fire. "He looked as if he would take great pleasure in tearing me limb from limb. I quailed before him!"

"Tall, and rather cadaverous?"

"That's the one! I've seen him once or twice, always alone and always wearing that awful jacket. He went off towards Carthew's Yard."

"That's the Pole," Emma said. "Stefan Something. No one can pronounce his last name."

"What's he doing here?"

"Working at the shipyard. I don't know much more about him than you do." Emma laughed. "You'd better ask the fount of all knowledge – Mrs Hoskings!"

"I will," said Rachel.

The conversation turned to the recent party, and to Marlene.

"She's agreed to come after Christmas," Rachel said. "I'll manage till then. She's going to work in the Neptune Cafe in Polvear in the afternoons, so it couldn't be better. She's a dear little thing, isn't she? And so sensible! When I think of myself at the age of fourteen – "

"She'll be fifteen next month."

"She seems much older. I think we'll get on very well."

"She seems to have fallen for Tess already," Emma said. "Which, I have to confess, is a fairly easy thing to do."

"You're going to warn me now about being over-protective and over-anxious," Rachel said, laughing at her. "Maybe I should get you and Stefan Whatsisname together. You'd cancel each other out."

"I'd be terrified, if what you tell me about him is true! I wonder why he's come to St Bethan? There's a story behind it, mark my words."

"Which you will ferret out?"

"Hm. I take exception to 'ferret'. Investigate is better."

"Investigate, then," Rachel agreed, laughing.

Conversation between them seemed to flow, easy and unstrained.

"Look," Rachel said at last. "I must give Tess her bath and bottle now – "

Emma jumped to her feet immediately.

"Heavens, how the time has gone! I had no idea it was so late. I must be off."

"Oh, do you have to go? Stay for pot luck! I'll rustle something up once Tess is in bed."

Emma, looking at her, saw her need and sat down again. Rachel, she recognised, needed company, needed to talk – and there was, really, nothing to make her rush home to the schoolhouse at the top of the hill.

"Well, if you're sure," she said.

With Tess duly bathed and fed, a more ordered, peaceful atmosphere descended on Gull Cottage. The 'something' that Rachel rustled up proved to be toasted cheese and baked beans – a repast that she surveyed, as she placed it before Emma, with an expression of disgust tinged with resignation.

"What a nerve, to give you something like this," she said, taking her place at the table. "Could you pretend it's lobster, do you think?"

"I'd really rather pretend it's smoked salmon, if it's all the same to you. I'm allergic to shellfish."

"Whichever. I suppose the day will dawn when we'll be able to indulge ourselves – though you don't appear to do too badly, judging from the spread you prepared the other night. I made an absolute pig of myself."

"That was the object of the exercise. I have a tame farmer in my power, you see. By the grace of God, I managed to get his far-from-bright son through his grammar school entrance, and he seems to feel in my debt for evermore. I'll bring you some bacon and eggs for your breakfast next time I come."

"How wonderful! My stomach's rumbling at the very thought." Rachel took a forkful of toasted cheese. "D'you know what I crave more than anything?" she said. "A slice of paw-paw! In Uganda we had it every day for breakfast, all pink and dewy, with a slice of lime and a touch of sugar. I would have killed for it when I was pregnant."

"I've never tasted it; never travelled at all. I've always longed to, though. Africa, in particular, has always held a great fascination for me. I envy you, being brought up there. You must know it in a way mere visitors can never do."

"Know it?" Rachel shook her head regretfully. "Oh no, Emma. I didn't know it at all. I loved it – or thought I did – but we lived a strange, detached kind of life in our little European enclave. It wasn't Africa. That was somewhere at a distance, red in tooth and claw, violent and pulsating and totally incomprehensible to us."

"You couldn't have been aware of that as a child, surely?"

"No," Rachel said thoughtfully. "No, I wasn't. But later I was – and I could never live there again."

"How old were you when you went back?"

Rachel smiled.

"I was seventeen," she said. "Younger and greener and more innocent than any girl has a right to be." She laughed a little. "It was a million years ago, Emma. Thinking of it, it all seems to have happened to someone else."

"Youth viewed in retrospect always seems like that."

"I suppose so. By the time I came back – " She paused, memories crowding in.

"You were older and wiser?" Emma suggested.

Rachel laughed again.

"Well, older, anyway. Look, do finish the beans. They'll only go to waste."

"Is there any more of that delicious smoked salmon?" Emma asked.

★

Empire. The dressing for dinner, the protocol, the dropping of calling cards – Rachel was astounded at the importance her mother placed on such rituals considering her nonconformist attitude when on leave in Warnfield.

"Do we have to?" she asked when her mother mentioned the necessity of signing the book at Government House, and was quite taken aback at the vehemence of her reply.

"Well, of course we have to," Kitty said explosively. "Honestly, you are a little goose, Rachel! You want to be asked to things, don't you? You don't want to be a social pariah? What on earth would one do in this place if one weren't asked to things?"

It was all too, too Jane Austen-ish, Rachel thought with lofty amusement; and if this had been all there was to Entebbe, then she would have been bored to tears in a week, as bored as her mother had been in Warnfield. But there was a great deal of fun to be had, too – and she needed fun. She seemed to have been starved of it for a long time and she rushed with open arms to embrace it, happily dancing at the Club until dawn lightened the sky over the lake, and agreeing, rather diffidently, to take the part of Edwina, the *ingénue* young sister of the heroine, in a somewhat insipid comedy called *Skylarks in Suburbia*.

This involved a considerable number of entrances through french windows, tennis racquet swinging, but mercifully few lines to speak. Somewhat to her amazement, despite doubts induced by the memory of her stage debut at Clearwater which still had the power to make her blush, she found herself able to manage the undemanding part quite adequately. The rest of the cast, being kindly disposed towards the young newcomer, had no hesitation in telling her so.

Her self-esteem burgeoned. She found it easier now to converse with her elders at dinner parties; she even flirted a little, taking discreet lessons from her mother who was adept in the art. Most amazing of all, she allowed herself to submit to golf lessons from a handsome young Administrative Officer called Clifford Bailey, whose hands lingered over hers as he demonstrated the correct grip.

Clifford Bailey was a young man considered by the matrons of Entebbe to be the answer to any maiden's prayer. Such a *nice* young man, they all agreed. The Bond gel would be doing well for herself if she could get him to the altar.

The Bond gel, after a steamy session in Clifford's car one moonlit night, thought differently. Kissing was acceptable. Rachel was getting a considerable amount of practice at it these days and felt, modestly, that she was now quite good at it and could possibly show Barney Rossiter a thing or two. However, the kind of insistent, intrusive, even painful fumbling that Clifford had considered appropriate was something different, even frightening. He had ignored her demands to be taken straight home, ridiculed her prudery, accused her of leading him on and giving him the wrong signals. She hadn't know how to deal with it, how to emerge from the situation with any self-respect; and the whole incident had shown her how ridiculously inexperienced she still was, how totally at sea in her dealings with the opposite sex.

The awful thing was that, though she had struggled and fought against him, there was no denying that, in retrospect, she'd found the whole incident exciting in a weird kind of way. Which was pretty despicable, because the truth of the matter was that not only was she *not* in love with Clifford, but she didn't even like him very much, winning smile and golf lessons notwithstanding. Quite apart from his venom at her rejection which had been unattractive in the extreme, she had discovered a mean and arrogant streak, well hidden by the surface charm, that was positively repellent.

Perhaps the whole thing was her fault, after all. Had she, in the phrase that was so often bandied about among the matrons of Entebbe, 'led him on'? Oh, why did everything have to be so confusing? How did people like Diana manage, flirting as they did with a dozen different young men at once?

"Don't give him another thought," Paula Garfield said comfortingly, when Rachel confided in her. "He's not worth it. I've always thought him a slimy piece of work. Have you seen him sucking up to the bosses' wives? It's enough to turn anyone's stomach."

Paula, who had quickly become a friend, was one of the younger wives whose husband held a junior position in the Public Works Department. Kitty Bond regarded her with a great deal of dubiousness for that very reason. There was a definite pecking order among the various Government Departments, with the Secretariat – naturally – at the top and the PWD at the bottom.

"You know, you can't be too careful in this life," she said to Rachel. "I do wish you'd be warned by someone who knows a great deal more about society than you do."

"You're beginning to sound just like Grandma," Rachel said angrily.

It was not a remark calculated to please her mother, already put out by the ending of Rachel's friendship with Clifford and inclined to say so, over and over. Rachel, however, continued to see much of Paula, whom she liked better than anyone else she had so far met. She liked her commonsensical attitude to life, and her irrepressible, irreverent sense of humour. If it were not for Paula, she now realised, life in Entebbe, for all the fun, would be frightfully tedious, with acres of time lying vacant and unused. A kindred spirit made all the difference and now, more often than not, they spent their afternoons together at the swimming pool.

"Mummy is absolutely maddening," Rachel confided to Paula when she had been in Entebbe for a full six months. "She always wants to know everything. Honestly, I had more freedom at school."

"You'd feel upset if she didn't care what you did."

Rachel sighed, but admitted the truth of this.

"Yes, I suppose so." She was silent for a few moments. "We seemed such friends in England," she went on. "Well, we're still friends a lot of the time. She can be so much fun when she wants to. But now all she seems to think of is finding me a suitable husband. *Why*, for heaven's sake?"

"She hasn't got enough to do," Paula said. "Planning a wedding would be marvellous entertainment. Or maybe she's jealous. Perhaps she wants to see you settled, out of harm's way."

"That's nonsense," Rachel said; but it was an echo of Judy's remark on board ship, and it made her uneasy. Surely it couldn't be true? Mothers weren't like that. Or shouldn't be. She was silent for a moment, then sighed heavily. "It's such a shame," she said. "For years I've longed and longed to come back to Entebbe, but now I'm here, my mother and I seem to do nothing but argue."

"Maybe you should try to find some kind of job – "

"I have. There isn't one."

"Well – " Paula hesitated. "Should you really be here, then? Look, this may sound like unwarranted interference, but I think you're wasting your time. You ought to be out in the real world – learning something, living life, not sitting here letting it all roll by. But until then, cheer up and think of the good things. After all, it's a beautiful place, the climate is wonderful, we have servants so that entertaining is easy – which reminds me! You're going to accuse me of match-making now, but I promise you I'm not! There's a chap from up-country coming down for a short spell. His name's Tom Whitcroft and he's going to be working for Bob for the next few months. Priscilla and Brian Martin are coming to dinner on Saturday night to meet him. Will you come too, to make up the numbers? He's a bit of a rough diamond, Bob says, but an interesting chap. Intelligent. I haven't met him yet, but he sounds the sort you

173

might enjoy talking to. Do say you'll come. I swear I'm not match-making!"

"You'd better not be." Rachel's fierceness was merely assumed, for the implied compliment hadn't been lost on her. She smiled at Paula, happy again. "Thank you," she said. "I'd love to come."

She found refuge in her journal that night.

'I can't help wondering what Red Rosie would say about this life I'm leading,' she wrote. 'It seems so purposeless, somehow. I've offered myself for Good Works, but nobody needs me, and I've read nothing worthwhile for ages. I hereby resolve to take myself in hand.'

In England, Mr Chamberlain flew back from Berchtesgaden, with his death's-head smile and his winged collar and his umbrella, to announce to the populace that he brought 'peace for our time'.

It was quite like old times, Rachel thought, as she listened to Tom Whitcroft holding forth at the Garfield's dinner table the following Saturday. He was a wireless buff, a great listener to the BBC, and utterly contemptuous of Neville Chamberlain and his policy of appeasement.

"He caved in," he said, his thin dark face showing his disgust. "Gave Hitler everything he wanted – and the Czech representative wasn't allowed to say a word. Nor was Russia. The poor bloody Czechs were just sold down the river – "

"Rubbish," snapped Priscilla Martin. She was a blonde vivacious girl with a wicked gift for mimicry, star of the Dramatic Society. She was also a notorious flirt, but had clearly not found it worthwhile going into action for Tom. "Nobody wants war."

"Have you looked at a map recently?" Tom asked her derisively. "The Rhineland's remilitarized to the west. Now Germany's snatched the Sudetenland to the east. If you imagine the threat's over, all I can say is there's none so blind as those who won't see."

And because of his accent – the accent, in Priscilla's view, of comedians and men with daft grins who played ukeleles – they were words that she garnered and relished and improved upon; so that 'Noon so blaind as them as worn't see' became a catchphrase, bandied about among the younger set long after Tom Whitcroft had returned to his home station at Masaka.

It was, of course, the accent that did for him as far as Kitty was concerned – that and the fact that he had, as she told Rachel after the first and only time that he came to the house, a working-class face. In vain did Rachel say that he was intelligent and had opinions she found interesting; her mother continued to assure her that she was committing social suicide by continuing to associate with such an impossible young man.

Rachel set her lips stubbornly and continued to enjoy Tom's company, not admitting even to herself that her mother's opposition in any way increased his appeal. He was interesting, she said – a whole lot more interesting than most of the people she was forced into conversation with at all the dinner parties she had to attend. Her mother should be glad, she insisted, that she'd met someone who at least encouraged her to find out what was going on in the world, and to read the more serious magazines that arrived spasmodically in large, out-of-date bundles.

Few others in Entebbe seemed to share Tom's disquiet. Did Gavin, Rachel wondered? Was he even now burning with righteous zeal on behalf of the Czechs, just as he had done for the Spanish Nationalists? And had he joined the RAF yet? He would, she felt sure, at the first opportunity – unless, of course, his fiancée talked him out of it. Or was she his wife by this time? She'd had no news of him since leaving England. Grandma wrote from time to time, but she made no mention of the family next door and Rachel was too proud to ask.

Oh, you fool, she said to herself. Stop thinking about him! It wasn't as if she loved him any more, was it?

Who would have thought that the Spring Ball would have been the catalyst that brought everything to a head? It started so innocently – a celebration of spring, Kitty told Rachel, with the Club decorated with garlands of spring flowers (paper flowers, of course) and a collage of skipping lambs and fluffy chicks all over the walls, and a competition for the best Easter bonnet.

"What's that got to do with Uganda?" Rachel asked.

"That's hardly the point. We're English."

"Mrs McTavish isn't. Nor Mrs Muir."

"British, then. Don't be absurd, Rachel! Anyway, we're going to start making the flowers next week. That'll be fun, won't it? It'll give you something to do."

"Mummy, I can't! I'm useless at that sort of thing."

"Well, you can cut out, or something."

"Over my dead body," Rachel said. "Honestly, I've never heard of anything more futile."

"What on earth has got into you?" Kitty's eyes were blazing. "There's no pleasing you these days. You seem to enjoy being as contrary as you know how."

It wasn't true, Rachel thought, as her mother swept angrily off the verandah. She didn't really enjoy much about Entebbe these days. It all seemed so petty and time-wasting and pointless. Take this so-called Spring Ball, for example. What did springtime mean to anyone in Entebbe? What on earth would the Africans make of it?

The stewards at the Club, in their long white khanzus and their red fezzes, watched everything that went on with flat, opaque, unreadable eyes. The plays, the reviews, the skits, the dances; the drinking, the flirting; the mighty Europeans with their hair down. What did they think – *really* think?

Nobody cared. Oh, people cared about building roads and schools and hospitals, about tending the sick and administering justice and planting trees and husbanding the land. They cared on a grand, cosmic scale.

Perhaps, Rachel thought, it was different for those who lived close to the people; the District Officers who administered justice and were witness to the daily struggle for existence. Perhaps they became more intimately involved. But here, in Entebbe, it sometimes seemed as if Africans did not exist as individuals but only as a crowd of film extras.

That night at dinner, with her father recently back from one of his up-country safaris, she ventured to voice some of these thoughts.

"I was thinking about the boys," she said. (Boys? Juma was old enough to be her father – even grandfather! Did he mind that he and his kind were called boys? Why hadn't it struck her before that to do so was ludicrous? Maybe she would ask Melika about it. She saw her quite often and sometimes sat with her under the huge tree on the greensward where the children played.)

"What about the boys?" Kitty asked. She sounded wary, clearly prepared for more criticism of her way of life.

"I was thinking that we are just like the Victorians, aren't we? They treated their servants as if they were somehow of lesser importance, without the same feelings and emotions as the upper classes. We're the same with the Africans."

Kitty gave a gasp of outraged laughter.

"Rubbish!" she said. "They wrap us all around their little fingers. The whole household revolves around Juma. I bend over backwards to please him. With what result? This very day he's told me he has to go back to Mbale to bury his father – *again*! That's the third time to my certain knowledge."

"Are you going to let him go?"

"Well, of course I am. I don't want to lose him, do I? I'm just illustrating the point that they've got us where they want us. Juma had better be back by the Spring Ball, because I intend to take a party."

Rachel found her heart sinking. Who would have thought it? Once she would have been thrilled at the prospect; now everything had gone flat, as unexciting as Tizer without the bubbles. She knew exactly who would be invited, what they would talk about. Suddenly it seemed unendurable.

A few days later, when she was walking with her father in the cool of the evening, she nerved herself to speak of her feelings.

"I don't think I can stay much longer, Daddy," she said.

For a few moments he continued walking in silence. She glanced at him sideways. He looked sad, she thought. Disappointed. But not altogether surprised.

"I thought, perhaps, that this would give us all a chance to get to know each other," he said.

"But it has!" She took his arm, pressed close to him. "It's been lovely. It's what I needed *then*. But now – "

"Now it's claustrophobic?"

"Yes. That's it, exactly. I keep thinking, is this *it*? Mummy wants me to find a suitable man and settle down here – "

"I suppose we both want that, really."

"But it's not what I want. There must be something else in life! I'm bored stiff, Daddy, that's the truth of it. Anyway, what suitable man? There isn't one. I could die, waiting!"

"I doubt that. You're growing into a lovely young woman, Rachel."

"Hark to my proud and prejudiced father!"

"Do you have some sort of plan in mind?"

"I want to go back to England. To London. Alice is working there now, living with her Aunt Susan. I met her once, at school. She's awfully nice, and she says that I could live there too. She'd be glad of the money, Alice said."

"And if war comes?"

Rachel said nothing for a moment.

"It may not," she said. "But if it does, I'd rather be there. Oh Daddy, I *must* be there!"

"Yes." His voice was reflective. He understood, Rachel saw, rather to her surprise. She heard him sigh again.

"You know, Rachel," he said, "I've always loved my job, loved living here. It's always seemed to me something worth doing.

Don't dismiss all that we've done as unimportant, or self-seeking, or trivial. For me, it hasn't been like that."

"I know," she said softly.

"I can see that for the women, for the families, then it's different, though. I wonder, sometimes, if it's all been worth it – worth the separation and all the pressures of living this rather artificial life. I suppose one can never be sure. One can only hope that something is gained and not too much lost. I can't imagine any other life that could have been so rewarding for me."

"But you see how I feel?" she asked him.

"I do." He glanced at her sideways and gave a short and rueful laugh. "But don't expect your mother to," he said.

11

---

*A*lice's Aunt Susan lived in Shawcross Street, Chelsea, not too far from Sloane Square. Number 29 was tall and thin with a flight of steps to the front door and area steps to the basement. It looked, Rachel thought, a little forbidding – an impression enhanced rather than lessened by the fact that it was identical to all the other houses in the street, give or take the odd brass knocker or window-box. Even so, her heart swelled with excitement. This, after all, was the beginning of a new life.

"Gosh, I've missed London," she said to Alice as, having paid off the taxi that had brought her from Victoria, she stood on the pavement surrounded by her luggage, inhaling the mingled aromas of smoke and petrol, cat-soured earth and summer heat. A man, sorting through parcels at the back of a delivery van across the road, was whistling 'The Lambeth Walk'. The whole cocktail brought back the summer she had spent with Sylvia – not the loneliness, but the rewarding voyages of discovery she had embarked on with such determination and eventual enjoyment.

"The last time I saw you, you were missing Africa," Alice pointed out, not unreasonably. Rachel laughed, but attempted no explanations.

Inside the house she found a comfortable, untidy clutter; an elderly dark-red carpet covered the hall and stairs, and there were far too many coats on a stand. A tall Chinese vase contained umbrellas and two peacocks' feathers, a pile of books on the bottom stair waited to be taken up to a more permanent home, and just outside the kitchen door was a green felt board pinned with notes and telephone numbers and reminders. On this, a plain white foolscap sheet of paper stood out. Its bold black message read: 'Alice. Eric rang.'

"Oh!" Alice grinned and tore it down. She stuffed it into the pocket of her skirt, looking both pleased and embarrassed.

"Who's Eric?" Rachel asked. "You haven't told me about him."

"All in good time!" Alice tried to look mysterious, but giggled instead. She had lost much of her puppy fat, Rachel noticed, and seemed a great deal happier than when she was at school; her face, however, did not lend itself to mystery. It was round, almost childish still, her little rosebud mouth as vulnerable as ever.

"Come on," she said now. "I'll take you up to your room. Aunt Sue is out for the moment. You're up two flights, so we'd better leave the trunk in the hall and just take up the small cases. Someone will be around to help us later."

It was, Rachel found in the days that were to come, that sort of a household. Someone was usually around. The key was on a string and could be pulled through the front door letter-box, enabling out-of-work musicians, wives on the run from violent husbands, refugees from Nazi Germany, Members of Parliament in search of a kind word, any and all manner of people to gain entry and help themselves to friendship and a cup of tea. Aunt Susan worked in an Agency that liaised between refugees and the Home Office, and her circle of friends and acquaintances seemed enormous.

Eric was one such, Alice told Rachel on that first day, as she sat on the bed and watched her unpack.

"Aunt Sue met him at some political function. He wants to go into Parliament," she said.

"What party?"

"Oh, Labour, of course."

"There are others," Rachel pointed out.

"Not for Eric. He's very earnest – "

"Oh, dear!"

"Yes, well . . . I feel a bit guilty, really, because I confess I stop listening sometimes and just look at his mouth. And his chin. It's sort of pointed, with a cleft – "

"His mouth?"

"His chin, idiot! And the tip of his nose has a super way of moving downwards when he smiles. Not that he does very often. Honestly, politics are all very well and I know we have to have them, but you can get tired of them. There's an awful lot of them in this house, I can tell you. Oh Rachel, it's so wonderful to have you here! I've got to know a few girls at the College, but there's

180

no one who speaks the same language, no one I want to *do* things with, like go to theatres or the pictures, or anything."

Rachel turned and grinned over her shoulder.

"It will be fun, won't it?"

"If only Julia – "

"Yes," Rachel said flatly. The loss of Julia could still hurt so piercingly that, from time to time, it took her breath away. "Tell me about the College," she added, changing the subject. "Will I like it?"

Her father had decreed that typing on its own was woefully inadequate to meet the needs of business life, and she was to join Alice for three months to learn the intricacies of shorthand and bookkeeping.

"No, of course not. You're bound to hate it, the same as I do, but what's the alternative? Teaching? Nursing?"

"Sword-swallowing? Bareback riding? You'd think there'd be something, wouldn't you?"

"What happened to the writing?" Alice asked.

"It – simmers," Rachel said. "I've decided that what I need is Experience of Life."

"Didn't you get that in Entebbe?"

"A bit, I suppose. I learned I didn't belong there, anyway. But where do I belong? I don't know!"

"You have to Find Yourself," agreed Alice earnestly. Rachel could almost see the capital letters. "It's terribly important. Eric Found Himself when he discovered politics."

Rachel perceived that, for Alice, finding Eric had been important, too. She knew what it was like to have the urge to bring the beloved's name into the conversation at every opportunity and experienced a surge of affectionate sympathy.

"Well, good for Eric if he's managed it," she said. "What do you want to do with your life, Alice?"

Alice sighed wistfully.

"Get married eventually, of course. It's the only fulfilling thing for a woman, isn't it?"

"Is that what Eric says?" Rachel asked guardedly.

"It's what *I* say! But of course, Eric agrees."

He would, thought Rachel. She didn't think, somehow, that she was going to like Eric very much.

There was general amazement, not least from Rachel's grandmother, that she should be sent back to an England which, on all sides, was making preparations for war.

181

"I think your mother must have taken leave of her senses," Grandma said, setting the telephone wires buzzing with her outrage.

"You can't blame Mummy. She didn't want me to come, but I couldn't go on wasting my time there, Grandma. I had to get on with doing something. Daddy agreed with me. After all, they'll be home themselves early next year."

"Next year? Next *year*? We'll be at war long before then!"

"Nobody knows that for sure. It might be over by then. Or it might not happen."

"Your grandfather says it will. And then where will you be? It's a well-known fact that London will be bombed to bits in the first week."

This, indeed, was the current speculation. Trenches were being dug in Hyde Park, and air raid shelters delivered and installed in back gardens. People in Entebbe, Rachel was forced to admit, didn't know the half of it. She presented herself at the local Police Station to be given a gas mask, to bring her into line with the rest of the population who had been issued with them at the time of Munich, and in August, when she had been in London only a month, there was a trial blackout.

And in spite of it all, she wouldn't have missed a moment of it. She was frightened, but there was a thrill, too; the thrill of being part of it, right here in London, where the news was immediate and the discussion constant.

Aunt Sue, to the rest of the world, was Susan Greaves. Rachel had tried calling her Miss Greaves, until her look of astonishment prompted her to ask if she would prefer to be called Aunt Sue.

"Why not Susan?" she had replied. "That goes for you, too, Alice. It's what everyone else calls me. God knows you're big enough and old enough."

She was a small, olive-skinned woman with warm brown eyes and a big smile, her grey-streaked dark hair pulled back in a knot at the back of her head. She dressed carelessly in men's shirts and hand-woven skirts, but in spite of the fact that she spent the minimum possible time on herself, she had style. Rachel admired her from the first. She liked her casual warmth, the friendly, no-nonsense way she treated her many visitors, her lack of pretence. She was brisk and efficient and could mix a salad or make a toasted cheese sandwich faster than Rachel had ever seen before, but beneath the efficiency and the forthright manner there was real kindness.

The house had been left to her by an uncle she had cared for until he died, but there was no money for its upkeep beyond her inadequate salary, and she made no secret of the fact that she was glad of Rachel's contribution. There were two more empty bedrooms, but though she allowed some of the droppers-in to stay a night or two under exceptional circumstances, she refused to let any more rooms on a permanent basis.

"Not to any of this lot, anyway," she said privately to Rachel and Alice. "If I'm to share hearth and home, it has to be to someone who'll pay the rent. These, on the whole, are not good payers."

They were, however, excellent talkers. Rachel, listening avidly for echoes of Red Rosie, was astonished to find a remarkable unanimity among almost all of them. None of the old attitudes seemed relevant any more. The days of the Peace Pledge Union were over. The Nazis, it was generally agreed by everyone no matter what shade of politics they preferred, were evil; and a war, sooner or later, was inevitable.

Grandma, on the telephone, begged her to visit Warnfield 'before the balloon goes up'.

"There'll be no travel afterwards," she said dolefully. "Railway lines are bound to be the first target, mark my words."

Though not everyone shared Mrs Bond's apocalyptic view of wartime Britain, it was true that no one knew what to expect. Sylvia, whom Rachel attempted to contact by telephone for courtesy's sake, had elected to stay on in Cornwall after her summer holiday.

Rachel dreaded going to Warnfield, dreaded the possibility of seeing any of the Rossiters. She knew nothing of their current doings. Grandma never mentioned them in her letters which, invariably, were concerned with items which she considered of more burning interest: namely, such matters as Doreen's insolence and her departure to work behind the sweets counter in Woolworths, and the vicar's distressing tendency to repeat everything three times, despite having been told, over and over, that his sermons were far too long.

Only once had the family figured, rather obliquely, in her litany of complaints. The grass verge outside The Laurels had, so Grandma wrote much earlier in the year, been 'ploughed up and totally ruined' by a car driven without due care and attention 'shooting like a rocket' out of the drive of the house next door. The driver, Grandma informed them, was apparently a friend of the Rossiters, an officer in the Royal Air Force, from whom, surely, more responsible behaviour was to be expected.

"Heaven help us all if he flies his plane in the same way as he drives his car," she wrote, adding with bitter sarcasm: "Who needs Hitler and his bombs when the RAF will devastate your property?"

"Three cheers for the boys in blue," Kitty had said as she handed over the letter for Rachel to read.

Rachel, equally unsympathetic, had spared little thought for Grandma's grass verge, but seized immediately on her mention of the RAF. It seemed to imply that Gavin had already joined, if the Rossiters were entertaining friends from the Service. Surely, surely, if he had married, even Grandma would have found it worthy of mention? Not that she personally cared if he were married six times over. It wasn't as if she was in love with him any more. Gavin Rossiter, she told herself, could do exactly as he liked, and good luck to him. She just would like to *know*, that was all.

It was the others – Alannah, Diana, Mrs Rossiter – she really dreaded seeing. Those last days in Warnfield had taken on the aspect of a nightmare, the participants grotesque and larger than life. The desolation she had felt then still made her feel hollow with grief.

"I'm a fool," she confided to Alice. "The chances of seeing them are remote. I'll go up next weekend."

"You can't! We're going out with Eric and Kenneth on Saturday."

"So we are." Rachel felt depressed. Nearly two months in London, and Kenneth was the only man who had asked her out – and that merely because he was Eric's friend and had been pressed into service to make up a foursome. He was an angular, awkward, bespectacled youth who tended towards Communism but was undergoing agonies of self-examination now that Stalin and Hitler had formed an unholy alliance. It did not make for lively social chitchat. "Do I have to?" she asked. "I don't think Kenneth likes me much."

"He does, I promise you. He told Eric. Anyway, you said you would and I can't cope with them both."

Rachel sighed. She didn't think Eric liked her much, either, and certainly she was not enamoured of him, finding him dull and pedantic and seeing little attraction in the cleft chin and strangely mobile nose that Alice found so fascinating. How inexplicable it was, this business of love. Alice was clearly enraptured, hanging on his every word, apparently oblivious to the self-importance and sheer egotism of his endless monologues. It was enough, she thought, to make any girl long for the spurious charm of a Clifford Bailey.

184

"All right, I'll come," she said, capitulating reluctantly. "But next weekend, I must go."

And she wrote on the notice board in the hall: 'Sept. 2nd and 3rd. Rachel in Warnfield.'

"Well," Grandma said, passing the cabbage. "Better late than never!"

She'd been saying it on and off ever since Rachel arrived on the train, which had been greatly delayed owing to the evacuation of children from London to the country. She was not, however, referring to the hour of the train's arrival, but to the fact that Rachel had been in the country two months before making the journey to Warnfield. This observation, in various forms, together with her remark concerning Rachel's inexplicable arrival in England at such a period in the country's history, had meant that there had hardly been time to talk of anything else. Now, as they sat at lunch, she produced the phrase once more just in case Rachel had not taken it in the first time.

"Now, now," Grandpa said jovially, wagging a finger at her. "Don't spoil things, Maisie. Rachel's here now, and very glad we are to see her. May this be the first of many visits."

"I hope so, Grandpa." Looking at him, Rachel felt, after all, a few pangs of guilt. He looked unexpectedly frail, his nose sharper, his flesh fallen away a little. Her grandmother, on the other hand, was unchanged, at least to the naked eye. Even the dress she wore was one that Rachel remembered well: small white leaves on a grey ground, with a white guipure modesty vest showing at the neck.

"It seems like only yesterday," Grandpa went on, "that you were here in your white blouse and gym slip! Such battles we had over the chessboard, didn't we?"

"You used to let me win."

"No, no. Well – " twinkling at her " – maybe sometimes, but only when you were very young. I soon learned to fight with the best." The light seemed to die out of his eyes. "And now we've a real fight on our hands, haven't we? That dreadful man – "

"Not Hitler, please. Not at the lunch table." Poland may have been invaded, diplomatic exchanges had reached crisis point, children were fleeing the cities, but the mention of the man who had caused all this chaos, Grandma implied, must not be allowed to sully a civilised meal. "Rachel dear, do tell me more about your father. He's so conscientious and works so hard, I can't help worrying about his health, especially in such a climate.

185

It's not as if – " she broke off sharply, cleared her throat. "More potatoes, dear?" she asked.

Not as if he has a wife who looks after him, she was about to say. Rachel could hear the words as clearly as if she had actually spoken them.

"Daddy's fine," she said. "And so is Mummy."

"Well, at least he's safe," Grandpa said. "He won't have to fight in this war."

"He'll *want* to." Grandma's eyes flashed belligerently. "He's not the kind to sit back and let others do the job. Last time he volunteered, Rachel, did you know that? He didn't wait to be called up. I was so angry – but proud too, of course, underneath it all. He looked a picture in his uniform." She sighed and shook her head reminiscently. "Saying goodbye to him at Warnfield station that last time was the hardest thing I've ever been called on to do."

"But he only went to Edinburgh," Grandpa pointed out, with a touch of amusement. "He was one of the lucky ones."

"We weren't to *know* that, were we?" Grandma reacted as if her son's patriotism had been impugned. "We weren't to know he'd be stuck in Scotland for the rest of the war. He obeyed orders, that's all, like everyone else. When I waved him off in that train, it could have been next stop Flanders."

"He would have been taking a somewhat eccentric route," Rachel remarked, in a neutral kind of voice.

Grandma looked at her pityingly. "Smile, Rachel, as much as you want to," she said. "You young people don't know what life's all about. You've no experience of the worry and the heartbreak – war's just excitement to you. Mark my words, you'll learn, you'll learn." She spoke almost as if this would be a process she, personally, would greatly relish – as if it were about time this generation suffered as hers had done. Rachel was conscious of a sudden chill, a goose walking over her grave.

"I expect we will, Grandma," she said.

Although it was warm, that afternoon and evening were spent indoors, making black-out curtains. Grandma had prudently bought a huge roll of black material when last in town – enough for Buckingham Palace, Rachel thought with a sinking of the heart when she first saw it – and together they measured and cut and sewed.

If Rachel had been called upon to nominate her least favourite way of spending an afternoon, sewing would probably have been top of the list. However, at least for the first hour or so, she was bolstered by a feeling of virtue, the consciousness that she was doing her bit, being of genuine help to her grandmother who, after all, had given her a home when nobody else would do so.

So she sewed with a good grace, and listened to Grandma's complaints about the vicar, and Miss Bickerstaffe of the haberdashery counter at Drake's Stores, who had promised to get in some navy ric-rac braid but had taken three weeks about it, and the boy from Hobbs Groceries who whistled in a particularly piercing and unmusical way, point-blank ignoring any requests to desist.

"What about the Rossiters?" she brought herself to ask at last. "Do you see anything of them these days?"

Grandma, busy with Rufflette tape, made a noise indicating disdain.

"As little of them as possible, thank you very much," she said. "If I'd known what sort of neighbours they'd be, I'd never have come to live here. Not content with ruining our grass verge with cars running out of control, it's been nothing but mess and noise around here for months. They've had some sort of elaborate air raid shelter built in their garden. There's been a lot of talk about it, actually. Of course, I'm not accusing them of using Council labour and Council materials, but you can imagine what's being said."

Rachel imagined; but not for long, for Grandma had further grievances.

"Mrs Rossiter is on some committee or other to do with billeting. She had the effrontery to call the other day to ask if I could accommodate three teachers from London, in case of wholesale evacuation. She said she didn't think I'd welcome children! I was put out, I don't mind telling you. What a thing to say! Anyone would think I was some sort of monster. I felt it was a slur, bearing in mind the years I'd had you! I said to her 'Mrs Rossiter, you make me sound like Herod – '"

"But would you welcome children?"

Grandma shrugged and pursed her thin lips.

"Well," she said defensively after a moment. "It's hardly a question of what I want. Your grandfather isn't as strong as he used to be."

"There you are, then," Rachel said. "Mrs Rossiter was only being considerate."

"Nonsense!" Grandma was having none of that. "She was making a point. Underlining the fact that when you were here, you spent more time at their house than you did at home."

"But Grandma – " Rachel began, then sighed. It was an old bone of contention, best ignored. "So you opted for the teachers, then?" she said.

"Certainly not! I have very little help in the house. No live-in staff any more since Doreen left me to go to Woolworths. Just Mrs Harkness three times a week, and heaven knows she's all but useless. And as I pointed out, I have a duty to my family. You could well need to come back here to live when the bombs start falling. And then there's Sylvia. I have to think of her – "

"She's staying in Cornwall."

"I know that now, but I didn't then. It's so *like* Sylvia to find herself a safe little haven – "

Not for the first time, Rachel felt that the nature of Grandma's conversation made responding to it highly complicated.

"What about Alannah? Is she still at home?" she asked quickly, hoping to get back to the Rossiters.

"You're not going to look her up, surely, after the way she treated you?"

"I just wondered what she was doing."

"Oh, she's here, all right. I happened to see her from the window only a few days ago."

"And Barney? Is he away?"

"The younger boy? I heard he went to Art College. In London, I suppose. He comes back from time to time in a dreadfully noisy little car – "

"And Gavin?" Rachel's head was bent over the never-ending hem of a bay-window curtain.

"In the RAF. It was his friend who ruined our verge. I sent your grandfather round to complain, and of course he let them get away with some kind of apology. What about compensation? I said. No mention of that, of course. I should have known."

"Did he get married?"

"Married?" For a moment, Grandma looked perplexed, having lost her thread. "Oh," she said at last. "The Rossiter boy! Not that I've heard. Now Rachel, do look what you're doing! You've tacked the top of that curtain to the bottom of the other."

"Oh dear! What an idiot!"

How she hated sewing. Even so, she felt, all at once, ridiculously happy. Which proved without doubt that she was indeed an idiot.

The following morning Mr Chamberlain's voice, tired and regretful, emerged from the wireless set to tell them that the nation was at war. So it was now a fact.

Even Grandma was silenced. Or almost.

"Well –" she said, hands gripping the arms of her chair. "Well!"

"At least we know where we are and what's to be done," Grandpa said.

The aroma of the weekend joint roasting in the oven brought Grandma back to more immediate concerns.

"Business as usual," she said briskly, rising to her feet. "That's what they used to say the last time. I must go and baste the lamb."

Rachel caught her grandfather's eye and he smiled.

"Brace up, my darling. We'll muddle through somehow. Right's on our side." His voice sounded frail and rather touching. Rachel nodded, wanting to believe him but at the same time remembering all that Tom had said about Germany rearming and taking over the Czech factories that supplied military equipment. Being on the side of virtue wasn't always enough. "I think," Grandpa went on, getting up from his chair, "that on this occasion I'm going to forget your grandmother's views about drinking in the middle of the day. I need a good strong Scotch. Can I get something for you?"

Before Rachel could reply, the air raid siren sounded, swooping up and down in a way that chilled the blood. Halfway between his chair and the drinks' cabinet, Grandpa stood transfixed.

"Did you hear that?" Kitchen spoon in hand, Grandma appeared framed in the doorway. "I knew it. I *knew* it! They'll bomb us out of existence – "

The noise of the siren died, and from the street, through the open window, could be heard stentorian tones:

"Take cover, take cover."

Forgetting her rules regarding the vulgarity of peering out of windows, Grandma went over and pulled the lace curtains aside.

"It's only that Sid Parker from the butcher's," she said. "A dreadfully common little man. You'd think they could find someone with a bit more authority. He looks quite ridiculous in that tin hat."

"Come away from the windows, Maisie." Grandpa, for once, was taking charge. "We'll sit under the stairs, as we'd planned. The canvas chairs are there, and a torch. Don't forget your gas mask – " He broke off as the doorbell rang.

"Oh, who can that be at such a time?" Grandma was fretful. "How very thoughtless."

"I'll go," Rachel said.

She opened the door to find, to her total astonishment, that Barney was standing in the porch. Stunned into silence, they gaped at each other. It was Barney who recovered first.

"Rachel! Good Lord! I didn't expect to find you here."

"Who is it? Come away from the door, Rachel." Grandma came up behind her. "This is no time for a social call! What on earth do you imagine you are about?" she said severely, seeing Barney. "We're supposed to be taking cover."

"That's why I'm here," Barney said. "My parents sent me round to ask if you'd like to come and share our air raid shelter. There's plenty of room in it, and its very comfortable. We thought that perhaps you hadn't had time to make your own arrangements." His eyes went back to Rachel. He seemed to be unaffected by the prospect of danger and was grinning widely, delighted to see her. "You'll come, won't you?"

"Are you sure – ?"

"We'll stay here, in our own home," Grandma said firmly; but Grandpa, as if the outbreak of war had brought out a streak of decisiveness hitherto undiscovered, overruled her.

"This is most kind of you, my boy," he said. "Come along, Maisie. Get your gas mask. We can't stay dithering here, and if the Rossiters are kind enough to offer us a place of safety, then we owe it to Rachel to take it. It's not as if we have only ourselves to think of."

"I'm all right. Don't worry about me," Rachel assured him. The thought of confronting Mrs Rossiter seemed, at that moment, worse than anything Hitler might throw at her.

Sid Parker's shouts could be heard once more as he approached the house, riding slowly back down the street on his bicycle, tin hat worn very straight on his head, ARP armlet much in evidence. He stopped when he drew level with The Laurels, seeing the small knot of people standing at the open door.

"What the 'ell do you think you're doing? Take cover!" he yelled.

"That's *quite* enough, Mr Parker!" Grandma was icily outraged; but at least she was galvanised into action, and without further argument, went to get her gas mask, turn down the oven, and join the others as they went next door.

"I don't believe any of this," Rachel said to Barney. "It's surreal!"

"I certainly can't believe you're here. I thought you were in Uganda."

"I came back a couple of months ago."

"*Here?*"

"No, no. London. Barney, what will your mother say when she sees me?"

190

"She'll be all right," he assured her.

And she was. Not frighteningly angry as she had been at their last meeting; not even coldly polite, but serene and smiling, apparently delighted to see her. She sat in an old wicker armchair imperturbably sewing her tapestry as if there had been no past rows or tears, no present air raid. Her calm was monumental, her air that of a Lady Bountiful welcoming guests to her castle.

"You were surely going to call on us before you went back to London, weren't you?" she asked when they were comfortably sitting in the concrete shelter, sipping the coffee Alannah made on an ingenious little camping stove. Rachel's experience of air raid shelters was limited, but she felt sure that this represented a highly superior model. The walls were bright with painted murals – undoubtedly Mrs Rossiter's work, judging by the impressionistic nature of them – and rugs covered the cement floor.

"Well – " she felt some embarrassment at Mrs Rossiter's question. She could, she felt, hardly say, 'You were so hateful the last time I saw you that wild horses wouldn't have dragged me'. "There wasn't, actually, very much time," she said. "I only arrived yesterday, and must go back this afternoon."

"There won't be any trains," Alannah said.

She, of all the Rossiters present, was alone in seeming awkward. She had greeted Rachel with polite surprise but with no intimacy. Their eyes had not met when Alannah had handed Rachel her coffee cup.

"Oh, I'm sure some will run," Mrs Rossiter said vaguely.

"Always supposing," Grandma said, "that London still stands."

"Now, now, Mrs Bond. That doesn't sound like your normal optimistic self." Mr Rossiter gave a private, conspiratorial wink in Rachel's direction. "We mustn't give way to gloom, must we?"

His manner was as lively as ever, and Rachel expected, any moment, the suggestion of a quick game of Adverbs, or even I Spy.

Barney, who had gone aloft once more to retrieve the gas mask he had forgotten on his first journey, came down the steps again.

"There's an old man with a white beard wandering around outside," he said.

"What a dreadful omen! Does he happen to have a scythe about his person?" Alannah asked – at which Rachel giggled and Alannah, for the first time catching her eye, joined in.

"That'll be old Jimmy Bancroft, poor old chap," Mr Rossiter said. "He's one of the doormen at the Town Hall. Tell him to come down, Barney. He's a funny old fellow," he explained in an undertone to the others. "Talks a lot – cleft palate – all alone in the world. He lives just round the corner. He seemed worried when I spoke to him yesterday so I told him to come if the balloon went up."

Mrs Bond pressed her thin lips together in disapproval, but naturally said nothing. If Mr Rossiter wanted to share his shelter with every Tom, Dick or Harry, that was, of course, up to him. For her part, she was not accustomed to mixing with Town Hall doormen on a social basis, still less funny old fellows with cleft palates, and had no intention of allowing this war to lower her standards.

Jimmy Bancroft proved to be a mine of information. Enemy bombers had been sighted over the southern counties of England, he told them – except that he said 'schighted over', which made Barney bite his lip and stir his coffee with great concentration. Gunsch, he told them, were already firing in Hyde Park. The entire Government was moving, lock, schtock and barrel, to Wooshter, or was it Leamington? (Maybe it was Schirenschester, Barney whispered to Rachel in Jimmy's voice, making her giggle again). And patientsch in all the London hoschpitalsch, not exschepting the dying, had been schent home to make room for air raid caschualtiesch. He had it all, he said, on good authority.

"Really!" Grandma, coldly scornful, was the only one present prepared to break the trembling silence which could, so easily, have erupted into hilarity. "I suppose Mr Chamberlain was in touch with you personally, this very morning?"

Barney, to create a diversion, went up to ground level once more to see what was happening. He returned a moment later to announce that the All Clear had gone and with jokes concerning the rapidity with which the good old RAF had been able to scare Hitler away, the party prepared to disperse. Jimmy Bancroft, with effusive thanks, tottered off down the garden, leaving Rachel, Alannah and Barney free to indulge their mirth.

"Come along, Rachel," said Grandma, clearly wishing to put a stop to this kind of childish unseemliness. "We're most grateful for your hospitality, Mrs Rossiter."

"You don't have to go for a minute, do you?" Barney asked Rachel, who glanced interrogatively towards her grandmother. Lunch, she was told, would be a little later than usual; half past one, and mind she was there on the dot.

"I think I ought to leave immediately afterwards," Rachel said.

"Getting back to London might be difficult. It was bad enough yesterday. It was a ridiculous day to travel, really."

"You could have come at any time over the past two months," said Grandma, with perfect truth, but Rachel made no reply. She had run out of pacifying remarks.

"I'll drive you back to London," Barney offered. "No trouble."

"Oh, I couldn't possibly – "

"Yes you could! I insist."

In the event, Alannah came too. The constraint between the girls was shortlived, past differences ignored, and Rachel found she was glad, in spite of everything. It had always been thus – childish quarrels, so important at the time, had invariably been forgotten when they next met.

But this hadn't been a childish quarrel, and she surely couldn't have forgotten, Rachel thought, herself remembering all too clearly the tears, the accusations, the coldness – even the letter to Miss Scrimgeour, for heaven's sake! How could they have forgotten?

Perhaps it was the war, she told herself. The smaller crisis had been swallowed up in the larger; and the same spirit that had urged the Rossiters to ask Grandma to share their shelter after so many years of sniping, had enabled them to erase the uncomfortable memories of almost two years ago.

Gavin, she was told, had joined the RAF at the earliest possible moment and was now flying Blenheim bombers up in Lincolnshire. He'd been home last weekend, but had been recalled by telegram and gone back immediately. So perhaps, Rachel thought, they realised they had been wrong. Gavin had been determined to fly, and nothing she had said could have influenced him, either then or now. But if so, she knew better than to expect them to admit it openly.

Perhaps this present friendliness meant they were sorry. She would give them the benefit of the doubt, anyway, for she knew that this was the best she could hope for by way of an apology. And it was good to be friends again! To giggle with Alannah who, for all her little ways, could be so funny when she tried. No one's perfect, Rachel thought. Life's too short and too uncertain to bear grudges.

"But what happened to Jacqueline?" she asked. "The last I heard she and Gavin were engaged and going to get married."

"They weren't at all suited," Alannah said. "We all saw it – "

"I didn't," Barney said. "I liked her."

"Ma couldn't abide her, and nor could Di. She was frightfully bossy, Rachel, always telling Gavin what to do. He saw it would be a disaster – "

"But Jackie chucked Gav," Barney pointed out.

"*Anyway*," Alannah said, dismissing the point as irrelevant. "They broke off the engagement, that's all that matters. She didn't fit in, that was the top and bottom of it. She kept wanting to drag Gav off to her family."

"How very unreasonable," Rachel said dryly, causing Alannah to give her a sharp look. "And Diana?" she pursued. "Where is she now?"

"Oh, Di did absolutely brilliantly at University," Alannah told her. "Well, we all knew she would, of course. And now she's doing some post-graduate research at Cambridge. Something to do with Minoan Culture. She was home last week, too, but she was anxious to get on with some particular bit of work so she went back with Gavin and he dropped her off. They're not so very far from each other."

"Is she going to teach or lecture or something?" Rachel asked, and Alannah laughed.

"I can't see it, can you?" she asked. "She'd be the world's worst teacher. I don't think she knows what she wants to do, exactly."

"Maybe she'll join the Army," Barney said, at which they all laughed. The thought of Diana subject to Army discipline beggared belief.

As for Alannah, she had left school at the end of last term, she told Rachel, leaning forward with her arms resting on the two front seats of Barney's Austin Seven. And she'd managed to get a place in the Rose Kelly Academy of Dramatic Art in London. Only she supposed it wasn't in London any more, because they'd said in the event of war they would be transferring to Cheltenham.

"The parents aren't at all keen, even on that," she said. "They feel we ought to stick together. It's funny how different parents can be, isn't it? I mean, yours have never minded you being miles away from them, have they?"

She hadn't changed, Rachel realised with some amusement. If she was going to be friends with Alannah, she would have to accept her as she was, tactlessness, egotism and all.

"The circumstances are different, you idiot," Barney said, ever defensive of Rachel.

"Aren't you terrified of being in London?" Alannah asked her.

"Not terrified, exactly." Rachel struggled for honesty. "I don't know what I'll be like if there really are air raids, but so far being in London is rather exciting, especially living where I am. Alice's aunt knows so many interesting people. We had two Members of Parliament for dinner the other night – "

"Now that's what I call gluttony," Alannah said; but she looked impressed, just the same. "I must say," she went on, "I'm dying to go to Drama School. Honestly, Rachel, I don't know how you can possibly settle for secretarial work – it's always sounded the dullest thing in the world to me. I've positively refused to have anything to do with it. But then, I've always known what I wanted to do, so I suppose it's different for me, in a way. For someone like you it's probably the best thing."

"Don't be so damned patronising," Rachel said. She spoke without heat and with the utmost good humour, but the remark caused Alannah to regard her with the same sharp interest she had shown before.

"You've changed," she said.

"She certainly has," Barney agreed, giving Rachel an apprecia-tive sideways grin. "She's a knock-out."

"You're too kind," Rachel said, returning the grin.

"I didn't mean just looks," Alannah said.

The kitchen of 29 Shawcross Street gave the impression of being full to bursting point, and the atmosphere was one of nervous excitement, even elation. Several people were talking at once: Eric, who appeared to know exactly what strategy should now be adopted by the Government; Rudi, who being Polish and having lost his home, had a different and more bloodthirsty approach; and Carla, a wild-eyed woman who had left her husband in Guildford and now did social work among the more deprived families of the East End. Her line was to trace, in detail, the mistakes made by the Conservative governments of the past which had led the world in general and Britain in particular into the folly of war.

Others – Alice, Susan, a French violinist (old) called Jules and another (young) called Paul – sat around the pine table drinking tea and eating bread and jam and arguing or agreeing as they saw fit.

Into this maelstrom came Rachel, Barney and Alannah.

"Thank God!" Susan called by way of a greeting. "Come and be a diversion. I'm going quite mad, being told on all sides how we should conduct this war. Come on, draw up a chair, if you can find one."

Introductions were made, tea was poured, plates provided.

"Oh, you're the *Rossiters*," Alice said. "I've heard so much – "

195

She pulled herself up short, remembering just what she had heard. "Anyway, I'm glad to meet you. Did you have the air raid warning? Wasn't it terrifying? I was still getting dressed and didn't know whether to finish or come down here as I was."

The babble broke out again. Everyone had a story to tell, even Jules, whose English was all but incomprehensible. Susan, looking resigned, cut more bread and butter.

"Well, I'm grateful for it," Barney said. "Because it was only when I went to ask the Bonds to come to our shelter that I discovered Rachel."

"Their shelter is quite incredible," Rachel told the assembled company. "You've never seen such comfort! Pictures and rugs and all mod. cons. – "

"Plus another shelterer who gave us real up-to-the-minute information," continued Barney, which led to an hysterically funny, if exaggerated, representation by Alannah of Jimmy Bancroft, which reduced all of them, even Jules, to helpless laughter.

Afterwards, Paul kissed his fingers in Alannah's direction.

"I 'ave 'eard, always, of ze Engleesh sang-froid," he said. "Now I see it! To cause laughter on such a day – " Words failed him and he gave an eloquent shrug. His dark, expressive eyes were full of admiration and Alannah rewarded him with a dazzling smile.

"The show must go on," she said.

"It's getting the show on the road that's the problem," said Eric, who felt he had been out of the limelight long enough. "What the Government should do is – " He was off again and Susan, catching Rachel's eye, shrugged with helpless amusement.

It was Barney who finally brought the peroration to a close by getting to his feet and announcing his and Alannah's departure.

"I promised my parents we'd be back early," he said. "Thank you for the tea, Miss Greaves."

"Thank you for your company. Come again."

"I'd like to, very much." His eyes sought Rachel's. "I live in London myself, during the term."

"You'll be most welcome. Any friend of Rachel's – "

"She's nice," Alannah said to Rachel who had come out into the hall to see them off. "Gosh, you're lucky, finding such a super place to live. Who was that *gorgeous* Frenchman? I didn't catch his name."

"That's Paul. He's a violinist. He doesn't live here. He and Jules live in a terrible place in Earls Court and just come to have baths every now and again."

"A thought strikes me," Alannah said. "If by any chance the

Rose Kelly doesn't move to Cheltenham and I need to find digs in London, do you think I might come here?"

A feeling of panic, a kind of claustrophobia, seemed to sweep over Rachel.

"That would be up to Susan," she said faintly.

"Maybe I'll get Ma to contact her, if the need arises. 'Bye for now."

She flapped a hand and made for the car. Barney let her go, turning halfway down the steps for a last word.

"Rachel – " he sounded tentative. "Will I really be welcome if I come again?"

"Of course," Rachel said. "You heard what Susan said."

"I mean, would you welcome me?"

For a moment Rachel hesitated, not knowing why. Surely she would welcome Barney? He'd always been a friend, hadn't he? Whatever reservations she might have about Alannah, she had never had cause to doubt Barney's friendship and there was no possible reason for this instinctive feeling that no good would come of encouraging him. "Yes of course I'd welcome you," she said, dismissing her doubts. "Come any time."

"I'll give you a ring," Barney said, and smiling, went to the car where Alannah waited.

It was, so everyone agreed, a funny kind of war. Nothing much happened, though all around was dramatic evidence that these were dangerous times. Hotels and shops were protected with high walls of sandbags, and above London floated the barrage balloons, shining silver in the sunlight of late September.

There were no more air raids; indeed, there never had been any, the warning on that first day of the war being a somewhat hasty response to an unidentified aircraft over the coast. However, gas masks were now an essential accessory and the traders in Oxford Street cashed in by selling fancy cases designed to cover the square, cardboard boxes. Rachel bought a plain and functional one in olive green with white piping – but couldn't help wishing, afterwards, that she had been a little more adventurous. Alice's scarlet case matched her new shoes and looked well against her navy blue coat.

Late September brought Barney back to London, and though petrol was short, he phoned Rachel at the first opportunity to suggest a run out to the country the following Saturday. They went, on a day of sunshine and scudding clouds, to Box Hill.

"This is wonderful," Rachel said, sitting on the grass with her arms encircling her knees, looking out over the surrounding countryside towards the South Downs. "Such space! I love it."

"I knew you would."

"It reminds me of *Emma* and the Box Hill picnic."

"I had a bet with myself about how long it would take you to mention her."

"How well you know me. I love seeing the English countryside spread out like this. Nothing must change it – not Hitler, not anybody!"

"I'll say not." Appreciatively, Barney looked about him. He had seemed strangely remote all afternoon, not talking very much, but now, for the first time, Rachel thought he looked more relaxed.

"Is something bothering you, Barney?" she asked now.

"Bothering me?" He sounded surprised. "No, of course not." He paused for a moment, apparently engaged in contemplation of the distant view of Dorking. "Well," he went on after a moment. "I suppose that's not strictly true. Yes, something is bothering me. Something like – what the hell am I doing at Art College when there's a war on? Of all the irrelevant occupations, it does seem to take the biscuit. Don't you agree?"

Rachel opened her mouth to disagree violently, then closed it again. Maybe he was right. He wasn't saying that art wasn't important, just that other things, at this moment, took precedence. She could imagine feeling the same herself, if she were a young man. On the other hand, there seemed a distressing familiarity about the whole question.

"Don't you inveigle me into your plans," she said. "I don't want to be accused of sending yet another Rossiter into the Valley of Death."

"I wouldn't dream of involving you!"

"You'll be called up eventually. Can't you wait until then?"

"I suppose so. God knows, I'm not in any hurry in one way. I hate the thought of the Army. I know I'll be a rotten soldier – "

"Why should you be?"

"Well, I've always been bad at doing things en masse. I've always been a loner."

"An unlikely claim for a Rossiter," Rachel said dryly. But she had to acknowledge that he was right. He was always the nonconformist among them.

"We have a lot to answer for, haven't we?" She sensed that he was looking at her. "As a family, I mean. We treated you so badly, and you've been very forgiving."

"That's not entirely true," she said. "*You* didn't treat me badly.

And I don't think I'm as forgiving as all that. Nothing will ever be quite the same again as it was before."

He was silent for a moment, wholly occupied, it seemed, with breaking a small twig into even smaller pieces.

"I've thought about you often," he said. "I was afraid I'd never see you again."

"Were you?" Rachel frowned in disbelief. She had not really thought it possible that her absence could have affected any of the Rossiters in any way.

"I used to imagine you having a whale of a time in Uganda, with hosts of dashing hunters dancing attendance, laying their trophies at your feet."

"Hunters!" Rachel laughed at him. "It wasn't like that."

"There must have been men, though."

"Well – " Rachel considered the question. "Some."

"Are you in love with anyone?"

"Good Lord, no! Would I have come back to England if I had been?" Barney said nothing in reply to this, but sat up straighter and grinned at her, his gloom apparently lightened.

"What about you?" Rachel continued after a moment. "Are you in love with anyone?"

"No," he said at once. Then amended it. "Yes."

Rachel, laughing, looked at him.

"Make up your mind," she said. He reached out and took her hand.

"I think I did that a long time ago," he said.

She sobered, and for a long moment looked down at their two hands joined on the grass. His fingers were quite short and blunt; not an artist's hands, one would have thought, but capable. Slowly she lifted her eyes and looked into his, those bright, blue eyes that she had once found so intimidating.

Was it possible? she asked herself. Was it Barney, all the time? He had teased her, laughed at her – ignored her quite frequently; but at the same time she had always known she could depend on him. And when she had opened Grandma's front door and seen him standing there, she had experienced a moment of pure joy.

He was a Rossiter, sure enough, and a staunch one; yet alone among them, he had taken her part when it came to a show-down.

"Barney?" Her voice was soft and full of wonder, full of questions.

One hand still clasping hers, he put his other at the back of her head and slowly, inevitably it seemed, they drew together.

And this time, unlike its childish forerunners, the kiss was not perfunctory but long, searching, exploratory.

But still, in the end, unexciting. At least to Rachel. Unmoved, and disappointed to find herself so, she drew away from him, only to see from his face that he had experienced a quite different reaction. His expression was luminous with love, his eyes full of happiness.

"There's never been anyone else but you, Rachel," he whispered, a catch in his voice. "Never! You must believe me. It seems too good to be true, that I've found you again."

"I'm glad too," she said. And she was. He was a good friend and she had missed him.

With a sudden change of mood, he gave a whoop of joy and leapt to his feet, and pulling her up beside him he put both his arms around her and hugged her tight.

"It's going to be all right," he said, his voice exultant. "I'll stay here in London until my call-up, just so long as you're here too. Oh Rachel, this changes everything! You're wonderful, do you know that? And you're my girl, aren't you? Say you are!" He was laughing now, his problems forgotten.

Was it possible, she asked herself again? Could Barney be the one? He was highly presentable and fun to be with. They laughed at the same things, shared so many memories. Maybe she was being silly and childish to expect more.

And it would be awfully nice, she thought, to be someone's girl.

12

*B*arney was rather dazzled by the menage at Shawcross Street. Rachel, introducing him to a political columnist in a popular newspaper, saw it and was secretly amused, feeling it put her, for once, one up on the Rossiters.

It meant that he exerted himself to be acceptable to Susan. Or perhaps, she thought, relenting a little, she was being unfair. Maybe he would have exerted himself anyway. Maybe the fact that he proclaimed himself in love with her was enough to subdue the normal Rossiter arrogance.

His efforts were rewarded, for everyone liked him. He endeared himself to Susan by uncomplainingly helping with the washing up – an activity totally ignored by many of the droppers-in – and making her laugh as he did so. He also fixed the bolt on the back door which had somehow dropped out of true and been impossible to shoot home for many months.

"I had no idea you were so domesticated," Rachel said admiringly. "You never were before."

"There wasn't the call. Actually, I quite enjoy it."

"Well, you've made a big hit with Susan."

"Good! That was the idea."

Rachel tried not to let Susan's approval affect her view of him, but subconsciously she was influenced nevertheless. She had always liked him; now, it seemed to her, that love was a distinct possibility.

Alice, also, was impressed by him.

"He's awfully attractive, Rachel," she said.

"Do you think so?"

"I certainly do! Those eyes!"

"Rossiter eyes," said Rachel. "Diana and Gavin are the same. They get them from their father."

"What a good thing you went to Warnfield that weekend and met up with them again."

"I suppose," Rachel said doubtfully, "I ought to go again."

In fact Barney had several times suggested going home for the weekend. Always she had resisted the idea, partly because the prospect of spending time with her grandmother held few charms; but, more urgently, she felt far too tentative about her new relationship with him to allow it to become public property.

"Why on earth?" Alice asked, when Rachel mentioned the matter to her. "I know your grandmother doesn't like the Rossiters, but she'll have to get over it if you're going to *be* one!"

"For heaven's sake, don't jump the gun! Nothing like that has even been mentioned. We just, well, go around together, that's all."

"I've seen the way he looks at you," Alice said. "The other night when we were all packed into the sitting room and Paul was playing that violin sonata, he was absolutely *devouring* you with his eyes!"

Rachel laughed dismissively.

"Heavens, Alice, you really will have to stop reading lurid magazines," she said. "You're beginning to think like them."

But she was pleased, nevertheless. It was good for her prestige to have such a devoted boyfriend, and there was added kudos in the fact that he was so presentable. Though Barney would never have Gavin's film-star looks, he was tall and straight, with good teeth and a friendly smile – not to mention the much-remarked eyes. And the lock of hair which still insisted on falling over his forehead was undoubtedly endearing. Compared to Alice's Eric, he was desirability personified.

"It's not just Grandma," she said.

It was, in fact, far from just Grandma. Going back to Warnfield with Barney would be making a statement to his family that she was not yet prepared for, and perhaps never would be; but any suggestion to Barney of dissembling when in the bosom of their respective families met with astonishment.

"But you're my girl, for heaven's sake!" he said. "Why should you want to keep it dark?"

'Because I'm not really sure that I'm in love with you,' she might have said; but she kept her silence. How could she not be sure, when everyone in the whole world told her how lucky she was? Maybe she was searching for something that didn't really

202

exist, except in the imagination. Maybe this was *it*, the thing that people wrote poems and sang songs about.

Certainly, she felt nothing but affection for him, liked being with him, was delighted to have him as an escort; even, up to a point, enjoyed his lovemaking. Not that he ever – well, he was pretty circumspect, really, though he'd been venturing a little further recently. Alice, regaled with details, as indeed she regaled in her turn, was envious. Eric, she confided, had very high standards and didn't seem to be interested in that sort of thing. He was, she said, more cerebral – which didn't prevent her speculating on what *might* happen, should his iron control falter.

"Not that I'd ever Go All the Way," she assured Rachel earnestly. "Not before marriage. Would you?"

Rachel was less dogmatic.

"I honestly don't know. I suppose it's possible to imagine being carried away."

"But wouldn't you be afraid that you'd lose Barney's respect? You wouldn't want to be known as That Sort of Girl, would you?"

"I wasn't thinking of Barney, exactly."

"Who, then?"

Rachel shrugged her shoulders impatiently.

"I don't know. Someone I haven't met yet, maybe. Oh, don't look at me as if I fling myself at the feet of every man I come across! It's just that I can't help thinking that I could meet someone, one day, who would make me throw caution to the wind."

Among Barney's friends, a raggle-taggle band made up in almost equal number of dedicated talent and preposterous poseurs, she was well aware that it was assumed that they went to bed together – not that there was a great deal of opportunity, since Barney shared a small bed-sitter in Bloomsbury with another student, Clive Chambers.

Clive played the role of artist far more realistically than Barney, Rachel considered, being thin and dark and tortured-looking, as well as hopelessly untidy. He talked openly about sex, discussing his needs and his conquests in a way that embarrassed Rachel.

Barney, ever the gentleman, told him to shut up in her presence, but once Clive had left them, he appeared to regard his friend's excesses more indulgently. "Take no notice of him. It's all hot air," he said. "He's just trying to shock you. Don't let him see he's succeeded."

"How Barney puts up with him, I'll never know," she grumbled to Alice. "He says the rudest things about Barney's work, but flies off in a huff if there's the smallest criticism of his."

"Doesn't Barney mind?" Alice asked.

"Not really. He doesn't have any great opinion of his own capabilities. Never did have! He still says he only came to Art College to please his mother." Rachel gave a sudden giggle of amusement. "He took offence the other day, though. He produced one of his mother's pictures. Clive laughed fit to bust when he saw it. He said it was the most god-awful daub he'd ever clapped eyes on."

"Gosh, how frightful! What did Barney say?"

"Not much. He just put it away without a word, all huffy and on his dignity."

"And was it a – " Alice, not used to such language, gulped a little. "A god-awful daub?"

Rachel laughed a little and shook her head.

"How do I know? I don't know the first thing about art. There was lots of splashy colour about, the same as always, but apparently the technique and the composition were all wrong, according to Clive. I'm inclined to take his word for it. Everyone seems to defer to him, as if he knows what he's talking about. Funny thing," she went on after a moment. "I've heard Barney criticise pictures for the same sort of thing heaps of times. It's as if all the Rossiters kind of suspend their critical faculties when it comes to their own family. I knew Mrs Rossiter was like that, but I never suspected it of Barney."

"Still, it's too bad of Clive to say awful things about his mother, even if she deserves it," Alice said. "Why does Barney put up with him?"

Rachel shrugged. "Convenience, I suppose. Lack of money. He'd love his own place, but he can't possibly afford it. And he likes Clive really, in a funny kind of way. He respects his talent."

"Well, it's not hard to see that you don't like him much," Alice said.

Rachel considered the question. She supposed Alice was right. Certainly she found Clive unattractive, even offensive, and would be thankful never to clap eyes on him again – but at the same time she welcomed his presence because it meant that a certain restraint was forced upon Barney.

"Life," she said somewhat obscurely to Alice, "is incredibly complicated."

"Mine isn't," Alice said wistfully.

Not for the first time, Rachel reflected that Eric was a pain of the first magnitude, but naturally kept her silence. Once or twice she and Barney had gone out with Alice and Eric, but Barney had implored her to enter into no more such arrangements. He and Eric, he claimed, had said all they ever wanted to say to each other within the first five minutes of meeting.

"You know what your trouble is?" Rachel said. "You're just not cerebral."

"No wonder I can't sing in tune," Barney remarked.

Alice, who finished her secretarial course a few weeks earlier than Rachel, had managed to find lowly work at the Ministry of Information, which had taken over the London University main buildings in Bloomsbury. She did little, she said, but carry files about from one office to another. No one seemed to know who was dealing with what, and no matter where she took the files, she was invariably told to take them somewhere else.

Rachel would cheerfully have settled for this, but was less successful when her turn came to look for a job. She finally managed, with a great deal of difficulty and many disappointments, to find an equally humble position in the typing pool of National & Domestic Insurance. It was not, she had to admit, quite what she had hoped for. Something more intimately connected with the war effort had been her goal, but such appointments seemed hard to come by – at least to someone of her limited experience.

"Insurance is very important. Day-to-day life has to go on," Susan assured her – but with sympathy and understanding, since a feverish desire to do what was generally known as one's bit had the entire population in its grip. She herself had moved to a job in the War Office, which gave her an oracle-like status in the eyes of all her friends and acquaintances. On all sides she was appealed to for up-to-the-minute news, predictions of future tactics and explanations of strategy – as if she now had a direct insight into the minds of the greatest powers in the land; and she became adept at noncommittal pronouncements that gave nothing away.

Rachel sighed.

"It's so incredibly dull," she said mournfully. "And the woman in charge of the typing pool is such a dragon."

"Look on it as practice, Rachel dear," Susan urged her. "Sharpen up your skills. Something will turn up, I'm sure. I'll keep my eyes and ears open for you, I promise. It's only too clear that the war is going on for some time yet, so your turn will come, you can depend on it."

Some said the war had barely started. Apart from raids against

German ships involved in mine-laying around the coast, the action seemed mostly to be confined to words. Hitler, in a Reichstag speech, had declared that he had no war aims against Britain and France and that warmongers like Churchill were wholly responsible for the present deplorable state of affairs. British bombers infiltrated enemy territory, but dropped propaganda leaflets, not bombs. The British Expeditionary Force, sent to France at the very onset of war, waited behind the supposedly impregnable Maginot Line for the Germans to make the first move.

Despite the official news bulletins from the BBC, rumours abounded. Germany was said to be on the brink of revolution, or about to invade Holland, or soon to make more peace proposals. It was, said Miss Pargeter, the typing pool supervisor whom Rachel had disliked on sight, what she would call a very peculiar war. Very peculiar indeed.

"Not like the good old Crimean," Pam Compton whispered to Rachel out of the side of her mouth. At which Rachel suppressed a giggle. Pam Compton was the only thing that made National & Domestic Insurance even partly tolerable.

"They don't make wars like that any more," she whispered back; and was the recipient of a disapproving glare from Miss Pargeter.

Disapproving glares were her stock in trade, and Rachel was the target for the worst of them when, towards the end of November, Barney phoned her at the office. Even at the best of times, Miss Pargeter's face was severe; matters such as girls who spent too long in the lavatory, girls who dawdled in the corridors, girls who failed to clean their typewriters, and girls who received private telephone calls, were inclined to sharpen her expression still further to the point where her thin lips all but disappeared and, Punch-like, her chin and nose seemed almost to meet.

"Kindly tell your friend," she snapped as she called Rachel over to her desk, "this is not the place for private chitchat."

"Don't bother," Barney said, as Rachel took the receiver and put it to her ear. "I heard that."

"Well, we're not supposed – "

"It's an emergency! Is it OK if I pick you up about six thirty tonight? I've arranged to meet some people in a pub."

Rachel's heart sank a little. There were, among Barney's friends, individuals whom she liked very much. Clive was not entirely typical. On the other hand, en masse she found them overpowering. They used a language she did not understand, talked of people and techniques about which she knew nothing, made in-house jokes that to her were incomprehensible. Among them, she was the outsider once more, with no identity other than Barney's girlfriend.

"You wouldn't rather go on your own?" she said.

"No, definitely not! I want you to come."

"OK," she said resignedly – for after all, being wanted was not something to be lightly ignored. "I'll be ready."

Inexplicably, the chosen pub was in Hampstead, not one usually patronised by Barney and his friends.

"We thought a change would be nice," he said easily.

"On a night like this?" Rain was dashing against the darkened windows of the bus. Outside, headlights reduced to pencil-thin beams and shaded torches did little to pierce the gloom of the black-out.

"Cheer up!" She could barely see his face, but knew he was grinning down at her. "It'll be fun."

"Who's coming?"

"Oh, people."

"Will Clive be there?"

"Mm? Shouldn't think so."

His voice was offhand; and as, at that moment, he was delving in his pocket for the fare, she did not pursue the subject. She didn't care very much anyway. It was always, with a few additions or subtractions, the same crowd.

Once deposited in Hampstead they dashed to the Hollybush, huddled together under one umbrella; but though there were many people inside who looked as if they might be artists, Rachel could recognise no one as they stood just inside the curtained threshold, shaking the rain off themselves, peering through the pall of smoke.

There was a fair sprinkling of uniforms; a mass of khaki just inside the door, and more at the far right-hand side of the long bar.

"There they are," Barney said, and reaching for her hand began to plunge through the crowd. He appeared to be making for an elegant blonde whom she did not recognise, noticing only the shining pageboy hairstyle and the black saucer-shaped hat with an emerald-green feather. She looked, somehow, expensive and out of place in this far from pretentious pub.

Beyond her was an Air Force Officer with his back towards them. He turned as they approached; and all at once Rachel felt as if she had been hit by a ten-ton truck.

Gavin. Gavin and Diana.

"Surprise!" Barney was crying. "See who I brought? It's our own little girl next door."

"Rachel!" Diana was coolly welcoming. "Hallo. How nice to see you again."

"Wow! Look at you!" Gavin opened his arms wide and hugged her. "You look wonderful. Isn't she lovely, Barney?"

"I think so," Barney said, grinning at her.

She couldn't speak, could barely breathe. For a brief moment it seemed as if she had turned to stone – as if all physical activity normally taken for granted had simply stopped in its tracks; then suddenly everything seemed to lurch into action at several times the normal rate. Her heart was thumping madly and she was breathing as if she had run a race.

Somehow she contrived to say the right things. She was, she said, with just the right amount of amused, if affectionate, detachment, frightfully impressed by the uniform. And Diana looked as if she had stepped out of the pages of *Vogue* (dismiss the memory of the wild-eyed fury who had all but forbidden her the house) – and just fancy Barney not telling her who to expect! Honestly, he didn't improve, did he?

Thank heaven, she thought, that she had taken Alice's advice and worn her new Stewart tartan wool dress with the white collar. She almost hadn't.

Drinks were ordered and taken to a table which suddenly became free.

"Why Hampstead?" she asked again, her voice very bright and social. "What are you two doing here?"

"Di's staying with a friend up the road, and I managed to get a forty-eight, so I'm staying there too," Gavin said. "Well, well, will you look at the girl? How you've changed!" He lifted his glass to her. "Here's to old times, and times still to come."

He had always turned heads, but now, in his uniform with the wings over the breast pocket, he looked, Rachel thought, like every woman's dream. He knew it, too. There were two girls at the next table staring at him, nudging each other. Briefly he looked at them before, smiling a little, he turned back to his own circle, like a film star mildly pleased by the idolatory of his fans but not making anything of it, accepting it as his due.

And quite right too, Rachel thought, breathless with wonder at being in the same party as such a god-like being.

"Well, Barney-me-lad," he said to his brother. "When's your call-up?"

"Any time."

"You'd do better to volunteer. They might send you to the Pay Corps or something equally ghastly if you don't."

"Leave him alone," Diana said. "Why should he join up before he has to? Just because you couldn't wait to show your manliness – "

Dangerous ground, Rachel thought uncomfortably. She should change the subject. But her mind was a blank and she could think of nothing to say. The thump, thump, thump of her heart was the only reality.

"And what is your contribution to the war effort, sister dear?" Barney asked sweetly.

"Standing By, duckie." Equally sweetly, Diana smiled at him. "It's the fashionable thing to do, didn't you know? It's something I'm awfully good at. Actually, now I have my doctorate I'm being pressed to lecture, at least for a couple of terms. After that, I'll think again." She took a small sip of her gin and orange. "Oh!" she went on, putting the glass down with a thump. "Have you heard the latest? Dad's thinking of enlisting!"

"*What?*" This was news to Barney.

"They want architects, apparently, because of requisitioning big old houses and turning them into Army HQ's and offices and things. I've told him he's quite mad. He'll send Ma into a decline."

"Rubbish!" Gavin gave his slow, devastating grin. "Ma is a tough old boot. Look how she created about me learning to fly. But she got over it."

Involuntarily Rachel looked at Diana, to find her eyes upon her. They exchanged a brief, blank glance before Diana turned to fumble in her bag for a cigarette.

"Give me a light, Gav," she said. He flicked a lighter and held it to her cigarette. The green feather dipped as she bent her head.

"Don't hand them around, will you?" he said, satirically.

"It was my last one."

"A likely story! Generous to a fault, is our Di." He grinned at her and in return she wrinkled her nose at him. They seemed so close, so friendly. Rachel wondered if they had outgrown the rows they used to indulge in. In his turn Gavin lit a cigarette, offering one first to her and then to Barney. Both shook their heads in refusal.

"Rachel," Gavin said, turning to her, "when was it we last saw you? Darned if I can remember. It seems ages ago."

"It was just before you didn't go to Spain," Rachel said after a moment, and he gave a short, amused laugh.

"Good Lord, yes! What a fiasco! Imagine getting mumps at such a juncture. I was absolutely mortified."

"No long-term effects, we're all thankful to say," Barney told her.

"Not nearly as thankful as I am, old boy."

He knew nothing, Rachel realised; nothing of all the trouble that had followed his announcement that he was going to Spain, and nothing about the cataclysmic effect on her life and her relationship with the rest of his family. No one had told him. Or if they had, he'd forgotten.

Diana remembered well enough. How could she not? She drew on her cigarette, looking at Rachel through the smoke with narrowed eyes. Her lips were curved in a small malicious smile.

"Actually," Barney said, "Rachel fought your corner and suffered for it, Gavin. I told you at the time."

"Oh, please! Don't let's drag all that up," Rachel said quickly. "It doesn't matter now."

Gavin blew her a kiss.

"My belated thanks," he said, dismissing the subject. "I say, what a pity young Lannie isn't here to make the party complete. How's she getting on? Anybody heard?"

She liked Cheltenham, Barney said, but had reservations about everything else.

"She says that she hasn't learned much yet."

"Cocky little beast," Diana said affectionately.

"She says she's going to shorten her name to Alannah Ross, so that it will be easier when it's up in lights."

"She'll make it, too," said Gavin. "Now!" He leaned forward with the kind of eager vitality that reminded Rachel of his father. "What are we going to do this evening? Let's find somewhere to eat and dance, shall we?"

"I'm skint, Gav," Barney said.

"I've just been paid. Let's eat, drink and be merry, for God's sake."

The implication of possible death was not lost on Rachel, but Gavin gave no impression of being weighed down by the thought. He stood up, reached for her hand, pulled her to her feet and stood smiling down at her.

"Gosh, it's good to see you again," he said. And as, speechless, she smiled back into those blue, blue eyes, she saw them cloud for a moment as if with sudden surprise. He tilted his head and frowned. He looked, she thought, as if he were trying to get her into focus.

Her heart, which had been behaving erratically from the moment she saw him, now felt as if it were turning somersaults. Her throat was dry and her head was whirling.

This, she knew without any doubt, was love. It wasn't imagination, wasn't anything to do with the affection she felt for Barney. That was all of the mind. This was of heart and nerve and stomach. This was a giant hand squeezing the gut and closing the throat and stopping the breath. How could she possibly have fooled herself, pretended that she was over him, even for a moment? Nothing had changed – not one thing!

No, she was wrong. Something had changed after all, for he was looking at her in a different way. There was a softness about his mouth, a look of uncertainty, as if for the first time he was truly seeing her. And, unbelievably, as if he were attracted to her. She had seen that look before, seen other girls melt before it.

"Come on, you two," he said to the others. "Before I whip this lovely creature away and keep her all to myself."

He put his arm loosely around her waist as if to guide her to the door and, to Rachel, his touch burned like fire.

Sometimes there were days enlivened by reports on fraudulent insurance claims, or claims of such a bizarre nature that it was possible to extract some amusement from them. The day following the meeting with Gavin and Diana was not one of them. Dull, routine letter followed dull, routine letter. Miss Pargeter found numerous careless mistakes in Rachel's work, and was sharply angry, slapping them down on her desk for her to re-type them.

"Perhaps, Miss Bond," she suggested acidly, "if you had a little less social life and went to bed at a reasonable hour you might be able to keep your mind on your work."

"Yes, Miss Pargeter," Rachel said dully.

Her mind, she had to agree, was very far from her work, split as it was between remembering all the glories of the previous night – every word Gavin had spoken, every look cast in her direction, every touch of his hand – and wondering what she was to do about Barney.

He had taken her home (in a taxi he couldn't afford, which made matters worse) and had kissed her goodnight. He had made no mention of the fact that she and Gavin had apparently got on so well, had danced together far too often and found so much to talk about.

He had seemed as affectionate as ever and said that he'd come round to Shawcross Street the day after next. He'd promised, he said, to go and see a mate in hospital the following night. One of his fellow students had fallen down a flight of steps in the black-out and broken his leg. The rest of them were taking it in turns to visit, as he had no family nearer than Sheffield.

She hadn't prolonged the farewells, guiltily thankful that owing to the unfortunate friend she had a day's grace. She tiptoed up the stairs, careful not to waken the sleeping household, and went to bed, there not to sleep but to indulge herself by thinking of Gavin. And Barney, of course. What on earth was she to do? She'd have to do something, that was certain. Even if she never saw Gavin again, she now knew without doubt how she felt about him.

Dawn had brought no solution; nor had the hours spent at the office. Surreptitiously she looked at her watch. Fifteen more minutes left of this ghastly day. She just about had time to type the letter to the Birmingham branch.

"Miss Bond?"

She was fitting her paper into the typewriter (top copy and three carbons) when she heard Miss Pargeter call her name as she came hurriedly through the swing doors from the outer reception area. What now? Rachel thought wearily, looking up. More mistakes? Take a hundred lines and stay after school, maybe.

"Yes, Miss Pargeter?"

Astonishingly, Miss Pargeter was smiling, her normally pale face quite pink and bright with animation.

"Miss Bond, you have a visitor. As a special favour, I'm willing to let you go now, even if it is a little early." She wagged a finger that was positively roguish. "Just this once, mind. We mustn't take advantage, must we? But nothing's too good for Our Brave Boys."

Had she gone mad? Rachel wondered.

"What about this?" she asked, indicating the paper in her typewriter.

"What's that? The Birmingham letter? Oh, tomorrow morning will do. Perhaps you could come in a little early. But run along now, dear, because the gentleman has to get back to camp quite soon."

Gavin, Rachel thought. In all his glory. It could be none other; and indeed, there he was, in Reception, making the whole dreary place crackle with excitement. The girl behind the counter was sorting through files in an important kind of way, taking great care not to look at him but at the same time self-consciously fluffing out her hair and tossing her head. And even Mrs Spooner who had a face like a dried lemon was smiling and wished Rachel a cheery 'good night, dear' in a way she had never done before; adding, saucily, "Don't do anything I wouldn't do!"

"And what, I wonder, might that be?" Gavin asked as he took her arm and led her into the dark night outside. Rachel giggled.

"Heaven knows! You've got a nerve, Gavin, coming here like that."

"My dear girl, what are so many dragons to one who dices with death? I thought maybe you'd have an early dinner with me. I've got to leave London about nine o'clock at the latest – hence the sob-story to Miss Thingummy."

"She said that nothing was too good for Our Brave Boys."

"Quite right too. I trust you're of the same opinion."

"In a modified form," Rachel said.

She felt quite pleased with her ability to converse lightly when inside she was in such a turmoil. She'd had a chance to powder her nose, apply lipstick and comb her hair when she went to the cloakroom to get her coat, and while she could have wished to be wearing something other than her black skirt and pale blue jumper for such an occasion, and regretted the fact that her hair wasn't newly washed, it might have been worse.

He took her to a restaurant in the City, not far from the offices of National & Domestic Insurance but a million miles away in atmosphere. It had red plush banquettes with high backs, pink tablecloths, and framed posters advertising Naughty-Nineties entertainments: lists of musical-hall turns superimposed on high-kicking, black-stockinged legs, huge hats and feather boas.

The food was unremarkable, but the waiter apologised only to Gavin as he served the tired vegetables, proffering wartime and shortages as an excuse. Other customers, Rachel noted, had to take it or leave it.

For herself, she could have been eating cotton wool garnished with wood shavings, so little impact did the food make on her. Afterwards she could only remember Gavin, his apparent pleasure in being with her and her pride in being with him, sitting by his side on a velvet banquette. People would think he was her boyfriend – even, perhaps, her fiancé.

He went on, she thought, about how much she had changed, but he had changed too, in a way that was hard to define. Now that they were alone together he seemed altogether quieter – almost as if the handsome, extrovert, archetypal RAF officer was merely a role he adopted for the outside world to see and admire. He had told her the previous evening that he flew regularly on the leaflet-dropping

213

raids over Germany, but when pressed to say what it felt like to fly over enemy territory, he seemed unwilling to make any kind of a drama out of it.

"It's bloody cold," he said. "So cold you ache with it. Could cry with it, sometimes. And all for what? Leaflets! Why not bombs, for God's sake? Still, I suppose it's all experience. It's flying."

"You love it as much as ever, don't you?" Rachel, studying him, tried to understand. "Do you remember telling me all about it when we met in Piccadilly?"

"Of course. I must have bored the socks off you about it. And Spain. Funny," he went on, "I was so sure about everything then. I'm still sure about some things but not, I truly believe, quite so didactic."

"I thought of you often when I was in Uganda. I met someone who was always sounding off about politics and policies and the awfulness of Chamberlain. I thought you were probably thinking the same."

"I think he's a good man, Chamberlain. Honest and honourable – too honest and honourable, probably. At least he bought us time. We need someone else now, though. God, how we need someone else!"

"Churchill?"

"Probably. We need his drive and sense of urgency. This inactivity isn't doing anyone any good. Are you glad you came back? What was it like, that time you spent in Uganda?"

This was new, Rachel thought, as he listened with apparent interest to her replies. As he himself had said, in the old days he had sounded off about numerous issues, but he had never seemed greatly interested in what anyone else had to say, least of all little-Rachel-Bond-from-next-door.

Now he listened, laughed at her jokes, asked supplementary questions. Perhaps he had always been like that with his successive girlfriends. How could she tell? Did it mean – ? She couldn't bring herself to speculate what it might mean. She only knew that she was happier here, with him, than she had ever been in her life before.

"What are you grinning at?" he asked her, catching her unawares.

"Was I grinning?"

"Like the cat who caught the canary."

"I was just thinking," she said artlessly, "how seldom it is that one's happy and realises it at the time. I mean, you look forward to being happy sometimes, only to find that you're not; and sometimes you look back and realise that you have been, only you didn't know it."

He smiled at her, his eyes warm.

"Complicated sentence construction," he said. "But I get the drift. Am I to take it that you're happy now?"

She was giving away too much, Rachel thought, but she couldn't help it.

"Yes," she said softly, smiling back at him. For a while he said nothing, but the look was there again; that puzzled, seeing-her-for-the-first-time look. He reached out and touched her cheek with a gentle finger.

"Dear Rachel," he said. "Dear little girl next door. How sweet you are! Thank you very much for growing up."

Could one faint from sheer happiness? Instead, Rachel smiled warmly back at him.

Barney called at Shawcross Street as promised the following night with the intention of taking her to a Deanna Durbin film she had wanted to see. Instead she suggested a walk and a talk.

The rain had started before they reached the Kings Road and they dived into a Milk Bar for shelter. It was not a particularly sanitary place, Rachel noted as she sat at a smeared table by the thickly curtained window. The ashtray was overflowing, and dirty glasses and a half-eaten bun on a plate still remained as a souvenir of the last customers.

Barney, returning to the table with two pallid coffees, pulled a face.

"This place has solved the problem of where the flies go in the wintertime," he said. "Why don't we go to the flicks? I don't fancy spending the evening here, and the rain looks as if it's set in."

"Barney, we must talk," Rachel told him.

Barney, taking the bentwood chair opposite her, looked wary.

"Could that be, do you think, the most ominous sentence in the English language?" he asked. Then, as she sat with bent head, finding it difficult to begin: "It's Gavin, isn't it?"

Rachel, lip caught between her teeth, looked up at him and nodded.

"I'm sorry, Barney. I'm afraid it always has been."

"I see," he said. For a while he stared down into his cup. "And Gavin?" he asked, not looking up. "Does he feel the same way about you?"

"I don't know, Barney. I only know how I feel."

He looked at her then, and her heart smote her. He looked so miserable, almost as if he were about to cry. And it was all her fault! She'd been guilty of leading him on, just like she had Clifford Bailey, only worse because Barney really cared.

"Oh Barney, I'm sorry," she said again.

Still he said nothing. He looked down again at his unappetising coffee.

"You don't know him," he said. "You don't know the first thing about him. He's a complicated sort of a bloke."

"Don't be ridiculous! I've known him for years and years. I fell in love with him the very first time I saw him."

Barney gave a small, hopeless kind of laugh.

"I know when I'm beaten," he said.

"So there you are," Rachel said to Alice, much, much later. "No more Barney."

Three short words; so easy to say to Alice, but so painful to convey to Barney. She'd felt like a criminal.

Alice, who had managed to buy some toffees now in very short supply, looked at her, one cheek as round as her eyes.

"You're an idiot," she said, indistinctly.

"Maybe."

"You are – there's no maybe about it!" She sucked furiously for a few moments in order to deliver some well-chosen words with greater clarity. "Barney is here, on the spot," she said at last. "Dancing attendance, you might say. It doesn't matter how marvellous and glamorous Gavin is, you can't get over the fact that he isn't *here*! And you don't even know how he feels about you."

Rachel said nothing. It was true that there had been no declaration, no promise of a further meeting. How could there be? Gavin was in the RAF, subject to all kinds of restrictions on his movements. But things had moved on in an indefinable way. There was in his manner an implicit understanding that the relationship between them had changed, the age difference reduced now to vanishing point. His goodbye kiss had not been entirely brotherly either, even if it fell short of a passionate embrace.

But none of this was of importance anyway. What mattered was the way she felt about him. How could she go on being 'Barney's girl' when she felt like this?

"If you ask me," Alice went on, "you're throwing away the substance for the shadow. I don't think it's fair on Barney, when he might be called up at any time."

"Being fair to Barney is what it's all about," Rachel explained with commendable patience. "I've always been mad about Gavin. It wouldn't be honest to pretend I felt remotely like that about Barney."

"Well, I don't think Gavin's behaved very well," Alice said priggishly. "I mean, taking over one's brother's girl isn't really *on*, is it?"

"Gavin didn't know anything about Barney and me. You can't blame him. Anyway, all he did was take me out to dinner. I expect Diana would have come too if she hadn't been doing something else." (And thank heaven for that, she thought.)

"It must have been awful for Barney when you told him."

"Actually," Rachel said thoughtfully, "he'd kind of guessed. He said he noticed that night we all met up in the pub that I came alight for Gavin in a way he'd never seen before."

Alice sighed despondently.

"I come alight for Eric," she said after a moment. "But I don't think he notices."

By Christmas, both Eric and Barney had gone to serve King and Country – Eric in the RAF somewhere in Leicestershire and Barney as a Private in the Royal Hampshires in Aldershot.

Rachel went to Warnfield to celebrate Christmas with her grandparents and spent the evening of Christmas Day next door with the Rossiters. Neither Gavin nor Barney were given Christmas leave, and though the Rossiters did their best to make the occasion as much like other years as possible, there seemed, to Rachel, a hollow feeling about it all.

Alannah was in complete agreement.

"I hate it without the boys," she said when Rachel came over to Kimberley Lodge to say goodbye before going back to London. "There just doesn't seem any point in it."

"Business as usual, the show must go on, are we downhearted?" Rachel chanted, running all the words together.

"Frankly, yes." Alannah yawned as if exhausted and took up a studied pose on the window seat in her bedroom. Her fine blonde hair was swept up, Edwardian style, wisps escaping to fall around her face. Her mouth was painted pillar-box red and, at this moment, looked discontented. "I'm glad you came, anyway," she said. "I'm desperate to talk. Tell me, do you know anything whatsoever about how I can get into ENSA? It's a branch of the Ministry of Information, you know. Didn't you say your friend Alice works there?"

"Yes, she does. And what's more," Rachel added proudly, "so

do I now. Alice told me they wanted someone for the Overseas Division, so I applied and I got it. Isn't it great?"

"Gosh, you never said!"

"No." Nobody, Rachel reflected with a touch of inward amusement, had given her much of a chance. Par for the course, she thought.

"Well, what about it? Can you do anything?"

"About what?"

"About *me*, of course! I would give," Alannah said dramatically, "ten years of my life if I could get into ENSA."

"I can't do anything, Lannie. I just type things for people."

"But you must know someone. Who's in charge of it?"

"ENSA? Heaven knows!"

"Can't you find out?"

Despairingly Rachel thought of the Ministry, with its far-flung offices in different buildings, its staircases, the rabbit-warren corridors, the utter impossibility of locating almost anyone.

"I don't know that I can," she said.

In an angry, sinuous movement, Alannah rose from the window seat and began striding up and down the bedroom. Rachel watched her with enjoyment.

"I thought they hadn't taught you anything at that school of yours," she said. "How come you've learned to do that?"

"What?"

"Getting up from your seat in one easy movement and swooping around like an enraged prima donna. It's most impressive."

"Well, yes, there's quite an art in it." Alannah's voice was now normal, undramatic. "There's an art in sitting, too. When you cross your legs, they're supposed to go in the same direction, not splayed out in different ones like yours are now. See, like that."

"Oh, very elegant!"

"Never mind all that. You will try to find out something, won't you?"

"About ENSA? I can't promise anything, Lannie. Wouldn't it be better to stay and learn your trade – "

"There's nothing, absolutely nothing, so good for teaching you the trade as actually working," Alannah said passionately. "Travelling around, taking plays to the forces, learning on the hoof – that's what will teach me the trade."

"Maybe you're right."

"I know I am. Oh, I wish I were in London! It's the only place to be. I wish I could come and live at your place."

"Susan's place," Rachel corrected her. "She says she doesn't want any more lodgers, I'm afraid."

She felt guilty about feeling so thankful. Gavin had been down once more since the time he had taken her to dinner, and she never knew when he might be able to come again. The last thing she wanted was to have Alannah on the spot – advising, analysing, wanting to *know*. The relationship with Gavin was a delicate one, far from resolved.

He seemed to like to talk to her. His last trip had taken place in cold, bright weather. Snow had fallen recently and still covered the vast acres of Richmond Park, where they walked all the way from Robin Hood Gate to Richmond Gate via Pen Ponds. The collar of his greatcoat had been up around his ears, and he had taken her right hand and held it inside his pocket. Her left hand in its too-thin leather glove had felt frozen, but she didn't care. Her feet were cold and wet, too, but she didn't care about them either. She could have gone on walking for ever, just so long as Gavin was there at her side.

He had talked and talked and talked; not in the didactic way he vowed he had forsworn, but musingly, reflectively, about war and bombing and the rights and wrongs of it. About how much he wanted to get on with it, but how he couldn't help wondering . . .

"Do you still read poetry?" Rachel asked him. "You used to like Auden and Spender – "

"Still do."

So at last she could quote to him the poem she had longed to present as a gift so many years before: " 'Through corridors of light where the hours are suns – ' "

" 'Endless and singing.' " He took up the lines, delighted that she knew and loved them. " 'Whose lovely ambition/Was that their lips, still touched with fire,/Should tell of the Spirit clothed from head to foot in song.' "

"That's flying for you," he said. "That's how I feel – 'clothed from head to foot in song'."

She glowed with the glory of her discoveries about him.

"That's wonderful. I'm so glad."

The look of strain that she had noticed when he first arrived had quite definitely gone, she thought, when she faced him over the table at the little teashop on Richmond Hill where they finally found their way.

Just imagine if Alannah had been there too! He would have wisecracked – they all would have wisecracked – and she would be no nearer knowing him than she had been before. Now she felt closer to the real Gavin, the man behind all the glamour, the adult, authoritative pilot who took seriously his responsibility to his crew and his country.

He was, she thought, so unlike the man he appeared to be. Oh, he exerted charm to get his own way, and he wasn't averse to a swagger here and there, and if he saw admiration on the faces that were turned to him, then he enjoyed that too.

But that wasn't all of him. She knew him now to be thoughtful, vulnerable; even afraid. How could she not love him?

It froze that evening. They went – where else? – to the pictures, sitting in far better seats than Rachel was accustomed to, with a box of chocolates to pass between them.

His arm was round her shoulders. All around them there were service men and girls in the same position. It didn't mean anything, Rachel told herself; but even so she was far more conscious of him than of the film. She didn't want it to end. If there were to be no more than this, she thought, then at least she would have had this little piece of him, this one weekend.

No – a thousand times no! She didn't want Alannah in London. Even so, she did, eventually, ask about ENSA, and managed to find an address for her to write to. Probably nothing would come of it, she thought; and forgot the whole matter when Gavin phoned a few days later to say that he would be coming to London once more on the following Saturday.

"About lunch time, I think," he told her. "If that's convenient."

Convenient? Rachel gave a breathless laugh. Her heart was hammering with excitement at the very thought and she could hardly speak. It couldn't, as it happened, have been more convenient, for Susan had already announced that she was off to Brighton to some conference or other, and Alice had been invited to a family gathering in Wimbledon with Eric, currently home on seven days' leave. She and Gavin, therefore, would have the house to themselves, which could lead to almost anything. Not that she expected – not that she would – well, she didn't think she would, anyway. Oh, it was ages until Saturday! Was it possible to *die* from sheer excitement?

The week passed somehow, a confusion of hopes and dreams and soaring emotions. By twelve thirty on Saturday she was dressed and pacing. She had opened a can of tomato soup which she knew to be one of Gavin's favourite things, and it waited in the saucepan, ready to be heated at a moment's notice. She'd made

220

an egg salad, too. She'd tried to buy ham but the corner grocer was out of it – or said he was – and she had rejected Susan's kindly meant offer of a tin of corned beef because Gavin had always turned up his nose at it. That was in the old days, of course. Maybe he was less finicky now.

It didn't look a very exciting meal, she thought, gazing at it without enthusiasm as she paused momentarily in the kitchen. Maybe she should have prepared something hot. It was just that a salad seemed easiest, since she didn't know exactly what time he would get there. Anyway, he liked egg mayonnaise, she remembered that very well, and it was too late to do anything else. He'd surely be arriving any time now.

She went and stood by the fire in the front sitting room, absently warming her hands – waiting, waiting. She'd lit it in case they decided to stay in that afternoon. She didn't know – couldn't guess – what would appeal to him, but if he wanted to sit on the sofa with her listening to records and – well, doing other things – then that was all right with her.

By half past one there was still no sign of him. The house seemed to wait for him, empty and expectant, with no sound but the ticking of the grandfather clock in the hall. Rachel waited, too, each minute that passed making her a little more anxious, a little more certain that something had happened to prevent him coming at all.

By three o'clock, she was seriously worried. Unable to read or settle to anything, she sat with her hands clasped tightly on the kitchen table in front of her, her eyes fixed on the salad which she could not bring herself to eat.

The phone shrilled through the empty house, causing her to jump with alarm and race to answer it, certain that it would be Gavin saying his leave had been cancelled, not knowing how she would bear it if it were. But it was only someone wanting Susan; nothing of any importance.

He'd been shot down, she was convinced of it. If he'd just been delayed, then he would have phoned. He'd never submit her to this waiting, not without a word of explanation, not in wartime when anything could happen. It was always the finest and the best – think of the poets in the last war, Rupert Brooke and Wilfred Owen, and – and – oh, lots of others.

There was a strangely hollow, fluttering feeling in her stomach. This couldn't really be happening, could it? It wasn't real. She couldn't face a world without Gavin. She sat very still at the kitchen table and tried to imagine it; tried to remember what it

221

had been like, all those months when she'd worked so hard to convince herself that she didn't love him after all – times when she'd laughed and danced and flirted and tried to fall in love with someone else, telling herself that she would never see him again, that he was gone from her life for ever and ever; but at the same time knowing deep within herself that he hadn't gone and never would, not while she had breath in her body. She hadn't thought then of death, of *his* death; had made no allowances for it – for its cruelty, the irrevocable quality of it.

The doorbell, when it rang, made her jump and catch her breath. She ran to answer it. Gavin, standing on the step, saluted with a flourish as she flung the door open.

"The late Flying Officer Gavin Rossiter, at your service, ma'am."

"Oh!" She was incapable of doing more than gape at him as if she could hardly believe the evidence of her eyes, so irrevocably had she consigned him to the grave. For one moment she thought she was going to faint, like a Victorian heroine, and put out a hand to steady herself against the wall. "Oh, Gavin!" she said, helplessly. "I'd given you up."

"Always a mistake," he said, bending to kiss her lightly as he came into the hall. "You can't keep a Rossiter down, you know."

With the door to the outside world closed behind him, she took hold of his lapels and looked into his face. Though he smiled, though his words were flippant, there were strains evident. His eyes were bloodshot, his mouth tense.

"I was so worried about you," she said softly.

He gave a grunt of laughter and pulled her close to him, rubbing his face against her hair.

"Strictly between us, I was worried about myself," he said. "Our little trip over enemy territory last night was not, as they say, without incident. I say, have you got any grub? I'm absolutely ravenous."

"Yes, of course. Come into the kitchen." Rachel ran to turn the gas on under the soup. It all seemed hopelessly inadequate, this small repast, now that he was there. How could she have thought it would satisfy him? "I remembered this was your favourite," she said, making the best of it. "You said once that it didn't taste like any recognisable vegetable, least of all like tomatoes, but that you liked it just the same."

"What a memory you have!"

"I hope it's enough. There's egg mayonnaise, too. I'm sorry it's cold, but I didn't know exactly when you'd arrive – "

"It'll be fine," Gavin said. "You shouldn't have waited for me."

Again she noticed the weariness behind his eyes, the deadness of his expression. She took her place at the table opposite him, passed him the bread and the butter, all the while looking at him anxiously.

"What happened, Gavin?" she asked softly, after a few moments. "Can you tell me?"

He gave another short laugh and shrugged his shoulders.

"I probably shouldn't," he said. "But what the hell? We were out on a leaflet raid last night over the Ruhr. It was just routine. We should have been back by two, two thirty at the latest. But coming back – " his voice seemed, suddenly, unutterably weary, as if he could hardly bring himself to recount his misadventures.

"You were hit?"

"No, not hit. I told you how cold it was, didn't I? Well, the wings iced up to such an extent that we went into a steep dive. It took the strength of both Jock and me to pull her out of it." Jock, Rachel knew, was his co-pilot. "When she did come out of it," Gavin went on after a moment, "we found that the rudder and elevators were stuck and the port engine on fire. All the time we were losing height like mad."

Rachel stared at him in horror.

"So what happened?" she asked at last when he fell silent.

"There was a lot of cloud cover. Because of the rudder we'd drifted a long way off course and didn't know where the hell we were. Finally, flying very low, we saw an airfield of some kind – a strip and hangars and huts and so on. Didn't have a clue which side of the Maginot Line we were, of course, but I didn't have any choice, we'd lost so much height. I had to put her down."

"And where were you?"

"In France, thank God, just over the border. It was getting on for three by that time. We had to wait until around nine thirty this morning for things to be fixed sufficiently for us to fly home. Then, of course, there were reports to be made – endless reports . . ." Wearily his voice trailed away, then picked up again. "I kept looking at the clock, seeing the time tick away, knowing you'd be waiting. I'm so sorry, Rachel. I guessed you'd be worried."

"It doesn't matter now," she said gently, dismissing those frightful empty hours that had echoed with her nightmares. "Eat your lunch. You must be exhausted. You can't have had any sleep."

"We managed to get a couple of hours' kip in France. I'll be all right."

But later, when she persuaded him to go into the front room to sit by the fire while she made coffee, she discovered when she brought the tray in to him that he had fallen asleep where he sat, stretched out in the winged armchair, arms hanging loosely over the sides and legs stretched out in front of him. His tunic was unbuttoned, his tie loosened.

For a moment she stood and looked at him. She had never seen him so helpless, so utterly without pretension. His exuberance, his vitality, his charm, his egotism – all had drained away, leaving him without defences, not a leader of men but a child once more.

Weak with love for him, she sat down to drink her coffee, feasting her eyes on him, noting again the curve of his mouth, the way his hair grew, the shape of his fingernails, just as if she had not, long ago, learned him by heart. The thought that he could so easily have been killed – could even now be no more than a heap of broken bones and torn flesh – was beyond bearing. The relief of having him here, safe, still living and breathing made her feel strange; sick and breathless and hollow inside.

For a while she sat and watched him sleep. He stirred once and muttered to himself. She felt guilty then, as if she were invading his privacy, and stood up, irresolute, before going noiselessly out of the room, back to the kitchen. She'd write a letter, she thought. It was high time she wrote home.

Three times she pushed open the door a crack to peer in and see if he had woken up and three times she saw that he had not stirred. She made up the fire, looking round at him anxiously when coal grated against coal, but still he slept.

On her fourth visit, she found that he was awake and sitting up, leaning towards the fire. He did not hear her cautious opening of the door. Instinctively she opened her mouth to speak to him, but was shocked into silence, the words shrivelling and dying. She thought, in that moment, that she had never seen such grief before, such utter desolation. She could see what he would look like when he was old and his good looks ravaged by sickness.

Something was wrong. Her heart seemed to lurch with fear.

"Gavin? Gavin, what is it?" Swiftly she went to him and knelt beside his chair. "You look awful! Are you really all right? Has something happened to you, something you haven't told me?"

"Hey, what's all this about?" He turned and smiled at her and the look was gone. "I always look like death when I wake up. You've drawn the curtains! What time is it?" He looked at his watch. "My God, it's almost seven! You shouldn't have let me sleep so long."

"You needed it." Rachel sat back on her heels, looking at him with a puzzled frown. Had she imagined that ghastly expression, then? Or was it born of the nightmare hours he had endured in the crippled plane, the responsibility he bore for his crew, something he must feel himself unable to share with any civilian? But she wanted to share it – wanted to share everything with him.

"Poor Rachel," he said, stroking her hair. "This is hardly the kind of day you expected, is it? Let's go out somewhere really grand tonight, shall we?"

"Not unless you want to. It's a horrible night. I'm perfectly happy to stay in, if you'd rather."

"When will the others be home?"

"Alice is going to be late and Susan isn't coming home at all."

He grinned at her and twirled an imaginary moustache.

"Ho ho! I have you at my mercy, my pretty wench."

"Completely," she said.

His smile slowly died; then he reached out and pulled her towards him, shifting a little so that there was room for her, too, beside him in the chair. For a long moment he seemed to study her face.

"You know," he said at last. "You could be the saving of me."

"Oh?" She gave a puzzled smile. "How's that?"

"Every man needs something to live for."

"But you have – "

"Everything to live for?" He gave a breath of laughter. "I know. But there are times – " He broke off, and very gently, almost thoughtfully, brushed her cheek with his lips, not finishing his sentence. Rachel held her breath, feeling as if all her nerve endings were concentrated in that one spot.

"Finding you again was the best thing that's happened to me for a long time," he went on after a moment. "I was always fond of you. You were such a funny, anxious little thing – "

"Thanks!"

"Well, weren't you? Always minding your manners and saying thank-you-for-having-me, and trying so hard at those ghastly games."

"But you enjoyed them! You were so terribly competitive and so good at them – "

"We weren't that good. We just didn't care. You cared so much it was painful."

225

"You make me sound such a ninny."

"You were endearing."

"Diana thought I was a ninny."

He pulled a face.

"Yes, well, Di would. She judges everyone harshly." He sighed. "Me, most of all."

"Nonsense! She adores you."

"Well, I suppose I adore her too, sometimes. Unfortunately." His voice diminished to a mere thread and his expression was sad. "And there are other times," he said, "when I hate her guts. Family relationships are the damnedest things, aren't they?"

"I – I suppose so." Rachel sounded uncertain. "I haven't actually had many of my own."

"Well, never mind Di," he continued after a short silence. What had he been thinking? Rachel found herself unable to make any guesses. "She's an unwelcome third at this moment. I want to concentrate on you."

Could she ever have imagined, in all her wildest dreams, hearing such heavenly music as those words? She closed her eyes in sensuous pleasure as his mouth sought hers; and this, she soon realised, was the kind of kiss that must surely signal the abandonment of brotherly embraces for ever. The kisses of all the other young men who had been tried and found wanting were forgotten. She felt his hand on her breast, tasted the sweetness of his searching tongue, gasped with the joy of it.

"Oh Gavin, I love you so much!"

As, tremblingly, they drew apart the words seemed to surface of their own volition, terrifying her with their boldness. What would he think of her now? No girl should be the first to say such things. That was one of the rules, the received wisdom, handed down from mother to daughter and friend to friend.

"Honestly?" he asked, as if there might be some doubt about it.

"Honestly. I always have. I'm sorry," she added foolishly – meaning the embarrassment, the burden, the feeling that he might be expected to do something about it.

But he was smiling, apparently not burdened at all. He touched her forehead, her nose, her eyelids with small, light, butterfly kisses.

"Then marry me," he said.

13

It was a Sunday in late March, with the sun shining out of a cloudless sky and daffodils and forsythia and all the pink almond trees that were such a feature of the gardens of Ranelagh Avenue shouting aloud the glories of spring. It was a day made for celebration, but beneath the delight Rachel felt at walking from The Laurels to Kimberley Lodge with Gavin by her side, there was an undeniable feeling of apprehension.

She was reminded of the time when, sick with nerves and dreading the scorn of the Rossiters, she had gone next door for the first time. She had been doubtful then of her reception. The doubts were even greater now.

"I can't believe they took it so well when you told them," she said to Gavin. "I can't believe that your mother was really pleased." She hadn't, after all, been associated with the Rossiter family for all these years without knowing that there was no one in the entire world good enough for Gavin.

"Why wouldn't she be? Just because she was a bit miffed with you that time, all those years ago – "

"Three years," Rachel said. "Not long, really." And 'miffed' was hardly the word, she thought, remembering the tears and the fury and the total rejection. How could anyone forget it? Gavin squeezed her hand.

"Cheer up, sweetheart! I honestly don't know what you're so worried about. It's all right, believe me. Look, Ma's waiting for us at the door – "

And holding her arms wide in their voluminous sleeves, Rachel saw, like some beneficent priestess.

"Come, come – let me give you a kiss, Rachel dear. Welcome

227

to the family – a *real* Rossiter at last!"

"Thank you." Rachel succumbed to her embrace. "Thank you very much. Are you really pleased? I thought – "

"That I'd bear a grudge? Oh no, child. That's not my way. I believe in letting bygones be bygones. All that's forgotten and forgiven – "

How very magnanimous, said the small cynical voice in Rachel's head. But it was swamped, drowned, by the welcome from Mr Rossiter.

"Look what I've got," he said triumphantly, holding aloft a bottle of champagne. "The last brace of bottles in Warnfield, I shouldn't wonder. I had to get something special to drink your health. Where are those girls? Give Di and Alannah a shout, Gavin."

Di and Alannah. Best to get it over, Rachel thought, resignedly. She couldn't begin to imagine what they would say, let alone think, but at least she was spared Barney's reaction. She felt guiltily thankful that he couldn't get home that weekend.

Alannah was the first to come downstairs, and seemed genuinely friendly.

"*What* a dark horse," she said when she had kissed Rachel. "But you were always crazy about him, weren't you? We used to have a bit of a giggle about it, Diana and me. It seemed such a hopeless cause! It never crossed our minds that he would ever – " she caught herself in mid-sentence and apparently realised that, even by her standards, she was about to be more tactless than was acceptable on such an occasion. She gave Rachel another hug. "But at least you're One of Us, aren't you? I couldn't be more pleased, honestly."

"Thanks, Lannie."

"Show me the ring. Oh, it's lovely! What a dear little diamond! Bags be a bridesmaid! When's the wedding?"

"Soon," Gavin said, his arm round Rachel's shoulders. He bent and kissed her lightly on the tip of her nose. "Very soon," he added.

"What's the hurry?" Placidly, Mrs Rossiter smiled at them from the large armchair in the window where, as always, she had taken her place, the queen on her throne. "You're both very young."

Gavin's face seemed to grow very still.

"Not as young as all that," he said. "Times aren't what they were, Ma dear."

"Don't you think I recognise that?" His mother's smile had died and her remark was gravely reproachful. "I worry about you

228

constantly, Gavin. Believe me, you're never out of my thoughts or my prayers."

"Wow – let joy be unconfined!" Diana said ironically, making her entrance at this point. "What's this? A wake or a celebration?" She looked stunning in a plain black dress relieved by a black and yellow scarf tied with the kind of jaunty expertise that succeeded in making Rachel feel dowdily schoolgirlish in the tartan dress that had, up to that moment, seemed fashionable and becoming. She smiled brilliantly at Rachel but made no attempt to kiss her. "Congratulations are in order, I understand."

"You congratulate the man and give the lady your good wishes," Alannah instructed fussily. "I read it in Mrs Beeton."

"Then congratulations Gavin, and good wishes Rachel." Again Diana smiled as she raised the glass that her father had given her.

"I am about to make a speech," Mr Rossiter said. "Oh yes I am – "

"Oh no, you're not," chorused the family automatically.

"Silence, *mes enfants*! We have all known and loved Rachel for a very long time," he continued despite the groans from his children. "She has always seemed like a member of the family, and I, personally, am delighted that now she will be one in fact. As for Gavin – well, he knows how proud we are of him. He deserves nothing but the best – "

"Which I've got," Gavin said, looking down at Rachel.

"Stop stealing my lines! I was about to say that."

"Can't we get on with the drinking part?" Diana asked plaintively.

"Here's to both you dear young people. To long life and happiness, and may the sun that's shining today shine on you both for ever and ever."

"Amen," said Alannah irreverently. "To Gavin and Rachel."

"Gavin and Rachel."

"I and my future wife," Gavin began, in tones of pompous mock-solemnity that had the party groaning again, "wish to express our heartfelt thanks to you all. We wish," he went on, his voice throbbing with drama, "to ask of you one crucial question. It is a question that strikes at the very heart of family life; a question that comes from the very depths of our being – and, of course, when I say 'our', I refer to my future lady wife and myself – and one that demands an honest answer." His voice reverted to normality. "When the *hell* are you going to fill up these glasses?"

Amid laughter, Mr Rossiter brought the bottle round once

more. It was going to be all right, Rachel thought, the hard, icy knot of nerves in the pit of her stomach beginning to unfreeze itself. Alannah had been nicer than she had expected, admiring of the ring, thrilled at the prospect of a wedding in the family. Even now she was speculating about bridesmaids' dresses. Not pink, she was saying. Please not pink. I look awful in pink.

"What about you, Di?" she asked her sister, raising her voice to reach Diana who still stood on the fringe of the small group as if reluctant to commit herself absolutely to the day's celebration.

"Me? What's it to do with me?" Diana's voice seemed to ring out across the room. Rachel, looking across, was struck by the look of contemptuous amusement on her face. "You can count me out," she said. "I'm not the bridesmaid type."

"My dears, there's plenty of time for all that," Mrs Rossiter said comfortably. "Plenty of time."

Gavin, catching Rachel's eye, gave her a small, reassuring, heart-warming wink.

It was going to be all right. She was almost sure.

Sending letters to Uganda was something of a lottery. Sometimes they arrived in reasonable time, sometimes they were delayed for months and sometimes they didn't arrive at all.

'I wonder,' Rachel wrote to her parents in the letter which told them of her engagement, 'when you will get this. Soon, I hope. How I wish you were here! I am so happy, and I want someone of my own family to be happy *with*! You are happy for me, aren't you? I wonder if you've got Gavin's letter yet, and what he said to you. He wanted everything to be very proper and above board, and said he was going to ask you for my hand in the time-honoured way. I trust you won't withold your permission. You'd better not! I do love him so.

'Grandma isn't best pleased because she "took agin" the Rossiters ages ago and nothing they do can make her change her mind. I pointed out how kind they were on the first day of the war when they invited us to their air raid shelter, but she said that one shelter doesn't make a summer, or words to that effect. They invited her and Grandpa to the celebration lunch, but she refused because of gastric trouble – which none of them believed for one minute! Still, her presence wouldn't have added much to the gaiety of nations. Barney was soldiering on Salisbury Plain and couldn't get home, but all the others were there and were very nice to me.'

230

She paused a while, chewing her pen. That was hardly the whole truth, she thought. Diana wasn't nice. Diana had more or less said the right things, but her smile was strained and her eyes had been hostile. Later, after lunch when Rachel had carried glasses out from the dining room, she had come across Diana and Gavin facing each other just inside the kitchen with the atmosphere crackling with tension, taut with remarks just uttered or about to be uttered. Seeing her, Diana had turned and without a word had left them.

Rachel had wanted to ask what was wrong, but Gavin gave her no chance.

"It's such a gorgeous day, we ought to go out somewhere this afternoon," he said brightly, taking the glasses from her hand. "What about Chuffington Common, for old times' sake?"

"Is Diana – ?"

"Oh, never mind her! She's in one of her moods."

He dismissed the incident lightly, but Rachel was under no illusion. Diana was dangerous. Diana had scuppered Gavin's engagement to Jacqueline. He hadn't gone into details about that particular episode in his life, but that much had been clear between the lines. And Mrs Rossiter, with her smug, platitudinous 'No hurry' remarks. Was she truly as delighted as she had maintained?

With Gavin to put his arm around her, to give her smiles and kisses, it was easy to be lulled into a false sense of security. She knew, however, that she had to keep on her guard. The insidious power of the family was not to be underestimated.

It was the week following her visit to Warnfield that Germany invaded Denmark and Norway – for those countries' own protection, it was said – and a naval battle raged off the Norwegian coast. It marked a new phase of the war, for at last British bombers were permitted to attack a target on the mainland of Europe and were dispatched to bomb Stavanger airport.

Though Gavin was not among those who made the flight, everything was in a state of change and confusion, and all leave was cancelled with personal matters forced to take a back seat. Rachel's spirits were raised in early May when he phoned to say that he hoped to manage a quick trip to London the following Saturday. She made a chart: so many days, so many hours, so many minutes – but at the last moment he phoned again to say he couldn't make it. He was being sent to another station, Chilbury, still in Yorkshire, but further east, transferring to Whitleys. There was no hope of leave just yet.

"Sorry, darling," he said. "I'm so sorry."

"Just so long as you're all right – "

"I'm all right. Longing to see you."

"Mm. Me too. When do you think – ?"

"Can't say. Things are hotting up."

"Take care."

"You bet. I love you, Rachel."

"Love you, too."

"Not coming?" Susan, passing through the hall, put a sympathetic hand on her shoulder. "Poor love! Bloody war."

"Isn't it just?" Rachel agreed.

T-Tango was the name of Gavin's new aircraft. She had a letter from him a few days later, referring to it as if it were a living, sentient being; and she learned about his crew, too. There was Griff, the first officer, an ebullient Welshman; Prof, the wireless operator, who had been a teacher – an old man of twenty-eight; Jimmy, the navigator, who had a girlfriend who was the spitting image of Dorothy Lamour; Mike, the rear gunner.

She became aware that Gavin had moved into quite a different phase of his life where T-Tango and the crew were all-important. She understood, she told herself. She absolutely understood. Personal relationships, love, marriage – all had to wait. At least he phoned and wrote to her when he could, and she wrote back. Every day.

Though she thought of him and worried about him constantly, her life had taken on a distinctly more interesting aspect lately and, day-to-day, she was not actively unhappy. For several weeks, when first appointed to the Ministry of Information, she had dutifully typed the reports dictated to her by Colin Milner – the ageing, sometime writer of thrillers, now employed not so much to thrill as to ensure that news favourable to the Allies was given the widest possible publicity overseas.

Rachel was, at first, much in awe of him. He was, after all, a real writer, someone she had actually heard of. Further acquaintance, however, demonstrated that though able, he was constitutionally lazy. He was, it transpired, only too happy to allow her to compile the reports and was delighted with the ability she showed.

"You can actually write the King's English!" he said, pleased and astonished.

"Of course."

"No 'of course' about it. Most people can't."

"I can't do anything else, really," Rachel admitted. "English was my only good subject."

"Nonsense! You have a good analytical mind. You can see what to put in and what to leave out."

"Can I go on doing it, then?"

"Certainly," Mr Milner agreed, visions of long lunches and soporific afternoons floating before him. "I'll have a quick run through and make a note of suggestions, and you can take it from there. I suppose I'd better see the reports and approve them before you send them upstairs."

"Of course."

It didn't matter to her that they went out under his name while her pay stayed at the very bottom of the typists' scale. At least life had become more challenging. She took pride in describing events economically, honing her sentences, selecting the right word. And when, as sometimes happened, Colin Milner took her up on some matter of syntax or scored his blue pencil through passages he considered could be better expressed, she took his strictures seriously and learned from them.

Worry about Gavin became part of everyday life, no more and no less than that suffered by most other women in the country. She had little direct knowledge of his activities, but since the invasion of Holland and Belgium and the bombing of Rotterdam by the Germans, any British scruples regarding raids on Germany had disappeared altogether. The nights of the leaflets were over. Now more dangerous missiles were dropped east of the Rhine and news bulletins frequently reported that 'one of our aircraft failed to return'.

Whenever she heard the dread statement, she felt certain it must, this time, refer to T-Tango. To the warning by Churchill, now Prime Minister to the relief of almost everyone, that he had nothing to offer but blood, sweat and tears, she felt she could add another promise. There was nothing, now, but the twist of fear in the gut that underlay everything – every action and every thought.

Gavin was long overdue for leave, but with the German Army marching inexorably through France, all leave was cancelled. Now there was Barney to worry about, for he had been sent to France at the beginning of May. No one knew quite what was happening there. On 20th May, Amiens fell in the morning and Abbeville in the afternoon; and less than a week later tens of thousands of British and French troops converged on Dunkirk to wait on the beaches under bombs and shell fire for the Armada of boats of all kinds that were to bring them home.

It was at the very beginning of June that Rachel, answering a ring at the doorbell, found Alannah standing on the doorstep. The clutch of fear intensified and she couldn't speak. It had to mean bad news, surely?

But Alannah was laughing.

"What's up?" she asked. "It's me, not a ghost! Aren't you pleased to see me?"

"Yes, yes of course. Come in. I just thought – "

"I tried to phone but there was a queue at the station and the one in the kiosk in Drury Lane didn't seem to be working."

"Drury Lane?"

"Yes – Drury Lane!" Inside now, bubbling with excitement, Alannah hugged her. "I got tired of waiting for an answer to my letter, so I bunked off college and came down. I've been there since crack of dawn, but at last I got to see Mr Fairman – the chap you said was more or less in charge, remember? – and he took down my particulars!"

"And?"

"He seemed impressed. He did, honestly! I swore I would do anything, go anywhere, could learn lines in less time than it takes to read them. He got me to read a bit of *Hay Fever*. I gathered they're trying to cast it – gosh, how I'd *love* to be Sorrel! And then he said what else could I do, so I did my lightning impressions of Shirley Temple and Gracie Fields and hundreds of others – even George Formby! He actually laughed at George Formby. Though I says it myself what didn't ought, my George Formby is really rather good."

"So what did he *say*?"

"Well, the usual. You know – don't call us, ducky, we'll call you – but he did ask if I would be free at a moment's notice and I said 'You bet!' He liked me, Rachel, I know he did. Listen, can I stay here tonight? I could share your room, couldn't I? Then I'll go there again tomorrow first thing and start pestering all over again. It's the only way."

"But what about – ?"

"I told the old Queen Bee that I simply had to go and see my fiancé who was wounded in France and just back from Dunkirk – which reminds me, Barney is OK."

"Oh, thank God!" It was entirely typical of Alannah, Rachel felt, that this news should have taken second place to the other.

"He's not home yet, but he phoned from Folkestone and he's fit and well. Expect him when they see him, he told Ma."

"What a relief for her, and your father. They must have been out of their minds with worry."

"I knew he'd be all right." Alannah spoke airily, looking into the

234

hall mirror and tucking little tendrils of hair into place. "Barney could always look after himself. He'd suit you a lot better than Gavin, you know."

Rachel stared at her.

"I happen to love Gavin," she said distantly.

"Don't we all know it!" Alannah grinned and flapped a hand at her. "Love's Young Dream just isn't in it! Listen, it is all right if I stay, isn't it? I know you've got a double bed in your room because I saw it that time I came before, so yah-boo, sucks to you, you can't pretend there's no room."

"Of course you can stay." Rachel took her arm. "But we'd better sort of ask Susan, just for politeness's sake. Come on, everyone's in the garden tonight. It's such a wonderful evening."

"Is that gorgeous French violinist there?"

"Paul? Good Lord, no! He went into the Free French Army ages ago. We can do a nice line in sailors, though. One of Alice's cousins is here – "

"Less drippy than she, I trust."

"Shut up! Alice is all right. Mind you behave yourself."

"Don't I always?"

She did, of course. She had always, like all the Rossiters, been able to switch on the charm when it suited her. Susan seemed delighted to see her again, and old Mr Spivey from across the road, who had taken a fancy to Susan and was now a constant visitor, sat up a little straighter and stroked his moustache. Rachel was, however, quite pleased to see that although Alice's sailor cousin was perfectly pleasant, his eyes still rested on Alice rather than the newcomer. In Rachel's opinion, Lieut. Keith Bessemer was a far more attractive propostion than the odious Eric. She only hoped that Alice recognised it too.

For a long time they sat in the narrow walled garden where the evening sun lingered, talking of matters large and small. Mr Spivey was wrestling with his conscience over the matter of the newly formed Local Defence Volunteers. He was too old for them. Too old *on paper*, he said, over and over; but not a bit too old in fact. He could defend the gas-works just as well as Mr Hubbard next door who'd joined up the day the force was formed and, even as he spoke, was drilling in the park with a broom-handle instead of a rifle because rifles were in short supply.

Age was relative, Mr Spivey said. Mr Hubbard, now, was an old man – bent, crippled with rheumatism, could hardly see a hand before his face, no matter what his birth certificate said. On the other hand, he, Wallace Spivey, was spry. Trim.

235

"Look at that," he said, banging his midriff with his clenched fist. "Not an ounce of spare flesh. Not an ounce."

What should he do? Perjure himself by lying about his age? Find some other war work? All he'd been offered was the job of collecting waste paper, he told them disgustedly. What kind of job was that for a man of his capabilities? Was that the sort of thing to make Hitler sit up and take notice?

"If you ask me," Keith Bessemer said, "I'd advise you to hold your fire. Air raids on London are bound to start soon, then you'll all be in it and there'll be jobs for everyone. I wish you and Alice would get out, Aunt Susan."

"My job is here," Susan said calmly.

"And so is mine."

Alice spoke bravely, with no evidence of the fear which Rachel knew was beneath the surface, for she had confided in her one night and had spoken of her nightmares.

"Everyone else seems so brave," she had said. "But I can't get it out of my mind. Just imagine houses falling down on top of you. Imagine being trapped!"

Now, however, she lifted her chin and smiled at her cousin, inviting his admiration. Rachel, mentally, rubbed her hands. It all, she thought, seemed to be going very well. She was thankful that Alannah hadn't succeeded in putting a spanner in the works of this budding romance; not, it had to be said, for any want of trying.

Susan was, of course, perfectly agreeable that she should stay there that night. It seemed to Rachel, as they prepared for bed, that the old relationship between them had been utterly restored and, despite all that had happened, she was glad that the friendship had endured. Even if she now regarded it with more caution, was less starry-eyed than in the past, she still valued it.

It felt quite like old times, listening to Alannah rattle on about her dreams and her hopes – how Mr Fairman had looked at her; how he had asked the woman with the clipboard to make sure she had her address; how (once more) he had laughed at the George Formby impression; how she, Alannah, was sure, absolutely *positive* that he'd rather fancied her.

"You can't mistake that look in the eyes, can you?" she demanded; and Rachel agreed that you could not. "Of course he was old," she went on. "Oldish, anyway. Nearly as old as Dad, I suppose."

"Your father's not really old," Rachel said as she climbed into bed.

236

"He's forty-six. But he has the kind of looks that wear well, don't you think?" Alannah wiped some surplus cream off her face and got in beside her.

"Like Mr Spivey?" Rachel suggested, and they both giggled.

"Imagine craving to drill with broom-handles and wear those pathetic armbands," Alannah said.

"He'd feel he was Doing His Bit. Everybody's the same. All right if I turn out the light?"

"OK. You know," Alannah went on out of the darkness, "I reckon Gavin will wear well, don't you? He's got Dad's sort of gloss and energy."

"I don't care if he does or not," Rachel said softly after a moment. "Just so long as he goes on *being*."

"Oh, he'll be all right. We're all survivors, we Rossiters. Look at Barney! An awful lot of his battalion got taken prisoner, apparently."

A sudden and totally unexpected rage gripped Rachel so that for a moment she was unable to speak. Who did they think they were? Did they honestly imagine themselves to be immortal? Was Barney inherently more worthy of being saved than his friends? Every night, to her certain knowledge, Gavin was in the most fearful danger – danger which Alannah seemed to dismiss without a thought. Yet it hadn't always been like that.

"You didn't seem to think that when he wanted to go to Spain," she said.

"Oh, gosh, that was ages ago! You're not still harping on that, are you? You really must learn to be less sensitive, Rachel. You'd think you'd know by now that it really doesn't *do* in our family. Tell me – " she leaned up on one elbow. "What have you and Gavin decided about the wedding? Have you fixed the date?"

"Not yet. There hasn't been much of a chance."

Alice sighed, and sank back on to her pillow.

"I suppose not. Poor Gavin! They're keeping him busy, aren't they? Di says he's looking awfully tired."

Rachel, in the middle of a yawn, became rigid with shock.

"Diana's seen him?"

"Yes. I think he spent the weekend before last with her. Yes, it must have been then, because last weekend she went home. I phoned up on the Saturday and she answered – that's when she told me about Gavin. Why?"

Couldn't she honestly see why? No, of course not. It would seem quite natural to her, that one Rossiter would spend the weekend with another Rossiter rather than come to London to spend time with an outsider, even if that outsider were a fiancée.

"No reason," she said stiffly. "Good night. I'm going to sleep now."

"'Night," responded Alannah, unaware of any hurt. "Roll on the morning and darling Mr Fairman. Oh, please God, bless Mr Fairman! He must take me, mustn't he? You do think he will, don't you?"

But Rachel, feigning sleep, said nothing.

When towards the end of June Gavin was finally rested and came to London on a weekend pass, Rachel taxed him with it. She had vowed to herself that she wouldn't mention it. Told herself that if she married a Rossiter, this is what it would be like; especially with Gavin and Diana, who had always been so close. It was just something she would have to learn to put up with.

Maybe, she thought, he had just driven over one afternoon; after all, Cambridge was nearer to Chilbury than London. But not *that* near! That theory wouldn't wash. He must have had at least a twenty-four-hour pass. And anyway, why hadn't he mentioned it? He had phoned her often enough and said how much he wished he could see her, hold her in his arms, kiss her; but never once had he said that he'd been able to spend time with Diana.

Somehow, despite her vow of silence, the words seemed to speak themselves.

They were lying on a grassy hillock that seemed a million miles from London, yet was no more than twenty miles away overlooking peaceful Hertfordshire woodland. Though the country held its breath, imminently expecting invasion, here it seemed unimaginable, totally ludicrous. A honeysuckle bush was close beside them with wild roses clambering over its higher branches, and the air was redolent with all the scents of summer, birdsong and the murmuring of bees.

Rachel had lain in his arms all afternoon, happy at last. Their lovemaking had been low-key, for from time to time others had walked along the footpath close by, and once a child's large rubber ball had come to rest in the small of Gavin's back.

Still it was a time of great sweetness and contentment. They had talked and kissed, made plans and kissed again. They must marry soon, Gavin said. Somehow he would find accommodation for her. He wanted her to be with him – and in addition, he wanted her to leave London. There would be raids, he was certain of it.

"That's what Alice's cousin said."

"Alice's cousin was right. Come on, fix the day – "

"It depends on you. When can you get leave?"

"I should think – say, six weeks from now? The first week in August? How about the 3rd? That's a Saturday."

"I don't think I've anything important planned," Rachel said with assumed offhandedness; and he laughed and held her close and told her to consult her diary, just to make sure there was nothing vital like a hairdresser's appointment which could interfere.

"The sun's given you freckles," he said, tickling them gently with a long stem of grass.

She reached out and touched the face, so much loved and now so close. Diana was right, she thought; he did look tired.

"Alannah mentioned that you saw Diana." There it was – the statement that had lain all afternoon in her subconscious.

"Did she?" He had been lying on his stomach, cap and tunic abandoned. Now he rolled over on his back and stared up at the sky, one arm shielding his eyes.

"You – you didn't mention it."

"Didn't think it important." Then, when she didn't speak, he removed his arm and turned his head to look at her. "Do you think it was important?"

"No. Well, not really." She half sat up and began, idly, to encourage a ladybird to move from a blade of grass on to her finger. "I did sort of wonder," she said at last, "how you managed to find the time."

"When I couldn't get to London? Now, come on, darling!" he reached for her arm and pulled her down to his level again. "You're surely not jealous of my own sister, are you?"

Yes, yes, Rachel wanted to scream. But she said nothing and could not meet his eye.

"Look," he said persuasively. "One night, I was scheduled to fly. Was intending to fly. But Griff let on to the CO that I'd been ill all day with a touch of God-knows-what. Delhi-belly, Montezuma's Revenge – call it what you like. The quack grounded me. Put me off-duty for twenty four hours. I didn't fancy hanging around the Mess feeling lousy, so I went down to Di's and felt lousy. OK? Understood?"

"Yes, of course." Rachel felt overwhelmed with guilt. "I just wish you'd said – "

"It was such a last-minute, off-the-cuff thing. I was back on the station by twelve the following day. I could hardly have been down to London and back in the time."

"No, of course not. Honestly, I'm not complaining, darling. It's just that I never stop thinking of you and worrying about you."

He pulled her into his arms once more, and covered her face with small kisses.

"Silly one! Nothing's going to happen to me."

"Of course not," Rachel murmured dryly. "You're a Rossiter, aren't you?"

Back in London, much later, he took her out to a French restaurant in the King's Road, where the owner and his wife were still in mourning for Paris which had fallen the previous week.

"Just imagine if it was London," Rachel whispered, seeing their stricken faces. "It doesn't bear thinking about, does it?"

"*Vive de Gaulle*," Gavin said, raising his glass towards the restaurateur, unleashing, at last, smiles and straightened backs and expressions of patriotic fervour.

"*Vive le* RAF," responded Madame from behind her cash desk.

Gavin rose, raised his glass once more, and bowed. There were more mutual expressions of esteem. He was smiling when, finally, he turned back to Rachel, taking both her hands in his.

"So much for the *entente cordiale*," he said. "Now about us. Let's take a run up to Warnfield tomorrow and get everything settled. We can ring Ma tonight to warn her."

"She's not going to like it."

"Then," Gavin said hardily, "she'll have to do the other thing. Don't worry about it."

"I'll have to ask Grandma about a reception."

"It'll be at our place, naturally."

"I don't know, Gavin. Grandma might be hurt if I don't ask her first."

Gavin groaned.

"Oh, Lor'! Maybe we ought to get a special licence and elope."

"I wouldn't mind."

He seemed to give the matter his serious consideration, then shook his head.

"No – no, we can't do that. The family would be upset. Especially Alannah! She seems to think we're arranging the whole thing so that she can be a bridesmaid. Besides, you'll want a splash, won't you? White tulle and a bouquet and all that?"

"I suppose so. That's not what's important, though." Even as she spoke, however, she felt a tremor of excitement. Yes, she thought. Oh, *yes*! Marrying Gavin was the important thing, not how it was done, that went without saying; but the thought of floating down the aisle of Warnfield Parish Church on Grandpa's arm was utterly beguiling, she had to admit. She could see it all – could see Gavin waiting for her at the altar, looking, as he always did, so wonderfully handsome in his uniform, and everyone else dressed to the nines. How her mother would love to be there, and what a thousand pities that her parents were so far away! The rows, the harsh words that had been uttered in Entebbe now belonged to the forgotten past. She owed it to them, she thought, to have the best of weddings and thousands of photographs. She could just imagine her mother showing them round to her friends in Entebbe; could imagine the pride with which she would display pictures of her daughter on the arm of such a devastatingly handsome hero.

"Don't worry about a thing," Gavin said. "I'll talk Ma round, see if I don't. And if the worst comes to the worst – well, I don't need parental permission, do I? Not like you, my little child bride."

"I am nineteen," Rachel said with great dignity. "And a half," she added, with slightly less. "You can't call me a child."

"I shall call you whatever I like," Gavin replied with mock ruthlessness. "Love, honour and obey, don't forget."

"Till death us do part," Rachel said softly.

She had made a bed up for him in one of the top rooms, on Susan's instructions. Did Susan really expect him to sleep there alone? Rachel thought about it as, sitting up in bed with her arms about her knees, she waited impatiently for the hush of night to descend on the house.

Alice expected it. Alice had popped in for a few moments before going to bed to say that Keith had phoned earlier. He was coming up to town the following week and wanted to take her out. Did Rachel think, she asked, that it would be fair to Eric if she went to the theatre with Keith? He was so nice, such good fun and he was, after all, a cousin. On the other hand, she had sort of promised to keep herself for Eric –

"Go," Rachel advised her without hesitation.

"Gosh, Rachel, you're always so decisive!" Alice had looked at her admiringly. "You know," she added a little shyly, "I've been meaning to say – I was wrong about you and Barney. I can see what you mean about Gavin. Barney's nice, but Gavin's something special."

"Well, I think so, anyway," Rachel agreed.

"I'm so awfully glad that you're happy, Rachel. And I must

say – " Alice bit her lip and went pink. "I must say, I do admire you," she finished in a rush. "I mean, I know how crazy you and Gavin are about each other, but you still stick to your principles."

"Oh?" Rachel raised her eyebrows in surprise and some amusement. "What principles are these?"

"Well, saving yourself for after marriage, and all that." Alice's voice was earnest. "I do realise it can't be easy."

"How do you know I have saved myself? It's not a thing one would be likely to advertise, is it? I mean, you'd hardly put an announcement in *The Times* in the Virginity Lost column."

Alice giggled in spite of herself.

"You mean you – oh, you're having me on, Rachel! You haven't, have you? Gone All the Way, I mean?"

Teasingly, Rachel grinned at her.

"Wouldn't you like to know?" Then, seeing Alice's expression, she took pity on her. "No," she went on. "Not yet."

"Well, good for you! It's always a mistake."

"That's what you've found, is it? In your experience?"

"Oh, shut up! You know I haven't. And won't, what's more."

But I will, Rachel thought. And soon. She hoped that she proved to be good at it. How could a girl know? How could you learn? Some people said it hurt a lot the first time; even Mrs Marryatt and Evelyn Home, those two oracles who had always been her mentors in such matters, often stressed to enquiring correspondents that the initiation into the mysteries of sex was sometimes disappointing.

She felt she would be good at it. She wanted it enough; wanted Gavin, anyway, and was fully prepared to exercise patience and fortitude and any other quality that might be necessary. Oh Susan, *please* hurry up and come to bed, she thought, as after Alice left her she did her best to will her lively landlady into tiredness, into switching off the radio, turning off the lights, and coming upstairs.

And at last she heard her; heard the tread on the staircase, and the click of the bathroom light; heard the bathroom door shut behind her, heard taps running and the flushing of the lavatory. Heard, finally, the sound of the bedroom door being closed.

She gave her half an hour after that. And then, with great caution, she opened her own door and looked out. There was no line of light under any door. No sound anywhere.

Slowly, cautiously, her bare feet silent on the carpeted stairs, she began to make her way to the next floor.

★

"It's no good," Gavin said at last, lying rigid beside her. "It's no bloody good. God, what's the matter with me?"

"It's all right. Honestly."

"No, it's not. How can you say that?"

Angrily, as if disgusted with himself, Gavin flung the bedclothes aside and went over to the chest of drawers, fumbling for a cigarette. The lighter flared, then dwindled, but not before Rachel had seen his face. It looked drawn and old, contorted by self-disgust.

Drawing on his cigarette so that the end of it glowed in the darkness, he went to stand by the uncurtained window. The moon was almost full and his profile was sharply defined.

Rachel felt a great sadness – not so much for herself, though she couldn't deny that her disappointment was great, but for him. He had wanted her so much. They had planned this at the restaurant, holding hands and smiling at each other with excitement.

He had drawn her into his bed and his kisses and caresses had quickly brought her to the point where any lingering doubts and fears were swept away. But as her passion mounted, his seemed to languish and die.

"Don't worry," she urged him now. "It doesn't matter. You're tired."

On the back page of Alice's magazine, she remembered, it had been clearly stated only last week that it was necessary for wives to be aware of the problems often suffered by their husbands. ('Wives', not 'women', for no unmarried woman would get herself in this position, if she took Mrs Marryat's advice.) Husbands, said Mrs Marryat, often suffered worry and stress which their wives, confined as they were to the daily round within the four walls of their home, were unable to comprehend. Sometimes the strains and tiredness consequent upon their work made it impossible for them to make love. Any wife worthy of the name would be patient and loving and understanding.

"What on earth are you going to think? You're better off without me."

"Gavin, it's all *right*. Why don't you come back and let me hold you? Let's be like we were this afternoon. I want to feel close to you."

"Do you still want to marry me? How could you?"

"Don't be idiotic! Of course I do. I love you, don't I?"

"I feel so damned useless."

"There'll be lots of other times. Maybe you're inhibited by being in someone else's house. All this creeping about."

She heard him sigh. He opened the bottom half of the sash window, ground out his cigarette on the sill and threw it out. For a few moments he stood motionless, leaning out, as if communing with the stars. Then he turned and looked towards the bed where she sat waiting for him.

"You're a girl in a million, Rachel," he said. His voice sounded strange, almost as if he were crying. He came and sat on the side of the bed, holding her hands. "God knows why you love me. I'm a pretty worthless type, if the truth were to be known."

"What nonsense!"

He gave one great sob and pressed the heels of both hands to his eyes.

"The last thing I want is to disappoint you."

"I know. Oh, Gavin! Darling! Don't be upset. Another time it will all be different, you'll see."

"I don't mean just this. I mean – oh, in all sorts of ways. I know how I seem. All brash and cocksure and the-world-owes-me-a-living kind of thing. But inside I'm not a bit like that. I'm – I'm jelly, Rachel. Just jelly."

She had a sudden vision of a bomber trapped in the criss-cross beams of searchlights, tracer bullets falling like rain.

"Who wouldn't be?" she whispered. "Come back to bed, darling. Come."

It was getting light when she crept back to her own room, leaving him asleep. He came down to breakfast looking and behaving just as usual and it was not until they were on their way to Warnfield that he referred to the incidents of the night.

"You were right, of course," he said. "It'll all be different another time. It'd better be!"

She kissed him.

"It will be. Don't give it another thought."

By the time they drove back to London, all the necessary arrangements had been made. Perhaps compensating for his previous night's shortcomings, Gavin was forceful and determined and would brook no talk of delay from his mother. He was brutal in his arguments.

"Ma, I'm risking my neck every night," he said. "I want to marry Rachel now, and I want her with me. Surely you can understand that?"

"But you're both so young!"

"Not that young. Twenty-four! I've got seventeen-year-old boys in my squadron who think I'm practically in my dotage."

"Gavin does have a point, Carina," Mr Rossiter said, rather

surprising Rachel by his support. "If he's old enough to fight for his country, then I think we should respect him when he says he wants to get married, and not put difficulties in his way."

"Put them in our way if you like," Gavin said flatly. "All that would mean is a special licence and a London registry office. You pays your money and takes your choice."

So Mrs Rossiter with her 'No hurry' talk was silenced. Gavin even managed to charm, moderately, Rachel's grandmother, and get her agreement to holding the reception in the garden of Kimberley Lodge, a marquee to be provided by the Council.

"It's bound to be disruptive," Gavin argued. "The last thing we want is to put you to any trouble."

"Well, I don't know – "

"Our garden will be at its peak just then," Grandpa said wistfully. "Still, perhaps you're right. You Rossiters are so much more practised at catering for numbers."

Alice and Alannah were to be the bridesmaids, and Rachel undertook to get a suitable pattern and samples of material from John Lewis's the very next week. And for Rachel herself, said Mrs Rossiter, beginning to get into the spirit of the thing in spite of herself, she knew the very women – her own pet seamstress who had made for her many, many times over the years and who would produce a wedding dress that would look as if it had come from a Paris couturier. At a fraction of the cost, of course.

"All we need is somewhere to live," Gavin said as they drove away from Warnfield. "I'll get on to that right away."

"I suppose I'll have to put my notice in."

Rachel felt a pang of regret at the thought of losing her congenial job, but it lasted no more than a second. How could she compare it with being Gavin's wife?

"Oh darling," she said softly. "I can't wait, can you?"

Meat and tea and fats might be rationed, but somehow a wedding breakfast was to be scraped together. Friends sacrificed stocks put down for Christmas, grocers turned blind eyes, farmers in the country were visited and proved to be generous with butter and eggs when it came to the wedding of an heroic RAF pilot.

Little by little, Mrs Rossiter collected the ingredients for a cake. Rachel, visiting Warnfield to be fitted by the dressmaker, was thrilled with the dress and excited by all the discussion regarding the great day, coming closer by the minute.

A telephone call from Gavin in mid-July brought her the best news of all. He'd managed to get hold of a tiny cottage, he told her – a bit primitive, standing on its own at the edge of a field, but perfectly suitable. It had been occupied by a fellow officer, now posted to Kent. His wife, a Scottish girl, was imminently expecting a baby and had elected to go back to her home in Edinburgh for the birth.

Rachel caught a train at the crack of dawn on Saturday morning and was with him by eleven o'clock. He took her straight out to see the cottage. It was plain, square, unadorned, without any fancifully romantic appurtenances such as thatched roof or roses round the door, but it had all the necessary conveniences. The bathroom had to be approached through the kitchen, but who cared about that? There was a front door to close against the outside world, that was the important thing.

It had a tiny living room and a short steep flight of stairs leading to the bedroom which looked out over the fields that Gavin had mentioned.

"The other bedroom's hardly worthy of the name," said the present occupant, who, heavily pregnant, had left her task of packing the kitchen equipment into boxes and had followed them upstairs. "Still, it's useful to put things in. There's not much storage space."

"You must be sad to go."

"Yes." The girl sighed. "Still, that's the way it goes. We've been happy here. I love the view from this window."

Rachel looked towards it once more. There was a field of ripening wheat directly in front, with a broad, grassy path to the side of it leading uphill towards a five-barred gate in a grey stone wall. Beyond the gate, the path curved around the side of a wood, one hill folding gracefully upon another.

"It's lovely," she said. "I know we'll be happy here too."

"You can bet on it," Gavin said, smiling down at her.

Any hopes Rachel might have cherished that there might, this night, be an opportunity to wipe out the memory of the last she had spent with Gavin were to be dashed, for he was on duty and she lay alone in the high white bed under the eaves of a cottage close by the pub. The sound of the planes flying overhead just before midnight made her feel much nearer him, much more immediately involved in his day-to-day danger.

Many hours later, she heard them coming back, but it was not until some time after that she knew T-Tango was safe yet again. How would she cope, going through that vigil night after night? It would take, she thought, a special kind of strength.

Back in London, the countdown to the wedding began. Alice's

dress was ready and pronounced beautiful. Alannah, as yet still at the Rose Kelly Academy, required one more fitting, so her mother reported. As for Rachel's own dress, Mrs Rossiter said that it was almost finished.

"You'll be up this weekend, won't you?" she said.

"Yes, I'll be there Saturday afternoon."

Saturday morning was her last day at the Ministry, for she had given herself one week at leisure in Warnfield before the wedding. It had seemed, like so many other things in life, a good idea at the time; however, once the final details of her dress had been decided, and a list made of all the wedding presents that had so far arrived, she felt strangely out of place.

Somehow, here in Warnfield, it seemed that the wedding was nothing to do with her and with Gavin. It had been taken over by others, its main purpose forgotten amid the welter of arrangements that had to be made. She knew such things were inevitable, but she longed to see him just once more before the day – to feel his arms around her again and to hear his assurances that being together was the only importance.

And she *would* see him! She would go by train to York and would get a bus from there to Chilbury. She knew the way now, after her last trip. Nothing could be easier. After all, she had settled the problems connected with the dress. It wasn't as if her presence was really required – in fact the opposite was the case. Even the few tentative suggestions she had made regarding the reception had been swept aside by Mrs Rossiter.

"I don't think you should go chasing after him," Grandma said dourly when she was told of Rachel's planned trip.

"Grandma, I'm marrying him! Any chase is over. And I'll be back on Wednesday."

There was no telephone at the cottage, so she was unable to tell him of her plans. She enlivened the journey by picturing his surprise. With any luck, she could be there by lunch time. If he'd been flying, he might probably still be in bed. Her heart raced at the thought. This time would be different, perfect, a forerunner of many, many other times.

The train was crowded with servicemen of all kinds; and if she hadn't known that happiness had made her pretty, then their reaction would have told her so. But though she smiled and replied to their overtures, she kept her distance, sat in her corner, and watched the countryside go by.

The train was so slow – much, much too slow! And there were far too many stops. But at last, inevitably, it arrived – and there,

247

right outside the station was her bus. She sprinted and caught it, and stood, strap-hanging, laughing with triumph and all those around smiled in sympathy.

It dropped her at the end of the lane. The wheat, she saw, was yellower than it had been on her last trip. There were bright poppies on the edge of the field and the sky was cloudless.

She could see the cottage ahead of her, and quickened her footsteps. The little wooden gate squeaked as she opened it. There was a tiny front garden, choked with weeds. She would do something about that – and she would polish the knocker and the doorhandle. Oh, there was so much she would do! It was going to be their place, their palace.

The door opened at her touch. There was no need for locks and bolts out here. Who would want to come in? Only friends, she thought.

"Gavin?" she called.

There was no answer. Perhaps he was asleep. She smiled to herself. She'd waken him with a kiss, she thought; Sleeping Beauty in reverse – the handsome prince being woken by the princess.

Quietly she went upstairs and pushed open the door to the bedroom; but this, too, was empty. He had been here quite recently, though. The bedclothes were pushed back, his uniform jacket was slung on a chair.

And also on the chair was an ivory satin dressing gown, unmistakably feminine. Rachel stared at it, bewildered. Her gaze travelled round the room. There was a blue enamelled brush and comb on the small dressing table; an open jar of face cream, a drift of powder.

Gavin must have let someone else use it, she thought. That was it, of course. He had lent the cottage for the weekend to one of his crew, perhaps. Well, she hoped they'd made good use of it. It was quite clear two people had used the bed – hopefully with more success, she thought wryly, than she and Gavin had enjoyed.

A sudden breeze gusted the curtains inward from the open window, and with it came the sound of laughter. Time she got out of there. She turned for the door, glancing as she did so towards the view that she had so admired on the previous occasion.

Her heart seemed to stop beating. Gavin and Diana were sauntering down the path, arms round each other. Like lovers. They looked happy, without a care in the world. As Rachel watched, they came to a halt and Gavin, laughing, stuck poppies in Diana's hair.

248

She couldn't move, couldn't turn her eyes away from them. She felt desperately, physically sick – sick with disbelief, yet somehow, beneath the disbelief, she recognised the truth and saw that it had always been there, waiting to be discovered.

Gavin and Diana. How could he? How *could* he?

She had no memory of going downstairs, but found herself, somehow, standing at the open front door. And still they came towards her, happily dawdling, engrossed in each other, unaware of her presence.

Then Diana looked up, stopped in her tracks and pointed. Rachel saw Gavin look towards her. His face seemed blank, wiped of all expression; then, giving a hoarse cry, he began to run towards her.

And she, weeping, waited for him.

"Well, at least she knows now," Diana said to Gavin.

"Just leave us a minute, Di." Gavin's eyes were on Rachel; but though all three of them were standing awkwardly in the small living room, he made no attempt to touch her and Rachel was glad of it. Once Diana had gone upstairs, however, he came closer. He reached out a hand towards her, but let it drop as she shrank away from him.

She was trembling, and had wrapped her arms about herself as if for warmth and comfort.

"Rachel," Gavin began falteringly. "I – I'm sorry. I don't know what to say."

What was there to say? She tried to frame the words but could not speak. Blindly she shook her head.

"Rachel, darling, please – let me explain."

"No." At least she managed that. "You can't."

"I didn't mean this to happen. I didn't know she was coming." Rachel sank into a chair, her head bent, not looking at him, not speaking. "Honestly, that's the truth." Gavin crouched down beside her. She looked at him then.

"What difference does it make?" she whispered. "You and she – you're lovers. It's horrible!"

"I know." He got up and walked away from her, towards the window. It had old-fashioned wooden shutters; so useful, the previous occupant had said. You didn't need black-out curtains. Idly he pulled one side towards him, then pushed it away again. "I know how this must seem – " He stopped, turned towards her. His face was wearing that haggard, tortured look she had seen before. He ran his hand through his hair, a gesture of desperation. "Don't you see," he went on, his voice rising, "I need you so badly! She won't leave me alone – "

Sick at heart, Rachel closed her eyes, saying nothing, and he too fell silent as if he were suddenly aware of how pathetic he must sound.

"I loved you," Rachel said at last. "I loved you so much. But I suppose, really, for you, almost anyone would have done."

"No, it wasn't like that." He came swiftly to crouch beside her again. "It wasn't, Rachel. You seemed so – so sweet. Complete. Contained. Oh, I don't know! I felt good with you, able to cope with everything. Don't leave me now."

She stared at him, without comprehension.

"You think I can marry you in four days' time?"

"Rachel, nothing's changed."

The tears began again, streaming down her cheeks, soundless and unheeded.

"You're wrong, Gavin," she said. "Oh, how wrong you are!"

14

Rain had been falling in a dismal, long-term way since early morning, and now the lights of Polvear which normally added a magic touch of festivity to the wintry evenings were no more than an insubstantial blur.

It had been a miserable day altogether. Tess had woken before five thirty that morning after a restless night and had been less than her amenable self all day, demanding and difficult to please. She was teething. There were two bulges in her top gum that looked sore and angry and Rachel felt the pain as if it were her own; more, perhaps, for she had the additional mental anguish of knowing that there was little that could be done to help matters, plus a lurking feeling of guilt at feeling even a moment's exasperation with the constant crying of a suffering child. Teething powders, warmly recommended by Mrs Hoskings, had little, if any, effect. Only time, she suspected, was going to heal, in this case as in so many others.

She was thankful when Tess went down for her customary afternoon nap, but the ensuing peace was wasted to a large extent for her writing had not gone well. Somewhere along the line, she realised, the book had taken a wrong turn – but where? Was it David, the rather raffish charmer with the heart of gold? She had a shrewd suspicion it was, and that she had caused him to act in a way that no raffish charmer would ever act. She hadn't *got* him, somehow. Didn't really know what made him tick. She wasn't, she thought gloomily, very good at men. Maybe she didn't know what made any of them tick.

Whatever her problem, it made for a highly unsatisfactory and frustrating afternoon, particularly as Tess had woken earlier than usual despite her premature start to the day. She was glad, at last, to draw the curtains, shutting out the dark and the rain, wishing as she did so that it was as simple to shut out her other nagging worries.

She had not, after all, told her parents about Tess. The letter she had finally written in reply to the one she had received from her mother had been apologetic, cheerful, superficial, but essentially unrevealing. Yes, she was working hard, she had said, and had taken Sylvia's cottage in Cornwall. She guessed they'd be surprised at that! It was just the most inspirational place to live, and a wonderful part of the country for them to stay when they came on leave. She was so looking forward to seeing them. Spring was beautiful in Cornwall, she had been led to believe, with loads of flowers all over the place. *With This Ring* was coming out in March, too. She'd hold the champagne until they arrived.

Not one word about Tess.

Later, she thought. She'd tell them later. When they were actually here, on the spot – away from Entebbe, where they had the opinions of friends and superiors to worry about. Then she'd tell them.

Tess seemed a little better after her sleep and was happily sitting in her high chair gnawing a rusk when there was a knock at the door.

Emma? Tess wondered, going to answer it. Or maybe Marlene. She'd given the girl a warm invitation to come any time, so that Tess would get used to her, and she had already dropped in once or twice.

But it was neither. Standing on the doorstep, his face shadowed by his peaked naval cap, was the man she had dubbed in her mind the Angry Pole. He looked not so much angry now as anxious and unsure of his welcome. In his hands he held a bunch of chrysanthemums wrapped around with soggy paper.

"Please," he said, holding them out stiffly towards her. "To apologise for other day."

"Oh!" Taken aback, Rachel was for a moment speechless, not yet quite prepared to unbend. "That's – that's very kind of you. Really, there was no need."

"Please." He thrust the flowers closer, and automatically she took them from him. "I was wrong," he went on. "Cruel. I am sorry. Forgive me." He gave a stiff little bow, turning to leave without another word.

"Wait," she said, relenting. "These are lovely. Thank you very much." She looked at him as, half turned from her, he waited on

252

the step. "Look, I know I was careless. I've had nightmares ever since. I can't tell you how grateful I was that you were there."

"The little one – she suffered nothing, I hope?"

"She's fine." For a moment longer Rachel hesitated. He looked cold and wet and rather tired, and his duffle coat was soaked through on the shoulders. She was surprised to see how young and vulnerable he looked. Somehow, at their last encounter, the intensity of his emotion had given his gaunt face an appearance of age which she now realised was false.

"Come in and see her," she said impulsively. "I've just made some tea."

She regretted the words the moment they were out of her mouth. She was in no mood for making conversation with a stranger, particularly with a stranger like this who seemed so odd and abrupt; and since Tess's sleep pattern had been so disrupted that day, she had made up her mind to start the bedtime ritual earlier than usual. This unexpected visit was bound to delay things.

And the cottage was a mess! She and Tess had been confined to the house all day because of the weather, and the living room was strewn with toys, with nappies airing on the fire-guard, a half-chewed rusk on the floor, and a general air of seediness everywhere. The whole picture would do nothing, she felt, to improve the impression of neglectful and incompetent motherhood that she had clearly given on their first meeting.

Still, too late now. He had accepted the offer with polite, if surprised, thanks, and was even now wiping his shoes with great care on the doormat. There was nothing for it but to go through with it with a good grace. It had, after all, been kind of him to bring the flowers.

He took off his cap and removed his coat, dangling it helplessly from one finger.

"Is so wet!" he said.

"Never mind. I'll hang it in the kitchen by the boiler."

He bowed again.

"You are very kind. More kind than I deserve. These days, I am sometimes not myself. I am sorry."

"Please, don't give it another thought."

(Why not? He'd been rude and offensive and horrible – but somehow, now that he was here, it was hard to see him as the same person who had shouted at her the other day.)

"Look, here's Tess," she said. "None the worse, as you can see."

Tess smiled at him engagingly, banging the tray of her high chair with a wooden spoon that Rachel had offered her when all else seemed to pall. "And I am Rachel Bond."

"Stefan Wisniowiecki." Yet again he bowed.

"I think," Rachel said, "I'd better call you Stefan."

For the first time his smile was something more than a nervous twitch of his lips.

"Please," he said. "Stefan is best, I think."

"I think so, too. Please excuse me. I must put these flowers in some water and hang up your coat in the warm. Do sit down, won't you?"

He had not done so, she found when she returned with the flowers and an extra cup, but was stooped over the high chair playing with Tess, making her crow with laughter. He straightened up as Rachel appeared.

"She is lovely child," he said.

"Well, I think so." She smiled at him, pleased as always by praise of Tess. She stood the flowers in their pottery jug on the mantelpiece, then busied herself with the tea things. "She's not always so angelic, though. She's been a little fiend all day. She's teething, poor child."

"Ah, teeth! A trouble coming, a trouble going."

"You have children yourself?" It was a casual question, made without looking at him as she poured the tea. "Do you take milk and sugar?"

When no reply to either question was forthcoming she glanced up at him. His face was thin, with high cheekbones and a strong, slightly curved nose. It seemed, at this moment, a harsh face, a face without warmth, the mouth drawn down in something like the angry snarl she had seen before. Then, as if with an effort, a polite neutrality returned and he smiled thinly.

"Milk, no sugar," he said, coming to sit at the table in the window. "Thank you."

There was a short and awkward pause. Rachel was angry with herself. From the days when she had lived in Shawcross Road and been in contact with Susan and her refugees, she knew that direct questions about families were to be avoided. Especially were they to be avoided with lone, bitter-looking men like this one. He'd lost a child – that much was clear as day.

Tess began to cry and Rachel, glad of the diversion, lifted her out of the high chair, putting her down on the floor amid the toys.

"The poor darling doesn't know what she wants today," she said.

"How old is she? Nearly one year? I thought as much." Stefan reached out a hand which Tess clutched with enthusiasm. "Is a frustrating age, no? They are learning that there is much to explore in the world, but as yet are not able to do so. They are like prisoners who look out of the window at sunlight and green fields but cannot reach them."

"Yes, I suppose you're right."

Rachel looked at him curiously. On reflection, he seemed an unlikely person to be a manual worker. There was intelligence and refinement in that hawk-like face. How old was he? Late thirties, early forties, perhaps. He looked, she thought, more like a musician or an artist.

"What in the world are you doing in St Bethan?" she asked impulsively.

He glanced at her, sharing with her the smile that Tess had coaxed from him. He wasn't, Rachel thought, at all bad-looking when he smiled; not, that is, if you liked the lean and hungry type of man.

"Working in boatyard," he said. "Don't tell me you don't know! In St Bethan, everyone knows everything."

"That's true. Yes, I knew that much – but why here?"

"Oh – " He turned back to Tess. "A long story, and not so interesting. This is nice house," he said, firmly changing the subject away from himself.

"It belongs to my aunt. I'm afraid you're not seeing it at its best."

"No? To me it seems like home. Warm and comfortable, with books."

"There were china ornaments on those shelves when we came, but I wrapped them up and put them away for safekeeping. I was afraid Tess would make short work of them now she's crawling. Anyway, I needed the space. I seem to have so many books – "

"You are author, they tell me."

"Who told you that?"

"The lady on the quay who was there when the pram ran away. She told me where to find you, too."

Rachel laughed, shaking her head with resignation.

"I've never spoken to her in my life before that day."

"But she is right? You are author?"

"After the day I've had, I'd hesitate to describe myself as such – I don't seem to have been able to construct two coherent sentences. But yes, on the strength of one book, not yet published, I suppose you could call me an author."

He did not reply, apparently engrossed in making a pink fluffy teddy bear hide in the crook of his arm only to pop up into view to the accompaniment of shrieks of delight from Tess.

"I, too," he said after a moment.

"You – you're a writer, too? *Really?*" Rachel looked at him with interest. "What sort of thing do you write?"

He held up his hands in an attitude of repudiation, still holding the pink bear.

"No, no. I am not a true writer. I write one book, no more. A textbook."

"On what subject?"

"On synthetic resins. Interesting, yes?" He cocked a mischievous eyebrow in her direction.

"If you say so," Rachel said, laughing. "Does that mean you are a scientist?"

"Of a kind."

"Then why – " on the brink of asking more questions that might seem intrusive, Rachel hesitated.

"Why do I make boats?" He spread his hands out before him. "For me there is much joy in working with wood. It is, for me, therapeutic."

"He seemed so different from that first time," Rachel said a few days later when Emma came to call and they were sitting drinking coffee together. "He was so kind and gentle and sweet with Tess – yet at the same time, you could feel a kind of – " she hesitated, her face screwed up with thought as the appropriate word eluded her.

"Bitterness?" Emma suggested.

"Maybe. No, I don't think that's quite the word. Sadness, I think. Even despair. Something very weighty and powerful, anyway."

"I know a little more about him than I did," Emma said. "I happened to meet Mrs Carthew the other day – Mrs Joseph Carthew, that is, wife of the chap who owns the boatyard. It seems he – your Stefan – had a horrendous war. He was in a prison camp at the end of it, starving and debilitated, and when he finally managed to make his way back home he found his wife and little girl had both died on some sort of forced march to Siberia. She said he was quite a wealthy industrialist before the war."

"He told me he'd written a book on synthetic resins. I think that's what it was, anyway."

"Plastics, in other words. Interesting! Apparently he succeeded in getting to England, and went to the home of some business

256

associate he'd had dealings with before the war. I don't know the full story. Anyway, he managed the journey, but then he collapsed – had a breakdown, mental and physical."

"Understandable," Rachel said.

"It seems he's a good craftsman as well as everything else, with a knowledge of boatbuilding. The friend happened to be someone who spent all his time sailing on the Pol before the war and he knew Joe Carthew very well, so through him your Stefan came down here. Mrs Carthew says he's still recuperating, really. His doctor thought that working with his hands in the peace of the countryside would be excellent therapy for him."

"Yes, he said as much. Poor man." Rachel was silent for a moment, thinking about him. "The bloody war," she said bitterly at last. "So many lives thrown into chaos! I guessed about the family, of course."

Emma seemed absorbed by her own thoughts.

"Sometimes," she said, "it seems quite despicable that I should have spent the war here, going on with my work so peaceably."

Rachel laughed at her.

"Don't be ridiculous! Children need teaching even in wartime. Perhaps most of all in wartime."

There was a touch of self-mockery in Emma's smile.

"Yes, I know. But I longed sometimes for a little bit more involvement – something more exciting. I had fantasies about being parachuted into occupied France, or being one of those women who plotted aircraft in the Battle of Britain. Still, I've only to hear a story like your poor Stefan's to realise that I had – and still have – much to be thankful for."

"He's hardly *my* poor Stefan," Rachel objected.

"Tell me," Emma said, leaving the subject aside and pursuing a further path of her own. "What did you do in the war, Rachel?"

For a moment it seemed that Rachel had not heard her. She added some milk to her coffee, offered Emma the plate of biscuits.

"Go on," she urged. "Have another. I've got plenty, thanks to an unprecedented burst of generosity on the part of La Pollard. The war?" she went on, after a small silence. "Well, for a while I worked for the Ministry of Information." She paused as if she was speaking of times long past that she could barely remember. "Then, in 1940, just before the Battle of Britain, I joined the WAAF."

"That must have been fun."

For a moment Rachel continued to look thoughtful; then she gave a laugh that was almost a sigh. "Yes, I suppose it was." Then, more certainly, "Yes, of course it was. A lot of it, anyway."

"What job did you do?"

"I trained as an RTO – Radio Telephone Operator. We talked the aircraft down. I was in Kent until the end of 1941, so we had our share of air raids – "

She paused again, remembering. She hadn't cared, she thought. She really hadn't cared. People had thought she was brave or reckless or stupid or all three, but the truth was that she hadn't cared one jot or tittle whether she lived or died, not at first. She had felt as if she were dead already.

Life had returned, however. She found, rather to her astonishment, that the world, post-Gavin, still held things to enjoy: friends, laughter, books and music.

"And then?" Emma prompted her.

"Then Bothley," Rachel said. "A bomber station near Leamington."

Dances in the Sergeants' Mess; silk stockings, for once, instead of the hated lisle, bought with precious coupons that were supposed to be used for essential non-issue items; hair combed down in a Joan Bennett style instead of rolled up, off the collar; a band, more or less in tune, thump-thumping out the beat of songs that she knew, even as she heard them, would always mean wartime and Bothley and the living-for-the-moment excitement that motivated them all.

There were tragedies, of course.

"Isn't Ken coming to the dance tonight?"

"He bought it over the Ruhr."

And Ron. And Ginger. And Scotty. And Titch.

All friends; but no one close. No one that touched her more than superficially. No one that she shed tears for.

"You're so hard, Ray," Mary said to her, the day they heard about Titch. He was a rear gunner with an enormous grin and a wicked sense of humour. They'd all loved Titch in their various ways. Rachel, in particular, was looked upon as a special friend of his, though they'd never done more than go for a few drinks together. Titch's heart, he had confided, was with the girl he left behind in Rotherham. Rachel, on the other hand, had no heart at all. Or so the other members of the WAAFery thought.

She smiled in response to Mary's accusation, the rather enigmatic smile that sometimes made others uncomfortable, unable to see what, if anything, had amused her.

"Rubbish! I'm not in the least hard," she said.

"Then I don't understand – ?" Mary – wholesome, innocent, unmade-up Mary, eyes still pink from the tears she had shed – blushed to the roots of her flaxen hair.

"Why I don't cry?" suggested Rachel. "How do you know I don't, in the dim watches of the night?"

She was looking in the mirror as she spoke, touching up her lips with Scarlet Flame lipstick.

"Well, do you?" Mary asked.

Turning from the mirror, Rachel smiled again.

"'Tears, idle tears. I know not what they mean'," she said. "Tennyson. Lord Alfred of that Ilk."

Mary, eighteen years old and fresh from school, felt a million years younger than Rachel who would be celebrating her twenty-first birthday in two months' time. She was greatly in awe of what she perceived as Rachel's sophistication and savoir faire even as she criticised her lack of feeling. She bit her lip and nodded thoughtfully.

"You're right, of course. I suppose it's the only way to be in wartime," she said. "The only professional way, I mean. It's just that it's so awful, when you get fond of people, and then you lose them – "

Rachel snapped her shoulder bag shut, straightened her tunic and swivelled her head round to check her stockings.

"Are my seams straight?" she asked. Satisfied, she looked back at Mary and smiled a rallying sort of smile. "Cheer up!" she said. "Live for the moment."

The smile remained as Rachel walked smartly away from Mary towards the Watch Office, but it changed in character, became thoughtful, self-mocking. Look who's talking, she thought. You weren't so bloody cheerful last year.

Strange, really, how the terrible events of the summer of 1940 seemed to have happened to someone else. In a way, they had. She was a different person now. She had been like Mary then – trusting and innocent and ingenuous. The whole thing was like a nightmare she could barely remember, frightening and fragmented, faces looming and fading, events out of sequence.

Had Gavin put her into a train at York? If so, how had

they got from the cottage to the station? She couldn't remember; she only knew that she had sat on the train with tears streaming down her face. A woman with fat pink cheeks had spoken to her – offered help, tea, coffee, sympathy. She didn't know if she had accepted; and if she had spoken, what she had said.

It had seemed, at the time, natural that Alice should meet her in London and bear her off to Shawcross Street; only long afterwards had she realised that Gavin must have phoned to alert her.

Susan had dealt with the Rossiters and her grandparents and the cancelled wedding. Suddenly her grandfather was there, in London, offering kind but ineffectual support; and as suddenly he was gone without her noticing his going.

A letter arrived from Mrs Rossiter, heightened emotion causing her normally confident, loopy writing to straggle down the page in uneven lines.

'I simply cannot imagine what has possessed you to behave in this unforgivable way, after everything was arranged (against my better judgment, I may say), and for such a frivolous reason! Can you imagine how upset Gavin is, having the wedding cancelled at such a late hour? And why? Because of his fondness for his sister! I am appalled and disgusted that such petty jealousy could motivate one who has been part of our family for many years and has therefore been fully aware of the closeness between us all. Did you truly imagine that you would be able to take the place of the family in Gavin's affections?

'There is no doubt in my mind that my son, and indeed my entire family, has had a most fortunate escape, which in no way lessens my anger at the thought that you, who surely might have thought herself the luckiest girl in the world to have captured the love of a fine young man such as Gavin, should have wantonly brought such heartbreak upon him at a time when he is risking his life for all he holds dear, and at a time when any lapse of concentration could mean the difference between life and death.'

"Petty jealousy?" Rachel repeated with astonishment to Barney when he came round to Shawcross Street some two weeks after the debacle. "Hasn't anyone explained to her – ?"

Barney, now in the uniform of a Second Lieutenant, looked miserable.

"You know Ma," he said. "She simply doesn't take it in. She believes what she wants to believe."

"You knew, didn't you?"

For a moment he said nothing. He stood, head bent, running his finger round and round the bevelled edge of a small table that stood in the sitting room.

"I – I kind of had my suspicions," he admitted at last, looking up at her. "I didn't know for sure."

"How could you let me – ?"

"I thought, maybe, it would all be all right. He told me he loved you."

"Did he?" It seemed unbelievable now.

"I'm sure he did, Rachel. I thought that once he was married he and Di would see that it wasn't on."

"Wasn't on?" Rachel repeated the words and gave a short, incredulous laugh. "What a masterpiece of understatement! It's disgusting, Barney. It's incest."

She saw him wince at the word, biting his lip. He looked at her then, and sighed.

"Oh, Rachel," he said helplessly. "I'm sorry. About everything. About you and me, and you and Gavin." He sighed heavily. "Especially about you and me. I have a kind of feeling there'll never be anyone else – " He broke off and shrugged his shoulders. "Oh well, too late now, I suppose."

"Much, much too late," Rachel agreed. "But if you felt like that, I can understand less than ever why you didn't say something. You put up no fight at all, did you?"

"I should have done. I can see that now, but you were so mad about him – "

"Yes," Rachel agreed sadly. "I always was. More fool me. I see now that there was always something weird about them, something I didn't understand."

"He wants to see you, Rachel."

"No!" Her response was immediate and implacable. "I couldn't, Barney. I couldn't bear it. Anyway, there's no point."

"He wants to explain."

"I don't want his explanations."

"I honestly think it was Di's fault."

"'The woman tempted me'? That won't wash, Barney."

"What are you going to do now?"

She was silent for a long time; then she sighed.

261

"I don't know," she said. "I've lost that job at the MOI that I quite enjoyed. Susan's being marvellous about the rent and everything, but I'll have to look around for a job soon. Maybe I'll join up."

"You could do worse," Barney said.

The Blitz had started by the time she had an opportunity to prove him right. Every night now she and Alice and Susan huddled in the Anderson shelter in the back garden dressed in what were popularly known as siren suits. They slept – or attempted to sleep – in deckchairs, wrapped in layers of blankets against the cold, fortified at intervals by tea from the several thermos flasks they took with them.

They never knew, each morning, if they would emerge to find the house standing; but in fact 29 Shawcross Street survived unscathed, apart from broken windows. Mr Spivey – so anxious to join the Home Guard – was killed outright when a landmine hit his house and its neighbour, and the street that ran parallel was almost totally destroyed.

At the end of September, she enlisted in the WAAF.

"Why the WAAF?" Alice had wailed when Rachel had come home with the news that the die was cast. "Of all things! You'll be surrounded by RAF uniforms – you might even be posted to the same station as Gavin!"

She was convinced that Rachel's choice of the Air Force over all other services had been born deep in her subconscious. Freudian influences were not ruled out.

"That's nonsense," Rachel said. "I didn't care where I went or what I did – with the possible exception of the Land Army! I stepped off the bus, and there was the WAAF recruiting office, so I went in. There's nothing more to it than that. It's a million to one against that I'll get posted anywhere near Gavin. And even if I do it won't matter. It's finished, Alice. Over. I'm not wasting another ounce of emotion on him or any other Rossiter."

Easily said; but the posting to Bothley towards the end of the following year had undoubtedly caused something of a setback in her erratic recovery. The sound of the bombers taking off on her first night caused tears to pour down her cheeks, just as they had so long ago during her first term at St Ursula's.

There were other similarities to boarding-school life. Because she worked shifts, in Kent she and the other RT operators had been given rooms that were shared by only one other girl. Here at Bothley she slept in the WAAF equivalent of a dormitory, with two long rows of iron beds, shifts or no shifts.

She found, despite those initial, infuriating, despicable tears, she could endure the communal life and the tighter discipline more easily than most. She put it down as much to her boarding-school education as to the new, hard, protective shell she had grown.

She discovered in herself a new, subversive attitude towards authority which amused the other girls, who seemed to turn naturally to her as a leader. If requests or complaints needed to be made, she it was who made them. She gained a stripe, then lost it again when she was discovered climbing in a window long after she should have returned to camp.

She it was who let the air out of the tyre of the car which was bringing some visiting top brass to inspect the WAAFery, thus gaining invaluable time for clutter to be thrown into lockers, papers tidied, lines of washing taken down. And it was she who was responsible for the libretto of the Christmas revue which poked dangerously anarchic fun at the top brass.

"You don't give a damn, do you?" said Penny, the girl who had become her closest companion.

Rachel smiled at that, and raised her newly-plucked eyebrows. She spent a lot of time on her appearance these days, and never lacked escorts for dances or the cinema. Her job meant that she was in constant contact with men of all ranks, and she treated them all with camaraderie and a mild form of flirtatiousness.

"She's a funny kind of Sheila," Dave Seldon complained to Penny. He was an Australian pilot with a handsome, open-air, guileless face. "I don't know what to make of her."

"Nobody knows what to make of her," said Penny. "She's nice, though. A good friend."

"Yeah," Dave agreed, but moodily. He wanted more than a friend.

It was, in fact, to Dave that she lost her virginity – a happening that would have astounded the entire station, had any but Dave known about it. It was generally assumed, from her air of sophistication, that she knew her way around; it was, however, an entirely false impression. Despite the friendliness and the flirting, she kept all men at arm's length.

It happened after her twenty-first birthday party in the January of 1942, for which Dave had commandeered an unused kitchen at the back of his billet, sufficiently far from the WAAF admininstrative headquarters to avoid objections regarding noise, the lateness of the hour, or anything else that could be dreamed up by what they all, universally, regarded as the kill-joy authorities.

It was a bitterly cold night, but Dave had lit the ancient boiler for the occasion. There were streamers and balloons strung from the cobwebbed ceiling, and a borrowed card table covered with the contents of assorted food parcels, including a fruit cake from Australia which he had decorated with twenty-one candles. There was a little wine, too, but only enough for one glass each with which to drink Rachel's health. After that it was beer or orange squash.

There was dancing to a gramophone, with everyone roaring out the words of the songs, and Paddy O'Toole doing his one-legged-Irishman-dancing-a-jig act without which no party was complete, and Jerry Wolstenholme reciting 'Napoleon's Farewell to Wigan' and Dave and two fellow Australians performing an Aboriginal War Dance.

"Enjoying it?" Dave asked Rachel, sitting beside her on a broken-down bed that had been dragged in as extra seating.

"It's a wonderful party, Dave. Thank you."

"You look gorgeous. Did you really like your present?"

"I loved it." He had given her a thin gold bracelet, delicately chased. "You were much too generous, though."

"Nothing's too good for you, you know that."

"You're sweet, Dave."

She smiled at him, wishing she loved him. He was so much in love with her, so eager to please, so handsome, so *nice*!

The music had changed to something slow and smoochy. Someone put the light out and there were whistles and catcalls until the door was opened to allow the muted light from the passage to filter in.

Dave pulled her to her feet, and holding her close they joined the other couples who were swaying, closely entwined, in the small space that was all that was available. She could feel his lips caressing her brow, feel the warmth of his breath. He smelt wholesome, she thought, like fields and open places. The great outdoors.

The party was thinning out as people went on duty, or to bed.

His lips moved to the vicinity of her ear.

"Jim's on ops. tonight," he said.

She drew her head back a little to look up at him. His face seemed the face of someone who had never entertained a base thought in his life. He was, she thought, a thoroughly good person – a little diffident and unsure of himself, perhaps, at least where she was concerned, but that was something in his favour. If there was one kind of man she couldn't abide, it was the handsome, swaggering, Lord-of-Creation type of man. Jim Hubbard was rather like that. He was an Australian, too, who shared a room with Dave.

"I hope it keeps fine for him," she said, knowing exactly what Dave had in mind.

"We could slope off," he said quietly. "No one would miss us."

For a moment she danced without speaking, her head turned away from him. Then she looked up at him once more.

"All right," she said coolly; and turning, walked rapidly to the door.

She had to turn to allow him to catch her up out in the passage, for she had no idea where his room was. She saw, by the greater light, that he looked dazed, almost disbelieving. She knew that he was several years older than she was, but suddenly she felt immeasurably older and wiser.

"Upstairs," he said. "There, to the right."

The house was an ex-married quarter, now occupied by six pilots, half of whom were on duty. No one was about. Only Dave, breathing a little heavily, biting his lips, anxious now; and Rachel, walking ahead of him, her head high like a Ziegfeld girl, her emotions in some kind of limbo, her footsteps in time with the thump, thump, thump of the beat from downstairs.

Dave could barely wait to kiss her, taking her in his arms the moment the door closed behind them. She had discarded her tunic long ago, down in the heat of the kitchen. Now he reached to unknot her tie. He was trembling.

"I'll do it," she whispered, laughing; and he laughed, too, and attended to his own tie and shirt buttons, drawing her down on the bed.

"God, you're lovely," he said thickly, kissing her face and neck and breasts. "I love you, Rachel. I'm crazy about you."

In reply she stroked his face and his hair and returned his kisses, hoping, hoping that desire would sweep her away, that this cold, detached creature that she seemed to have become would disappear for ever.

Dave's passion mounted. She gasped as he entered her, but with pain, not with delight. She found the whole process uncomfortable and messy, and really rather puzzling. Why did people make such a song and dance about it? There must be more to it! Maybe she just wasn't very good at it. Maybe Dave wasn't very good at it. Suddenly she wanted to giggle. Mrs Marryat, where are you when I need you? she thought.

The almost maternal tenderness she felt for Dave, who after-wards lay as if exhausted in her arms, took her by surprise. Was this what it was all about?

"Darling!" Dave propped himself up on one elbow, pushing her hair away from her face. "Was it good? Oh God, I love you so! Was it good?"

And she smiled at him and lifted her hand to his cheek.

"Yes, it was good," she lied.

"Then tell me you love me. Let me have it in words, Rachel."

She hesitated for less than a second.

"I love you, Dave," she said softly.

There seemed, quite simply, nothing else she could say, nothing else remotely appropriate.

Back in her own bed she stared sleepless into the darkness and asked herself how on earth it had all happened. She could give no sensible answer. Why had she said that? Why had she *done* it, for heaven's sake?

Sheer curiosity? Perhaps. Because she was a twenty-one-year-old virgin, and it was high time? Well, that had something to do with it, too. But most of all it was in the hope that only in this way would she be able to feel again – be like other people, warm and responsive and properly alive; a real person, instead of this automaton who seemed always to be an onlooker, always on the sidelines.

The very real danger that she might have become pregnant didn't hit her until the following day, but somehow she knew that she had no cause to worry. And indeed, all, later, proved well.

The next time they met, Dave asked her to marry him, sketching out the future he saw for them as they sat in the Golden Lion, side by side with their hands joined.

"I'm going to carry on flying after the war," he said. "There'll be a great demand for it in Australia, the distances are so huge. You'll love it in Perth. It's a beaut place. Whaddya say, Ray?" His grip tightened. "Are you going to make me the happiest man in the world?"

"Dave, I don't know!"

"But you said you loved me."

"So I do." In a way, she wanted to add, but managed to restrain herself. "Look, we can't talk in here – "

"Where, then? It's bloody freezing outside. Look, all you've got to say is yes or no!"

"No, it's not!" Sadly she turned and looked into his eyes, wanting to be the girl for him – tempted, almost. He'd never treat her badly. He'd be kind, devoted, the best of husbands and fathers. And, she added to herself as she continued to look at his broad, handsome, guileless face, she would be bored in a week. "I'm not ready, Dave. The time's not right."

He looked at her, sighed, gave a short, mirthless laugh.

"No, well, guess you could be right, at that. I could be history by tomorrow night."

"I didn't mean that."

"True, though. OK, let's leave it for the moment – but let's plan a forty-eight together, shall we? I'm due for one. I want to go to London, see some of the sights. We could book into a hotel, get tickets for a show."

"I'm not sure," Rachel said; and felt like a murderess when the light went out of his eyes. "I promised I'd spend my next leave with my friend Alice," she explained.

"What's Alice got that I haven't?"

"I was at school with her. We've been friends for ever."

"Where does she live? London? Well, that's no problem. You could see her. We could take her out for a meal, or something."

Rachel gave her enigmatic smile, but said nothing. She knew that the Rachel who was Alice's friend was in no way like the Rachel who had become Dave's lover, and that inviting her to meet him, laying herself open to Alice's bewildered scorn, was out of the question.

"I'll have to think about it," she said.

They lost another plane and its entire crew that night. Jim Hubbard, Dave's room-mate, failed to return and later his Lancaster was reported shot down over the North Sea.

Losing Jim was a terrible blow to Dave, Rachel knew. Aircrew always put on a show of calm, philosophical acceptance, but Jim was a friend and a fellow Australian. He and Dave had been together a long time. And Dave could be the next. He didn't need any diagrams drawn to show him that.

The next night at the Golden Lion, Dave talked about Jim, on and on; about their exploits when training, the near-misses, the jokes. The time when he lost his way over France and surrendered to a gendarme, thinking he was in Germany. The time when they double-dated and Jim walked off with his girl, leaving him with the bespectacled, buck-toothed, earnest prude who had to be home by nine thirty.

"I'll go to London with you, Dave," she said, when at last he fell silent.

Jim was, momentarily, forgotten.

"You will?" Dave seized both her hands. "That's terrific! I'll find a really beaut hotel, wait and see – private bathroom, the lot. Nothing but the best for you, Ray."

"Well, don't break the bank."

"I don't care if I do."

He looked, she thought, as if she had just presented him with the keys of the kingdom and was conscious, not for the first time, of a feeling of panic. She didn't, for some reason, feel wise any more.

They went on leave on Saturday 14th February of the coldest year anyone could remember. It had snowed all the previous day, and the fields on each side of the railway track were the purest, unbroken white. Rachel had civilian clothes in her case and intended to change into them at Charing Cross, before arriving at the hotel. Dave had, with considerable difficulty and only after phoning six hotels, managed to book a room in the name of FO and Mrs David Selden, a deception which Rachel accepted as inevitable but tried not to think about.

Increasingly, as the time approached, she found that she was having to gear herself up, persuade herself that she was doing the right thing.

It had seemed right at the time, that night when he was so low in spirits. She had managed, then, to persuade herself that she had only to act as if she loved him to make it come true.

All that had happened was this increasing unease, the feeling that she was being unfair to him and untrue to herself. But it would be even more unfair, she told herself, to duck out of it now, with everything booked and his excitement running high.

"You're very quiet," he said to her as they sat side by side on the train. "You're not having doubts, are you?"

"Don't be silly," she said. "It's going to be a super weekend. I'm looking forward to showing you London."

It was mid-afternoon when they arrived, already growing dark; but not too dark for Rachel to stare in astonishment at an almost life-sized poster that confronted her the moment she stepped out of the train. There, before her, was a picture of Diana Rossiter dressed in the uniform of an officer in the WRNS, hand lifted gracefully to shade her eyes as she gazed out to sea, lovely face glowing with dedication. Beneath her was the legend: 'Answer the Nation's Call: Join the WRNS'.

"Good Lord," Rachel said, standing and staring. "I know that girl."

Dave whistled. "She's a corker," he said in awed tones.

"I didn't even know she was in the WRNS."

"Maybe she isn't. She's probably a model or an actress."

"The last I heard she was lecturing on Minoan Culture at Cambridge."

"On *what*? Wow! she doesn't look like an egghead."

Rachel smiled as she turned away from the poster. Girls, to Dave, came in two distinct categories, eggheads or dolly-birds. She, she was aware, was a dolly-bird, and he would be put out if she attempted to be anything else. Quote poetry at your peril, my girl, she said to herself.

For that reason she had pressed to see *Blithe Spirit* at the Piccadilly, and kept quiet about *The Merry Wives of Windsor* at the Strand, which would have been her first choice.

The newspaper placards were shrieking the news about Japanese advances in the Far East as, having settled into their hotel and eaten at the Coventry Street Corner House, they walked up Shaftesbury Avenue.

"Dave, I must buy a paper – "

"Come off it, Ray! We don't want any bad news now."

"My friend's parents are there."

"Missing the beginning of the show isn't going to help them, is it?"

He was right, of course. Rachel turned her back on the headlines and tried to forget them, at least temporarily. It proved an easy thing to do, since she adored the show, even if it had been her second choice. The wit and the laughter made her forget not only Singapore but her own personal unease.

"Enjoying it?" Dave asked her as the curtain came down for the interval.

"Very much," she said. "Isn't Margaret Rutherford wonderful? I loved that bit – oh, my heavens!"

Her hand flew to her mouth and her eyes were the size of saucers.

"What is it?" Dave looked over his shoulder, following the direction of her eyes. "Someone you know?"

Laughing, Rachel ducked her head in an attempt to make herself invisible.

"I've just seen my uncle," she said. "Look, that rather portly chap making his way up the centre aisle with the blonde."

"Your uncle? Well, I'm damned! Don't you want to go and speak to him?"

"Not in the least. I never knew what to say to him at the

269

best of times. I shall look the other way and pretend I never saw him."

"Good. I don't want to share you with anyone."

She didn't know why this statement should irritate her so much. The unease, dormant for a while, flared into near panic. She pretended absorption in the programme, fighting down the mad desire to run.

What was wrong with her? Dave was sweet, and very handsome, and he never stopped telling her how marvellous she was, how much he loved her. No one had ever loved her as much as he did. She ought to be grateful.

He didn't know her, of course. The Rachel he thought he loved didn't really exist, had never existed. He loved the smooth and soignée face she saw in the mirror, not the girl inside.

For who could possibly love that girl? She was cold, dead, without feeling. She neither deserved it, nor could she return it.

She was glad when the curtain went up again and once more she was amused and distracted, with all such questions buried deep. It was, after all, only for two nights. She'd cope with that, then try to extricate herself, with as little hurt to Dave as possible.

Maybe this calm and philosophical mood would have continued if Dave hadn't occupied himself during her absence in the bathroom at the hotel by turning on the radio, so thoughtfully provided.

"This place has got everything," he said happily. "I reckon I struck lucky when I found it, don't you? You know who recommended it to me? It was the old dragon that works in the Admin – "

"Shut up a minute," Rachel said, her face expressionless.

It was the calm, measured tones of the BBC late news bulletin that had caught her attention. Lazily Dave reached out a hand and switched it off.

"You look gorgeous, Ray," he said. "Come on to bed. We don't want the news – "

But she had leapt to switch it on again.

"Leave it," she snapped. "I want to listen."

Singapore, said the disembodied voice, was about to fall, and the Japanese were now in virtual control. Many British nationals were known to be captured, their fate unknown.

"And Australians," Dave said, a touch of belligerence in his voice. "They've got thousands of Australian troops out there. Typical Pom attitude – "

"I must go to Alice," Rachel said. "Her parents are there. She'll be distraught!"

"Aw, come on, Ray!" Dave propped himself up on one elbow. "Have a heart! It's late! You can't go anywhere now."

"I could phone her."

Defeated, Dave lay back on the pillows once more.

"Sure, why not? Help yourself."

Alice answered the phone on the second ring. Rachel knew immediately, from the sound of her voice, exactly how her face would look, how her delicate, childish mouth would be trembling.

"Alice, it's me, Rachel. I've just heard the news."

"Oh!" Alice drew a long, shuddering breath. "Oh Rachel, it's awful, isn't it? And there's nothing anyone can do – nothing. Only wait and hope. They say one ship got away last week with a lot of British nationals on board."

"Then they might be safe."

"They might. But – " she paused and Rachel heard the sob in her voice. "Dad wouldn't leave, not until everyone else had gone. And Mummy wouldn't leave without him. I can't feel hopeful."

"Is Susan with you?"

"No, she had to go to Bristol."

"You're on your own?"

"Well – Captain Blackwell was here earlier. He's the War Office man who's taken the two rooms at the top of the house. I told you about him – "

"Is he with you now?"

"No. He had to meet someone and take them somewhere. I don't know where. I didn't take it in. He's not coming back tonight, anyway." She sounded frightened, and very lonely.

"Where's Keith?"

"At sea. Somewhere in the mid-Atlantic by now, I expect. Rachel – " Her voice strengthened a little. "We're engaged. He bought me a ring last week, when he was home."

"Alice, that's marvellous news. Keep thinking about that! Don't let yourself get down."

"But – but – " Rachel heard an unmistakable sob. "He's in danger, too. I can't stop worrying about all of them. Oh Rachel, I wish you weren't so many miles away."

"I'm not," Rachel said. "I'm in London. Alice, don't cry! Listen, do you want me to come over?"

"Oh, *would* you? That would be wonderful! But it's awfully late – "

"Not that late. There are still cabs about the place."

"You're an answer to prayer!"

"See you soon."

Rachel put the phone down, turning to look uncertainly at Dave, who was staring at her as if he could hardly believe his ears.

"What the hell – ?" he began.

"Dave, I'm sorry, but you heard all that, didn't you? I must go."

"*Now?* For God's sake, Ray!"

"I'm sorry," she said. "Really sorry. Look – try to understand. Alice and I have comforted each other ever since we were little kids at school, both with parents overseas. And later, she was marvellous to me when I needed her. Now she needs me. She's worried to death, and all on her own. I must go to her."

"Dammit, *I* need you," he said, suddenly savage. He swung his legs over the bed and stood up, reaching out for her. "You can't do this, Ray – "

"I'm sorry!"

"What's the good of being sorry? Don't you know how I've looked forward to this?"

"Yes, I do know – and I don't want to hurt you, honestly, but I have to go."

"Why can't it wait until tomorrow?"

"It can't, that's all." She evaded his clutching arms and began snatching up the clothes she had discarded only a few minutes before. "She's got no one else at the moment. I'm going, Dave."

"Go, then." This was a harsh, ferocious Dave she had not seen before. "Get the hell out of it – "

He threw himself into the satin-covered armchair and watched her pack her case with a stony expression, his mouth distorted, his breathing heavy. He was smoking, taking short sharp drags at his cigarette, saying nothing.

When she was ready to leave she went over to him.

"Shall I phone you tomorrow?" she asked him.

He stared at her, his expression unaltered.

"I shouldn't bother," he said. "I know now how much I mean to you, and that's bugger-all. If you go now, you go for good."

She returned his look, but sadly. She sighed, then gave a small, hopeless shrug.

"Goodbye, then," she said; but hesitated a moment even as she turned to leave. "I really am sorry, Dave," she added softly. "I didn't mean to hurt you."

"Just get out," he said wearily.

It occurred to her as she walked down the thickly-carpeted corridor towards the lifts that the porters and the receptionists, if any were still on duty, would think she was doing a moonlight flit. She would have to plead a sudden call to a bed of sickness, say her husband was still in the room and would be staying on –

Husband! Oh, thank God, she thought, a sudden breathless joy sweeping through her. For the moment Alice was forgotten. Thank God, thank God, thank God – she was out of it! Maybe not with honour, but out of it. She should not, she admitted humbly, ever have got into it in the first place.

She need not have worried about questions being asked, for the lobby was still busy. A small crowd of American army officers were occupying the receptionists, and the uniformed porter was out on the street trying to whistle up a cab for an elderly Frenchman. Seeing his lack of success, Rachel decided to begin walking. There was muddy, city-streaked slush still covering the pavement and banked up by the side of the road, but the night was clear and bright and she knew the way like the back of her hand. She could cut down to the Kings Road through Wilton Place and Belgrave Square – she'd walked it a hundred times.

It seemed longer than she remembered, and the case became heavier with every step. It was after half past one when she turned at last into Shawcross Street; but she knew, the moment she saw Alice, that she'd done the right thing.

"I just can't believe this," Alice said, when they had hugged in greeting. "Tonight, before you rang, I was wishing you were here – and suddenly, there you were. It was just like a miracle. What on earth are you doing in London?"

Rachel looked at her and saw the strain that the bad news and the loneliness had had on her. Her face had lost its look of childish innocence. Alice, she could see, had grown up.

"It's a long story," she said. "I'll tell you some time."

"Come into the kitchen. It's warm in there and I'll make some tea. You don't mind sharing my bed, do you? I'll make up another if you like – "

"No, no, that's fine. I could sleep anywhere, I'm so tired."

"You don't look tired. You look marvellous! Honestly, Rachel, you're so – so *groomed* these days. Like a film star, or a model or something."

"It's still scruffy old me underneath, I assure you. But talking of models – have you seen that new recruitment poster for the WRNS? It's all over the place."

"Mm." Alice was busy lighting the gas, putting on the kettle, already looking better. "Why?"

"It's Diana Rossiter – "

"*No!* Is it? I didn't know. I never met her. Gosh, you always said she was gorgeous – "

"I stepped out of the train, and there she was! I had the shock of my life."

Alice pulled a face.

"You should have thrown a rotten tomato at it, or drawn on a moustache, or something. I knew she was in the WRNS – something very high up at the Admiralty, but – " she stopped in mid-sentence, her face reddening.

"How did you know that?" Rachel asked curiously. Alice bit her lip.

"Oh gosh, I'm such a fool," she said miserably. "I asked Susan if she thought I ought to mention it in my letter to you, and she said better not. She thought it would just upset you all over again." She groaned. "I'm such an idiot, Rachel, so scatty. Trust me to let it drop!"

"Let what drop, for heaven's sake? Come on, Alice, you might as well spill all the beans now you've started."

"Yes, I suppose I might." Alice sighed penitently. "It's nothing important, really. It happened when Keith was home. We were sitting here quite late one night with Susan, drinking cocoa, when Captain Blackwell put his head round the door and said did Susan mind, he'd bought a colleague back with him to sleep on his settee. They'd tried several hotels, he said, and couldn't find a bed for love or money. So of course, you know Susan – she invited them into the kitchen for cocoa too, and said what nonsense, they mustn't think of using the settee, and rushed around making up a bed for him in one of the spare rooms."

"And that was Mr Rossiter?"

"Yes – well, Captain Rossiter, actually! Wasn't it amazing? He's working at the War Office now, something to do with requisitioning buildings, the same section as Captain Blackwell. We didn't know who it was at first, of course – didn't even catch the name, but gradually it came out that he was an architect, and came from Warnfield and had four children, so it didn't take much to put two and two together."

"Did he know about me? I mean, that I'd lived here and that you were my friend?"

"Well, I told him, of course. He knew you had lived here, in Shawcross Street, but didn't know the number. I suppose I was

274

a bit – well, hostile, at first, but he was awfully sweet about you, Rachel. Awfully sorry it happened. I couldn't help feeling – well, nothing was his fault, was it?"

Rachel gave a brief laugh at that.

"Maybe not," she said. "On the other hand, he was all part of the Rossiter conspiracy – the 'Aren't We Wonderful, Nobody's Like Us' conspiracy. It contributed, I imagine. Tell me, what's Gavin doing now? Did he say?"

"Only that he was flying Lancs. Alannah's with ENSA. She's been touring Scotland with a company, doing lots of different plays in repertory. Marvellous experience, he says – "

"Of course," Rachel murmured.

"Barney's in the Middle East."

"I know. He wrote to me at Christmas."

"You know, Rachel – " Alice poured the tea and pushed a cup towards her. "I can't help thinking it was an awful shame you didn't stick with Barney. I always liked him."

Rachel sipped her tea, looking at Alice over the top of her cup.

"So did I," she said. "But it was Gavin I loved." She put her cup down. "What are we doing talking about me? You haven't shown me your ring yet, or told me anything about Keith."

"There!" Alice displayed her left hand. "Isn't it gorgeous? I always loved sapphires. Keith is so sweet! He writes the most wonderful letters, and I write to him, every single day. We're going to get married on his next leave."

"I knew he was right for you."

"We went to see his parents in Winchester – my uncle and aunt. I thought they'd disapprove because we're related, but they didn't. They seemed really glad he'd chosen me. And Rachel – " Alice lowered her eyes, fidgeted with her teaspoon as if unsure how she should continue. "Rachel, I must tell you." Still she hesitated, biting her lip. "On the way back we stayed the night at a lovely little Wiltshire pub. Do you think that was awful of us?"

She looked up appealingly, her eyes wide and questioning, as if she really wanted to know. Rachel laughed. Alice was such an *infant*, she thought.

"Of course I don't!"

"As husband and wife, I mean," Alice went on, as if Rachel hadn't quite got the point.

"Alice, you love each other, you intend to get married. Where's the harm?"

"Well – " she looked down again. "It's not the way we've been brought up, is it? I mean, I never thought I would. I never intended to."

"Did you enjoy it?" Rachel asked lightly. "That's the main thing."

"Oh, Rachel!" Alice was glowing now, her eyes bright. She reached across and clasped Rachel's hand. "Oh, Rachel, it was wonderful! Wonderful! If we never have anything else, we'll have had that night."

"You'll have lots more," Rachel said softly, aware, suddenly, of wanting to cry and despising the cheap sentimentality that prompted such a desire. She got up from the table, took her cup to the sink. "You know, Alice my love," she said. "I'm dead on my feet. Is there any chance of bed in the near future?"

"Of course, of course! I'm a selfish wretch, keeping you talking like this."

"But you do feel a bit better?"

"Lots, thanks to you." Alice came close and hugged her. "God knows what news tomorrow will bring, but at least I'll have you to share it with. Thanks for coming."

"I wouldn't be anywhere else," Rachel said. "Now, bed."

But once there, she found to her annoyance that she was unable to sleep.

She thought of Dave. She'd behaved badly from beginning to end, she could see that now. Poor Dave.

She thought of Barney. Was Alice right? Should she have stuck with him? How could she have done, when she loved Gavin so? Liking might be important, but it wasn't enough.

And, with a small twisted smile, she thought of Alice. Little did she think she could ever be envious of Alice.

But that's just what I am, she thought forlornly. That's just what I am.

15

It was mid-November when Stefan called with his floral peace offering, but the end of the month before Rachel saw him again.

The book was running away with her, wanting to get itself written. Any moment she could spare away from Tess, she rushed to her typewriter, often working far into the night. She knew she was pale, short of exercise, short of sleep; but a kind of exaltation had her in its grip, interspersed with agonising periods of sheer panic when she felt certain that what she had written was without interest, totally worthless, and that no one, ever, would want to read it.

"You must let up a little," Emma urged. "Make more use of Marlene. She's only too happy to have Tess on Saturdays or in the evenings."

"I just can't wait for her to start work properly after Christmas," Rachel said. "It's going to revolutionise my life."

She took note of what Emma said, however, and one Saturday in early December – a day so clear and bright that it seemed to have been borrowed from spring – she decided to explore the countryside that had tempted and intrigued her from the beginning but had so far been inaccessible in the company of Tess and the inevitable pram.

Marlene came soon after lunch, and Rachel quickly made her escape, heading a little way up the hill, then turning to where steps rose steeply between the cottages, first this way and then that. There were children playing, two women talking at a front door, stocky men in caps and sweaters and seaboots clumping down towards the ferry. There was, she gathered, a football match in Polvear. They smiled and wished her good day, not so reserved now as they had been at first. They were beginning to accept her, in spite of the disgrace of her unmarried state. She'd been right to think that time would help. St Bethan felt like home now.

Or was that merely an illusion? Maybe the people greeted her because they were kind. To them she was, and perhaps always would be, a 'furriner', and a sinful one at that. But *oh!* – she stopped and gasped as she reached the end of the steps and came out on to the path that ran high up above the river – how could anyone not wish to be at home in this place?

It was, of course, the same river that she could see from her windows, but viewed from this angle and in this light it looked unfamiliar – wider, more serene, its surface smooth as satin.

The sight of it was a piercing happiness made suddenly sweeter by the appearance of three swans flying up-river, the beating of their wings as perfectly synchronized as any *corps de ballet*. This is *it*, she thought – not analysing her meaning, not attempting to put it into words, merely recognising that this was perfection.

She savoured it a little longer, then continued on her way. For a few yards she was hemmed in; to her right a stone wall, green with moss and ivies and springing ferns, and to her left the thick band of woodland that lay between her and the river, shimmering between the trees in a series of blinding silver flashes. There were holly bushes thick with berries, and blackthorn, and the lichen-clad trunks of oak and beech, the odd shrivelled leaf still clinging stubbornly to their branches. The path here was wide but muddy. Head down, she picked her way cautiously, so that when, suddenly, the way opened out once more, she was taken by surprise by the sight of Stefan Wisniowiecki standing as transfixed by the view as she had been a moment earlier.

Still dazed by so much beauty, she greeted him, looked, and marvelled and turned to smile at him.

"What can one say?"

He smiled, too, and shook his head as if he, too, were lost for words, and it struck her how much better he looked than when she had last seen him. He seemed younger and happier. Was all this heavenly beauty responsible for that, too, she wondered? For it was not merely that there was more flesh on him, the deeply scored lines from nose to mouth less apparent; he looked less hag-ridden, less likely to give the jerky, disconcerting bows that accentuated his foreignness. One could even imagine a dawning air of serenity.

His smile grew more mischievous.

"Where is baby?" he asked. "In river perhaps?"

"Ouch! That's unkind!" But a good sign, surely, that he could joke like this? "I'm playing hookey – truant," she added, seeing his look of perplexity. "I've run away from my duties and left Tess with a friend. On a day like this, I just had to walk."

"I, too." He looked at her hesitantly. "You go down to creek, I think? Is it, perhaps, that you want to be alone?"

"Not at all." Rachel wondered, even as she spoke, what on earth had got into her. She *did* want to be alone! She wanted time and space to enjoy the sights all around her; and time to think, too. Time to work out that conversation between David and Catherine that was so crucial but was proving difficult. Oh, well – nothing to do now but make the best of it. "Why don't we walk together, if you're going that way?"

"You are most kind," he said; and for the first few minutes conversation between them proceeded on this formal level. Was he enjoying St Bethan? Yes, indeed, everyone was most kind. And she – did her work progress satisfactorily? Yes, thank you – at the moment it was going well.

It was impossible, afterwards, to remember quite how or when it all changed, at what precise moment the conversation between them became urgent and absorbing, and far more fundamental, causing them to stop in their tracks as they pursued an argument. She forgot David and Catherine and every other character in the novel and was glad – glad to an astonishing degree – that she was walking with Stefan Wisniowiecki.

The sky paled, and the air grew colder, but unaware they stood at the creek's edge and talked of life and love and war. He had lived in Warsaw, he told her, but his family had owned a cabin in Mikolajki, to the north of Warsaw, close to the Mazurian Lakes.

"That's where my heart was," he said. "I could never wait for school to be finished, so that we could pack up and go there for our holidays. It is more lovely than I can tell you – and not so different from this. There was creek like this . . ." His voice trailed away, then turning, he bent to pick up a stone that he sent skimming across the water. "So much is like, Rachel. I may say 'Rachel'? There were cormorants and herons there, just as here, and boys who make rafts and boats just like boys of St Bethan." He laughed as if the thought of them made him happy. "And they annoy mothers by forgetting mealtimes and fathers by growing up and rebelling, I think, yes?"

"Is that what you did?"

"Not so much. I struggle a little, but at finish, I do what

they wish." His twisted, inward smile seemed, she thought, a little rueful.

"You regret that now?" she asked.

He shook his head.

"No, no, not at all. I wish it, too. I study chemistry at Warsaw Polytechnic and for few years afterwards we work together, my father and I. It was good. We came to understand each other, to be friends, and for that I am thankful now for after early weeks of 1940, we never saw each other again."

Rachel hesitated for a moment. Did he want to talk? Would it seem like prying?

"What happened?" she said at last, shyly, not pressing. For a moment he was silent. He stared out over the creek, but she knew it was not this stretch of water and these seabirds he could see.

"My father had factory in Warsaw," he said at last. "It manufactured small things. Light-fittings. Ashtrays. Tubing. Things that screwed into other things. Things that could be made from synthetic resins. He was chemist – a clever, inventive man, always experimenting. We had comfortable life. My mother was – was lady." His face lit up with amused affection as with a gesture he contrived to illustrate the refined elegance of his mother. "Her father was high Government official. Important man! She was cultured, spoke good French, played piano. She dress me in velvet suits, but other boys laugh and my father plead for me. We were not really grand, you understand, but comfortable. It was natural for my father to want his only son to go into business."

"But you had other ideas?"

"I was boy who live and dream boats. I long to build them and sail them and spend all my life close to lakes. My mother and sister and I stay at cabin for all of summer, with my father coming from time to time. Later, as I grew older, I spend holidays there working in small boatyard, much like Joe Carthew's. It belonged to old man called Jan." He paused for a moment, smiling, remembering Jan. "An old, wise man, he was." He hunched his shoulders. "Stooped, like this. Eyes no good. But great craftsman. He tell me – told me? – 'I have no son. Come and work with me here and learn craft well, and when I go this yard will be yours.'"

"It must have been a hard choice."

He nodded, slowly and thoughtfully. "At home there was much argument. At last I agree to study and give factory trial. All the time I was student, I still returned to Jan and yard whenever I could. But before end of my studies, I met Irina." He had only to speak of her, Rachel noted, for his voice to change. He seemed to catch his breath before continuing. "She was music student in Warsaw – "

"So you decided to stay?"

"Boats were my life; music was hers. She could not have lived in Mikolajki, away from music. Besides, she was offered place in orchestra. Violin, she played . . ." his voice trailed away before picking up again. "But we still kept cabin and sailed each summer . . ." This time his silence left a sense of almost unbearable desolation.

Rachel was aware suddenly of the chill striking through boots and gloves. The sun had gone altogether now. She shivered and hunched her shoulders.

"Oh, you are cold," Stefan said, coming back to the present. "You should not let me talk so much. We must go."

Not unwillingly, she began retracing the steps they had taken down to the creek, up the steep and narrow track that led to the path above the river. They climbed for a while, in single file and in silence.

"You didn't say what happened afterwards," she said when he came alongside her as the path widened at the top. "Do you want to talk about it? Or does it hurt too much?"

His face, half turned from her, was a series of harsh, downward curves.

"I was rounded up and sent to Germany as slave labourer in 1940," he said at last. "My sister Bronia married Jewish doctor just before war. Joseph, his name. He was good, kind man. We liked him very much, though he was of different race. At first he could continue work, but things grew worse and worse. All Jews were ordered to ghetto – my sister too, of course."

He paused again and drew a long breath, but before she could speak, he had taken up the story again.

"By that time I was in Germany, working like slave. Like dog. All this I hear after, from friend who was sent to same camp. My sister was expecting baby. My parents would not let her go to ghetto, so they hide them, Bronia and Joseph. For many months, they hide them in storeroom of factory. But they were betrayed."

"Who would betray them, Stefan? Who could do such a thing?" At Rachel's horrified question, he gave a short, mirthless laugh.

"Who knows? Someone, perhaps, with grudge against my father. Every man in authority who employs and fires labour must have enemies, I think. Or perhaps it was someone who hated Jews. Oh yes, there were many in Poland who did so.

Or perhaps it was someone who wanted to gain favour with Germans. Who can tell? All that is certain is that they were found and arrested. All died in Treblinka – my mother, father, my sister and her husband."

Instinctively, she took his arm.

"Stefan, I'm so sorry."

For a moment he stared bleakly at the wide sweep of the glassy river and all the heartbreaking beauty that was spread before them.

"It meant that Irina and Nadya, our little girl, were alone in Warsaw. Her parents were dead and she had no one in the city. I got word to her to go to relatives in mountains, close to Russian border. I thought it would be safer and more comfortable." He paused again. "It was not," he said flatly. "They, too – "

"Don't talk about it now," Rachel said gently. "Later, perhaps."

Slowly he nodded. "Perhaps," he said after a moment. "Is still too near, I think. Some things I am able to speak of with sadness but without – without anguish? Yes? Anguish is word?"

"That, I think, might begin to describe it," Rachel said dryly.

"Other things – " he hesitated. "Of other things I cannot speak." He looked at her and managed to smile. "Don't look so sad, Rachel. So many suffered, but life goes on and must be lived. Soon I will feel this, perhaps. After all, I came through. I survived – oh, perhaps not as man I was, but I am here, yes? Already I have plans."

"That's good," Rachel said.

They walked for a while in silence and when he spoke again it was if he had deliberately moved into another gear, forcing his mind away from past tragedies. His voice sounded stronger and more vibrant.

"I tell no one," he said at last. "But I tell you, today. I say to you, I think, that factory worked with synthetic resins? That I wrote book? There are many different kinds. My poor, boring book concerned possible use of six, and there are more."

"You mean – like Bakelite?"

"Bakelite, yes, is one kind of plastic. There is future for boats in such material, Rachel."

"Bakelite boats? You mean, like ash-trays, only bigger?"

"Now you make fun – but you are not so wrong. Ash-trays are made from moulded resin. Make resin that is harder and stronger material – resin that will not melt in hot sun, or break easily in pieces, and make moulds that are bigger and of different shape, and you have boat. Not big boats perhaps. Not ocean-going yachts

– though who is to say what future will bring? But small pleasure boats, almost certainly. Boats that little boys can save money to buy, and families, and old men who want to go fishing."

His dark eyes were alive again, the sadness banished for the moment.

"It sounds wonderful! Not," Rachel added hastily, "that I know the first thing about it."

"I try to tell Joe Carthew that such scheme is possible, but he laughs and thinks I am madman. I understand him. He is a man who loves building in wood, as I do myself. There is nothing like it. Of course I agree that wood is best. For this other I must go back to chemistry."

"Well, good for you!" Fired by his enthusiasm, .Rachel turned and smiled at him. "You'll do it, I'm sure."

It was his turn to catch her arm and pull her to a halt.

"Thank you. Thank you," he said.

"For what?" she asked, but he did not answer. For a moment they were still, standing and looking at each other as if for the first time; and for the first time she felt a stirring of sexual interest, an awareness of tension. Was she, she wondered, like Desdemona, loving him for the dangers he had passed through? It was possible.

But she had no wish to fall in love. Nor was she doing so, she assured herself. Not now, not ever. This threatened awakening of emotions long dead, this ridiculous fluttering of the nerves, must be subdued at all costs. It was enough to note with clinical interest that the arrangement of eyes and nose was rather striking, now that he had a bit more flesh on his bones. His eyebrows, she saw, grew in a rather spectacular way, like two dark wings, and his mouth –

Her thoughts shied like a nervous horse at the thought of his mouth, but still she could not look away from him. It was a strong face, she thought, intelligent and humorous and alive – the face of a man who would survive and triumph. A man a woman could be proud to love.

"My goodness, it's awfully cold," she said, digging her hands in her pockets and setting off once more at a brisk pace.

"Please," he said after they had gone a short way. "Do not speak of plan to anyone, Rachel. It is too – " Vaguely he waved his hand in a circular motion above his head. "Too much in air. I tell you so you will see I do not live in past. Others would think me mad, I think, not just Joe."

"Well, I don't," Rachel said, composed once more. "I'm sure

you know what you're talking about – and how well you say it, too! Your English is wonderful."

"No, no, not good! I learn at school, long ago, and afterwards meet others in same business, English and American. Now I read to improve my language. Trollope, Dickens, Jane Austen. These were always in our house, in translation of course, thanks to my mother. As a race, we love books, but so little I know of modern writers. You will advise me, yes? Which modern writers should I read?"

The subject of books and writers happily occupied them all the way home; and afterwards, long after they had parted, Rachel was conscious of a feeling of – what? Excitement?

Forget it, she told herself. Concentrate on other things. She had found his company mentally stimulating; that was enough. Falling in love was dangerous and in this case could bring her nothing but more heartache, since it was abundantly clear that he was still mourning his wife. It was too great a risk. Anyway, she didn't have the time or the energy left over from her writing; and it was the writing that was the important thing, now that she had Tess to provide for.

Still the thought of him recurred at intervals during the rest of the day.

"We shall meet and talk again – yes?" he had said as they parted.

"I hope so. Anyway, there are the books you're going to borrow. You must call to collect them. I wonder – " she hesitated for a moment, then made up her mind. "I've a friend, Emma Laity, coming to supper on Wednesday. She's the schoolteacher here. Won't you come too? I think you'll enjoy meeting her."

"Thank you. I would like to come."

Mentally she revised the menu. Omelettes wouldn't do, she thought. Not for a man. Fish pie would be better. She'd try to get a nice piece of fish. Maybe go over to Polvear . . .

The evening went well, as she had somehow known it would. Stefan's presence provided a stimulus to conversation, a focal point.

We two women are both on top form, Rachel thought, halfway through the evening; and was wryly amused by the reflection, thinking it cast an illuminating and none too flattering light on their manless state – though Emma, to be fair, was not as manless as all that. She had many friends, many interests. That particular evening she was fired with enthusiasm about

284

a CEMA sponsored play that was being staged in Truro the following week.

"What's 'CEMA'?" Rachel asked. "I've never heard of it."

"That, my dear, is because you've lived until now in the metropolis where you have theatres to right and left. CEMA is Council for the Encouragement of Music and the Arts. It's a sort of peacetime ENSA, sent out to the poor deprived peasantry. We've had some good companies down here. This time they're doing *Arms and the Man*. Why don't you come?"

"We could go together, yes?" Stefan said, smiling at Rachel.

He, too, seemed in the best of spirits, his lively face with its dark deep-set eyes full of warmth and humour. On the walk he had proved himself a good conversationalist, but somehow she had not imagined he could be so amusingly entertaining as he had been that evening.

"Why not?" she replied, getting up to clear away the plates. She paused for a moment as she put them down in the kitchen. Careful, she warned herself. Watch yourself. Don't be disarmed by an attractive smile and a pair of sparkling eyes.

She had to admit to herself, however, that the prospect of this outing pleased her out of all proportion to its importance, and it proved, in the event, as enjoyable as she had hoped. Stefan was as friendly as ever and came back to the cottage for coffee. They did not touch on personal matters, talking mainly of Poland's history, but somehow, as they said good night and he left the warmth of her home to return to the yard where he lived in a bare, converted room that had once been a store, she knew that intangibly their friendship had advanced.

She felt surprised and thankful that here, in this unlikely place, she had met such a friend – and it was, she assured herself, only as a friend that she regretted the comfortlessness of his present quarters. She found herself brooding about it, long after the time when she should have gone to sleep. She couldn't let him spend Christmas there, she thought.

With the approach of Christmas, Izzy Pollard grew ever more self-important, dispensing jars of mincemeat and boxes of biscuits and tins of sliced peaches to her favourites as if no one need imagine that the mere possession of sufficient points in a ration book entitled them to any such favours. Emma, who had made arrangements to spend the holiday with her late husband's parents, pressed on Rachel a chicken which had been given to her by her tame farmer.

"Cook a super Christmas dinner for Stefan," she said. "The poor man's as thin as two boards."

"How did you know I'd invited him?" Rachel asked indignantly. "Honestly, this place is the end! I suppose he told Mrs Carthew, who told you."

"Not at all," Emma said. "He told Mrs Carthew, who told Mrs Hambly, who happened to mention it to Betty Pearce when she came to the school to collect her grandson, who of course, aware of my friendship with you, passed it on at the earliest opportunity. Simple. You realise, of course, that you have the entire village agog."

"Oh, really!" Rachel hardly knew whether to laugh or to be angry. "Well, they can gog all they like! For heaven's sake, one trip to the theatre, one fish supper, a couple of walks – what does it add up to? We're friends, that's all."

And friends, Rachel told herself, were all they were likely to be. He spoke of his wife from time to time, briefly and in passing; but she was not deceived. He still felt her loss and grieved for her constantly. He had no photograph of her, but had mentioned, once, that she had been dark and slightly built.

He had given no other details, and Rachel had asked him for none, but there were times when she felt Irina was present with them – a small, delicate ghost with a cloud of dark hair, full of grace as she lifted her violin and tucked it under her chin. It was Stefan's unswerving love that conjured her up, she felt certain. And she, who had surely made enough mistakes regarding men, was not going to be fool enough to fall in love with this particular one.

She continued to enjoy his company, however; and so did Tess, for he had endless patience with her and appeared to like nothing more than to play the repetitive games she enjoyed so much. He was good-humoured, undismayed by the tears or the temperament without which no child would be human.

"Where is father?" he asked her once. "Does he see her?"

"No," she answered briefly, in a voice that brooked no further questions.

"That is sad," he said after a moment. "If I were her father – "

"Well, you're not, are you?" she snapped; and half humorously, half taken aback, he had sucked in his cheeks, raised his eyebrows and said no more.

Easygoing though he was, Rachel had clear evidence that the angry man of their first meeting was not so very far below the surface. Soon after the walk to the creek, they had met by arrangement to explore the cliff path, and had scrambled down to a rocky cove where they had found two small boys tormenting a gull with a broken wing. Stefan had shouted at them, and raised an arm as if he would strike them, so threatening that they had taken to their heels and fled. He was shaking, Rachel saw as he passed a hand over his face when they were gone, muttering to himself in Polish.

"Unforgivable," he said to her after a few moments. "Unforgivable. They were children, only. I cannot stand seeing any helpless creature hurt, but this loss of control I thought in past. It is not – not *I*, Rachel! What must you think of me?"

"What do I think of you?" Rachel had laughed as she looked at him. "Well, I can hardly be under any illusions, can I? I thought you were going to give me a fourpenny one that first time we met."

"Fourpenny one?" He frowned, not understanding. She had hoped to make him smile, but saw she had failed.

"Hit me, I mean. Stefan, don't be daft," she went on. "If I didn't like you, I wouldn't be here, would I?"

He smiled at that as if with relief. He looked younger all the time, she thought. How old was he? Thirty five, maybe? She found herself unable to guess, and admitted to herself that she was curious. Only because he was something of an enigma, she thought hastily; not for any other reason. Sometimes he seemed to possess the wisdom of the ages, as if he were a whole generation removed from her. This loss of control that he deplored so much was almost a relief. At least it proved that he was human.

Enduring such spartan living accommodation as he did, he was appreciative of the efforts she made to produce a Christmas dinner. He came bearing bottles of wine, and small presents – a book for her, a doll for Tess.

"Is so beautiful!" he said, looking round the room at the tree she had decorated, and the streamers and swags of holly and cards above the fireplace. So few cards to show for twenty-five years on this planet, she had thought as she set them out. There was one from her mother and father; one from Sylvia and Rex, with a scrawled message below the names to say they hoped she was keeping warm and enjoying the cottage. One from Alice and Keith, now married and living in Edinburgh. One from Susan, sent from Germany where she had a job with UNRRA, working with Displaced Persons. One from Nancy and George, and another from Emma. One from her editor, one from her agent, one from Beattie.

Only to someone like Stefan, she thought, would this seem like abundance.

When Tess was in bed, worn out by the excitement of her first Christmas, they sat down to the meal that Rachel had prepared. All, to her relief, had turned out well. The chicken was succulent, the potatoes crisply roasted, the brussel sprouts still had a bite to them. She'd been worried about the stuffing, that the herb content was too much, but it had been all right. Better than all right. Conversation was easy and unforced. It was, after all, turning out a far better Christmas than she might have expected.

"More wine?" He leant towards her to refill her glass. "That was delicious, Rachel. I have not had such a meal since – oh, I can't remember!"

"The chicken was courtesy of Emma."

"But you stuffed it and cooked it, and did all the rest. And as for the pudding – ! Well, I have made a mutton of myself."

Rachel giggled, feeling slightly light-headed.

"Glutton, I think you mean. Unless my cooking has made you feel like a dead sheep."

"Dead – ?" He clapped a hand to his head. "Such a fool! Glutton I meant."

"I think coffee might be a good idea, don't you? Why don't you sit by the fire, and I'll bring some in?"

He insisted on helping her to clear the table, but she refused all offers of help with the washing up. When she returned to the sitting room, she found him sitting by the fire, apparently lost in thought. Silently he watched her as she put the tray down and poured the coffee.

"So little I know of your life," he said as she handed him his cup. "I see cards and I know you have friends and family, but you do not speak much of them."

"Well, there's not much family to speak of," she replied lightly. "I've told you about my parents in Uganda. The aunt and uncle who own this cottage are in America – and that's it. Tess is my family now."

He seemed to brood on this a little, but there was something in the quality of his silence that made her aware that questions were on the tip of his tongue.

"If you are thinking about her father – " she began defensively.

"No, no!" Hastily he denied such a thing; then he shrugged his shoulders. "Well, perhaps. But I think only that it is sad for you to be alone. But soon your parents come home, yes?"

"Yes." There was a note of hesitancy in Rachel's voice as if she were, after all, less than overjoyed at this prospect, and he looked at her narrowly.

"What is wrong? You do not wish to see them?"

She gave a brief, unhappy laugh.

"The question is, will they wish to see me, once they know about Tess?"

"You mean they know nothing? You have not told them? But why, Rachel?"

"Haven't the guts," she said, adopting a flippant note. "That's the long and the short of it. Oh, they'll have to know eventually, of course, but sufficient unto the day. Now you see me for what I am," she went on, as he continued to look at her, frowning, not saying a word. "Lily-livered and pusillanimous."

"I don't know those words – "

"I'm a coward, Stefan. I lack courage. I'm scared. No doubt there are other ways of saying it, but that's the essence."

"No! Is nonsense!" He laughed disbelievingly. "Is not easy for woman on her own with baby. You manage well. You are brave."

Rachel sighed and sipped her coffee in silence for a moment.

"Some things I am brave about," she said. "Other things scare me to death. Things like – will my parents ever forgive me for doing this to them? They'll be hurt and humiliated and angry."

He leaned towards her, his dark face intense.

"You are wrong, Rachel." She could see he was having difficulty in finding the right words to express himself. He knocked his head in frustration. "How shall I say? You must be – more fair to them. They, perhaps, are not so small as you think. Yes, perhaps, they will be upset. But can't you trust their – their – " he paused, struggling. "'Compassion' is word, yes?"

"Maybe," she said.

"If they love you – and I am sure they love you, they will not make this a reason to stop. This is meaning of family."

"Mm." Rachel looked sceptical. His concept was too simplistic. Losing his own family had made him over-sentimental, that's what it was. As far as her family was concerned, hadn't Alannah always said – ?

Damn Alannah! She didn't want to think what Alannah had always said. The evening had taken a wrong turn, with all this talk of families. It was dangerous territory for both of them.

"Emma's planning an enormous New Year's Party," she said brightly. "I do hope Marlene's going to be able to sit in for me. Have you been invited yet? I know you will be. Emma's talking about making it fancy dress, and I've been racking my brains about what to wear. Have you got any good ideas?"

Stefan had bought some small cigars with him and thoughtfully he lit one, drawing on it with his eyes still fixed on her. He blew out the smoke so that it wreathed around him, hiding his expression.

"No," he said. "Rachel – " The smoke cleared and she could see his eyes, dark and intense and troubled. "Is not my business to advise – "

She abandoned the bright conversational manner and gave him a small, twisted smile.

"But you're going to do it anyway?"

"Rachel," he said again. His voice was gentle, and he hesitated a little. "Your parents will, I think, be more hurt the longer you keep this secret. And for your own sake, too, you should tell them, not allow them to come and be confronted by grandchild they know nothing about."

"Perhaps you are right," she said at last. "I'm sure you are right. But for God's sake, let's talk about something else. Would you like more coffee?"

"Thank you. Is good. You buy here in St Bethan?"

"Good Lord, no! There's a little shop near the church in Polvear . . ."

The conversation drifted to other things and did not return to that particular subject; but as if it had cast a shadow, there was no sparkle in the evening now.

They spoke of Emma's party, but without a great deal of interest. They compared Christmas traditions, English and Polish. Stefan described ice-sailing one year on the Mazurian Lakes; she told him about the Rossiter's parties and pantomimes.

They were like two old pensioners talking about the good old days, she thought, and suddenly she found herself deeply depressed as if the day should have built up to a climax more exciting than this.

What the hell did I expect? she demanded of herself.

She didn't know. Not bed, that was certain, or any kind of commitment. She wasn't ready, and clearly nor was he. Perhaps he never would be.

He rose to go, and she made no protest. He had done his best, no doubt; but she had the distinct feeling that, as the evening progressed, he had become increasingly weighed down by memories of other times, other Christmasses.

"I thank you so much," he said when he was about to leave.

"It would not have been good to be alone. Not for you, I think, nor for me. We are both Displaced Persons – yes?"

"Perhaps," she said, conscious suddenly of the prick of tears behind her eyes. Damn it, what was wrong with her? It must be the wine. She'd had too much and it had made her over-emotional.

"But you have parents still," he said, taking her two hands to give added emphasis to his words. "That is big thing, Rachel. Please don't hurt them more than you have to."

"All *right*!" She snatched her hands away, her impatience real enough even though she laughed at him and attempted to turn it into a joke. "Point taken!"

After he had gone, she went into the kitchen and with a sinking heart surveyed the sink full of dishes, gearing herself up to tackle them, knowing that the next day would bring its own quota of chores. She picked up an encrusted saucepan that ought to have been put to soak, looked at it with hatred, and crashed it down on the draining board.

"*Bloody* Christmas," she said, the tears that had been threatening for the last few minutes suddenly spilling over.

She turned her back on the mess and returned to the sitting room where she found there was still half an inch of wine in one of the bottles. Sniffing, wiping away the tears with her fingers, she poured the remains into her glass and sat down with it on a footstool close to the dying fire.

"Fool," she said bitterly to herself. "Bloody idiot. For God's sake, pull yourself together."

She sniffed some more, and fumbled in her pocket for a handkerchief. She had Tess, hadn't she? And the book was progressing, wasn't it? She had friends, enough to live on – she was *lucky*, for heaven's sake!

It wasn't as if she wanted that sort of here-we-go-round-the-mulberry-bush, Rossiter-ish Christmas, that suddenly seemed to bloom in her memory as if it had been nothing but fun and good cheer. It hadn't been like that at all.

It had been an illusion, a lie. Without substance. As so much had been. Including Alannah's cruel and frequent remarks about the Bonds' lack of family feeling. That wasn't true either. They did care for each other, even if it were in a different way from the Rossiters. It was crazy to play Alannah's words over and over in her head like an old record.

All, all was a lie. But, in a strange and perverse way, the Rossiters had set a standard. Impossible not to think that this was the way a family ought to be. That somehow she had missed out.

Rachel stared into the fire and seemed to see them all, closely linked, laughing, admiring each other, forgiving each other. Would her parents forgive so easily?

She yawned, tired now. Bed, she thought; and to hell with the washing up. And to hell with the Rossiters.

And to hell with Christmas, she thought as, a little unsteadily, she climbed the stairs. Next year she'd abolish it altogether. But then she remembered Tess, and knew that she wouldn't.

Emma's New Year's party went ahead as planned, but the weather was bad and roads were icy, so that many of her guests failed to make the journey to St Bethan and no one was anxious to make it a late night.

From the beginning it was clear that Stefan had shaken off the sub-fusc mood of Christmas, as indeed she had herself.

"Did I nag?" he asked Rachel as they walked up the hill to the schoolhouse, her arm through his.

"A bit," she admitted.

"Oh, well." He smiled down at her. "I cannot help being so right, I think. Is my wonderful nature."

"So wise, and modest with it," Rachel mocked him.

Emma had decided not to make the party fancy dress after all. Stefan wore grey flannels and a tweed sports coat, newly bought, and succeeded in looking both more English and more foreign than usual. Rachel noted that women who would not have given him a second glance had they seen him in his donkey jacket and seaman's cap were hanging on his every word; but he looked across at one point and winked at her as if to say – just look at me, don't you find this amusing? And she had grinned back. For once, there seemed no sign of Irina anywhere. There was dancing to records collected from Emma's friends and acquaintances, the dining room cleared for the purpose.

"Embrace me, you sweet embraceable you," crooned Frank Sinatra; and looking up at Stefan, feeling his arm around her waist, finding him looking at her with a softness of expression she had not seen before, Rachel was conscious of a twist of excitement and longing. Was love possible, then? Was it at all possible? She felt breathless at the very thought of it. It frightened her to death, yet sent a shiver of delight through her body.

Oh, the potency of cheap music, she thought, forcing herself down to earth. Noel Coward certainly knew a thing or two.

There were the usual screams of excitement and kisses as 1947 came into being and the chimes of Big Ben were relayed over the radio. Stefan, being the darkest man present, was detailed to do the first-footing.

"Isn't he gorgeous?" said a young, redheaded woman, a schoolteacher from Falmouth. "Such a fascinating accent! I could listen to him all night."

When, later, Stefan deposited her at her door, Rachel reached up to kiss him lightly on the cheek.

"I shan't ask you in," she said. "It's much too late, for one thing; and for another, I have every intention of writing a letter before I go to sleep tonight. A letter to my parents. *The* letter! It's my New Year's Resolution."

By the porch light she could see his smile, the upward slant of his cheeks, the dark bright eyes. He bent his head and kissed her. A reward for being good, she thought. But then his arms tightened around her and he kissed her again, and this time there was hunger in it, and passion, and delight; and for a moment she lost herself in it, drowning in sweetness and joy, all fears swept away, sure that the waiting was at an end. And then, as suddenly, he drew away, his expression unreadable.

Irina, she thought, with a sinking of the heart. Always there. Why can't she see that I'd never come between them, never want to?

"You do good thing, Rachel," he said softly. "I am pleased with you."

She gave a small, trembling laugh.

"You sound like a schoolmaster talking to a promising pupil," she said. "Or a vicar, maybe."

His smile seemed both gentle and regretful as he lightly stroked her face. She was pleased to notice that his breathing was uneven.

"I do not feel like vicar," he said. "No, not at all like vicar." He was silent for a moment, not smiling now, and his hand was cold against her cheek. "Happy New Year, Rachel."

"Happy New Year, Stefan."

For a long moment they looked at each other in a silence that seemed to vibrate with words trembling on the brink of expression. He said no more, however, but turned and left her. For a second or two she stood looking after him. She gave a breath of laughter that ended in a sigh, then she shook her head and sighed again.

She would try to put him out of her mind for the moment. She had to. The most difficult composition of her life lay ahead.

16

Winter clamped down on the entire country, bitter and remorseless, made even harder by shortages. The long-suffering British public was exhorted by the Government to save electricity, heat only one room, cut down on the bath water. Meantime bread rationing was introduced, the meat ration cut. Austerity was the word on everyone's lips.

The weeks passed without a letter from Uganda. Sometimes Rachel was quite sure that this was because her parents had cut her off completely; at others, she knew it might well be because the mail was delayed. It happened all too frequently.

It was hard not to succumb to depression, not to fear the worst, even though good things were happening. *With This Ring* was to be published in March, and already seemed to be generating a certain amount of interest. The present book was developing well. Marlene was proving a great success. Tess was healthy, happy, almost walking. Why didn't she, then, feel more at peace with herself?

That was an easy one to answer. Until now she had, in a strange way, taken pleasure in the slow growth of her relationship with Stefan and their dawning dependence on each other. There had seemed no urgency in it. They were loving friends, good companions, and if there were times when a word or gesture had made her suddenly hungry for more, times when she had begged the frail, dark ghost to disappear once and for all, for the most part the relationship had suited her pace as much as his. It was as if she knew a long-sought treat was waiting for her at the end of the road, but recognised that she was not yet ready to savour it. She, too, had been through a period of mourning, after all.

Time, she had felt, was on her side. Sometimes she could swear that he was on the point of losing his icy control, as on New Year's Eve. Sometimes he seemed almost luminous with wanting. Soon, soon – oh, surely soon, the memory of Irina would become bearable and he would be able to love again without fear of faithlessness? She sensed it coming; had even thought, that night when he told her about Anna, that there was an air of excitement about him that signalled the waiting was at an end.

What a poor, deluded fool she had been, imagining her only rival to be a ghost! Anna was beautiful, he had told her – as fair as Irina was dark. He had smiled when he spoke of her.

"She was – *is*, I hope, like quicksilver, all movement and gaiety," he said. "And so talented! She sang like an angel. Back in the old days in Warsaw, she had only to walk into a restaurant for all heads to turn. Irina used to tease her – say that no other woman could be noticed when Anna was there, but they were good friends, with much in common. I hope the war did not touch her too badly."

"I hope so too," Rachel had responded; but she was unable to control an instinctive tremor of unease as she made the required response. Did he realise, she wondered, how his voice had changed and lightened as he spoke of her? How foreign he seemed, suddenly? How full of joy, that this Krasinski family he had known in Warsaw had turned up in London – mother, father, and beautiful blonde daughter?

"I shall see them when I am there next week, of course," he said. "We shall have so much to talk about."

And Rachel had smiled and agreed and wished to die. A ghost was enough to contend with. A live blonde with shared memories was too much.

It was a bitterly cold day towards the end of February that Emma called in for a friendly chat, having battled down the hill in the teeth of wind and icy rain.

"I sometimes think," she said, unwinding a long woollen scarf, "that life is rapidly becoming insupportable. However, I suppose it's marginally less insupportable today than it was yesterday. At least the school is closed and the poor little mites don't have to sit in their coats and hoods attempting to work. All the outside WCs are frozen solid and we've no heating at all. I must say it's blissfully warm in here," she finished, subsiding gratefully at the kitchen table.

"It's the only room that is. Coffee?"

"Lovely. Thanks."

"I have to keep the boiler on because it heats the water, so here is where Tess and I live and move and have our being. Sorry about the festooned laundry. At least Stefan has made me this super pulley thing so I can hoist it all up above our heads."

"Useful fellow," Emma said dryly.

"Mm." Rachel was giving nothing away. "He's in London at the moment, lucky chap."

She felt a pang of longing as she spoke, not only for Stefan. Even the most ardent fan could not say that St Bethan was at its best in February; and though she knew quite well that the temperature in London was even lower, still there was something appealing about lights and shops and theatres and libraries.

"Oh?" Emma looked alertly interested. "Why?"

In spite of low spirits, Rachel felt amused. Emma was both kind and intelligent, but she was undoubtedly as bad as the rest when it came to gossip. She was utterly well-intentioned, quite without malice, but she did love to *know* – and to pass it on. If Rachel let slip the information that Stefan was seeing a man about plastic boats, it would be all over St Bethan in no time flat, one more piece of evidence that, say what you will, 'furriners' were all mad as hatters. Still less could she bring herself to speak of Anna. The village would either pity her, or say it was no more than she deserved, neither of which could she bear.

"Oh, it's just some business," she said vaguely. "He's going to the Embassy. Something to do with his residency. And then he's going to look up some Polish friends."

She saw Emma's quick probing glance and wondered if her voice had betrayed her feelings.

"When's he coming back?" Emma asked.

Rachel did her best to shake off her fears.

"He wasn't entirely sure. Sunday, maybe. It depended on his friends."

"You must miss him. Cheer yourself up by coming to the play on Saturday."

"Which play?"

"Oh Rachel, I told you – *Pygmalion*! It's another CEMA thing. Why don't you come? There'll be plenty of tickets this weather."

Rachel considered the matter, but declined with thanks. Tess was teething again and had had a few bad nights recently. And the book was so close to being finished now, she really wanted to work flat out. And the weather was so appalling –

"Well, another time," Emma said. "The weather's a killer, I agree. I don't suppose many will turn up at all."

"Now you make me feel guilty!"

"Not at all. Stay and get the book finished. Then you'll be able to kick up your heels a bit."

By seeing *Pygmalion* in a draughty hall? Rachel smiled grimly, but made no comment. Think of the glories of the river, she urged herself; and the coming of spring. Winter wouldn't go on for ever – even this one, which was beginning to seem endless, and which, undoubtedly, was the cause of the feeling of depression that she seemed powerless to dismiss. Even if Stefan chose to stay with Anna, she still had Tess, still had her writing. Her life wouldn't be over. It would just seem like it for a little while. She would recover, bounce back. Oh God, she thought, I am so sick of bouncing back!

When she went to collect her Sunday paper the following morning, she ran into Emma on her way to church. She hadn't missed much, Emma said. The play hadn't seemed quite up to the standard of previous productions. To her mind, the actress who played Eliza had missed the whole essence of the thing and had played her strictly for laughs.

"Not what I would call a very intelligent performance," Emma said. "And the hall was only half full. Oh Lord – it's raining again!"

Rachel dashed home through the icy sleet, pushing the pram before her. Both Marlene and Mrs Hoskings had flu and had failed to report for duty that week. Perhaps she was going down with it. Maybe that was the reason she felt so dispirited.

She was struck, on her return, by the general awfulness of the cottage. She'd been too busy writing to do household chores, but she couldn't escape them for ever. Dusters would have to be wielded, carpets hoovered. Tess, safe in the large playpen that Stefan had made for her, played with her toys and sang to herself, content for a while to be left to her own devices as Rachel went rather grimly about her work.

Where was Stefan now? He would almost certainly be with the Krasinski family this Sunday morning. Later, they would probably go out for a meal, to some restaurant where all eyes would follow Anna –

"And how do you feel about that, Irina?" she asked, directing her question to the far corner of the sitting-room ceiling. "Would you give him up more easily to your friend Anna?"

Probably not; but he might give himself up. He was better now, on an even keel, not the nervous, hag-ridden man she had first known. Had she been merely an instrument in his recovery, no more important than his work at the boatyard and the peace of

St Bethan? Would he now move up to the next rung in the ladder of his rehabilitation, leaving her behind?

She paused, duster in hand, conscious of rising panic. He wouldn't – surely he wouldn't? She'd been too patient, that was the trouble. Oh, why hadn't she flaunted herself a bit more, played the sex card? She'd wanted to, often enough, but she felt he'd needed time.

And she'd needed time, too. She couldn't deny that. Seeing Barney again had stirred up all kinds of emotions and memories she had thought long dead. They were quite a pair, she and Stefan, when one considered the matter, with enough complexes between them to keep an analyst occupied for years. She resumed polishing the table, forcing down the panic. She was an idiot to worry. Naturally he had been excited about seeing old friends. Who wouldn't be? But still he would come back from London and would rush round to see her, bubbling over with news of all his doings.

"Because he does tell me things," she said to the hovering Irina. "I am important to him. I'd be much better for him than Anna – can't you see that? She's the past. I'm the future."

There, she said to herself as she progressed with her duster to the mantelpiece. Totally mad. That proves it. Imagine talking to a Polish ghost in a Cornish cottage!

She was going stir-crazy, that was the trouble. She'd spent too many days confined to the kitchen. Well, to hell with government directives! She was going to light the fire in the sitting room today whatever They said. There were logs and driftwood in the fuel store and soon she and Stefan could go and beachcomb to get some more. Maybe. Again she fought down panic. Oh, it couldn't all be over, could it?

Tess was getting fed up with the playpen and was demanding more attention. Rachel looked at her watch. A few minutes play, she thought, then lunch, then bed. Then, with any luck, she could count on a couple of hours at the typewriter. She might even finish today – now that would be something to tell Stefan on his return!

The programme proceded as planned; but as she played with Tess, prepared lunch, fed them both, Stefan still dominated her thoughts. Setting all her more personal concerns to one side, this trip of his had enormous implications. He was meeting a boat designer who had shown interest in his radical new ideas, and all depended on Stefan's ability to persuade him that they did, indeed, have possibilities.

And if they did, who knew what would happen? Anna or no Anna, his interlude at Carthew's Boat Yard would be over. A new life would await him somewhere else.

Lost in thought, she held a spoonful of strained beef and carrot just out of Tess's reach, resulting in vociferous complaints which recalled her to her maternal duties with a jolt.

"Sorry, darling," she said humbly, in the face of Tess's blue, accusing stare.

She had just finished mashing a banana for the second course when the doorbell rang. She caught her breath, unable to move for a moment, transfixed by joy. *Stefan!* Who else would it be? It had to be him, come home early after all. Oh, what a fool she'd been ever to doubt him! He'd seen Anna, and still come home to her. Joyfully she rushed to the door.

"Surprise, surprise! Look who's here!"

It wasn't Stefan. For a moment Rachel stared without recognition at the girl with the Veronica Lake hairstyle and the scarlet lips who stood on the step. Slowly her smile died.

"Alannah!" she said faintly.

"In the flesh! Darling, it's pouring with rain, in case you hadn't noticed! Are you going to leave me outside to get soaked through?"

"No, no of course not . . ."

Helplessly Rachel's voice trailed away. Alannah was already inside, looking round the room, exclaiming, admiring.

"What a marvellous room! Such a divine view! Darling, how clever of you to have found it. How *are* you? You look – " she hesitated. "Marvellous," she finished, unconvincingly.

Rachel, clad in the corduroy trousers and thick, baggy sweater that she had almost thrown out the previous winter, swore inwardly. Alannah looked aggressively fashionable in a long, tight-waisted black coat with a little black bowler hat with a veil.

"Alannah, how in the world – " she began, then stopped as she realised the truth. "Of course! You were in the play," she said. "*Pygmalion*. In Truro. My friend saw it last night."

"Really? Darling, why didn't you come too? The place was half empty – pearls before swine simply wasn't in it!"

"But how did you get *here*?" Rachel asked dazedly. "Surely not by bus and ferry – "

"No, no! Oh darling, no, of course not. Someone else in the company was going to stay with his aunt in St Austell for the night, so he kindly offered to drop me off. Barney got your address from the woman who's living in your house in London."

299

She was about to continue, but Tess forstalled her. She, it seemed, had decided that enough was enough, and that now was the time to complain bitterly at her mother's desertion.

The roars of rage caused Alannah's pencil-thin brows to shoot upwards.

"What on earth – "

"That's Tess," Rachel said. "Excuse me."

She went through to the kitchen where Tess, in her high chair, had succeeded in smearing herself and much of her sur-roundings with mashed banana. Alannah, framed in the door-way, dainty and detached, surveyed the scene with ill-concealed horror.

"My God, what's this?" she asked. "Are you in the baby-farming business?"

"Tess is mine. And no," she went on, anticipating the next question. "I'm not married."

Rachel didn't look to see the result of her announcement, but lifted Tess from the chair and set about wiping her hands and face. "She's due for a sleep," she said. "If you'd like to go in and sit by the fire, I'll get her settled. Do take your hat and coat off," she added politely, as Alannah continued to stare at her, apparently bereft of words.

With Tess tucked up in her cot, she returned downstairs to find that Alannah had accepted the invitation to take off her outer garments and was looking at herself in the mirror over the fireplace with every evidence of satisfaction. She turned as Rachel came into the room, her expression changing to one of compassion. With arms outstretched she moved gracefully towards her and embraced her closely.

"Oh, you poor darling, I'm so terribly sorry," she said, her voice throbbing with sincerity. "I had no idea! How absolutely frightful for you! How on earth do you cope? Now listen to me!" She took hold of Rachel's shoulders and gazed earnestly into her eyes. "I want you to know that it won't make the slightest bit of difference."

"Difference to what?" Rachel asked.

"Why, to *us*, of course. To being friends!"

Rachel stared at her for a moment with dawning amuse-ment.

"That's a great relief."

"I mean, what are friends for?"

"You tell me," Rachel said. "Would you like some coffee? Have you had lunch?"

She went into the kitchen and Alannah drifted after her hovering in the doorway once more.

"We stopped at an hotel on the way. Darling, it is all right if I stay the night, isn't it? I mean, you can give me a doss-down somewhere? I've brought my jim-jams and my toothbrush in my little bag. You see Terry – that's the man who gave me the lift – he's staying the night at his aunt's house and can't pick me up until tomorrow."

Rachel, setting out cups and saucers and teaspoons, froze for a moment before continuing the task.

"I see," she said.

"Darling, you should see the ghastly little guesthouse where they've put us in Truro! I absolutely jumped at the chance of getting away. I would have phoned, but Barney didn't get the number and you're not in the book."

"It's under 'Courtney'. The cottage belongs to my Aunt Sylvia."

"Oh, I see. That explains it. I wondered why you'd come to such a godforsaken neck of the woods."

"I like it," Rachel said, forgetting the nostalgic dreams of urban delights that had taunted her recently. "This is ready now. I'll bring it through."

"It smells wonderful, darling."

"What's all this 'darling' business?" Rachel asked with some amusement as they settled themselves in front of the fire.

"Oh, everyone's 'darling' in the theatre."

"So it's all going well, is it?"

"Oh yes, I adore it! Of course, this CEMA business isn't exactly the West End, but it's wonderful experience. I'm sure it will lead to something."

"I hope so." Rachel poured the coffee and handed a cup to Alannah. "What part are you playing?"

"In *Pygmalion*? Eliza, of course. In Falmouth we're doing *The Devil's Disciple*. I'm Judith in that. Eliza is more fun. You should have come to see us."

"Well, it's a bit awkward – "

"Oh, yes." Alannah gave a small, embarrassed laugh. "I suppose it must be."

"Well," Rachel said after a short silence. "Tell all! How's everyone?"

"Tell all! I like that! You're the one with things to tell." Putting the cup down on a table by her chair, Alannah leaned forward. "You know, darling, you can confide in me. Why didn't Barney tell me about this baby of yours?"

"Barney didn't know anything to tell."

"But he came to your house – "

"He didn't see her."

"And you didn't say a word! You always were a secretive little thing. Who's the father?"

"No one of any importance."

"Oh, poor Rachel. I really am sorry!"

"So you've said before. You needn't be, honestly."

"But it's every girl's nightmare, isn't it, getting caught like that, finding yourself pregnant? Why on earth didn't you have it adopted?"

Rachel looked at her without answering, a faint smile on her face. I could have written the script, she thought.

"Believe it or not, I wanted to keep her," she said.

"I suppose you were madly in love with the father?"

"Not in the slightest. But I still wanted her. I wanted someone to love, someone that was a part of me." She got up and put more wood on the fire. "Maybe that was selfish," she said as she came back to her chair. "I don't know. I just know that I couldn't give her up."

Alannah still gazed at her, frowning. She shook her head as if she found the whole thing totally incomprehensible.

"What a dreadful tragedy," she said. "I mean – " She shrugged her shoulders. "You can't get away from the fact, darling. You've ruined your life." She shook her head sadly as she turned to pick up her cup. "And it absolutely knocks Ma's little plan on the head," she added, incomprehensibly.

Rachel frowned. "And what little plan might your mother be hatching?" she asked.

Alannah gave her embarrassed laugh again.

"Oh, it was nothing, honestly," she said. "It was just that – well, Ma's worried, and she thought you might help. Not that it's at all possible now."

"Oh?" Rachel's voice was cold.

"Well – " Alannah laughed awkwardly. "It's Barney, you see. We're worried about him. I mean, *really* worried!"

"Why?"

Alannah chewed her lip in indecision.

"It's sort of telling tales out of school," she said at last, "but you are almost family, aren't you?"

"Not that I'm aware," Rachel said.

"Oh, you know what I mean!"

"What's wrong with Barney?"

302

"Well – " still Alannah hesitated, then took the plunge. "He's been sort of odd since he left the Army. Unsettled. Disorientated. Didn't you think so, when you saw him?"

Rachel considered the matter.

"I thought he seemed – nervous," she said. "Did he go into the antiques business? He was talking about it when I saw him and seemed enthusiastic – "

"God, no! Ma managed to talk him out of that. I mean, imagine going into business with Guy Seamark! He's a frightful drip. Do you remember how he used to moon over Di? And then he married a common little creature you'd expect to find serving in Woolworths!"

"But he knows his antiques, Barney said."

"It would have been an awful risk. The parents advised against it, quite rightly in my view, so Barney took a job in a shipping firm. An awfully good job, actually, but he never really settled in it. It only lasted a couple of months and then he handed in his notice. Then he tried being an estate agent, but that was even worse. *Then* he put every penny he possessed into some doubtful property deal with Reggie Baker. Remember him? Daphne Baker's brother? We thought the Bakers were all right, but they weren't at all and poor Barney lost all his savings, such as they were. Now he doesn't seem to know what to do. He's – well, we're kind of worried that he's drinking too much. He's got in with a really fast set."

"That doesn't sound like Barney," Rachel said, astonished.

"It doesn't, does it? Reggie was such a bad influence. Ma blames him for everything."

You don't say? Rachel thought, but manfully contrived to leave the words unspoken.

"Where am I supposed to come in?" she asked instead, totally bewildered.

"Well, we thought you might help," Alannah said. "But of course, that's out of the question now. The baby's rather put you out of court."

Rachel put a hand to her head and closed her eyes.

"Forgive me," she said, "but I seem to be missing some vital piece of the argument here. What the hell has Tess got to do with anything?"

"Oh Rachel, don't pretend you don't know! I'm talking about you and Barney. You know perfectly well he's always been in love with you."

"Well, maybe once, when we were very young, but not now. Not since – since Gavin."

There. She'd spoken the name. Alannah remained unmoved.

"You're wrong. He told Ma he was in love with you. He said he always had been and that there'd never be anyone else. He'd tried going out with other girls – God, Daphne Baker never leaves him alone! – but it's no good. It's you he wants."

"Really," Rachel said, without expression.

"He said that it wasn't any good, that you wouldn't look at him after what had happened with Gavin, and that anyway you were all fired up about your writing career."

"Go on," said Rachel.

"Well, that's it, really. I wasn't there myself, but apparently he managed to convince Ma that you were the only girl he'd ever wanted. We talked it over just before I came on this West Country trip. She feels that in spite of everything, you're the only person who can straighten him out, so she suggested that I should come and invite you back. For Barney's sake."

Rachel stared at her.

"Does he know about this suggestion?"

"He knew I intended to see you. I had to get your address from him. But for the rest – well, Ma said we'd better leave that until I'd sounded you out."

Still Rachel stared at her, shaking her head in disbelief.

"I just don't believe I'm hearing this!" she said. "Your mother is actually asking me back – "

"Well, I don't suppose she'd be so keen on it now," Alannah said. The look on Rachel's face seemed to disconcert her and she seemed to be floundering. "Surely you understand? Having the baby alters everything."

"Why?" Rachel asked coldly after a moment.

"Why? How can you ask that? Surely you must see that you've totally ruined any chance you might have of marriage and a normal sort of life? What man wants to take on somebody else's child?"

"Widows marry," Rachel pointed out.

"*Illegitimate* child, I meant. It's different. It's such a disgrace. I don't know how you can look the world in the face! My God, I'd want to shoot myself! Not that I'd have to. My mother would do it for me. As for Daddy – well, he'd go after the man with a horsewhip."

Rachel's mouth was twisted in a small tight smile.

"Nonsense! Your father would wash his hands of the matter and your mother would assume it was an immaculate conception and apply to have you beatified. Your mother cannot admit that any of you are to blame for anything."

304

Alannah's pale face grew pink.

"If you're talking about Gavin – "

"And Diana," Rachel pointed out. "Gavin and Diana. Yes, I suppose that's what I'm talking about." Until that moment she had held herself in check, forced herself to see the funny side; said to herself that really, only a Rossiter could possibly behave in this way. Now the bitterness flooded over.

"Leave Tess out of it for the moment," she said. "How your mother has the – the *gall* to send you here with this kind of half-baked proposal, I really can't imagine." She was aware that her voice was trembling. "Can either of you believe that I want anything more to do with any of you after what happened? Did I have one word of sympathy from her when I was in the very depths of despair? Like hell! It was all my fault for making mountains out of molehills!"

"Well, if you're going to rake up the past – "

"Did you come anywhere near me? Not a bit of it! If ever there was a fair-weather friend – "

"I was busy. I'd just been called up into ENSA."

"Rubbish! You could have written. Phoned. *Anything!*"

"I'm going!" Alannah jumped to her feet. "I came here with the best of intentions. You're still bitter about Gavin, that's the truth of it. I'm right, aren't I? You've never got over him."

"Oh yes, I have, Lannie. Believe me. It took me a long time, admittedly, and I made a number of mistakes along the way, but I'm over him now. I don't go for weak men any more. That's why, Tess or no Tess, Barney is not for me. I like him. I wish him well. But no power on earth would make me get involved with a Rossiter, ever again."

"There's no need to be so offensive." Alannah was shaking with rage as she made a grab for her coat. "I wouldn't dream of staying here now."

Without moving, Rachel watched her as she pulled on the coat and began to do up the many buttons that ran from neck to hem. Outside the winter afternoon was darkening and the rain lashed against the window.

Rachel felt the anger drain out of her. Alannah couldn't help being a fool, she thought. Emma was right when she had said that she was unintelligent. Add insensitive and overweeningly self-satisfied and you got somewhere near describing her.

And yet – how potent the past was, after all! Could one ever totally dismiss it? Pretend there had never been affection, or warmth or goodwill or shared laughter? She sighed.

305

"Where are you going, Lannie?" she said.

"I've no idea! I'll get back to Truro somehow."

"I don't think the ferry will run in this weather."

"Then I'll have to go by road. Call me a taxi."

"You're a taxi."

It was an old Rossiter joke, never very funny, but now it stopped them both in their tracks. For a while they stared at each other then, gently, almost wearily, Rachel laughed, shaking her head.

"Maybe you ought to go outside and we'll start all over again," she said.

17

What else could she have done, in view of the appalling weather? It was only for one night, Rachel said to herself as as she went upstairs to get Tess, now awake after her short sleep. Just one night. That was all. It wouldn't really hurt, would it? There was no reason, really, for this feeling in the pit of the stomach that no good would come of it. After all, Alannah had clearly demonstrated her total lack of interest in Tess as a person. Babies were outside her experience – nasty, dirty things to be disregarded whenever possible.

However, the banana-smeared Tess who was borne off so unceremoniously to her cot after lunch bore little resemblance to the clean, brushed, golden-curled infant who was brought down again clad in a pink woollen dress lovingly knitted by Mrs Hoskings.

"She's really rather cute," Alannah said with some surprise, watching Tess's efforts to haul herself upright by holding on to the arm of a chair. "Poor child! I hope she won't suffer too much."

"Because of me?" Rachel raised her eyebrows in polite enquiry.

"Well, of course because of you! There's bound to be a stigma."

How unfailingly did Alannah go for the jugular, Rachel thought, the familiar feeling of inadequacy creeping over her like frostbite.

"I shall do what I can to guard against it, of course," she said stiffly.

"One would have thought you might have considered it at the time."

"I did," Rachel said, her jaw clenched.

Alannah, supremely unaware of any offence, leaned towards Tess and waggled a long manicured finger, scarlet-tipped.

"Who's a little cutesy-wutesy, then? Come and see your auntie," she cooed; adding, in Rachel's direction and in a totally different voice as Tess gazed at her in smiling indifference, "With those eyes, she could almost be a Rossiter, couldn't she?"

"There are other blue-eyed men in the world, you know."

"I realise that! It's interesting, isn't it, how some women always fall for the same physical type?" Alannah abandoned her efforts to woo the unresponsive Tess who was enthusiastically rooting in a box of toys, and instead reached out towards Rachel and squeezed her arm. "Poor Rachel!" she said. "Honestly, I can't tell you how sorry I am that everything turned out this way. You must believe me."

Tess had managed to totter the few steps necessary to bring her mother the pink rabbit. Rachel swept her up in her arms and buried her face for a moment in her daughter's soft, sweet-smelling curls.

"It's turned out a lot better than anyone expected," she said. "Including me. But what about you, Lannie? Is there a man in your life?"

Alannah sat back and sighed, her compassionate expression giving way to one of acute misery.

"Oh, Rachel, it's so awfully complicated," she said. "Terry – that's the man who gave me the lift – he absolutely adores me. Idolises me, one could say. He begged me to go to St Austell with him, but I said no, I had to come and see my old friend. After all, friendship is friendship when all is said and done, and of course there was the matter of you and Barney – " She halted at the sight of Rachel's warning expression. "All *right*," she said defensively. "I won't go into that any more, I promise."

"What about you?" Rachel asked, putting Tess down on the carpet and building a tower of large, soft bricks so that they could be knocked down and built again. "Do you idolise him in equal measure?"

Alannah's face twisted with the agony of it all.

"That's what I keep asking myself, darling," she said. "I mean, he's frightfully handsome in a *louche* sort of way and the women in the audience go simply wild about him, but I don't think he'd go down at all well with the family. He's just the sort of man that Ma loathes."

"What sort is that?" Rachel asked politely.

"Oh – " Alannah shrugged. "You know. He's a bit of a

nonconformist. He hardly ever wears a tie, and he *will* wear a suit jacket with corduroy trousers. And he always insists on bringing a huge tankard of beer to the table because he hates wine. And, to be honest, he does swear rather a lot. And smoke," she added. "Ma's really turned against smoking. Honestly, Rachel, how could I ever take him home?"

"I do see the problem." Rachel bent to build up the brick tower again, hiding her smile. "On the other hand, your mother was never exactly conventional when it came to dress – "

"She has her standards. This aunt he's gone to see in St Austell – you'll never believe it, but she used to be in a circus, on the high wire. Can you imagine?"

"They sound a colourful family."

"But just imagine allying oneself – oh, stop it, Rachel! It's not funny."

"I know," Rachel said penitently. "I do understand how you feel – but it does seem to me that if it weighs so heavily, it must mean you don't really love him."

"Oh but darling, I do!" Alannah wailed. "At least, sometimes I think I do. But then at others – you see, I couldn't ever marry anyone who didn't fit in, could I? Not like Di."

"I thought Diana had made a brilliant marriage."

"Well – " Alannah made a dismissive kind of gesture. "At least Tom is a gentleman and went to public school and all that. Terry is, well, different. Wonderful in many, many ways – all credit to him for making something of himself – but I just can't imagine him at Kimberley Lodge. The family *matters* so much to me," she went on earnestly. "To all of us, really. I do realise it's hard for you to understand, because the relationship between you and your parents is so very different – "

"So you've always been at pains to remind me," Rachel said, an acid note creeping back into her voice. "Time for tea, I think, don't you?"

She picked Tess up and took her through to the kitchen, putting her in the high chair. She tied a bib around her neck and swathed her lower half in a Harrington square before giving her a biscuit.

Alannah, who had followed her and now stood in the doorway once more, watched this ritual with fascination tinged with horror.

"Heavens, it's awfully *constant*, isn't it, darling?" she remarked. "I don't know how you cope."

"One learns," Rachel said.

"I'm not sure that I want to. Di doesn't."

"What about her husband?"

"Oh, he wants kids of course. It would be a different story if he had to have them."

"Do you really not like him?"

"Well, we all thought he was marvellous at first, but he's changed. He's frightfully selfish. He insisted on spending Christmas with his family in some godforsaken part of Yorkshire and we didn't see Di at all."

"But don't Diana and – what's his name? Tom? – live locally? You must see a lot of them all the year. Maybe he thought – "

"We know perfectly well what he thought! He told Ma in no uncertain terms and now he doesn't let Di come round at all."

Rachel looked astonished. "I find that hard to believe, knowing Diana."

"Well, she hasn't been home for ages, Ma says. She'd never stay away off her own bat, so it has to be Tom's fault. I'm sure she's utterly miserable."

"She needed someone strong," Rachel said. "It sounds as if she's got it."

"Ma's frightfully upset."

"I can imagine." How upset? Rachel wondered as the kettle shrilled and she went to lift it off the stove. Red-eyed, streaming-haired upset? Writing-of-vitriolic-letter upset? It seemed very likely. Her heart went out to Tom.

Alannah was silent. Rachel filled the teapot, and turning with it in her hand, saw she was contemplating Tess once more, frowning slightly.

"It really is an extraordinary thing," she said. "It's just struck me – Tess looks exactly like Di in that photograph on the little table in the corner of the dining room. You remember it, surely – the one where she and Gavin are sitting together in a big wicker chair. She's holding a teddy bear."

Rachel's hesitation was almost imperceptible.

"I vaguely remember it, now you've reminded me," she said.

"She was about two, I think," Alannah went on.

"Why don't you take the tray through and see if the fire needs another log?" Rachel said, ignoring the matter of the photograph. "I'll just give Tess her juice and be with you in two shakes."

She continued to ignore it when she joined Alannah, resolutely talking of sleeping arrangements.

"I'll put my sheets on the bed in Tess's room, and put clean sheets on my bed for you," she said.

"That's sweet of you, darling," Alannah said; and, to Rachel's

310

relief, appeared to forget Tess's appearance, preferring instead to enlarge on her brother-in-law's shortcomings.

She continued to regard Rachel's efforts to entertain Tess with a wary and astonished eye. Prolonged discussion of any topic was difficult, even impossible, which did not prevent Alannah expatiating at length on the problem of Terry, various rivalries in the Company, and the tedium of having to play Shaw all the time – why not a Restoration comedy, for goodness sake? Or even a modern farce? She adored playing farce. Rachel would hardly believe, she said, how people who had seen her in farce during the war had come up to her in High Streets all over the country to thank her for making life bearable during the dark days of the war. 'Miss Ross', they said, 'we don't know how we could have carried on without you.'

"So really Churchill – indeed, the entire country – has much to thank you for," Rachel commented.

"Well, in all modesty, I think you could be right," Alannah said. "I do wish you could have seen me in *Rookery Nook*, Rachel. I really brought the house down – and you know what they say! Laughter is the best medicine."

"Perhaps," Rachel ventured innocently, "too good a medicine for unmarried mothers?" Alannah pondered the question for a few seconds before smiling thinly.

"I suppose that's meant to be funny," she said.

"Only mildly," Rachel assured her.

"I hope you won't get bitter, Rachel. That would be the worst thing in the world for little Tess."

"I'll bear that in mind," Rachel said gravely.

Inevitably Alannah returned to the problem of Terry; should she or shouldn't she take the plunge and invite him to Kimberley Lodge? Rachel did her utmost to show interest while continuing to build more towers, point out pictures in a book which involved the singing of a number of nursery rhymes, tuck up a fluffy dog in a cot which Tess rocked happily for at least three minutes before climbing on to her mother's lap and demanding a see-saw.

"Don't despair," Rachel said with genuine sympathy, appreciating how tedious her divided attention must be as Alannah looked at her watch for the umpteenth time. "It'll soon be time for bath and bed."

"Is it always like this?" Alannah asked.

Rachel laughed.

"This is a good day! Now admit it – she hasn't grizzled once."

"I'd hate to be here on a bad one, darling," Alannah said.

Inevitably, bedtime eventually came and silence fell on the house. Rachel came downstairs, conscious, as she cleared away the toys that still littered the floor, that Alannah had moved to the mantelpiece again and was now studying a photograph of Tess, taken by Stefan.

"You know, it is remarkable," she said. "She really is the image of Di."

"You're imagining things," Rachel said briskly. "I've fixed the beds. If you need another blanket, there's one in the cupboard, but I think you should be all right. Now, would you care for a drink? I can offer you a glass of white wine. There's nothing else, I'm afraid."

"I'd love some wine," Alannah said. "We have rather earned it, haven't we?"

Rachel was aware, as she poured the drinks, that she was the subject of a long and speculative glance, but she made no acknowledgement of it.

"There you are," she said, handing Alannah a glass. "An unobtrusive, shy little wine with an understated bouquet."

"Cheers," Alannah said absently. She sat down on one of the chintz armchairs and took a sip, her eyes still fixed on Rachel.

"Do you like liver and bacon?" Rachel asked. "I've got enough for two. Or there's eggs and cheese, if you'd rather – "

"Rachel," Alannah said abruptly. "Are you being straight with me? *Is* Tess a Rossiter?"

Rachel gave an exasperated laugh.

"Honestly, Lannie, you're paranoid!" she said. "Just because she's got blue eyes!"

"But it's such an unusual sort of blue. And it's not just that." Putting her drink down, she got up and took the picture off the mantelpiece. "Look at this. See the chin? It's exactly like that photograph of Di!"

"I thought all babies were supposed to look like Winston Churchill," Rachel said lightly. "Maybe they come in two varieties: those who look like Winston Churchill and those who look like Diana Rossiter."

"You're being absurd!"

"No, Alannah. It's you who are being absurd. Just a little bit of elementary arithmetic will tell you that what you're thinking is impossible. Tess is thirteen months old."

"I can't work that out." Alannah sounded cross, as if it were an outrage to imagine that she could.

"Well, add nine to thirteen," Rachel said, with exaggerated

patience. "That makes twenty-two. Now count back twenty-two months, and you'll have a rough idea when she was conceived."

"That's no proof of anything. Some babies are premature, some are late. Or so I'm led to believe."

"Not that premature or that late."

"If Ma knew that Gavin had had a child – "

"Stop it, Alannah! I swear I never saw Gavin after the summer of 1940. I couldn't have borne to. Look, I don't want to talk about this."

"Barney, then." Alannah had returned to her chair and lifted her glass to take a sip, but now lowered it to regard Rachel suspiciously over the top. "*Was* it Barney?"

"How could it have been? Barney was in the Middle East."

"He came home early in 1946."

"A year ago!" Rachel's voice was taut with anger. "I've already told you Tess was born in January, 1946. She was conceived – not that it's any business of yours – on VE day, which was the 8th May, 1945. I came up to town with a friend and we joined in the celebrations – a little too enthusiastically, you might think. We'd all drunk far too much, and I'd had practically nothing to eat all day. It was sordid and horrible and I couldn't be more ashamed – but, miraculously, Tess was the result. Okay? Satisfied? Inquisition over? Now I'm going to see about supper. In the absence of any other directives, I propose to cook liver and bacon."

She was upset, and didn't care if she showed it. She had a right to be, she told herself, venting her anger on the potatoes she was peeling at the sink. She should have let Alannah walk out into the wind and the rain when she threatened to. Who but she would go on and on like that? And why the hell couldn't she try to be helpful for a change? She hadn't lifted a finger to help pick the toys up, or offered to peel the spuds or set the table or *anything!*

"Rachel – " Alannah had followed her out to the kitchen. "I didn't mean to make you cross, honestly. Goodness, you are a prickly sort of person these days."

Rachel said nothing, but threw a peeled potato in a pot of water with unnecessary force before picking up the next one.

"Look, I'm sorry," Alannah said. "It was just that – well, it seemed so strange, that's all. You can't blame me for being curious, can you?"

"It's none of your business," Rachel said tightly.

"No – no, I see that now. Honestly. I am sorry, Rachel. Don't go on being cross, *please!*"

313

Rachel sighed and leant an elbow on the draining board for a moment, a half-peeled potato in her hand.

"You're impossible, Lannie, d'you know that?" she asked, in a voice that had more or less returned to normal. "You've always been impossible! You don't give a damn about other people, do you? You just ride roughshod over everyone."

"I've said I'm sorry," Alannah said.

"So you have." This, in itself, was something of an achievement, Rachel thought as she continued peeling the potato. In fact, now she considered the matter, she couldn't ever remember such a thing happening before. She glanced round at Alannah, rather expecting her to look offended, but instead was surprised by the expression of unhappiness which she could see on her face.

"Forget it, Lannie," she said, more gently than might have been expected only a few moments before. "Just keep off the grass, that's all. It really is none of your business."

"I know. Sorry."

Rachel continued to peel in silence for a few moments. Why wasn't Alannah happy? Terry, perhaps. And, reading between the lines, it seemed that she wasn't making a spectacular success of her role in this particular play. And then there was Diana's defection, and Barney's problems. It could be any or all of those things.

Or perhaps none. Perhaps it was nothing but her imagination. Briskly, she finished with the potatoes and turned her attention to a cauliflower.

"You'll never guess what I found the other day," she said. "There's a trunk of old books and papers dating from schooldays upstairs. I never unpacked it properly, but I was looking for a book of essays I thought might be there, and what should I find lurking at the bottom but *Hurrah for Dymphna*."

Dissension and apologies alike were forgotten as Alannah clasped her hands and shrieked with joy.

"I don't believe it!"

"I'll rake it out after we've eaten. I couldn't resist reading it right through, and d'you know, some of it isn't bad at all. I laughed like anything at that Prizegiving chapter where Miss Whetton-Wyndham gets caught up in the mayoral chain and has to be cut loose by the evil handyman with his hacksaw."

"Oh, I remember it! And what about the fathers' race incident on Sports Day – "

"And the time when Ethel Craddock won the cross-country by hiding behind a cowshed and popping out just yards from the finishing line!"

314

"And that dreadful head girl's little homily when she discovered the itching powder in her knicker-linings. What was her name? Helen something, wasn't it? Helena, that was it." Alannah adopted a solemn and self-righteous tone. "'Now remember, girls, never *ever* in the knickers!' Oh, we did laugh, didn't we?" Equanimity restored, Alannah leaned against the door-jamb and laughed again. "And now you're a proper writer, just like you said you'd be."

"You didn't think I could do it," Rachel said dryly.

"Oh, I did! Really, I did. You were going to write and I was going to act."

"And Barney was going to paint. Remember that picture he gave me? That's in the trunk too."

She hadn't laughed when she'd seen that, Rachel remembered. It had made her sad, reminding her as it did of lost innocence, and a time when Kimberley Lodge seemed a wonderful place full of wonderful people.

"Oh, I'm so awfully glad I came," Alannah said. "We did have some good times, didn't we?"

And some bad, Rachel reflected; but we won't talk about them. She was surprised to find herself feeling a little sorry for Alannah, conscious that somehow the pendulum had swung for the first time, putting her in the ascendency. Why hadn't she registered before, she wondered, how really *dim* Alannah was beneath all her surface self-assurance? But at least she'd proved a distraction from dark thoughts about Stefan, which could only be a good thing.

The level of the wine bottle went down as they ate their supper and reminisced. Recklessly Rachel stoked the fire up. They could hear the wind whistling around the house. It sent gusts of smoke down the chimney and caused the rain to batter against the windowpane. It was a night when it was good to be indoors.

The phone shrilled, startling them both.

"Rachel?" It was Stefan. Suddenly it was hard to breathe and her heart was pounding. She angled herself away from Alannah so that her expression would give nothing away.

"Stefan? How are you?"

"Missing you." Who could imagine that two simple words could give such joy?

"Me, too," she said. She would have said more if she had been alone. "I have a friend staying tonight," she added, to explain her guarded response.

"That is good. Rachel – " his voice strengthened, full of excitement. "I have such wonderful news. Wonderful! Everything has gone well."

"With Marine Engineering?"

"Of course. What else?"

What else? Didn't he know? Couldn't he imagine? She hadn't invented Anna, had she?

"That's marvellous, Stefan. Congratulations. And what – what about your friends? Have you seen them?"

"Oh, yes. We have meal together last night. It was good to meet with them again and talk of old times. It was – I think, cathartic is word, yes?"

"It could be."

"Seeing them again made me understand, somehow, how far I have come. You understand me?"

"Yes, yes." Oh, how she hoped she did!

"I am so glad I made effort to see them, for soon they go to Canada. They are so excited! New job, new life – "

"You didn't wish you were going too?"

For a moment he was silent, and when he spoke again he sounded puzzled.

"You cannot think that! You must know that all I care for now is here, in England. Rachel – ?" He sounded anxious as she made no reply. "Rachel, you are there?"

"Yes," she said softly. "Yes, I'm here."

"We talk tomorrow. I shall be home then. Maybe not until evening, but as early as possible. I come to see you then, yes?"

"Yes," Rachel said, forgetting to be guarded. "Oh, yes, Stefan. Come as soon as you can."

"I have so much to say, so much to ask you." He seemed to catch his breath a little and his voice quickened, became urgent. "Oh, Rachel! So much I want to say that is too important for telephone."

"Then, tomorrow," she said, and did not care that her voice betrayed her feelings. Home, he had said. He was coming home.

"Who was that?" Alannah asked curiously as Rachel retook her seat. "And why are you grinning like a Cheshire cat?" She didn't wait for a reply. "I was telling you about Terry," she went on. "You see, darling, the problem is – "

On and on she talked – what Ma might say, what Daddy might think. Rachel put on a listening expression and thought of Stefan.

Tomorrow. He would be here tomorrow. Oh, she wanted him so; wanted him, mind and body – all of him, all of her, for ever and ever. Was it possible?

Yes, she thought. It was possible. It was more than possible.

There was, it seemed, a future for him in this strange business of molded resin boats, something for him to offer a woman. He was the kind of man who would need that.

As for Anna – it seemed she was no threat. Perhaps she never had been. Please, please Lannie, stop talking, she thought, hiding a yawn. She longed to go to bed, longed for tomorrow to come quickly, longed for the waiting to be over, to be done with all pretence of patience.

"What happened to your friend Alice?" Alannah asked, just when Rachel thought she was winding down.

"She worked at the Ministry of Information all through the war, and married Keith in – oh, the summer of 1943, it must have been. You met him," Rachel went on, suddenly remembering. "That night – you remember it, Lannie – that night you bunked off college and came up to town looking for a job with ENSA."

"And we sat outside and talked about the Home Guard. Yes, I remember! He was in the Navy. Rather smashing, as I recall. Well, lucky old Alice! Who'd have thought she had it in her."

"They're living in Edinburgh now. Keith's gone back to University. They're supposed to be coming down here at Easter."

"There was a funny old man there that night – remember him? He wanted to falsify his age so that he could join the Home Guard and drill with broom handles."

"He was killed. His house got a direct hit."

"Oh Lord, how frightful! Was there much damage in that part of London?"

"A fair bit. The church at the corner has gone, and that block of flats in the next road. And remember that terrace of shops just before you turn into Shawcross Street? They were hit by a V2 and totally flattened. God, how I hated those things! They were so silent and so deadly. Much worse than the bombs."

"But the house itself escaped, did it? Yes, of course it did!" Alannah gave her knee a small, annoyed slap. "How could I have forgotten? Daddy lived there right at the end of the war, just for a week or so. Wasn't that a fantastic coincidence? He had a friend who worked with Alice's aunt. What was her name? Groves? Graves? *Greaves*, that was it! It's all coming back to me now. Dad had to move out of his flat because of a fire – nothing to do with the doodlebugs, it was after they'd finished. He was about to leave the Army anyway. Well, his friend asked Miss Greaves if Dad could have a room there until his demob, and she said yes."

"She was always kind," Rachel murmured vaguely; and saying

something about putting the kettle on for hot-water bottles, she got to her feet and went to the kitchen.

She filled the kettle and put it on the stove and went to the cupboard where two hot-water bottles dangled by a string from a hook on the inside of the door.

"There's a metal one, if you'd like an extra," she called to Alannah, raising her voice so that it would reach the sitting room. "I can't abide it, myself. It's a vicious thing that burns you as soon as look at you, but you're more than welcome. It's certainly cold enough. I do hope the weather's better tomorrow. It's such a nuisance when we're confined to the house all day. Tell me, what time is Terry coming for you?"

There came no reply from the living room. Rachel stood still for a moment or two, listening to the silence, her imagination running riot. What was Alannah doing? Sitting staring into space? Adding up, speculating, remembering? She went to the door of the kitchen to see for herself and slowly let out a long, relieved breath.

She had taken up *Hurrah for Dymphna* once more, and was leafing through it. Conscious of Rachel's presence, she looked up, smiling.

"D'you remember Daddy laughing at this?" she said. "He was lying in a deckchair in his panama hat, and we sat on the grass and read to him, and he laughed and laughed. I can see him now, can't you?"

The kettle shrilled, and swiftly Rachel went to deal with it, saying nothing.

18

Rachel had felt it an answer to prayer when she'd got back from her abortive trip to London with Dave to find that she was to be sent to Morecombe on a course to update her skills. Dave, not surprisingly, was avoiding her, but it was impossible not to bump into him sometimes and the sight of him made her feel embarrassed and ashamed.

"You used him as a plaything," said Penny, to whom she had confided everything. "You toyed with his emotions." At which they both collapsed in giggles, which made her feel a great deal better. Dave would get over it; and at least, she thought, it redressed the balance a little. When it came to toying with emotions, Air Crew were past masters.

While she was in Morecombe, her grandfather died. It was not entirely unexpected as he had been ill for several months, but she wept for him, remembering the many times when only his affectionate kindnesses had made life at The Laurels worth living.

No leave could be granted, she was told, while the course was in progress, and she had been unable to get away to the funeral, a dereliction of duty which her grandmother never wholly forgave. Even so, Rachel went to Warnfield from time to time out of a sense of duty, always afraid that she would encounter one or other of the Rossiters. She never did.

"Mr Rossiter – *Captain* Rossiter, I suppose I should say – is in London," Grandma said on an early visit, in tones of great scorn. "What he imagines he is doing to help the war effort I cannot imagine, sitting behind his desk in the War Office. And Alannah, they say, is entertaining the troops. I ask you!"

"She's only acting in plays, Grandma," Rachel felt it fair to point out.

"That's as may be. Mrs Rossiter, of course, is floating about the place in some uniform or other, too. WVS, I think, whatever that might mean. Something to do with canteens, I believe. I never see her."

"Have you – have you heard anything about Gavin?" Rachel asked at last, with great diffidence.

"Not a word. Still in the land of the living as far as I'm aware. You're not still hankering – ?"

"No, no, of course not."

"I should hope not, indeed!"

The fact of his continued existence was as much as Rachel ever heard about him – but this, she told herself, was all she wanted to know. The childish obsession was over. She had grown up, moved on. And moved on from ridiculous experiments like Dave, too. One day there would be someone. For the moment, she'd wait.

She'd been posted to Scotland after the course, to a bleak, remote airfield scoured by winds blowing direct from the Polar cap – a period which she had enjoyed nevertheless, entirely due to the congenial company she found there. She found herself writing plays and skits, making people laugh, relishing the applause. She gained a certain amount of fame, as opposed to the notoriety she had attracted at Bothley. With the CO's encouragement she applied for a commission, but later had second thoughts and withdrew the application. She was happy as she was, she said.

Her grandmother died suddenly at the beginning of 1945. This time Rachel went to the funeral and was surprised at the regret she felt for an era ending, as well as for a life that had known little joy. If ever it could be said of anyone that she was her own worst enemy then Grandma was the one.

This, she thought as she stood in the bitter wind by her grandmother's grave, was really the end. No more Rossiters, and no more Warnfield, ever again.

Her grandmother's will decreed that her estate was to be divided between her two children, Ivor and Sylvia, but a small legacy had been left to Rachel, which both surprised and touched her. It was no fortune, but at least she had the means now to buy somewhere to live after the war. After the war! The phrase seemed to conjure up some sunlit, verdant dream world full of smiling men and women at peace with each other and themselves. Victory had been an impossibly distant goal for so long, it was hard to imagine it achieved and accepted.

Sylvia didn't come to her mother's funeral. She had flu, she told Rachel on the phone; was absolutely knocked out by it, quite incapable of travelling so far, but proposed writing to Mrs Rossiter to ask her to keep various items from The Laurels until she felt able to collect them.

"I don't suppose she'd mind doing that for me, would she?" Sylvia said. "Bearing in mind all the years she and mother were neighbours. Do give her my best wishes when you see her."

"I doubt that I will," Rachel said; and indeed, there were no Rossiter representatives at the funeral.

She travelled back to Scotland, only to find that she had been promoted to sergeant and posted to West Greely in Berkshire.

"The Transport Section!" she said disgustedly to Nancy, the girl who had become her closest friend. "What do I know about bloody transport? I've never been on a non-operational station in my life! I wouldn't have withdrawn my application for the commission if I'd known they were going to muck me about like this."

"Cheer up," Nancy said philosophically. "It can't be for long, can it? Demob must surely be just around the corner. It's all over bar the shouting."

She was right, of course. Though bitter fighting was continuing, it was all swinging the Allies' way now. By mid-March they had crossed the Rhine and were storming eastwards, the German army crumbling before them.

At home, the black-out was lifted, the Home Guard disbanded, and the minds of members of the forces turned to demobilisation. Rachel knew exactly what she was going to do once she was free of the Air Force. She was going to go to London and establish herself as a freelance journalist. Already she had written a few articles and short stories for women's magazines which had been accepted. She felt strong and confident and full of hope. If she bought a house with Grandma's money, she thought, she could let a couple of rooms to ensure a small income and then she wouldn't need to get some boring nine to five job to tide her over the lean times, but could devote her time to writing.

"You're looking extraordinarily gruntled today, sweetie," said Ronnie, AC1 Ronald Havering, sashaying through the door of her office and arranging himself on the edge of her desk. "What's tickling you, may I ask?"

"Lovely after-the-war thoughts," Rachel said. She leaned her elbow on the desk, cupped her chin in her hand, and beamed at him. "What are you going to do, Ronnie?"

Ronnie rolled his eyes heavenwards.

321

"Don't ask. Go back to designing sets at Covent Garden, one *hopes*, but have the old hands lost their cunning, one asks oneself?"

"Of course they haven't." Rachel gave him a shove. "Go on, get off my desk and let me get to work. God, this is boring! Roll on demob."

"You ain't just whistling Dixie, sweetheart," Ronnie said in an atrocious American accent, as he sashayed out again.

Rachel laughed as she watched him go.

"I don't think he's at all funny," said Cynthia Brocklebank, the girl at the next desk who had been ostentatiously immersed in typing a report throughout this exchange, lips pressed tightly together. "I think he's disgusting."

"Really?" Rachel affected polite surprise. "What makes you say that?"

"You know perfectly well what I mean. He's one of *them*."

"Well, at least you needn't worry lest your irresistible charms send him wild with desire, need you?" she said sweetly.

Cynthia went scarlet, a shade which clashed painfully with her carrotty hair and purple lipstick. Seeing it, Rachel wrestled with her conscience for a moment, then sighed resignedly.

"Look, I'm sorry, Cynthia," she said. "I shouldn't have said that. Ronnie does camp it up, I know, but there's no harm in him. He's a good friend."

"Well, you've got a very funny taste in friends, I must say," said Cynthia, feeding more paper into her machine as if it were an offensive weapon being primed for the kill. "Very funny indeed."

In fact, coming to West Greely so late in the day as far as the war was concerned, Rachel had found it more difficult to make friends than she had done elsewhere. It was hard to rouse herself to make the effort to socialise since no kindred spirit was immediately obvious; and anyway, there was her writing. It was taking up more and more of her free time.

The lack of friends didn't bother her. Peace was coming, even if it seemed sometimes to approach at a snail's pace. By mid-April, the extent of the Nazi atrocities began to emerge as first Belsen and Buchenwald were liberated, and then, later in the month, Dachau. Newspapers were full of the horrors encountered by Allied servicemen entering the camps, and though everyone in the civilised world was aware of the details and had been sickened and revolted by the reports, Cynthia insisted on reading each one aloud at every available opportunity.

"Can't you just shut up about it for one minute," Rachel finally grated through clenched teeth, unable to get the reports and pictures out of her mind, night or day.

"Well, really!" Cynthia, once more, had taken offence. "You can't close your mind to these things."

"But you can stop behaving like a ghoul. Think of some good news. Think of the Russians capturing Berlin. The end can only be a matter of days now."

Even in the Pacific, things were looking up. At the beginning of May, Rangoon fell to the British. Rachel talked to Alice on the phone and found her in good spirits, certain that her parents would soon be leaving the camps where, separated from each other, they had been imprisoned by the Japanese. And Keith, too, now in the North Atlantic, was expected home shortly.

"Isn't it wonderful?" Alice said. "To think of the danger being over! I've never been so happy, Rachel."

The shops had been selling victory flags and bunting since the beginning of April, but it was the fifth of May before the Germans finally surrendered, and the evening of the seventh before it was officially announced that the following day would be designated Victory in Europe day.

On the morning of the seventh, Cynthia crashed into the office waving a miniature Union Jack.

"It's ever so exciting," she said. "People think it's going to be tomorrow, but nobody's certain. Whenever it is, there's going to be a bonfire in the Parade Ground and a dance at the NAAFI. They're putting out the flags now."

"Let joy be unconfined," said Ronnie, who happened to be in the office before her. His voice was flat and expressionless. Cynthia bridled. There was, Rachel thought, looking at her with interest, no other way of describing it.

"Well, you might not be glad the war's over, but others are," she said.

"Of course I'm glad, you silly mare," Ronnie said irritably, adding, in Rachel's direction: "Gordon Bennett, how can you stand it? Let's go to London to celebrate, shall we, you and me? There'll be great goings-on up there." He lowered his voice. "I'll nick one of the staff cars – "

"Ronnie, you can't!"

"Rachel, I can! There's that one that's just been repaired. It's not officially back on strength yet. Go on – be a devil, just for once. Where's the harm?"

Rachel thought about it for a moment. "Okay," she said. "Why

323

not? I could do with a bit of excitement. I've had enough of West Greely to last a lifetime, and that's the truth."

Meeting her in the village the next morning, Ronnie waved away her persistent fears regarding the car.

"Don't give it a thought, sweetie," he said. "We're entitled to the odd perk. By the way, you won't mind if we pop in to see an old friend of mine before we join in the celebrations, will you? She was an opera singer, a fascinating old girl, loves nothing better than a party. Everyone goes there – you never know who you'll meet. She lives quite close to Covent Garden. Vida, her name is. Vida Morell. If you haven't heard of her, your parents would have done. We'll have to try and get some bottles from somewhere."

"Just so long as we don't miss the high-jinks at the Palace – "

"Lord, no, dearie. There'll be bags of time."

Traffic was light until they approached London, with no indication that this day was in any way different from any other. It was not until they approached central London that the crowds appeared, heading in the direction of Whitehall. People looked happy but dazed, as if they hardly dared believe that the fighting was over and the victory theirs. Street traders were selling flags and Churchill buttons and rosettes, and all the shopfronts were decorated with a mass of red, white and blue.

The crowds grew thicker as they drove down Piccadilly and the Circus itself was alive with flags and bunting and the sound of a piper, dressed in his full regalia. Excitement was building. Rachel could feel it – outside, in streets, and within herself, too.

"You're quite sure we're not going to miss anything – ?" Rachel asked anxiously.

"No, no! Calm yourself, sweetie. Winnie's not going to the Palace until this afternoon. Time for a few jars first."

"Your friend won't mind us just dropping in?"

"Mind? Vida mind? Of course not! I told you, she loves a party. I must get a bottle, though."

It wasn't easy. All the provision shops were temporarily open but were packed to the doors, and any form of alcohol, it appeared, was like gold dust. Ronnie finally paid the exorbitant sum of £5 for a bottle of gin ("Don't worry about it, dear," he said to Rachel. "Easy come, easy go. I had a nice little flutter on the gee-gees last week.")

Vida greeted him with rapture when finally they arrived at her dusty, velvet-draped, over-furnished flat in Floral Street. They weren't the first guests to present themselves. Already there was a large red-faced man with side-whiskers and a gin-soaked, wheezy laugh; a baby-faced sailor who greeted Ronnie with even more rapture than Vida had shown; and a Brylcreemed Air Force officer attached to a platinum blonde who had the largest eyes Rachel had ever seen.

The bottle of gin was welcomed as warmly as Ronnie had been, and drinks urged upon them immediately.

"No, no, it's not a *bit* too early," Vida assured Rachel, surging up to her in a flurry of black velvet and face powder. "You've a fair bit of catching up to do, my dear. Let me give you some of my fruit cup. You'll love it, I promise you."

Rachel accepted a glass with thanks, thinking that she had never seen such an odd-looking woman in her entire life. She was dressed entirely in black, and her hair, too, was dense ebony, quite straight on either side of her chalk-white face, and cut squarely in a fringe across a bony forehead. It was impossible to hazard a guess at her age, but, Rachel thought, she must be well over sixty – perhaps over seventy. Her dress had the dropped waist fashionable in the twenties, and her shoes were pointed, with fancy buckles. Her mouth was a slash of vermilion, the lipstick applied with, apparently, no reference to the actual shape of her lips.

All those present were in some way connected with the theatre, past or present – and presumably future, too, in the case of Ronnie and the sailor, introduced as Binky, and the airman and his girlfriend.

Rachel stood and sipped her drink, on the sidelines, as it were, listening to the shrieks and the gossip and the speculation; thinking how much she would prefer to be outside with the crowds, knowing what was going on, being part of the celebrations instead of shut away with this collection of oddities.

"This must be awfully boring for you," said the airman, strolling languidly across to join her. "Let me top you up."

"No, I really think – oh," she realised it was too late for protests. "Thank you. What's in this, do you know?"

The airman winked. He had a long face with delicately modelled lips that twitched with amusement.

"Vida's secret recipe. Goes down a treat, doesn't it? Cheers."

"Cheers. I always feel a bit wary about these mixed-up things – "

"I always thought WAAFS were a tough breed. Don't disappoint me, I beg you." He extended a limp hand. "Neil's the name, by the way. Neil Faraday. Remember it, won't you? It'll be up in lights before too long."

He smiled at her, holding her hand overlong, and she smiled back at him, recognising the tactics as those of a professional charmer. But at least he was talking to her. Another couple had arrived – a short, Italian-looking man with his plump wife – to be greeted by screams of welcome from Vida and warm embraces all round.

"Recognise him?" Neil asked, with a jerk of his head towards the short, dark man. "That's Enrico Rinaldi – "

"The tenor? Goodness me." In some surprise, Rachel saw Rinaldi throw his arms around Ronnie. How, she wondered, did a set designer come to be on these sort of terms with an operatic star of such magnitude?

She voiced her astonishment to Neil, who winked.

"Our Ronnie has friends in high places," he said. "Never underestimate Ronnie. How do you come to know him, by the way?"

"We work together. We're both at West Greely, in the Transport Section. What about you?"

"Oh, I'm on Lancs. Chilbury. Hey, you're empty again. Let me give you a refill."

This time she made no protest. Chilbury. Dared she ask? Just how he was – that's all she wanted to know. Stupid, really – Gavin must surely have moved from Chilbury years ago. The chances of this man knowing him were negligible.

She took a sip of her new drink, giving herself courage.

"I don't suppose," she said after a moment, "that you came across a friend of mine? Gavin Rossiter?"

His response was immediate.

"I should say I did!" He shook his head. "Poor old Gav – yes, I knew him well. It was a damned shame – "

Rachel stared at him. Her face felt strangely stiff.

"He – he's dead?"

"Didn't you know? It must have been about – ooh, three or four months ago, I suppose. He'd actually left Chilbury. He was training, not flying ops. any more. Some bloody incompetent fool wrote him off – and himself too, of course. Damn shame, when you think of all the missions he did over Germany – here, are you all right? D'you want to sit down? Drink up, and I'll get you another."

"No, really – you're very kind. I'm all right. It was a shock, that's all. I thought – I thought he'd come through."

The dull morning had given way now to sunshine. Dust motes danced in the shaft of light that filtered between the looped velvet curtains. Rachel looked around the room, at the faded striped wallpaper and the gilt-framed pictures and the heavy mahogany furniture, all dulled with dust and hazy with cigarette smoke. More people were arriving, shrieking, embracing. None of it seemed real. Perhaps it was a dream, she thought. Perhaps this wasn't happening. Perhaps all these strident, gesticulating people and the white-faced witch were figments of her imagination.

Time seemed to contract and expand. How long had they been there? How many of these deceptively harmless drinks had she downed? She found herself unable to guess.

Neil was talking, bringing the girl with the eyes across to meet her. Pamela, her name was. She was a dancer, he said.

"Chorus," Pamela elaborated. "Back row, more's the pity."

"Not for long, darling," Neil assured her, and put another drink in Rachel's hand. "Pam's terrific," he said. "Absolutely terrific. I'm willing to bet any money – "

"I must go," Rachel said, interrupting him. "I must get out of here – get some air."

She found herself out on the street, heard someone call her name, and saw Ronnie hurrying after her.

"What's up, sweetie?" he asked. "You look like death."

"I needed some air."

"And something to eat, I should think. It's well past anybody's lunch time. Let's see if we can get something."

But it was so far past lunch time that they walked all the way to Trafalgar Square without finding anywhere still open, even going as far as the Coventry Street Corner House. That had such a long queue it seemed unlikely that anyone joining it at that late stage would ever gain entry.

They bought packets of crisps and sat on the steps of the National Gallery to eat them, looking down on the milling crowds in Trafalgar Square – at the lions, draped with revellers, and the hurdy-gurdy that played on, at roistering servicemen and women, at all the old and young, rich and poor, who had come to celebrate.

Rachel felt detached from it all. Poor Ronnie, she thought. She ought to give him some explanation. But somehow the words wouldn't allow themselves to be spoken.

"We ought to get up to the Palace," Ronnie said. "There's bound to be a terrific crowd there. About four, they say they'll come out on the balcony."

In the distance, the chimes of Big Ben could be heard, striking three. There was a crackling and a strange whistling sound from a loudspeaker somewhere out of sight towards St Martin-in-the-Fields, and then Churchill's unmistakable voice could be heard.

"Yesterday at 2.41a.m. the representative of the German High Command and Government, General Jodl, signed the act of unconditional surrender of all German land, sea and air forces. Hostilities will end at one minute past midnight tonight – "

For Rachel, the rest passed unheeded as silent tears streamed unchecked down her face.

"Hey!" Ronnie put his arm round her. "Brace up, sweetie. We all feel like shedding a little tear, you know. Patriotism *does* that, don't you find? I've only got to hear the distant strains of 'Land of Hope and Glory' to utterly dissolve, but *utterly*!" Tenderly he wiped her eyes with his handkerchief – fine linen, Rachel noticed despite her tears, and exquisitely laundered. "Time to foot it featly down the Mall and cheer the great man in the flesh, not to mention Kingy and Queeny and the adorable princesses. Tell you what – " He reached into his pocket and pulled out a hip-flask. "I was keeping this for emergencies. Have a swig, sweetie. It'll work wonders."

"Will it?" Rachel felt doubtful. She also felt that she had consumed quite enough alcohol – but maybe Ronnie was right. Anything was worth trying. His day would be ruined as well as hers, if she didn't pull herself together pretty rapidly.

She did, indeed, feel better after the prescribed swig; better, but strange, as if she were walking several inches off the ground. Things were slightly out of focus, softened round the edges – and that seemed to include the news about Gavin, too, for suddenly the sadness was cushioned. It was only what he had expected, she thought. Looking back, it seemed as if he had always known it would end like this.

They were so far to the back of the crowd outside the palace that the figures of those on the balcony were like manikins – recognisable as the King and Queen and Winston Churchill, with Princess Elizabeth in ATS uniform, and Princess Margaret dressed in blue, but so distant as to appear unreal.

Rachel and Ronnie were standing among a group of sailors, who were loud and bawdy and very funny. Rachel found herself laughing as helplessly as she had cried not long before.

But this isn't *me*, she found herself thinking. Where am I? What am I doing?

After a while, they moved off to Whitehall in answer to the rumour which said that Churchill would appear on the balcony of one of the Government office buildings to address the crowd. The sailors came too, joining them in a long, linked, unruly line to dance the Palais Glide, all the way across the park to Horse Guards.

Whitehall was already packed, but somehow they managed to sidle through the crowd to get close to the Ministry of Health, said to be the chosen building and now surrounded on two sides by a dense crowd. One of the sailors – the tallest and the brawniest, whose name, he told her, was Fred – grabbed Rachel's arm and pulled her over to the pavement directly opposite the building.

"Come on, boys – lift her up on my shoulders," he shouted to the others.

"No – I can't – oh! – " She was up there, swaying a little as Fred adjusted to her weight, and laughing wildly at the precariousness of her position.

The view was wonderful from this vantage point. She could see the balcony opposite, and crowds stretching all along Whitehall from Trafalgar Square at one end to Parliament Square at the other. The noise was unbelievable, like nothing she had ever heard before – a kind of soughing susurration as of a great wind, sweeping from one end of the thoroughfare to the other and erupting into a giant roar as Churchill and a group of other dignitaries came out on to the balcony.

Everyone was cheering as they recognised the face of the man who had for so long been the inspiration of the entire nation; the noise so great that it seemed the whole of London must be uniting in this one, overwhelming outburst of adulation.

The sudden silence that followed was equally stunning as the crowd waited to hear his words. I must remember this, Rachel thought to herself, owlishly wise. This is important. This is history. If only she didn't feel as if her head belonged to someone else! It seemed such a waste of a wonderful occasion.

"This is *your* victory – " Churchill began, in those gravelly, unmistakable tones, the rest of the sentence lost as the roar erupted again.

The crowd loved him and interrupted him constantly with cheers, but at last, with a final 'God bless you all', he was gone.

Rachel was gently lowered to the ground.

"Thanks, Fred," she said, clutching at him, feeling her head swim. "I reckon I had the best view in London."

It was then that she looked around for Ronnie, only to discover that he was nowhere in sight.

"He was next to me coming through the park," one of the sailors said. "Reckon he got detached in the crowd, somewhere."

They looked for him for a few moments, but it was clearly hopeless; in any case, Rachel wasn't at all sure that she wanted to find him. He'd said earlier that he intended going back to Vida's flat later on, which was a prospect that filled her with horror. She thought longingly of Alice and the house in Shawcross Street, and of the feeling of sanctuary she knew she would find there. She'd take a taxi –

"You'll never get one, love," Fred said. "Stick with us! We're going to look for some fish and chips."

Her stomach churned with hunger at the thought of it. But they didn't find a fish shop. They didn't even look for one until they had made several attempts to climb Nelson's column.

By this time an hysterical gaiety had them all in its grip. Fred persuaded Rachel that it would be a criminal act to leave the festivities now – what would she tell her grandchildren when they asked what she'd done to celebrate the end of the war, and she said she went home and had an early night?

So she stayed, and was hoisted to sit on one of the lions, from where she conducted a spirited rendition of 'There'll Always be an England'; and once back on the ground, she sang and she danced. All the way down the Strand she danced, three sailors to her left, and three to her right, all arm-in-arm; but then, suddenly, they too were gone and she was dancing with two American GIs, one of which she recognised as having perched next to her on Nelson's lion.

"Say, baby," he said. "You're great! You should be in pictures, you know that? D'you want a drink?"

"I want some *food*," Rachel said; and was grateful for the chocolate bar he produced.

He produced beer, too, which they shared around sitting on some office steps close to where a huge bonfire was blazing in the middle of the road, its sparks flying heavenwards.

"Gee, I'm glad I'm here, gee I'm glad I'm here," his friend kept repeating like a mantra, a wide, blissful smile on his face.

"Gee, he's glad he's here," the other said to Rachel. He moved a little closer. "Say, you're cute, d'you know that? My name's Chuck. What's yours, baby?"

"I don't think I can remember." Unsteadily, Rachel got to her feet and pointed dramatically. "Is that a taxi I see before me, handle towards my hand?"

"Come again?"

"I want a taxi. Please, please Chuck, get me that taxi!"

"No, gee, don't leave us – "

She ran towards the taxi, but was beaten at the last min-ute by a city gentleman in striped trousers and bowler hat who was driven off in triumph in the direction of Leicester

Square. She turned, despairing, to find that Chuck had followed her.

"I must go," she said. "I must find a taxi." And to her intense shame, she found she was crying again.

"Aw, come on, honey – " Chuck was embarrassed by her tears.

"I'm sorry, I'm sorry." Rachel delved into her pockets and found her handkerchief. "Don't worry about me. I must get a taxi – "

"There's one!"

Anxious now to speed her on her way, Chuck lunged across the street and hung on to the door of a cab which was just being paid off, turning to snarl threats at yet another GI who was attempting to wrest it from him.

"It's for the lady," he shouted. "C'mon, baby – get in."

Thankfully, Rachel did so and gave the Shawcross Street address. The cabby was talkative. What a day! he said over and over. What a day! She wouldn't believe some of the sights he'd seen.

Rachel could see two of him. She closed her eyes, then opened them again quickly, putting out a hand to steady herself as the whole world seemed to rock sideways. She'd never felt like this before – never so out of control, so helpless and miserable.

"The world is dark," she found herself saying in sepulchral tones, at which the cabby turned round and looked at her anxiously.

"We'll soon get you home, love," he said. "Nearly there. Look, this is Sloane Square. Nearly there."

She was drunk. Pressed into the corner of the cab she faced the fact, and was ashamed. What on earth would Susan think of her? And Alice? VE day was no excuse, nor was the news about Gavin. She had seen this coming, felt herself slipping away from reality, and had done nothing. The day had somehow gathered momentum, run away with her. It seemed to pass before her eyes in a series of pictures: Vida's flat, sitting on the steps with Ronnie, meeting the sailors outside the Palace, dancing across the park. Had any of it happened?

"Here we are, love," the cabby said, in the rallying tone used exclusively for drunkards or the mentally unstable. "That'll be five-and-six."

She gave him a pound note and turned towards the house, collecting herself for the walk across the pavement, ignoring the cabbie's attempt, admittedly halfhearted, to present her with the change. She took a breath. Perhaps, she thought, if she exercised great care, they wouldn't know –

Slowly and deliberately she walked towards the house and rang the bell. Alice would be glad to see her, she told herself, as she waited for an answer to her ring. Alice would welcome her, in spite of her shameful condition. Alice was a good friend. An old friend. Old friends forgave things.

But it was not Alice who opened the door; nor Susan. She stood transfixed, sure she must be hallucinating, that this was just one more surreal happening in a totally surreal day.

"Mr Rossiter!" she said faintly.

"Rachel, my dear!" He reached out both arms to welcome her inside. "What a wonderful surprise – and just when I was feeling so lonely, too!"

"Alice – ?" began Rachel.

"Alice has rushed down to Southampton. She had a phone call from Keith this morning to say he'd just put into port. And Susan's in France – "

She put a hand to her head and swayed a little.

"I was hoping to stay the night. I'd better go."

"Nonsense, nonsense!" He was all kindness, all benevolence. "Susan would never forgive me. The room next to mine is always known as Rachel's room. Besides – " He gave a low, indulgent chuckle. "It doesn't look to me, my dear, as if you're in any fit state to go anywhere."

"I didn't expect – what are you *doing* here, Mr Rossiter?"

"Living here, pro tem. Come into the kitchen. I'm just getting myself some food – nothing much, just bread and cheese, but I've a bottle of champagne to wash it down. I was going out after I'd had a bite, just to find a bit of life in town, but how much better to share an evening like this with an old friend."

When she made no reply, he took her by the shoulders and laughed again, looking into her face.

"How you've changed," he said. "You're quite the little glamourpuss, aren't you? But what have you been up to, you bad girl?" Humorously he chided her. "Just as well your sainted grandmother can't see you now – "

Her only reply was a sob.

"Hey, come on! It's not as bad as that. You can be forgiven! It is VE Day, after all – "

"Oh, Mr Rossiter!"

Her head dropped to his shoulder as the tears overwhelmed her, sobs coming from deep within her, racking and painful. She was a child again, helpless in her grief, all her defences stripped away. He held her even closer, stroked her hair, lifted her chin.

"Darling child, what is it?" he asked her, his voice caressing. He sounded so kind, so concerned. He kissed her gently. "There, there, nothing can be as bad as this."

"It's Gavin," she managed to say at last. "I've only just heard."

19

Rachel, in the unfamiliar, narrow bed in Tess's room, lay
sleepless, remembering.

She had put the past behind her, built a new life. Brooding and blaming seemed an unproductive exercise, destructive
both to herself and to Tess; but this night, with Alannah's words
ringing in her ears, the memories came whether she wanted them
or not.

They were dim and fragmented. She could remember sobbing
on Hugh Rossiter's shoulder, and the warmth of his arms around
her. He hadn't kissed her again. Not then. For a while he had
held her and stroked her hair; but then, all at once, his paternal
tenderness had turned into something else – and she had responded.
She had to admit that.

She had responded!

She had opened her mouth to him, wound her arms around
him, strained close to him. Why? Why?

That memory faded, and another emerged. The bedroom. Walls
tilting, advancing, receding. Hands – experienced hands – taking
off her clothes; and a voice, full of tenderness, soothing, reassuring,
laughing a little at her helplessness.

She had protested then. She was sure, afterwards, that she had
protested, and remained sure. The voice went on.

"So lovely! Darling child, you've become a beauty! How can I
resist you? Don't blame me for wanting you. Let me love you,
let me kiss you – here, and here. You want it too! Darling child,
you know you do."

And the panic, and the weight of him, and the sinking into
nothingness. And the waking next day to a hammering head

and a dry, foul-tasting mouth and the rush of horrified remembrance.

She'd taken a bath – had scrubbed herself as if she never could get clean; had drunk coffee and eaten cornflakes; and all the time there was this sick weight in her stomach compounded of shame and anger and fear. Slumped at the kitchen table, unable to rouse herself to move, her eye had fallen on an envelope on which her name was written. She picked it up and studied it. She had never seen his writing before. It was graceful, artistic; an architect's hand, of course.

'Darling little Rachel,' he had written.

'I have to be off to Warnfield at the crack of dawn this morning, so am writing to say bless you, sweet child. You made a tired, lonely old desk-warrior very happy!

'Last night was a wonderful experience that must remain our secret. I know you will understand, and hope that you will sometimes think of me with affection.'

Affection! Almost two years later the bitterness was as great as it had ever been; and the shame. How could she? she thought now as she had thought then. After all, she had been no child, whatever Hugh Rossiter had chosen to call her. Who would have thought that a twenty-four-year-old WAAF sergeant could have been so stupid?

She forced herself to breathe deeply and slowly. It was pointless to dwell on it, all over again – but how right she was to want to keep clear of all Rossiters, when only a few hours in the company of one of their number made her feel like this!

Think of something else, she urged herself. Think of Stefan; increasingly, it was hard to imagine how any other man could ever have attracted her. Think of the book, now forging ahead satisfactorily. Think of Tess, so bright and pretty and happy. Like Diana? Oh, God, no! She'd never grow up like Diana. Rachel herself would see that she didn't. What about heredity, then?

To hell with heredity, Rachel thought as she had thought so many times before. Tess wouldn't have a mother like Mrs Rossiter, would she? A mother who would take every opportunity of underlining at all times her superiority over lesser mortals.

The urge to smash that superiority was as strong as ever. How sweet revenge would be! Imagine admitting the truth to Alannah – showing her, once and for all, what a sham it was, this ideal, loving family façade that she had always flaunted.

335

It wouldn't be difficult. She was halfway there already; could even, possibly, have worked it out for herself in the still watches of the night. She might be unintelligent, but she wasn't *that* unintelligent.

Oh yes, Rachel thought. Revenge would be sweet. The truth would wipe the smug, self-satisfied smiles from their faces for ever. In particular, Mrs Rossiter's face.

Carina Rossiter. Rachel said the name over to herself. Hers was the blame. She it was who had encouraged the narcissism that had resulted in the unnatural love between Gavin and Diana. She had forced Barney into art college, saddling him with her own ambitions which he was incapable of achieving. She had made Alannah into the self-regarding creature she was.

As for her own life, there was no end to the misery Carina Rossiter had caused. And now, with the supreme egotism of which only a Rossiter was capable, she had invited Rachel back into the fold; until, of course, the next time she offended. Then, no doubt, there would be another withdrawal of approval, another tirade of abuse.

How sadly, Rachel thought, would Carina Rossiter shake her head when told by Alannah that she had an illegitimate child, that she was a Fallen Woman, a suitable subject for charity and pained regret. Would she say that it was inevitable, given her insecure background? Given *that* kind of mother? Thank God her sons had escaped marriage to such a creature, she would say.

Oh yes, Rachel thought. There was no doubt about it. Revenge would be sweet indeed.

She slept at last and woke to the sound of Tess singing to the pink rabbit and making all the unselfconscious Tess-noises that her mother delighted to hear. The wind had lessened and although it was not fully light, it was possible to see that the clouds were much higher and lighter. It was still very cold.

Shivering, she gathered up her clothes and Tess's, and took her downstairs so that they could wash and dress in the warmth of the kitchen.

It was many months since she had relived that night in Shawcross Street. She'd had the sense to see that bitterness was destructive, that she had to turn her face to the future, and she had done so. Now, however, the disgust and panic had come flooding back; and much as she tried to concentrate on Tess's needs, the past had her in its grip and refused to let go.

Rachel remembered the revulsion; the panic when she realised she was pregnant, the fluttering disbelief. She had drunk gin,

336

jumped down steps, taken hot baths – had even contemplated abortion, but was frightened by the tales she had heard and unsure how to go about it.

So the baby had stayed. She had left the WAAF, bought her house in London, and with Nancy's help had coped with the sneering looks of other women at the antenatal clinic, and the cold, brisk patronage of medical staff. There was one nurse in particular –

Oh, why remember? She had Tess.

"You have a lovely little girl, Mrs Bond," they said – for all mothers were given the courtesy title of Mrs, with or without a ring – and Tess had been wrapped in a blanket and given to her then and there, still unwashed. And Rachel had looked at her and loved her, and wept with joy at her perfection and with relief that the ordeal was over, and she had vowed then and there that nothing and nobody would take this child away from her.

Lost in her thoughts, absentmindedly feeding Tess, it dawned on her that the sound she had heard and disregarded a few moments before was probably the sound of the mail arriving. She left it until Tess had finished the last spoonful, then went to investigate. Unhurriedly, still lost in the past.

And there it was. The long-awaited air-letter from Uganda – and in her father's hand. Her heart sank a little. Her father had only ever written on important occasions; stilted, pedantic little notes to congratulate her on passing an exam, or perhaps to accompany a birthday cheque. It was her mother who had fired off the chatty, inconsequential letters that had kept her in touch over the years. This, she knew before she had touched it, was written because this was an important occasion and he had something momentous to say.

She could hardly bring herself to open it. She brought it through to the kitchen and put it down on the table while she peeled and cut up an apple for Tess, just as if the letter had no significance. Her heart was racing, high up in her breast, almost in her throat. Suppose – suppose –

She snatched at it, possessed suddenly of an impatience to know the worst, and tore it open, holding her breath. Then, slowly, as she read, she gave a long, relieved sigh.

'My dearest Rachel,

'We have only just returned from a month's safari to find your letter waiting for us. By mistake it came by seamail, which explains the long delay.

337

'I cannot pretend that your news was not the greatest shock to us – but oh, my poor child, our hearts go out to you! You may have acted unwisely, but in our view you have paid the price and both your mother and I are saddened by the thought of all you must have been through, all without the support of your family.

'Whether you were wise to elect to bring Tess up on your own rather than agree to adoption may be debatable but I cannot do other than say it shows a degree of courage which I find admirable. Why, I wonder, did you not find the courage to tell us at the time? I suppose I can understand your trepidation, but surely you know that though we may not approve of everything you do, and though due to circumstances we have been unable to be as close over the years as we may have wished, you are our much-loved daughter and will never be any other.

Oh, dear of him, dear of him, Rachel thought in the Cornish vernacular. A little pompous, a little pedantic, but loving too, his heart in the right place. How could she have doubted him?

'Your mother, is writing to you at greater length. There are so many questions she wants to ask and comments to make, but I thought, in view of the long delay in response to your letter, that I must get this off at once.

'Today we received notification that we have confirmed passages on the *Dunottar Castle*, sailing on 3rd March via the Cape, arriving Tilbury on 5th April. We shall indeed look forward to seeing spring in Cornwall, as well as meeting our granddaughter. And of course, our excitement at the thought of seeing you again after so long cannot be expressed.

He signed it 'Your always affectionate father', and added a P.S.

'Be prepared for some criticism of your choice of name. Your mother apparently was taught by a nun called Sister Theresa long years ago, and has hated the name ever since! I cannot help but disagree. I consider the diminutive, Tess, quite charming.'

Rachel leaned back and laughed at this. Of course there would

338

be criticism, she thought; and questions and comments. There was not the smallest doubt that there would be arguments, too, that she and her mother wouldn't always see eye to eye. But it really didn't matter. That was the most important thing of all. It didn't matter. It didn't alter anything. None of them were perfect, but it didn't stop them being a family, and a loving one at that. Stefan hadn't been impossibly idealistic after all.

"You look as if you're in good spirits," Alannah said, coming in at that moment.

"Yes. I've just had a letter from my father. They're coming home very soon."

"They can't be too pleased about your current situation."

"They're living with it," Rachel said. She got up, folded the letter and stuck it behind a plate on the dresser. "What can I get you for breakfast? I've plenty of eggs. I get them from a farm at the top of the hill."

"God no! I couldn't face eggs. Just coffee, please." Alannah sat down heavily. "I had a simply frightful night," she said.

Rachel looked at her. She had no makeup on, and looked pale and plain, with dark circles under her eyes.

"Was it the wind?" she asked. "We get an awful lot, I'm afraid."

"No," Alannah said heavily. "It wasn't the wind. Not altogether, anyway. I was doing some thinking. Putting two and two together. Rachel, you've got to be honest with me."

"Hang on – I'll give Tess her drink. Here you are, sweetie – yum-yum-yum."

"Will you *please* stop the baby-talk and pay attention to me for once? Rachel, listen! I've got to know! Just as I was going to sleep, it suddenly came to me. Dad spent VE day in Shawcross Street. He told us. I was at home the day after when he came back to Warnfield. He said that there were things to clear up at the office in the morning, so he thought he might as well stay in London and see what was going on, but it was all such a scrum that he went back to Shawcross Street and listened to it all on the wireless."

"Very sensible," Rachel said, still attending to Tess, her face hidden.

"But was he with you? That's what I want to know. Turn round and look at me, Rachel. Was he with you?"

Sweet, sweet revenge, Rachel thought. With one word, it could be mine. She's handed it to me on a plate.

She thought of her misery and bewilderment when she was made an outcast, blamed for Gavin's decision to go to Spain.

The constant belittlement, the remarks that suggested that she was unloved, the lack of support in the greatest crisis of her life.

And she thought of Hugh Rossiter. Of how she had turned to him for comfort and he had taken advantage of her helpless, drunken misery.

Words, she thought, couldn't begin to describe what she thought of Hugh Rossiter.

She took a deep breath.

"No, Alannah," she said. "I spent VE night with a group of sailors and two GIs. So there you have my sordid story."

"Oh!" Alannah drew the exclamation out, as if now she understood, all questions answered. "So that's it! An American!"

Sorry, Chuck, Rachel said to herself. It's a far, far, better thing you do –

"An American with blue eyes," Rachel lied. What did one more lie matter? Or perhaps it wasn't a lie. She couldn't remember noticing Chuck's eyes. "So could we leave this entire subject, please?"

"Well, I knew it couldn't be Daddy, really," Alannah went on. "I mean, he wouldn't, would he? You're younger than his own daughter. And anyway – well, when you think how devoted he and Ma have always been it simply wouldn't make sense for him to look at another woman, particularly at – well, I mean to say, he just wouldn't, would he? Put everything in danger, I mean. Because it would absolutely kill Ma if she thought he'd been unfaithful. Not that he would be."

"Of course not," Rachel agreed.

Suddenly she felt radiant with happiness, as if a weight had been lifted from her, as if all the anger and bitterness and fear and regret had rolled away. And the envy, she reminded herself. That had gone, too – gone for ever. Why should she envy anyone? It was her own imperfect family that had stood the test, wasn't it?

"The wind has dropped. I think it's going to be a nice day," she said; and at that moment the front doorbell rang.

"Oh, my God!" Alannah crashed her cup down in its saucer. "That'll be Terry, and I haven't got my face on yet. Stall him for me, there's an angel." She fled upstairs, leaving Rachel to answer the door. But it wasn't Terry. It was Stefan, and he was smiling.

"I could not wait to see you," he said simply. "I caught night train."

"Oh, Stefan!" It seemed only natural that she should reach out to greet him, and in a moment he was over the threshold and in

340

her arms. "It's so good to have you back," she said as they hugged each other. "But I'm not ready – I'm a mess – "

He drew away a little and looked at her, then bent his head and kissed her cheeks and lips and the tip of her nose.

"You are not mess, you are beautiful!" His expression was tender, full of love. "I changed my mind. Second thoughts, yes? I was impatient. There seemed no point to sleep in hotel, so I sleep on train – arrived at six this morning. I stop off at apartment for wash and shave. Joe is thinking I come tomorrow for work, not today, so I come straight to see you. Is so much to tell you. And to ask you."

Smiling he looked into her eyes; then bit his lip and shook his head, as if in doubt.

"Oh, Rachel. I hope, I hope. Please may I hope?"

Yes, yes, *yes*, she longed to shout, but unaccountably she felt close to tears – she, who hadn't cried for so long, who was too strong for tears, who despised them. Yet she could feel them now, swelling her throat, filling her eyes.

"You weep?" Stefan asked, surprised and dismayed. He held her close then and she could feel his lips on her hair.

"With happiness," she said, luxuriating in it for a moment.

"Then I may hope?"

"It depends what you're hoping for," she said softly, looking up into his eyes, reaching to lay her hand against his face. "I hope, too – but Stefan – " she pulled away from him, sniffed a little and wiped her eyes, smiling at him, at her own foolishness. "Alannah's upstairs, that friend I told you about. She'll be going in a minute."

"Then all can wait until then. So much I have to tell you! And all so good."

"Me, too. Stefan, my father wrote. It's just as you said. They forgive me."

He tightened his arms round her and held her close once more.

"Didn't I say? They love you. I love you. You are much loved."

"And you," she whispered, as he bent to kiss her. There were no tears now; just a blissful sense of homecoming and rightness, and a silent but soaring trumpet-song of joy.

"Where's my Tess?" he said at last.

"In the kitchen, in her chair."

He went through, and plucked Tess out of the high chair, holding her aloft at arms' length while she squealed with delight.

"She's missed you, Stefan." Rachel said.

"Ah!" He lowered Tess and held her in his arms, ducking his head as she made a grab for his hair. "I, too, have missed her. But no more. No more partings, yes?"

Alannah came back into the room at this point, hair shining and her makeup freshly applied. Rachel introduced her to Stefan who, despite holding Tess, managed to acknowledge the introduction by one of his exotic, courteous bows.

"Miss Rossiter," he said. "I am honoured."

He had bought himself a new coat in London, a fawn-coloured, military-type mackintosh, and he wore it with great style over a dark-blue high-necked sweater. He looked, Rachel thought, rather dashing, a touch piratical. Alannah clearly was impressed and could barely conceal her astonishment that Rachel – poor, poor Rachel, always such an object of compassion – should attract a man such as this. It was, Rachel thought, one of the more satisfactory moments of her entire life.

Alannah flashed her best smile, fluttered her lashes.

"I'm so glad to have had the chance to meet you," she said. "You know, Rachel and I have been friends for a long, long time – how long is it, Rachel?"

"Ages," Rachel said.

The doorbell rang once more, and she went to answer it. This time it was Terry, who was much as she had imagined from Alannah's description. He was untidily dressed, with thinning hair straggling over his collar, but might, she thought, have been quite good-looking in a raffish kind of way were it not for the bad-tempered scowl on his face.

"Is Alannah ready?" he asked peremptorily, not wasting time on polite greetings. His voice was attractive, she had to admit that. Probably behind footlights, made-up, playing a part someone else had written for him, he would have a certain charm. Right now, however, the charm was somewhat difficult to discern.

He was annoyed and impatient, and didn't mind showing it, acknowledging Alannah's introduction with an ungracious nod, hardly bothering to speak to Rachel at all but addressing all his remarks to Alannah.

"These bloody lanes! I've been stuck behind a farm tractor for miles. Couldn't pass anywhere. I could have been back in Truro an hour ago if I hadn't had to make this detour."

"Rachel." Alannah embraced her and held her for a moment. "It's been wonderful to see you, and your lovely, lovely baby. Thanks for putting me up."

342

"I'm glad you came," Rachel said; finding, rather to her astonishment, that she meant it. Stefan, it seemed, wasn't the only one who had been engaged in exorcism. "I hope that everything works out all right with Barney."

"Come *on*, Alannah," Terry called, down in the street now and waiting impatiently beside the car.

"I must go. Thanks again."

"Goodbye."

They watched her go, Rachel with Stefan beside her, and Tess in his arms. They waved. Then, when the car was gone, they closed the door and went back to the kitchen.

Like a family, Rachel thought.